MY POLL

AND

MY PARTNER JOE;

OR, PRETTY POLL OF PUTNEY.

A NAUTICAL ROMANCE.

BY THE AUTHOR OF

GALLANT TOM; THE SMUGGLER KING; THE DEATH SHIP; JACK
JUNK; RICHARD PARKER; ETC., ETC.

LONDON:

PUBLISHED BY E. LLOYD, 12, SALISBURY SQUARE, FLEET STREET.

PREFACE.

The Author and Publisher of MY POLL AND MY PARTNER JOE, tender their united thanks to the Public for the Patronage it has bestowed on their work; the sale has been prodigious, thus ecouraging their humb'e servants to again endeavour from time to time to cater to the public taste, as well as at the same time elevate the Public taste and morals.

The writer has given facts throughout, with very little more embellishment than was necessary for the style required by the novelist.

The Author and Publisher take leave of their indulgent readers with the sincerest gratitude for past favours.

MY POLL AND MY PARTNER JOE;

OR,

PRETTY POLL OF PUTNEY.

BY THE AUTHOR OF "GALLANT TOM," "THE DEATH SHIP," "JACK JUNK," &c.

CHAPTER I.

OLD BATTERSEA.—THE CROWN AND CROSIER.—HARRY HALLIYARD.

BRIGHT, smiling, refreshing spring had succeeded the dark, cold, and dreary months of winter, and nature had assumed its most inviting aspect. The flowers put forth their sweetest blossoms, the verdant lawns and meadow-lands were clothed in their richest mantle of green; the stately trees waved their bright foliage in the gentle breeze, and the feathered songsters of the grove carolled forth their most mellifluous notes, contributing their

gladsome part to the charms of the season.

The little village of Battersea, at the time of which we are writing, was one of the most pleasant spots in the vicinity of the now overgrown metropolis; and adjacent to the Hard, or landing place, stood an old-fashioned public-house, known by the sign of the Crown and Crosier, the worthy host of which, old Will Wallit, was as jovial a fellow as ever cracked a bottle, or smoked care away in a pipe of tobacco.

The Crown and Crosier, as may be supposed, was principally frequented by watermen, but by none who held so high a place in the esteem and admiration of all who knew them as Harry Hallyard, the Pride of Battersea Hard, and his warm friend, honest Joe Tiller. They were partners in a trim built wherry, and both loved the beautiful and innocent Mary Maybud, or, as she was more commonly called, 'Pretty Poll of Putney,' an orphan girl, living under the protection of old Sam Sculler, the warm friend of her late father. Mary could not be insensible to the manly qualities of Joe Tiller, she esteemed him as a brother, but to Harry Hallyard her whole heart and soul were devoted; and Joe would have hated and despised himself could he have acted with treachery towards his friend, and, therefore, there was nothing left for him to do but to cherish his love in silence, and to hope that the time might come when he should be able to subdue it altogether, and to fix his affections on some other damsel who might be equally worthy of him.

One afternoon, about the middle of April, there was a number of persons assembled in the parlour of the Crown and Crosier, drinking and smoking, and amongst the rest old Sam Sculler (who was busily engaged in perusing a newspaper), and one Mr. Watchful Waxend, a psalm-singing, drunken cobbler, who gloried in the title of 'The Bishop of Battersea,' and whose eccentricities afforded considerable amusement to the denizens of that place. At the moment we introduce this worthy to our readers he had been saying something which excited roars of laughter from his companions, at which Waxend appeared to be rather vexed; and fixing upon them a look of remonstrance, he said—

"Ah, you may laugh, you profane scoffers, but I stick like wax to my religious spirit."

"Ay," replied Will Wallit, the landlord, "that you do, Mr. Waxend, and to my full-proof spirit, too." The guests all laughed.

"I tell you what it is, my friends," stammered the Bishop, who had imbibed on that occasion somewhat more than his usual quantity of the gentle stimulant, "you're all going by steam to the diabolical oven—drinking and sotting from morning till night. Here, Wallit, fill my pot. You'll be thirsty enough in the next world, and no beer: there they allows none to be drunk on the premises."

"Here's your beer, Master Watchful," said the landlord; "money!"

"Oh, stick it up," replied Waxend; and then turning to the watermen, he continued—

"Don't trust me, but read the psalms of Thomas Paine, and the commen—com—en—tatories of Julius Cæsar."

He was proceeding, when at that moment Joe Tiller entered the room, and seemed to be in his usual merry mood.

"Harry Hallyard not here yet?" he said;

"Then I must forth again to wander by the river,
To see if I my par-ten-er and kind friend can diskiver."

"Ah, Master Joe," observed the Bishop, "you're a poet; why don't you turn your thoughts to holy subjects? why don't you do as somebody did—write a legacy in a country churchyard?"

"An elegy, you mean," replied Joe.

"Well, I know," returned Waxend, "some people call 'em t'other way. All the world's a rot," he added, drinking; "ah! you little think how drinking wears out the soul."

"So much the better for you cobblers," returned Joe Tiller.

"If drinking wears the soul away,
    Why, add a little leather;
For till our welting does decay,
    We'll drink and stick together."

"Bravo, Joe—capital!" shouted the guests.

"That would make a capital psalm," observed Waxend. "I'll uplift my voice.

"' If drinking wears—' "

"Hold your tongue, Master Waxend," said Sam Sculler, rising from his seat; "I've got athwart of the account of the great battle of late; here's a full list of the killed."

"Is Dan Leadeye there?" asked the landlord.

"No," answered Sculler.

"Or Sam Scupper, or Charley Coil? or Mick Marline?"

"No, no," replied Sculler.

"I'm glad of that," remarked Wallit; "they left a long score unpaid. Now, I shouldn't mind if Ben Binnacle was popped off; he was the only one as paid his shot afore he sailed, and I've got his shore togs in keeping."

"Ah!" suddenly exclaimed Sam Sculler, starting up, "what's this—Harry Heartley dead—Harry? Poor fellow, poor fellow!"

"What!" said Joe. "Harry that you were bound for? That's bad news, Master Sculler; he'll never come back to pay his debt."

"No, Joe," replied the old man, in a melancholy tone of voice, "and if they come upon the poor old waterman, why, they must e'en sell his boat, and make a beggar of him at once."

"That'll be too hard," remarked Joe, "let's hope better; no one would be Philistine enough to rob a poor, white-headed old man of his last crust."

"Philistine!" said Waxend; "ah, the Philistines were common robbers— all Dick Turpins, every one of them."

"You're too much learned for us, Master Waxend," remarked Tiller; "but I will say it's a hard law—

"For, if a man is taken to prison,
And stripped of everything that's his'n,
'Twere better for him to stop his wizen."

"Capital—capital!" cried the guests.

"Bravo, Master Joe!" said the landlord, "why, I declare, you're quite the Byron of Battersea."

"Yes," answered Joe, modestly, "I does a little poetical poetry; it comes natural to me."

"Yes," observed the Bishop, mounting on a chair, and drinking, "the spirit naturally gets over us. Hear me preach."

"No, no; no preaching," said the watermen, pushing him off the chair.

"Come, don't be cast down, Master Sculler," said Joe. "Where's Harry Halliyard? I've got a little present for him; something as I've been writing about his pretty Poll—his Poll," he added, with a sigh. "Well, he deserves her, for a better lad with a truer heart never feathered an oar."

"Right, lad," coincided old Sculler. "Harry's the pride of the Hard, and Mary's the prettiest, ay, and the most industrious wench on either side of the river. It's a pleasure to see her little fingers go stitch—stitch—stitch—hem hem—hem, from morning till night. She's been a daughter to me since her father died. Poor fellow, his was a brave end. Well, as I was saying, she's looked up to me because I was his friend, and a neater cabin than old Sam Sculler's ain't to be found near the Thames: all her work. And now, if these harpies come for poor Heartley's debt, they'll sell up all the sticks, and leave the old man without a rag of canvas to weather his days. Well— well!"

As the poor old man gave utterance to these words in the most melancholy accents, he pressed his hand upon his aged and wrinkled brow, and sighed deeply.

"But," observed Joe, "they won't do that, Master Sculler. Come, come, be of good heart. But, as I was telling you, I've written a something about Mary."

"Let us hear, Joe," said several of the guests.

"Here it is," replied Tiller, taking a paper from his pocket, "I——"

"Ah," interrupted Waxend, "them charity schools is a good thing."

At which observation, which seemed to tickle their fancy for the moment, the whole of the company laughed heartily.

"Ah, laugh away," remarked Joe, nothing at all abashed, "they are a good thing. How many children they save from depravity! How many do they teach the difference between a brute and a man! I learnt in one, and I should think I was unworthy the charity shown me, if I ever stooped to deny it; for, mark ye, my lads—

"When the mountains so high are kivered
    with snows,
What a very cold wind from the top of 'em
    blows!
But when great ones and rich ones are kind
    all the while,
What a very warm sun's for the poor in
    their smile."

"Good lad—good lad!" ejaculated Sculler, admiringly.

"When the mountains so high," sung the drunken Bishop, at the top of his voice; "common time—When——"

"Stop, stop!" said two or three of the guests; "let us hear Joe's verses."

"Now, lads," observed Tiller, reading—

"Near Putney Bridge there lived a maid,
    More bright than May-day morn."

"Oh, stop, stop!" interrupted Watchful Waxend, "I've heard something like that in a hymn, long metre—

"On Richmond Hill there lived a lass,
    More bright than May-day morn."

"Oh, fie, Joe—fie!" cried the company.

"Well," returned Joe, somewhat offended, "I'll never write no more. I'm no pirate; I never steals another man's ideas. At all events, you can never be robbed."

This retort was more than they could reply to, and they retired to another part of the room, just as another individual made his appearance. This was a man of anything but prepossessing aspect or demeanour, and all eyes immediately became fixed upon him. He was a man about forty years of age, of middle stature, but muscular proportions. His complexion was dark, with large black whiskers, and shaggy eyebrows; features coarse, irregular, and repulsive, and the expression of his eyes was of that description which excited a disagreeable feeling to gaze upon. His dress consisted of a large pea-coat, red waistcoat, rough blue cloth trousers, a glazed hat, and buckles to his shoes. We have been thus minute in describing him, as he is destined to hold a very conspicuous part in our narrative. He advanced slowly, and took a seat, at the same time eyeing the company sullenly. The landlord bowed to him.

"This is the Crown and Crosier, is it not?" he interrogated.

"It is, sir," answered Wallit; "the best house above bridge for comfort and respectable company."

"So I perceive," returned the stranger, sneeringly, and eyeing the company with a contemptuous look. "Bring me some rum. I have business in this neighbourhood."

"Can I assist you in——" inquired the landlord, officiously.

"You can," interrupted the uncouth visitor, surlily; "bring the rum, and be hanged to you."

Wallit made his exit, muttering and grumbling to himself. Waxend, whose curiosity was excited, now drew his seat nearer to the stranger, and addressing himself to him, said—

"Sir, were you ever among the niggers?"

The stranger started, and looking fiercely at him, demanded, "Why do you ask?"

"You'd make a capital slave-driver," replied the Bishop.

"Dare you insult me?" cried the stranger, sternly.

"Don't wax wrath," returned Waxend, "or I shall bristle myself up. Hear me preach."

"Psha! fool!" exclaimed the man, thrusting the officious Bishop back; who, being overloaded with drink, lost his equilibrium, and fell over his seat. The watermen who were assembled rose tumultuously.

"Come, come, sir," interposed Joe Tiller, "you are forgetting yourself. This is the Bishop of Battersea, and—

"If the church is knocked down with such gaiety,
Why, there'll be pretty pickings for the laiety."

"Am I among madmen here?" demanded the stranger fiercely. "Oh, here's the rum!" he added, as the landlord re-entered the room. "Hark ye, landlord, is there one Sculler, a waterman, living in these parts?"

"My name's Sculler," answered old Sam, coming forward, "Sam Sculler."

"You had a friend named Heartley?" said the strange visitor.

"Ah, poor fellow! I have just read of his death," replied the old man.

"Then you must be aware he can't pay a certain debt that he owed," returned the man, "and that you are bound for it—here's the agreement; and so, old gentleman, hand over the rhino."

"Great Heaven!" exclaimed the poor old man, violently agitated, "I'm a ruined man!"

"This rum's not so bad," observed the stranger, coolly, and drinking, and without seeming to take any notice of the emotion of Sculler.

"You will give me time to look about me?" said the latter, eagerly.

"I want the money," was the stern reply of the stranger, and at the same time he retired to the window which overlooked the Hard, and beckoned to some one outside. "You must talk to this gentleman about time."

As he spoke, there entered the room a man of the most singular appearance. He was a dirty-looking fellow, wearing a ragged great coat, a misshapen old white hat, and a pair of top-boots, from which his toes were plainly visible.

"That's your prisoner," said the stranger, addressing him, and pointing to Sculler.

"Oh, my lapstone!" remarked Waxend, "what a gentleman! Baalim and his ass! Oh, ye captivators of corpuses, hear my voice!"

"Silence!" commanded the uncouth stranger, in the sternest accents, "or I'll spoil your voice for a month to come. Where's the money?" he inquired, addressing himself to Sculler.

"If you insist on your demand," replied the latter, "I am a beggar."

"Away with him," was the unfeeling order.

"You see, my old cove," said the man who had just entered the room, "here's the parchment,—no gammon about it,—all regular. So, you'd better out with the yeller 'uns, and stash all patter."

"I must sell my boat," said the poor old man, despairingly.

"To be sure," said the fellow, who gloried in the name of Snatchem; "you must put up the floater. Take my advice; I'm th' honestest chap as is,—has a feeling for the misfortunate. Never resist the law; if a man claims your vestcoat, let him have it, or you'll lose your kicksies in trying the argument."

"Away with him!" once more commanded his companion.

"This is too bad," observed Joe, whose indignation was aroused; "what, lads, will you see old Sam Sculler, whose hairs are grown white in honesty and industry, dragged like a dog to a jail? Let go your hold!" he added crossing over to Snatchem, and fixing upon him a threatening look,

"Don't resist the law," remonstrated the latter individual. "Take my advice, if a man kicks you, rub the place; for, if you strike again, ten to one if you has witnesses as to who was the degressor."

"Down with them! down with them!" shouted the watermen, assuming a most threatening and determined attitude.

"Look to your prisoner," exclaimed the stranger. "Stand back, I say!"

As he thus spoke, he thrust poor old Sculler over to Snatchem, threw himself between them and the approaching watermen, and levelled a pistol at the latter. Waxend immediately jumped upon a chair, terribly alarmed.

"I'm a man of peace," he said; "hear me preach!"

"Quick, quick! away!" commanded the stranger, addressing himself to Snatchem, who forced the old man towards the door; but at that moment Harry Halliyard rushed suddenly into the room, and darting hastily forward, he knocked Snatchem's hat over his eyes, seized his companion's pistol, hurled him to one corner of the room, and levelled it at him.

"Ahoy!" cried the young waterman, "what boats are foul here? an old wherry run down by a coal barge! Damme, stand back!"

"Who the devil are you," demanded the unwelcome visitor, sternly, "that board strangers like a red squall, without leave or notice?"

"Who am I?" replied Harry. "I'm the happiest dog on the Thames; got the best craft, and the prettiest sweetheart; will pull a match with any man between bridges; know how to serve a friend, 'specially an old one; always pay my rent; can wash my own shirts; and hate lawyers.—Now, who the devil are you?"

"Don't resist the law," said Snatchem,

pushing up the hat from his eyes;
"take my advice."

"So I will, lad," answered Harry,
again knocking his hat over his eyes.
The watermen followed his example,
and the miserable Snatchem got terribly
hustled about.

"Don't, lads, don't," said Sam
Sculler, interposing. "Hark ye, Harry,
you are a fine fellow, and I know will
listen to reason. This is Harry
Heartley's debt ; he, poor fellow, is
dead, and——"

"Harry dead!" interrupted our hero;
"poor Harry! But who's this gentleman that's come to shoot us all ?"

"I demand payment of the debt,"
replied the stranger.

"When the devil demands his due,
look out," observed Watchful Waxend.
"You'll be saying you knew me, but
I'll send notice that I never kept such
company."

"A truce to this foolery," said the
man; "am I to be paid, or must the
man go to prison ?"

"Why, look ye, sir," answered Harry,
"if your demand be a just one it would
be folly to resist."

"That's right," remarked Snatchem ;
"take my advice."

"It would be in vain to resist, as I
have said," continued Harry, "but you
would never be so stone-hearted as to
strip an old man of the hard earnings of
sixty years of weary toil, and that, too,
for a debt not his own? To pay your
demand he must sell his boat, then what
remains for him? He must go to the
workhouse, the last resting place in the
world you would send him to."

"All the preaching in the world won't
talk me out of my debt," returned the
stranger determinedly; "my money : or
a prison for him."

"Shame—shame!" shouted the persons present.

"Hold, friends," ejaculated Harry,
"here, I will be bail for him, and Will
Wallit, here, will be bound with me."

"Ay, that I will," replied the landlord.

"Thank you, lads, thank you," said
Sculler, gratefully.

"And," said our hero, turning to the
stranger, "do you hear? do you and
your devil's imp beat down to the old
man's house in half an hour; and if my

Poll is what I think her, we'll board you
in the smoke of a salute you little
expect. Lead the way, landlord. Sculler, cheerly, old heart. 'Tisn't every
squall that capsizes a boat. Cheerly—
cheerly !"

Thus saying, the kind-hearted Harry
hastily quitted the house, amidst shouts
of admiration from the persons assembled.

———

CHAPTER II.

MARY MAYBUD AND ABIGAIL HOLD-
FORTH.—AN ACT OF NOBLE GENE-
ROSITY.—A MAIDEN'S REWARD.—
HAPPY PROSPECTS.

WE must now introduce the reader
to Mary Maybud, who was seated at
needlework in the comfortable little
parlour of old Sculler's house, and rather
a pretty rustic looking girl standing
before her. We must not trust ourselves
to describe the charms of Harry Halliyard's sweetheart ; let it suffice to say
that they were perfection itself.

"And so, you see," observed the
female who was standing before her.
"seeing you at work, ma'am, I thought
I'd make bold to ask you."

"Well, but my good girl," remarked
our heroine, "London is a large place,
and the industrious never need starve in
it. What trade are you ?"

"I'm a shoe-binder, ma'am, from
Bullock Smithey," replied the damsel ;
"I'm a girl of moral perpensities, can
sing a psalm, or beat a carpet ; and as
for turning a corner in the binding way,
leave me alone for neatness."

"But what made you come away
from your own town ?" asked Mary.

"There it is," answered Abigail (for
that was her name), "one of my moral
perpensities got the better of me—I
fell in love."

"And not being able to meet a return
you ran away from the object ?"

"No, I run'd after the object. He
was obliged to emigrate through a misfortune : a wicked hussy swore a filia-
tion to him."

"Then you should endeavour to
forget him," returned Mary.

"I can't forget him," returned
Abigail, "and I thought it was best to

come away, for fear they should swear something of that sort to me."

"I am sorry I cannot serve you," said Mary. "I am an orphan, and obliged to work for every meal. I am content to do so, because I think, somehow, that the bread we have earned must eat the sweater. I am a stranger, too, to London; I never travel further from Putney than just down the river in Harry's boat to Westminster Bridge—yes, I once made a voyage to Hungerford Market. So, you see, my good girl, I could direct you but badly. But if you had written to this lover of yours——"

"I did, bless you!"

"Then you know his directions?"

"Oh, yes," replied Abigail, "the girl at the huxter's shop wrote three times for me, and I saw the letters carefully directed, 'Mr. Watchful Waxend, London.'"

"So, so," said our heroine, aside, "Mr. Watchful. You had better look in again towards evening," she said to Abigail; "I have an old friend here who can perhaps advise you."

"I'm much obliged to you," returned the latter; "be so good as to say that I can turn my hand to anything: I can hem and seam, and trundle a mop; nurse a baby, or turn a mangle; I can bind shoes, and make hay; milk a cow, or sing a psalm; and don't forget to say that I'm a girl of strong moral perpensities." With these words the loquacious damsel curtseyed to Mary, and hurried from the room.

"So, so," said our heroine, when she was gone, "here's a discovery for the Bishop of Battersea, as my Harry calls Waxend! Oh, dear! I wish our marriage was over! And yet I'm sure, if Harry were to ask me, I should put it off for another year. Harry's to row for another wherry in a month. La! if he were to win that, as he did the last! that might alter affairs. Mr. and Mrs. Halliyard, with two boats of their own! I'd have one with a white awning fringed all round, and a flag at the stem, for Richmond parties, and 'tother for everyday work; Joe should row that. I like Joe, because he's Harry's friend, and he's so good-natured and poetical, and because he's so kind to me; yes, he should row the everyday one, and my Harry should

sit like a king in the other, and then, when there happened to be no company, he should just pull me and the little ones down to——La! what am I thinking about? We have neither got the boat nor the little ones yet."

At that moment Joe Tiller entered the room, and advancing eagerly towards the beauteous and innocent maiden, he said—

"Ah, my pretty Mary, I've been longing all the day to have a peep at your blue eyes. Why, what's the matter?"

"I don't like your singing about Poll this, and Poll that," replied Mary, pouting. "My name's Mary."

"I mean no disrespect, Mary," said Joe, "but ain't you called Pretty Poll of Putney?"

"Oh, yes," returned our heroine, "and there's a parrot at the public-house; she calls herself pretty-poll of the King's Arms."

"Well, well," said Joe, "forgive me."

"Oh, kill not my heart with a frown from your eyes,
For if you look angry, the poor flutterer dies."

"Well," observed Mary, mildly, "I'm sure I do not frown—I'm not angry, Joe; only, you see, Harry is in a fair way to be a most respectable proprietor of boats, and he wouldn't like his wife to be called Poll Halliyard this, and Poll Halliyard that. Decent people must have decent comportment."

"Very true, Mary," coincided Joe Tiller; "every word you say is wisdom.

"There's some folks speak wisdom and sense every minute,
Some, when they open their mouth, put their foot in it."

But here, Mary, I've brought you a present," he added, taking a ring from a paper. "Here's a ring, a keeper. When Harry gives you a plainer ring, but of more value—ha! then, Mary, put this on—his friend's present, as a guard to protect his own. Harry loves you dearly, Mary, but not more than Joe loves you—as—as a friend."

"Yes, Joe," returned the maiden, in her sweetest accents, "I know you do, and I'll wear your ring, and dance with you at our wedding."

"Will you, though?" said Tiller, elated.

Before our heroine had time to return any answer, the voice of her lover was heard shouting without—

"Yo ho! the pretty Mary, there!"

"Oh, here he comes," said our heroine, and then playfully imitating him, she cried—

"Yo ho! there, the saucy Harry—yo ho!"

"Yo ho!" repeated Harry. "Now a long pull, old one."

"I forgot to tell you," observed Joe. "Don't be alarmed; Harry sent me forward that you mightn't be alarmed, but poor old Sculler——"

"What—what of the old man?" gasped forth Mary, in an agitated voice.

"Is going—to—to prison."

"To prison!" repeated the astonished girl, and at that moment her lover entering the room, she ran towards him, ejaculating—

"Oh, Harry, the old man, my dear Harry! Ah!" she added, as Sculler made his appearance, and embraced him, "you are not gone, then? What—what is the meaning of this?"

She had scarcely spoken the words when Brandon (for that was the name of the repulsive looking stranger), Snatchem, and several of the watermen who had been guests at the Crown and Crosier, also entered the room, and Mary could not help trembling as an irresistible feeling of apprehension came over her.

"What men are those?" she eagerly demanded. "Is it true—is it true?"

"Come, come, my lass," replied Harry, "cheer up. Why, you are as troubled as Chelsea Reach in a gale. Only shipped a little of the bilge water of misfortune: you and I must lend him a hand to bale him dry. Hark ye, lass, come here."

He took her hand, and leading her to another part of the room, they soon became immersed in private conversation.

"She's a pretty 'un, isn't she?" said Snatchem to Brandon.

"Silence!" commanded the latter, peremptorily, and at the same time fixing one of his blackest and most disagreeable scowls upon him.

"Got a nice little ankle," continued Snatchem, "a small waist, but a particularly nice little article of a foot; not like a pick-axe, as much behind as before."

"Fool! hold your tongue!" said his companion, surlily. Harry now come forward, at the same time saying to his sweetheart—"Go and fetch it, then, Mary, will you? There's a little queen; and I'll talk a bit to these visitors."

Mary departed from the room, and Harry addressing himself first to old Sam Sculler, said—

"Come, old heart, we're on the right tack, so just listen to me. Hark ye, my black looking friend," he continued, crossing to and eyeing Brandon, who met his gaze with ferocious defiance; "it strikes me, after all, that you're a sort of a kind of a pirate. The paper you've brought is right, but how the devil did you run foul of it? Come, show your reckoning, as they say at sea. Who are you?"

"Who am I?" replied Black Brandon sternly. "I am one who thinks the frog of the river looks well when he questions the shark of the sea."

"That observation's true in your log," returned our hero, coolly;— "shark, indeed; but when we get the shark in the shallows, let him look out."

"The frog would look pretty in the Atlantic," retorted Brandon, significantly. "I never forget an insult."

"Tell me how I may insult a callous heart like yours," said the young waterman, "and I'll do it, that your memory may last for ever. Ah! here comes the best girl in the world, with a load of ammunition that shall founder your cockle-shell."

Mary now re-entered the room, bearing in her hand a canvas bag.

"Give it me, my lass," said her lover. "Look at that girl; she's life and all the world to me; even your iron soul must tell you I'm a happy fellow, for she loves me. Bless her blue eyes! they are Heaven's stars to me."

"Harry—Harry! remember!" said Mary, blushing.

"I must talk to 'em Mary," he replied, "and just now my heart feels like a member of parliament—it could speechify till a dissolution · but, hang it girl, I hope to more purpose. Well, as I say," he continued, addressing himself to Brandon, "we love each other; we were both poor. I won a wherry; it enabled me to earn and to save money; she worked hard, too. We agreed to marry when we had saved thirty pounds; there's the sum," throwing the bag at the feet of Brandon. "Your debt is thirty-two: will you take it? No; there's the black demon of avarice grinning in every feature of your ugly phizog. But there, sir," he added, throwing down another bag, "I have earned a pound to-day, that makes thirty-one, and if you don't take that, and discharge the old man, damme, I'll give you a pound's worth of drubbing to get a full receipt."

As Harry spoke, he threw of his jacket, and placing himself in a fighting attitude, he showed that he meant what he said; but Mary, who was alarmed, interposed.

"Stay, Harry, stay!" she said. "It were a pity an humble and honest man should ever foul his hands by contest with either a tyrant or a rogue. I don't mean to say, sir, that you are either one or the other. But there's another pound, earned by honest labour; take your full demand, and quit the house, before the gallant spirit of my lover bursts the bounds of prudence, and makes you do it by the window."

Black Brandon bit his lips, and frowned fiercely upon them: but he, nevertheless, took up the money, and laying down the paper, he said—

"This is all I want; you can talk about honesty when I am gone. It's not a saleable commodity, and I know nothing about it. But, hark ye, sir," he continued, turning to Harry fiercely, "I have already told you I never forget an insult. We shall meet again. Come, Snatchem!"

"She's a very pretty one for all that," said the latter, "though there is a bit of the brimstone, too."

Harry turned and moved towards Brandon, but he rushed hastily from the room, and left them to themselves.

"Why, old man," observed Harry, turning to Sculler, "the tears are in your eyes; give us your hand. Poll and I have only to wait another year or two, and you are happy."

"But I have prevented your being so," said Sculler.

"Pshaw! never mind that," said Joe Tiller. "Harry, you're a noble fellow —Mary, you're a queen. I'll help you; —I'll never go to the Crown and Crosier; but every farthing I can save you shall have. We'll soon have the thirty pounds.

"With a long pull, and a strong pull, we'll shoot the bridge in style,
And we'll have the thirty pounds, yet be merry all the while."

"What a happy man I am!" ejaculated our hero, "though the shark has sheered off with the gold. Hang the mopusses! what care I for the world's ups and downs, while I've my Poll and my partner Joe?"

"You were made for each other," said Sam Sculler, "and I am the cause of a continued separation."

"Not so," returned Mary; "the money we have paid was Harry's—my earnings were but trifling; and I love him more for sacrificing the means of our marriage than for earning them; for that sacrifice was made for you, my second father. Oh, Harry, why should we not struggle as well together as man and wife, as singly? If you think my hand a reward sought-out for your noble devotion, take it—I will be yours even to-morrow."

"Eh, what! mine—to-morrow? My dear Mary!" exclaimed her lover, half mad with joy, and kissing her; "run, Joe, run down to Tommy Tearepsalm, the parish clerk, tell him I am to be married to-morrow;—run, old man, run to Will Wallit, tell him to send me in a store of grog; we'll be merry to-night.—Mary mine! what will old dame say? Married to-morrow! Cut and run. My dear Mary—bear a hand —bear a hand!"

He took the arm of the beauteous Mary as he spoke, and in ecstasies hurried from the house, followed by his friends.

CHAPTER III.

THE FESTIVITY AT DAME HALLIYARD'S COTTAGE.—THE INTERRUPTION.—BLACK BRANDON'S REVENGE.—THE PARTING OF THE LOVERS.

IT was a neat and pretty cottage that our hero and his aged mother resided in; and before it was a beautifully arranged little garden, looking over the river. And what an excellent old woman was dame Halliyard! so proud of her son, and so fondly attached to the innocent and gentle Mary. At the time we introduce her to the reader, we find her busily engaged outside her dwelling spreading a table, near which was seated on a stool, smoking and drinking, the Bishop of Battersea.

"And so," said the dame, addressing herself to her companion, "Harry said I was to welcome some friends?"

"Yes," answered Waxend, and drinking; "welcome them with a joyous spirit. I feel that thou hast made me welcome. I should like a little heeltap, a little more wax on the thread."

"You shall have it," said the dame, replenishing his glass, "though you're rather s'rang now."

"The juggling of the spirit," he returned, "is mighty within me; I want to preach, and I can't till I've finished my pipe."

"And, so, my boy, (bless him!)" remarked Dame Halliyard, "is going to have a merry-making? Well, well, I suppose Mary and he have made up the match. Some mothers wouldn't like a young wife coming home, and turning them out of office; but I know the wench—a better doesn't breathe by the old river."

"Ah!" sighed Waxend, "women are troublesome spirits."

"What do you mean?" demanded the dame, sharply; "you never suffered by them."

"Haven't I, though?" returned the Bishop; "their love has been my ruin; I looked too much after the flesh. I worked very hard at my trade, but I couldn't help leaving a few *waxends* about."

"Pooh!" said the dame, "you should have got married, as my Harry means to do. There's everything ready for him; there's his pipe, and Mary's favourite mug, and old Sam Sculler's backey-bax. Oh, what a happy old woman I am to have two such children!"

"Mother! Dame Halliyard! ahoy, there!" now shouted the welcome voice of Harry outside, and directly he and Mary, Sculler, Joe, and several watermen made their appearance.

"Oh, my dear boy," said the old woman, advancing eagerly to her son, "welcome, all of you! Mary, my lass, give us a buss; well—eh, when is it to be? have you agreed? Um! can I have a new cap made? Hark ye, old Sam, you and I'll dance a jig at the wedding."

"That we will, old lass," replied Sculler. "Ah, you don't know!"

"Why, what's the matter?" inquired the dame, eagerly.

"Come here," said Sculler. drawing her aside.

"Well, Mary," said her lover, "here's my Lord Bishop, all ready to marry us. How does your reverence feel to-day? Is the spirit strong within you? We've news, news that will shake it."

"Thank your good mother," replied Waxend, very drunk, and looking at his glass, "it's pretty strong; "I had it waxed a little more."

"Master Watchful," said Mary, drily, "were you ever in love?"

"Twenty-seven times," answered the Bishop.

"Oh, shameful!" ejaculated our heroine.

"Do you know a place called Bullock Smithey?" asked Harry.

"I have heard of it," answered Waxend, rather staggered.

"Were you ever in love there?" inquired Joe.

"The spirit was strong."

"Did a girl ever swear—" said Harry.

"Don't mention it," interrupted the Bishop.

"A girl from Bullock Smithey is here," observed our hero.

"Here!" exclaimed Waxend, alarmed, "then I must fly."

"But she will see you," said Joe Tiller.

"She shan't," he returned—"it's not mine; mine are like wax dolls, with hair like bristles, and eyes as sharp as an owl. I'll fly! I'll not be made a victim of. One more sup, and I'll exile myself as far as Tuttle Street. Farewell, Battersea—I'll—I'll not be sacrificed!"

Thus saying, the Bishop of Battersea staggered away in great terror, amid the laughter of them all.

"Boy," observed Dame Halliyard, coming forward, and taking the hand of her son, "you've done a noble action; hang the pence, Mary and I will soon save it up again; there's a grunter yet in the stye—the wherry's tight and light—you are strong and willing, and Mary's active and industrious. As for me, I suppose I shan't be able to reckon much on myself after a little. Baby's clothes are tedious things for an old woman—eh, boy? Eh, Mary? Ha! ha! ha!"

"Come," said Harry, "let us be merry; take a seat, dad. Joe, run yourself ashore. Mary and I moor together. Mother, what matters it which way the wind blows, so that our hearts are true, and we have no leaks in our conscience? Fill out a bumber—let's drink a health to Mary—I'm so happy we're to be married to-morrow."

"Fill! fill!" said the dame; "I'll drink that—I'll drink that."

While they were thus busy regaling, a boat appeared in sight, filled with sailors, and soon afterwards Black Brandon and another man cautiously landed, and the former having pointed to our hero and Joe Tiller, said to his companion in a low voice—

"Those are the men—fine young fellows."

He then retired. The sailors approached silently. Harry snatched a kiss from his sweetheart, and was about to drink her health, when the man who had landed with Brandon tapped him on the shoulder, and he started, and stared with amazement to find himself surrounded by strangers, whose appearance was by no means prepossessing.

"You must come with me," said the man.

"Who are you?" demanded our hero, rising hastily.

"The king wants men," was the laconic reply.

"What do you mean?" asked Harry.

"You'll make a devilish good sailor," answered the man, "and must serve him."

"Pressed!" exclaimed Harry and Joe in a breath.

"Pressed!" gasped forth the terrified Mary. "Oh! no, no!"

"He'll come back an officer, my girl," said the seaman, "and he'll have his friend with him."

"No, you're out of your reckoning there," returned Joe Tiller. "I serve a fire-office; here's my protection."

The man looked at the paper which Joe presented to him, and then said—

"All's right—you're safe."

"And must he go?" ejaculated our heroine, in a voice half choked with emotion; "oh, sir, for pity—"

"Pity!" answered the fellow, "it arn't among the articles of the press service, my pretty dear."

"Right," observed Harry; "fiends incapable of pity first gave birth to the idea, and by fiends only is it advocated. What! force a man from his happy home to defend a country whose laws deprive him of his liberty? But I must submit. Yet, oh! proud lordlings and rulers of the land! do ye think my arm will fall as heavily on the foe as though I were a volunteer?—No! I shall strike for the hearts of those I leave weeping for my absence, without one thought of the green fields or flowing rivers of a country that treats me as a slave."

"Duty is duty," returned the man, "and must be done."

"Ah!" said Joe Tiller,

"So says the thief when he serves the devil,
And does it the readier, 'cause its evil."

Mary was almost fainting, but her lover pressed her with the fondest emotion to his bosom, and stifling his own feelings as well as he could, he said—

"Come, Mary lass, cheer up! I'll return an admiral—be faithful to you in every clime. This little lock of hair shall be the sheet anchor of our constancy. Bless you, mother, I must go."

"You must, boy," replied the poor old woman, drying her tears, and stifling her sobs. "I know you wish to do your duty as a man; but, for the sake of the young lass, and the old lass, too, don't be rash, my Harry. Be a hero— I know you will. God bless you!"

"Dear mother!" our hero with difficulty ejaculated,—"Mary, bid me good bye—a kiss, lass! You will be true to me?"

Mary pointed solemnly towards Heaven, but she had not the power to speak.

"All's over!" continued Harry, after a brief pause, "I'm ready, lads.—Joe, you are my friend;—take care of the wherry—protect Mary and my mother—be to them as I would. God bless you! Mary!—I have your promise, Joe?"

"You have," answered the latter, fervently.

Harry pressed his hand, as he cried, in a broken voice—

"Farewell! Mother!—Mary!—God bless you all!"

It would be vain to seek to describe the agony of poor Mary and Dame Halliyard; they still clung to Harry, and by the most piteous looks they eloquently appealed to those who were insensible to every feeling of humanity. Black Brandon now once more made his appearance on the scene, and advancing to the man who had led the others on, he said—

"Why do you stand palavering there with the swab, Bowse? Seize him!—You see," he added, turning upon Harry a fiendish look of triumph, "I never forget an insult!"

"Ah, villain!" exclaimed our hero, "art thou here?"

He darted fiercely upon Brandon, but he was overpowered by numbers, and dragged away, Mary fainting in the arms of Joe Tiller. We must draw a veil over the scene which followed.

CHAPTER IV.

HARRY HALLIYARD ON BOARD THE POLYPHEMUS.—HIS GALLANT CONDUCT.—BLACK BRANDON AGAIN.—THE SLAVE SHIP.—ZINGA THE NEGRO.—THE CHASE.—THE ENGAGEMENT.—THE DEATH OF BLACK BRANDON.

FOUR years have elapsed since the occurrence of the events recorded in the previous chapter, and during that period Harry Halliyard had eminently distinguished himself on board of the Polyphemus, one of the finest vessels in the British navy, and he was the darling of the crew, and the pride of his captain and the officers.

In turning over the pages of history, we contemplate with enthusiasm the martial prowess of our ancestors, who were called to defend not only their own liberties, but those of mankind. Britain has maintained her proud supremacy among nations through a long series of ages; trampled down stern oppression, that threatened and (with her own glorious exception) had well nigh spread abroad universal anarchy; and crowned the glorious work by giving peace to the world and freedom to the slave. All honour to our wooden walls, and the bold hearts that have ever throbbed within the hardy sailor's breast. Harry Halliyard proved himself to be one of the bravest and most generous Jack tars of unconquered and unconquerable old England. Fear was a stranger to him, danger he smiled at; he was as bold, courageous, and intrepid as a lion. No care or sorrow disturbed his mind, except when his thoughts wandered to the lovely lass he had left behind him; and even then, the hope that he should shortly behold her again buoyed him up, and endowed him with patience and resignation during their painful separation,

On the quarter-deck of the Polyphemus were assembled Captain Oakheart, Lieutenant Manly, and the other officers of the vessel

"Gentlemen," said the captain, "the duty for which we are assembled, though a painful, is an important one. To preserve the necessary discipline, we are compelled to reprimand a brave man for an action that confers honour on the British flag; yet, while obliged to condemn, we shall applaud and honour in our hearts one of the best seamen that ever trod a plank—one of the most fearless spirits that ever handled a cutlass. His very courage must be restricted with severity, or his example and extraordinary success will banish subordination from the fleet"

Harry Halliyard now made his appearance on deck, guarded by a party of marines, and bowed respectfully to the officers.

"You have been four years on board the Polyphemus," said the captain.

"Ay, your honour," answered Harry.

"You were a volunteer?"

"No, your honour," returned our hero; "I was a pressed man—pressed the day before I was to be married to the prettiest and best lass in the world."

As the hardy and honest-hearted young seaman thus spoke, he took the lock of hair he had received from his sweetheart from his bosom, and kissed it fondly.

"You are a brave fellow, Halliyard," observed the captain.

"Thank your honour," replied the former, "there's no scarcity of 'em aboard this craft."

"Right," coincided the captain; "I am proud of my crew, but brave men should never forget obedience to their superiors. You have forgotten your duty. You have been promoted since you came on board;—you are a petty officer, and Mr. Manly has ever been your friend; yet you have proved yourself ungrateful."

"Oh, your honour!" ejaculated Harry, "don't say that—it cuts me to the soul! Do you think I can ever forget that Mr. Manly did all that he could to get me my pretty Poll's letter that was lying for me at Trieste, when we were up the Mediterranean? And he would have got it, too, but sudden orders came for us to join the fleet in the West Injees. My log wouldn't be worth keeping if I hadn't got that in large letters. And then your honour's been so kind to me since I've been aboard, that you've almost made me forget the cruel law that took me from a young bride. So, what with your kindness, and the ship (bless her!) being called the Polly—Polyphemus, keeping me constantly in mind of somebody at home, I've begun to be almost happy. Ingratitude! May I spring a leak, and go down in the black sea of contempt if ever I take such a villanous cargo on board!"

"And yet, Halliyard," said Captain Oakheart, "you have dared to disobey orders. Mr. Manly, state your charges against him."

"I must preface," remarked Manly, "that in thus complaining of him I am performing an imperative duty, with which no private feeling dare to interfere. He will respect me the more for a conscientious discharge of it when I publicly avow that he has twice saved my life."

"Oh, your honour," returned our hero, "say no more of that. I'd have done it even for Sulky Sam, the cook's mate, though he is the most disagreeable swab in the whole ship's crew."

"Proceed, Manly, with your charges," desired the captain.

"After orders had been passed to lie close," continued the lieutenant, at the same time it was quite evident how painful to him was the duty he had to perform, "we having in the night crept in and anchored under the enemy's guns, he secretly persuaded twelve of the crew to a breach of discipline. They lowered themselves over the side into the ship's boat, and, at the imminent hazard of the lives of all, and the destruction of the commodore's plans, they attempted the cutting out of an armed store-ship, loaded with ammunition and supplies."

"Avast there, your honour," cried Harry, hastily, but respectfully, "there's a bit of an error in your charge. We *did* cut her out, and brought her clear off, in spite of the fire of all their batteries, and the bellowing and blazing of their flotilla to boot. And, if your honour only remembers the prisoners we brought in—there were just two to a man—six and twenty Spaniards, and we without a scratch, except Georgy Gunnel, who would be so venturesome as to fight six——"

"Still you were wrong," interrupted Captain Oakheart.

"Wrong, your honour?" repeated our hero; "begging your honour's pardon, a great deal of it was your honour's fault."

"Mine!"

"Ay, your honour, with respect be it spoke. Don't you remember when you had me on the quarter to give me a little jobation, because in the action of the day before I took the trouble to go and fetch the Frenchman's flag to tie round Mr. Manly's wound; don't you remember that, as I was standing by, you pointed out where the store-ship lay, and said it would be a good thing, a glorious thing to disappoint the enemy of all the powder and stores on board ? Ah! I see your honour recollects. And you said, too, it was an impossibility. Now comes my fault. Says I to myself, I don't think so ; I know about a dozen as would do it, and, as our chaplain says, damme, if I don't try! And so I axed them, and they said yes; and we tried it, and we did it, and that's all I can say about it, your honour."

Captain Oakheart could with difficulty conceal his enthusiastic admiration of the indomitable courage of the intrepid and generous-hearted seaman; but he replied—

"Now, mark, what might have been the consequence had you failed : we were in the presence of an enemy of superior strength; the policy of the commodore was to hem them with their heavy vessels in shore : day by day we had been creeping on them, till, on the night in question, we had taken up a position which, with every advantage on our side, must have brought them to a battle. Now, as I observed before, had you failed, our resources and position would have been known, and the prospects of the war totally destroyed in consequence."

"But as it was, your honour," said Harry, "they thought the devil was among them, and standing, at all hazards, out to sea, dropped, like pigeons, into the commodore's hands. Your honour will admit that, although you punish the cause——"

At that moment a midshipman hastily made his appearance, exclaiming—

"Sail on the larboard quarter, your honour."

"What is she ?" interrogated the captain.

"Can't make her out," answered the midshipman.

"Jump aloft, Halliyard !" ordered Captain Oakheart; "take my glass; you've a quick eye : report her build."

"I'm a prisoner, your honour," replied Harry.

"We'll take your parole for the present."

"Thank your honour," he remarked, going, but suddenly returning, he added, "I suppose, your honour, I mustn't board this craft, whatever she is, till— till I can lay my grappling irons on her!"

"Gentlemen," said Oakheart, when our hero had departed to obey his instructions, "each to his quarters ; we will resume when this business is over."

The midshipman again made his appearance hurriedly.

"Halliyard reports a brig," he observed, "armed, a good sailer —no colours."

"My life on it he is right," ejaculated Captain Oakheart. "Be brisk, gentlemen, we may have warm work in store. To your quarters—quick ! quick !"

The officers obeyed, and soon all was bustle and active preparation on board the Polyphemus. The vessel was indeed a suspicious and awkward-looking craft, and between the decks of which we must now conduct the reader. It was a slave ship, commanded by Black Brandon, and numerous unhappy wretches might be seen chained to the floor, guarded by a seaman, heavily armed, walking to and fro, carrying a whip. Black Brandon, with a glass, was standing at one of the open ports, on the look out. His brow was stern, and his whole demeanour determined, though excited.

"Curses on her !" he exclaimed, "she walks the water like a witch ;—are all the black cattle on board ?"

"Ay, ay," replied a sailor.

"Where, in the name of the fiend, is Bowse ?" demanded Brandon. "She keeps the weathergage in spite of us ; and yet the Black Bet is no skulker on a wind. Hark ye, ye nigger animals, if I hear the least noise, or see the least signs of grumbling among you, I'll make shark's meat of every one of ye. Ah !" he added, again looking out of the port with his glass, "her sails rise above the water as fast as the cloud of a white squall."

A poor slave, heavily ironed, and the mournful expression of whose features plainly showed the intense agony of soul he was enduring, now issued from the hold, and creeping up to Brandon, he fell on his knees at his feet.

"What the devil do you want ?" demanded the ruffian fiercely.

"I would ask mercy, master," answered the poor fellow; "poor Zinga begs his wife."

"Your wife, fool !" returned Brandon. "She's in my cabin ; and had she been kinder, you might have had your arms and legs at liberty."

"I'll wear your fetters, master," said Zinga, in piteous accents; "see, they eat into my flesh, yet I will be happy; let me have my wife, my Zamba!"

"You thought to escape me, did you?" said Brandon.

"I followed but the impulses of nature," returned the slave, humbly. "Three years ago you tore me from my country, from the presence of my parents and the arms of the maid who is now my wife; regardless of my shrieks and cries, you dragged me away to slavery. My heart was broken, and if I murmured, the lash was my only answer. Yet, master, I did not seek revenge; I could have had it. Yes, one night when you were sleeping, my knife was at your throat, but I thought of the words that the good white man said to me at my own home, when he taught us his religion, and I conquered the temptation. Well, I served you faithfully: you again sought my country to make more slaves; I fled to join my Zamba: was it a crime? Oh! give her to me, and I will be your slave for ever! In pity to my agony spare her—give her to my arms unharmed!"

"Back, beast!" replied the miscreant, fiercely, and striking him violently. Zinga staggered, but wound up to a pitch of frenzy, he made a weapon of his chain, and rushed towards him, and was about to strike him, when Brandon drew his sword, and presented it at him; a seaman drew a pistol and cocked it, and was about to fire, when the blood-thirsty monster preventing him, cried—

"Stop, if we throw him overboard, his carcass may betray us to those bull-dogs. Give him the whip, and keep an eye upon him. Let us get clear of this hell-cat in chase, and his hours are numbered."

The seamen immediately obeyed the inhuman orders of Brandon, and applied the whip to the back of poor Zinga with brutal severity. Zinga groaned and writhed beneath the torture inflicted, till, overcome with pain, he crouched piteously at the feet of Brandon, who felled him with another ferocious blow, and then burst into a loud laugh, while the seaman thrust Zinga among the other slaves.

Ben Bowse now entered with a glass in his hand.

"What news?" demanded Brandon.

"I've made her out," answered Bowse, "though her hull isn't above the water, for I know the cut of her jib. 'Tis the Polyphemus sloop, she as I was boatswain of, and deserted from when I fell in with you. We must make more way than we do now, or she'll walk over us: 'tis the fastest craft in the service."

"She's a flying devil!" said Brandon, looking out. The distant report of a gun was now heard. "Boom!—she's began to talk; we must lighten the Pet. Boom again! Ah, chatter away. If we can keep out of the reach of her long speechifiers for another hour we may double her in the dark. Some of our heavy metal must go overboard."

He hurried away as he thus spoke.

"It'll be all of no use, Master Brandon," said Bowse, looking out. "See, her sails flap! She's about to take a longer reach."

Another report of a gun was heard, and our old friend, the Bishop of Battersea, but so metamorphosed that it was almost impossible to recognise him, now made an appearance.

"Oh, Lord! oh, Lord!" he cried, much alarmed, "I wish I was at Battersea! I'd better have fathered all the children of Bullock Smithey, than been kidnapped here, and treated like a white nigger. Now I shall be shot at like a piece of wax stuck in the middle of a target."

A great noise and confusion was now heard on the deck.

"There goes Black Tommy overboard!" said Ben Bowse.

"Oh, dear!" remarked Waxend, turning to the negroes; "they'll be coming down here for some of you black Tommys soon."

Loud shouts and noise again proceeded from the deck.

"There goes his brother Bill," observed Bowse.

"My spirit sinks!" ejaculated the Bishop; "when they have settled all the bills, they will dot and carry one with me. Oh, Mr. Bowse, who is it they are throwing overboard? How many is there before it comes to my turn?"

"P-haw, fool!" replied Bowes, "it's the two guns, our heavy thirty-two pounders. Ha! she feels it, but not enough. Right, Brandon; better lose our metal than our lives."

"Right," said Waxend, "I'll lose anything rather than life."

Black Brandon entered hastily, more excited than he had been before.

"She nears us fast," he cried; "will it never be night? Curses on her! I've ordered Rasper to cut eight inches into her ribs; let her shake a bit, so that we can run under the rocks of Martinique: d—n the repairs!"

"Oh, if he was to cut eight inches into my ribs!" said Waxend.

"Bravo, Bet!" cried Brandon, again looking out; "she'll better them yet."

At that moment a loud crash was heard, followed by the report of a gun.

"It's all over with us," said Brandon. "No, curse it, no!—the black cattle shall feed the fishes first, every mother's son of 'em. Ah! hark ye, Bowse; do you take charge of the papers, tie a shot to them, and if we're spoken to let the fishes read 'em. What now?" he demanded of one of his crew, who entered hastily.

"They've carried away the quarter-bulwarks," answered the man; "shall we heave to?"

"The first man that speaks of surrender I'll scatter his brains upon the deck!" replied the ruffian, fiercely.

"I'll hide myself," observed Waxend, "for I'm sure to speak of it."

He got into a large empty cask, as he muttered these words to himself, and stooping down concealed himself.

"Stay," said Brandon, speaking to Bowse, "a thought strikes me. It's getting dark; pick out one of these niggers—we'll give him a floating bath; if they shorten sail to pick him up, we gain time; if they don't, the sharks will get him."

"Oh, lor!" muttered the alarmed Waxend, peeping out of the cask, "they'll be mistaking me for a nigger."

"Bowse, I have it," observed Brandon "bring me the woman from my cab."

Bowse directly made his exit, and Zinga, starting forward, again knelt at the feet of Black Brandon.

"Master!" he ejaculated, in tones of the most earnest supplication, "you will give me my wife? oh, master! mercy, master!"

"Ay, ay," laughed Brandon, ironically.

"Oh!" cried poor Zinga, mad with joy, "Master! good master!"

He had scarcely given utterance to the words, when the sailors brought Zamba forward, and the scene which followed was sufficient to move a heart of adamant to pity. They rushed into each other's arms, and gave expression to the powerful emotions that agitated their bosoms in the most mournful and convulsive sobs.

"Tear them asunder!" commanded Brandon, fiercely, and the sailors obeyed.

"No, no!" exclaimed Zinga, piteously, "you mistake! Master Captain has given me my Zamba, my own Zamba! Master will make Zinga happy!"

"Tie her in an empty hogshead," said the villain; "let her gently over the side; they'll hear her shrieks."

The men seized her: she screamed frantically; Zinga broke desperately from those who held him, and rushing into her arms again, embraced her. But they dragged her shrieking away, her unhappy husband clinging to her until he was forced away by the sailors.

"You are a white man," he said solemnly, turning to Brandon; "can your own God forgive you?" He sank insensible as he spoke. Brandon turned away indifferently from him, and again looked out. The shrieks of poor Zamba were soon heard, as they were wafted on the air, and amid the shouts of those on deck. They grew fainter and fainter, till they were lost in the distance, and she was seen through the port-holes floating fast away.

"'Tis done," said Brandon, with a fiendish look of triumph.

"'Tis a bad act," observed Bowse, who had just entered with the papers which the slave captain had ordered him to take charge of.

"'Tis good policy," returned the miscreant. "See, they shorten sail to pick her up!—Now's our time!—One or two more, and we defy them!—Are all the papers there?"

"They are," answered Bowse.

"We gain upon them!" cried Brandon; "yes, they are changing their course to snap at my black bait. I'll upon deck. Have the husband ready for the gudgeons.—And, d'ye hear, if it comes to the worst, you know what to do with the papers?"

"Ay, ay," replied Bowse. Brandon then departed, and the former looked out.

"All right," he said, "the poor thing will be saved—ah! them Polyphemus lads are of the right sort.—What a fool have I been to leave her! I mustn't live to be found out."

Zinga now recovered faom his state of insensibility, and rushing to the port, he cried in frantic accents, as he strained his eyes over the deep in the direction which his beloved Zamba was being hurried away.

"Ha, she is there!" he exclaimed, "I see her arms raised for help; and, as the wind comes, I hear her wild shrieks! My brain will burst.—Ah! the ship is shortening sail!—they put out a boat! —they near her!—one moment more, and—oh, misery!—the cask is filling!— they will be too late!—my eyes will start!—she sinks—she's lost!—no, no! —a sailor plunges into the waves!— I cannot see them now!—yes, he rises! —she is in his arms—they take her into the boat,—she is saved!" he added, sinking on his knees, clasping his hands vehemently together, and raising them gratefully towards Heaven. "Thank God! thanks! thanks!"

There was a momentary pause, which was almost instantaneously followed by a terrific crash. Then there was a loud report of cannon, intermingled with shouts and lamentations, and the slave ship had received a fearful shock, which it did not seem likely she could long survive. Bowse now tied the papers to a ball, and placed them near the hatches.

"The game's up," he said; "they've shot away her mast!" He snatched up the papers, and throwing them through the port into the sea, added—

"Now, then, to die like a man!"

He then hurried away with the sailors and made his way towards the deck. Waxend, when he saw that they were gone, crept cautiously out of the cask, and faltered out—

"Bless my soul, how hot I am! My flesh melteth, and my spirit waxeth faint! They've shot away the mast:

I wish they had shot away the master. There! they're at it again. What a row they're kicking up about these papers! They seem of consequence. I'll take one or two of them for my own private reading when I'm at home at Battersea. Don't mention Battersea; I'm likely to be battered at sea here."

He took some of the papers and hid them in his bosom, and the report of guns and a great noise was again heard, and Bowse re-entered hastily.

"The game is completely up," he said, "in another moment they will board us. Again, I say, I will die like a man."

"And again I say I'll live like a man," remarked Waxend, as Bowse again hurried from the place. "There seems to be a deal of *wetting* going on; I hope one side will get *leathered*. Oh, Bullock Smithey—Battersea, anywhere but here!"

The noise and confusion increased every moment, and it was perfectly deafening and distracting. The sailors crossed the place hurriedly and evinced the greatest possible excitement. Zinga arose from his kness, looked around him anxiously, and in vain tried to release himself from his chains. The Polyphemus might now be seen through the port-holes of the Black Bess, and it was evident that the decisive moment had just arrived; another instant elapsed, when a tremendous crash was heard, which seemed almost to shake the slaver out of the water; this was followed by loud shouts, the report of fire-arms, and the clashing of swords, and then a number of the crew of the Polyphemus entered in desperate combat with the ruffians belonging to the Black Bess. Harry Halliyard encountered Brandon, whilst Lieutenant Manly was engaged with Bowse. The combat was most furious and determined, and for some time was engaged with equal skill and courage on both sides; but at length Bowse was disarmed, and rushing past desperately, jumped through the port into the sea. Black Brandon was cut down by the heroic arm of Harry, who turned from him, when the villain took the advantage thus offered him to draw a pistol which he discharged at Harry, but fortunately it had no other effect than to knock off his hat, and the hardy young seaman turning to him, said—

"Missed, you black-looking, piratical robber !—you'll swing for this. There they are," he continued, addressing himself to Lieutenant Manly, and pointing to the negroes. "Poor souls ! chained all of a row, like so many bullocks at Smithfield. May six of my days be banyan days, if I arn't as great a mind to let that ugly soul adrift on its downward passage to—but no ; I'll leave him to the gallows."

"Let the hold be searched," said Manly, "and let the manacles be struck off these poor creatures."

Harry went to the hatchway and looked down, while the sailors were releasing the slaves. Black Brandon, making a powerful effort, suddenly rose, and with a small dirk was about to stab our hero in the back, when Watchful Waxend, peeping from the barrel in which he had concealed himself, snatched a pistol from the belt of a sailor who was passing, and discharging the contents at the miscreant, shot him in the head. Brandon shrieked, and fell weltering in his blood.

"There's a ball of wax for you, my boy," said the Bishop, looking knowingly from the cask. Harry turned his head, and fixed a look of disgust and triumph upon Brandon, who raising himself on his elbow, said, in a hoarse and hollow voice—

"It's all over—run down at last by a Peter-boat ! Well—well, do hanging this time, Halliyard ; you don't recollect me, but I remember you. I never forget an insult."

"Ah !" cried our hero, starting, "I recollect that voice. Those words !—is it possible ?"

"Ay, ay," replied the dying ruffian, "I did a good thing in getting you pressed ; made a neat rod for my own hide. Well, it's all over—the Black Bet and her captain will go to Davy Jones together.—Put me over to the sharks.—Ha, ha ! I never forget an insult !"

With another hysterical laugh, the inhuman wretch fell back, and his guilty life was brought to a termination.

"Let this ship be cleared of the dead," commanded Lieutenant Manly ; "turn all hands upon deck."

"But the poor woman, your honour," observed Halliyard, "that we picked up ; she may have a friend or a brother among these ebony gentlemen."

"Right !" coincided Manly ; " pass the word for the negro woman."

Zamba's voice was immediately heard outside, and Zinga, rushing forward, and looking anxiously at Harry said—

"Zamba !—my wife !"

"Your wife !" repeated our hero, eagerly.

Zinga by his looks and actions gave his assent. Harry rushed away, and instantly returning with Zamba, they threw themselves into each other's arms in a transport of delight. They then in an ecstasy of gratitude prostrated themselves at the feet of Lieutenant Manly and Harry.

"Lord love my eyes," cried the latter, "the poor creturs are lovyers ! She's the Poll of his heart ! Tip us your black fin, my honest fellow ; there's one at home I'd give the world to hug in my arms as you do your brown fair one here. Here's a bit of her silky hair ! It's my breast-plate in the hour of battle, and my library of comfort in the darkness of the night-watch."

"Halliyard," observed the lieutenant, "I shall leave you as prize-master, while I go to report to the captain. This poor fellow," he continued, introducing Waxend, " saved your life ; you must look to him. Come, bear a hand, lads."

"Ay, ay, your honour," replied Harry ; then turning to the Bishop, he added, "follow me my lad, and we'll overhaul your log. And, do you hear, boys, let the wounded be looked to ; let the niggers go free upon deck. Dance, you black angels ! No more captivity ! The British flag flies over your head, and the very rustling of its folds knocks every fetter from the limbs of the poor slave."

CHAPTER V.

OLD ACQUAINTANCES.—MARY'S LETTER.
—THE SLAVERS FORT.—THE PLOT.—
A PERILOUS ADVENTURE.—THE AT-
TACK.—THE   TRIUMPH.—TERRIFIC
EXPLOSION.

"Now, my lad, who are you ?" asked our hero of Watchful Waxend, when they had entered a cabin. "You saved my life, and I thank you. I'll do the same for you another time, but—why—there's something about the build of your figure-head as strikes me—did you ever cross my latitude afore?"

"I don't know what you mean by your latitude," answered Waxend, "but I've crossed your door-way at Battersea many a time to see the old dame—capital punch she used to make; haven't had a drop since."

"Why, surely—no—it can't be the Bishop!" cried Harry. "What! Master Watchful Waxend turned pioneer and slaver?"

"I was a slave myself," replied Waxend; "I was kidnapped on board one night when the spirit had moved me; I fell asleep at Wapping, and I've had nothing but whopping ever since."

"Give us your hand," cried our hero, "it does one's heart good to see anyone from the dear home. Well, and how was my Poll? pretty and constant, eh? and the old lass, old mother, and Joe, eh? how are they?—speak, lad, speak!"

"So, I—I—I will, when you've done jogging so," said the Bishop.

"Why don't you give me fire then?" demanded Harry, impatiently. "My heart's up in my mouth! My dear Mary!" looking at the lock of hair he prized so highly. "Let out a roof of your jawing tackle, my lord Bishop, or you'll get monkey's allowance. How are they all? How's Poll?"

"I can't tell you; I've been away these three years," replied Waxend.

"Oh, lord, oh, lord!" cried his companion, disconsolately "no news anyway; not one letter have I had, and I've wrote a dozen."

"Oh, yes, stop a bit; I've got one for you."

"Eh? From Mary—where is it, lad? How did you get it?"

"Why, she gave it me to take to the Admiralty the night before I was kidnapped. I popped it into my portmanteau, and stuck it in with a ball of wax, and so I've kept it ever since. Here it is."

Eagerly did Harry seize the welcome letter, and as he glanced at the superscription, his feelings nearly overpowered him.

"Bless her little fingers!" he said.

"How it smells of cobbler's wax! Never mind; let's see what she says."

He opened the letter and read as follows—

"My dearest Harry," (bless her!)—"we haven't none of us had no letter from you," (why, I wrote a matter of four afore this was writ) "and I do nothing but cry for fear of some accident." (bless her pretty eyes, my poor Mary!) "Oh, Harry, you are inconstant, sure." (I'll be d———d if I am!) "Your poor old mother asks the letter-man every day whether he expects one from you to-morrow. Joe's very kind, and works like a good one for the old dame," (God bless him!) "She's crying over my shoulder now. Do write—I can't see the paper; excuse blottings. My dear Harry, I must give over. My heart will break if you don't write. Do soon, my dear, dear, own Harry, and God bless you!—' MARY."

"P.S.—Mother's and Joe's love, and mine a million times."

Thus the letter concluded, and Harry pressed it again and again with the most fond and powerful emotion to his lips.

"Thank you, lad, for bringing this," he said to Waxend; "thank you—thank you! Bless them all!"

He shook the hand of Waxend fervently, and unable to restrain his feelings, tears started down his manly cheeks.

"Why, Harry—Harry!" said Waxend.

"Ah," returned the former, "I am not ashamed of these drops; when the heart's brimful of love and happiness, it must run over somewhere, and where and why shouldn't it at the eyes? I don't think a man has less fire and courage in him for having a little of the water of affection."

"Here's something may serve to brighten you up a bit," observed Watchful, giving him Brandon's papers, "may serve, as I say, to put a little more wax on the thread."

"Ah!" exclaimed Harry looking with surprise at the papers. "Where?—eh—what? Correspondence with the enemy! Map of a secret cave or harbour beneath the rock of Martinique?—place of communication with the fort—list of pirate signals—all's right!"

Zinga now entered the cabin, and advancing towards our hero, said—

"It was you, sir, who saved my Zamba's life: I owe you my gratitude. The object nearest to your heart is glory; I can put the pirate's horde into your hands; I have been his messenger to the rock for near two years. Do you prepare a strong cable, by which you can ascend; put me ashore, I will enter the fort as if from him, I will lower a rope from above, and—you understand?"

"I do, my brave fellow: the rock's ours. You shall be a general for this, and you, Waxend, an archbishop! Not a moment must be lost! We are right off the rock now; the enemy will know this vessel. Here we have the signals, and let British courage do the rest. Huzza! Damme! I'll plant the British flag on their fort before the moon sinks. Bear a hand, lads; old England for ever!"

Thus saying, they departed to prepare to put their designs into execution.

The moon was shining brightly, when our hero and his brave companions started on their extraordinary and perilous adventures. The Slavers Fort and stronghold was situated on the top of the lofty rock of Martinique, and was approached by a flight of steps hewn out of the solid rock. A rampart run round it, in which was a pole with a lamp near the bottom with a cord attached to it. The height was so great, that it was enough to turn the head giddy to gaze at it. A sentinel, heavily armed, was on duty at the time of which we are writing.

"The Black Bet has taken a long sweep this time," he said to himself; "it's my turn for a cruise next—better than being coped up in this dog-hole. I thought I made her out this afternoon; if so, she'll be for running under the rock to-night. Let me see: this is four hundred feet above the sea, yet I can almost fancy I feel the spray. Yaw—aw! and by the booming of the cave beneath, in spite of the moon's smiling, I should say it would be a rough night. Yaw—I'm devilish sleepy!"

A signal like a boatswain's call was now heard.

"What devil's bird is that chirruping?" said the man. The same signal was repeated twice, and he ran and looked over the rampart. "'Tis Brandon," he said; "there's the signal light of the Black Bet under the rock. I must show the lamp for 'em to hoist the portcullis in the path below." He raised the lamp by a cord to the top of the pole. "There's a wind rising, and Brandon's not the man to hug the shore. We shall lose our supplies. Yaw—I'd rather turn in than be prowling here with a storm brewing. Yaw!"

There was a knock, and opening the door, Zinga entered with a wallet.

"Oh, it's you, Master Nigger, is it?" said the sentinel. "Well, what luck this trip?"

"Good, Master Beargruel, good,' replied Zinga. "Here's a bottle; drink, whilst I deliver my message."

The man took the bottle eagerly, and drank heartily, and while he was thus occupied, Zinga drew a rope from his wallet and made fast the end to a stanchion, which he dropped over the rock.

"I was as glad to see that light below as if I had a fortune," remarked the sentinel.

"'Tis a fearful night," said Zinga, looking over the rampart.

"It is," said the sentinel, still drinking.

"Hark how the wind howls!" observed the negro, and he then added aside: "if their hearts should fail, 'tis too much for mortal courage to contemplate."

"Here's your bottle," said the sentinel, turning to Zinga.

"No, keep it till my return," replied the latter."

"Yaw—right!" and Zinga left the spot. "That black's got a white soul," continued the man. "I—I'm very sleepy. Another pull at the bottle may wake me. I wish I was aboard the brig —I—I—aw—yaw; I—capital!—yes, yaw!"

Overpowered, he then threw himself on the steps, and was soon wrapped in a sound sleep. Zinga now returned cautiously.

"The opiate in the brandy has taken effect," he said: "now to my task."

He pulled up the cord which he had lowered, and secured the cable which was attached to it, with sticks run through it, and fastened it securely in the stanchion. He then stooped and looked over the rock.

"The rope is pulled," he said; "they will make the attempt. It is a fearful peril. I see by the torch in the boat which the preserver of my Zamba holds that they have begun to mount; he is the last to cut off all retreat. Each has his cutlass in his mouth, and, with a raging sea beneath them, five and twenty souls are trusted to a single rope. The howling wind below dashes them against the rock! I can gaze no longer; my heart sickens at their danger, yet, like the basilisk, it fascinates me to the fatal spot. They pause! does one heart shrink? The word is passed from man to man, What do I see? Halliyard is mounting over the shoulders of those above him; the wind almost extinguishes his torch! He with his cutlass compels the men to mount. Ha! they fall! No! 'tis but the torch! they are in darkness—still they mount! Should the rope give way—it has worn with their weight upon the rock—should it break! No, no, they are here!"

At that moment our gallant hero appeared on the cable, waving the Union Jack. He sprang over the battlements, followed by his companions, and shook hands with Zinga, who pointed to the sentinel whom one of the sailors had raised his sword to strike, but Harry prevented him.

"No, no; the poor fellow sleeps," he said; "all fair and above board." He secured the arms of the sentinel, and placing him against the rampart, he tried the door of the fort.

"So, fastened!" he said; "perhaps this fellow has the keys." He searched him. "What's to be done?" he added; "I have it."

He shook the sentinel, who started up amazed and confused, and the sailors retired.

"What's the matter?" demanded the man, waking, "and who the devil are you?"

"Silence!" said our hero, "I am from Brandon."

"Oh, good! I'll inform Sebastian and the rest."

"Do so," said Harry.

The sentinel went up the steps, and giving three knocks at the door of the fort, a guard put his head from above; the sentinel gave the pass-word, "Brandon and the Black Bet!" the guard retired; our hero motioned all his men forward, and they ranged themselves on each side of the door.

"Ah!" said the sentinel to Harry, "what does this mean?"

"That you are in our power," he replied, seizing him and putting a pistol to his head. "One word, and you die!"

"I don't fear death!" replied the man.

The door was now thrown open, and the pirates rushed out.

"Treachery!" shouted the sentinel, but he was too late: our hero snatched up his firelock and discharged it at the pirates, one of whom was seen at the top of the rampart bearing the tri-coloured flag. A general conflict then ensued; a shell was thrown from the ship below, and it fell among the combatants, spreading death and destruction around. The scene now became truly appalling. Harry, with that indomitable courage and presence of mind which ever characterised him on the most trying occasions, seized the shell and hurled it into the fort. Confusion and dismay immediately followed. A terrible explosion took place, and the fort was instantaneously blown into the air, carrying with it a number of the lawless wretches who inhabited it.

In all these gallant proceedings the sailors of the Polyphemus fought with remarkable bravery, but our hero was ever foremost and most distinguished. He was completely blind to and reckless of all danger. Among those who were destined to feel the invincible power of his arm was the commandant of the fort, whom he encountered and attacked. The commandant was a brave man, and fought desperately; for some time the combat remained doubtful, but at length Harry's sword penetrated his body, and he fell dead at his feet.

The pirates were now completely subdued, and but few of them survived the dreadful conflict. The fort burst into flames that ascended high into the sky, and illuminated the ocean for miles around, rendering it one of the most grand, but awful scenes that could well be imagined. Our hero boldly dashed through the fire, and rushing to the top of the fort, seized the pirate with the tri-coloured flag, hurled him into the sea, and hoisted the British standard, amidst the enthusiastic cheers of his companions. The triumph was now comple e, and the conquerors having achieved their object, returned to the Black Bet. They found her, however, in a sinking condition, and having launched the boats, they proceeded without delay to the Polyphemus and left her to her fate.

CHAPTER VI.

MORE PERILS AND DANGERS.—THE FIRE AT SEA.—DESTRUCTION OF THE POLYPHEMUS.—DEATH OF ZINGA AND HIS WIFE.—THE RAFT.—THE FEARFUL SITUATION OF HARRY, THE CAPTAIN, MANLY, AND OTHERS.—THE RESCUE.

HARRY and his companions reached the Polyphemus in safety, where they received the unqualified thanks of Captain Oakheart and the other officers, for the almost unexampled act of bravery and daring they had performed.

"Halliyard," said the captain, "you are a fine fellow, and you shall not go unrewarded for this."

"Ah, as for that, your honour," replied our hero, "I do not know that I deserve any reward for such a trifle, though, to be sure, we have shipped a few of the greatest rascals that ever lived to old Davy. If your honour is satisfied, that's enough for me, and I only wish that it may not be long before I shall have such another piece of sport. But your honour forgets that I am a prisoner."

"No," returned the captain, "you are forgiven. Your recent conduct more than compensates for your offence."

"Thank ye, your honour," said Harry; "and if ever I neglect my duty, hang me to the yard-arm, and make shark's meat of me with pleasure."

"The late stronghold of these rascals doubtless contains some treasure which it may be worth the taking," remarked Captain Oakheart; "so we will run the Polyphemus under the rock and examine it, and then hurrah for old England again !"

"Hurrah, your honour !" cried our hero, tossing his hat into the air. "Lord—lord, how the very name of that dear place, after so long an absence from it, sets my heart agoing. My pretty Poll, dear old mother, and friend Joe, too, I shall see them all again ; and I'll get spliced in the turning of a handspike, that is, if my Mary is true, and to doubt that would be to render myself one of the veriest swabs and rascals that ever lived. Oh, I shall be so happy !"

"I hope you may," said the captain, "for you richly deserve to be so, my fine fellow. Be ready to attend me to the rock in about an hour."

"Ay, ay, your honour," answered the brave young seaman, "I am ready this instant, if your honour pleases. This has been one of the best day's sport we have had for some time ; for have we not destroyed Brandon and his daring crew—set the poor creatures whom he had in his power free, and blown the fort to the devil ? See, your honour, how proudly the British flag floats in the air, surrounded by the devouring flames, which yet refuse to injure it. Oh, it is a glorious sight !"

Thus saying, Harry Halliyard bowed respectfully to Captain Oakheart, and the other officers present, and made his way below.

In about a couple of hours the Polyphemus was under the rock of Martinique, and they proceeded to examine the scene of the late dreadful combat. They were well rewarded for their trouble. Considerable were the stores and treasures they discovered amongst the ruins, though much had been destroyed by the terrible conflagration and explosion which had taken place.

"Halliyard," remarked Captain Oakheart, "this has been a fortunate adventure for you. Your share of the prize will be sufficient to forward your prospects in life ; and I do not flatter you when I declare that such a reward is no more than your great merits richly entitle you to."

"Oh, your honour," replied our hero, "indeed, I know not how to thank you for the high opinion your honour is pleased to entertain of me. As for fortune, all that I covet it for is to make my pretty Poll a lady ; for she is a fair craft who would do honour to any commander, whatever his station might be."

"And, I suppose, Halliyard," said the captain, "if you should ever obtain fortune enough you will quit that service to which you are now such an honour, rather than endure the pain of a separation from your wife?"

"Avast, there, your honour," replied Harry, "axing your honour's pardon, but I think you have taken the soundings of Harry Halliyard's character rather wrong, if that is your idea. God bless my king and country, say I, and the service; I am too much attached to it ever to abandon it whilst I have the means to lend it a helping hand, and I know that my Mary (Heaven love her!) possesses too noble and loyal a heart to wish me to do so. As for separation, (though it will be painful enough) we shall each of us take too large a cargo of love aboard to care the cracking of a biscuit about that; for, whatever danger may surround him, the Great Commander aloft will never suffer the honest heart to run foul of the shoals and quicksands of destruction, or to founder in the black sea of misfortune."

"Well spoken, Halliyard," complimented his captain, "with such sentiments as those you have just now expressed, and which I am convinced spring sincerely from your heart, you have nothing to fear. You shall wed your pretty Poll, and if Providence spares my life, I will do myself the pleasure and the honour of being present at your union."

"Bless your honour for that promise," ejaculated Harry. "Oh, what a happy fellow I ought to consider myself, dear heart. God watch over and preserve my beloved Mary, my dear old mother, and my faithful friend and partner Joe, and suffer me to arrive safe again in happy old England, and I would not exchange situations with the first lord of the Admiralty."

* * * * *

The whole of the treasure is removed on board—the white sails are spread—the anchor is weighed, and each heart that beats beneath the blue jackets of the brave crew of the Polyphemus is elate with joy and hope, for the noble vessel is on her way towards the white cliffs of England, and bright and cheering are the anticipations they form of the happy meeting they shall have with friends and relations on their arrival there, after so long a separation. For several days, there was nothing to dampen the ardour of their hopes. The weather was beautifully calm, the wind favourable, and the vessel careered over the bright surface of the deep like a thing of life. There was little labour for the ship's company to perform, and they passed a delightful relaxation from the perils and fatigues they had experinced, in mirth and harmony; in spinning those wondrous yarns for which our bold sons of the ocean are so celebrated, and in picturing to each other the joys of home. But at length a sudden and fearful change came o'er their prospects. The weather became wild and tempestuous; with what frightful speed the black and ponderous clouds were driven through the heavens; how awfully did the voice of "Rude Boreas" bellow, and the tremendous roaring and heaving of the sea was sufficient to appal even the stoutest of the bold hearts of that gallant vessel. It was frightful to gaze upon the black boiling waters—to notice the foaming waves as they seemed to rise to the clouds, and to witness the vivid flashes of lightning that with their lurid glare at intervals illumined the whole of the terrific scene. Still the Polyphemus was so good a vsssel, and so skilful and experienced were the crew who manned her, that, for some time, not the least fears were entertained that she would be unable to weather the storm. At length it was discovered that she had sprung a leak, and made water very fast, and considerable alarm for he safety were now excited. Most of the hands were obliged to work at the pumps, and some of the heaviest metal was compelled to be thrown overboard, in order to lighten her, and to prevent her from foundering immediately. The lightning blazed still more frequently and awful than before; but still, in spite of the leak and that there were more than two feet of water in the hold, the noble vessel dashed on, poised on the crests of the billows, which rose and fell in wild chaotic madness; now swelling into the semblance of a mountain ridge, and tumbling and breaking over the ill-fated ship, threatening to overwhelm her or to dash her to pieces every instant.

Still the hardy crew abated not the

least in their exertions and perseverance, but, on the contrary, the more apparent the danger became, so did fresh courage seem to take possession of them, and the feats they performed were actually miraculous. At length came a flash, more terrific than any that had before preceded it. Great God! it had struck the ill-fated ship, and in a moment "Fire—fire!" was shouted from every hoarse throat, and all was horror and confusion. So sudden was the calamity that all were paralysed, and for a minute or two were unable to render that assistance which might have prevented it from extending. The fire was all aloft, and terrifically it was raging there. The destructive element ran along the ropes, crackling and hissing as if in exultation, as it were, and communicating with the broad sails, and quickly reducing them to tinder. Instantly spars, mainmast, and mizen mast were in a blaze, and such a strong hold had the scorching flames obtained, that it resisted all the desperate efforts of the officers and crew to subdue, and threatened the certain and speedy destruction of the noble vessel. Anon, and one of the blazing masts fell on the deck, killing two of the seamen, and with the rapidity of thought the fore part of the vessel fell a prey to the devouring element, and the horror of the scene that then prevailed completely beggars all attempt at description. For miles and miles around, as the large flames shot up into the midnight sky, was the wide waste of troubled waters illuminated, and distraction and despair was upon every sturdy face.

"All is lost!" cried the captain, in a frantic voice, for he had completely lost his presence of mind; "to the boats—to the boats!"

Quickly one was lowered over the burning ship, but before any person could enter it, it was dashed far away upon the crests of the mountainous billows, and smashed to pieces by the breakers. Oh, what an awful moment was that! Several of the unfortunate beings, in the frenzy of their despair, leaped into the stormy gulf, only to meet with an immediate death! The only remaining boat was now launched, and so many were the frantic creatures who at once sprang into it, that it was in-

stantly capsized, and the whole of them were uselessly struggling for their lives in the deep. Among the rest was poor Zamba, and that in the sight of her faithful and devoted husband. For a moment she was lost to the view, but soon she arose again to the surface, and raised her arms in supplication for that help which no human being could offer her.

"Zamba! my wife! my own Zamba!" cried Zinga; "I will save or perish with you!" As the words escaped his lips he leapt into the ocean, and was seen desperately and manfully struggling with the waves to gain the object of his anxiety. He reaches her—he grasps her form with one arm, and endeavours to swim towards a floating spar with the other. Vain effort! Wave after wave overwhelms them, and they are lost for ever!

Fiercer and fiercer raged the fire, setting every effort to subdue it at defiance. The unfortunate ship was now, in fact, in flames almost from stern to stem. Huge beams and masses of timber were flying outwards and upwards, and on every side amid the howling voice of the tempest were heard the wild shrieks of despair.

In the meantime, our hero and two or three more of the crew, who were more cool and collected than the rest, were busily engaged in constructing a raft from such materials as they could lay their hands on, and being now finished, it was launched, and himself, the captain, Manly, Waxend, and several more leaped upon it, and committed themselves to the mercy of the waves. They were soon dashed far away from the burning ship, though their peril was so great that there seemed to be but little chance of preserving their lives. The sea washed so furiously and heavily over them that it was with difficulty they could maintain their positions on the raft; and, certainly, the awful scene which prevailed around them was sufficient to daunt the most hardy spirit. The tempest had but little abated, and from the broad glare of light emitted by the unfortunate burning vessel they had just quitted, as for as the eyes could stretch, they could not discover the slightest glimpse of land. Although they might, by their exertions, prolong life for a certain period, the fate which awaited them ultimately seemed to be almost inevitable.

Harry still maintained his position under the trying circumstances to which himself and his hapless companions were exposed; though when his thoughts wandered to those beloved beings from whom he was so widely parted (which they constantly did), his feelings were of the most intense description; and whilst he exerted himself to the utmost for the preservation of himself and his companions, he offered up mental, but fervent prayers to Heaven for their welfare. He took from his bosom the lock of hair presented to him by his Mary, and again and again did he press it to his lips and bedew it with his manly tears.

But now their attention was called to the unfortunate vessel from which they had just escaped by a smothered roar that escaped from it, which seemed to convulse the very air and ocean around, and had a palpable effect on the frail craft to which the remnant of the crew had committed themselves. But an instant, and all the fire, low and aloft, disappeared with a hissing sound; this was followed by a huge white cloud of steam; then came the sounds of cracking and rending timber, a more dense cloud of smoke than before floated into the heavens; it evaporated, and whilst the shipwrecked seamen gazed anxiously towards the fatal spot, all signs of the vessel had vanished.

The work of destruction is complete," said Captain Oakheart, in the most melancholy accents; "the flames have reached the powder, she has exploded, and the noble Polyphemus shall never more ride the broad expanse of waters, or strike terror into the hearts of the enemy. Alas! alas!"

"Ay, your honour," remarked Harry, "it is a sad job, and peace to the souls of the brave fellows who have perished on this awful night, say I. But do not despair, your honour. The poor Polly—Polyphemus I mean. Ah! never mind; a stout heart, a strong arm, and confidence in the Great Commander aloft, and we shall yet be able to weather the storms by which we are at present surrounded, and cast anchor in the port of safety at last. And see! the storm is abating—the wind lulls—the waves go down—our raft rides steadily and freely; in about another hour we shall have the glorious light of day, and then, with the blessing of Heaven, we shall be able to steer to some port of safety, and where we shall find relief from our present dangerous and dreadful situation."

Captain Oakheart took the young seaman's hand, pressed it cordially within his own, and expressed his thanks by his looks.

The storm had indeed abated; the wind had almost ceased to howl, the flashes of lightning were less frequent and terrific, and the vast expanse of waters was comparatively calm to what it had been before. Still the situation of the unfortunate seamen on the wreck was most deplorable. They were completely drenched to the skin, and almost perishing with cold and the extraordinary fatigue they had undergone; and as far as the eye could penetrate through the darkness, they could distinguish no signs of land, neither could they form any accurate conjecture of the course in which they were being drifted, and had no other alternative left them but to consign themselves into the hands of the Omnipotent. All that they could preserve in the hurry of their escape from the burning vessel was one small cask of salt provisions, a few biscuits, and a limited quantity of rum; and, as there were twelve of them in number, that, of course, could not last them long; therefore, if they were not fortunate enough to be speedily picked up by some friendly vessel, death alone stared them in the face. Still did Harry Halliyard, by his example, inspire his companions with courage, and enable them to exert themselves for their preservation in a manner which they could not otherwise have done.

The storm at last entirely subsided, and the raft went steadily on its way, affording the hapless seamen some slight portion of rest after the many trials it had been their hard lot to encounter. Daylight at length broke upon the ocean, and they gazed with anxious eyes to see whether there was any chance of deliverance; but the prospect was as dismal and cheerless as could well be imagined: nothing but sea and sky presented themselves to their observation, and not the least signs of any vessel. They fixed a spar in the centre of the raft, from the top of which they hoisted a shirt, so that it might attract the attention of any ship which might hove in sight, and then, having partaken very slightly of the rum and the biscuits, they huddled together, leaving one man in charge of the raft, and endeavoured to compose themseves to sleep. But the mind of Harry Halliyard was too busily occupied to suffer him to rest, and with folded arms he contemplated the blue waters of the deep, whilst his whole thoughts were fixed on those beloved beings whom he had left behind him, and whom it was now so doubtful he should ever behold again.

In this manner several hours passed away, when suddenly our hero descried land at a distance, and aroused the captain and his other companions in misfortune with the welcome intelligence. The raft was being drifted by the wind right in the direction of it, but they had no means of descrying the exact character of it, and, therefore, they awaited the result in doubt and the most painful suspense. As they approached it nearer, however, they had an opportunity of observing it more distinctly, and they felt their hopes somewhat diminished, for it presented not the least signs of habitation, and, therefore, their chances of relief were but limited. But they kept up their spirits in the best way they could, and once relieved from the perils of the deep, they trusted that Providence would not forsake them. In about another hour, the raft floated gently and immediately under it, and it not being very high, they landed without much difficulty. Anxiously they gazed around them, but as far as their eyes could stretch, they could not perceive the least signs of a human dwelling, and, with the exception of a few straggling trees here and there, it was completely barren. Quite worn out with the fatigue and privations they had experienced, they stretched themselves on the earth, and resigned themselves to rest. They slept several hours, and when they awoke the afternoon was far advanced, and the sun was shining scorchingly upon them. What would they have given for some

fresh water! but, unfortunately, they had not been able to preserve any from the wreck, and that rendered their situation the more deplorable. They again partook sparingly of the rum and biscuits, and feeling somewhat refreshed, Harry and two more of the unfortunates proposed to travel further into the island to reconnoitre, leaving their companions behind them. They took with them a small empty cask, in case they should be lucky enough to meet with some fresh water, and they started on their errand. But the further they proceeded the more wild and cheerless did the island appear to be, and it was quite evident that it was wholly uninhabited, and had probably never before been trodden by the foot of man. They returned by a different route to the spot where they had left their companions, and were fortunate enough to meet with, on their way, a spring of pure water, at which they slaked their burning thirst, and then filling the cask they had brought with them, they made their way back. Captain Oakheart and the others received the intelligence with more composure than might have been expected, and having partaken of the fresh water they all set to work to erect themselves a rude tent to shelter them from the scorching rays of the sun, or the inclemency of the weather, as it was quite uncertain how long they might be compelled to remain in this desolate place. In this manner the day wore tediously and hopelessly away, and night set in, without anything at all occurring to inspire them with the least hope. It was a lovely night; the moon shone forth in full splendour, dancing merrily on the blue waters, which, lately so fearfully convulsed, were now as calm and unruffled as an infant's slumber, scarcely displaying a ripple. They could see for many miles across the ocean, as clearly and distinctly as at noon-day, but not the least signs of any approaching vessel met their gaze to inspire them with hope or to gladden their hearts, and after watching until they were fairly exhausted, they returned to the tent for the night, leaving one man on the look-out.

The night passed away, and the morning broke upon them, without any prospects for the better presenting itself to them, and their spirits drooped, for it seemed as though Providence had deserted them, and that their fate was inevitable. We should, however, become tedious were we to detail minutely all that befell them, and the dreadful thoughts of agony and despair that crowded upon their minds. Three days and nights elapsed, and still their situation remained the same; but now, to add to their horror, the scanty stock of provisions which they had been enabled to preserve from the wreck was exhausted, and a terrible death by starvation stared them in the face. Two more days passed, and they had nothing but the water from the spring, and they were completely worn out. Three of their companions sunk under their dreadful sufferings, and died, and Captain Oakheart was so much exhausted, that it seemed impossible that he could survive much longer, unless relief arrived, and of which there did not seem to be the least chance at present.

The sixth day came, and dark and ominous were the looks that the sufferers bestowed upon each other. It was awful to contemplate their livid and ghastly countenances, their blood-shot eyes, and their wretched and emaciated forms, which had all the appearance of premature old age; and they could scarcely have been recognised as the same men who but a few days previously had performed such feats of courage and daring on board of the unfortunate Polyphemus. And now the expression of their countenances became more ghastly, and strange mutterings passed from one to the other, which seemed to betoken some approaching and dreadful crisis. At length one of them suddenly started up, and in hurried, yet desperate and determined accents, exclaimed—

"It is impossible to endure this suffering any longer; we must not starve; it is a fearful alternative I have to propose, but the horrible circumstances in which we are placed will offer an excuse for it.—I, therefore, suggest that we should cast lots, to see which amongst us shall die, in order to prolong, if not to save the lives of his companions."

There was a shudder of horror amongst the unhappy men at this revolting and frightful suggestion, and a death-like silence for some moments ensued, and each one looked anxiously at his companion, as if he would read his answer in the expression of his features. Poor Watchful Waxend, (who had hitherto borne his misfortunes and sufferings with much more fortitude than could have been expected from a man of his temperament) was in a dreadful state of alarm; his teeth chattered in his jaws, and he trembled violently in every limb.

"Gen—gen—gentlemen," he faltered out, "you surely cannot think of doing as this good man proposes—cast lots which shall be butchered? What a cannibal idea! However, if you are determined, and it should be the awful fate of Watchful Waxend to come to such an *end*, I only wish to caution you that every particle of my body is rank poison, so you must take the consequences if you make sandwiches of me, that's all! Oh, Battersea! oh, Bullock Smithey! I shall never behold you again!"

"It is indeed a dreadful alternative," observed the captain, "and it must be avoided if possible. The Almighty surely would visit us with His most terrible retribution if we were to perpetrate such an inhuman and monstrous deed. I will never give my consent to it."

"Nor I," observed Lieutenant Manly. "I am fully prepared to perish of hunger rather than resort to so frightful a means of prolonging existence."

"Right, your honour," said Harry; "not that I, having so often faced death in all its most terrible shapes, am afraid to die; but let us await patiently, and bear up against our misfortunes a little longer, and, my word for it, we shall yet be saved."

"No, no, no!" shouted the other five seamen in a breath, with looks of determination, and brandishing their knives fiercely, "anything rather than perish of hunger! The lots! the lots!"

It was in vain that the captain, Manly, Harry, and Waxend remonstrated, and tried all the force of argument and persuasion; the majority were against them, and as they had no means of defending themselves, or resisting the dreadful proposition, they were forced to yield. The lots were drawn.

and the fatal paper fell to the fate of Harry Halliyard.

"Well," he said, in a faltering voice, "it can't be helped; though I never thought that such a fate would have befallen Harry Halliyard, after all the perils and dangers he has encountered and escaped. It would have been better had I died in battle, or found an ocean grave; but to be thus—Oh, my poor Mary! what will be your anguish when you hear of the untimely and dreadful death of him who loved you so fondly? My poor old mother, too, and Joe!—But, damme, I will not snivel. I will meet my death like a man. Mary, mother, Joe! God bless you all, and——"

"Halliyard, my brave fellow," interrupted Captain Oakheart, much affected, "you must not perish thus! The idea is monstrous. Reflect," he added, addressing himself to the men, "and pause ere you commit a deed which will destroy your souls for ever. Who among ye can have the heart to perform this hideous work of blood?"

"It cannot be helped, captain," replied one of the seamen, "we are driven to desperation, and I trust that Harry will forgive us. We must again draw lots to see which of us shall perpetrate this dreadful deed of necessity."

"Well—well," said our hero, with all the firmness he could muster on so trying an occasion; "I am content. I am content. I can only die but once. But there is one request that I have to make of your honour."

"Name it, my poor fellow," replied the captain; "and I swear that if ever it should lie in my power I will comply with it to the very letter."

"Thank you, thank you, your honour, and God bless you!" said the young seaman, in a voice almost choked with the power of his emotions. "It is this: should you ever be fortunate enough to return to England (which I trust to Heaven you will) I beg of you to seek out my poor Mary, and my aged mother, and break to them the intelligence of my death, as gently as you can; but do not tell them by what means I died; say that I fell in battle, and that my last words were uttered in a blessing upon their heads. Tell my—my—my Mary—pardon these tears, your honour—

tell my Mary that my heart was faithful to her to the last, and that I died in the hopes that, though it was not permitted us to be united on earth, I felt confident that we should be in heaven. Comfort my poor old mother, and give my love to Joe. Promise only that you will do this, and I can die happy."

"I do indeed promise you, Halliyard," said the captain. "But can nothing save you?"

"No, your honour," replied our hero, firmly, "my doom, it seems, is sealed; but after what you have promised, I am satisfied. Harry Halliyard's log will be overhauled when he mounts aloft. Good bye, captain; farewell, Mr. Manly, remember me in your prayers. My worthy Bishop, your hand. God bless you—God bless you all!"

"Oh, Harry," said Waxend, wiping the tears from his eyes, "I must have a heart as hard as a lapstone if I could stand this. They will not surely take your life? But if they do, I promise you that I will not eat a morsel of you, for if I did, I am sure it would choke me."

"I am ready," said Harry, baring his breast. "Ned Clewline (for I see it has fallen to your lot to do this business) I forgive you. Strike sure, and get over it as quick as you can."

He knelt down as he spoke, and taking from his bosom the lock of Mary's hair, he pressed it fervently to his lips, and then raised his hands and eyes solemnly towards heaven, as if in prayer. A painful silence ensued, the captain, Manly, and Waxend averted their looks, and Clewline approaching Harry, raised the knife in the air, and was about to inflict the fatal blow, when at that instant his hand was arrested by an exclamation from Manly.

"Hold, hold, on your life!" he cried, "the Almighty has interposed to save him! A sail—sail!"

Clewline immediately dropped the knife, and Harry, starting to his feet, rushed towards the spot where Manly and the captain were standing, and then, sure enough, he beheld a vessel in the distance, and apparently steering in the direction of the island. Again he sank upon his knees, he clasped his hands together, and exclaimed—

"Saved—saved! God be praised!

I shall yet see my beloved Mary again!"

We need not attempt to describe the frantic joy of the unfortunate beings, who were so lately driven to despair, at the prospect of speedy deliverance that was now before them. They rushed backwards and forwards like madmen, rending the air with their cries, and waving their handkerchiefs on high, with the hope of attracting the attention of the persons on board the ship. It glided over the ocean swiftly, and every moment approached nearer, and at length the report of a gun convinced them that they were seen. Immediately afterwards they saw a boat launched, and making its way to the island, and they once more sank on their knees and returned their thanks to Providence for their fortunate deliverance from what had seemed to be a certain and terrible death.

In a short time the boat, which was the long one, and manned by four sailors, reached the island, and the men stepped on shore.

"What ship, my lads?" inquired the captain.

"The Invincible, bound for England, was the reply. "Captain Beaufort commander."

"Ah!" said Captain Oakheart, "my friend. This is fortunate."

He then briefly explained his name, and what had happened to them, and stepping into the boat they were rowed away from that island on which they had all expected to perish. The feelings of joy and thanksgiving they experienced we will leave to the imagination of the reader ; but no one was more extravagant in the expression of it than poor Watchful Waxend, who had given himself up for a dead man, and who could now scarcely persuade himself that he was not labouring under the influence of a dream.

CHAPTER VII.

THE INVINCIBLE.—THE ENGAGEMENT WITH A PIRATE.—DEATH OF LIEUTENANT MANLY. — THE VOYAGE HOME.

THE boat having quickly got alongside the Invincible, they were received with every kindness by the captain and the officers on board, and every and immediate attention was paid to their urgent necessities ; the vessel then proceeding on its course.

It was not till the next day that they were sufficiently recovered from the hardships they had experienced to enter into any explanation, and Captain Oakheart then related all the particulars to Captain Beaufort, of the daring adventures they had met with during the time they had been absent from England, introducing our hero, and paying a well-deserved compliment to his prowess and able qualities as a seaman.

"Your hand, Halliyard," said Captain Beaufort, most familiarly ; "in spite of the difference of our stations, I feel it an honour to grasp the hand of a brave man. From what your captain has just now stated to me, I am certain that you are an honour to the service, and your merits will, no doubt, meet with the reward they deserve to do."

"Thank you, your honour," replied our hero, "I'm sure I ought to feel as proud as a Rear Admiral, at least, to receive such compliments as these. As for what I have done, I don't see as how I can take much credit to myself, but I only rejoice to think I have had the power to do it. How grateful am I to you for having rescued my captain, Lieutenant Manly, myself, and my shipmates from death ; and I only hope it may be in my power to make some return for it before we reach England. The poor Polyphemus to meet with such a fate, after all the hard service she had seen! I could cry for her the same as if she had been my own mother. Lord love your honour, she was a craft! No washing-tub, but a trimmer vessel never ploughed the waves."

"Yes, it was indeed an unfortunate event that the Polyphemus was destroyed in the manner she was," said Captain Beaufort : "but the brave fellows who perished with her are much more to be lamented."

"True, your honour," returned Harry, "God rest the souls of the poor fellows, say I ; but I was much attached to the Polyphemus, especially because her name so much resembled the name of one, who is more precious to me than my own life, at home. Pretty Polly —my Polly! Bless her heart, I know she is thinking of me at this very moment, and weeping her bright blue eyes out, for fear she should never see me again, and, indeed, I was afraid that she would not myself, after we were cast away on that desolate island, and I was about to be made food for my shipmates instead of the sharks. But we should never despair; we shall reach happy old England in safety, I trust, and then my Mary and I will make all sail to the church, and—oh, dear!—oh, dear! my heart is so full at the thought that I know not how to express myself."

"Well, Halliyard," said Captain Oakheart, "I sincerely hope that your anticipations may not be doomed to be disappointed; for if your sweetheart is half so good and so pretty as you paint her, she is indeed fully deserving of so brave and honest a man as yourself, and I wish you every happiness."

"Thank ye, your honour," returned Harry. "Half so good and so pretty as I have painted her! Lord love your honour! I am not half artist enough to paint her as she deserves. She—she's a perfect angel! and that's the long and the short of it. I only wish your honours could see her, and if you did not acknowledge that she is the most cap—cap—captivating (don't they call it?) lass in all England, may I never go aloft, or handle a cutlass in the defence of my king and country again."

Captain Oakheart and his friend Beaufort smiled at the simple energy of the honest-hearted young seaman, and after again complimenting him, they dismissed him to enjoy himself with his shipmates below.

"Ah, Mr. Halliyard!" said Watchful Waxend (who had got an allowance of grog) when he entered the cabin, "what a blessed change is this! I thought it was all up with us; I never expected to see Battersea or Bullock Smithey again. And as for you, when Clewline had got his carving-knife at your throat—wheugh! it freezes the very blood in my veins to think of it."

"Well, your reverence," replied Harry, "it is all over now, so it is not worth while to think any more about it, though it was a rough squall while it lasted, to be sure."

"Yes," remarked Waxend, "and I fancy you'd have had a rough *squall*

when you felt the keen edge of Clewline's knife. Turn you into butcher's meat! Oh! the very idea gives me a rumbling in the inside."

"Well, take another tack, shipmate," said our hero, "and do not stand there palavering any more about it. We are now bound for old England, and there we shall be able to bring up with a favouring gale, and cast anchor in the port of happiness and pleasure."

"And if ever I leave Battersea again," said the Bishop, "may I be *leathered* to death on my own lapstone. No, I trust 'after many raving years,' as one of Dr. Watts's hymns says, I'll e'en settle down, do the amiable, and take unto myself a wife."

"Bravo, Watchful!" cried Harry, "there's nothing like the good ship, matrimony, when you can meet with such a mate as my Poll."

"And my Abigail Holdforth," added Waxend. "I begin to think that I acted wrong in deserting her at Bullock Smithey, and the punishment I have since endured, the many hardships by sea and land, have been nothing more than a judgment on me. Oh, Abigail! lovely Abigail! should we ever meet again, and thou art faithful to me, we will bind ourselves together like sole and upper-leather, and to the last we'll stick like wax to each other."

"Well said, my old friend," observed our hero; "and Poll shall be your sweetheart's bridesmaid."

"No! shall she though?" ejaculated Watchful. "Well, that is very kind of you."

"Kind!" repeated Harry, "belay your lingo there, shipmate; all fair and above board; you saved my life, and one good turn deserves another, don't it?"

"Yes, Halliyard," replied the Bishop, "you had a narrow escape there: that rascal Brandon meant to have stuck his awl into you, and no mistake; and I think I gave him a tidy welting for his pains. Mr. Watchful Waxend never expected to distinguish himself in the manner he has done, and I shall now have something to preach about, and from a good text, too, when we arrive at Battersea."

"Ay, ay, messmate," said Harry, "that's the way to talk. Overboard with dull care, say I. I am so merry, so light of heart, have such a cargo of hope on board, that I feel as if I wouldn't care whether King George (God bless him!) were my father. Lord! what a day it will be in Battersea when we cast anchor there, and are moored alongside our sweethearts and friends! We will set all the bells a ringing, the marrow-bones and cleavers a rattling, every table groaning with the weight of good cheer, the fiddlers scraping, and every man and woman, old and young, married and single, jigging away!"

"Yes, Mr. Halliyard," remarked Waxend, "you draw a very lively picture in anticipation—a very lively picture indeed; and I only hope that it may be realised, that we may reach England in safety. But you are a better judge of these matters than I am; do you think that we are not likely to have any accidents on the voyage? Any storms, or battles, or——"

"If we are lucky enough we shall."

"Lucky enough!"

"Yes, I hope we shall."

"You *hope* we shall!" repeated Waxend, with a very lugubrious expression of countenance; "hope we shall! Then all I have to say is, that I pity your want of taste."

"Taste, you lubber!" cried our hero; "a true British tar always shows his taste the best by giving the enemy a taste of his quality. Why, he is never so much at home as when he is engaged in a tempest, or in drubbing the foe."

"It's all very fine for you to say so, Mr. Harry," returned his companion; "but, if I must speak the candid truth, I never feel myself so much at home as when I *am* at home, half-seas-over, or drubbing the *leather !*"

"Ha, ha, ha!" laughed our hero; "your reverence is a hero; however, every man to his fancy. Just tow yourself alongside of me, and I will pilot you to as jolly a set of fellows as ever cracked a biscuit, a bottle, or an enemy's head! Heave a-head, my hearty! yo yeo!"

Thus saying, Harry Halliyard seized his arm, and hurried him away to the place where a number of the ship's crew were enjoying themselves.

For three days the Invincible proceeded on her homeward voyage without anything particular or worthy of being recorded taking place; but on the evening of the fourth day the man on the look-out reported a sail a-head; a brig, hoisting no colours, and making all the sail she could.

"A pirate, my life on it!" said Captain Beaufort, looking through his glass. "Stretch every point of canvas! give chase! the wind is in our favour, and if the gallant Invincible does not deceive me, as she has never done yet, we shall quickly be upon her, and make her give a good account of herself."

"Hurrah!" cried Harry Halliyard, who was on deck at the time, "then we shall soon have a fight!"

"Oh, dear! oh, dear!" said Watchful Waxend, who was standing by his side at the time, "I feel very ill;—I do not like fighting;—'tis against my religion:—I am a man of peace:—may I not be permitted to retire below for an hour or two?"

"Bravo! bravo!" shouted Captain Beaufort, "we gain rapidly upon her; she cannot escape us!"

One shot, then another proceeded from the Invincible, which the brig was nothing loth in answering, and the two vessels now approached so near to each other that they had every opportunity of distinguishing their different powers. The brig was a fine built craft, appeared to be well manned, and to carry some heavy metal; but still, in comparison with the Invincible, she was no match, and the latter calculated on an easy conquest, in which, however, she was deceived, for the brig, finding that all chance of escape was at an end, stood up heroically, and was evidently determined to make a desperate resistance. The fight commenced, and bravely and fiercely on both sides it continued for some time; but there was no resisting the superior calibre of the Invincible. Terribly did her guns tell upon the pirate brig, which staggered and reeled about from the shock, and was evidently about to sink. One more terrible broadside from the brig, however, told with terrible effect upon the Invincible, and Lieutenant Manly sank bleeding and mortally wounded in the arms of our hero. The next moment there was a loud shout from the crew of the pirate brig, and down she went, head-foremost.

the dark waters closing over her, and leaving not a vestige of her in sight.

CHAPTER VIII.

PORTSMOUTH IN ALL ITS GLORY.—SAILORS ASHORE. — HARRY HALLIYARD, CAPTAIN OAKHEART, AND WATCHFUL WAXEND.—HAPPY PROSPECTS. — THE COACH. — HEY FOR HOME.

PORTSMOUTH was all life and gaiety. Every public-house was full—fiddlers were playing, sailors and their lasses were singing and dancing; mirth, drinking and jollity were the order of the day. Jew duffers were carrying on a roaring trade, victimising the intoxicated sailors with their trumpery wares, to decorate their lasses, which was well understood between the latter and the Jews, who allowed them a liberal percentage on the articles they were the means of disposing of.

No house was more thronged than the Seaman's Friend Inn, which overlooked the high road and the quay beyond, with the docks and the numerous stately vessels lying in arbour, and here might be seen Mr. Watchful Waxend, all in his glory, now rigged as a sailor, with a girl on each knee, and a long pipe in his mouth. He had evidently been taking sundry potations, but he continued his carousal with the same gusto as when he had begun. At the same time of our introducing the reader to this scene, several of the sailors, in voices far more stentorian than musical, were engaged in singing a chorus, of which the following are the words—

'Sailors lead a jolly, jolly life,
   While roving on the ocean;
In every port they have a wife,
   Of every girl a notion.
      Fol de rol, &c."

"Yes, my loves," said Mr. Waxend, addressing himself to his fair companions; " to be sure, you shall have as much grog as you can swim in, but as for the rings, and broaches, and things you want, I'll give you them next time we come to Portsmouth."

The girls no sooner heard this than they quitted the Bishop's company,

evidently vexed and disappointed, and retired to the sailors who were buying of the Jews.

"Oh, dear!" said Watchful, rising from his seat. "Yes, they'd soon bring the cobblers all to an end. Hallo, Jack!" he added, speaking to a half intoxicated sailor, who was reasonably amusing himself by frying his watch in a pan; "if you hadn't kept you watch better at sea, you wouldn't have been able to make so free with your time ashore."

"Bravo! Bishop of Battersea!" shouted the sailors.

"Bishop of Battersea!" repeated Waxend. "I wish I was at Battersea. But I've given up the Bishop line now; it's a bad trade, and I'm anxious to mix in respectable society. They cured me aboard the slaver of preaching. You see, none but the niggers would listen to me, and I thought it was all nonsense to preach to them as didn't understand; though to be sure there are some in the line who arn't fit to preach to 'em as I does. Come, strike up a tune, old Rosin! give me a hornpipe—common time."

The sailors were merrily dancing, when the voice of Harry Halliyard was heard outside, and he was heartily welcomed by all as he entered the room.

"Yo ho, lad!" he cried, grasping Waxend by the hand; " here I find you. Rather queerish anchorage, though; lots of rocks and quicksands, eh ?" pointing to the girls, and then, looking significantly at the duffers, he added—" and swarming with sharks, too. When I landed I could have knelt down, but every one was looking. My heart kept tittaping —tittaping! and the tears of a whole lifetime seemed swelled into a large lump just here. So I pressed Mary's lock of hair with the iron grip of a seaman to my heart—crowded all sail, and without seeing a single landmark, made this harbour; but how I managed to steer clear of the chaiseses and the posteses, I'm jiggered if I know."

"I've seen two or three London-looking chaps about here," observed Waxend, "and so I——"

"Eh ?" interrupted Harry, eagerly, " did you ask 'em about Mary, and Joe, and the old house ?"

THE PRESSGANG—BLACK BRANDON'S REVENGE.

"I was going to do it," answered Waxend, "when one of 'em says to the other—'Damme, what a orrid smell of tar. I never could abide the wo—tar, damme!'—So, you see, after that I thought it was no use axing them about a waterman's home; for their manners convinced me that they were no better nor lords or linendrapers, or some such sort of people."

"Well, well; have you made soundings about the coach?"

"Ay, ay," replied Waxend

"Then," said Harry, "I'll only just beat about here till the captain bears down with a few gimcracks that want stowage, and then crowd all sail for London. But have you secured the berths?"

"Ay, ay."

"What's the name of the craft we're to go by?" asked our hero.

"The Nonpareil," answered his companion.

"The Nonpareil! I wish it had been the Polly, or the Poly—phemus; but, never mind, the Nonpareil will answer for my Mary. So, do you hear? heave a head, and just make a minute of the exact time they weigh anchor."

"To be sure I will," said Watchful, "and ask all about her rate of sailing; there's a fair wind, we shall soon be at Battersea."

With these words Watchful Waxend departed on his errand.

"I'm there now," soliloquized our hero, when he was gone; "I can see the old mother, with her bellows in her lap, listening to Mary, as she reads my last letter about coming home; I can see the tears standing in the wrinkles of her dear old cheeks; and I can hear Mary's voice quivering a bit, as she comes to that part where I tell her that I love her more than ever—Joe, in the corner, with his pipe, fancying he's shaking hands with his old friend Harry, and puffing out the smoke to hide his quivering lips. I can see 'em all there; and the old wherry, and Sculler picking gooseberries in the garden, and the old clock behind the door, ticking louder, as if to welcome me. I can see 'em, I can see 'em!—What a fool I am! I am crying like a boy!"

The noble-hearted fellow hastily dashed away the manly tears that had started to his eyes, and just at that moment one of the Jews approached him and said—

"Von't you puy noting for the pretty dears?"

"No," replied Harry, impatiently, "I'll buy nothing. I'll take her home no wishey-washey trinkum-trankums, no base metal, covered with a little finery, like the ugly figure-head of the Saracen's phizog, with a gold beard; but I'll take her the pure coin of an unaltered affection, and the hard earnings of five years of toil and glory."

"Very nice," said the Jew, "but you'd petter take dem de earrings, or de shoe buckles, ma dear."

"Mary," continued Harry, as the Jew retired, "would give all the finery in the world for one word of love. My eyes! I'm so happy! my heart is as merry as a newly made middy, and I feel running before the wind of joy with all the sails of content filled to bursting."

"All right!" said Waxend, who now returned; "in half an hour they'll take the peg out of the last—Pooh! I mean weigh anchor: or, vulgarly speaking, be ready to start in that time."

"Hurrah!" shouted our hero. "Eh, here, shipmates. Some of us have been five years together—let our parting be a merry one. Order some punch; I'll pay for all.—Let us have a dance! Drink success to our ship, and then home to our sweethearts and wives. The Invincible! and the memory of the good ship Polyphemus!"

The sailors all responded cheerfully to the toast, and shouted heartily,

"Fill again!" said Halliyard, "I wish the captain would bear down. Now, my lads, Captain Oakheart, and the memory of the brave Manly!"

This toast was drunk with equal cordiality, and the shouts were renewed with redoubled vigour, when Captain Oakheart made his appearance.

"Thanks, my brave fellows," said the captain. "I'll give you a toast anon. Halliyard?"

"Your honour," answered our hero.

"I shall see you in London soon," remarked the captain. "If you call at my banker's, you will find that your friend, Lieutenant Manly, has made you his heir. You saved his life twice, Harry; but your arm could not save him from the grim tyrant in the last action; and, as he had no relations, you will now come into possession of three hundred a year."

"Oh, gemini!" exclaimed the astonished and overjoyed seaman, "three hundred a year! Was there ever such a sum?"

"Don't let wealth spoil you," said Captain Oakheart, "nor your pretty Poll, but tell her that your captain, who admires your honest integrity, will be her father on the day of marriage, and give her, too, the best protection, a good husband."

"Oh your honour," returned Halliyard, "I'm all over gratitude. Won't Poll be proud, not of the money, though I thank and bless the good lieutenant for it, (heaven rest his brave soul!) but to think that your honour, a captain just posted, should—Oh, my heart! what a jolly day we will have of it!"

"Come, my lads," said Captain Oakheart, "fill me a glass of punch! In the meantime," he added, speaking to Waxend, "in the meantime, my good fellow, here is a purse of fifty guineas for the papers you furnished us in the slaver."

"Oh, thank your honour," answered Watchful, taking the purse, and bowing awkwardly to the captain. "My eye, won't I buy a stock of leather and wax!"

"Here's our country," said Oakheart, taking the glass which our hero offered him, "and may she always have sons as brave in battle and as humane in victory as the lads of the late Polyphemus!"

Loud applause followed this toast, and then Captain Oakheart took his leave. The coach now stopped at the door, Harry and Waxend took a hasty but hearty leave of their companions, and then took their seats on the coach, at the same time one of the seamen mounted to the roof and commenced a hornpipe amidst the uproarious shouts and laughter of the spectators; the guard blew his horn merrily, and away went the coach on its way to London.

CHAPTER IX.

MELANCHOLY CHANGES.—DISAPPOINTED HOPES.—THE DESERTED HOUSE.— THE ASTOUNDING INTELLIGENCE.— MY POLL AND MY PARTNER JOE.

ALAS! how sad was the change that had taken place at home since the departure of Harry, and how little did he anticipate the shock that was in store for him; the annihilation of all those bright hopes that had sustained and buoyed him up in every danger. But the melancholy secret will be explained in the due course of our narrative.

Joe Tiller and Sam Sculler were in conversation together in the house of the former. Five years had made a considerable alteration in the appearance of the old man, but Joe had undergone little or no visible change, and he was as good-tempered and poetical as ever.

"And so we are to pull the gentleman down to the bridge, are we?" said Joe.

"Yes," answered Sculler, "and we must make haste to; he said he would be ready in a few minutes, so come along."

"No," said Tiller, "I cannot go without seeing Mary; there's no persuading her out of her melancholy—

All day she sits in tears, as sure as my name's Tiller,
Like a crying cherry-bum, or else a weeping willer.

I'll be bound, now, she's gone down to the old churchyard, to sit by the side of old Dame Halliyard's grave. She's always there; and as for a smile on her face—

They're as scarce to be met with as oysters in June weather,
And as difficult as strawberries in winter time to gather."

"Ah!" said old Sculler, "the poor dame was a mother to her, and how she used to watch the old woman, as she faded day by day! Why you might see her sink inch by inch into the grave."

"Yes," coincided Joe, in melancholy accents, and shaking his head; "and poor Mary got as pale as a winding-sheet, (bless her!). I *must* see her for a moment, and then I'll go to work. Work's my comfort. I don't know how it is, but I feel a something hanging over me; it's very foolish, but—

When the blue devils is wexing your brain,
You way drive them away, but they'll come back again."

"Well, then," observed Sculler, "run down to the churchyard and look for her; I'll go to the Hard and prepare the boat."

"Agreed," said Tiller, going to the window, and looking out. "Ha! here she comes. Look at her dear eyes! They're quite red; yet she seeks to hide them from me, as if my *symphonies* didn't inform me."

Mary now slowly entered the room. Alas! how sad was the change that time had wrought in her appearance. Her form was wasted—her cheeks were ashy pale, and the expression of her once sparkling eyes showed too painfully that care and sorrow had fixed their seal upon her heart, and blighted all her hopes and prospects. The sombre character of her dress (for she was clad in half mourning) added to the general sadness of her appearance. No person could look upon her without experiencing feelings of the deepest interest and sympathy. She advanced towards Joe with a forced and melancholy smile, and giving him her hand, said—

"Did you want me, Joseph?"

"I was just waiting to say a word to you before I went down to the Hard," answered Tiller. "You are still fretting; you shouldn't take on so, Mary—it's breaking my heart."

"I won't, then, Joe," she replied, "for you're so very kind to me. I will endeavour to be cheerful—it is my duty to be so; but I've had a dream, and I've been down to mother's grave, and I couldn't look upon the flowers I've planted there without crying a little, they seemed so like her own dear, bright old eyes. Besides, there's a strange flower grown up among them—I didn't put it there! It came up of itself, like a message from the dead. It's a—yes, Joe, it's a Forget-me-not!" Sobs for a moment choked her utterance, but at length she proceeded;—"a Forget-me-not!"

"Well, well," returned Joe, with visible emotion, though he tried to conceal it, "we never can forget her."

"Oh, never!" ejaculated Mary, fervently. "I hope it will not die, pretty bud, to come of itself! I'll water it every day. Do you know as I looked at it, I heard her dead voice say the words, as sure as I stand here. So you must forgive me for being a little melancholy."

"Yes, Mary," replied Joe. "I'm rather low myself to-day; I had a dream: I thought my boat was run down, and I had a narrow escape of my life."

"Heaven forbid it!" exclaimed our heroine, anxiously; "you are my last friend!"

"I was a fool to let it annoy me," said Tiller, after a pause,—

"Because 'tis a maxim, you see, my dearest Mary,
  That if we dream of one thing, it's sure to come contrary."

"There's one thing I'm dreaming of that won't come contrary," interposed old Sam Sculler; "if we don't go down to the boat, the gentleman will hire somebody else to row him to the bridge, and it's a guinea job."

"Right," replied Joe.

"And if we lose a guinea,
  I know who'll be a ninny.

I don't know when I shall be home, Mary, but Sculler will come with me. Come, cheer up a bit; go out and buy a few trinkums; call on Mrs. Strop, the barber's wife, she'll talk you into spirits. God bless you!

Come along, my old chap, and let us diskiver,
  If the customer's ready to go down the river.

Good by, Mary! good by!"

Kissing her, Joe and his companion departed; and Mary stood for a few minutes wrapped in deep and melancholy meditation; but at length she said—

"I have called on Mrs. Strop already, and I've seen a newspaper. The ship that saved a portion of the crew of the ill-fated Polyphemus has come home—but where is he?"

The intense agony of her feelings stifled her voice for a moment or two, and tears coursed each other down her cheeks.

"Stay—stay, Mary!" she at last continued, "you mustn't think in this way now—yet there can be no crime in loving the dead. I loved Harry living, and I can't do wrong in loving his memory. I passed by the Hard, and I saw the wherry. Joe hasn't taken out his name, for I could see it through the bit of crape he has nailed over it. I looked, and looked, till I couldn't see boat or river; my head swam, and my heart beat. I am a silly—silly girl! he ought to have died with his mother—but I feel I'm burning away. Ha! ha! I'm strong, but it won't last for ever—no—no!"

She was interrupted by hearing the voice of Abigail Holdforth singing without.

"Oh, here comes this silly girl to annoy me," Mary observed. "I have no spirits for her prattle."

Abigail now made her appearance, dressed in the height of vulgar fashion.

"Just comed up to Battersea for a breath of hair," said the loquacious damsel. "Lunnun is so smoky! We, who gets our livelihood in the fashionable quarters, to be sure, is better off than them as vegetates in the purloins of the Mansion-house; but to me, a native of the delightful city of Bullock-Smithey, it's all very condense and mistificatory. So I took advantage of having to measure Mrs. Fubsey, the great malster's wife (who lives within a short distance), for a new Parisian corset, to rustificate for a day, or rather for half a day; for I've got to take home Miss Jemima Jumper's, the dancing master's daughter's new yellow silk frock, and there arn't a stitch done. But I would come to see you, for you know you recommended me into a first-rate Magazin des Modes. I never forgets that to your good nature I'm indebted from the first. But you don't look well. As Mrs. Cackle, the poulterer's wife says, there's a melancholy conglomerfication about you—What's the matter?"

"I'm—I'm not well," answered Mary, who was afraid that Abigail would kill her with talk.

"Do you like this dress?" asked Abigail, turning round and showing herself off to the best advantage. "Pretty taste, isn't it? You can't think how the fellers did stare at me! One sailor gentleman in particular; it struck me I had seen his face afore. At first I thought it was your Harry, but——"

Mary started at the mention of that beloved name, and turned ghastly pale.

"Oh, do not," she implored—"do not! This is cruel!"

"I beg you r pardon," replied Abigail. "I didn't thin k—But I must go to Mrs. Fusbey's. La, she is such a prodigious size round! Oh, now I think of it, there was somebody with the sailor gentleman very like Watchful Waxend! but I was on the coach, and it couldn't be he. Well, good morning. I must go, or Miss Jumper won't have the yellow silk frock, and the Magazin des Modes will lose its charackter for punctuality. Good-morning, my dear; remember me to all; good by. Comment vous portez vous to you. Mrs. Fusbey will be in such a way! Bye—bye!"

She curtseyed, and at last made her exit, much to the relief of our heroine, who felt much agitated by some of the observations she had made us of.

"The sailor gentleman she saw!" she said. "That's like my dream! In my sleep I thought Harry had come back; there he was with his manly face tanned by the sun, but looking better than ever, and his mother was crying with joy. And he was dressed like an officer, and opened his arms for me, and I tried and tried, but I couldn't move near him; yet I heard him speak my name, and I felt sure that he loved me. And this was dreaming! Oh, I wish the sleep had lasted! Yes, how I wish I could have died in that dream. But I awoke, and I——"

Overcome with her emotions, she sunk on her knees, and clasped her hands together.

"Oh, my heart!" she groaned. "Harry—Harry!"

Covering her face with her hands, and sobbing bitterly she hurried from the room.

* * * *

The house that poor old Dame Halliyard and her son had resided in, was deserted—the shutters were closed, and the whole aspect of everything connected with it told too plainly the melancholy event that had happened. Alas! what a sad, sad return was it for the gallant young seaman, after five years of toil and danger; what a fearful disappointment to the sanguine hopes he had formed, the bright visions of the future his fond and ardent imagination had conjured up, was in store for him. But we will not anticipate our story.

Watchful Waxend, having been sent forward by his companion, after they had dismounted from the coach, arrived at the house, the desolate appearance of which he surveyed with astonishment and perplexity.

"Well, this is all very odd," he said to himself. "I've been round the house, as the riddle says; but every window is as close as a clicker's seam, and Harry is waiting for me all this while in the road. He wouldn't come, for fear of frightening the old dame and Mary. He needn't have been afraid; they've gone out for some frolic on the water. I haven't seen a soul I know. Well, I'll go down to the Crown and Crosier; old Wallit will remember me, for I owes him two-and-ninepence. But first to find Harry, and then—"

"Avast, lad!" cried Harry, tapping him on the shoulder. "Why didn't you come? You don't know how my heart has been keeping reckoning of all the time you've stayed. Have you seen 'em? May I go in? Belay there! I'm taken quite aback! What's the meaning of all these dead lights being hung out? Have they shifted their anchorage? Have they fallen foul of any misfortune? Where's my Poll? Where—where's the old mother? Speak! say out what intelligence you've got, or I shall founder with the trembles!"

"The house is shut up," said Waxend.

"I see—I see!" impatiently replied our hero.

"I've been round it, and can't find a hole to peep in at."

"Well—well!"

"So I conclude——"

"What—what?" eagerly demanded Harry, and his heart beat so violently against his side that he could scarcely contain himself.

"Why," answered his companion, "that Joe's giving 'em a bit of a nautical discursion on the river."

"Right, lad, right!" coincided our hero, feeling somewhat relieved; "that's it! My heart was up in my throat! There's no accident happened to the old craft, that the young one's been obliged to sail from her moorings? No —no! Joe would take care of that—! know him—Joe's a true heart. It's hard, though, within sight of port, to be blown out in this fashion. What's to be done?"

"I know what I shall do," answered Waxend; "I shall bear down to the Crown and Crosier, and old Sculler's."

"Good," agreed Harry; "they'll spin you a yarn. Crowd all sail, while I tack about these latitudes. I can't leave the old spot. Come, lad, bear a hand, and be back in the turning of a handspike."

"I'l be back before you can wax a thread," said Watchful, going; but suddenly returning, he added—"You stay here, my boy! I'll hoist a signal that shall put a sparable in your heel, and I'll stick to you like wax!" He then hastily departed.

"No," said our hero, looking anxiously upon every object around him, "I can't leave the old house, though there is nobody to welcome me. I thought I should have been scrunched up with kissings and huggings and handshakings before now. And here, after five years of danger, no one knows me; the old house shuts its door against me; and there's no Polly—no mother—no friend! Well, well," he continued, after a moment's pause, "they didn't expect me. My eyes! how glad they will be to see me when they do come! What a fool I am!—I don't know who lives here," he said, crossing over to the opposite house; "but they'll give me some chart to steer by. I'll knock and ax a question."

He knocked, and then again surveyed the old house with feelings of the deepest emotion.

"Yes," he said, "there's the old garden, and the little dock where I used to launch all the small craft I cut out of the bits of wood I got from Charley Chips, the carpenter. Ah! my pretty Polly was a young one then! La! how she used to laugh to see 'em slip away top-sided down the river! Bless her!"

It was at the house of Mary that our hero had knocked, and at that moment she issued from the door, and without particularly noticing him, in a timid voice inquired,

"Was it you that knocked at our—"

"Ha!" exclaimed Harry, starting, "that voice!—Mary!"

He advanced a step or two, but she receded from him, gazing at him all the while, completely petrified.

"Mary! my own Polly!" ejaculated her lover, in a voice half choked by the power of his feelings, "don't you know me?—Harry, my girl—Harry!"

"Ha!" screamed the poor damsel, frantically, and as if awaking from a dream. "Alive! Harry! my Harry!"

She sprang into his arms, and, overpowered by the tumultuous feelings that rushed upon her, she instantly fainted. What words can describe the emotions of the young seaman as he pressed her lovely form to his bosom?

"Gently, my tender one!" he said, in a broken voice. "But I hardly know myself whether my senses won't desert the flag. Lord love her pretty pale face! Joy's colours, 1 see, are white. Polly, lass, cheerly—cheerly! Come, don't shut the port of your pretty peepers to give your sailor his welcome, like the old mother's house, there! Mary —my precious Mary! Ha! her recollection's heaving to; there—there!"

She partially revived, and looked vacantly around, as if striving to recollect.

"I thought——" she faltered.

"Mary!" exclaimed her lover.

"'Tis he!" she cried, in a delirium of joy. "'Tis so, then!—My dear Harry, you alive, and——"

She again rushed into his arms, but, recollecting herself, she screamed, as she started, shuddering, back.

"No!—don't come near me!—Don't touch me, Harry!—Don't touch me, I say!—It is past!—Oh, cruel deceit!— Don't touch me!—I dare not—I—Oh! my brain is bursting!"

"Good God!" cried the astonished Harry, seizing her arm, "what does this mean?"

"Oh! for mercy's sake!" gasped forth the poor girl, "unhand me—1 am—I cannot speak the word! Let go —let go!" she added, struggling wildly. "I shall go mad!—There—there!" she ejaculated, as she broke from him."

"Oh, pity me! when you know all, pity me!"

With these words, pressing her fair hands to her forehead, and sobbing convulsively, she looked distractedly into the house.

"When I know all!" cried our hero, completely thunderstruck and bewildered; "what all? Is this my fond Mary, that—Oh, I'm dreaming!—Not come near her!"

At this moment old Sculler approached the spot.

"Avast heaving, old man!" said Harry. "A word or two with you."

"Don't stay me," replied Sculler, "I've got important business to——"

"I must have a word with you," interrupted our hero. "Don't you know me, old boy? Why you arn't altered a bit."

"Why no!" exclaimed Sculler, staring at him as if he had encountered an apparition. "What! can it be Harry Halliyard?"

"It is," answered the latter, hastily.

"We thought you dead," said Sculler, in a faint voice.

"Why's the old house shut up?" demanded Harry, eagerly. "Where's my mother? Why does Mary fly from me? Tell me quick, old man; my brain's on fire."

"Oh, unhappy business!" sighed Sculler, "when he knows all!"

"When I know all?" repeated Harry, impatiently. "What is there for me to know? Out with the worst; my mother——"

"Lies in yonder churchyard," rejoined Sam, solemnly.

"Dead!" gasped our hero, staggering back appalled. "Poor old mother— and I not here to close her eyes! Mary?" he added, after a pause.

"Mary is—I—I can't tell you."

"Oh, do, old man, if you have any mercy—if you have any recollection of your green days," supplicated Harry; "those days when your heart loved, and —speak—speak!"

"It must be told," said Sculler, struggling with his feelings. "Mary is —*Mary is married!*"

Had a thunderbolt at that moment descended upon the head of Harry Halliyard he could not have been more astounded than he was at this fatal intelligence. The blow was struck—his hopes were blasted for ever! The cup of happiness was dashed from his lips just at the moment when he fondly anticipated to drain it to the dregs. He stared at the old man wildly as he cried in a hoarse voice, while every limb was convulsed with the power of his emotions—

"God!—married? Mary, that 1 have loved so truly, married?—Oh! ha—ha —ha! it's a lie. You may as well trifle with a hungry shark. Come, tell the truth. Yet she wouldn't come near me. I'm surely going mad! Who's her— her—you know what I mean."

"Her husband?" answered Sculler; "Joe, your partner Joe."

"Oh!" groaned the wretched young man, staggering, and nearly falling "is —is this——"

He tried, but in vain, to finish the sentence, but at length a passionate burst of tears came to his relief, and he threw himself upon the shoulders of poor old Sculler.

"My poor, noble Harry!" said the old man, "I won't attempt to comfort you—words would be in vain; but they were not to blame—I am their witness."

"Not to blame!" repeated Harry, with sarcastic energy—"not to blame? Oh, no, falsehood isn't a fault; treachery isn't a crime. I have been five years away, but I have never for a moment forgotten her; I have worn this lock of hair upon my heart day and night, in the battle, the storm, and the calm, ever since, and her name, my mother's, and his, have been oftener on my lips than my prayers, and dearer to me than the life I ventured! Well, I come back—I—I find her false, the friend I loved a villain, and my poor mother cold and dead! And all through their treachery. No—no—no, they are not to blame! I—I—Curse it! I wish the tears didn't come up in this way—they're fire! Here—here, take my money—take my watch—take all! I earned all for their sake, and now I have lost them!"

He was hurrying away, but Sculler detained him.

"Stay, Harry," he said, "you shall see Joe."

"See him!" repeated our hero; "yes, I will, and—but where can I find him? I——"

"He will be here in an hour or two," answered Sam; "calm the tempest of your feelings, and——"

"Calm!" interrupted our hero, passionately; "you might as well try to hush the voice of the thunder as to stay me in my determination, old man. I will search him out though it be at the farthest extremity of the globe, and—Oh, Mary! Oh, my brain!"

With these words, before the old man could again attempt to detain him, he rushed wildly from the spot, and was immediately hidden from the view.

"Unfortunate youth," said Sculler, as he gazed after him, "how heartily do I pity you. Mary, too! alas, alas, how will this terrible and fatal business terminate?"

The old man sighed deeply, and then slowly entered the house.

————

CHAPTER X.

THE PAINFUL INTERVIEW.—THE DISTRACTION OF MARY, AND THE HASTY DEPARTURE OF HARRY.

WE must now conduct the reader to a neatly furnished apartment in the house of Joe Tiller and his unfortunate bride, from which a glass door opened and commanded a view of the well arranged little garden, the river, and the opening shore beyond. Poor Mary, who for some time had remained in a state of unconsciousness, was now partly recovered, and was endeavouring to peruse a newspaper. Her manner was wild and hurried in the extreme; her cheeks were ghastly pale, upon which the tears still trembled, and her whole frame was convulsed and agitated.

"I can't see!" she ejaculated, with trembling eagerness, "my eyes flash fire—I wish I could cry!—I did see it here.—No, no!—Ha! there, dead! dead!—and yet I have seen him—I have heard him call me his Mary, and I have lived to know myself another's!—Oh! if I could but sink into his mother's grave, and he never know—but he will know—and he will loathe me—he will curse me! Oh, do not, do not, Harry, curse me!—no—no! the old woman begged it with tears in her dying eyes—he won't believe me—he laughs! Oh, God!—I—I would I could die at your feet, Harry, that you might see my heart!—I was true; I—oh, don't spurn me—I—"

She fell insensible from the chair just as old Sculler entered the room.

"Poor, broken-hearted girl," he said feelingly, as he approached her. "She breathes!"

At that moment he turned his head, and was surprised to find Harry Halliyard peeping in at the glass door, and supporting himself by the door-post.

"Look here, Harry," said the old man, in a low voice, and beckoning him. "The poor thing's fainted!"

Harry advanced, and gazed upon her for a moment with an expression of countenance which no language can adequately describe, and Sculler being about to raise her, he hastily prevented him.

MARY SHOWS HALLIYARD THE FALSE NEWS OF HIS DEATH.

"No, no," he said, "let her lie still. Retire for a minute or two, and leave me to my own sad meditations."

Sculler obeyed, and then our hero, gazing sorrowfully on the beauteous and inanimate form that was stretched before him, said—

"There she lies in her pale beauty, like a moonbeam on the stilled waters of the ocean. What a pity that she should be as cold as the one, and as fickle as the other! All my world is in that little spot of earth! Oh, if she could conceive how I love her! Even *her* changing heart would weep for me. But she can't—no, no! she knows nothing of the lively hopes, and the sweet longings of a real love!—Even now—false to me —another's!—my soul is pouring out of my eyes in adoration! I will raise her from the ground—it is a coarse bed for so tender a flower.—I cannot resist the impulse—she will not know that I have stolen that which is now another's—'twill be the last—the last—the last, and for ever !"

Frantically did he press warm kisses upon her pale lips again and again, when he was interrupted by the return of Sculler into the room.

"I think her recollection's leaving to," said Harry, raising her. "Here, take her, old man, take her !"

Sculler raised the unfortunate damsel in his arms, and Harry, overpowered by his emotions, turned away, and wept bitterly.

But in a few moments Mary recovered, though her mind evidently wandered, and she knew not what she said.

"It is true !" she cried, "he is dead, and—mother, don't say so!—I—oh, my brain !"

Looking round wildly, she beheld Harry, and on seeing him she exclaimed —"No, it was no vision ! no creation of the disordered imagination ! Oh, God ! the fatal truth is, alas, too palpable ! I remember all now !"

As she gave utterance to these wild and broken sentences, while her looks were frenzied, she rushed to the table where she had placed the paper in which he was reported to be dead, she held it up to Harry, and in the greatest agony pointing out to him the paragraph, she threw herself on her knees at his feet, and looked up imploringly in his fact, sobbing as though her heart would break all the while.

"'Tis the paper with the account of your death," she with difficulty gasped forth; "read ! read ! and——"

"What of that ?" said Harry, averting his looks, and speaking partly to himself; "had she loved, she would have hoped it was false; she would have gone down to her grave—to her grave—as——"

His emotions overpowered him, and he could not finish the sentence.

"Would to Heaven I had," groaned our unfortunate heroine, still kneeling to him, and fixing the most piteous looks upon him, "would to Heaven I had, Harry ! How did I prove my love? —though 'tis sin in me to speak of it now. Two, three, four years elapsed,

and no letters from you ; but I never doubted—no, great Heaven is my judge I did not. I tried to prove my love for you by performing all the duties of a daughter to your mother. Still time went on; at last the news came that you were killed—we saw it in the newspaper—Joe got the list from the admiralty—there we saw it again.—I won't say how my heart was bleeding as I watched your poor old mother dying with the news—she and I wept together, and prayed for the peace ! I saw she was sinking, too; she trembled to leave me; for your sake she pointed to Joe as a protector—for your sake she begged, and, to let her die in peace, for your sake, Harry, I consented—I became a wife——but I still loved—I still wept in secret, though duty made me silent. Go, it is a broken heart now, and my hand is another's, but 'tis yours till the grave—till—oh, pity !—oh, pity and forgive !"

She could say no more; the maddening anguish of her soul found vent in convulsive sobs, and she sank exhausted in the arms of Sculler.

"I do ! I do !" said Harry, wildly, and striking his manly forehead in a paroxysm of the most unutterable despair; "but can't believe you—no—I have stayed to tell you that there is money—I have earned it for your sake —and if you wish to —not quite to kill me, you will use it."

"Oh, no, no !" cried Mary.

"You will, Mary !"

"Oh, spare me !" she implored.

"You will obey me," returned her lover, in a determined voice, "if you wish me to forget—forget !—oh, that's as impossible as that I should ever cease to love. But you may have need of it—the shoals of adversity ar'n't always to be avoided—even now you are among the breakers. There it is," he added, throwing a bag of money on the table. "And now I forgive you—but him—oh! I would not curse him—God bless you !"

The last words were scarcely audible, so intense was his agony, and he was about to hurry away.

"Oh, pity !" again supplicated the hapless damsel, on her knees, and clinging to him.

"I do ! I do !" he cried; "and do

you pity me. My heart is now a wreck, and I care not how soon this poor hulk founders. Farewell, Ma—Mrs. Tiller— Ha, ha, ha! Oh, God! My reason is all aback!—God bless you!—we shall never meet again; but whoever finds my lifeless corpse, will be sure to recognise poor Harry Halliyard by the precious lock of hair which they will find in his bosom, pressed nearest to his heart!"

"Harry! Harry! for God's sake, what would you do?—Oh, hear me!" shrieked Mary: but it was too late, he had rushed wildly from the house, and though it was but the work of an instant, he was far out of sight and hearing.

"Gone! gone!" gasped forth our heroine, pressing her hands upon her forehead, as if to recall her scattered senses. "Oh, God! my heart must surely burst! Harry—Harry—return! Oh, this is most cruel! Great Heaven! why do you not at once strike me——"

"Mary! Mary!" interrupted Sculler, "hold! give not utterance to such awful words as these, but endeavour to calm your feelings. It is a terrible blow to you both; but the first burst of his anguish over, reason will resume its seat in Harry's mind, and he will endeavour to resign himself to the will of fate."

"Oh, never! never!" sighed our heroine; "it is impossible! The wound inflicted in his manly heart is too deep ever to be healed. Whither has he gone? His last words!—they ring awfully in my ears!—and, hark! a storm is gathering—the moon is obscured by dark and ponderous clouds— and Heaven's wrath is spoken in the voice of the thunder! Harry—Harry— where art thou?—and yet—Oh, God! —my brain is distracted—I know not what I say!"

She sank exhausted on a seat, and poor old Sculler hung over her with looks of the deepest compassion, but was at a loss what to say, or how to impart to her the least consolation.

And now the storm burst forth with the greatest violence. The aspect of all around fully accorded with the melancholy feelings that pervaded the bosoms of the hapless Mary and her aged companion. The moon was completely obscured by dense clouds; the darkness which prevailed was almost impenetrable, and was only interrupted at intervals by the flashes of the electric fluid, which shot across the dark canopy of ethereal space with an effect at once terrific and sublime.

Our heroine continued in much the same state of mind, and the suddenness of the storm had a depressing effect upon the spirits of Sam Sculler.

"Joe will have a drenching," he remarked, "I hope that no accident will happen to him."

"Joe—Joe," said Mary, with a vacant look, and still pressing her hands upon her aching temples, for her senses wandered, "he—he is my—I dare not utter the name. Harry!—where is he? Why did he so suddenly leave me? I—oh, God—oh, God! how will this awful business terminate? He cursed me, did he not? and I am wretched! The cup of my misery is full to the brim."

"No—no—no, my poor lass," said the old man, soothingly, "do not take on so; he forgave you—he pitied you, and——"

"But whither has he gone?" interrupted our heroine, anxiously; "why did he not remain to confirm his words? He is driven to despair, and in such a state of mind, what rash and desperate act may he not be tempted to commit? Oh, Harry, after all the years of toil and danger that you have experienced, what a sad return is this for you to make your native land. Your poor mother mouldering in the silent grave, your friend estranged from you by circumstances over which neither he nor any of us had any control—and he believes me false to him! He looks upon me as a heartless, degraded being! He hates— he despises me! Oh, Heaven, my poor brain! Would that I were dead! Harry, dear Harry, the sight of you, and the knowledge of the despair to which I have unwillingly consigned you, ought to have stretched me a corpse at your feet."

"Mary," replied Sculler, solemnly, "again I enjoin you not to presume to arraign the all-wise though apparently severe decrees of the Supreme; your words shock me, and can have no other tendency to add to rather than decrease your misery. Hope for the best, my child, and depend upon it, that, sad and dismal as your prospects now certainly seem to be, a bright sunshine will supercede the clouds that now obscure your destiny."

Mary made no reply, and seemed to be unconscious of what her aged companion had been saying; but at that moment the voice of Joe Tiller was heard singing merrily as he bent his way towards the house, notwithstanding the raging of the storm, and she started and trembled convulsively in every limb, and was compelled to hold by the back of a chair to support herself from falling.

"Joe!" she ejaculated, and her lips quivered as she pronouced that name; "what a feeling of horror does the sound of his voice now impart to me! What can I do—what can I say to him? How reveal to him the dreadful, the fatal truth? I dare not meet him. Hah!—hark, he comes! Assist me, Heaven, for I know not how to act!"

"Retire into another room for a short time," said Sam Sculler; "be it my painful task to break the fatal intelligence to him, and although the shock to him will naturally be a severe one, I trust that poor Joe will have the fortitude to bear it as a man. Come—come."

She suffered the old man to take her arm, and he lead her gently from the apartment to another room, and then, closing the door after him, he returned, and awaited the entrance of Joe Tiller with as much composure as he could assume.

He had not to wait long, for Joe immediately afterwards entered, shaking the wet off him.

"Dear heart!" he said, "what a rough night it is, to be sure; who would have thought it, after such a lovely day as we have had? But it's no use to grumble about trifles, for—

After a storm comes a calm, so they say,
And I hope we shall have it without more
    delay.

Ah! my old friend, you are here, then? But—eh?—how's this—what's the matter with you, old man? You look as dull as the night. Where's Mary? No doubt she's been most anxious for my return, for—

The heart that loves true can ne'er be elate,
If only deprived for a time of its mate."

"Joe," said Sculler, after a pause, and scarcely knowing how to begin, "I have something to impart to you, which no doubt will equally shock and surprise you; and I must request you to muster all your fortitude to hear it."

"Eh! what?" ejaculated Tiller, "I don't understand you.—There is nothing happened to my dear Mary, is there? Why is she not here to welcome me as usual? Answer me—speak! and do not keep me in suspense!"

"Harry Halliyard——"

"Ah! why do you mention his name at this particular period? Poor Harry—Heaven rest his soul!—I trust that he is now at peace!"

"Would to God he were!" returned old Sculler, impatiently. "But the truth must be told, and the sooner the better. Harry, then—Harry—d—n it! I cannot speak it!—Harry is——"

"Well, this is strange!" said Joe; "your boat seems to have run aground, old man—Harry is what?"

"Alive!"

"Alive!" exclaimed Tiller, starting back, and staring at him incredulously; "you are dreaming, Sculler. Come, come, old man, arouse yourself, and talk something like a rational being. Poor Harry!—did we not read the account of his death in the newspaper? and did I not get the list from the admiralty to confirm it?"

"True—true!" answered Sam, "but both were, by some strange accident, wrong—Harry lives!"

"Lives!"

"Ay, and has returned to England—to Battersea—here!—I have seen him—Mary has seen him, and spoken to him—and——"

"Say no more!" interrupted Joe Tiller, turning ghastly pale, and trembling so violently with the emotion of his feelings, that he could scarcely prevent himself from falling: "you distract and bewilder my brain!—But you are attempting to play a hoax on me, merely to try the strength of my fidelity. Come, come, this is too bad, Sculler—you do not speak the truth."

"As God is my witness, I do," replied the old man. "Harry Halliyard, but a short time since, was in this room, and heard from my lips and those of Mary the fatal truth.—He forgives her—pities her; but has rushed away distracted, I know not whither."

"Am I awake ?" cried Joe, rubbing his eyes, and still looking at Sculler with amazement and incredulity. "Harry Halliyard, my friend, my partner, alive, returned, and I the husband of Mary! Oh, it is impossible!"'

"It is true," answered Sculler.

"True! true!" repeated Tiller; "then the blow is struck which destroys my happiness and that of her who is far more precious to me than my own existence, for ever! My dream—my fatal dream is realized.—My boat is run down, and I am lost for ever!—Oh, Mary!"

The poor fellow laid his head upon the shoulder of Sculler, and was completely unable to restrain the power of his emotions any longer.

"Be calm, Joe," said Sculler; "this unexpected event must be a severe shock to your feelings, I know, but still it is the will of Heaven to put you and your wife to the trial, and you must learn to submit."

"Submit!" replied Joe, bitterly; "oh, how calmly you can talk, because the circumstance does not affect you. But think not that I regret that Harry has escaped from the fate which we thought had befallen him. —No, Heaven knows how sincerely grateful I am for it. But have we not annihilated all his hopes by this unfortunate marriage ?—And must he not look upon me as a base and treacherous villain?—How can I meet him ?—He will not listen to the explanation I have to offer him, and which you know to be true—and Mary loves him, too—and now—Alas! alas! how horrible and overpowering is the thought! My dream of happiness is at an end—There is nothing left for me but to fly, and hide myself in obscurity.

Then farewell, my trim-built wherry,
And all my friends and hopes so merry,
I new must seek some other quarter,
Or quickly make a hole in the water.

But Mary!—where is she?—Why is she not here to communicate to me the fatal intelligence ?—Has she fled with him, and abandoned me to the misery and despair of my own thoughts ?—I—"

"Oh, Joe! in mercy do not thus wrong me by such suspicions, and add to the agony which already distracts my brain!" exclaimed our heroine, darting from the room to which she had retired, and rushing into his arms, "I am your wife, and though I have now nothing to give you but a broken heart, never—never will I abandon you while the purple stream of life continues to circulate throughout my veins. Oh, Joe! had you but seen him, and witnessed the agony, the madness of his despair, how must it have wrung your generous and manly heart! Picture to yourself what his sufferings must be!—After five years of toil and danger, he returned home but to find the hopes he had most fondly cherished blasted for ever!—his poor old mother resting cold and dead in the silent grave—her he loves so fondly the wife of another, and—I shall choke!—Harry—Harry! Break, break, my heart, and let me in death find a release from my miseries!"

Convulsive sobs stifled her further utterance, and she hid her head in the bosom of Joe, and gave vent to her overwhelming feelings in a passionate torrent of tears."

"Oh, Mary," said Joe, in a broken voice, "I—I dare not call you wife—what a terrible and unexpected blow is this for us both! Heaven knows how much I feel for you, and how I hate and loathe myself. And yet I was not to blame; we acted only in obedience to the dying injunctions of the poor old woman; and it has been my constant study to prove to you how much I loved you, and to render you happy. Tell me, Mary, have I ever by a single word or deed given you cause to regret our union, or created in your breast one pang of sorrow ?"

"Oh, never, never, dear Joe!" replied our heroine, fervently; "I should, indeed, be most ungrateful and unworthy did I thus accuse you. You have been the most kind and affectionate husband, and borne patiently with me when sorrow and melancholy rendered me but a sorry companion for you; and for that my heart must ever be indebted to you, more, much more than I can by words express."

"But it is all over now, Mary," sighed poor Joe; "there was a time when—I dare not trust myself to give utterance to my thoughts. But—we must part, Mary; fate wills it, and—"

"Part, Joe?" interrupted the distracted damsel, looking in his face with an expression that was sufficient to penetrate to his very soul; "what dreadful meaning is there in those words? Are you not my husband?—have I not at the altar of God sworn to be faithful to you? and I must be a wretch indeed, unworthy to live and unfit to die, could I break those solemn vows."

"But, Harry," faltered her husband, in accents of agony, "can you ever again be happy with me, knowing that he is in existence? I feel that it is impossible. I know my own unworthiness, and must resign myself to my fate. I will leave you, Mary; I will, like him you love, abandon myself to the perils of the deep, with the hope that some friendly ball may quickly lay me low, and thus again leave you free and unfettered to unite your fate to that man who has so just a claim upon you. Yes, Mary, we must part, but may I cherish the hope that when I am far away you will sometimes bestow a thought of kindness and affection upon poor Joe Tiller?"

"My God!" groaned Mary, looking piteously in his face, "this is too much to bear! You torture me, Joe, by those expressions. I am your wife by every sacred tie, and dare not, must not, encourage any other thoughts but of you. Remain, then, firm, and we may yet become contented and resigned, if not happy."

"Oh, Mary," returned Joe, "this generous expression of your feelings overpowers me. Poor Harry—poor Harry!—but whither has he gone?"

"Alas!" sighed our heroine, "I know not; but from the agony of his feelings, and the words he made use of when he rushed away from my presence, I fear that he may be hurried into the perpetration of some rash act. Oh, Heaven forbid that my dreadful forebodings may not be realised. Would to God that I was satisfied of his safety, and——"

"I will myself go in search of him," interrupted Joe, hastily, "and will not return until I have discovered him, and endeavoured to impart consolation to his lacerated mind."

"You, Joe—you!" said Mary, "in such a storm? No—no, it must not be. Providence, I trust, will watch over him from committing any rash or desperate act."

"Nay, Mary," returned Joe, "you must, indeed, let me have my own way in this painful business; it is not the terrors of the tempest that can deter me from performing my duty towards my beloved and unfortunate friend, and I cannot rest until I have seen him."

"Oh, I fear the consequences should you meet, excited as he at present naturally is," ejaculated Mary. "Do not go. Whither can you seek him?"

"Nay, Mary," said Joe, "surely you cannot think so meanly of Harry Halliyard as to believe that he would harbour feelings of hatred and revenge against his friend, who never did him any wilful injury by word, thought or deed; and who has only been the cause of his present misery and bitter disappointment through a supposition of his death, and the dying injunctions of his mother? I must see him, and come to some explanation of this melancholy business. Come, cheerly, cheerly, Mary, and all may yet be well. Sculler will remain with you while I am gone, and fear not that I shall soon return, and with some intelligence to remove your present doubts and apprehensions. One kiss, Mary, and then to depart on my errand. Bless you! my poor lass—bless you—bless you!"

Our heroine could not return any answer, but she trembled excessively, and a sickly sensation came over her, which she found it impossible to conquer, when Joe embraced and kissed her fondly. Then resigning her to the care of old Sam Sculler, he hastily took his departure.

The storm became more violent; the heavy peals of thunder shook the house to its foundation, and the lightning blazed awfully into the apartment in which our heroine and her aged companion were. Sculler respectfully and compassionately approached her; but her looks were wild, her eyes fixed on vacancy, and she seemed to be almost unconscious of his presence.

"Come, Mary," said the old man, at last, "had you not better retire into another room, where the horrors of the tempest are not so apparent?"

"No," replied Mary, hastily, and arousing from her lethargy, "no, I will remain here! The battling of the infuriated elements is in strict unison with the tempest of passions that now struggles within my breast. Rage on—rage on! The deafening voice of the thunder can impart no feeling of terror to me—it is music to my soul! I can view the forked lightning's vivid flashes with indifference; they cannot equal the fire that scorches up my brain! The very wreck of nature could have no terrors for me, so that I might be included in the destruction! Life! oh, it is now a bitter mockery to me—a curse! for all that rendered it precious is lost to me for ever. Oh, Harry! where are you now?—shall I ever more behold you?—No, no—he said so, and virtue forbids me to encourage such a thought!"

"Mary," observed Sculler, "you must not give way thus to despair. Heaven will acquit you of all blame, and——"

"No, no, no!" interrupted our heroine, wildly, "I am all to blame!—It is I who have destroyed the happiness of one of the noblest of human beings, and annihilated those hopes which my oft repeated vows of constancy had led him to encourage.—I have deceived him—basely, cruelly deceived him; and whatever fate may befall him, it will be upon my head! Oh, what a wretch have I been!—How monstrously have I abused the confidence of that faithful heart! Harry—deeply injured Harry! you can never forgive me, and I feel that I deserve it not. You must hate and despise me—and even now methinks I hear you invoke the most terrible curses on my head. Curse on—curse on!—This devoted heart merits all the maledictions you can give utterance to. There is——"

"Oh, forbear, Mary," interposed Sculler; "you cannot, surely, know what you say, or you would never thus so cruelly and unjustly reproach yourself. Harry Halliyard possesses too noble and generous a heart to entertain any such thoughts against you."

"Oh," replied Mary, bursting into a paroxysm of tears, "he does indeed possess a noble heart, and I have been false to him, and am now properly punished for my base duplicity."

"How can you thus wrongfully accuse yourself, Mary?" said the old man. "I and others can bear ample testimony to the fidelity of your attachment to him, and to the anguish of your feelings when you heard that death had deprived you of your hopes."

"No, no!" she cried, in an agony of despair, " had I really loved him with the sincerity that I professed to do, nothing could ever have induced me to give my hand to another. Oh, it is in vain that you seek to console me, old man; I feel myself to be a being unworthy of sympathy. Oh, my heart! how torturing is the anguish that now corrodes it, and from which I feel there will be no relief but in the grave. Would that my cold remains were mouldering there now! Poor Joe, too! what dreadful misery is inflicted on him through becoming connected with me. Had we never known each other, these horrors would not have taken place. I have proved a curse to all who have become acquainted with me!"

"What madness is this!" exclaimed Sculler; "arouse yourself from it."

"Madness!" she repeated, wildly. "Ay, you may well call me mad! It is no wonder that my poor brain should go distracted with such an accumulation of horrible thoughts crowding upon it. Poor old dame, could you now witness the misery and desolation that is spread around! Joe and Harry, too, should they this night meet, how terrible may be the consequences. God grant that they may not do so, for I fear that in the excitement of his feelings poor Halliyard might be impelled to commit some act of violence, and——"

"Oh, no," returned Sculler, "there is no fear of that; Halliyard will not suffer his passions to overpower his reason; he cannot forget his past friendship so readily, but will listen to the explanation which Joe will have to give."

"And can anything, think you, reconcile him to that which has taken place?" said Mary. "Oh, no, it would be folly—it would be worse than madness to suppose so. I feel convinced that the cup of my misery is nearly full, and the sooner the final blow is struck the better."

"You must persevere, Mary, and banish these dismal thoughts from your mind," replied the old man; "gloomy as your prospects even now are, there are happier days iu store for you."

"Cease, old man," ejaculated Mary, impatiently, "nor seek to buoy me up with any such delusive hopes. Happiness!—oh, it never will again be mine—it is impossible. There was, indeed, a time when I was most happy—when my heart knew not what care and anxiety were—when my path was strewed with flowers — when all was fragrance, and serenity, and content around me; and I fondly hoped that it would last for ever, that nothing would occur to disturb the tranquillity of my life. Alas! time has too painfully convinced me of the fatal delusion. How dreadful is the change that I am now doomed to experience! And yet you talk to me of future happiness! Yes, happiness in the next world, but never again in this."

"Would that I could persuade you to think otherwise," said her companion; "this is, indeed, a severe trial of Providence, but support it with fortitude and resignation, and you will be enabled some time or another, probably before long, to triumph over all the troubles which now surround you. Come, retire into the next room from the contemplation of the storm, which cannot but serve to add to the melancholy of your present thoughts. Joe will, I dare say, soon come back, and then set your doubts and fears at rest."

"Ah, no," replied our heroine, "I cannot entertain any such expectations; when I remember the dreadful state of agitation in which poor Harry left me I dread to see him, for something seems to assure me that my worst apprehensions will then be confirmed. Alas! alas! what a night of terror is this! even the tempest seems to mock at my sufferings, and between its pauses I could almost fancy that I heard the curses of Halliyard invoked upon my head. Oh, why did we ever become acquainted? for I feel myself quite unworthy the love of one so good, so noble, and so honourable, and had he never seen me, he might now have been happy. Harry—Harry, I can never survive this dreadful shock, and I look anxiously for death as my only release from misery so utterly insupportable."

She wrung her hands in the anguish of her despair, and Sculler again exerted himself to the utmost to console her, but with little or no effect. He, however, did at last persuade her to retire into the inner apartment, where she threw herself upon a seat, and covering her face with her hands, she became completely absorbed in her own gloomy meditations, and entirely insensible to all that was passing around her.

CHAPTER XI.

HARRY'S DESPAIR.—THE MEETING BETWEEN HIM AND JOE TILLER IN THE OLD CHURCHYARD.

WE have before described the state of our unfortunate hero's mind when he quitted the presence of her who possessed his whole soul's affections, and for whom he would at any time have sacrificed his life, but who was now lost to him for ever; and it may very well be imagined that the longer he reflected upon it, the more powerful and overwhelming became his angish and despair. The heroic seaman, who had never yet shrunk from dangers in their most appalling form, was now subdued—his spirit crushed—his hopes destroyed; and being now alone, and no one to observe him, his feelings burst forth unrestrained, and he wept like a child. He proceeded onward with hurried and disordered footsteps until he had got to some distance from the house where the affecting scene we have described in the previous chapter had taken place, and his mind was too much bewildered and distracted to notice or to care whither he was going. In the confusion of his mind he had forgotten all about his old friend Watchful Waxend, and, indeed, he was anxious to avoid his society altogether, and seemed as if he would wish to fly from himself. Strange and uncouth voices seemed to mutter in his ears, and his brain became giddy and bewildered. The facts were too astounding and appalling to bear the semblance of reality, and it was with the utmost difficulty that he could persuade himself he was not labouring under the influence of a dream. His Poll—his pretty Poll—his long-affianced bride, the

THE ATTEMPTED MURDER AND ROBBERY BY HUGH BRANDON.

wife of another man, and that man he whom he had ever esteemed as his friend, and in whose honour and fidelity he had at all times placed the most implicit confidence. By Heaven, it was impossible! He must have deceived himself—his senses wandered—he must be labouring under some strange and fearful delusion! At length he paused, and looking around him, had no recollection as to where he was. Everything was strange to him; nothing whatever was familiar to his eye; but that was not much a matter of surprise, considering the number of years he had been absent from his native place, and the far different scenes he had mingled in during that period. He pressed his hand upon his forehead for a moment, and then looked back through the darkness in the direction from which he had come, with a melancholy expression which spoke at once, far more eloquently than language could have done, the painful struggle that was going on in his breast, and showed how deeply the poisoned barb had penetrated his warm and generous heart.

"Cast upon a lee shore," he said, at last, "a complete wreck—not a single timber left on which to float the smallest cargo of hope. The pretty Polly, too, who was to convoy me to the port of happiness, deserted her colours, slipped her cable, stuck to the enemy—no, no, the—the *friend*; ha, ha, ha!—Well, well, Harry Halliyard has lost his reckoning at last, and has forgot how to box the compass. What a fool have I been to trust in the promises of one of the fair craft—I might have been aware that they are as hollow as an empty cask, and as deceitful as the weather. But my Polly—my dear Poll, for whose sake I have braved all the perils of the ocean, and never once cried peccavi when death stared me in the face, (for the thoughts of her, and my confidence in her constancy, doubly nerved my arm, emboldened my heart, and always cheered me on to triumph) to jilt me thus!—Oh, what a precious lubberly boy have I been! But, avast! avast!—Polly is too true a heart ever to turn mutineer—Joe could never turn pirate, and rob his old shipmate of his best, his only treasure!— It is all a hoax—I must have taken too much grog aboard, and been troubled with a fearful dream! Let me open my ports, and look upon daylight!— No—no— all is dark—I am cast alone upon a barren rock, with nothing but a stormy sea around me, and without rudder or compass to steer by. I have seen her—I have spoken to her—she is married!—Yes, those were the words, and they thunder in my ears like the roaring of ten thousand stormy seas! Oh, Mary! Mary! cruel lass! your false and fickle heart has caused your poor, faithful, confiding sailor, to founder in the ocean of despair!"

He paused, for his feelings overpowered him, and his heart was full to bursting. Again he gazed wildly and vacantly around him, and for a few minutes his brain was so bewildered that he had no idea where he was, and only a confused notion as to what had happened.

"And after shipping such a cargo of happy expectations," he resumed at last, "to cast anchor safe again in the harbour of home, with plenty of shiners in my sack, and as rich as a prince—after having arranged in my own mind all the plans for the splicing, and got the promise of the good captain to pilot my fair vessel to church, to be thrown all aback, and cast adrift on the quicksands of a woman's inconstancy, and through the treachery of a friend, in whose hands I would have trusted my life, certain that he would never hoist false colours. Oh, d—n it! this is more than any mortal man can bear with patience! And yet they were not to blame! Ha—ha—ha! Oh, no, *he* was not to blame for persuading *her* to mutiny; *she* was not to blame for yielding to him! Why what a lubber they must take me for to think that they can deceive me by such a yarn as that! They read of my death in the newspaper; they saw it in the admiralty list. Why, it's all a lie! How dare any one enter such a thing in their log when I am alive, and—damme! it would be a bad day's work for 'em, if they tried to play such tricks as them at the cost of Harry Halliyard! I—I damme; I would enter an action against 'em—I—I would board the sharks! I—I—what am I palavering about? I must have gone mad! But no, I remember one thing—that Mary is false, and that Joe is a villain. Yes, and I will bear down upon the pirate, too, when he little expects it, and pour such a broadside in upon him, that shall send him to old Davy in less time than the boatswain could pipe all hands. The infernal shark! He to rob me of my Mary! Oh, let me but come athwart his hawse, and may I be hanged up to the yardarm the next moment, or flogged to death by marines, (which is one of the most scurvy deaths that a seaman can die), if I do not call him to such an account, that he will be scuttled and sunk to the bottom of the ocean of shame in an instant. But," he added in more gentle tones, "how beautiful and innocent she looked as I held her in my arms, and with her pale cheeks, and eyes teeming with tears; surely falsehood could never hoist such signals as those. Bah! what a swab I am! she was only hoisting false lights to deceive me, and to consign my poor vessel to the shoals and breakers. The captain she now sails under knows well enough how to teach her, and I dare say that they are both now laughing merrily enough at my expense; and to think how they have gulled and cheated me! And I have left them the prize-money of five years of hard toil and danger to complete the joke! Well, let 'em have it, and welcome, and much good may it do 'em. Harry Halliyard has no use for money, now; though I should think if they have not tossed conscience overboard altogether, every coin of that money they touch will serve to remind them of the black treachery with which they have acted towards me, and raise such a rough sea of thought in their breasts that they will find it a hard matter to weather. Gold! no— what do I now value it? I never prized it only for the sake of my Polly, because I thought it would make her a lady, and considered worthy of the friendship and society of her superiors. But it is all over now—there is not a hope left for me in the world! I must never behold her again, for the sight of her would unman me, and render me as weak and soft as my own upper-works must have been ever to be tricked and cajoled in the manner I have been. Oh, Mary! Mary! you will surely live to repent this."

His voice again faltered, and he remained silent for a few moments, and communing with his own gloomy thoughts, perfectly regardless of the storm, which had now commenced, and soon raged around him with the most terrific fury.

"And then to spin the base yarn that it was by the advice of the old dame, and in obedience to her last words, that they committed the guilty act! What a shameful falsehood is that! Could the old woman ever beg for the destruction of the hopes of her darling son, and that, too, at the very moment when her soul was summoned up aloft?—Oh, it's impossible! Poor old mother! and even you are taken from me—your cold remains are now mouldering in the dark cockpit of the grave, and I shall never behold you on this earth again!—I am left alone, without a home, without one single being to smile upon me, or to bid me welcome! Oh, Harry! Harry! better, much better would it have been for you had you long since have been made food for the sharks, than to be left to a fate like this! But what's this? —my pumps at work again!—pshaw! what a fool I am—I have become as weak as a powder-monkey—I—I—"

In spite of all his efforts to the contrary, the noble heart of the young seaman overflowed, his tears burst forth in a torrent, and he was unable for some minutes to give utterance to another word, and, in fact, his mind was so bewildered that he scarcely knew where he was.

The terrors of the scene increased; the storm became perfectly frightful: but still the young seaman stood regardless of its fury, and abandoned himself entirely to the intense agony of his own thoughts. Suddenly, however, he started from his lethargy, and folding his arms, as he gazed at the battling elements, he exclaimed:

"Ay, roar away! The tempest blows great guns, and the engagement becomes more fierce every instant—but it has no terrors for Harry Halliyard—no, he has lost the sheet anchor of hope, and, boarded by the foe, despair, all weather is alike to him! There is a fiercer storm raging within his breast than that which shakes the heavens. Mary!—why do I trust myself to repeat that name? and yet there is something about it which, in spite of what has happened, makes it constantly float in my memory, and rise to my lips. Oh, that so fair, so trim-built a craft, should ever hoist false colours, and make a wreck of that heart that was so faithful to her. But —but—I cannot curse her.—Curse her! no—no—I—I—d—n it! pirate or mutineer, although she has deserted that flag of which I thought she once was proud, and sails under the command of another captain, I can never cease to love her until I have finished the cruise of life, and my shattered hulk is moored in the bilboes of the grave. Oh, how happy we once were—before her heart knew deceit, and her Harry was all the world to her! But, no—I only deceived myself—she could never have loved me, or could she have acted as she has done ? What a lubber I must be to believe her ! Oh, Mary ! Mary ! what misery has your cruel conduct caused to that man who would have sacrificed his life, his very soul to serve you, and who could have knelt at your feet every moment and worshipped you."

He gazed upon the dark waters of the river, which were ever and anon illumined by the lurid glare of the forked lightning's flash, and as he did so, he continued—

"Roll on, ye dark waters, roll, ye stormy billows, mountains high ; your mournful howling is music to my soul and the storm which convulses you is in strict accordance with my feelings. You seem to invite me to return to you, and in the distance to which you will bear me from all that I can ever love, mayhap to drown the remembrance of—No—no, I can never forget ! That is as impossible as I can forget my duty to my king and country, or hoist the yellow flag at the sight of an enemy. Everything is entered in my log in characters that nothing can destroy. I thought, after all the dangers and hardships I had encountered, to lay myself up in the port of matrimony, and with Poll for my chief mate, Joe for my lieutenant, old Sam Sculler for my cockswain , and a crew of jolly and honest hearts on board, to pass the remainder of my days undisturbed by squalls, and clear of the breakers of trouble. But it seems I have made false soundings ; it is all over now, and there is nothing left for me but to weigh anchor, spread all my canvas, and go to sea again. Yes, that must be it ; the blue waters of the deep must be my future home, the gallant ship my future mistress. D—n it, Harry ! you must not founder in the ocean of despair altogether ! Overboard with care, say I ! I—I will think no more of the—the pretty, dear, d——d faithless Polly ! She—oh, it's a hard task—it's a hard task !"

He dashed away his tears, struggled manfully with the wild tempest of his feelings, and then rushed away from the spot, through the fierce raging of the storm, and totally unmindful as to where he was going. His brain was bewildered, and various and conflicting were the thoughts that rushed tumultuously

through it ; but he had no settled purpose, and, in fact, cared but little what became of him. At first he thought of joining Watchful Waxend at the Crown and Crosier ; but he was in no state of mind to listen to the badinage of that eccentric individual, or to enter into any explanation of the circumstances that had taken place, though there was no doubt that he had become acquainted with them before this, and he, therefore, hurried on, his only anxiety being to get as far away as possible from the spot which contained Mary and her husband. In this manner he continued to wander for some time, the storm all the time abating nothing of its fury, but, on the contrary, seeming to increase ; when, suddenly looking up, as the noise of the people passing him aroused him, he found himself in the streets of Westminster, though how he had got there he could not form the least conjecture, nor did he trouble himself to think about it ; for, wretched and deserted as he now considered himself to be, all places were alike to him. He found himself close to an old-fashioned public house, from which loud sounds of merriment proceeded, and being wet, wretched, and weary, he entered it, determined to seek to drown the present misery of his thoughts in drink, and completely reckless as to what became of him.

He made his way to the room from which the sounds proceeded, and which contained a motley assemblage of half-intoxicated individuals, two or three of whom, from their appearance, were sailors. They were all carousing merrily ; the landlord, a rubicund-nosed, fat-bellied individual, smoking a long pipe, being one of the company, and seeming to enjoy himself heartily. On the entrance of Harry, the guests paused in their merriment, and eyed him for a moment, and having apparently satisfied themselves as to his character, they gave him a most cordial welcome, which compliment Harry returned with his usual familiarity, and for awhile the recollection of his misery was banished from his mind in the contemplation of the scene and the persons before him.

"What cheer, shipmates !" he cried, extending his hands to them with as much freedom and hearty good will as if they had been on intimate terms for years; "so, you have got the grog aboard, eh? And a good thing too, on such a rough night as this; I have been tossing about for some time in the storm, and didn't know if I should be able to weather it out or not, for, you see, my vessel is in rather a crazed condition, so, I thought I might as well put in at this port, where, if the skipper has no objection, I will remain till the morning, that is, if he can find a berth for me, which, perhaps, he can, as I am not very particular."

"All right, my lad!" said the landlord; "and let me tell you you could not have cast anchor, as you call it, in a better place, or amongst a more jovial crew of good fellows. What shall I have the honour of doing for you?"

"A crown-bowl of punch for every man in the room," replied poor Harry; "a cargo of backey—plenty of pipes! Harry Halliyard will pay for all, and d——n the expenses!"

"Hurrah!" cried the whole of the guests, vociferously, and again shaking the distracted and bewildered seaman by the hand; "you are one of the best fellows as we have seen here for many a long day."

"Harry Halliyard!" ejaculated one of the men partly to himself; starting at the mention of the name, and fixing a hasty but scrutinising glance upon him.

"Ay, messmate," replied our hero, "Harry Halliyard, of his majesty's ship, the late Polyphemus, and as noble a craft as ever ploughed the deep, or poured a broadside into the enemy! I am not ashamed to own my name, for I defy any man to produce a black mark agin me, and I wish that every man could say the same with a clear conscience, when he comes to be overhauled."

The man who had spoken muttered something to himself, which, in the noise that prevailed, did not reach the ears of the company, and then resumed his seat in the chimney corner, still eyeing our hero narrowly. He was an ill-looking fellow, apparently about fifty years of age, with a dark complexioned countenance, repulsive features, and large black whiskers. He was dressed in a large pea-coat, with coarse canvas trousers, and his waist encircled by a broad leathern belt.

"Oh, here is the grog," said Harry, when the landlord made his re-appearance in the room. "All right! Now we will have a jolly night of it; never was in better spirits—capital spirits. What should I have to trouble me? Just returned from sea, after buffeting about for five long years—lots of prize money, as rich as a nabob; and would not care if his gracious majesty, King George, (God bless him!) was my father. Drink, messmates, drink, and send dull care to old Davy. We won't have the old shark here! Come, I will give you a toast. Here's to the girl of our heart, to her that is faithful to the lad who loves her; and confusion to the jade who would ever desert him, and rough seas and no help for all false friends and treacherous swabs."

"Bravo!" shouted the guests, drinking the toast most heartily.

"So," observed the man whom we have already described, "you have only just come ashore then, messmate, and have had a successful cruise, eh?"

"Successful!" repeated Harry, sporting a bag full of gold and notes; "you may say that, my old trojan; and here is something in proof of it which will do some of your eyes good to see. But push the grog about, lads; there is plenty more when that is gone, and Harry Halliyard will pay for all."

"And so you were one of the crew of the Polyphemus?" said the man before alluded to.

"Ay, shipmate," replied the young seaman, "and rare sport there was on board of her, I can tell you. Didn't we bang the foe? Then we destroyed a set of piratical rascals, and took possession of their stronghold on the rock of Martinique."

"Ah!" ejaculated the man, and a dark and sinister expression passed over his features, which he tried to conceal from the observation of Halliyard, as he added—"That was a bold achievement, no doubt, shipmate. But was not the Polyphemus afterwards destroyed by fire?"

"True," answered our hero, "and a sad job it was, for the British fleet could ill afford to lose her, after the service she had done. The poor Polyphemus! She was a gallant craft, and had never yet struck her colours to the foe, however powerful they might be. Oh, that another Polly had been as true as she was! But, I say, messmate, now I come to look at our figurehead, it strikes me that I have seen you somewhere before. Are we not acquainted?"

"Not at present," said the man, "but I trust we shall be so better by-and-bye," he added, with another peculiar look, of which Harry Halliyard took no particular notice.

"Ay, I trust so," returned our hero, "for I love a honest-hearted fellow as I love my life, and I would never see him want while I had a shot in the locker. Drink away, my lads! drink away!"

The company present did not scruple to accept of this invitation, and the grog passed merrily round, amidst the most uproarious shouts of mirth, Harry quaffing glass after glass, until his senses began to reel and his brain was fevered. The man with whom he had held the brief conversation we have described seldom removed his eyes from him when he thought he was not noticing him; and the expression of his countenance fully showed that there was something of a dark and guilty nature passing in his mind.

It was now past two o'clock, and our hero having recovered himself a little, arose from his seat, and addressing himself to the landlord, said—

"So, you say you can find me a berth on board this craft, old boy, eh?"

"Yes, my lad," answered the host, "two or three of the company present are staying here just now—but I have still a spare room, where you will find yourself in as snug quarters as you could wish, I can tell you."

"All right!" said Harry, "then just you take me in tow, and pilot me to it, d'ye hear? for I feel myself half-seas-over, (it is not three-water grog that you sell) and I think a turn in would do me no harm. Good night, messmates, good night! Heave a-head, old boy!"

Thus saying, Harry Halliyard shook the hands of every person present, and then followed the landlord out of the room, and up the stairs to the room he had mentioned, and left the guests to disperse at their leisure. They all did so with the exception of the man who had addressed himself so particularly to our hero, and when he found himself alone, he arose from his seat, advanced to the door, and having listened attentively, seemingly to ascertain that no one was at hand to overhear him, he said—

"So, Master Halliyard, we have met at last, and under the most fortunate and favourable circumstances. He has plenty of money about him, which must be mine, together with the gratification of my revenge. He little imagines who I am, and how much cause he has to dread me. If fate does not frown upon me, this night my brother's death, and that of my comrades at the fort, shall be avenged! When all have retired to rest, I can easily make my way to the chamber—the quantity of drink he has taken will cause him to sleep soundly, and then the deed can be accomplished without difficulty. He cannot offer the least resistance.—If he does, he will have to pay for it with his life, that's all!"

At that moment the landlord returned into the room, and as he entered he remarked—

"There, I have stowed him away comfortably enough in the room up stairs; and I think, after the quantity he has had to drink, he will go to sleep without rocking. I hope I shall be able to persuade him to remain at my house for a week or a month, for he is one of the right sort; I never saw a man bleed so freely. What say you, Brandon?"

"Ay," replied the latter, "he appears to be a generous fool, sure enough, and he has got plenty of money, a little of which would do neither you nor I any harm! But I think I shall follow his example, and retire to bed, for I feel rather drowsy and weary. Good night, Welden!"

"Good night, Master Brandon," responded the landlord; "I suppose I shall have no occasion to call you in the morning?"

"No," returned Brandon, "I do not expect that I shall feel inclined to rise very early, and I shall require no one to arouse me."

"Very good," said the landlord, and Brandon quitted the room, yawning as he went, and affecting to be overpowered by sleep.

Harry Halliyard, on reaching the chamber which was allotted to him for his repose, threw himself in a chair, and now that he was alone, in spite of the drink he had taken, and the influence of sleep that was upon him, his thoughts again wandered to the melancholy and unforeseen circumstances of his fate, and he became as truly wretched as he had been before.

"What a poor crazy vessel I now am," he soliloquised; "I must shortly go to pieces altogether, and become a complete wreck! Oh, Mary! cruel lass! it is your falsehood that has done all this! May the Great Commander aloft forgive you.—And yet, poor girl, if she has spoken the truth, is she not to be pitied? But, no, after what has taken place, I must be a land-lubber, indeed, to believe her. There is no excuse to be offered for her—had she loved me as fondly and as truly as I do her, she could never have been persuaded to have given her hand to another, even though she were convinced that my body was placed under hatches. Shiver my timbers! the thought of this will drive me mad! Here's a berth for Harry Halliyard, after five years of absence on the perilous deep; and when he had fondly anticipated that he should have been moored in a happy home, and gladdened by the smiles of the girl of his heart!—Well, well, it is no matter what becomes of me now—I do not care the cracking of a biscuit, or the turning of a handspike, whither I steer. I have been cast away on the desolate island of despair, and the sooner I perish altogether the better. Here is the lock of her hair, which I have prized beyond everything else in the world but her to whom it belonged—but why should I treasure it now, since she has so cruelly, so basely deceived me? It will only serve to remind me of my misery!—I will cast it from me, and—but no, I cannot deprive myself of this little memento of her former love. It is all I have in remembrance of her, except a broken heart; and I shall never behold her again. Oh, Mary!"

He pressed the lock of hair to his lips again and again, sighed deeply, and then sunk into a melancholy silence, which continued for several minutes, and during which period the poignant anguish of his thoughts and feelings may be far better imagined than the most eloquent pen could possibly pourtray them. At last, being overpowered by sleep, fatigue, and anxiety of mind, he threw himself on the bed in his clothes, without taking the precaution to lock the door, and soon became unconscious of all around him.

About a quarter of an hour elapsed, when the door was silently and cautiously opened, and the ruffian Brandon entered the chamber, bearing a dark lantern in one hand and a knife in the other. He closed the door after him, and then shading the lantern, he advanced on tiptoe towards the bed on which the unconscious Harry Halliyard was lying, and listened.

"He sleeps!" he muttered to himself; "it was lucky he did not use the precaution to fasten the door. Everything is favourable to the accomplishment of my designs. How little does he dream that the brother of Black Brandon now stands over him, and that his life is in his hands. But I will not take it at present unless I am compelled. Another time I shall probably have the opportunity of gratifying my revenge: at present it will be enough for me to secure his money, and that will afford me a rich booty. Now to business—I have not a moment for delay!"

As the ruffian thus spoke, he commenced searching the pockets of the sleeper for the money, but he could not find it, it having dropped on the floor in the hurry with which our hero had thrown himself on the bed.

"Confusion!" he exclaimed, "it is not here! and yet I am certain that he returned it to his pocket after displaying it below. What can he have done with it?—I must search again!"

He did so; but in the hurry and agitation of the moment he handled the person of Halliyard more roughly than he should have done, the spell of sleep was broken, and Harry started alarmed, confused, and surprised, from his bed, and a broad flash of lightning which at that instant gleamed in at the window fell full upon the countenance of the villain, and revealed to our hero his features.

"Hollo!" he cried, "what devil's work's afloat now?—Hold hard, mate!—you have made a mistake, and steered into the wrong berth—tack about, and

—ah! what is it you, my black-whiskered friend?—What brings you here?—You do not speak!—I begin to suspect that you are a pirate—so clear the way —sheer off—or, damme! you will have my grappling irons upon you in less time than you could cry Jack Robinson!"

"D——n!" cried the ruffian, fiercely; "discovered!—foiled!—Then, Harry Halliyard, you have but one course to adopt, and this it is—die!"

As he gave utterance to these words, he raised the knife in the air, and was about to plunge it in the breast of our hero, but before he could do so Harry grasped his arm, wrested the knife from his hand, and hurling him to the other side of the room; he was about to follow him up, when the miscreant, with the quickness of thought, threw up the window, and although it was a considerable height from the ground, he leaped out, and Harry hastening to it, was astonished to find that he had alighted in safety, and quickly recovering himself, he fled along the street at the top of his speed, and was almost immediately hidden from the view in the darkness.

"What ho! ship ahoy!" shouted Harry, "there are pirates on board! Captain, ahoy!"

Thus shouting, he rushed from the room down the stairs, and alarmed all the inmates, who started from their different chambers, with the landlord (who was dressed) at their head.

"Hollo!" demanded the astonished host, "what, in the name of wonder, is the matter?—why are you kicking up this disturbance, my good friend?"

"Why!" repeated Harry; "why isn't it enough, quite time enough to pipe all hands and prepare for action when the enemy is aboard? That respectable-looking gentleman who was sitting in the chimney corner to-night has just been in my berth, with the intention of overhauling my pockets, and laying his grappling-irons on my gold, I suppose; but I awoke too soon for him, and he has made his escape by leaping through the port-hole."

"Is it possible?" said the landlord.

"Possible!" repeated Harry; "to be sure it is! do you think that I am throwing the hatchet? I tell you he was in my room not five minutes ago,

woke me by examining my clothes, and would have murdered me too, only I happened to wrest the knife from his hand, and he then thought it more safe and prudent to sheer off as quickly as he could."

"I am astonished," said the landlord. "I would not have had this happened upon any account, for mine is a very respectable house, and this might injure its reputation. But have you lost your money?"

"I don't know," replied Halliyard; "but I haven't got it in my pockets, so I suppose the infernal shark has sheered off with it. Ah, now I remember that I dropped it on the floor, when I threw myself on the bed, and I would not trouble myself to pick it up again, thinking it would be safe till the morning. Bear a hand, mate, and we will go in search of it."

The landlord made no answer, and they made their way to the chamber, where they had the satisfaction of finding the money safe on the floor, where our hero had dropped it.

"Ah!" cried Harry, "the lubber is disappointed; no doubt he thought to capture a rich cargo of shiners, and that would have been rather provoking. As it is, there is not much harm done; but the infernal swab had better not come athwart my hawse again, or I will pour such a broadside in upon him as shall shake every timber in his black-looking hull."

"Well," said the landlord, "I could never have believed this of him."

"Hark ye, my old boy," remarked our hero; "if you suffer such a chap to enter his name in the ship's company, you may chance to get overhauled in such a manner as you won't like."

"Indeed, my friend," observed the host, who was evidently much alarmed, "I had not the least suspicion that he was the character he has shown himself to be, and I am extremely sorry for what has happened, and congratulate you on the preservation of your money and your life."

"Avast heaving there, mate," replied Harry, "there is enough of such lingo as that: but have you known the swab long?"

"Why—why," returned the landlord, hesitatingly, "not—not very long, and

THE ATTEMPTED SUICIDE IN THE CHURCHYARD.

after what has happened, I can assure you that I have no wish to cultivate his acquaintance."

"Well, I must say that I do not think it would be much of an honour to you," said Harry. "But do you know the name of the craft?"

"His name?" answered Welden. "Oh, yes, the only name that I know him by is that of Hugh Brandon."

"Brandon!" cried our hero, with a look of astonishment. "Why, splice my timbers, this is a rum go! Brandon! why, that was the name of that rascally pirate, the captain of the slaver; and now I recollect that the ugly figurehead of this fellow resembles his as much as ever I saw. Do you know whether this Hugh Brandon, as you call him, ever had a brother?"

"I have heard him say that he had," returned the landlord, "and that he perished at sea; but what he was, he never told me."

"Ah!" cried Harry, "'tis the same, and no wonder that this scoundrel should seek my life. What brings him cruising in these latitudes?"

"I don't know," answered Welden, "but I understood that he had not been long from sea, and that he had only come to London to visit some relations before he rejoined his ship."

"Visit his relations!" repeated Harry, "then they must be the devil and some of his imps. But I am sorry that he has escaped, for he may have the chance to do some more mischief. However, should I ever come cross him again let the lubber look out for squalls, that's all I've got to say. He must have been one of the fellows at the fort, and how he managed to escape I can't think."

"Had you not better retire to rest again?" inquired the landlord.

"No," replied Harry, "this bit of a squall has spoilt my rest; so I will just cast anchor in the room we occupied to-night; and hark ye, bring me a jorum of your stiffest grog, none of your three-water stuff, mind, for I feel inclined to splice the mainbrace again, and will thus occupy myself till daylight."

The landlord assented, and leading the way down stairs, our hero took his seat by the fire, and the host departed from the room to procure what he had ordered, with which he soon returned, and having exchanged a few words with him, he once more made his exit, and left him to his own reflections.

The late event that had just taken place for a short time diverted the thoughts of our hero from the melancholy subjects that had before engrossed them; and his singular meeting with the brother of Black Brandon caused him not a little astonishment; but soon all the agony of his feelings was revived with redoubled and overwhelming force, and he arose from his seat and paced the room backwards and forwards in a state of the greatest agitation. The storm had ceased, and a gloomy silence, which was scarcely less appalling, reigned on everything around, and was not at all calculated to diminish the melancholy feelings that pervaded the breast of our hero.

"Mary," he said, "if your heart feels but half the misery that mine does now, I do indeed pity you. But, no; it has become as cold and insensible as a rock, and mayhap you are now only laughing at the poor, fond, silly lubber, whom your falsehood has cast adrift to buffet with the waters of misfortune, without rudder or compass!—And another is moored in those arms where I only hoped to find a haven of happiness! Even now, your lips are pressed fondly to those of him whom I considered my friend, my partner—your *husband*! (oh, God!) and not one thought do you bestow upon the poor sailor but one of scorn, if not of hatred! My senses are all aback—I know not what I say!—But no, I cannot, will not judge her so harshly! She must indeed be a wretch, if she can entirely forget that man who has ever shown his pure devotion to her! How piteous were her looks! what anguish seemed to rack her soul at our last meeting!—Could that be hypocrisy?—Oh, no! Mary, I will endeavour to believe you; though, alas! everything looks so suspicious against you. But I must not continue to cruise about in this latitude—I dare not trust myself to remain here, yet I hesitate to depart! I must be firm— she is another's bride, and I must weigh anchor, and set sail to some other part of the world, where I may learn to forget her! Oh, what a swab I am to talk in that manner! Forget her?—that is no more possible than that I can stay the fury of the tempest, or bid the mighty waters of the deep to stand still! And must I never look upon that lovely face, which has been constantly present to my imagination during my long absence from home, again?—No, I must not; for now that she is the wife of another, it would be sinful for me to seek to do so. But Joe!—Ah! I must, and will see him—pour into him the full broadside of my reproaches and indignation, and then, farewell to old England for ever! Again will I brave the perils of the deep, regardless what dangers I may have to encounter; and if it is not my fate to perish by the battle or the tempest, I will seek some lonely isle, where I can hide myself from the sight of my fellow-creatures, and indulge my melancholy thoughts alone and uninterrupted. Poor Harry Halliyard is now all aback, and cares not how soon his mizen-topsail is hove to the mast!"

He paused, overcome by his emotions; and although he struggled all in his power with his feelings, he was unable to obtain the least degree of consolation, or to come to any conclusion as to the course he should in future adopt. He could not make up his mind not to behold Mary again; and yet, at the same time, he dreaded and shrank from the interview. He also pictured to himself the sufferings she was at present enduring; for notwithstanding all that she had stated to him should be false, and that her union with Joe Tiller was her own voluntary act, he could not believe that she could have become so entirely insensible to every proper feeling as not to sympathise with him in his misery and despair; and when he remembered the condition in which he had left her, he began to think that he had been almost too impetuous and uncharitable, and he trembled with apprehension lest anything should have happened to her.

Such were the torturing and conflicting thoughts that continued to rack the brain of our hero for several hours after the occurrence which has been described in the previous pages; and it was in vain that he endeavoured to gain the least tranquillity. Daylight at length appeared, and the landlord soon afterwards entered the room, and asked him if he would like to partake of breakfast. Harry, however, excused himself, for he was in no humour to eat, and after having exchanged a few words with the host, and settled his score, he quitted the house, and once more slowly, and in the same dismal state of mind, bent his steps towards the neighbourhood of Battersea. On arriving there he hesitated what to do, but at length he walked towards the spot where our heroine resided; half resolved to again present himself before her, and then to bid her farewell for ever; but on arriving in sight of the house his heart failed him, and he paused and reflected, pressing his hand upon his forehead, and feeling all that maddening

despair and anguish which might have been expected under all the circumstances. He at last ventured to approach the parlour window, but the blinds were drawn, and he was unable to see into the apartment; he listened, but all was still, and a terrible thought that something fatal had happened crossed his mind. Good God! he reflected, and the blood froze in his veins as he did so, should the shock have been too much for her strength to support, and death had overtaken her! The thought was too dreadful for encouragement, and he strove to banish it from his mind; but still he remained rivetted to the spot, and was completely bewildered, and at a loss how to act. With what bitter anguish did he contemplate the now deserted house of his poor old mother; and the melancholy thoughts which that engendered were almost overpowering, and caused the tears to start to his eyes.

"Dear old mother," he ejaculated, "I shall never more hear the sweet tones of her gentle, soothing voice, or behold your smile of affection as you gazed with maternal pride upon your son. How short does now appear that portion of the voyage of life which I have already weathered; and yet how rough have been the storms that I have experienced. All the scenes of my childhood, those happy days when I was only a little cockboat, no higher than a marline-spike, now rush upon my memory, as clearly as moonbeams reflected on the ocean. Would that I were a child again, surrounded by all the blessings that were then my lot, with the poor old dame fondly watching me with anxious care, and Mary innocent as innocence itself, with her rosy cheeks and her merry laugh joining me in my playful sports, and knowing no one on earth whom she loved more fondly than myself. What a change, a fearful change has now taken place. I can scarce believe it is reality. Mother dead!—Mary false to me and the wife of another! It is enough to drive me mad! But, avast—avast, Harry!—you must not suffer your pumps to be set agoing again. She— she is unworthy of a thought! She is a —Oh, God, it is no use; false or true —wife or no wife, I can never cease to love her as fondly, as fervently as I have ever done, while I am still alive. But, my poor mother," he added, after another pause. "I have not yet paid the proper tribute of a son to your memory. Old Sculler told me that your poor bones moulder in the old churchyard yonder, and thither will I steer my way, and invoke on her grave the blessing of her sacred spirit."

With these words, Harry Halliyard, endeavouring to stifle his emotion as much as he could, and once more fixing an anxious glance upon the residence of Mary, slowly quitted the spot, and bent his steps towards the old churchyard in which the mortal remains of his mother were deposited. He had not, however, proceeded many paces, when some person abruptly crossed his path, and looking up his astonishment may be imagined when he beheld the villain Hugh Brandon.

Brandon was evidently no less confused and astonished than himself, and he started back a few paces when he recognised him whom he had doubtless little expected to see, but at the same time he exhibited not the least alarm, but stood gazing at him with a scowling brow.

"Ah, you infernal shark!" cried our hero, "so I have borne down upon you again, have I? This time, if you escape me, my name's not Harry Halliyard, and I hope I may never mount up aloft, or heave the lead!"

As he gave utterance to these words, he was rushing upon Brandon, to seize him by the throat; but the latter, with the utmost coolness and deliberation, drew from one of his coat-pockets a pistol, which he presented at the head of our hero, who started back, at the same time laughing triumphantly and sarcastically.

"You, see, Master Halliyard," said the fellow, in the most disagreeable tones, "that I am better prepared to meet you than you anticipated. I would remind you that you have no child to deal with; therefore, if you would prolong your life for a short time, you will sheer off, and save me the trouble of quieting you for ever. The time has not yet exactly arrived for Hugh Brandon to seek his revenge on the destroyer of his brother. We shall meet again under far different circumstances, and then I——"

"Avast heaving there, you picca-

rooning Malay Junk! You talk about running down a gallant gun-boat like Harry Halliyard?—You—you—you be d—d!"

"You may swagger, my fine fellow," replied Brandon, but the time will come when you shall find to your cost that the threats of Hugh Brandon are not to be despised."

"So," said Harry, "you are the brother of that infernal rascal whom I was the means of destroying, eh?—A pretty, side-going, land-crab you are ;— you and honesty steer as wide apart as cowardice and a British tar. You are no more fit to live in this merry country than weevils in a seaman's biscuit; so, damme, part company before in spite of that popgun of yours, I give you a lurch into port that shall settle you down in the old one's locker."

"Ha, ha, ha!" laughed the ruffian scornfully. "Fool! what effect think you your empty threats will have upon Hugh Brandon? I hold the power in my hands to quiet you in a moment, but again I tell you that I seek a more deliberate and terrible revenge, and I will not fail to have it, too; and that in such a form that it shall make even your stout heart shrink appalled to sue to me for mercy!"

"Sue to you, you infernal-looking swab!" cried Harry, half resolved to rush upon the villain, and inflict summary punishment upon him; "why you—you are one of the devil's flying fish! Don't look at me with your rat's eyes, you grampus, or, may I go down in a Nor-wester, if I don't put the cat on your back to frighten them out of your head!"

"Ha, ha, ha!" again laughed Hugh Brandon, scornfully, and still presenting the pistol in a threatening manner towards him; "a puddle in a tempest! I suppose, now, you are what one would call a right-down salt water hippopotamus! a half sea-horse—half shark!— However, I only waste time by standing here palavering with you. Remember my words—we shall meet again at some future time, and then, beware of the vengeance of Hugh Brandon, the buccanier!"

"Why, you infernal Gorgon!" cried Harry Halliyard, "and dare you threaten me?"

"Threaten you!" repeated Brandon, with a look of contempt; "threaten you! Ay, and what's more, I will dare to execute, too. But already my feelings of revenge are partly gratified."

"What mean you, you black-looking grampus?" demanded our hero, at the same time fixing upon him a stern look.

"Your hopes have been disappointed," replied Brandon, with a malicious and exulting expression of countenance; "your pretty Poll, as you call her, pretty Poll of Putney——"

"What of her, you lubber?" hastily interrogated Harry, at the same time his feelings became every moment more excited, and it was not without the greatest difficulty that he could conquer his emotions, or keep them within the bounds of reason; "how dare such a rascally pirate as you mention the name of that fair vessel? Let me overhaul your papers.—What do you know of my Polly?"

"What do I know?" repeated Hugh Brandon, with a sardonic grin; "why I know that she has deceived you—jilted you—that the hand and heart you thought of possessing are bestowed upon another—that you have been played with, tampered with, like a weak fool as you are—that, in consequence, you are as miserable as a tar without flip—that you have parted from the sheet-anchor of hope, and are drifting about among the shoals and quicksands of misery and despair—and therefore do I exult. Harry Halliyard, it is Hugh Brandon, the brother of that man whom you were the means of destroying, who tells you this, and who now once more promises you, that he will never rest night or day, sleeping or waking, until he has had an ample and terrible revenge upon your head. Think not that he is destitute of the power to accomplish his wishes; you do not know him yet, nor the secret and certain means he has of accomplishing any designs upon which he may have fixed his mind. Beware! beware!"

"Why, you d——d, black-looking figure-head of the devil!" cried our enraged hero, as he rushed upon the daring ruffian, and seizing him by the throat, wrested the pistol from his grasp, and then hurled him to the earth several feet from him. "you dare to get your jawing tackle on board of me, and to taunt me about my Mary!—Damme, I have you in my power now, you must cry peccavi, and I have as good a mind to ship your piratical craft to the old one's locker before your time, as——but no—I will show you that the true British tar can show more mercy to you than you deserve;—take your worthless life, but tack about, crowd all sail, and sheer off, or, may I never see salt water again if I do not pour such a broadside in upon you as will send you to the devil in less time than I could cry Jack Robinson! Sheer off, I say—or I will not leave you a timber to float with! These are no quarters for piratical vessels to cruise in safely."

Hugh Brandon slowly gathered himself to his feet, the ferocious expression of his countenance showing the rage and disappointment that agitated his guilty breast; whilst our hero presented the pistol he had taken from him at his head, and his looks were sufficient to convince any one that he was resolved to put his threats into execution, if the villain did not immediately obey his commands.

"D——n!" cried Brandon, eyeing Harry Halliyard at the same time with looks of the most deadly malice, "am I again foiled and defeated? Harry Halliyard, for the present the triumph is yours, but, mark my words, the time will yet come when you shall have bitter cause to repent this. We shall meet again, if not on land, on the broad waters of the deep, and then tremble; you will find that the shark—the devil's flying-fish can bite! Beware—beware—beware! and remember that Hugh Brandon, like his brother, never forgets an insult."

With these words the ruffian shook his fist in a threatening manner at our hero, and turning round, hurried from the spot, and was almost immediately out of sight.

"What an infernal swab, to be sure," said Harry, when he was gone; "I do not know whether I have acted wrong in suffering him to sheer off as I have done without a drubbing, especially after the threats he uttered against me. However, it's as well as it is; what have I to fear from such a lubber as that? But should I ever come athwart his hawse again, I will so belabour him that he will never be able to put to sea again. And he, too, knows all about me and Mary, and taunts me about her falsehood. Oh, that is worse than all! To think that I——But no: avast, Harry, you must not think, or you will lose your reckoning altogether, and drift out of the right course. Mary—Mary, what a wreck has your inconstancy made of everything connected with me!"

He paused for a minute or two, and gave free vent to the powerful emotions which struggled in his breast. But at length he made a strong effort to conquer them, in which he partly succeeded, and then bent his footsteps towards the old churchyard. With a sad and heavy heart did the young seaman enter it, and as he did so, the most dismal thoughts took possession of his mind, and for a few moments his brain was so bewildered that he scarcely knew where he was. The solemn silence that reigned in that sacred receptacle of the dead was sufficient to add to the depression of our hero's spirits, and he gazed around him with a melancholy expression of countenance, while manly tears, in spite of all his efforts to the contrary, started to his eyes. He knew the spot where his poor old mother always desired that her remains should rest, and not doubting that her wish had been complied with, he slowly advanced towards it, the place being readily pointed out by a large drooping willow, and the next moment Harry Halliyard was standing by the side of his mother's grave. Green was the turf above her cold and mouldering remains, and fresh were the flowers that blossomed o'er it, and which were so carefully and anxiously attended to every day by the hapless Mary. Prominent among them was the Forget-me-not, which Mary had described to her husband. A plain and simple stone at the head of the grave merely recorded the name of the deceased, and the date of her death.

Harry solemnly knelt down by the side of the grave, and for a few moments his feelings completely overpowered him, and he could not give utterance to a single syllable.

"Poor old mother!" he at length ejaculated, "and is your time beaten vessel moored here at last——and shall I never see you again, or be gladdened by your affectionate smile? It was hard, too, that your fine old craft was not permitted to ride at anchor till my return. But no, why should I murmur or complain—is she not better off? Oh, yes; for though her body's under hatches, her soul has gone aloft. Poor old mother!—poor, dear old mother! Your son now kneels by the cold and silent grave which contains your revered remains, and supplicates the blessing of your spirit."

His eye now suddenly fell upon the Forget-me-not, and he started, and gazed more intently, while emotions of the most indescribable nature struggled in his breast.

"Ah! what is the meaning of this?" he exclaimed; "who planted this flower here? or did it spring up spontaneously? —Forget-me-not! What a powerful significance is there in the name!—Forget you, mother! oh, that is as impossible for me to do as to turn my back upon the enemy, or to blubber in a gale of wind. But Mary—can she ever gaze upon this simple flower without bitterly reproaching herself for her cruel and faithless conduct towards me?—Oh, yes; for her heart has become insensible to every feeling of shame, and she was sailing under false colours when she pretended that Harry Halliyard was the only lad in the ship who did, or who could possess her heart. And yet, what a lubber I must have been to have suffered myself to be so deceived. But who could have thought that my Poll, my pretty Poll, would ever have turned mutineer? Lord! there wasn't a glance of her pretty eye that didn't say, I'll stand by you, Harry!—There wasn't a grasp of her pretty hand that didn't defy poverty and danger. And as for her lips!—oh, what a lot of eloquence and fine language there was locked up in their soft touch! But now! oh, God! what has she become?—Where are all her promises?—her solemn words? How has she deceived me!— Fool that I was to believe her! Pshaw! why do I not banish the jilt from my thoughts?—She is unworthy to occupy them; and yet it is impossible for me to forget her! Oh, what a heavy sea of misfortune, treachery, and disappointment have I shipped, and is it not a wonder that I have not already foundered? Why should I struggle to keep this shattered hulk afloat any longer, since I am thus deserted by the crew, and left to steer the vessel as I can? It would be much better for me were I bound for eternity, and—" he added, as a terrible idea flashed upon his brain, and he gazed at the pistol which he had taken from Hugh Brandon, "have I not the means in my possession to bring at once this stormy voyage to a termination? But a moment, and all is over! I have hundreds of times boldly faced death in its most frightful shapes, and shall I shrink from it now?—No, I will not. Mary—Mary! with my latest breath I bless and forgive you, and pray that Heaven will continue to watch over and protect you from every danger that may threaten you! and may you find the same fond regard, nay, adoration in the man on whom you have bestowed your hand, as you would have done in him whom you have so cruelly deceived; whose hopes you have annihilated, and whose life you have destroyed! Mother, dear sainted mother! supplicate Heaven for mercy on my soul—and now farewell to all the world; I am outward bound!"

With a desperate and determined hand the unhappy young man raised the fatal weapon towards his head as he spoke, and another instant the awful deed would have been accomplished, when his arm was suddenly and powerfully arrested by some person from behind, and a well known voice at the same time exclaimed—

"Hold! rash man! what awful and guilty deed would your desperate hand commit? Forbear, Harry!"

Startled by the well known accents of the voice, Harry Halliyard turned hastily round, and his emotion and astonishment may readily be conceived when he beheld Joe Tiller.

"Ah! villain! pirate! land-shark!— is it you who dare to cross my path, and in this solemn place, too?" he cried, fiercely; "traitor!—I—"

"Hold, Harry Halliyard!" interrupted Joe, calmly; "I am neither villain, pirate, land-shark, nor traitor; but still your warmest friend, and one who is ready to make any sacrifice for your sake!"

"Liar!" cried Harry, passionately, "dare you look me in the face after what has happened, and still have the boldness to make these assertions?"

"Be calm, Harry," expostulated Joe Tiller, "and listen patiently to the explanation I have to offer you. I merit not such harsh and ungenerous language from you as that you have addressed to me. I am not to blame! —Mary, poor girl, Heaven knows, is not to blame, and——"

"Not to blame!" interrupted our hero, impatiently; "it is the same palaver that old Sam Sculler preached to me even when I had the evidence of my eyes and ears. But do you take me for a loblolly boy altogether, and think to sport as you like with me, taking me for a gudgeon? Beware, Joe Tiller, if you do, for, may I be run down by a peter-boat, if I do not teach you such a lesson that you will have good cause to retain in the log-book of your memory as long as your vessel continues afloat."

"Harry Halliyard," said Tiller, in a voice of deep emotion, "by our past friendship, by the number of years that we have known each other, I beg of you again to listen calmly and patiently to me, and I am certain that you will then, when you have heard my explanation, have the good sense to acknowledge that however unfortunate and fatal circumstances have been, that not the least blame, as I said before, can by any possibility attach to myself and Mary; and that in no one instance have we ever deceived you."

"Avast—avast!" ejaculated Harry, and still fixing upon him a look of the utmost indignation and reproach, "lest my impatience should ship its cable, and I should board you in the turning of a handspike! Is not Mary your wife? Have you not broken all the solemn promises you made to me when I went to sea, and when I believed you indeed to be my most ardent friend, and I placed the same confidence in you as if you had been a dear brother? Have you not, like a rascally pirate as you are, watched your opportunity to bear down upon the fair craft when her commander was away, and, either by threats or persuasions, persuaded her to change her colours to you? And yet you would make me believe, if you could, that you have not deceived me, and—"

"Harry—Harry!" interposed Joe Tiller, "how cruelly do you wrong me by entertaining such suspicions as those you have expressed. Could you but read my heart, you would find that it still beats with the same sincerity and warmth of friendship towards you that it always did, and that no one can feel more poignantly, more acutely than I do the fatal circumstances that have taken place, but which have been occasioned entirely in error. We had every reason to suppose that you were dead, and——"

"'Tis false!—belay your jawing-tackle, I will not believe a word of it."

"What obstinate madness is this, Harry," returned Tiller, "when there is the newspaper and the admiralty list to prove it."

"Had Mary really loved me with half the fervour and sincerity that she pretended to do," remarked Harry, "the very supposition of my death would have strengthened her affection; she would have cherished my memory too fondly ever to have given her hand to another, and that man—he whom I had trusted and esteemed as a brother. Oh, it has been a base deed; and as I gaze upon you, Joe, I feel something rise in my breast which I dare not name, and yet I have no power to control. Weigh anchor and sheer off, and never you again attempt to sail in the same latitude as I do, or there will be some mischief done. As for Mary—oh, how I tremble when I utter that still loved name ; yes, Joe Tiller, I say again that still loved name, though she is your wife, and I have no further claim upon her ; may she never experience the troubles, the pangs, the insupportable agonies which her faithlessness has inflicted on me. We shall never meet again ; I must once more to seek the blue waters of the ocean, and with the hope that they may soon close for ever o'er my head, and thus end that life which, by the faithlessness and heartlessness of those I loved, has now become hateful to me. Stand back, Tiller, my brain is turning, and the more I gaze upon you, fiercer, and more uncontrollable become the feelings that have taken possession of my mind, and I know not what fearful deed I might

not be tempted to commit, which might bring destruction upon the soul of Harry Halliyard ! Stand back, I say !"

"Harry, stay—stay, but for a moment, and hear me !" ejaculated Joe Tiller, grasping his arm, and detaining him, whilst at the same time he fixed upon him a look of the deepest sympathy and gentle appeal; "I cannot, indeed I cannot, suffer you to leave me thus, and with these terrible and false impressions upon your mind against poor Mary. The poor old woman believed you dead, and fearing the danger that would threaten and surround Mary, in all probability, when left without a protector, she suggested, knowing that I loved her with as pure and ardent a passion as yourself, that Mary should become my wife. She hesitated, poor girl, for some time, and declined to give her consent, so fondly and so faithfully did she cherish your memory, Harry ; but when your lamented mother died, the poor old dame on her death-bed, and with almost the last words that she spoke, solemnly implored her to yield. Is it likely (and can you blame her for so doing) that she could resist ? She——"

"'Tis false—false as hell itself !", again interrupted Harry, impatiently ; "I will not believe a word of it; it is a base fabrication, got up merely to stifle my reproaches and suspicions. Reason itself denounces it as a barefaced lie !"

"Harry Halliyard," returned Tiller, in the most solemn accents, and at the same time fixing upon him a penetrating and expressive look ; "we are now both standing beside your mother's grave, and I call upon her sacred spirit to attest——"

"Avast — avast !" interrupted the young seaman, whose brain was excited to the frenzy of despair, and he scarcely knew what he uttered, or what he did ; "I will not listen to you—I will not be duped by any of your idle inventions. Let go your hold ! Take your grappling irons off me, and let me begone, or it may be worse for you, in the state of mind I am now in, and with such a tempest of violent passions as those that are at present raging within my breast ! Let me begone, I say ! Ah, do you still seek to board me ? Nay, then, since you will madly provoke me to do it, take that, and with it the curse

THE PIRATE'S ATTACK ON PRETTY POLL.

of the broken-hearted Harry Halliyard!"

As he thus spoke, he hastily released
himself from the hold of Joe, and deal-
ing him a violent blow, which felled him
to the earth, he rushed hastily from the
spot, with all the air of a madman.

It was a moment or two before Joe
could sufficiently recover himself to rise
upon his feet, and when he did so his
brain was bewildered and confused, and
he could with difficulty only believe in
the reality of what had happened. His
agitation when he did so, however, may
easily be imagined.

"Struck!" he muttered to himself,
"and by Harry Halliyard! Called a
villain and a liar, too. By Heaven, this
is almost too much for human patience
or forbearance to endure. But—but

I must not suffer the excitement of my feelings to overpower my reason. Poor Harry, how greatly are you to be pitied! I am still your friend, your most sincere and ardent friend, though you now look upon me as one of the most base and treacherous of mankind. Alas—alas! what will become of my poor Mary? she can never be happy again with me, knowing that Harry Halliyard is still living; and nothing but the most fearful misery is presented in the most vivid and unmistakable characters before my eyes. I shudder to think of it. Oh, why did I ever consent to make her my wife? And yet I so fondly loved her. Alas—alas! poor Joe Tiller, your boat is capsized, and all hope of happiness for you is at an end—

I'll go and hide myself in some forest dreary,
And by my death release my lovely Mary."

With these words Joe Tiller slowly quitted the churchyard, and with a sad heart, and almost dreading to meet the looks of Mary, he retraced his steps towards home, pondering deeply upon all that had taken place between him and Harry Halliyard, and sincerely anxious to know what would become of him.

CHAPTER XII.

THE STRUGGLE OF THE HEART.—HARRY HALLIYARD'S DETERMINATION.—MEETING BETWEEN HIM AND MARY, AND THE CONSEQUENCES.

IT may, perhaps, be needless to inform the reader that the despair and anguish of mind which Mary endured suffered not the least abatement, but, on the contrary, rather seemed to increase in violence, and so agonising were the thoughts that continually crowded upon her brain, that reason almost forsook her seat, and she raved at intervals in the most incoherent manner, turning a deaf ear to all the remonstrances and advice of Joe, who exerted himself to the utmost to console her, and to inspire her with hope and confidence; but at the same time his own anguish of mind, as may naturally be supposed, was almost insupportable, for he saw plainly enough, now that it was discovered Harry Halliyard was living, that all his prospects of happiness were at an end, while at the same time he had the greatest reason to fear that Mary would not be able to support a shock so sudden and unexpected, but that she would die of a broken heart, and thus he should be left, as it were, alone in the world, and without a friend from whom he could look for sympathy or consolation.

The form of the unfortunate, but noble-hearted Harry Halliyard was never for an instant absent from the imagination of the hapless Mary, and she shed scalding tears when she reflected upon all the melancholy, and almost unprecedented circumstances of the case. She avoided the presence of her husband as much as possible, for although she pitied and esteemed him for the kindness and affection with which he had ever behaved towards her, she could not help gazing upon him with feelings which almost amounted to disgust and horror.

"Oh, Harry!" she sobbed, when she was alone, Joe having departed from the house in the morning with the hope of meeting with the object of their anxiety: "oh, Harry! what a dreadful trial for us both is this unexpected discovery; and what, oh, what will be the result of it? You believe me false, and must, therefore, look upon me as a wretch unworthy of anything but the greatest abhorrence. Horrible thought!—how it freezes the blood in my veins and distracts my brain as it occurs to me with such overwhelming force that I can with difficulty save myself from sinking under it. And he will curse me!—Oh, no, no, no! Heaven, in your infinite mercy, do not suffer him to do that! You know that I am not to blame—you know with what fervour and sincerity I have ever loved him, and the dreadful agony of mind I have endured during the time I thought he was no more; how incessantly and fervently I mourned his memory. Harry, dear Harry! do not, oh, do not curse me! Would to Heaven I had died when the report of his death reached my ears —what unutterable misery would it have saved me, and even his mind would not have experienced such excruciating agony as it now does, for he would have been convinced that my heart remained faithful to him to the last, and he would still have placed the same unlimited confidence in the friendship of Joe that he had hitherto done. But now, how sad, how terrible and alarming is the reverse! Oh, Halliyard! can I think of the words you uttered when we met last night, the looks of mingled agony and reproach you fixed upon me, without shuddering?—It is impossible! What has become of you?—whither have you gone?—what fearful and desperate act may you not in the frenzy of your despair be urged to commit? God! the thought will drive me mad! This awful suspense is more tedious and insupportable than all! Heaven guide and protect him, and avert any calamity which may at present threaten him. Oh, how keen were the reproaches which he heaped upon my head—how scornfully he rejected my asseverations of my innocence—and yet, when he separated from me, did he not say he pitied and forgave me?—He did, and with that assurance I will at least endeavour to find some degree of consolation. But can he sincerely pardon me, and try to forget what has happened? Alas! I dare not flatter myself with any such sanguine hopes, which are only too likely to turn out fallacious. Harry! did you but really know the sincerity of the feelings which glow within my breast, the strength of my emotions, and the anguish of my despair and regret, you must, you would indeed pity me, and you would probably then try to reconcile yourself to that terrible misfortune which there are now no means of remedying. Oh, why did you leave me in the abrupt manner you did, and without giving me any idea as to when we should see each other again? But, no, I must not now encourage such thoughts as those; they are sinful now that Fate has made me the wife of another. We must never more meet—did he not say so when he tore himself away? and dare I hope that his assertions will not be realised?—I dare not; for honour and virtue forbid that I should do so; and though my heart should break in the effort, I must still struggle with my feelings."

She paused, and for several minutes gave the most unrestrained indulgence to the overwhelming load of grief which pressed upon her bosom, and rendered her one of the most truly wretched beings in existence.

"Poor Joe, too," she continued, "what a sad disappointment will this be to your hopes—how dreadful will be the suspense and anxiety of mind you will have to endure now that it is discovered that Harry Halliyard is still living, and you know how fondly my heart is devoted to him. You have been an earnest, an untiring, and affectionate friend and husband to me, and I should indeed hate and despise myself could I feel anything but the most unbounded gratitude towards him for it. He has been deserving of a much better fate than I fear is now in store for him, and which will imbitter all his future days. Harry—Harry! so conflicting are the thoughts which rapidly succeed each other, that my brain is distracted, and I know not what I do. God of mercy! look down upon me, for I shall otherwise be guilty of some awful deed; for to long support this unutterable torture of mind is impossible!"

With agonised and uneven footsteps, she traversed the room, and it was all in vain that she endeavoured to obtain the least relief to her feelings. Joe had now been absent from home for some time, and Mary awaited his return with no inconsiderable degree of anxiety; though she almost wished that he and Harry Halliyard might not encounter each other, fearful as to what the consequences might be from the great excitement under which the latter would doubtless be labouring. He believed that Joe had acted the part of a villain towards him, and in the state of mind that he was at present, she was well convinced that not all the explanations her husband could give, or all the arguments and remonstrances he might offer, could persuade him to the contrary. Should Harry seek revenge, she shuddered to think what might be the terrible result, and her anxiety and suspense at the prolonged absence of Joe Tiller every moment became the more painful. Had she been aware that at that very time Harry was standing outside her dwelling with a heart full to bursting, anxious, yet dreading to see her, what would have been her feelings? How eagerly would she have rushed to meet him, though prudence and rectitude forbade that she should no so, and there was no knowing the consequences of which it might be productive. But surely Harry's manly heart, if he and Joe should happen to encounter each other, would not suffer him to proceed to violence, or to be guilty of anything which might afterwards give him cause to regret. He would not turn a deaf ear entirely to truth and reason, but hear the explanation which Tiller had to give, and which must satisfy him at once that they were not to blame for that which had so fatally taken place, but that they had acted merely in obedience to the dying injunctions of his mother, and under the impression that he was no more. But could that explanation impart the least consolation to her lover, or compensate him for the loss of her hand? She too well knew the strength of the young seaman's feelings, and the bitter disappointment, nay, total annihilation his hopes had received, to imagine for a moment that it would; and when poor Mary pictured to herself the sufferings she knew he must be enduring, the anguish of her mind was increased tenfold, and she could not without the greatest difficulty contain herself. She continued to pace her chamber backwards and forwards in the most distracted manner, and whichever way she directed her thoughts, the most dismal images and melancholy forebodings presented themselves to her imagination and completely banished all chance of tranquility from her breast. In this manner another hour passed away, when there was a hasty tap at the outer door, and Mary, hastening to it with trembling steps, opened it, and gave admittance to her husband. She could see in a moment, from the agitated expression of his features, that he had something of an unpleasant nature to communicate, and she almost dreaded to question him. He took her hand, and gazed affectionately in her face, and then ventured to imprint a kiss upon her lips, at which our heroine could not help involuntarily shuddering when she thought of Harry, and pictured to herself what would be the agony, the disgust, and indignation of his feelings could he have witnessed it.

"My dear Mary," said Joe, "how ill, how haggard, and how melancholy you do look. I am afraid that you have still been abandoning yourself to all the violence of grief and despair; but I do not wonder at it—it was presumption on my part ever to think that one so humble and unworthy as myself could ever obtain possession of your heart, when the image of Harry Halliyard was so firmly ingrafted there. I see plainly what my fate will now be, and I must endeavour to resign myself to it. Mary, you cannot love me, your brain must be distracted, and your heart torn with anguish, now that Halliyard has returned, and, although I know full well the dreadful suffering it will cost me, I will endeavour to support it with the fortitude that becomes a man. We must part, Mary."

"Part!" she repeated, fixing upon him a look of mingled astonishment and pity. "Part, Joe? Know you what you say, or do you no longer love me? Am I not your wife? Can you then think so meanly, so basely of me as to imagine that I can ever forget the duty I owe you, or cease to remember with gratitude the uniform care, attention, and affection you have ever bestowed upon me? Oh. Joe, do not wrong me by entertaining such suspicions of me, as those to which I have alluded; for, indeed, it has ever been my constant study to endeavour to convince you by my conduct how little deserving I was of them."

"I know it has, Mary," coincided Tiller, fervently, "and pardon me, I beseech you, if I have appeared to wrong you by encouraging any such groundless surmises, though if you will believe me, Mary, I solemnly declare that I have not; but Harry——"

"Ah! what of him?" eagerly demanded Mary; and her heart palpitated so violently against her side that she could scarcely support herself; "what of him?" she repeated; "have you seen him?"

"I have," replied Joe, in a melancholy tone of voice; "but a short time since we encountered each other by his mother's grave."

"His mother's grave!" sighed our heroine, and tears started to her eyes; "it was a solemn place to meet. Poor old woman! what would have been the agony of your feelings had you been now living, and knowing——but pardon me, Joe; I will not finish the sentence, which might sound harsh and ungenerous to your ears. But say, what happened between yourself and poor Harry? Surely you did not meet in anger?—He could not turn a deaf ear to your words of explanation—he must listen to the voice of reason."

"Alas, Mary!" replied her husband, "it grieves me to have to tell you that all I could say, every argument and remonstrance I could make use of, had not the least effect upon him; nothing whatever could banish the impression he has suffered to take possession of his mind. He believes that I have deceived him—that I have acted as a villain towards him—and he even called me so, and refused to listen to the explanation I had to offer."

"Oh, Harry! unfortunate Harry!" ejaculated our heroine, "where, oh, where will this terminate?"

"I would fain conceal from you the truth, Mary," observed Joe, "but I feel that I should be wrong by so doing. Had I not arrived at the spot at the time I did, he would, in all probability, now have been no more."

"No more!" gasped forth our heroine, with a shudder of horror; "what mean you?"

"The fatal weapon was raised to his head," replied Joe; "another moment, and, in the frenzy of his despair, he would have terminated his existence."

"Oh, God! surely he could never be guilty of so rash, so dreadful and desperate an act."

Joe shook his head mournfully, and remained silent.

"You do not answer me, Joe," said his wife, in a faint and agitated voice; "alas, then, have I not reason to fear the worst? Heaven arrest his hand, and watch over and protect him. He, then, believes me false—he thinks that I could never have loved him—and I feel that he must curse and hate me, and despise me in his heart!"

"Oh, no!" returned Joe, "it is impossible that he can do so; and when he has recovered from the state of excitement into which this unexpected discovery, and the annihilation of his hopes has naturally thrown him, reason will, I trust, resume its sway, and he will become firm, and resign himself to his fate, cruel and severe though it be."

"Would to Heaven that he might!"

ejaculated our heroine, fervently; "but how can I flatter myself with any such a hope, after what you have told me? You say that he met you in anger, that he refused to listen to your explanation; even at his mother's grave he would not believe your assertions; that he called you villain, and——"

"Alas, Mary!" returned her husband, "it is too true; nay, more——"

"What? what?" breathlessly demanded our heroine.

"Oh, I dare not give utterance to the painful truth," said Joe. "Oh, Harry! Harry! how little has the sincere friend of your youth, he who has regarded you as a brother, and who would willingly now make any sacrifice to serve you, deserved that which he has experienced at your hands?"

"Explain yourself, I implore you, Joe," said our heroine; "your hesitation does but keep me in suspense far more painful than certainty. What meaning do your words and your looks of agitation imply?"

"Mary," replied her husband, in a voice half choked by the power of his emotions, "he not only called me villain, and other opprobrious epithets with which I will not shock your ears, but he struck me!"

"Struck you!" repeated Mary, looking at him with an expression of mingled astonishment, terror, and incredulity; "no, no, no—you cannot mean what you say! Harry Halliyard could never have suffered his passions so far to have obtained the mastery of his reason as thus to unman himself. You must have allowed your excitement to deceive you."

"Would that it were so," answered Joe; "but, alas! it is too true. He struck me to the earth, and, hurrying from the spot, left me to the anguish of regret and degradation. Oh, Mary, I could have endured anything but that without a murmur of complaint; but to receive a blow from that man whom I have, Heaven knows, never injured by word or deed, at least not wilfully so, wounds me to the very soul."

"Oh, Harry!" sighed our heroine, "grief, despair, and disappointment, must surely have deprived you of reason. Never could I have imagined that you could so far have committed yourself. Will nothing convince you of the truth?"

"And yet, Mary," remarked Joe Tiller, after a pause, during which he seemed to be struggling with his feelings, "I forgive him, from my very soul I forgive him; and I trust that when he comes calmly to reflect upon all the painful circumstances, he must admit that he has acted with precipitation and injustice towards me, and will exert himself to reconcile himself to that fate with which it has pleased Heaven to visit him."

"My brain is distracted," sighed our heroine, pressing her fair hands upon her forehead; "where has he gone? I shall never behold him again, and in such an alarming state of mind as he is at present, what desperate act may he not be urged to commit? Alas—alas! I feel that my troubles have but just begun, and I shudder to contemplate the future."

"Nay, my poor Mary," returned her husband, looking upon her with the utmost affection, and the deepest commiseration, "do not thus give way to despair, for to witness your agony grieves me more than all. In spite of all that has taken place, I do not fear that Harry Halliyard will be able to soon recover himself—to view all that has happened with a merciful and unprejudiced eye, and to act accordingly. I will again seek him out, and will not rest until I have persuaded him of the truth."

"Seek him out," repeated Mary, "and his mind excited and enraged as it is against you? Oh, no—no—no, that must not be, I tremble to think of what the consequences might be should you meet again. He believes you false and treacherous; his temper once excited is impetuous and ungovernable, and God only knows to what desperate lengths the anguish of his mind might urge him Alas—alas! what a dreadful trial is this!"

"And I am the cause of all, Mary," said Joe; "had I not yielded to the solicitations of the poor old dame, and the strength of the passions that glowed in my breast towards you, all this misery might then have been spared. Harry Halliyard would have returned to find you faithful and affectionate as ever, and

you would have received the happy realization of those bright hopes you had for so many years, sanctioned by virtue, justice, and reason, encouraged, and I should still have retained the same place in his warmest regard that I had formerly done—

But now our fate with gloom is overcast,
And all the sunshine of our hopes is past."

"Joseph," said Mary, fixing upon him a look which spoke at once the sincerity of her mind, and the power of the emotions which held at the present time such dominion in her breast, "why do you thus reproach yourself? You, indeed, are not to blame. We were both deceived, and acted only as prudence and obedience to the last wishes of the poor old woman dictated. I esteemed you, Joe, warmly, regarded you as—as I would do a brother, for well did I know your honest heart, well had I experienced your many noble and manly virtues; but I know you will forgive me, and not respect me the less, if I candidly acknowledge to you that I could not love you with the same ardent passion that Harry had created in my breast. But it is past now, and my lips may not give utterance to those sentiments which it was once innocent and holy for me to encourage. You are my husband—I know you love me; you have ever been most kind and affectionate, and studious of my happiness, and I should indeed blush for and despise myself, while, at the same time, I should be unworthy the name of woman, did I for a moment shrink from the performance of my duty to you as your wife. I can never forget Harry Halliyard, but whenever you find me abuse the confidence you have reposed in me, or injure you by one unholy thought or deed, may the most severe but just retribution of Heaven descend on my head, and render me an outcast from society, despised and loathed by every one altogether."

"Oh, Mary, beloved Mary!" cried her husband, deeply affected by the energy and earnestness of her manner, and fully convinced, as he had ever been, of her truth and sincerity, "you are too generous, too kind and indulgent, and self-sacrificing. It overpowers me, and I know not how to reply; I feel at once my own unworthiness, and the superior merits of Harry Halliyard; why, then, has fate made me the unhappy instrument of crushing those bright hopes you have for so many years indulged in, and bringing upon you both such irremediable misery? Would to Heaven that we had never known each other, for was it possible for even the most insensible man who had once beheld the beauteous and guileless Mary without paying to her the homage of his heart? To say that I love you, Mary, would be to characterise my glowing sentiments by far too cold a name; I have ever adored and worshipped you as some unearthly being; my whole thoughts, my every anxiety has been for your welfare and happiness; there is no sacrifice that I would not cheerfully and eagerly make, which should seem at all calculated to contribute to it; and now —I dare not trust myself to finish the painful sentence, to give utterance to the torturing feelings that at present distract my brain, and hold their stormy dominion in my mind. I will in future be to you a brother, protector, friend, but, though the struggle will cost me dear, I will endeavour to cease to forget you as a wife. This home, and all that it contains, is yours, but I will no longer occupy it, though it shall at all times be my constant study to watch over and protect you from danger, and to contribute all in my power towards your welfare and happiness. Probably my death will soon release you from——"

"Forbear! forbear!" interrupted our heroine, in a voice of the deepest possible emotion, "your words torture me, and shock me. Oh, can you really love me, and yet think so meanly and so basely of me as to imagine that I can ever abandon my duty to you as a wife? Alas! what an erroneous opinion have you formed of my character if you suppose me capable of any such conduct. You are my husband, and death alone can dissolve the solemn bonds that unite us together. It is my duty, since fate has so willed it, to endeavour to forget that there is such a being as Harry Halliyard in existence: or, at least, to remember him only as a friend, a brother. It would be sinful in me to encourage any other thoughts; and let the consequences be whatever they may, I will conquer my feelings. Harry, too, will see the necessity of yielding with patience to the stern decrees of Omnipotence, and no longer encourage thoughts which can only be productive of misery, if not of shame to us all."

"Noble-hearted lass!" cried Joe, embracing her with the fondest transport, and the expression of his features plainly showing the enthusiastic admiration he entertained of her character, "how shall I find words sufficient to convey to you an idea of the nature of my feelings?— How little have you deserved the awful and untoward fate which has befallen you; and never can I sufficiently testify to you my gratitude for your generous self-devotion. But I must see Harry Halliyard again, and endeavour to effect a reconciliation with him. Heaven knows that I bear him no vindictive feeling, but that, on the contrary, he has my warmest sympathy and deepest commiseration, and that there is no sacrifice that I would hesitate to make, even at the risk of my own life, to serve him, and to ameliorate the anguish of his despair, which this fatal and unforeseen disappointment of his hopes has naturally engendered in his mind. Come, Mary, gloomy though our prospects at present are, they may yet brighten, and we may learn to look back upon the past, if not without regret, at least without that bitter anguish of soul which we now experience."

"God grant that we may!" ejaculated our heroine, emphatically; "though much I fear that poor Harry Halliyard will never again be the happy individual he formerly was. His behaviour at your meeting, and the manner in which he parted from you fill me with the utmost alarm; for to what rash act may he not be urged by the frenzy of his despair? Too plainly can I read the thoughts which are at present occupying his mind, and I tremble for the consequences of which they may prove to be productive. Your timely arrival at the spot, according to your own account, only prevented him from laying violent hands upon himself."

"True," coincided Joe Tiller; "but still, I trust, when reason resumes her sway, that he will think better of this, and endeavour to reconcile and tranquillise the feelings which at present occupy his mind."

"But he will not believe that I am innocent," said Mary; "he considers that I have treated him with the basest ingratitude and duplicity, and the ardent love he once entertained towards me must be changed to scorn and hatred. He will heap his curses on my head, and——"

"Oh, never, Mary!" interrupted her husband. "It would be monstrous to entertain such a thought. Harry must be convinced of your innocence, though the power of his feelings for the present prevents him from acknowledging it: and when they have in some measure subsided, he will resign himself to that fate which is now unavoidable, and by absence seek to bury in oblivion that which has so unfortunately taken place."

Mary shook her head mournfully, and it was quite evident from the agitation of her features that the feelings which struggled in her breast were of the most painful description.

"But I must never behold him again," she said, after a brief pause; "virtue, prudence, and propriety forbid it: and when he is far away, perhaps again exposed to all the perils of the deep, the uncertainty of the fate which has befallen him will be a constant source of the most torturing anxiety to me; and even while I am encouraging such thoughts, how severely must my conscience reproach me for the injustice with which I am acting towards you, Joe!"

"Do not let such thoughts trouble you, dear Mary," replied her husband; "I cannot expect that you can forget him, but I am convinced that you could never wrong me, and it shall be my constant care to compose your mind, and to reconcile you to your destiny; so,

Pray, my dearest Mary, do not fret,
For though Dame Fortune frowns to-day,
    we may be happy yet.

Come, come, make a bold effort, my dear lass; banish the gloom of your present thoughts, and view the future on the brightest and most sunny side. I will find Harry Halliyard out again, for, after all, I do not think he will be able to form the resolution to quit this neighbourhood for the present; and when his excitement has in some measure cooled down, I do not fear that I shall be able to convince him that what I have stated is true: that we believed him to be dead, and that in uniting our fates with one another we only acted in obedience to the dying injunctions of his late lamented mother, and for the best."

"Would to God that I could think so!" said our heroine; "my mind would then indeed feel some slight portion of relief; but, alas! when I take all the painful circumstances into consideration, I cannot but entertain the greatest doubts and most dismal forebodings. I tremble, too, at the thoughts of you and Harry Halliyard again encountering each other, for, wrought up to a perfect pitch of madness as he is through the disappointment of his hopes, Heaven only knows the fearful extremes to which he may be impelled."

"Oh, my dear Mary!" returned Tiller, "entertain no such apprehensions, for indeed they will turn out to be groundless—I feel convinced that they will. For your sake, if he sincerely loves you, as he has ever professed to do, Harry will stifle his passions, and at length calmly listen to the voice of reason. Can he any longer refuse to believe the truth of our statements, after the unquestionable proof we can give him?—He must indeed be uncharitable if he did; and after the years that we have been acquainted, and so intimately connected together, I must then, indeed, acknowledge to myself that I have been most grossly deceived in his character. But I do not encourage any such ideas, and I am certain that you, Mary, must banish them from your mind upon mature reflection. Come, my dear lass, compose yourself, and put your trust in Providence, who will not suffer you to be disappointed in any hopes you may form as to the happy termination of this painful business. I must leave you for awhile; for you know that I must not neglect my business on the river, and old Sam Sculler, I have no doubt, has been most anxiously waiting for me at the Hard. I shall return again in an hour or two, and I then hope to see you in better spirits, and to find that the roses have once more resumed their place in your cheeks. Good-bye, my love, and God bless you! Cheer up—cheer up; for, as Milton says, in his Paradise Lost, I think:

THE PAINFUL INTERVIEW BETWEEN MARY AND HARRY.

"There's many a dark and cloudy morning,
  Turns out to be a sunshiny day !"

With these words poor Joe Tiller embraced his wife affectionately; but her emotions were too great to suffer her to return any answer, and he quitted the house, and left her to her own melancholy meditations. When he was gone, Mary threw herself disconsolately in a chair, and for several minutes remained silent; and her brain was so distracted and bewildered that she was almost unconscious as to where she was, or what had taken place. A copious flood of tears at length came to her relief, and she arose from her seat, and walking to the window, looked out upon the scenery beyond, almost expecting to behold the object of her thoughts; but the coast was quite clear, and she returned again to her chair.

"Generous-hearted husband!" she

soliloquised, "how sincerely do I feel for you! But still, though I know it is almost criminal in me to do so, I find that it is impossible for me to banish my beloved and unfortunate Harry from my thoughts. And can I feel surprised at his conduct, after taking all the circumstances into consideration? Oh, no; well do I know the bitter, the almost insupportable anguish of mind he must be enduring, and the conflicting thoughts and torturing doubts he cannot help encouraging. He must now indeed feel himself, as it were, alone in the world, deserted by all, and especially those who were far dearer to him than his very life, and where can he look for consolation? Can I be surprised if the violence of his despair should hurry him to the perpetration of some rash and fatal act? I cannot; I shudder with horror as the thought rushes upon my aching brain. What a sad, a terrible reception is this for him to meet with after so many years of absence. Would to Heaven that I could behold him again, for surely he could not turn a deaf ear to my supplications!— he could not believe me so entirely lost to all sense of shame and honour as to seek to deceive him, as if in bitter mockery of his misery. Ah, no! Harry Halliyard, I am certain, possesses too noble and generous a mind to do that, and must forgive and pity me. Did he not say he did on parting with me? And yet his interview with Tiller shows how fearfully he has changed his mind. I cannot help dreading to meet him, although, at the same time I am so anxious to do so. Alas—alas! what will be the end of this? though I have too much reason to fear the worst. Harry, Harry, I could lay down my life, and oh! how gladly, how willingly, too, to restore you to happiness, and yet you believe me false, and must look upon me with scorn and loathing! That thought of itself is sufficient to drive me to madness, and I know not how to support myself under the accumulation of misery that presses upon my mind. Would to Heaven that I had died ere his return, and even then when he heard that I had been united to another, would he not have cursed my memory? God of Heaven! he surely could never have had the heart to have done that. My brain is so bewildered by the different thoughts that crowd upon it, that I scarcely know what I utter. What can ever impart to me the slightest degree of relief? Surely, no situation in the world can be so miserable and deplorable as mine is now!"

She paused for a few minutes, and pressing her hands upon her temples, she gave herself up to the agony of despair.

"But," she at last resumed, "how terrible, how insupportable is this suspense! Where is he now? Perhaps he has already terminated his existence, which he was only prevented from doing this morning by the interposition of my husband. My blood chills at the thought, and yet is it not, alas! too probable to be easily rejected? I must see him again, if possible, in spite of the consequences, and then on my knees I will supplicate to him for mercy and forgiveness, and should he then reject my earnest appeals, his heart must indeed have become insensible to all those tender feelings of compassion with which it once throbbed. But no, I cannot believe that he will remain inexorable. My tears and supplications cannot fail to make some impression upon him, and to convince him that I am not that heartless and faithless being he now considers me to be. Dear Harry, though cruel fate has decreed that we should not come together, you, and you alone can ever possess my heart's warmest, most devoted affection, and nothing whatever can change my sentiments while the purple current of life shall continue to circulate through my veins. But hold!" she added after a pause; "to what guilty words is my rash tongue giving utterance? Am I not the wife of another? Of one who loves me fondly, and whose whole thoughts and wishes are devoted to my happiness, and shall I be base enough still to cherish my hopeless passion? Of what monstrous ingratitude and injustice am I guilty! The curse of Heaven will surely pursue me if I do not abandon such unholy thoughts! Harry, you must henceforth be only as a stranger to me, and I must struggle to forget all the happy moments of the past. But what a painful and arduous struggle will it be. How, alas, can I ever hope to accomplish the task? I must not see you again, lest in the moment of despair my resolution should fail me, and I should be guilty of that which would entail the most indescribable shame and misery upon my devoted head. How dreadful is my destiny, yet there is no alternative left me but to endeavour to resign myself to it, and to seek to become calm and patient under the heavy trials to which I am subjected. Calm and patient!—oh, what a bitter mockery do those words convey to an unhappy being in my wretched situation! God of Heaven guide me how to act, for I am completely lost and distracted."

Again she paused, and sobbed as if her heart would break, but not one ray came to her relief, and she gave herself up entirely to all the horrors of her fate, which seemed to be almost to overwhelming for human nature to endure. Once more she walked to the window, and she then perceived that Abigail Holdforth was approaching the house, which was a source of great annoyance to her, for she was never in a worse state of mind to listen to her garrulous and insipid conversation. The next minute she knocked at the door, which our heroine opened, and she entered the room in her usual state of bustle.

"How d'ye do, mem?" she commenced; "very dull and lug-grubiest, as Mrs. Pointer says. Ah, well! I do not wonder at it after what has occurred. What a wonderful thing, to be sure! The dead alive!—quite a romance! Dear me, who would have thought it? And he looks so handsome, too—he's an officer, too, so I hear; and has got a mint of money! What a pity it is that Mr. Tiller didn't die of a broken heart; or that the law does not allow a respectable woman to marry two husbands if she thinks proper; but that would be *beggar me*, I suppose, which is reckoned a very serious offence; so, as Mrs. Frizzle says——"

"My good girl," interrupted Mary, "for Heaven's sake do not go on so. If you knew the agony of my mind, I am certain you would forbear."

"I beg your pardon, mem," replied the loquacious damsel; "I am sure I would not say anything to wound your feelings for the world, for I should think, since I have become the proprietess of a

Magazin des Modes, and mingle in nothing but the most fashionable society, I know myself too well for that. But it is really very remarkable, and take it altogether a very melancholy affair; and I shouldn't at all be surprised if Mr. Halliyard was to commit homicide, don't they call it? which would be very rash and silly on his part, because the crowner's jury, as he is a nautical man, would be almost certain to bring it in fell in the sea—(though, for the life of me, I can't see how they could if he died on land), and then they would run a stake through his body, and bury him in the cross road, because he is crossed in love, I suppose. Well, for my part—"

"Abigail! Abigail!" expostulated our heroine, in a voice of the greatest agitation.

"Well, well, mem," returned the former, "I did not mean any harm. It is a sad job, to be sure, as I said before, and I am very sorry for you; so I could not help calling to pay my respects, and to offer you any little consolation in my power. Oh, mem, what do you think?—I have had such a sweet revenge upon Master Watchful Waxend for his deceit and treachery—the ungrateful little brute! I can't think what could possess me ever to fancy such a low, vulgar fellow! Wheugh! I shall never get the smell of the filthy cobbler's wax out of my nose! So now he returns from sea, and because he happens to have scraped together a paltry guinea or two, he thinks to take the proprietess of the *Magazin des Modes* by storm. But I have disappointed him, and have let him see that I can marry his betters. About a month ago I became acquainted with such a delightful little man, a French *frizeur*, doing an extensive and fashionable business—Monsieur St. Jacques St. Lercrou is his name; and from the first moment he beheld me, he fell desperately in love with me and I with him, and ever since then he has been paying his *devours* to me, and I have made up my mind to marry him, for I'm sure we cannot be off making a rapid and splendid fortune by our joint businesses; and how very beautiful and elegant it will sound—Madame St. Jacques St. Lercrou! Poor little Waxend!—I expect it will break his heart, and serve him right, too. But, dear me, how the time slips away when one is talking, and I had almost forgot that I have got to call upon Mrs. Tick, the fashionable pawnbroker's wife, to measure her for a new dress, and she is very particular about punctuality. Good day, mem; remember me to Mr. Tiller. I do not think your present husband is a very long-lived man, and when he is gone you can marry Mr. Halliyard, that is if he don't go to sea again and get drownded, and then there will be no harm done, you know. I will call and see you again in a day or two, for I dare say you are very dull down here without some agreeable society. Good day, mem, good day! Bless my soul! I shall never get to Mrs. Tick's at the time appointed."

With these words the loquacious girl curtsied herself out of the room, much to the relief of poor Mary, whose mind had been distracted all the time she had been present. She again threw herself on a chair, and once more her thoughts wandered to the melancholy subject which had before so deeply engrossed them. It was in vain that she sought to find some relief; and, in fact, her anxiety and anguish increased every moment instead of abated, and it was with difficulty that she could restrain herself within the bounds of reason at all. She now walked once more to the window, and gazed anxiously in the direction of the river, with the hope of seeing Harry, though why she should expect him there she could not very clearly imagine; but not a single human being met her gaze, and after the lapse of a few minutes she returned disconsolately to her seat.

"He will not come — he will not come!" she ejaculated; "but why should I expect him?—why should I imagine that he will now venture near me, since I am the wife of another? But yet it is hard that we should not meet again, while he has the fatal impression on his mind against me. Surely it would be some melancholy consolation to me to be able to disburse his mind of the fatal prejudice he entertains against me, to convince him how little myself and Tiller have been to blame in this sad affair, and to receive his forgiveness and blessing. His blessing? Ah,

no, I dare not hope that he will ever bestow it upon me, and, perhaps, even now he is invoking curses upon my head. Dreadful thought! I tremble with a feeling of the most unconquerable horror as it occurs to me; and all the misery of the future that is in store for me is vividly presented to my imagination. The contemplation appals me, and I look in vain for anything to inspire me with hope. Would that I knew where to find him, methinks I could not resist the temptation to go forth to meet him, and throw myself on his mercy, let the consequences be whatever they might. But away with such ideas! it is criminal to indulge in them, and I know not the danger with which they may be fraught should I give way to them. My doom is sealed, I am the wife of another, and I should be acting with the basest injustice and ingratitude towards my husband, from whom I have ever experienced such kindness and affection, should I not seek to banish his image from my memory. Vain task, how utterly futile is it for me to attempt to accomplish it. This poor broken heart must case to beat, and my limbs be stiffened in the cold embrace of death, ere I can cease to remember the fond and noble-hearted Harry Halliyard, to whom I have been bethrothed from the earliest days of childhood. Oh, what blissful days were those! No care, no anxiety, no thought of sorrow ever disturbed my mind. Happy days of innocence, never to return! How little, oh, how little did I anticipate the horrors of the future that were in store for me, or my reason must surely have deserted me, or death at once speedily have put an end to my sorrows. Would to Heaven that it had, what many anxious hours of the most indescribable misery would it have saved me, and Harry might now have been happy in the love of one more worthy of him, and ceased to have remembered that there was ever such a being as Mary in existence. But could he ever have loved any other woman with half the fervour that he did me? Oh, no, too well do I know his noble and manly heart to believe that he would, and it is that conviction which makes his present suffering too painfully apparent to me now. But it is passed, our doom is sealed, we are irrevocably separated, and grim despair, with all its attendant horrors, frowns upon us on every side. God help us! for situated as we at present are, and without the least prospect of relief, I know not what will become of us. My very soul sickens and shrinks appalled at the contemplation. Would that I were dead—would to Heaven that I were dead, for there is no hope for me on this side of the grave, and I seem to be fated to involve in misery all who unfortunately become connected with me!"

She buried her face in her hands, and burst into a paroxysm of the most overwhelming and uncontrollable grief, convulsive sobs escaping her heavily loaded bosom, and a flood of tears streaming down her pale cheeks. She was unable to collect her thoughts for some time, and scarcely knowing where she was, she staggered into the inner room, and throwing herself on a sofa, she abandoned herself entirely to the anguish and despair of her feelings, and in this deplorable condition we will at present leave her.

Mr. Watchful Waxend was returning from the Crown and Crosier, in something more than his usual state of inebriation, and, at the same time, it was quite evident that he had in the course of the day heard something which did not at all tend to exhilarate his spirits. He had not seen Harry Halliyard, however, since the astounding discovery had been made which we have detailed in the previous pages, although he had been made acquainted with all the particulars, and he began to feel alarmed lest in the anguish of his despair he had been induced to lay violent hands on himself, for our worthy acquaintance, the Bishop, notwithstanding all his numerous eccentricities, and apparent carelessness of disposition, really entertained a sincere friendship for the young seaman, and would willingly have done anything in his power to serve him, as we think his conduct has pretty clearly shown.

"Harry, my boy," soliloquised Watchful, "we are a poor, unlucky pair of worn-out sparables, and the couple of souls that we thought would stick to us like wax to boot, have turned out nothing more, after all, than a pair of slippers. What two confounded pumps they must have taken us for! Isn't it enough to make any one wax wrath to think of it?

I wonder where Harry is? I must see him, for now that all our hopes are blasted there is nothing left for us to do but to mingle our sorrows together, and once more to commit ourselves to the dangers and perils of the briny deep. Oh, the inconstancy of woman! But who would have thought that Abigail would have deserted her Watchful Waxend, for a little, ugly, French barber? What a barbarous idea! He had better not come near me, that's all, or I shall bristle up and commit *suminary* punishment on him by skewering him alive, like a cockchafer, on my awl! Ha, here he comes;—now for a row."

At this moment the object of his wrath, who was a squat, ludicrous looking little Frenchman, made his appearance, and they interchanged mutual glances of jealousy and indignation with each other.

"So, you ugly, deformed little Polly Woo Francay,' began Waxend, looking daggers at his rival, " I have met you at last, have I? Now do you not think you are a pretty fellow to try and rob me of my Abigail, to whom my heart has been devoted so——"

"You, Monsieur End-de-Vax?" replied the Frenchman, shrugging his shoulders, and fixing upon him a look of the most ineffable contempt; "pooh! you are nobody!"

"Nobody!" repeated Watchful; " I'll make you swallow all the frogs in Battersea, you ugly hemigrant!"

"Swallow?" cried his antagonist. "Sacra! I sall make all de bull run down you neck, you foreign cokeyney."

"What!" said Waxend, doubling his fist, " I have as good a mind to kick you as——"

" Pooh !" interrupted Monsieur St. Jean, nothing daunted; " I would pull your eye and black your nose."

" Why, you insignificant, little French poodle," retorted Watchful Waxend, "to dare to insult a seaman in his most gracious majesty's royal navy in this manner! Oh, if it wasn't for the law, wouldn't I pummel you! But hark you —do you mean to persevere in paying *devours*, as you call 'em, to my Abigail? Do you think to rival me in grace and——"

"Oui!" interrupted Mousieur St. Jacques, "look at me; talk of de grace.

Whoo! dare is de grace for Mamselle Abigail, and she know it, and sall admire it."

"Grace!" repeated the Bishop, scornfully. "Why your leg's like a mile-post, and your body like a beer barrel."

"My leg!" laughed the Frenchman; "I have turn all the ros bif I eat into von vera fine calf—ha—ha—ha!"

"Yes," replied Waxend, pointing sarcastically to his wig and pigtail, "and you garnish your calve's head with a dish of cauliflower and a stick of beet-root."

"No," returned the other, "it is de froth of de portere dat I carry in my barrel, and as for de odere, you may get de *beat*-root if you not hold your tongs."

"I don't use tongs, you little nondescript," retaliated Waxend; "but do you mean to say that Abigail Holdforth has become so lost to all sense of shame as to consent to throw herself away upon such a fellow as you?"

"We, Monsieur Lapstone," replied his rival, "she sall throw herself avay, and we sall valk to de church, and to-morrow, next veek, instanment. Dere, sare, you put that in your smoke and pipe it—ha—ha—ha!"

With these words the little Frenchman fixed upon him a most provoking look of contempt and triumph, and ironically bowing to him, abruptly made his exit.

"Well," said Watchful Waxend, when he was gone, "who would have thought it would ever have come to this? It's all over, that's very clear! My thread of happiness is brought to an end. But it's no use fretting about it. Abigail Holdforth is a deceitful little minx, and it's plain that she could never have loved me, so, perhaps, she is better lost than found, after all. This is her revenge, I suppose, for my running away from Bullock Smithey. Never mind! Sorrow's very dry, so I'll e'en return to the Crown and Crosier, and endeavour to revive the inward man with another jug of old Wallit's best. But, eh? No—yes it is! It is Harry Halliyard coming this way just in the nick of time. Poor fellow! how dull and wretched he does look, to be sure! But I do not wonder at that. His Polly to become the wife of Joe Tiller, after all the vows of constancy she had made to him! Well, I'll never believe in woman again!"

Harry Halliyard, with a sad and disconsolate air, and buried in deep and melancholy meditation, now made his appearance, and Watchful Waxend drew himself aside, and observed him for a few moments in silence.

"My ship's completely water-logged," soliloquized our hero, "and it's not possible that she can float much longer. Well, it's no matter; I have lost my chief mate, and so the sooner the vessel goes to pieces the better. Why did the pirate bear down upon me and board me at the very moment when I was about to slip my cable? It would have been all over now, and Mary might have been brought to her senses, and have been forced to admit the cruel way in which she has served the faithful heart which was so fondly devoted to her! But it is not too late now. There is nothing more left for me to toil for, and so I may as well finish the cruise of life at once, and——"

"Oh, don't say so, Master Halliyard," interrupted Watchful, coming forward, "there are sometimes more ports than one in a storm, you know; and although you are at present driven out of your latitude, if you only take the pilot Hope on board, you might find safe anchorage yet."

"Ah, Master Waxend!" replied Harry, "is that you? How is it we have parted company for this last day or so? Give us your flipper, shipmate. I suppose you have heard all about it? —all about the—the—d—n it! I cannot speak it!—The words would choke me!"

"Yes, Harry," answered his companion, "I have heard everything about your Mary—no, she is not your Mary now; she is the wife of——"

"Avast, avast, mate!" interrupted Harry, in a voice of the greatest excitement, "or my senses will be cast altogether adrift! My fair craft has struck her colours to the enemy—lowered her flag to a peter-boat, and I am completely run down, even in sight of home!"

"It is a bad job, Master Halliyard," remarked Waxend, "but do you not think that, perhaps, they are not so much to blame, after all? It is said that it was supposed you were dead, and that the poor old dame, on her death-bed—"

"It is all false!" interrupted Harry, impatiently. "I will not believe it! Do you think that I am such a lubber as to be deceived by such a yarn as that? And even if it were true, had she really loved me as faithfully and fondly as I do her, and Joe had been the sincere friend that he ever pretended to be to me, could they have acted in the way they have done?—No! they could not! Oh, they have indeed acted with the basest ingratitude towards me, and I am now one of the most wretched beings in existence!"

"Ah! Master Halliyard," replied Watchful Waxend, "I am, indeed, truly sorry for you, and I only wish it was in my power to serve you; but I am as bad off as yourself—we are two unfortunate individuals."

"We! What do you mean?"

"Why, that my fair craft, Abigail Holdforth, has been hoisting false colours all along, and that she has deceived me also, and has suffered herself to be taken in tow by a French buccanier."

"Ah!" ejaculated Harry, "is constancy in woman, then, all a lie?"

"Yes," returned Waxend, "I have found, to my cost, that they are all no more to be depended upon than an unwaxed thread!—But as for your talking about foundering altogether in the ocean of despair, pardon me, but I must say that it is little better than madness. You have got plenty of money now, and——"

"Money!" interrupted our hero; "what think you I care about it now? I only valued it for her sake, and now she is false to me, I view it only as so much useless dross!"

"Well, Master Halliyard," returned Watchful, "you know best, I dare say; however, money is a very handy thing, after all. For my own part, I have made up my mind what to do."

"And what is that?"

"Why, to make my way to Portsmouth without delay," answered the Bishop, "and see whether I cannot get a ship. That is much better than committing suicide, and not half so painful or so dangerous an experiment, in my simple opinion."

"Right!" coincided Harry, suddenly arousing himself, "a true British tar never cries peccavi to trifles; so we will set sail together, and once more on the bright blue waters of the deep try to get the weather-gauge of care, and to forget the misfortunes that have befallen us ashore."

"Ah! now, Master Halliyard, you speak like yourself," remarked his companion, "and you shall find me stick to you as close as sole and upper-leather."

"Crowd all sail, then," exclaimed our hero; "weigh anchor; overboard with thought; weigh anchor, I say, and for Portsmouth ahoy! But, avast, Harry," he added, after a pause, "take in a reef, and steady boy, steady. Can I go, perhaps never more to return or to behold her again, without one word at parting?—I must see her pretty figurehead again, though she now—She would not refuse me this last request; and even Joe cannot, I should think, object to it. But I must see her alone—no other ears but our own must listen to our words of parting—no eye but that of God witness the painful scene. Waxend, you are my friend; think you, then, that it would be wrong in me to request her to see me for the last time?"

"Why, no, Harry," answered the former; "taking all the circumstances into consideration, I do not think that it would, and I don't suppose that there is much fear of Master Tiller bringing a *Crimp Cod* action against you. But how do you propose to make her acquainted with your wishes?"

"I have it, shipmate," replied Halliyard; "I will just write a few lines to her, asking her to meet me in the old churchyard to-night. Yes, there cannot be a better place for the scene than where the bones of my poor old mother rest. It shall be so—so let us steer our course without delay to the Crown and Crosier, where I will write the letter, and you must endeavour to deliver it into the hands of Mary, and receive her answer. Are you willing to do so?"

"To be sure I am," answered Waxend, "and I have no doubt that I shall be able to execute my mission with my usual ability."

"Come along, then, my jolly tar," said Harry; "this meeting over, let us hope that we may once more weather the storm, and cast anchor in the port of peace and content at last. Oh, Mary! Mary! did you know my feelings at the present moment, I think you could not help pitying me. She will not, surely, refuse me this last sad request?—No, no; she must indeed loathe and despise me even worse than I think she does if she can. Come along, Waxend, let us get this painful business over, and then we will crowd all sail for Portsmouth."

"Ay, Master Halliyard," returned the former, "and I care not how soon we do so, I assure you, since Abigail Holdforth has jilted me in the manner she has done; for if I remain here much longer I shall certainly be the death of that Mounseer, my rival, and it would be a mortal shame to get hanged for such a hignorant, hugly little himigrunt as him."

With these words they hurried from the spot, and without entering into any further conversation at present, they made their way to the Crown and Crosier. Here they retired into a private room, in order to escape from the noise and interruption of the persons assembled in the house; and our hero having procured writing materials, sat himself down to accomplish the task he had imposed upon himself, whilst Watchful Waxend resigned himself to his pipe and his jug, and endeavoured to while away the cares and anxieties which pressed upon his mind.

To the simple-hearted young seaman the task he had to perform was no easy one to accomplish, and his feelings, as might be expected under the circumstances, were of that description as to nearly overpower him. He could proceed but slowly, for his mind was bewildered, and he knew not how to address the unfortunate object of his affections. Line after line he wrote, and then, dissatisfied with what he had done, he erased them again, and throwing the sheet of paper aside, he commenced a fresh letter; but at length he finished it, after being occupied for full an hour, and having folded and sealed it, he delivered it into the hands of Watchful Waxend, and started him on his errand, with strict injunctions to him to deliver it into the hands of Mary

safely, and endeavour to obtain from her a favourable answer. When he was gone, poor Harry Halliyard paced the room for a few minutes in a state of the greatest agitation, and reflected upon what he had done, and the probable result of it.

"Should she refuse me," he said "then, indeed, my despair will be complete, and I shall feel that I am all alone in the world, and the sooner that my voyage is over the better. Refuse me? No, she surely cannot have the heart to do that, even after all that she has done. It is the last favour, I dare say, that I shall ever ask her, and it is not much to grant. Ah, Mary, that it should ever come to this! That I should at last find myself in the bilboes of misery, neglect, and despair, and compelled to beg for a little mercy, some small indulgence, like a tar who has got himself into disgrace, and knows not whether he is to be strung up to the yard-arm, or receive the punishment of the cat. Well—well, I have not deserved it, and so that is some small consolation. But should she consent, how can I meet her? Will not the sight of her, and the knowledge that she is the property of another, and that she is lost to me for ever, overpowers my senses? I almost regret that I have sent to her at all, for will she not look upon me with scorn for having done so, and only laugh at my sufferings? Pshaw!—no, that can never be! Her heart must have become as cold and insensible as a rock, if she can do so. Her heart!—she cannot possess a heart, or she could never have deceived her faithful sailor, the companion of her childhood in the manner she has done. How can I believe her asseverations of innocence? They are only bitter mockery to my feelings. She has cajoled me—jilted me; Joe Tiller could only have possessed her affections, or she would never have been so ready to have bestowed upon him her hand. The thought is madness!"

He struck his forehead as he thus spoke, and then again traversed the room with disordered steps, while his mind was in such a bewildered state that he scarcely knew what he was about. In the meantime Watchful Waxend proceeded on his way to the residence of our heroine, at which he

JOE BEARS THE INSENSIBLE MARY HOME FROM THE CHURCHYARD.

shortly arrived, and then hesitated for a moment how to act, for his errand was a most delicate and important one, and should Joe Tiller happen to be at home, he knew not how he should be able to accomplish it.

The reader will remember the condition in which we left Mary, and it was some time ere she could recover herslf or could obtain the least compo-sure. The image of Harry Halliyard, as may be expected, was never absent from her mind for a single moment, and most dreadful and agonising were the apprehensions and forebodings that distracted her brain as to the fate that would befall him, especially after what had occurred between him and Tiller, and the rash and desperate act he was then about to commit.

"Heaven protect him!" she earnestly ejaculated, clasping her hands vehemently together, and sighing deeply; "Heaven protect him, arrest his hand when he would be impelled, in the frenzy of his despair, to commit some violent act, and give him fortitude to support the terrible disappointment it has been his hard lot to experience. Oh, Harry! surely you cannot believe me the false and heartless being that I may appear to be! Reason will resume its sway over your brain, and you will no longer doubt the truth of that which I have stated. You will not—cannot curse me!—Oh, no! I know your noble and generous heart too well to imagine that. It would drive me to absolute madness could I make up my mind to believe you could form so cruel and unjust an opinion of me. God knows how faithful has my heart ever been towards you—there your image was too fondly enshrined for anything ever to displace it. But what do I say?— Am I not committing a sin by daring to give utterance to such words as these? —Oh, yes; I am now the wife of another, of one who loves me, and who has ever behaved to me with the most unbounded affection and attention, and this is surely not the return I should make for it. Oh, Joe! would to Heaven that we had never met; for then all the dreadful consequences that have since taken place might have been avoided, and I might have become the wife of that man to whom my vows were plighted in early childhood! Cruel Fate! surely your decrees have been too severe!"

She pressed her hands upon her aching forehead, and sobbed convulsively, as if her heart would break. In this painful manner the afternoon wore away, and the evening set in, but still Joe Tiller remained absent from home, and Mary began to fear that he had again encountered Harry Halliyard, and that something serious had happened between them, especially after what had transpired at the interview they had recently had with each other. She could well appreciate the excited feelings of Harry, and how little prepared he would be to listen to the voice of reason and persuasion; and led on by the impetuosity of his emotions, what fatal excesses might he not be tempted to commit! So powerful and torturing became her doubts and apprehensions, that she was several times half-resolved to issue forth from her dwelling; and to go in search of her husband, but still there was something seemed to restrain her, and she remained where she was.

"Oh, God!" she earnestly ejaculated, "I beseech you to avert the dreadful catastrophe I apprehend, and prevent my husband and the unfortunate Halliyard from coming into collision with each other; for, alas! should they do so, I shudder with an almost insupportable sensation of horror to think what may be the consequences. Harry is far too prejudiced against us to listen patiently to any explanation that can be given, or to believe the statements made; and I fear that, notwithstanding the warm friendship which Tiller bears towards him, and the deep and sincere sympathy which he feels in his unfortunate fate, and the cruel disappointment to all his bright-formed visions of happiness, he has had to experience, will never be able to brook the bitter reproaches and unjust accusations he will too probably heap upon him. This morning Harry called him villain and traitor, and struck him to the earth, and in spite of Joe's efforts to conceal it from me, I am too fatally convinced that his indignation and resentment must be aroused, and that it will need but little more to urge him into such a retaliation as they would both have the greatest cause afterwards to repent, and which would at once complete the misery of us all. Oh, how terrible is this suspense! Oh, that something would occur to bring about a satisfactory and amicable arrangement of the difficulties by which we are at present surrounded; but, alas! it would be little better than madness to imagine that such will ever be the case."

She now took from her bosom a miniature likeness of Harry, which, from the time he had given it to her, she had worn next to her heart, and as she pressed it again and again with frantic fondness to her lips, her tears flowed fast, and the hysterical sobs that heaved her fair and gentle bosom were almost overpowering. As she gazed upon the resemblance of the well-known features of the handsome young seaman, the excitement of her feelings arose to an almost insupportable degree, and she beat her breast with all the vehemence of the most unspeakable and indescribable grief and despair.

"Unfortunate youth," she again soliloquised, and convulsive sobs almost choked her utterance, "how happy were we at the time when you presented to me this precious token of your affection, how sanguine and buoyant were our hopes and expectations; who could ever have expected that they were doomed to be so fatally and so cruelly disappointed? Days of blissful innocence and peace, fated never to return! God! what horrible thoughts distract my fevered brain as they arise to my imagination, and I contemplate the present awful alteration in our circumstances, and the prospects that are spread before us."

She paused, for grief again choked her utterance, and she could proceed no further. She returned the miniature to her bosom, and walking to the window, gazed eagerly from it, with the hope of seeing her husband approaching; but she was doomed only to be disappointed, and the anguish and suspense of her mind increased.

The moon had arisen, and was shining brilliantly on all around, and imparting a tone of tranquillity and happiness to everything upon which her silvery and lucid beams fell, which was little in accordance with the feelings that agitated our unfortunate heroine's bosom, and she averted her looks from the scene, and gave herself up entirely to the indulgence of her misery and despair. She was at length interrupted in the midst of her gloomy meditations by hearing a knock at the outer door, and she started from her lethargy, and her bosom throbbed with expectation and revived hope.

"Oh, thank Heaven!" she ejaculated, as she hurried towards the door; "my prayers have been heard; it is Tiller who has returned, and all is at present safe."

She opened it, but started back with amazement and disappointment on beholding Watchful Waxend.

"Good evening to you, Mary—I beg your pardon, Mrs. Tiller, I mean," he said; "I hope you are quite well, though, to be sure, you look ill and sad enough,

which I do not wonder at, after what has taken place; but that's neither here nor there. Is Joe at home?"

"No," replied Mary, "he has been absent from home for many hours, and I thought he would have returned ere this."

"Well," remarked Watchful, "that is fortunate."

"Fortunate?" repeated our heroine, with a look of astonishment; "what mean you, Mr. Waxend, and what brings you here?"

"Oh, Mrs. Tiller," returned Watchful, "it is an errand of importance, I assure you, so let me advise you to compose yourself, and listen to all about it. Harry Halliyard——"

"Ah!" interrupted Mary, eagerly, and her lips trembled as she spoke, "what of him? Have you seen him, and——"

"Yes—yes; and in a sad way he is. It is a bad job, Mary, a very bad job, and God knows what will be the end of it; and then there's my Abigail, too, whom I——"

"Speak—speak! do not keep me in suspense! Poor Harry! Oh, tell me, has anything serious happened to him?"

"Why, what a strange question that is to put to me," returned Waxend, "after what has taken place."

"Do you come from him?" demanded our heroine, impatiently; "this equivocation is insupportable."

"Yes, Mary," he answered, "I do come from him, sure enough, and I bring a message from him; that is, I have a letter for you."

"A letter for me and from Harry?" ejaculated Mary, eagerly; "he, then, has not forgotten me—he does not entirely despise me. Oh, give it me!—but no, what would I do? I must not now receive any communications from him without the knowledge of my husband."

"And if you do not, Mary, you will break his heart, that's all about it," observed Waxend; "it contains his last request, and after you have complied with it, you will never behold him again."

"No more behold him!" sighed Mary, with a look of agony. "Oh, God! But give me the letter, there sure can be no harm in perusing the last words that I may ever receive from one whom I have so fondly loved."

Waxend placed the letter in her hand, and as she gazed eagerly at the well-known characters of the superscription, the tears almost blinded her, and convulsive sobs, that were quite heartrending to hear, heaved her bosom. With trembling hands she hastily broke the seal, and unfolding the letter, she proceeded to peruse the contents, and as she did so, her countenance underwent the most powerful and painful changes, and it was quite evident that the emotions which agitated her breast were of the most conflicting and torturing description.

"Grant him a private meeting in the old churchyard?" she gasped forth; "oh, it is impossible! Prudence and justice to him who is now my husband forbid it. And yet, Harry, can I refuse you this one last request, when you are going once more, with a broken heart, to brave the perils of the deep, and we may never meet again? Can I decline your last sad farewell, and probably to receive your forgiveness? Oh, no, I cannot!"

"That is just my opinion, Mary—Mrs. Tiller I mean," remarked Waxend. "Then I am to say that you will come?"

"No—" hesitated the poor damsel, and pressing her hand upon her forehead. "Yes—yes, I will be there at the time appointed; that is, if my husband do not return before and prevent me, I——"

"Pardon me, Mary," interrupted Waxend, "but had you not better go with me now, and that will prevent any disappointment of the kind you have mentioned."

"No—no," returned Mary, "I must have a few minutes to prepare myself for the trying interview, and then I will hasten to the place of appointment, in spite of the consequences that may follow. Go—go, my friend, and deliver my message, and tell Harry that in half an hour at the farthest, if nothing occurs to prevent me, I will meet him at the willow tree in the old churchyard."

Watchful Waxend waited for no more, but, very well satisfied with the result of his mission, he quitted the house and hurried on his return to our hero, whom he had no doubt would be waiting most anxiously and impatiently to see him.

When he was gone, poor Mary proceeded once more to peruse the contents of the important letter, and, as she did so, her tears again flowed fast, and painful sighs escaped her heavily surcharged bosom. Every word which our hero had written there went to her heart like a dagger, and, if possible, made the misery of their situation, the utter hopelessnes and cheerlessness of their prospects the more apparent to her.

"And he is going far away!" she sighed; "he is once more about to expose himself to all those dangers from which, after so many years, he has just escaped; and blighted as are his prospects, how reckless will he be of those perils which he might otherwise avoid, but which in his despair he will now probably court as a happy release from the misery of his fate. Oh, Harry! noble-hearted youth! how my heart bleeds for you, and how willingly would I sacrifice my own life, could I rest assured that by so doing I could restore you to that happiness and peace of mind from which you never deserved to be estranged. That, however, it would be even worse than madness to think about. But what have I promised to do?—Meet him secretly, and unknown to my husband?—Will it not be criminal in me to do so?—And what may not be the dark suspicions it may engender in Tiller's breast?—Let me pause ere I be guilty of that which may plunge me and all who are connected with me, in greater misery than that which we now experience! Alas! it is useless for me to attempt to abandon the idea; it is probably the last request that he will have the opportunity of making, and it would be cruel of me to refuse it. Give me courage, great Heaven! and grant me protection, as you know the purity of my motives. There is not a moment to be lost; the evening is advancing; in a short time my husband will probably return home, and then all chance of my fulfilling the promise I have made to Halliyard will be at an end. Let me be firm, and trust to Providence to support me through this trying interview. I will just write a few lines to Joe, to excuse my absence and quiet his fears, and then to make my way to the solemn and sacred place of assignation."

With these words she once more pressed the letter of him she so fondly loved vehemently to her lips, then carefully depositing it in her bosom, she hastily wrote a few lines to her husband. which she left upon the table, and putting on her bonnet and cloak, she emerged from her dwelling, and with trembling footsteps, and a mind so bewildered that she scarcely knew what she was about, she made her way to the old churchyard, frequently pausing and looking back, fearful that Tiller might be watching her.

The moon continued to shine brightly over the scene, so that she had a distinct view of every object around her, but perceiving nothing to alarm her, she pursued her way with more confidence, and could now distinguish the place of her destination a short distance before her. And now she was compelled to pause to take breath and to collect her thoughts, and again the most dismal doubts and forebodings crowded upon her imagination.

"What am I about to do?" she said; "may not my conduct of to-night be the means of bringing destruction upon myself and my husband?—Why should Harry seek a private meeting with me? If he wished to bid me farewell, and to assure me of his forgiveness, why should he hesitate to do so in the presence of Joe? Let me pause ere it be too late. But why should I suspect him? Oh, too well I know his soul of honour, and that he would hate and despise himself could he for a moment contemplate anything which he should have reason to blush openly to acknowledge. Dear, unfortunate Harry! I will trust you, let the consequences that may follow be whatever they may!"

Emboldened by these thoughts, she drew her cloak closer around her, and once more proceeded on her way; but she had not advanced many paces when she was startled by observing the dark shadow of a human form upon the ground, and hastily looking up, she could scarcely repress a scream when she beheld the tall figure of a man of the most repulsive features (for they were clearly revealed in the moonlight) standing before her. We have, however, no occasion to describe him minutely, when we inform the reader that it was the villain Hugh Brandon.

He was gazing at her with a rude expression of countenance that was particularly alarming, and before our heroine could recover herself from her terror and astonishment, he advanced towards her, and grasping her by the wrist, said—

"So, fair damsel, we have fortunately met, for I have long been anxious to see you, and to cultivate your friendship."

"Unhand me, man!" gasped forth Mary, in a faint voice, and trembling violently; "why do you thus boldly obstruct me? I know you not—who are you?"

"Oh, that matters not," answered the ruffian, with a half-sardonic grin, which made his countenance doubly repulsive; "it is sufficient for me that I know you as the beloved of Harry Halliyard, formerly of the Polyphemus, and the wife of the waterman, Joe Tiller. We have well met, I say again, for I have a word or two to ... with you. Nay, start not, nor gaze u... me with such looks of scorn and disgust, for I am not the sort of man upon whom they are likely to have the least effect. Harry Halliyard and I are enemies, for he has done me mortal injuries that I can never forget or forgive; but you, so fair, and——"

"Release me, villain!" again cried the now completely horror-struck damsel, and at the same time struggling violently, though it was all to no purpose, "your looks and words strike terror to my soul, and convince me of the villany of your purpose. Release your hold, I say again, or my screams shall summon assistance, and vengeance will descend upon your head!"

"Ha—ha—ha!" laughed the fellow scornfully, "such threats will make no impression on me, I assure you, my dainty damsel; your cries would only be wasted on the air, for there is no one here to fly to your aid, and Hugh Brandon is not the man to be intimidated by trifles."

"Brandon?" repeated our heroine, looking more narrowly upon him, and shuddering; "those features, too—oh, God!"

"Ay," he returned with a malicious look of exultation, "no doubt my features are familiar to you, and must be very agreeable to you; it is not the first time we have met. You must go with me."

"With you, ruffian?" exclaimed Mary, still endeavouring to release herself from his rude grasp; "miscreant, forbear. Oh, help—help!"

"I tell you again your cries are useless," said the fellow Brandon, grasping her arm more fiercely, and with his other arm encircling her waist; "from the first moment I beheld you, your charms made a lasting impression on me, for, ruffian though I am, I am not insensible to female beauty. But it is a waste of time to stand parleying here—so, come, come; this night shall make you mine, and gratify my wishes and revenge at the same time."

"God of Heaven!" ejaculated our heroine; "is there no one to rescue me from this monster in human form? Help—help—help!"

"Resistance is in vain," he cried, as he attempted to drag her towards the banks of the river; "you are mine—you are mine!"

Still did the unfortunate damsel resist with all her might, and rent the air with her cries for assistance, but her strength was almost exhausted, and she was scarcely able to save herself from fainting, so overpowered was she by terror, when at that critical moment the shouts of men in the distance saluted her ears, and eagerly looking in the direction from whence they proceeded, she beheld two men hastily approaching the spot. Brandon saw them at the same moment, and in a voice of fury exclaimed, as he recognised one of them in the moonlight—

"Ah, by hell it is he! The game is up—foiled! Curses light upon him! but we shall meet again, and then beware!"

As he thus spoke he released his hold, and rushing from the spot, in a contrary direction to that in which the men were coming, he was almost immediately out of sight. Mary again gazed eagerly towards the men who were approaching, and recognised the manly form of Harry Halliyard in the clear moonlight. Overpowered by her feelings, she uttered a faint cry, and immediately sank insensible upon the earth. With the speed of lightning our hero approached, followed by Waxend, and raising the insensible form of her he so fondly loved in his arms, he gazed with mingled feelings of transport and regret in her pale but beauteous face.

"Mary—Mary," he exclaimed, in a voice of the deepest emotion, and which showed the power of the feelings that at that moment were struggling in his manly breast—"My Mary, and to be thus borne down by that black-looking pirate. Poor lass—poor lass! How pretty she looks even in her melancholy paleness; I—I—oh, how my heart beats as I once more press to my bosom that lovely craft which is no longer mine! I feel it going at the rate of fifty knots an hour, and yet I am all aback, and have neither rudder nor compass to steer by. Mary—Mary! She does not hear me. Oh, that one so taut and trim should ever disgrace her flag! One kiss; she will not know I stole it, and, therefore, cannot reproach me for the liberty. Liberty!—damme, that word sticks in my throat like a piece of salt junk. No matter; I cannot deny myself this small indulgence."

With the most fervent affection, he pressed warm kisses again and again upon her lips, and then strained her delicate form more closely to his bosom.

"She does not revive," he said, "that infernal shark has so alarmed her, that—but we must not remain here, or we may be interrupted. We are not far from the place of appointment, so while she remains unconscious of my presence let me convey her thither. Oh, Mary—Mary, my heart is so full, that I know not what I am about."

As he spoke he once more kissed her, and then raising her gently in his arms, he hurried from the spot towards the old churchyard, followed by his faithful though eccentric friend, Watchful Waxend. On arriving there, he placed her on a gentle mound of earth, beneath the branches of the old willow tree, and gazed with mingled feelings of delight and melancholy despair upon her. Mr. Waxend retired to some distance from them, so that he might not cause any interruption to the tender and affecting scene which he knew what was about to take place.

Our heroine still remained insensible, and Harry continued to gaze for some time intently upon her pale features, without being able to give utterance to a syllable, while the various emotions which at that moment struggled in his breast may be much better imagined than we can possibly describe them.

"How beautiful she looks in her insensibility!" said the honest, warm-hearted young seaman, at length, and dashing hastily away a manly tear that had started to his eye; "just like a vessel becalmed, with the bright moonlight shining over her. Oh! is not this enough to make a complete wreck of my crazy vessel? Can such a lovely and innocent face as this mask the greatest falsehood and duplicity?—Can she have deceived me in the manner I suspect her to have done?—It is impossible! And yet, shiver my timbers! has she not deserted the ship's company, and now sailing under another commander, after having duly signed her name in the books?—It is too true; and I must be a swab indeed if I could persuade myself to the contrary. Mary, I—I—I—damme! in spite of all, I feel as if I could love you better than ever, if that were possible, in spite of all that has happened, and that's all about it; and—but, ah! see, she revives. Mary!"

The poor damsel opened her eyes, half raised herself from the grassy mound on which she had been reclining, passed her hands in a bewildered manner across her forehead, and gazed vacantly around her as she said—

"Where am I? What place is this? I have had a strange vision—methought that I had left my home, and wandered forth in search of——Ah! Harry—Harry!"

She started hastily to her feet as she uttered these wild and incoherent words, and throwing herself convulsively into his arms, sobbed aloud, as if her heart would break with the extraordinary excitement she was undergoing. Harry strained her to his heart, and for a few moments he was so completely overpowered by the tumult of conflicting and overwhelming feelings which were struggling in his bosom, that he could not find power to give utterance to a syllable.

At length, however, Mary, as if recollecting herself, suddenly released herself from his embrace, and starting back a few paces from him, while she looked at him with a mingled expression of love, pity, and dread, exclaimed—

"No, no, no! I must not now! Virtue, justice, and prudence forbid it! Rash woman! what have I done? My husband! Oh, Harry! pity me!—I—I have never deceived you—I have loved you, still love you, faithfully, ardently! but Fate has ordained that another should possess my hand, and we must part, part, alas, for ever in this world! Oh, my heart will surely break in this dreadful struggle! Pity me, pity me, Harry!"

As she thus spoke, she covered her face with her hands, and the tears streamed fast between her long and taper fingers. Harry ventured slowly to advance towards her, but his heart was so full that it was some moments ere he had the power to speak.

"Mary!" he said, at length, in a broken voice, "and is it thus we meet, after so many years of separation, and during which time the thought of your love and constancy have been the sheet-anchor of all my hopes? Had I found you placed under the hatches of death, and knowing that you loved me fondly and truly to the last, though that would have almost made a complete wreck of my heart, still I might have reconciled myself to it; but to find that you have slipped your cable, and attached yourself to another service, without so much as bestowing a thought upon the poor mariner who was willingly and cheerfully encountering every danger for your sake, flattering himself with the fond idea that, after all, he would be moored safe and happy in your arms. Oh, Mary! you have indeed been cruel to that man who would freely have spilt the last drop of his blood if he had thought that by so doing he could have spared your heart a single pang. But it is almost over now! I am outward bound—I enter upon another cruise, without ballast, and caring not how soon I may split upon a rock and go to pieces altogether. I—I have taken the liberty of asking you to see me once more, that I might bid you a last farewell—you have granted my request, and I thank you, but——'

"Harry!" interrupted the distracted damsel, again throwing herself into his arm and looking up piteously and imploringly in his face, "your words drive me fo madness! Why, oh, why do you thus torture me? You believe me false !—oh, how cruelly you wrong me! Heaven knows that during the long time we were separated your image was never for a moment absent from my thoughts, and hourly were my prayers offered up to the Fountain of Grace for your preservation from danger, and that we might meet again, never more to part; absence did but add strength to the passion I felt for you, and even now—but, oh, spare me—spare me! Heaven forbid that I should give utterance to the words.—We believed you dead—here on your mother's grave I swear it—what right had we to doubt the truth of the report, after the apparently satisfactory proofs we had received? and it was then, and not till then, when, unwillingly, I resigned my hand to another, though it was impossible that it could be accompanied by my heart."

"Ah, Mary," ejaculated her lover, "it is there—in that one act is the proof of all your infidelity, for, had you sincerely loved me, though you believed that my body had been made food for the sharks, you could never have smiled upon another."

"Harry, it was, I repeat, only in compliance with the dying prayers and injunctions of the poor old dame, your mother, that I did so, and——"

"Avast—avast," interrupted Harry, "you must, indeed, think me a complete sea-gull if you imagine that I am to be deceived by any such a yarn as that—to suppose that the old vessel in which I was first rated would ever——"

"Halliyard," exclaimed Mary, kneeling down over the old woman's grave, clasping her hands together, and raising them and her eyes solemnly towards Heaven, "hear me while I swear, and solemnly invoke the spirit of your sainted mother to attest the truth of what I utter, that every word I have stated is in accordance with the fact. My heart was still yours—I loved, I adored your memory, supposing you no more; but to quiet the last anxious moments of your poor old mother, I gave my consent to that, which, alas! for us all, has terminated so fatally. Do

you any longer doubt me? You cannot. But if you do——"

"Mary—Mary !" interrupted our hero, in a voice of the most overwhelming emotion, "I pity you—I—I forgive you; but unless my mother's voice from the grave assured me of——"

"Hold !" cried the frantic damsel, hastily drawing a paper from her bosom, and thrusting it into his hand; "be convinced now ; here — here — here's your mother's will, where she leaves the sticks in the cottage, and the wherry and all, to poor Joe to marry me. You'll see how she urges it for your sake. Read, Harry, read! That is her voice from the grave."

She could say no more, her emotions overpowered her, and burying her face in our hero's bosom, she burst into a paroxysm of hysterical sobs and tears. Harry looked at the will, and at a glance he perused the whole of the contents, and as he did so, his manly heart was almost full to bursting. The mist that had before obscured them was, however, in an instant removed from his eyes, and he said, in accents which fully told, far more powerfully and eloquently than any language could possibly have expressed it, the nature of the feelings that were at that moment passing in his soul—

"Poor old mother! these are indeed your well known characters, and I can no longer doubt ;—it's, alas, too true !"

"Ah !" exclaimed Mary, eagerly, and looking up in his face with such an expression of features as it would be impossible for our feeble pen to do justice to, "you believe me, then ?—you do no longer doubt me—you acquit me of falsehood and duplicity, and I am comparatively happy! You will forgive me, Harry, and——"

"My poor lass," interrupted her lover, in a voice half choked by the violence and intensity of his grief, "I do indeed forgive and pity you, though this is the fatal ball which ere long must lay me low. But it is over—we must part, Mary, and for ever."

"For ever, Harry ?" repeated the hapless damsel, with an uncontrollable shudder of horror, throwing he fair arms around his neck, and fixing upon him such a look through the tears that dimmed her eyes, as penetrated to his

THE SMUGGLERS' KEN AT WESTMINSTER,

soul; "that dreadful word! Are there no means of avoiding the stern decree?"

"Yes—yes," replied the young seaman eagerly, as a sudden thought flashed across his otherwise bewildered brain; "there are means; and if you will but consent to avail yourself of them, we may yet be happy."

"Name them—name them!"

"Let us together seek some distant clime; I have plenty of money; I am rich, Mary—place yourself under my protection, and——"

"Halliyard!" interrupted our astonished heroine, withdrawing herself from his arms, and fixing upon him a mingled look of incredulity and reproach, "can it be you that thus advises me? No—no! my ears must have deceived me! Abandon my husband?"

"If you really love me as you profess to do, you will not hesitate," replied Harry; "I seek no more than to have you constantly in my presence, and to listen to the soft music of your voice, to bask beneath the radiance of your affectionate smiles;—I will be to you a brother, a——"

"Hold, hold! my astonished ears must not listen to language so unholy as this, and never did I imagine that it could escape from the lips of Harry Halliyard! Desert that man whom in the presence of the Almighty God I have sworn to be faithful to, who has ever behaved to me with such affectionate indulgence, and who would shudder at the bare thought of entertaining a doubt of my honour and truth? Horrible, revolting thought! Halliyard, that fatal proposition decides me. The mist is removed from before mine eyes—I see at once the fatal imprudence I have been guilty of in consenting to this painful interview—I—I love you, Harry—I must ever love you, and pray for blessings on your head. But I must leave you, there is danger in your presence. Farewell! we must meet no more!"

"Be it so, Mary!" replied our hero, with a burst of emotion which no language can describe; "your words have sealed my doom, and convinced me what a lubber I have been ever to believe that I had taken your heart in tow! Continue to live with the husband of your choice, and console yourself with the thought that he whom you so cruelly deceived is no more afloat to trouble you with his presence! I—I—I hasten to complete my fate, and—"

"Hold—hold!" cried the distracted woman, once more throwing herself into his arms, and her brain seeming to whirl round as the words escaped her lips. "What would you do?—Would you thus rush unbidden into the presence of your Maker, and your last words invoke a curse upon my head? Horrible thought! Gracious Heaven, teach me how to act! Husband!—Tiller!—Oh, God! my brain! Harry—Harry! I cannot control the feelings that rise within my breast, though perdition be the consequence! I yield! I am yours! —I am yours!"

The extraordinary agony and excitement of her feelings were too much for human nature to support, and with a groan she once more sunk insensible in the arms of her lover, who was scarcely in a better situation than herself.

CHAPTER XIII.

THE TERMINATION OF THE INTERVIEW IN THE OLD CHURCHYARD.—THE DEPARTURE OF HARRY HALLIYARD. —THE RECOVERY OF MARY.—HER DISTRACTION AND MEETING WITH HER HUSBAND.—HUGH BRANDON'S PLOT.

WE must do adequate justice to the varied emotions that filled our hero's breast, as he held the insensible form of Mary in his arms, and gazed upon her pale and inanimate features. His brain was, in fact, so bewildered that he could scarcely persuade himself that he was not under the influence of some extraordinary and torturing dream; but still the last words which his beloved and unfortunate Mary had uttered continued so ring in his ears, and he at last became convinced of their reality.

"Mine—mine!" he ejaculated; "did I hear aright? Mary mine!—my constant companion for the future—mine to love and worship? Oh, blissful assurance! I—I—I—Mary, my dear lass, arouse yourself from this lethargy, and convince me that my senses are not labouring under a delusion. Mine!— But, avast, Harry! whither would the madness of your feelings steer you? Is she not the wife of another?—of one to whom the dying injunctions of my mother consigned her? and should I not be a villain to plunge one so fair and innocent into crime, and persuade her to desert him?—No, no! I must have been mad to have given utterance to such a wish; and let me now reflect calmly. Honour, virtue forbid the guilty connexion; and let me, therefore, avoid it while I have the power. She is now unconscious of all that is passing around her; let me, therefore, away while she is in that condition, lest, when she recovers, my resolution should fail me. Poor lass—poor lass! what a sad fate is hers! But why do I delay, when every moment is fraught with such danger? One kiss on those pale ard lovely lips—it will be the last; and then, most loved of all earthly beings, farewell for ever!"

With what frantic ardour did he kiss her, and press her insensible form to his bosom; then gently placing her on the spot where she had formerly reclined, he stood and gazed at her for a few moments in silence.

"Bless you!—bless you, Mary!" he said, at length, "and may Heaven give you fortitude to bear this dreadful trial, and induce you to pardon me for the guilty errors into which, in the frenzy of my despair, I would have plunged you. I—I can never cease to love you with the same intense spirit of adoration that I do now, and my last thoughts, my last prayers must be for you. Oh, God! what will become of me when I am far away from her presence, and know that I can never more be gladdened by the light of her eyes? To know that she reposes in the bosom of another, and that it will be sinful for me even to think of her? Think of her! is it possible that I can ever obliterate her from my memory? As well might I endeavour to dry up the waters of the mighty deep, or seek to control the elements in their wrath. But why do I remain here? Let me at once tear myself away, and abandon myself to my destiny. I have nothing now to live for; all my hopes are crushed, and the sooner I am no more the better. Mary, Mary, one more kiss, and then farewell for ever!"

He stooped down, and again and again imprinted warm kisses upon the lips and cheeks of the still insensible Mary—fixed one look of the most unutterable agony upon her, and then covering his face with his hands, and sobbing like a child, he rushed frantically from the spot and rejoined Watchful Waxend, who had been waiting most impatiently for the termination of the painful interview.

"Why, Master Halliyard," said Waxend, "what a state of agitation you are in, to be sure. Ah, I thought this meeting would not be productive of any good to either of you. But you are surely not going to leave poor Mary lying there in that sad condition, after bringing her from her home at such an awkward hour? It is very ungallant, I must say, and——"

"Avast, avast!" interrupted our hero, impatiently, and in a tone of voice that showed the agitation of his feelings, and was sufficient to silence the officious loquacity of his companion, "my mind is distracted!—I shall go mad, or become a contemptible wretch if I any longer remain here. Poor Mary, we have met for the last time, but may the blessing of Heaven descend upon her head, and enable her to support with fortitude the dreadful and heavy trials to which she is exposed."

"Ah," said Watchful Waxend, with a serio-comic expression of countenance, "those are my sentiments to the very letter. My Abigail Holdforth, we have met for the last time, but as for the blessing, when I think of that confounded ugly little French hemigrant, I cannot say that I wish her many of them; wicey wersy, as Shakspeare says."

"Let us begone," said Harry, "or my resolution will fail me; and should she recover before I have quitted the spot——"

"Begone!" said Waxend. "Where? To the Crown and Crosier?"

"No—no, you lubber," cried our distracted hero; "far away from this latitude altogether, for there are breakers ahead, and we have already sprung a leak. Away! Crowd all sail to Portsmouth—anywhere, rather than remain in this quarter. Oh, Mary—Mary! we are parted for ever, and Joe Tiller can now continue to hold possession of you undisturbed."

He cast one more anxious look towards the spot where Mary was lying, and then again covering his face with his hands, and giving utterance to the most painful groans, he hurried from the old churchyard, followed by his companion, Mr. Watchful Waxend.

It was not for some time after our hero had left her that Mary was restored to her senses, and when she was, she raised her head, and passing her hands across her aching forehead, gazed wildly and vacantly around her, unconscious for the moment where she was or what had happened. Her limbs trembled beneath the chilling influence of the night air, and the clear moonbeams, which were strongly reflected on the spot where she had been lying, dazzled her eyes, and, if possible, her brain became more bewildered than it had been before. But at length the recollection of where she was flashed upon her, and, starting to her feet, she gazed with astonishment around her.

"This sacred place," she added, "where repose the ashes of the dead—how came I hither, and at this hour of the night? what awful mystery is this? It is the silent grave of the poor old woman, too! What can it all mean?—have I been here since the morning, and, overcome by melancholy meditations, sunk into insensibility? Where is Tiller?—How is it that he has not been in search of me, alarmed at my prolonged absence from home? I know not what to think, but—ah! the painful truth now flashes upon my memory; I remember all. I came here to meet Harry Halliyard; forgetful of my duty to my husband I consented to a secret interview with him—And I saw him—I listened to him—I—I yielded to his persuasions, and consented to abandon husband, home, virtue, everything for him! My God! what a guilty wretch have I been! But where is he?—Has he only been trifling with my feelings, and abandoned me to misery and contempt! Harry—Harry! oh, where art thou?—Whither hast thou fled? Surely it was most cruel of you to desert me thus! Harry—Harry! listen to me, and since you have caused me to err so much, have pity on me, and counsel me for the best. How, oh, how shall I again meet my injured husband?—What excuse can I make to him for my absence from home?—Will he not load me with his reproaches, and, probably, heap his curses upon my head? I shall go mad!—I shall go mad!"

She now rushed wildly from the spot on which she had been standing, and with trembling footsteps wandered over the churchyard, sobbing bitterly in the intense and insupportable anguish of her feelings. Then she called again upon the name of our hero, but the mournful sighing of the night-breeze among the branches of the old yew trees and the drooping willows was the only answer she received; and a sickly feeling of terror and despair stole over her and almost overpowered her.

"Gone! gone!" she sighed, wringing her hands; "he has taken advantage of my insensibility, and left me to my fate. We shall meet no more, and he will remember me only with loathing and disgust, since I was so ready to yield to his wishes, and to desert that man to whom my fate, in the sight of Heaven, is indissolubly united. But, no, I remember, now!—He was convinced of my innocence—he acknowledged it, and forgave me, and invoked a blessing upon my head.—But then, to desert me in the manner he has done, without imparting to me one word of consolation, or guiding me how to act in the terrible difficulties by which I am surrounded! oh this is most cruel in the extreme, and can but add to the anguish and suspense with which my mind is afflicted. My God! when I remember the fearful words he uttered—the maddening despair of his feelings, what dreadful thoughts and forebodings flash upon my brain! Should he lay violent hands upon himself my misery will be complete. But why do I tarry here? why do I not return home, and at least endeavour to dissipate the fears of my husband? But how can I explain my extraordinary conduct?—Is it possible that I can deceive him?—and will he not look upon me with suspicion? But I must pass the painful ordeal, let the consequences be whatever they may. My limbs fail me, and I seem as though I were fixed to the spot as if by some terrible spell. How ghastly is everything around me!—My limbs tremble with the cold—I can proceed no further. —Oh, Heaven help me!"

As the unfortunate woman gave utterance to these words a cold shuddering came over her, her brain turned giddy, strange and frightful forms seemed to dance before her eyes; again she lost all recollection as to where she was, or what had taken place, and slowly seating herself on one of the tombstones, and burying her face in her hands, she sank into a state which was very little better than insensibility.

We must now return to the cottage. Joe Tiller, having been detained by business much longer than he had expected, did not return home for more than an hour after Mary had taken her departure to the old churchyard, and he was accompanied by his friend and partner, old Sam Sculler. They were both somewhat surprised not to behold a light burning in any of the windows.

"Why, how is this?" said Joe. "Mary would never retire to rest, I should think, before my return home."

"No," answered Sculler, "but she has most likely retired into one of the inner rooms, and that accounts for our not seeing any signs of a light in any of the windows."

"Ay," coincided Joe, "that must be it. Poor girl, it was a pity to leave her in the state of mind that she was when I was compelled to go to the Hard on business, and I daresay she has been most melancholy in my absence and anxious for my return. I will knock at the door and apprise her of my return."

He knocked at the door accordingly, and having waited a few moments without its neing opened, they both became more surprised than before. Joe knocked again, but still no answer.

"Well, this is very strange," he remarked, "she must have fallen asleep, and does not hear us. I hope nothing has happened, though."

"Oh, do not alarm yourself," returned old Sam Sculler; "you will find her safe enough, I'll warrant. You have a key, have you not?"

Joe replied in the affirmative, and taking it from his pocket, and applying it to the lock, he opened the door, and they entered. Not perceiving her in the front room, they entered all the others hastily, but when they could not find Mary in either of them, they were indeed astonished and alarmed.

"Not here?" said Joe, in a tremulous voice; "absent from home at this time of the evening, and so seriously indisposed as she was? How is this to be accounted for? My heart misgives me."

"Nay," observed Sculler, "do not fear, she is not far off, I dare say; she has probably only gone into one of the neighbours to pass the time away till your return, for it must have been very dull for her moping by herself."

"It is very unusual for her to do so," replied Sculler; "however, we will inquire of the neighbours."

They did so, and not being able to gain any intelligence of her, they returned to the house, completely bewildered, and not knowing to what conclusion to come or how to act.

"Something particular must have occurred to cause her to absent herself from home in this extraordinary manner," remarked Joe; "what to think of it I don't know. My God! should she have again seen Harry Halliyard, what may not have happened!"

"That is not very likely," answered Sam; "the poor fellow, I do not think, will have the heart to venture here in a hurry, if ever he does again."

Joe, feeling more agitated every moment, now hastily struck a light and the first thing that met his observation on doing so was the small strip of paper which his wife had left behind for him on the table, on her leaving the house. He hastily picked it up and read the contents.

"This is more strange and unaccountable still," he said; "she writes merely that the fineness of the evening has induced her take a walk, thinking that the air will revive her, and that she will not be absent long. Mary never acted in this way before, and my mind is not at all easy upon the subject."

"Well," observed Sam Sculler, " I must say that it is very imprudent for her to do so, considering how poorly she was; but there is not much fear of any harm coming to her, and it is not likely that she will be long before she returns."

"I cannot remain in this state of suspense any longer," said Joe, "so I must go forth in search of her, though I cannot form any idea of the direction she has taken. I must chide her for this. You had better remain here, Sam, in case I should miss her, and she should return in the meantime, when she would be alarmed at not finding me at home."

Sam Sculler nodded assent, and Joe, issuing from the cottage, bent his way in the direction she was mostly accustomed to take in her rambles; but the further he advanced, the more his mind misgave him, and he could not help still fearing that something serious had happened, or Mary would never have been absent from home at such a late hour of the evening, and when she must have been expecting him every minute. He wandered about for some time in every place where he thought it was most likely he should find her, but not perceiving the least signs of her, or meeting with any person of whom he could make any inquiries, he paused, and considered how he should act.

"Imprudent girl!" he said, "to take such a whim into your head as this, when you might be fully aware how much it would alarm me. Should any accident have befallen you I shall go distracted. What course can I possibly take now? She surely cannot have paid a visit to the old churchyard at such a strange and unseasonable hour of the evening as this. And yet, something seems to strike me that I am not altogether wrong in that conjecture; and I cannot any longer endure this state of suspense. Her conduct is indeed most unusual and unaccountable, and I cannot resist the influence of certain misgivings that beset my mind. I will immediately

To the old churchyard, so cold and dreary,
To see if I can find my dearest Mary."

Having given utterance to these words, Joe Tiller hastily bent his way to the old churchyard, where he arrived in a few minutes, and entered its silent and solemn precincts by the old ivy-covered gate, instinctively making his way towards the grave of the poor old dame. Seeing nothing of his wife, (for, as we believe we have previously stated, she had, on discovering that Harry had departed, and in the despair of her feelings, seated herself at some short distance from the spot where they had met, and, worn out with anguish and anxiety of mind, had sunk into a state of utter unconsciousness,) he called upon her name, and his fears increased every moment. But he received no answer to his cries, and again he paused.

"What can all this forebode?" he said, as he still cast his eyes anxiously around him. Oh, Mary—imprudent girl! what could ever induce you thus to alarm me? Surely something must have happened to you! Should you have encountered Harry Halliyard in his present excited state of mind, he might have prevailed upon you to—— no, no, no! I dare not trust myself with such a thought. I wrong my Mary to suppose that she could ever be guilty of anything that should call a blush of shame into her cheeks; and Halliyard, in spite of the bitter disappointment he has experienced, is far too honourable to tempt her to wander from the path of rectitude and virtue. I—I—I know not what to think. But it is useless for me to remain here—let me return home without delay, where I shall probably now find her, and receive every satisfactory explanation from her."

He moved from the spot on which he had been standing, and walked towards the other end of the churchyard, looking eagerly around him as he did so, and he had not advanced many paces, when he thought he distinguished in the pale light of the moon something crouching down upon the earth, which bore some resemblance to a human form. Inspired with mingled feelings of hope and misgiving, he hurried towards the object of his curiosity, and his emotions may easily be imagined when he discovered our heroine, seated in the attitude we have described her, her elbows fixed upon her knees, her face buried in her hands, and apparently inanimate and insensible to all that was passing around her. For a few seconds Tiller was so overcome with astonishment and alarm that he was completely petrified to the spot; but quickly recovering himself, he hastened up to the spot on which his wife was seated, and eagerly placed his hand upon her shoulder. She was cold as ice; and, still more agitated and terrified, he called frantically upon her name. She returned no answer, and evidently did not hear him, and all the most fearful forebodings which he had before entertained now arose to his imagination with tenfold force, and in a voice half-choked with emotion and the overwhelming power of his apprehensions, he ejaculated—

"Good God! she is dead!—Her form is cold and inanimate—she hears me not! Alas—alas! what have I done to deserve this terrible infliction? Oh, Mary! beloved, but most unfortunate Mary! what could have induced you to wander to this lonely place at such an hour, and ill and melancholy as you were? Dead!—dead! taken from me in this unexpected manner, and so suddenly, too! Oh, no, it is impossible! Mary—Mary! oh in mercy hear me! speak to me, and remove these horrible doubts, or I shall go mad!"

Gently, but in a state of agitation which we must fail to do adequate justice to, he removed her head from her hands, and looked anxiously in her face, and its pale and ghastly appearance, and the fixed and glassy expression of her eyes, which were wide open, redoubled the horror of his feelings.

"God of Heaven!" he exclaimed, clasping his forehead in despair, "my worst fears are realised—the terrible blow which annihilates all my hopes is struck—she is no more! The brightest spirit that ever inhabited female bosom is fled for ever! Mary is dead! and I —oh, Heaven! this is too much for human fortitude to endure! Let me die—let me perish by the side of her cold and inanimate corpse, and end at once this insupportable misery!"

He wrung his hands and beat his breast in the most indescibable state of agony; then again covered his face with his hands, and the convulsive sobs that escaped his breast were quite pitiable to hear. For a few moments he stood transfixed to the spot, and gave free indulgence to the violence of his grief; but at length he again suddenly aroused himself, as another thought flashed across his brain, and stooping down, and resting poor Mary's head upon his shoulder, and pressing his hand upon her heart, he found that it still beat, but so lowly that it was scarcely discoverable.

"All-merciful Father!" he cried, in accents of delight and gratitude which may readily be conceived, "I thank Thee! She lives—she breathes, and it may not yet be too late to restore her! Mary—Mary! 'tis your husband calls upon your name. No, she hears me not. Her strength is too much exhausted to permit her to do so. Alas! what can have happened to reduce her to this awful state? But there is not an instant to be lost! Could I remove her to our dwelling, she may be restored to sensibility, and the worst fears I now entertain be banished from my breast. Now, Providence, give me strength, I humbly beseech Thee, and all may yet be well."

He fervently kissed her pale lips and cheeks, then raising her frail and delicate form in his arms, he bore her from the old churchyard, and with a strength and determination to which the power of his emotions and the agony of his despair greatly added, he hurried away towards his house, never pausing to rest until he had arrived within a short distance of it, when he stopped, and resting his beloved, but inanimate burthen on his knee, he once more looked anxiously in her pale features, and placed his hand upon her heart. It still beat at the same low pace, and she remained in much the same condition, and with renewed alarm he again raised her in his arms, and hurrying towards his residence, he soon arrived at the door, at which old Sam Sculler, who had been in a state of great anxiety, was standing; and beholding him approach, bearing the insensible form of our heroine, who had all the appearance of a corpse, his alarm, as may be supposed, was greatly increased, for he imagined that she was no more.

Joe Tiller said not a word to him, but rushed hastily past him into the parlour of the cottage, where he placed the form of his wife in a chair, and gazed upon her, and hung over her with looks of the most unspeakable despair.

"Gracious Heaven!" exclaimed the old man, "what terrible calamity is this? Poor Mary——"

"She still lives," interrupted Joe, "but I fear that she is too far gone to recover. I—I found her in the old churchyard, and—but call in the aid of a doctor without delay, or she will be lost to me for ever."

Sculler waited to hear no more, but hurrying from the cottage, quickly returned, accompanied by one of the neighbours, a motherly sort of a woman, who advised that Mary should be immediately placed in bed, and bottles of warm water applied to her feet, while one of her boys was instantly dispatched for the nearest medical man, who, fortunately, resided but a short distance off. Tiller, having committed his wife to the care of the good woman, by her she was immediately placed in a warm bed in her own chamber, and Joe having thrown himself disconsolately in a chair, gave himself up entirely to the anguish of his own feelings, old Sam Sculler being, however, enabled to elicit from him the peculiar and alarming circumstances under which he had found her in the churchyard.

"It was very imprudent," observed Sam, "for Mary to wander to that dreary place at such an hour, and considering the state of mind in which she was at the time. The coldness of the night air, and the dismal thoughts which the place was naturally calculated to engender, have been too much for her strength to endure; but still, I trust, now that you have so fortunately discovered her, and she is so well attended to, no serious consequences are to be apprehended, and that she will soon be restored to sensibility."

"Alas!" sighed Tiller, "I fear that something more serious has occurred to her than we have at present an opportunity of ascertaining or conceiving. Poor Mary——"

He was interrupted by the arrival of the doctor, who immediately hastened to the chamber to which our heroine had been conveyed, in order that he might apply such remedies as should seem necessary, and thither he was attended by the anxious Joe, Sam Sculler remaining below to hear the result.

Mrs. Arnold, the neighbour who had been called in, had applied such simple remedies as her knowledge had suggested, and they were productive of the most promising results; our heroine breathed more freely, and much of the natural placidity of her countenance was restored, though she was still perfectly unconscious and inanimate as Tiller had first discovered her. The doctor, however, gave it as his opinion that she was merely suffering from the effects of the cold, and having prescribed certain antidotes when she should a little revive, he, for the present, took his leave, promising to call again in a short time.

Joe Tiller continued to watch by the bedside of his wife in the greatest anxiety of mind, and to form various conjectures as to what had been the cause of her present painful and alarming condition, and what might be the probable results; but it was some considerable time ere Mary evinced any symptoms of returning sensibility, and the patience of her husband became almost exhausted. At length, however, she respired more freely than before, and breathing a deep sigh, turned slightly on her side. Joe could not suppress a faint cry of gratitude to Heaven, and desiring Mrs. Arnold to retire from the chamber for a short time, he took her hand within his own, and called tenderly upon Mary's name. She, however, returned no answer, and seemed to be ignorant of his presence, or as to where she was, though she muttered some incoherent words which he could not understand.

"Poor girl—poor girl!" ejaculated Joe, "her mind wanders; the shock, whatever it may be, she has sustained, is too much for her; she knows not what she says. Mary—dear Mary! oh, speak to me! look upon me! Know you not who I am?"

She slowly opened her eyes as Joe thus spoke, started slightly, and gazing vacantly around her without appearing to notice him, ejaculated in a low and melancholy voice—

"Methought I heard him speak again; and that he uttered the word farewell, and for ever! But, no—he could not, would not leave me thus, and when I had promised to resign everything for his sake! I am labouring under some wild and agonising delusion. Oh, my poor brain!—Where am I?"

"My beloved Mary!" exclaimed the agitated Tiller, still retaining his hold of her hand, and looking anxiously in her face, "do you not know me? You are safe—you are in your own house—with your husband!"

"My husband!" she gasped forth, and fixing upon him such a look that penetrated his very soul with dread; "no, no—it must not, cannot be, after what has happened. I shudder with shame to look upon you. Oh, Halliyard—Halliyard! where art thou?"

"Halliyard!" repeated Joe; "oh, why do you mention his name on this occasion? For Heaven's sake compose yourself, Mary, and——"

"Compose myself, Tiller!" she interrupted; "oh, no, that is impossible; and you should loathe and despise me. I have disgraced you—wronged you."

"Fearful words!" exclaimed Tiller, in the most distracted accents, and gazing eagerly into her pale face; "you cannot know to what you give utterance."

"It is true," she returned; "oh, I have been most guilty, when you shall know all the fearful truth. I met Harry, by appointment, in the old churchyard; and there I listened with too fond in-

THE AFFRAY BETWEEN HALLYARD AND THE PIRATES.

dulgence to his melancholy and despair; I agreed to fly with him—to abandon you, my husband—everything for his sake, and——"

"Oh, God!" groaned the thunderstruck and distracted man, clasping his forehead, and a multiplicity of conflicting thoughts rushing like a tempestuous sea across his brain; "is it possible that I can hear aright? Surely my ears deceive me? Could Harry Hallyard act so base a part—and you, Mary, could you for a moment contemplate——"

"I did—I did!" groaned our heroine, interrupting him; "I agreed to everything—to become the companion of his flight, even this night, that very hour.—And you should curse me—hate me—turn away from me, as one who has broken the solemn and sacred oath she pledged to you at the altar."

Tiller groaned, and could make no reply; the whole painful truth was at once displayed before him, and he saw clearly the misery and utter hopelessness of his prospects. He turned away his head, and covering his face with his hands, the feelings which at that moment struggled within his breast were almost overpowering. He was, however, aroused from this by hearing a deep groan of agony from Mary, and turning towards her, he beheld her again insensible, and writhing convulsively. Distracted, he called upon her name; accused himself of being her murderer; and enfolding her in his arms, endeavoured to recal her to sensibility. His cries of anguish reached the ears of Mrs. Arnold, and she re-entered the room, and was scarcely less alarmed than himself on beholding the condition of Mary. She immediately resorted to such means as the urgency of the case suggested to restore her, and requested Tiller to leave the chamber for the present, and seek to compose his feelings, but this he strenuously refused to do, until the doctor opportunely returned, and having stated it as his decided opinion that any further excitement to Mary, in her present condition, might be attended by the most dangerous, if not fatal consequences, Tiller was prevailed upon to comply; and with a sad and almost bursting heart he quitted the chamber and retired to the room below, where old Sculler had been most anxiously waiting to see him, and to learn what had taken place at the meeting between him and his wife. On beholding the terribly agitated state of Joe, the old man naturally apprehended the worst, and he questioned him accordingly, and by degrees he elicited from him the fatal acknowledgment which Mary had made, adding, in a frenzied tone of voice—

"You will thus perceive that my hopes are blasted for ever, and that I can never more expect that Mary will look upon me with feelings of love, if with those of common esteem and respect. Harry Halliyard possesses her whole adoration, her very soul; and so powerful is the influence that he exercises over her, that there is no sacrifice she will hesitate to make for his sake, even to the destruction of all my happiness, and the abandonment of me to the utmost misery and despair. Alas! why did we ever know each other?—or what cursed fate induced the poor old dame to urge and enjoin our union, when we all believed that Harry was no more?"

"Nay," remarked Sculler, "indeed you must not thus give way to those feelings of horror and despair, Joe. Mary and Halliyard will think better of this, and both of them repent of the momentary indiscretion of which they have been guilty, and time will teach them to forget each other save as friends."

"Oh, no," replied Tiller, "that I feel to be impossible; their passion is too deeply ingrafted in their hearts for anything ever to eradicate it; and should they meet again?"

"No," observed Sculler, "that I consider is very unlikely. Indeed, it seems most probable that Harry has already repented of the rash and unjust temptation he held out to your wife, or would he not have taken advantage of her insensibility to have removed her from the spot to some place of safety, where he might have had every opportunity of putting his designs into execution? My word for it, he has abandoned his wild and guilty hopes altogether, for too well do we both know his honourable heart to suppose that he could long encourage them. Harry Halliyard seek to take advantage of the innocence of Mary, and to dishonour that man whom he had ever a right to consider as his best friend!— Oh, that, I am convinced, is utterly impossible. Depend upon it, he would sooner encounter death in its most terrible form than he could do so. He is now far away from here, and in order to endeavour to conquer the anguish of those feelings which naturally at present hold possession of his breast, he will not again return to this neighbourhood until he can rest satisfied that the anguish and disappointment of the past are at least partly forgotten, and there is no fear of any further misery being occasioned."

"But can Mary ever forget?" said Tiller, in a melancholy tone of voice; "and will she ever be able to recover herself from the dreadful shock her feelings have t..is night sustained? Will not the image of Harry Halliyard be ever present to her imagination? and will she not always imagine that I look upon her with eyes of suspicion after what has taken place? I can never hope that she can love me, or even view me with feelings of common respect, after this."

"Hold, Tiller," remonstrated his aged companion "you do your wife an injustice, believe me, by encouraging any such ideas as those. Mary must regard you with feelings of the warmest esteem and gratitude, at least, for the uniform kindness, attention, and indulgence you have at all times bestowed upon her, and I do not doubt, if you do but persevere, that you may yet both be content, if you cannot be supremely happy. Come, come, arouse yourself, man, and do not thus give way to those feelings of despair."

"Ah, Sculler," said Joe, "how easy is it for you to advise; but I feel that my boat is capsized in deep water, and that she never will be able to float again. I shall never more have the heart to ply at my calling, for all the hopes that stimulated me to acts of industry are gone, and I have no one now to share my prosperity with me, or to bless me with the smiles of approbation and encouragement. Oh, Mary! what a wretched being have you made me now! But to think of abandoning me—of flying to the arms of Harry, and——"

"Do not let that thought torture you in such a manner," interrupted old Sam Sculler, "for the mind of Mary must have been bewildered; she could not have been conscious of what she said when she gave her consent to anything so revolting. And Harry, too, must have been mad to have made the guilty proposition, of which he afterwards so soon repented, as the abrupt manner in which he quitted Mary sufficiently proves. No doubt, he now bitterly upbraids himself for his rash and culpable conduct, which would have been sure to have been productive of consequences that it is now dreadful to reflect upon. As I before said, I have no doubt that he is now far enough from this neighbourhood, and will take good care for the future to shun the danger into which he was about so precipitately to plunge himself."

Joe Tiller was about to make some reply, when the doctor interrupted him by entering the room, and Joe eagerly inquired of him as to the state in which he had left our heroine.

"She has received a severe shock," replied the doctor, "but is at present comparatively calm, and in a state of stupor."

"Oh, tell me," demanded Tiller, eagerly, "is there any danger?"

"No," answered the doctor, "there is no immediate danger; but I will not be answerable for the consequences if she is the least excited. All that can best be done is to keep her as quiet as possible."

With these words he took his leave, promising to visit her again in the morning, but desiring that he should be immediately sent for if any unfavourable symptoms should make their appearance. When he was gone, Tiller evinced the same agitation he had done before, and it was as much as all the efforts of old Sam Sculler could do to pacify him.

"I will immediately make inquiries in the neighbourhood," he said, "and endeavour to ascertain whether or not he has departed, and if he has done so, that must, at any rate, quiet your apprehensions, I should think."

"Oh, no," answered Joe, "I do not believe that he has departed; or if he has done so, nothing whatever can eradicate his image from the memory of Mary, or appease the anguish he has this night caused in her bosom, and thus will my misery be completed, and all my hopes annihilated. Harry Halliyard, you have been guilty of that which nothing in the world—no penitence can ever repay."

"Be calm, Joe," again expostulated his companion, "and all will yet be well."

"You talk to me in vain, Sculler," said Joe, impatiently; "what prospect is there now before me? Nothing but one of the blackest description. But I must once more see Mary; to be kept in this state of agony and suspense while I know that any danger threatens her is intolerable."

"Nay, Tiller," said his companion, "you have heard what the medical man has said; had you not, at least, better defer visiting your wife again till the morning?"

"No," answered Joe, "it is impossible that I can do so. But I will be careful not to excite her, and will endeavour to conquer my own feelings while I am in her presence."

It was in vain that Sam Sculler sought to persuade him to abandon his purpose, and finding he was determined, he gave up the task, and quitted the cottage with the intention to make the necessary inquiries he had promised, as to whether or not Harry Halliyard was still remaining anywhere in the neighbourhood.

With a heavy and foreboding heart Joe Tiller entered the chamber of his wife, and found her in exactly the state which the doctor had described, and Mrs. Arnold watching anxiously by her bedside. He advanced towards her, and gazed with the deepest and most unspeakable emotion upon her pale features, which bore the expression of intense mental suffering, though she was entirely unconscious of all that was passing around her. Mrs. Arnold, on his entrance, respectfully retired from the room, and left him to the indulgence of his own feelings, after having cautioned him how to act, should Mary recover from her state of insensibility, and informing him that she should be close at hand if her services should be required. Tiller then approached nearer the bed, and gazed even with more intense anguish than before upon her countenance, and even ventured to imprint a kiss upon her lips, but so sound was the state of torpor in which she was wrapped, that it did not in the last disturb her.

"Oh, Mary! beloved Mary!" he ejaculated, "how terrible is the fate which has befallen us, and how much more fortunate would it have been had we never known each other, since it has been productive of so much irreparable misery to us both. But, oh! did she but know the intensity of the passion with which I love her, and the misery I am now enduring, she would surely pity me. But she loves me not, that is too painfully evident, or, after having solemnly become mine in the sight of Heaven, she could never have consented to abandon me for another, though that one possessed her heart. Fool! how

could I ever have flattered myself with the hope that she would, when I knew how fondly they were for years devoted to each other? In spite of everything, I should never have consented to her sacrificing her hand to me, when I knew full well, at the same time, that it could not be accompanied by her heart. But why was Harry ever permitted to return again, since it has been productive of such misery to us all? We might have been happy, and time might have tended to ameliorate her grief and regret, if it could not have taught her entirely to forget. Mary—dear Mary! I feel that it will be utterly impossible for me to stifle the love I bear for you in my bosom, though you may probably look upon me with scorn, or even hatred. How beautiful she looks even in her paleness, and I wonder not that Harry should be unable to conquer the sentiments he entertains towards her in his breast. I feel as if I could even now kneel down and worship her as some angelic being. But what have I not to fear from Halliyard, since he could persuade her to desert me, and to lead a life of dishonour? And she yielded to his base proposals! Oh, how horrible and agonising is that thought! By Heaven! the deed should not go unavenged! And yet it must have been in a moment of madness that he did so; and if he has not become entirely insensible to every feeling of honour, his conscience must bitterly reproach him for it afterwards. Yes, that will be a sufficient punishment for him; and if he has any sense of shame or regret, he will never again venture near the spot which contains me and Mary.—But still he has implanted that in her breast which nothing can ever eradicate; and the easy manner in which she yielded to his guilty proposals shows too fatally the powerful and guilty influence he possesses over her feelings. Can this be the conduct of Mary—my wife? The thought will drive me to madness! Oh, I feel too well convinced that all my hopes of future happiness are destroyed for ever, and that there is nothing left for me but to fly from her for ever, and to hide myself in some place of obscurity where I shall be unknown to every one, and where I may indulge the bitter, the insupportable and unutterable anguish of my sorrows alone. But to desert her, never more to gaze upon that fair form, that angelic countenance, or to listen to the heavenly music of her voice again! the very thought is intolerable, and is enough to rack my brain to frenzy! No, I cannot leave you, Mary, even though your lips should declare that you hate and despise me, and breathe a curse upon my head! Though your heart, I now feel convinced, beats not for me, I live—I breathe but in your presence, and must brave all the consequences sooner than I can depart from it."

At that moment a gentle sigh escaped from the bosom of the still insensible Mary, and the name of Harry was uttered in a low tone of melancholy anguish. Joe started at the sound, as though a dagger had at that moment pierced his heart, and gazed more eagerly and earnestly towards her; but there was little or no alteration in the expression of her countenance, and she still remained in a state of insensibility.

"Ah!" he exclaimed, "that name, it still occupies her thoughts, and doubtless his image now haunts her imagination, and she probably pictures to herself the time when she may have the opportunity of flying to his arms, and abandoning me to all the horrors of misery and despair. Oh, how maddening is that thought! What can I do?—How shall I act to escape from the horrors by which I find myself surrounded on every side? There are no means of avoiding my fate, or of ameliorating my anguish. Whichever way I turn how black and threatening is the prospect before me! Harry Halliyard, you, whom I once esteemed to be my best, most sincere and devoted friend, have by this night's conduct been guilty of that which no future compunction on your part can ever by any possibility repay. You have vitiated that heart which was once the abode of every virtue, as pure as those of the angels in Heaven itself; and the curses of the Supreme should surely pursue you for it. But, Mary! oh, I cannot, dare not reproach her for that over which she, alas! has no control. May Heaven help and guide her in the terrible dilemma in which she is placed. But Halliyard has obtained a power over her which I much fear that nothing will be able to destroy, and which in the end will terminate in the destruction of us all."

He turned away his head from the contemplation of the pale countenance of his wife, and covering his face with his hands, for a few moments he gave unrestrained indulgence to the anguish of his feelings, and the convulsive sobs that escaped his bosom shook his whole frame, and must have excited the deepest commiseration in the breast of all who witnessed them. Then he knelt down by the side of the couch, and taking the hand of Mary in his own, he fervently implored the Almighty to give them both patience and fortitude to endure the heavy trials with which it was His will to visit them. Again he arose to his feet, and scarcely knowing what he did, again and again he imprinted the most ardent kisses upon her cheeks, without arousing her from her apathy, or in the least disturbing it, and unable any longer to endure the contemplation of that which caused him so much anguish of feeling, he rushed from the chamber and proceeded to the room below, where he found Mrs. Arnold, and being anxious to be alone, he desired her again to return to Mary, and to give him immediate notice if she should recover her senses, or should any unfavourable change take place. He folded his arms across his chest, and paced the room backwards and forwards in the most disordered manner. Never before had Joe Tiller felt half the anguish of soul which he at that moment experienced, and his brain seemed as if it would go distracted. It was almost impossible for him to gather his thoughts together to any reasonable point; and such was the bewildered and disordered state of his mind, that the most frightful forms seemed to dance before his imagination, and to grin upon, and mock at his misery.

"This is the most terrible trial of all that it has been my lot to encounter," he soliloquised; "and how shall I ever find strength or fortitude to support it? The bare contemplation of my miseries almost unmans me, and I know not what course to adopt by which I may hope to find relief. Oh, God! surely there is no act of my life that deserved this, and, therefore, I am the less prepared for the infliction. But what will be the sufferings of Mary when she is restored to consciousness? Will not her strength sink beneath the accumulated anguish of her thoughts and her feelings? And how am I to meet her, and again hear her repeat what took place at the interview between her and Harry Halliyard, and hear her once more avow, as she probably will, the love she bears him? The words will madden me; ard yet I cannot, dare not reproach her for that over which she has no control. I feel plainly enough that the troubles I have yet to endure are tenfold more severe than any it has hitherto been my lot to encounter, and I shrink from them with a feeling of horror fast approaching to cowardice. Would that I could fly from myself, and bury the past in oblivion; but, alas! that is impossible. Reflection does but impress them still more visibly upon my memory, and I could be guilty, methinks, of any desperate act to terminate all. Mary, I can pardon, I can freely pardon you for that which you have this night done, could I be certain that you would for evermore banish such thoughts from your mind, and at least endeavour to become resigned and contented in the lot to which Providence has destined you, and view me with the regard and esteem that are due to your husband, even if you could not love me. But, alas! it would be folly in me to flatter myself with any such hopes, and, therefore, there is nothing to which I can possibly look forward to but the greatest misery and anxiety of mind."

He paused, and once more pacing the room with agitated steps, gave himself up to all the intensity of anguish and despair, which every moment seemed to increase instead of abating. But he was suddenly aroused from his painful lethargy by hearing a knock at the door, and, opening it, Sam Sculler, whom he had not expected to see again that night, entered the room, and eagerly inquired after Mary.

"Alas!" answered Joe, "she is much in the same condition; still insensible, poor girl; and, perhaps, that is a blessing to her, for what will be the agony of her feelings when she is restored to a state of consciousness? But how have you succeeded in your errand, Sam?

Have you heard anything of Harry Halliyard?"

"I have," replied Sculler, "and it is as I expected; he and Waxend went to the Crown and Crosier after they had left the old churchyard, and from all they stated there, they are now on their way to Portsmouth. So that, you see, Joe, there is nothing further to be apprehended from Harry."

"Nothing more to be apprehended from him!" repeated Tiller. "Oh, Sam, I entertain a very different opinion to that which you appear to do upon that subject, even if it be true that Halliyard has gone to Portsmouth."

'If it be true?" repeated Sam Sculler. "What reason is there to doubt it?"

"I have every reason to doubt it," answered Tiller, "and to believe, on the contrary, that it is a mere subterfuge on his part to blind and deceive me, in order that he may the more readily accomplish the designs he has in contemplation—to watch his opportunity for getting Mary in his power. But even admitting the truth of his going to Portsmouth, and entering once more into the service of the navy, has he not already been guilty of that which nothing whatever can atone for?"

"What mean you?" inquired the old man.

"Has he not destroyed Mary's peace of mind for ever?" replied Joe—"has he not persuaded her to consent to that which casts a stigma on her character as a wife, and must render me for ever doubtful, miserable, and suspicious?—Oh, Sculler, he has done that which ages of penitence could not repay. Think you that Mary could ever forget him? and, overwhelmed by shame, her future life will be an endless source of misery and self-reproach to her, while I——Oh, I shudder to think of it! Would that I were dead, that would terminate all. There would then be no further obstacle to the union of Harry and Mary, and——"

"Joe," interrupted the old man, "are you mad, to talk in this wild manner?"

"Mad!" reiterated Tiller—"yes, I am mad; and can you wonder at it?—I must indeed have been more than man if, with the events of the last day or two —the last few hours, I could have retained my senses. To find that Harry Halliyard still lives—that he has so far forgotten himself as to seek to tamper with the virtue of her whom I love and cherish far dearer than my own existence, and that she is willing to yield to his allurements—sacrifice me—abandon me, everything for his sake—Sculler, think you I can ponder over this without becoming a madman?"

He covered his face with his hands, his emotions quite unmanning him, and sobbed like a child, and old Sam Sculler was almost equally agitated, and so bewildered that he knew not what to say in answer to his observations, or which might be calculated to afford him consolation. Joe was, however, in that excited state that he would not leave him; and thus the time wore drearily away till the morning, Mary continuing in the same state of apathy during the night, but without any more unfavourable change taking place.

The day was just beginning to dawn, and Joe Tiller was sitting disconsolately in the arm-chair which had always been occupied by the dame when she was alive, his head resting upon his hand, and old Sam Sculler standing watchfully over him, when the attention of the old man was attracted by a rustling sound outside, and immediately raising his eyes towards the window, he started, and gave utterance to an exclamation of surprise. Joe was aroused, and starting to his feet, demanded—

" How now ?—What's the matter ?"

" Nothing—nothing," answered Sam, " it is gone now ; it could only have been imagination."

" What do you mean ? It must have been something more than usual that could thus alarm you," said Joe.

" Well—well," returned Sculler, " I will tell you; I thought I beheld one of the most ugly and repulsive faces that I ever saw in my life staring just now in at the window. But I must have been deceived."

" No—no," said Tiller, " you were not deceived; how could you be ? Some villany is afloat ! Let us endeavour to fathom this mystery."

As he spoke he rushed to the door of the cottage, followed by old Sam Sculler, and opening it, they both gazed eagerly beyond and around them as far as their eyes could penetrate, but could not discover a single object which was at all calculated to excite the least curiosity, and they then returned to the room.

" Well, it is strange," remarked Sculler, " but I could almost have sworn that I saw the countenance of a ruffianly looking man staring in at the window upon us, and eyeing us both with looks of the most malicious expression. It strikes me, too, that I have seen him somewhere before, but where I cannot for the moment recal to my mind. However, I must have been mistaken, that's very certain. We have no one to fear. Certainly, no robber would think of coming to the residence of a poor waterman to commit his depredations."

" No," returned Joe, " I feel satisfied that you were not mistaken, and that there is some mischief afloat, at which Harry Halliyard is——"

" Nay," interrupted the old man, " be not ungenerous, Joe; you can never, I am sure, entertain so severe an opinion of Harry as to believe that he would for a moment contemplate any such base design."

" He would tear Mary from me," cried Tiller, " and plunge me into the gulph of misery and despair; and being thus worked up to a pitch of desperation, there is nothing at which he would stick to accomplish his base purposes."

" Nonsense," replied Sam Sculler, " the very idea is absurd. Harry has evidently repented of the temptations he held out to your wife, or would he not have availed himself of the opportunity to bear her away, when he could have done so without any fear of interruption during the time of her insensibility in the old churchyard? Come, come, arouse yourself and be a man."

Joe Tiller was prevented from making any reply by the entrance of Mrs. Arnold, who informed him that Mary was restored to consciousness, was more calm and collected than might have been expected, and desired so see him immediately.

" Heaven be thanked for this !" he exclaimed. " But, oh, how shall I meet her ?"

" Compose yourself," replied Sculler, " and, depend upon it, all will yet be well ; but if you should attempt to say anything that may at all tend to excite her, you may beware of the consequences. No doubt, the explanation she will have to offer will be most satisfactory."

"God grant that it may," returned Joe, "though much I doubt it."

And pressing the hand of his aged friend, he left the room, and hastened to the chamber of his unfortunate wife, where we will leave him for the present, and the scene that followed, and take the reader once more to the old public house, in Westminster, where our hero met with the exciting adventure that we have related in one of the preceding chapters.

It may, perhaps, be unnecessary to state that this place was the well known resort for some of the most desperate, worthless, and depraved characters, which infested the metropolis and its vicinity at that time, and the landlord, though he possessed great skill in concealing the fact, and had hitherto escaped detection, was as deeply implicated in most of the nefarious transactions as any of his customers: in fact, a moment's consideration will convince any one that it was almost impossible for him to be otherwise. In his den were concocted some of the most daring burglaries and highway robberies that were committed in London, and here, too, the depredators always found a safe place of concealment, for there was scarcely a room in the house which did not contain either a secret trap or door, which communicated with underground apartments or cellars, where they might defy detection; or if they were closely pressed, there was a long subterranean passage that led immediately to the water side, and from whence escape was easily available.

During the time that he was in London, or while he had any nefarious designs in contemplation, this house was invariably the place in which Hugh Brandon concealed himself, and its locality to Battersea rendered it particularly desirable to him at the present time, while he was endeavouring to carry out certain designs against Harry Halliyard and our heroine, of the nature of which the reader will be able to form a pretty shrewd guess from what has been already related, but which will be more fully explained anon. It may be sufficient for our present purpose to state that he was at the time to which our narrative now refers goaded on by a spirit of revenge against our hero, and a guilty passion which the charms of Mary had excited in his breast, and that he resolved to leave no means untried, however desperate they might be, to accomplish his wishes.

It was long past midnight, and in a dirty-looking room in an obscure part of the house were assembled, drinking and carousing, cursing and swearing, and indulging in libidinous jokes, *ad libitum*, as desperate a conclave of hardened ruffians as remained unhanged, or could possibly be imagined. The means of entrance into this room was by a secret spring in the door, and there were such ready means of escape, that the guests could vanish in an instant, and before any stranger could possibly obtain admission. At the time to which we call the attention of the reader, one of the fellows was engaged in singing a flash song, to the chorus of which his companions lent their aid in the most vociferous manner. The following were some of the words—

> "Oh, what can match the *gonuf's slum*?
>   Fal de ral iday!
> He'll crack a nob, or he'll crack a *drum*,
>   Fal de ral iday!
> And at length if grabbed by the traps he be,
> Vy, it's only a dance on Tyburn Tree
>   Fal de ra riday!
>   Fal de ra riday!"

This most splendid and characteristic poetical production was done ample justice to by the villains present, and the applause which followed at its conclusion was of the most uproarious and deafening description.

"Well done, my lads," said Bung (who was the proprietor of this respectable hostelrie), "well done, *Peep o'-day*," addressing himself to the individual who had favoured the company with the stave from which we have just quoted; "I do like you, because you allus shows pluck, never, by any *consekenze*, sniver, but allus comes up to th' mark, upright as the Tyburn prop, and down as the knocker o' Newgate. A werry pretty song, that, werry pretty indeed, such as it does a cove's beater good to hear, specially ven the swag has met the occilar!"

"Bravo, Bung! a very pretty

THE PENITENT AND THE PARDONER.

speech!" remarked one of the gentlemen present; "kevite refreshing! Vot a pity it is as you wasn't made a chaplain, or an ugly—ordinary, I means, for you've got such extra-ordinary powers."

"Ha, ha, ha!" laughed the worthy Mr. Bung; "right, Slug, right, my cauliflower; and so has my double stout, as you well know, to your adwantage. Vell, gentl'men (pardon the liberty I takes vith your characters), I perposes a toast."

"Ay, ay, a toast from old Bung!" shouted numerous voices.

"Vell then, gentl'men," replied the host, staggering, and propping himself up by the side of one of the tables, "I perpose a toast which I know you will all most *cord*-ially *despond* to:—Here's the Rogue, the Road, and the Rowdy!"

"Bravo, Bung!" again shouted the whole of the persons assembled, and at the same time tossing off the contents of their glasses in high glee.

"But where is Hugh Brandon?" said one of the company. "It is past his time of being here, and——"

"Oh," interrupted another of the ruffians, "it's all right, 'pend 'pon it; he's too flymy to be trapped ashore, as he has always steered clear of the sharks at sea! Hows'ever, his company would be very agreeable just now, and——"

At that moment a peculiar whistle was heard, which was almost immediately followed by three knocks at the door of the room in which this precious assemblage were congregated.

"That's him," said Bung, the landlord. "open *seaze'em he.*"

The spring was touched, and the door flying open, Hugh Brandon entered the room, and nodding hastily and generally to the company, he threw himself into a seat near the fire, and taking up a tumbler unceremoniously in his hand, he quaffed off the contents at a gulp.

"You're late, Hugh!' said the fellow whom the landlord had designated Peep-o'-day; "you've had business to attend to, I suppose?"

"Business!" repeated Brandon, with an oath; "yes, I have the devil's business and my own to attend to, and very little luck."

"Been after the *safe?*" inquired one of the ruffians.

"Safe be d——d!" replied Hugh: "I have other game in view just now. But, old Bung! why do you stand there, for all the world like a kid waiting his batch at hot-roll time? Replenish the board, you old son of a grampus, and be d——d to you. The vessel can never float without sea-room; let's splice the mainbrace, and then to talk about business."

"Bravo, Hugh!" said Bung; "you are th' most civilest, perlitest, damned —that is to say that I never neglects duty, but vill obey orders in less time than it would take to *top* a kid!"

Bung vanished instantaneously, and almost as quickly returned with a plentiful supply of grog and tobacco, to which the whole of the guests helped themselves with the utmost freedom.

"Seen anything of the young seaman, Hugh?" inquired the landlord.

"Seen him! yes," answered Brandon, with a frown; "d——n him! I've been yard-arm and yard-arm with him, just at the time when I had laid my grappling-irons on the fair craft who has now cast him on a lee shore. It was my misfortune to be compelled to strike to him on this occasion, but it will be his turn to cry peccavi the next time we meet."

"Ah!" remarked Bung, "Pretty Poll of Putney is a fine lass, and would make no bad partner for you on board your craft, I should think, Hugh."

"Where I intend to stow her, or lose my life in the attempt," said Brandon. "The 'Wasp,' as you know, now lies off Portsmouth, and is known only to the lubbers as the 'Ellen,' from Barbadoes. I have heard sufficient to-night to know that Harry Halliyard is bound for Portsmouth, in order to ship himself again, and if I do not secure him a berth on board my craft that he little expects, it will be strange to me. But I must also have this Mary in my power; her charms have created a certain passion in my breast, and it must be gratified, and my revenge against Halliyard at the same time. I listened to the conversation of her husband and old Sam Sculler this night, outside the cottage, and I have already concocted a plan for her abduction which I think cannot fail."

"Ah!" exclaimed two or three of the company, eagerly; "what is it, Hugh?"

"I have no doubt that you will be all ready enough to assist me in my plans," observed Brandon.

"Certainly—certainly!" replied every voice—"what is your plan?"

"Jack Oarsby," replied Hugh, turning to one of the guests, who was dressed in the garb of a waterman, "you and I are old acquaintances, we have done some business together many a time before now, and I think I could depend upon you?"

"Ah, that you may, Brandon, my lad," returned Oarsby; "and if you find I deceive you, why, you are welcome to scuttle my nob immediately, and I will offer no resistance. What is it you want of me?"

"You are a waterman," answered Hugh, "at least that is the profession you ostensibly follow, and are recognised by the land lubbers?"

"Very true," coincided Oarsby; "what then?"

"You are acquainted with Joe Tiller, and old Sam Sculler, and Mary, also, knows you, and believes you to be a respectable man?"

"Quite right!"

"Now," observed Hugh Brandon, "if I could by any means trepan her to this house, the job would be as good as done. I might keep her here concealed until I had an opportunity, and then I should find very little difficulty in shipping her aboard of my craft."

"Right—right," again agreed Jack Oarsby; "but how's that to be done?"

"Why," replied Brandon, "I will tell you; that is, if you will only listen to me for a moment."

"Proceed: I am all attention."

"What, then, I propose, is this," said Brandon.—"When Mary Tiller has recovered from the shock she has at present received, being now, as I heard to night, confined to her bed, you should watch an opportunity when Joe is out of the way, and by some stratagem, which I will presently concoct, decoy her to this crib. The rest leave to me. Are you agreeable?"

"Quite so, my lad," replied Oarsby; "and, from what you have said, I think there can be very little doubt of the stratagem succeeding."

"None," returned Hugh, "give us your hand; that's a bargain. Now then, Harry Halliyard, I will have ample revenge for the injuries you have done me, and prove to you that I, like my brother, Black Brandon, *never forget an insult.*"

"Bravo—bravo!" shouted old Bung, the landlord, whose nose was as rubicund as a half-burnt flambeau; "H— Hugh speaks like a dev—an—gel I mean! He, like his brother, never forgets *to* insult. She's yours, my— my — bo — bo — boy!— she's — here's luck!"

And with that Bung buried his nose in the tumbler, making the contents hiss again, and resigning himself to his usual seat, left the other worthy persons present to discuss the matter.

"And so Halliyard's gone to Portsmouth, and has resolved to enter again into the service, since he has lost his true love, as he fancied her to be, eh?" said Oarsby.

"Yes," replied Brandon, "but if he is not disappointed in entering into his majesty's service it is very strange to me. He and I must become much better acquainted just yet, and let me once get him on board the Wasp, and his pretty Poll also, as my mate, if I don't put him all aback, why, my name's not Hugh Brandon. Ha—ha—ha!— But he got the weather gauge of me to night, and I must steer a different course the next time—go upon another tack, d'ye understand me?"

"Ay—ay; but you may as well give us some insight into your plans?" said Jack Oarsby.

"Well, then," replied Brandon, "this is simply what I propose at present. You are old pals, all of you, and I know you will be ready to lend me a helping hand, especially as you know you will lose nothing by the bargain. When Mary has recovered sufficiently to be about, which I daresay will be in a day or two, and you know that her husband is out of the way on his usual business, which, of course, Jack, it will be no difficulty for you to ascertain, you must make your appearance at the cottage with some tale of an accident which has occured to her husband, at Milbank, or thereabouts, I will invent the yarn, and by that means it strikes me that you will find very little difficulty in decoying her hither. Do you understand me, Oarsby?"

"Perfectly," replied the latter, "and, I think, taking my ingenuity and skill in such matters into consideration, there is very little doubt of the success of the plot."

"None whatever," returned Brandon, "as we understand each other so well."

"Then that point is settled," said Jack Oarsby, "and when once you have secured Harry Halliyard and his pretty Poll on board the Wasp, you may consider your triumph as complete. But are you sure of meeting with him before the vessel on board of which he has entered has set sail?"

"Oh, yes," answered Hugh Brandon, "I have arranged all my plans in that respect. I have spies there with whom I will communicate immediately, and who will watch his every action. He cannot, I think, escape me. Oh! I will have such a revenge as shall fully gratify me for the injuries he has done me; the death of my brother, Black Brandon, and the destruction of the daring hearts that sailed under his flag. Success is mine!—I feel confident of it. But come, the grog is all out. Here, Bung, you old swab! Replenish; d'ye hear?—and let's have a jolly hour or two of it."

"Ay—ay, Master Brandon," said the host, starting from his seat, with wonderful celerity on hearing the instructions of Hugh. "There's nothing like drinking! Nothing to be done without it. Drinking comes over everything; and as for my double stout, damme, it's so strong, that when you once get the jug to your lips, if half a dozen dray-horses can force it away from it again, I'll be bound to—But no matter, you know it, and, therefore, it's of no use for me to tell you all about it."

With these words Bung departed from the room to execute the order he had received from Hugh Brandon; and having returned with the grog, the ruffians continued their carouse with renewed spirit; and having made the reader acquainted with the designs of Brandon, we will leave them for a short time, and hasten to scenes which may probably prove far more interesting. Several days must be supposed to have elapsed since the incidents occurred that we have recorded in the previous pages. Harry Halliyard, and his faithful companion, Watchful Waxend, have arrived in Portsmouth; what occurred to them on the journey it would be tedious and unnecessary to relate; it may be sufficient to state that they had engaged themselves on board his majesty's vessel, the Porpoise, which was under sailing orders in the course of a few days; and with all these premises, we leave them as well as the other characters for a short time, and proceed to the next chapter.

CHAPTER XIV.

THE "SEAMAN'S FRIEND."—PORTSMOUTH AGAIN.—A TRUE SPECIMEN OF ENGLAND'S TARS.

THERE was a jovial party assembled at the "Seaman's Friend," Portsmouth, the lion of which was Ben Bowsprit, the boatswain of the good ship Porpoise and who was always ready at any moment either to crack a joke, to assist a friend, or drub an enemy. Amongst the guests, too, was a nondescript sort of a being, who gloried in the name of Barnaby Blowcoal, who had by some strange accident been one voyage on board the Porpoise, and had been seasick, and sick of sea ever since.

At the time we introduce this worthy to the reader, he was seated in one corner of the room, with his elbows resting upon the table—his head leaning upon his hands, and his face presenting as ghastly a specimen of misery and suffering as could very well be imagined.

"What! still on the doctor's list, eh, Barnaby?" said Ben.

"Oh, yes," replied Barnaby, "I've been ill ever since old Neptune came on board and shaved me. Oh, dear!—oh, dear! what with the ducking and the drinking, I'm sure I've been labouring ever since under the *information* in my *infernals*."

"Well—well," said Ben, "you are all right again. Come, come, bring up."

"Bring up!" repeated Barnaby, with a most doleful expression of features, "don't mention it! I've done nothing else for months past."

"I mean, belay—bring to," said Ben.

"Ay," observed a corporal of marines, who was present, "as you were."

"As I were?" returned Barnaby. "Lord, I only wish I was as I were. I got a fortune of three hundred pounds left me, just after your ship left from Sheerness, two years ago. You, Mr. Ben Bowsprit, being gone, I proposed for Betsy Blossom—she turns up her nose; her father says yes—she runs away. Juniper Jumps, the parson's clerk, disappears at the same time, owing me one pound nine for rent. Misfortunes never come alone; I fell in with you at Spithead—came aboard—have a jollification—get drunk—feel very ill next day—can't get up for three days after—find I am out at sea, with no *inside* left, and only one kivering for my *outside;* and here I am, safely booked for another cruise, when I ought to be at home. Oh, my innards!"

"I dare say," remarked Ben, "that my Betsy steered for London, thinking somehow or the other, though I don't know how she could do so, to fall in with me. I'll not believe a word about the parson's clerk. But come, let's be merry; see the advantage of being a traveller, Barnaby; in time you'll get used to the sea."

"Not I," returned the cockney; "I'll never live in sight of it again:

> The only *sea* that I would *see*, I'll *see*
> In pictures,—never roam;
> Then while I *see* all foreign *seas*,
> I still shall *see* that I'm at home !"

The whole of the company laughed heartily at this; and at that moment a natty but delicate-looking lad, who was known by the name of Ralph Reefer, entered the room.

"Master Ben," he said; "oh, Master Ben, a word with you."

"Well taut, Master Ralph, my trim tiger," replied Ben; "what do you want? Is Master Marline's shirt not gone to wash, or Davie Deadeye's clothes-bag out of order? Some hurricane of that sort, eh ?"

"Did I ever make an illnatured compliment, Master Ben ?" said Ralph, with a look of reproach, "even when we were aboard ship ?"

"Never !" returned Ben; "give me your flipper! You are the truest and best lad in the ship, as far as your strength goes; you have been a good lad to me, though I can't think how you should take a liking to a rough foul-weather-Jack, as I am."

"'Tis because I find," replied the lad, in a hesitating voice, and partly covering his face, "'tis because I find though the outside be rough, Master Ben, you have a heart as tender as a woman's. I liked you above a bit before I knew you at sea."

"You did !" said Ben, with a look of surprise; "well! and how ?—eh? when? Did you know me at the Pigtail and Barrel Organ, in Ratcliffe? or the Cathead and Taffrail—whoo! I mean the Stem to Stern, in Wapping ?"

"I'll tell you *how* I knew you by and by," answered Ralph, significantly. "I came to speak to you about the prisoner, Reuben Somerville."

"Oh, he's all right, bless you," replied Ben, "though they will not let him leave the ship. He's a favourite from bow to binnacle! Seaman, or jolly—officer, or powder-monkey would do anything for Reuben; he preaches larning to the chaplain, till his reverence gets mopsy, and goes to sleep; talks about the heathen gods and goddesses to the middies, till there isn't a scrap of their berth uncovered by poetry; takes observations, and makes charts for the captain; and though he is so new to a nautical life, can hand, reef, and steer with the oldest master aboard. My eyes! I expect the admiralty will give me a pension for crimping such a sailor."

"Ay," said Ralph, "and he's as good as he's clever. What was his offence ?"

"Love, love did it all, bless you !" answered Ben; "he was drawing at the captain's table something his honour had bid him, when, all at once, up comes the name of the Traitor, one of the ships of the fleet; so his honour says, 'Sir Archibald Musgrove, the principal secretary to his lordship the ambassador, is aboard of that ship.' 'Ah !' says Reuben, starting. 'Yes,' says the captain, 'with his wife; some girl he brought from Yorkshire.' 'Wife !' shrieks Reuben, (I was there.) 'So she calls herself, but I happen to be Sir Archibald's relation; 'tis some girl he has seduced from Yorkshire.' ''Tis false !' says Reuben. 'False !' says the captain; 'her name is Singleton.' 'Liar!' screamed Reuben. 'Liar !' says the captain; oh, my eyes, what a row was there !—and so poor Reuben was clapped, to cool his passion, in the bilboes."

"Did you know this girl ?" asked Ralph.

"To be sure I did; a trim craft enough.—You knew her, too, Barnaby."

"Who ?" demanded Barnaby.

"Amy Singleton," replied Ben; "a taut-built vessel—rather too fond of a display of her clean and thin spars, and——"

"Stop a bit," interrupted Barnaby; "I never *seed* her show her legs, except once getting over a stile, and then I thought 'em precious good 'uns."

"I don't mean that, bless you, you're out; but you see when we seamen look out for a seaworthy craft, it's a very different thing to the one as we'd choose for a holiday cruise; in one case, we take her into dock, unrig her, look to her in'ards and out'ards, copper ho bottom——"

"Lord! lord!" ejaculated Barnaby, turning up the whites of his eyes.

"Well, we do," continued Ben, "give her a lick of tar, and a dab of paint—then start her for the voyage: in the other, so that she carries flying colours aloft, has a light pair of heels, and won't run under the water, she's very well for a trip. Now, in my mind, there's no two animals so like each other as a ship and a woman."

"How do you mean?" asked Ralph, with some curiosity.

"Why," returned Ben, "first, there's no two things in the world as a sailor's so fond of. Next, they're both to be guided, (wind and weather permitting), so that they have a good man at the helm. Next, they are both fond of flying-gear aloft, and always sail best when they are well-rigged. Next, they are our best friends in the storms of life, for, when the wind whistles loudest, and adversity threatens most, the one bears you like a swallow o'er the billows of the ocean, the other guides you, like an angel, o'er the rocks and shoals of poverty; and when it comes to the last—*last* struggle, man may desert the vessel as she founders, *but she perishes in his service!*—and so does woman, blessing him as she sinks, and praying for him as she dies."

"God bless you, Ben!" said Ralph, fervently, and throwing himself into his arms.

"Hollo! belay, youngster!" cried Ben, with a look of astonishment, "what signal's flying now?"

"Oh, he wants a vessel of his own," said Barnaby, "regularly coppered about her undermost."

"Hush!" said Ben, "some one is coming; and, as I live, it is the skipper, and that young lubber of a middy, Fred Wayward. What can bring them here?"

Captain Oakum and Fred Wayward now entered the room, and the former, addressing himself to the midshipman, said—

"How now, sir?—What do you want?"

"The ship nearest is the Traitor, sir," replied Wayward; "a boat is putting off."

"Good!" said the captain.

"Your honour," said Ben, coming forward, and bowing.

"Well, boatswain!" said the captain.

"You'll forgive me, your honour," continued Ben, hesitating, "for what I am going to say, but poor Reuben, sir, he's fretting all the skin off his ankles in the bilboes."

"He deserves it, sir," repeated Captain Oakum, sternly.

"Why," returned Ben, "so he does, your honour; but when a man's mad, why—why—why he's mad, and your honour can afford to forgive him."

"Afford?"

"Yes, afford, your honour."

"Ben Bowsprit," said the captain, "you take advantage of my good nature. You were born on my father's estate, you were my playfellow, and you are a good and trusty seaman."

"I know it, your honour," returned Ben; "that's why I says what I do; there isn't a man here as wouldn't die, rather than disobey you, and yet we never saw a cat aboard, or endured the degradation of the lash."

"The young man has insulted me personally," said the captain.

"Ah, that's it, your honour," replied Ben Bowsprit; "nobody but yourself could have afforded forgiveness; if he had have insulted the lieutenant, you would have punished him for the dignity of the service; if he had insulted me, why, insubordination cannot be overlooked; but you who are beyond insult, you can afford to forgive what madness could have alone tempted him to say."

"Madness?" said the captain.

"Oh, bless your honour," said the honest seaman, "on that point he's as mad as a powder-monkey in a boarding party."

"Well—well," said the captain, after a pause, "I will consider of it."

"All's right," said Ben, aside.

"I hope so," observed Ralph.

"I'll just say a word," remarked Barnaby. "Captain Oakum, sir, you know I'm a gentleman on my travels—that is to say, I'm travelling against my will. Yes, though I've an independent fortune, bless you, I'm not without having *talons*, so, if you'd let my friend Reuben off, I'll teach all your children to dance and fiddle for nothing."

"Silence, sir!" commanded Captain Oakum, sternly. "Bowsprit, you will come on board anon."

"Ay—ay, your honour," replied Ben, "and God bless you!"

The captain then departed from the house, and left the seamen once more to themselves.

"There goes one of the noblest vessels that ever ploughed the ocean of life," said Ben; "the man who would not do his duty by him deserves to be strung up to the yard-arm without judge or jury. Poor Reuben! he will soon be out of the bilboes, I'll warrant. Lord! how glad I am, to be sure. But, ah! here comes our new messmate, Harry Halliyard, as trim a sailor as ever trod the maindeck, though he is so very melancholy. I suppose he has some love affair on his mind, like Reuben Somerville. What a thing that love is, to be sure. But here he comes, and that strange craft who joined the ship's company at the same time as he did; though, to judge from his figure-head, I am at a loss to think what use we shall be able to make of him when we get him aboard."

Harry Halliyard and Watchful Waxend now entered the room, and after having returned the greetings of the persons assembled, he seated himself in one corner of the apartment, and seemed to become absorbed by the melancholy reflections that occupied his mind. Mr. Watchful Waxend, however, who was not altogether so gloomily disposed, and who seemed to think that in his case, at, any rate, the old maxim was the best namely, to endeavour to keep his spirits *up* by pouring sprits *down*, quickly gave orders for a jorum of grog and a pipe, which being brought to him, he sat himself down by the side of the fire, and seemed fully determined to enjoy himself in the best manner he possibly could.

"Why, Harry, my hearty," ejaculated Ben, "you seem as dull as a tar without flip. Cheer up, messmate! get the weather-gauge of care, throw the blue devils overboard, weigh anchor, and crowd all sail for the port of happiness."

"Ah, Master Boatswain," replied our hero, "it may be all very well for you to spin such yarns as that, but if you had been cast away on a lee shore as I have been, all your best hopes foundered, the sailor's best sheet-anchor, the girl of his heart, taken away from you, and that by a pirate whom you had thought your friend, and who was sailing under the colours of a fair trader, mayhap you would be as dull as I am. If you had ever been in love, Master Bowsprit, you——"

"Ever in love!" interrupted the boatswain, "shiver my timbers, Harry Halliyard, you are sadly out of your reckoning, and have taken wrong soundings, if you think that I am such a lubber as never to have felt that sweet sensation. Why, next to fighting, it is a thing that is dearest to a seaman's heart. I am in love from stem to stern, and that with one of the fairest crafts that ever sailed the ocean of life. Match my Betsy Blossom, if you can, and may I be disgraced and dismissed the service as one of the veriest swabs that ever the cat laid its claws upon."

"But she never deserted her colours?" said Harry; "never proved false to you?"

"False to me!" repeated Bowsprit; "my Betsy false to me! damme! why, you might as well expect to see the ocean disappear, as such a circumstance as that to take place; though the lubbers did endeavour to persuade me that she had slipped her anchor, and was scudding about in strange seas. But do you think that I believed 'em?—Not I! I must have been as soft as a powder-monkey if I had. Bless you! my Betsy, I know, is as true to me as the needle is to the pole; and if any man was to dare for to go for to say to the contrary, damme! if I wouldn't make a hulk of his vessel in less time than you could cry Jack Robinson. But cheer up, Harry, if her you loved has jilted you in the manner you say, and has lowered her flag to the enemy, why, all I can say is, that she is not worth a bad biscuit, and I would think no more of her. There are more ports than one, and more pretty girls with honest hearts than there are ships in His Majesty's service; so once more I say, steer clear of the shoals of despair, never hoist signals of distress while you have a timber left to float with; and there is fair weather yet in store for you. In a day or two the Porpoise will set sail, and then I know, when you are once more on the bright blue waters, your heart will be as light as a feather, and you will think no more about the craft that has cut away from her moorings than I would about a stale quid o' backey."

"Not think of her!" repeated our hero; "avast—avast heaving, Ben; she is anchored too firmly in my heart, in spite of the manner in which she has deceived me, for me ever to forget her."

"Ah!" remarked Waxend, after having taken an extra swig, "and so is my Abigail Holdforth, though she has turned me up for that little hinsignificant Frenchman, and that's the whole truth of the matter. Oh, this love! what a terrible thing it is, when it takes such strong hold of a sensitive individual's senses."

"Well, Harry," observed Bowsprit, "I must leave you for the present, for the captain's on board, and I promised to attend him shortly. There's a little bit of important business to be transacted to-night.—I have interceded for Master Reuben, who, you know, is at present in the bilboes for insulting the skipper, and I have no doubt he will be at liberty again in a short time. Poor Reuben, you know, is crossed in love, like yourself, and his senses are sometimes taken aback in consequence. The only difference is that his sweetheart is true to him, though there has been every obstacle to their union. In the first place, Amy's brother George is as d——d a shark as ever remained unhung—a poacher, a thief, and everything else that is bad. He is the mortal enemy of Reuben, and the tool of Sir Archibald, our skipper's relation, who entertains a guilty passion for Amy, who, they say, is in his power, and has become his mistress; but I do not believe a word of that. However, I must not stand palavering here. Good night, Harry, if I do not see you again; keep your spirits afloat, and all will yet be well. Come, shipmates! Let us weigh anchor for the ship."

Thus saying, and having shaken our hero heartily by the hand, Ben and the others departed, and left Harry and Waxend to themselves.

"Well," remarked Waxend, "that Master Bowsprit's a devilish good-hearted sort of a fellow, and I have taken quite a fancy to him. Why don't you drink, Halliyard? I find it an excellent remedy for the blue devils; and if it warn't for

that, I should never think of tasting a drop, for there is nothing, you know, that I so much detest as intemperance. Now, if your Polly——"

"Avast, you lubber!" interrupted our hero, passionately; "if you dare to mention that name without proper respect, may I never go aloft again, if I do not pour such a broadside into you as shall shake every timber in your crazy carcase!"

"Bless my soul, Master Harry!" returned Waxend looking at him with evident symptoms of fear, "how very hasty you are, to be sure; why any one would think that you were going to swallow me at a mouthful, and all because I merely said that——"

"Belay your jawing tackle, you swab!" cried Harry, "or else go upon another tack, or you may chance to encounter such squalls as you little expect."

"Well," said Waxend, "I'm sure I meant no harm, and I'm very sorry if I have offended you. I am a poor disconsolate lover like yourself, and, therefore, we ought to sympathise with each other. However, I will say no more upon that subject, since it seems it is not agreeable to you. Well, here we are in Portsmouth, entered on board the gallant Porpoise, (what a very remarkably pretty name!), and in a day or two we shall be once more braving the perils of the briny, and far away from our native land. Hurrah! Britannia rules the waves; and all I have got to say is in the words of Pope, that I hope in our forthcoming cruise she will be so kind and condescending as to rule 'em straight."

"Yes, Mary," ejaculated Harry, in a melancholy tone of voice, "in a few short days, I shall again be far away from my native land, and once more braving those perils and hardships it has before been my lot to encounter, though I had flattered myself that I should now have been able to have cast anchor in the port of matrimony, and should have been moored safe in your arms. We may never meet again. I can scarcely wish it, since all the fond hopes that I had cherished in my bosom are annihilated, and I find that you—oh, I cannot speak the word! But will she ever bestow a thought upon me?—

THE PIRATE'S TOAST.

Will she not offer up one prayer to Heaven for me? Oh, yes; she must! I cannot believe that she has become so callous as to entirely discard me from her memory. But no, she is not false to me!—She still loves me! Our meeting in the old churchyard ough to have convinced me of that. And did she not agree to accompany me?—to be the future partner of my fortunes wherever I might go?—to abandon her husband, everything for my sake? And can I any longer doubt the sincerity of her passion? Ah, no!—I must be a lubber unworthy of existence could I do so! Oh, Mary, what a wreck has fate made of both our hearts! And why did I not avail myself of the opportunity that was afforded me? She would have been my companion, and——But, avast, Harry;

on what course are you now steering? Would you, after so many years of true seamanship, now run foul of the breakers of dishonour?—Shame on you for suffering such thoughts to enter your mind! She is the wife of another, and as such, can never be anything to me; and it was wrong of me to seek to persuade her to abandon him whom she had sworn to love, honour and obey. But I must have been mad at the time, and knew not what I was saying or doing. Poor lass—poor lass! what must be the anguish you are now enduring? What will in future become of you? God bless you, Mary, and protect you."

"Ah, Master Halliyard," said his companion, "so I say, and most cordially too. My case is a very hard one, you know; but grieving's a folly, and since Abigail has acted in the manner which she has done towards me, I feel the spirit within me—Here, landlord, replenish my glass, and let it be a dash or two stronger than the last. Harry, my friend, why don't you drink, and, as our boatswain says, send dull care to the devil?"

"Belay your nonsense, Master Waxend," returned our hero, "and leave me to my own course; I am in no humour to-night."

"Well, well, as you please, of course," said Watchful Waxend; "but for my part I always find sorrow so very dry that I should crack like a badly welted shoe if I wasn't to wet it. Besides, we may as well be as cheerful as we can the short time we remain in England, and so uncertain as it is whether we shall ever see it again. In a few days we shall set sail in the gallant Porpoise, and should she meet with the same fate as the Polyphemus, we might not chance to have such a lucky escape as we did before; and that, I mean to say, would be a *burning* shame; I must confess that I feel quite *warm* upon the subject. But I say, Harry, there is one thing I wish to ask you."

"And what is that?" demanded the latter, impatiently.

"Why, what is your opinion of that vessel they call the Helen, which rides at anchor a short distance off?"

"What should be my opinion of her, but that she is what her papers show her to be, a fair trader?" replied Harry

Halliyard. "What's in the wind now?"

"Oh, nothing, Master Halliyard, nothing," returned Waxend. "You know that if there is anybody that detests scoundrels more than another it is myself; but I have heard several of our shipmates express no very favourable opinions as to her real character; and certainly her crew are the most ugly-looking and uncultivated set of sharks that I ever met with; and I never accidentally meet with one of them but I feel a sort of a sensation of all-overishness come across me which is very disagreeable. Another thing that seems very strange is, that I have never yet been able to find any one who has seen the skipper."

"Bah! you swab!" cried our hero; "what outlandish notions have you got into your upper-works now? Do you think it is not all fair and above board? It would indeed be a bold thing for any craft that would not bear overhauling to cast anchor in the very sight of his majesty's fleet."

"Well, it may be so," said Watchful Waxend; "however, I must acknowledge that I have my doubts upon the subject, and that's all about it. Last night, too, I had a very remarkable dream about that vessel, which——"

"A dream!" interrupted Harry, ironically. "Ha, ha, ha!"

"Ah! you may laugh, if you please," returned Waxend, "but I can only tell you this much, that my dreams are mostly very prophetic. I thought that we were far out at sea, when we espied a strange-looking vessel in the distance, to which we gave chase, and coming within hail of her, we discovered it to be this same so-called Helen; but immediately on our saluting her she hoisted the black flag, and poured in upon us such a heavy broadside that it made our vessel reel and stagger like a drunken man. The combat became terrific, but I thought in my dream that the pirates were more than a match for us, and boarding us, I discovered in their captain—who do you suppose?"

"Why, how should I know?"

"No other than Hugh Brandon!"

"Hugh Brandon!"

"The same. I saw him as plainly as I see you now."

"Nonsense!"

"But I tell you it was no nonsense; and what is more, screaming aloud for help on the deck of the pirate ship, I beheld your Mary."

"My—my Mary!" repeated our hero, in the most agitated tone of voice, starting to his feet, and seizing the terrified Watchful Waxend by the collar. "Have you done this to torture me, and to sport with my feelings, you lubber? My Mary in the power of a pirate, and that pirate my mortal enemy, the brother of Black Brandon, who—damme! if I have not a good mind to—"

"Harry—Mr. Halliyard—my dear friend!" stammered out Waxend, struggling to release himself from his hold; "wh—wh—what the devil are you about? Do you want to throttle me?"

"Well, well," said Harry, more calmly, and releasing him; "it was wrong of me to kick up such a breeze about such a trifle as this. It was only a dream, and—but what are you looking so sheepish about, now?"

"As I live," whispered Watchful, and pointing significantly over his shoulder, "there—there is one of them."

Harry Halliyard turned round as his companion said this, and beheld that during their conversation another man had entered the room, and had seated himself at a table opposite to them, but seemed to be watching them narrowly. He was a person of coarse and forbidding features, strongly built, and habited as a seaman, but our hero had no recollection of having seen him before.

"Good evening, messmate!" he said, advancing towards him; "you said so quietly that I had no idea of being within hail until my friend here gave me the signal. What ship, my lad?"

"The saucy Helen," replied the man, "as brave a craft as ever breasted the billows in a storm."

"Ay," said Harry, "she looks a tidy craft enough; axing your pardon, I cannot say as much for those of her crew that I have seen."

"Indeed," returned the man, with a half-sinister grin; "perhaps you may become better acquainted with them by-and-bye, though I do not know whether or not that will cause you to alter your opinion."

"And may I ask you where you are bound for when you leave here?" interrogated our hero.

"Newhaven," was the reply.

"Your skipper keeps himself very secluded," observed Harry.

"That's his business," was the larconic reply; "he is not fond of paying idle visits, and when he does so, it is to some purpose."

"Well, you need not be quite so sharp, shipmate," said Harry: "I'm not at all inquisitive, and I don't know that I have any particular wish to become acquainted with him."

"Perhaps not," returned the man; "and probably you may be introduced to him sooner than you expect."

"Well, that is not very likely, at any rate," remarked our hero, with a smile, "and I do not see that it is a matter of much consequence. Will you drink?"

"Ay," replied the man, taking up the glass, "and I will give you a toast, too:

"'Here's to the bold, the daring, and free,
Whether on land or on the sea!'"

"Bravo!" cried Halliyard, "a very good toast—

"'Here's to the bold, the daring, and free,
Whether on land or on the sea!'

You are not a bad sort of a fellow, I think, after all; and if we were not so soon to part company, and to sail in different latitudes, I might wish that we might become better acquainted."

"Oh, as for that matter," said the man, "there is no knowing what may happen, and we may meet again far away from hence, and under very different circumstances."

"Well, perhaps we may," returned our hero; "and all that I can say is, should we do so, you will never have cause to regret taking the flipper of Harry Halliyard of the Porpoise."

"Perhaps not," answered the other; "but I must sheer off, for I have other business to attend to, besides sitting palavering here. Good-night, Harry Halliyard, of the gallant Porpoise; good-night to you, my figure-head of a fire bucket on a handspike."

With these words the rather uncouth seamen hitched up his slacks, and with a peculiar expression of countenance as he gazed upon our hero and Waxend, he quitted the house.

"Figure-head of a fire bucket on a handspike," said Watchful, when he was gone; "there's a pretty name to give a respectable, able-bodied seaman like myself! What a cannibal, to be sure! There's not much to covet in his appearance, I'll be bound for it, and if he is not one of the men I saw in my dream on board the pirate vessel, I am much mistaken."

"Bah!" said Halliyard, "have your senses gone adrift altogether? You must never judge a craft exactly by its figure-head."

"Well, that may be all very true, Master Harry," said Waxend, "though to tell you the truth, I am not sorry he has gone, for I felt anything but comfortable all the time I was in his company."

"Why, what a lubber you are, to be sure," remarked our hero; "any one who did not know you would take you to be as green as when you first smelt salt water. But come, stow away your grog, it is getting late, and we must sheer off to the place where we are moored while we remain ashore."

"Now, what a very restless man you are, Master Halliyard," said Waxend; "I don't know what's come to you lately, but we have no sooner got the grog aboard now, but you want to weigh anchor. For my part, I do not think that we could do better than remain here at the Seaman's Friend, where there is such excellent stuff for the inward man, and I know we can be accommodated with the best berths in the ship. It is a very dark and uncomfortable looking night; I do not half like my dream, and——"

"Avast!" cried Harry, "what the devil do you think I care about dreams? Do you take me to be such another loblolly boy as yourself? Sheer off, I say, or, damme, I will pour such a broadside into you as will make you tremble again!"

"Gently—gently, Master Harry!" remonstrated Waxend; "do not be rash. Of course, I am not going to disobey orders, since you are so determined; but, oh, my dream!—I only hope that no harm may come of this."

Halliyard waited to hear no more, but impatiently pushed him out at the door, and followed him quickly, and hurried away from the tavern, in the direction of the house at which they were lodging during the time that they remained on shore. The night, as Waxend had said, was particularly dark and gloomy, and the wind blew cold and piercing from the ocean; but Harry took no heed of this, for his thoughts were occupied too much another way, and he hurried forward, followed by Watchful Waxend, anxious to arrive at his lodging. In their way towards the place of their residence, they had to pass a most lonely and unfrequented part of the country, and they had not proceeded far, when they were suddenly startled by hearing the sound of a shrill whistle near them, and they looked around them with astonishment, and some degree of alarm, but they saw nothing whatever to gratify their curiosity.

"Halloa!" said Harry, "what breeze is blowing now? That's certainly not th' bo'swain's whistle, for it is not likely that he would pipe all hands in such a place as this. There's something not right, and, confound it, I am not armed! But what should I apprehend? There is no one who can mean me any harm in these parts, and, therefore, I am all right."

"All right!" repeated Waxend; "I only wish we may find it all right, that's all; but my dream——"

"D—n your dream!" interrupted Harry, passionately, "what has that to do with the present moment? Come, let us crowd all sail, and take no further notice of this."

Watchful Waxend muttered something to himself which his companion did not hear, and they again hastened on their way; but they had not proceeded many paces, when they found themselves suddenly surrounded, as if by magic, by a number of armed men, whose ferocious looks immediately told the desperate nature of their designs. Our hero, however, stood undaunted, and faced them boldly, while poor Mr. Watchful Waxend trembled with fear, and his teeth chattered in his jaws, though he was unable to give utterance to a syllable.

"How now, you picarooning sharks!" exclaimed our hero, clenching his fists, and standing in a menacing attitude before them; "what do you mean by bearing down upon us in this manner, without so much as firing a salute for us to heave too? Let's overhaul your papers, and——"

"Stop the lubber's lingo," cried one of the ruffians, who seemed to be the leader; "we have them secure enough now, and have no time to lose; place your grappling irons upon him, and that lubberly boy there by his side."

"Boarded by pirates!" cried Harry; "yard-arm and yard-arm with the enemy!"

"Oh, my dream!" exclaimed the terrified Waxend, "I told you it would come true, but you would be so obstinate, and now you see the consequences. Gentlemen, we beg of you to——"

"Avast—avast!" cried our hero, in still more determined accents than before. "What's the use of standing palavering to such fellows as these?"

"Seize them!" commanded the fellow who had before spoken, and they advanced towards them more closely.

"Sheer off, ye lubbers, or shiver my timbers, I will scuttle some of your nobs, though I have nothing more than my fists to defend myself with."

As he spoke, he dealt desperately about him right and left, and felled two or three of the ruffians to the earth, while Watchful Wavend renderd all the assistance that his courage would let him, which was little enough, indeed; and, at length, surrounding them in a body, they were secured, and bound hand and foot, they were raised on the shoulders of two or three of the fellows, who raised a loud shout of triumph as they did so.

"The game is ours!" cried the leader; "fortune has favoured us well; away with them!—Quick! to our rendezvous!"

"You infernal swabs of the devil!" cried Harry; "a pretty triumph this is to boast over two unarmed men. Only set my arms at liberty, give me the means of defending myself, and, damme, may I never more go aloft, if I do not beat the old caboose of you, three at a time!"

"Ha—ha—ha!" laughed the miscreant who had before spoken, "how the mongrel cur snarls now he finds himself secure in the bilboes. But heed not what he says. I warrant that we

shall soon make him tame enough by-and-bye."

"Who are ye," demanded Halliyard, "that you thus dare to attack and assault two of his majesty's seamen?"

"Oh, you will know all anon," answered the fellow; "away with them!"

"Gentlemen," remonstrated poor Waxend, who, as may very well be imagined, was in a terrible state of alarm, "only consider now, what it is you do. Remember, the law——"

"Thrust a gag in that lubber's mouth and stop his patter," commanded the leader of this desperate set of ruffians but before they could do so, Waxend struggled violently, and called at the top of his voice for help, and the fellows were somewhat startled when they heard a shout at a short distance in reply to it.

"Ah!" cried the captain of the gang, "some persons approach to the rescue; but if we are quick, they will be too late. Away, my lads, and fear not!"

Again the shouts sounded on the air, and appeared to approach nearer than before, and Harry struggled hard to release himself from those who held him, but in vain. The men took a contrary direction to that from which the sounds seemed to proceed, and they had not gone far, when they beheld to their dismay and confusion, as well as the darkness would permit them, a body of men, far outnumbering their own, advancing from an opposite side, and making rapidly towards them.

"Confusion!" cried the leader, "we are foiled! It is the coast-guard!— What can have put them on our scent? It would be madness to venture to encounter them, for they far outnumber us, and defeat would be almost sure to follow. This time we fail to triumph, but another opportunity may be afforded us, and then we will succeed or perish in the attempt. Away! Let us escape, or we know what the consequences will be sure to be."

With these words the ruffians threw our hero and Waxend to the ground, and made a precipitate retreat from the spot, taking a different direction to that in which their pursuers were advancing. The persons approaching fired several shots after them, but whether with any effect or not could not at the time be ascertained, and soon afterwards the ruffians disappeared in the distance, and the individuals who had so timely come to their rescue advanced to the spot where Harry and his terrified companion were lying. They proved to be, indeed, several of the coast-guard, who being near the place where the daring, and desperate outrage was committed, when they were fortunately attracted by the cries of Watchful Waxend to the spot, and thus came in time to save him and our hero from, perhaps, a fate of the most terrible description. They quickly unloosened the cords which bound the limbs of Harry and his companion, and raised them to their feet.

"Thanks, my lads, for this service," said our hero; "you just hove in sight in the very nick of time, or them d—d rascally pirates, I expect, would have sent us both to Davy Jones's locker."

"Why, it is Harry Halliyard, of the Porpoise," said one of the men: "what is the meaning of all this?"

"That I can't tell you," replied our hero; "all that I know is that we were suddenly run down by a crew of as villanous-looking pirates as ever I beheld, and that if it had not been for your fortunate arrival, I have no doubt that they would have had us safe in the bilboes at the present time."

"And have you no knowledge of them?" asked the sergeant.

"Not I," answered Halliyard; "I never remember to have seen any of the sharks before, and I have not the least wish, I can tell you, after what has taken place, of becoming better acquainted with them."

"Were they dressed as seamen?"

"Yes, they were full rigged as such," replied our hero, "but it is not likely that any true British tars would have been guilty of such an outrage as this."

"And can you not form any idea as to the cause of it?"

"Lord love you, how can I?—For I'm sure I never gave any reason for any persons to bear such a rascally ill-feeling towards me; though I cannot help thinking that there is some one particular at the bottom of it all."

"Ah! it makes good my dream," observed Waxend; "and——"

"Oh, shiver your dream!" inter-rupted Harry; "what has all such nonsense as that to do with it?"

"Well," said the sergeant, "I am glad that we arrived so fortunately to your rescue, but it is a pity that the rascals have escaped us; however, I hope we shall be able to discover them yet, and to bring them to justice. No doubt they have some place of concealment not far from the neighbourhood."

"Very likely they have," returned our hero, "but it don't much matter, I don't suppose they will trouble me again, since they have been so fairly defeated this time; and in a few days the Porpoise will set sail, and then I shall have other enemies to encounter than them, and with whom I shall feel more at home. Come, Waxend, this bit of a breeze has blown over now, and as there is no particular harm done, we may as well set sail for home."

"You had better allow us to accompany you home," said the sergeant, "in case any of the fellows should be still lurking about to do you some mischief."

"Ay, do, your honours," said Waxend, "and thank you, too; for you know we are no match for them, and should they encounter us again, we should be murdered, to a dead certainty."

"Thank you, my lads, for your offer," said Harry, "but I do not wish to give you any such trouble; and as for those cowardly swabs, only give me arms, and I have not the least fear of meeting them."

"What rashness!" observed Watchful Waxend; "do not heed what he says, gentlemen, he don't know what he is talking about. *Arms* indeed! I fancy, for my own part, that *legs* would be of the most service, to run away from such desperate ruffians as them."

"Your resistance would certainly be of little avail with them," said the sergeant; "and when there is no necessity for it, it would be madness to run the risk."

"Well," returned Harry, "there is, perhaps, a good deal of truth in what you say, so I will accept of your offer. Weigh anchor, then, and let us hope that no more squalls will arise to-night, though I should dearly like to have a turn with those infernal sharks; and I have not the least doubt but that, if it came to a fair stand-up fight, I should soon be able to make them cry peccavi."

The sergeant made no reply to this, and they then departed towards the house at which Harry Halliyard and Watchful Waxend were at present residing. They examined the spot where they had fired at the villains in their retreat, but could discover no traces of any mischief having been done, and they therefore concluded that they had escaped uninjured, though they could not imagine who they were, and what were their motives for committing so daring an outrage. They then proceeded on their way, and soon arrived at the lodging of Harry and his companion, where they left them.

Our hero and Waxend on entering their lodging reflected seriously upon what had occurred, and the danger from which they had been so providentially rescued by the coast-guard, and Harry was unable to form any reasonable conjecture as to the cause of it, or what the motives of the ruffians could have been for committing such an outrage.

"Take my word for it, Master Halliyard," observed Waxend, "an idea has just struck me; take my word for it, I say, that Hugh Brandon is at the bottom of all this. Those fellows have been employed by him, depend upon it, to trepan you and get you in his power, or my name is not Watchful Waxend.

"Well," returned our hero, "there is certainly something rather probable in that, especially after the threats he held out against me. But the villain is foiled, and should I ever again come athwart his hawse, I will bring him to such an account as he little expects. The black-looking picarooner! he dared, too, to lay violent hands upon poor Mary, on the night we appointed to meet each other in the old churchyard. I have a long account to settle with him."

"That man we saw at the Seaman's Friend, too, to-night," said Waxend, "I strongly suspect, knows all about it. I did not half like his looks and the observations he made use of. He is one of the crew of the Helen, also, and should he prove to be connected with this plot, there will be still stronger grounds for suspecting the real character of the vessel to which he belongs."

"Avast heaving, shipmate," said Harry; "we must not be too ready to jump to conclusions. However, I must make further inquiries into this, and should it turn out to be as you seem to imagine, there is not much fear of justice being done, and the ruffians meeting with their deserts. But, come, it is time that we sought our hammocks, and to-morrow we can talk further upon this subject."

Waxend made no immediate reply, but after a moment or two's reflection, he said—

"After all, Master Halliyard, I cannot help thinking that there is much more in my dream than you seem to imagine, though I hope it will not come true. Brandon is your mortal enemy, and it seems from what has taken place, that he has formed some sort of a guilty passion for Mary, and should he have done so, he is evidently a man of that desperate character that he will leave no means untried, when you are out of the way, to get her in his power, and——"

"Hold, you swab!" interrupted our hero; "your various suppositions almost choke me. Hugh Brandon dare to raise his thoughts to my Mary! Shiver my timbers! if I thought the infernal shark could dare to do so, I would not rest until I had discovered him, let whatever might be the consequence, and wreaked my vengeance on his head. But, psha! why do I give way to such fears? Mary is secure from his power, and may set all his designs at defiance."

"I don't know that, Master Halliyard," returned Waxend; "Hugh Brandon is a desperate man, and I am much mistaken if there is anything that he would hesitate to do to accomplish his wishes."

"Well, I do not fear," said Harry; "the black rascal may have dared to raise his thoughts to Mary, poor girl, but the great commander aloft will keep a constant look-out for her safety, and frustrate any designs which he may have in contemplation. Dear Mary!—but no, avast, Harry, you are drifting in troubled waters;—you must not now dare to call her by any such names. As the wife of Joe Tiller—Bah! how that word sticks in my throat! But—but— I must not think of it, or it will drive me to madness. Well, Waxend, we have escaped from these fellows, and, therefore, we ought to entertain no further care upon the subject. I'll warrant that they will not venture the same trick again in a hurry."

"I hope not," said Waxend, "for I have not the least wish to see their d—d ugly physiognomies again, I can tell you. Besides, I am a man of peace, you know, and although I am not at all afraid to meet the enemy, I have, nevertheless, at no time, the least objection to his keeping a respectful distance."

"Why, you chicken-hearted, loblolly boy," said Harry Halliyard, "arn't you ashamed to stand there palavering in that sort of a manner, and call yourself a seaman?—Seaman be——"

"Hold hard, Master Harry," interrupted Watchful; "belay there, if you please. Have I not proved myself to be a sailor every inch of me? although I admit that there are times when I feel a little qualmish. But that I can't help; it's all owing to the nervous system. Loblolly boy!—Come, I like that! And is this the reward I get, after distinguishing myself in the manner I have done? Oh, the ingratitude of the world! Loblolly boy! Who settled the business of Black Brandon, and saved your life? Didn't I stick to you like wax? and now you turn round and——"

"Well, well, never mind, shipmate," said our hero, "I did not mean what I said; I know you are a good sort of fellow enough, especially when the *spirit* moves you, and that I much am indebted to you. So, give us your flipper, and we will say no more upon the subject."

"To be sure I will, Master Halliyard," said Waxend. "Lor bless you, I do not mind what you say to me, for I know you are my friend, and that you do not mean any harm; all that I wish is that my dream may not come true. But I have some strong misgivings that it will, that's all about it."

"Shiver your dream!" returned Harry, "I do not value it a biscuit. My Polly (bless her heart! I cannot help still calling her so) get on board a pirate craft! Why it is as unlikely as that I should become Lord High Admiral of England, and of that, you know, there is not much chance, at present, at any rate. However, there must be some inquiry made into this affair of to-night, and should the perpetrators of the outrage be discovered, they will be adequately punished for their tricks, there is no fear. But enough of this; good-night, Master Waxend, and more pleasant dreams to you, say I."

"Yes, so say I, Harry," replied his companion, "and I only hope that the dream I have already had may not be realised, that's all. Good-night."

With these words they separated, and each retired to his chamber. When Harry was left alone, however, and after he had retired to bed, he remained for some time awake, and reflecting upon all the exciting circumstances of the night, and it was in vain that he endeavoured to reconcile his mind to them.

"There is much more in what Waxend has said," he soliloquised, "than I have thought prudent to acknowledge. The infernal sharks, what did they mean by laying their grappling irons upon me? I never saw such a rascally looking set of fellows in my life, and no doubt that it was their intention to have shipped me to old Davy. I cannot help also being of Waxend's opinion that Brandon is at the bottom of all this, for he has threatened me with his vengeance, and I dare say that he will not fail to keep his word, if he should ever have the opportunity of so doing. His vengeance—ha—ha—ha! what have I to fear from such a fellow as him? In a few days I shall be far away again on the bright blue waters, and then if I should chance to encounter him, I fancy that he will have no cause to congratulate himself upon the meeting. But should he entertain any designs against Mary, which the daring outrage he committed against her gives me such good reasons to suspect, there is no knowing to what length he may not be emboldened to go, and Joe Tiller may not be able to protect her from him. Poor lass! I fear that there are yet many troubles in store for you, and I shall be far away and unable to assist you to—But avast, Harry, why do you suffer yourself to talk thus? What right have I to interfere, if even it were in my power? What is she now to me? What right have I even to think of her, now that she is the wife of another? The wife of another! The very thought distracts

"One shot, then another proceeded from the Invincible, which the brig was nothing loth in answering, and the two vessels now approached so near to each other that they had every opportunity of distinguishing their different power."—*See p.* 21.

me! Oh, Mary—Mary! Fate has raised a gulf between us, the very contemplation of which drives me to despair. Would that I had perished ere I could become acquainted with the fatal truth! But to forget her!—that is impossible. When I can cease to forget to cherish her image in my memory, the needle must cease to point to the pole. She is anchored so close to my heart that nothing whatever can cast her away. I—I—my top-lights are getting misty again, and I feel as if I could blubber like a child. What a fool I am! Ah! Mary, poor lass! I feel that we have met for the last time. How dark and stormy is the ocean you will in future have to battle with; and where will you find another like Harry Halliyard to be your pilot and guide?

Can you be happy with him who is now your husband, now that you know I am living? If you are sincere in the professions you have made to me, it is impossible that you can; and it is that thought which makes me even more miserable than I should otherwise be. My poor old mother! little did you imagine the mischief you were doing when you enjoined the union of Mary and Tiller. But let me not reproach your memory. No, Heaven forbid! You acted for the best, and with no other idea than that of securing for Mary a protector who would watch over her safety and be ever studious of her happiness; and to whom could you better confide her than my own and long tried friend and partner, Joe? I feel that I have acted with injustice towards him, and judged him too harshly; and what a villain should I have been had I suffered her to abandon him, and thus attached the indelible stigma of dishonour to her name. It was monstrous for me to persuade her to such a course, and many are the pangs I fear it will cost her. Mary—Mary! my brain becomes bewildered while I think of you, and I scarcely know what I do. Heaven bless you, and watch over your safety when I am far away, and should you sometimes bestow a thought upon my memory, oh, let it not be coupled with any feeling to the prejudice of him who has ever, and must continue to do with his latest breath, loved you so ardently, so sincrely. But despise and detest my memory! Oh, no, I feel assured that it is impossible she can ever do that, but, on the contrary, she must pity me, and pray for that happiness which I fear can never more be mine."

As he thus spoke, he took from his bosom the treasured silken lock of Mary's hair, and having gazed attentivey at it for a few moments, while manly tears, in spite of all his efforts to the contrary, started to his eyes, he pressed it fervently and with the deepest emotion to his lips.

"Precious relic of all I still hold most dear upon earth," he soliloquised, "how fondly will I continue to treasure you, and when the grim enemy, death, shall lay me low, you shall be found pressed nearest to my heart; and should no sacrilegious hand remove you, you shall accompany my cold remains to my ocean grave."

With these words, the young seaman returned the precious memento of his Mary's love to his bosom, and turning on his side, he tried to compose his mind to sleep. He at last succeeded in doing so; but when he did, the most painful visions crowded upon his busy and disordered imagination. Now he fancied himself at sea, and the gallant vessel on which he was on board battling with all the horrors of the storm, which raged with terrific fury, and threatened universal destruction every moment. In vain were the exertions of the seamen, the unfortunate ship was completely unmanageable in such a tempest; the tall masts were snapped asunder like glass, and every vestige of rigging was torn away, and the timbers severing, the water rushed in in every direction with a hideous roar, and the next moment she went to pieces, and he found himself struggling in the surging waves, and panting for breath, but still making the most desperate efforts to save himself. Through the mountain waves he struggled with the strength of madness and despair, towards a rock, which he perceived by the lightning's flash in the distance, but little indeed was the progress that he was enabled to make, and death seemed to be inevitable; but still he persevered, and notwithstanding the horrors by which he was surrounded, a certain feeling of hope sustained him. Suddenly, however, even above the furious voice of the tempest, the frantic shriek of a female saluted his ears, and casting his eyes in the direction of the rock, from which it seemed to proceed, he beheld by the broad and lurid glare of the lightning, standing on its summit, two human forms, one of which was the gaunt figure of a man, and the other that of a delicate female, who was struggling in his grasp. The reader may judge of the agony and horror of the dreamer when he recognised in that of the man the ruffian, Hugh Brandon, and in that of the female, his beloved Mary, who stretched her arms towards him, and again and again she shrieked aloud for that help which it was impossible for him to render her, whilst the miscreant Brandon laughed aloud and triumphantly at her useless cries; and, oh, madness! Harry distinctly saw him again and again pollute her lips with his odious kisses! With redoubled strength he imagined in his dream that he endeavoured desperately to reach the rock on which they were standing, but every wave seemed to drive him further back, and each moment he became more exhausted, and it seemed impossible that he could keep up much longer. At length the cries of Mary were heard no more, she sank exhausted and apparently senseless in the arms of the miscreant who held her, and with a hideous laugh of exultation he bore her from the spot, and in an instant they were both hidden from the sight. Madness now seemed to seize upon the brain of our hero—a mist arose before his eyes—his body seemed to spin round as if he were caught in the vortex of a whirlpool—strange noises thundered in his ears—the wild waters of the deep rolled above his head, and in the horror of the moment the fetters of sleep were broken and he awoke.

Such was the powerful impression that this remarkable dream had made upon him that, for a few moments, he could scarcely persuade himself but that it had actually taken place, and he could not imagine where he was.

"Release her from your grapnels, you infernal shark!" he vociferated, rising up in his bed, and with his fists clenched, and every sinew distended with the power of his excitement; "release her from your hold, and sheer off, or, damme, if I don't pour such a broadside in upon you as shall send you to old Davy in the turning of a handspike! Mary—Mary! my poor lass! I am here! I come to save you, and—— but where is she?—Where am I?—What does it all mean?—What's in the wind now?—Pipe all hands, and clear the deck for action! Lord! lord! what a fool I am to be sure; it—it is only a dream!"

He started from the bed as he thus spoke, and again gazed anxiously and with the greatest emotion around him, but his brain was so confused that it was several minutes before he could reflect calmly.

"It was only a dream," he said at length, "but such a one as is calculated to fill my breast with the utmost doubt and apprehension. I saw my Mary as plainly as if she were standing before my eyes at the present moment, and struggling in the arms of that daring and infernal miscreant, Hugh Brandon, and I was prevented from rendering her any assistance. What can have conjured such a vision as this up in my mind? But is it ever fated to be realised?—Heaven forbid. Mary once in the power of such a hardened and desperate villain as Hugh Brandon, her destruction would be inevitable! Oh, Mary! though we may never be destined to meet again, may Providence protect you from a fate so terrible as that. Pshaw! why should I suffer it to make such a serious impression upon me?—It is all in consequence of the disturbed state of my mind that it has been presented to my imagination. I must endeavour to think no more about it, for should I do so, I should become as weak and as superstitious as Watchful Waxend, and that would be unworthy of Harry Halliyard, who has hitherto been undaunted at real dangers, much more imaginary ones. And yet 'tis strange that this dream should occur to me so soon after the one which was presented to the imagination of Waxend, and they should correspond so remarkably. Pshaw! it is scarcely worthy of a second thought. It is not likely that I shall ever behold the poor girl in such a painful and perilous position. Providence will protect her from all such dangers as that. I care not what becomes of me, for I am now a wreck, and it matters not how soon I founder altogether; but God preserve that unfortunate being whom I must ever so ardently love from all harm; and if I could be assured that that prayer would be granted, methinks that I could be comparatively happy. Come, I must endeavour to shake off this sad feeling, and try to look forward to the future with hope. Hope! —what hope is there for me? Is not Mary lost to me for ever? And there is nothing now left to tempt me to live. It would be a happy release from misery should I in the first engagement with the enemy be laid low. But what a poor snivelling milksop have I become! Can this be Harry Halliyard, the pride of the ocean, who talks thus? My rudder and compass are all wrong, and I must take in a reef, or I shall be driven on the quicksands of despair and destruction altogether. Hugh Brandon can never get Mary in his power, and I must be a chicken-hearted swab to imagine such a thing for a moment. Let me arouse myself, and be prepared to act like a man in any emergency, and not like a loblolly boy. What would my shipmates think of me if they were to see me in this state? Damme, if I arn't ashamed of myself; and yet I should surely not be ashamed to encourage such feelings as those which now hold posssssion of my breast. Mary, my most anxious thoughts should ever and must ever be of thee! You were the companion of my childhold, the sheet-anchor of my hopes from the days of my earliest boyhood, and though those hopes are now annihilated, and I am cut adrift on the wild and tempestuous ocean of life, is it likely that I can ever banish you from my memory, and become as insensible as a ship water-logged? No—no, that is impossible, and time and absence will but make you more precious to me, though we never can be more to each other than we are at present."

He dressed himself, for he knew it would be useless for him to attempt to compose himself to sleep again; and having thrown himself into a seat, he remained absorbed in the same melancholy description of reflections, and awaited impatiently the arrival of the morning, that he might, by society and change of scene, probably be able to banish the gloomy thoughts that at present distracted his brain. But in spite of all his efforts to the contrary, all the particular circumstances of his extraordinary dream continued to haunt his imagination in the most vivid colours, and the longer he reflected, the more uneasy he became.

CHAPTER XV.

THE PIRATES.—THE STRATAGEM OF HUGH BRANDON SUCCEEDS.—MARY TREPANNED TO THE OLD TAVERN IN WESTMINSTER.

THE daring ruffians who had committed the villanous outrage against our hero and Watchful Waxend, after making their escape from the coast-guard, hurried on by the most unfrequented and lonely paths towards their secret rendezvous, which was situated in a remote part of the neighbourhood, and was so well chosen for their purpose that it created not the least suspicion in the minds of those whom they had every reason to fear; and so great was their apprehension of being pursued, that it was not until after they had got some distance from the scene where they had made the attack that they ventured to pause to see whether there was any one behind them. As far, however, as their eyes could then penetrate, the coast was quite clear, so that they imagined that the individuals who, so unfortunately for them, had come to the rescue, had given up the pursuit, and that they had nothing more to fear.

"Curses light on this misfortune," said one of the fellows, addressing himself to his companions, "we are defeated just at the moment when he thought that our triumph was certain."

"Ay, Bullruff," answered another of the ruffians, "you may say that; and d—d unfortunate and vexatious it is, too, to be thus disappointed. It is not likely that we shall have such another chance again, for the Porpoise sails in a few days, and then this Harry Halliyard, whom Brandon is so anxious to get in his power, will be safe enough from our clutches. He will be in a rare rage when he comes to hear of our failure."

"Yes, you may say that," returned Bullruff, "and I only wish he had been here, instead of loitering his time away in London, then he would have been satisfied that we were not to blame. For my part, I cannot see what he wants in town, when his presence is so much needed here."

"Why," replied the other, "as for that matter, you know, he has taken a fancy to this pretty Poll of Putney, as she is called, the former sweetheart of Harry Halliyard, and he has formed a plot to get her in his power, which he has probably succeeded in doing by this time; and should he have done so, we may expect him down here in a short time with his fair prize, and then she will be secure enough on board the Wasp, and I suppose we shall sail from this neighbourhood as soon as possible, though not before it is high time, for, if I may judge of all I have heard and seen, people begin to look upon our craft with suspicion."

"Ay," coincided Bullruff, "and this outrage may not tend to lessen their suspicions. Besides, I am tired of this sort of life, and am anxious once more to be upon the ocean. Had we gagged that lubber in time, and knocked the senses out of Halliyard, we should probably not have been interrupted in the execution of our plot."

"Perhaps not," said his companion; "however, it can't be helped now, and we must make the best we can of it."

"Yes, it is all very well to talk, Dogsby," said Bullruff, "but the question is how are we to satisfy the skipper that we were not to blame?"

"Well," remarked Dogsby, "it is no use for him to grumble about it, for had he been present he could not have helped it any more than ourselves. But come, let us away to our retreat, where we can discuss this matter in safety. We have been lucky, at any rate, in giving the fellows the slip."

"Ay," coincided the other, "and it is not very likely that they can have any suspicion as to who we really are. It would have been madness for us to have stayed to offer them any resistance, since they so far outnumbered us, and our defeat would have been almost certain."

"Very true," answered Dogsby; "of course, under all the circumstances, we have acted the wisest plan, though we have failed in our object. It would have been a glorious thing for the gratification of the vengeance of the skipper had he got this Harry Halliyard, whom he has so much cause to hate, in his power."

"Ay, it would have been so; but another opportunity may yet present itself, and then leave Hugh Brandon alone, he will not fail to pay off all old scores."

"True," said Dogsby; "he never has neglected to do so yet, but I have my doubts whether or not he will be able to do so in the present instance."

"Oh, I don't know that," answered Bullruff; "there are many chances and mischances at sea, and something may yet occur to favour the wishes of Brandon. The only thing I blame him for is for not having gratified his vengeance when he had him so completely at his mercy in the old tavern. However, if he gets this Mary Tiller in his power I suppose he will be satisfied for the present."

"Yes, I should think he would. She is a very handsome woman, I am told."

"Yes," returned Bullruff, "they say that there is not a more handsome lass in England, and, therefore, the skipper may consider himself a very lucky man if he succeeds in securing her."

"No doubt he will," said Dogsby; "but it will be necessary for him to use every precaution, in order to secure her on board the Wasp."

"Oh, leave him alone for that," replied the other; "but no doubt that Brandon has maturely arranged all his plans, and has no fear of being able to accomplish them. However, we tarry here, and there may be danger in our doing so, after the alarm which our attack upon Halliyard and his companion has naturally created."

"And what can be the skipper's reason for wishing to secure that lubber, Watchful Waxend as he is called, as well as Harry Halliyard?" asked the ruffian Dogsby.

"Why," answered Bullruff, "if all be true that I have heard, he is the very fellow who fired the fatal shot at Black Brandon on board the Black Bess."

"Indeed!" said Dogsby; "then I do not wonder at the skipper being anxious to settle accounts with him. But come, let us away."

Bullruff returned no answer to this, and the ruffians then made their way towards the place of their secret retreat, where they soon afterwards arrived, and having given the well-known signal, entered by a private way.

The place to which we now wish to direct the attention of the reader was an old farm-house, of considerable extent, and which presented nothing particular in its external appearance to attract attention or excite suspicion. It was a wild and rambling place, and being situated in a dreary and little frequented part of the country, was admirably adapted for the purposes to which it was put. The man who occupied this house was known by the name of Farmer Harville, and being a person of most reserved manners, and rather eccentric habits, his society was not much courted, though those who were at all acquainted with him were inclined to believe him a respectable yeoman, who had probably experienced some troubles and vicissitudes in life sufficient to induce him to prefer living as retired as he possibly could. We need scarcely inform the reader, we presume, that Farmer Harville was intimately connected with Hugh Brandon and his crew, that he shared in the booty they obtained, and that in his house the pirates always found a safe and secret retreat, whenever they were in England. There they had not the least fear of any interruption ; and even if it should happen that their privacy should at any time, by accident, be intruded upon, there were secret places in the old farm-house in which they could find immediate concealment, and no one could have the least suspicion that it contained any such inhabitants.

Harville, as we have before stated, having given the ruffians admittance, conducted them in silence along a dark and narrow passage, and having descended a flight of stairs at the extremity he unfastened a door at the foot, and led them across a small open space to another one opposite, and from the chinks of which lights glimmering, showed that it was either inhabited, or had been recently used. This door being opened revealed a large apartment, rudely furnished, but with every degree of comfort, and in which several coarse-looking men were assembled round a table, drinking and smoking, and some of them engaged in playing at cards and other games. They arose on the entrance of the pirates and greeted them, which they returned in the same rough but cordial manner.

"So," said Harville, "you have returned safe ; but it seems that you have not succeeded in that you went upon ?"

"No, curse it !" answered Bullruff, "fortune has not favoured us to-night, though we were as near as could be in accomplishing our purpose."

"Did you succeed in encountering Halliyard and his companion ?" asked Harville.

"Certainly," replied Bullruff, "we could not well do otherwise, after Will Harrop having put us upon the right scent."

"How is it, then, that you have failed ?" demanded Harville.

"Why," returned the other, "we had secured them both, and were bearing them away, when we were surprised by a number of the coast-guard, and were compelled to take to flight, for it would have been useless for us to stand to resist them."

"It is very fortunate," remarked Will Harrop, who was the man whom our hero and Waxend had seen at the Seaman's Friend ; "they have, then, escaped ?"

"For the present, at any rate," said Dogsby.

"And just at the very time when their capture seemed certain ?" said Harville.

"Yes."

"The skipper will be greatly enraged and disappointed when he hears of this," remarked Harrop.

"No doubt," coincided Bullruff, "but it cannot be helped ; it was no fault of ours. But another opportunity may present itself, and then we may, perhaps, be more successful."

"I much doubt it," said Harville, "for this adventure will put Halliyard on his guard, and in a day or two the Porpoise is to set sail, is she not ?"

"She is," answered Bullruff, "but there is no knowing what may occur in the meantime."

"Do you think that any of the coast-guard recognised you ?"

"Oh, no," replied Bullruff, "there was no chance of their doing that, for we were too far away from them."

"That is fortunate," said Harville ; "then they can have no suspicion as to who were the perpetrators of the outrage ?"

"Only from the description which Halliyard and his companion will be able to give of our persons," returned Bullruff; "and I don't suppose that they will have any recollection of having seen us before. I only wish that Brandon had been here to see after his business himself, and then he would have been satisfied that there was no one to blame in the matter."

"Well," observed Harville, "he will be here before long."

"Ah! how know you that?"

"Why, I have received a letter from him since you were away from the house," answered Harville, "in which he desires me to prepare for his arrival here probably in a few hours."

"Indeed?"

"Yes; he has been far more successful than you."

"What mean you?"

"Why," answered Harville, "this pretty Poll of Putney, as she is called, Harry Halliyard's sweetheart, and the wife of Joe Tiller, is in his power, and at the old crib in Westminster."

"You surprise me," said Bullruff; "he has indeed been lucky. How has he managed this business?"

"He has not had space nor time to inform me," replied Harville, "but we shall know the whole particulars when he comes here. Her strange abduction will, no doubt, cause the greatest excitement in the neighbourhood where she resides."

"That it will be sure to do," said Bullruff. "But how will he manage to convey her hither in safety, and without detection?"

"Oh, I dare say he has made every arrangement as regards that," returned Harville; "Hugh Brandon seldom fails to accomplish anything he undertakes."

"True; and once on board the Wasp, she will be secure from discovery."

"She will; and the triumph of Brandon will be all but complete. If all be true that is stated, this damsel is a prize that is well worth running any risk to obtain possession of."

"No doubt of it," said Bullruff, "and the skipper will know how to make use of the advantage he has obtained."

"Certainly," coincided Harville; "leave him alone for that. But come, you doutless need some refreshment after your evening's adventure. Fill your glasses, comrades; I think we cannot do better than drink to the health of the skipper and his fair mistress."

The ruffians required no further pressing to comply with this request, and they immediately filled their glasses to the brim.

"Bravo!" shouted Bullruff, raising his glass to his lips. "Here's to the health of our captain, Hugh Brandon, and his fair mistress, Pretty Poll of Putney!"

The pirates drank the toast with the most uproarious glee, and Harville having once more filled his glass, said—

"Another toast, my lads, to which I know you will all heartily respond;— Here's to the Wasp, and may every success attend her in all her future cruises!"

This toast was also drunk in the most cordial manner, and they then resumed their seats, and seemed resolved to enjoy themselves in the most extravagant manner.

"The introduction of this damsel on board the pirate craft will no doubt make a wonderful alteration," remarked Harville; "and will stimulate the skipper to fresh acts of daring."

"I hope it may not divert his attention from the more important part of our business," said Bullruff.

"Oh, there is not much fear of that," said Harville. "Brandon never suffers anything to interfere between him and duty. Could he but succeed in getting Harry Halliyard also in his power, his triumph and revenge would be complete."

"True, it would be so," coincided Bullruff, "but I rather suspect there is not much chance of his being able to do so now. The only thing that surprises me is how he has managed to obtain possession of Mary. What anguish will it cause Halliyard, should he become acquainted with her disappearance."

"It will," answered Harville.

"But when the captain has arrived, and his fair prize is safely on board," continued Bullruff, "no time must be lost in weighing anchor, and crowding all sail from this coast; for should any suspicions be excited respecting our vessel, we should be discovered, and our career would then be quickly brought to an end."

"Oh, there is no fear of that," observed Harville; "everything is in readiness on board the Wasp, and you can, therefore, set sail any hour you please."

"And I do not care how soon, for I feel completely out of my element when on shore, and do not like to remain idle while there is booty to be obtained for the seeking on the ocean."

"Well said," remarked Harville; "such ought ever to be the sentiments of a pirate; but you will, no doubt, soon be employed again to your heart's content. Come, my lads, drink away, and enjoy yourselves; we must never lag behind while there is plenty of good cheer in store."

The ruffians needed no second invitation, and they continued at their carousal till a late hour of the night, when they separated, and retired to their chambers, and here we will leave them and return to our heroine and her husband.

It was several days before our heroine recovered sufficiently to leave her chamber, and when she did, she was very little better than a shadow of her former self, and it was quite distressing to notice the melancholy and despair of her looks. It would seem from the wild and rambling observations which she made at times, that her reason was somewhat affected, and Joe entertained the most painful and fearful apprehensions as to what the future consequences might be. Although the agony of his feelings may readily be imagined, he never once made any allusion to what had transpired between her and Harry; and whenever her mind wandered to that subject, which it almost constantly did, he did all in his power to divert it from it, and to endeavour to prove to her that instead of upbraiding her for it, he sincerely pitied her. But all his praiseworthy efforts were of little or no avail, and most keenly did she reproach herself for having for a moment dared to encourage the guilty and ungrateful thought of abandoning that man whom she had sworn at the altar of God to love, honour, and obey, and who had ever behaved to her with the most unbounded affection, and had at all times been so studious of her happiness.

"Oh," she would ejaculate, in the most melancholy accents, whilst tears of the bitterest anguish would stream down her pale cheeks, "I have been most cruel, abandoned, and ungrateful to you, my husband, for a moment so far to forget myself as to think of deserting you, my husband, and following the footsteps of one whom honour and jus-

tice now forbid me even to think upon save in the character of a once dear and respected friend. Surely a curse will pursue me for it, and must make my future days those of the bitterest misery and most poignant regret. Would that I were dead! would that I were dead, and that——"

"Oh, forbear, Mary, for Heaven's sake," interrupted Joe, "for such words as those should never escape your lips, and do but serve to wring my heart. Banish all remembrance of the circumstance from your brain, and believe me that you shall never once hear me reproach you with it, or remind you of it by a single allusion."

"Banish it from my memory, Joe!" repeated his wife, looking piteously up in his face through her tears; "oh, that is impossible! I must have indeed become quite insensible to every feeling of honour and of shame if I could. I blush, I tremble to look you in the face after what has happened; for though you may attempt to conceal it, I know that you must look upon me with feelings of disgust, nay, loathing."

"Oh, Heaven forbid!" exclaimed Tiller, fervently. "Mary — dearest Mary! indeed you do me a great injustice by entertaining such an opinion of me. I should, indeed, have been most unworthy of your hand could I have failed to appreciate the strength of that love you entertained for Harry Halliyard, or not to deeply sympathise with you in the bitter disappointment it has been your hard lot to experience."

"And it is that conviction of your sympathy," returned Mary, "that should have urged me more than all to esteem and venerate, and to act with fidelity towards you; but, on the contrary, what is the return that I have made?—Did I not listen to the voice of the tempter? and had it not been that remorse, I suppose, came upon him, I should even now have been far away from this place, and living in a state of——"

"Cease, Mary!" again hastily interrupted Joe; "do not, I implore you, give utterance to the disgraceful word. Halliyard, I am certain, could never seriously have contemplated such a crime, and his brain must have been distracted when he gave utterance to

BLACK BRANDON AND BOWSE ON DECK OF THE BLACK BET.

the words of temptation. His having fled before you recovered your senses proves at once the truth of my surmises, and no doubt that he bitterly repented, and upbraided himself for having so far committed himself. Believe me, Mary, that I bear no ill feeling towards him, and that I wish him prosperity and happiness wherever he may go; and should we ever meet again, which I trust we shall under far more propitious circumstances, I will never reproach him for what has happened, but, on the contrary, will seek to bury the past in oblivion."

"Oh, Joe!" ejaculated his wife, "your generosity is too great, and makes me feel more keenly the manner in which I have committed myself. Alas! nothing whatever, I am convinced, can sufficiently repay the fidelity of your feelings, or atone for the injustice I have done you. But it is impossible that you can ever forgive me or Harry for the base ingratitude and cruelty of our conduct towards you, and I feel that we deserve it not."

"Mary," returned Tiller, solemnly, "I think you have known me long enough, and have been enabled sufficiently to penetrate the true sentiments of my heart to feel convinced that I cannot act the hypocrite, and that whatever I say, comes sincerely from the bottom of my soul. Not forgive you? Oh, I must indeed be most callous to every proper sense of feeling and generosity could I not do so. Come, come, let us talk no more upon this torturing subject, but seek to forget it, and to looked forward to the future with the hope of content, if not of real happiness."

"Happiness!" sighed our heroine; "alas! that can never again be mine; and what makes me more truly wretched than all is the knowledge of the unmerited misery I have inflicted upon you."

"Think not of it, Mary," replied her husband, struggling with his feelings in the best manner he could, in order to console her, "think not of it, and you will never find anything in my conduct towards you to cause you one moment of pain or self-reproach. Let me but once see you calm and resigned, and I will be happy."

Mary threw herself on his bosom, and the sobs that escaped her overcharged breast spoke far more than any language could possibly have given utterance to. But although Joe struggled whilst in the presence of his wife to stifle the real feelings that agitated his breast, it was impossible that he could entirely banish the anguish to which all the painful circumstances of the case naturally gave rise, or forbear from entertaining the worst apprehensions for the consequences that were yet likely to ensue, and when he was alone, he gave free indulgence to his feelings, and most keenly did he in secret reproach Harry Halliyard for the advantage he endeavoured to take of the love which he knew Mary still cherished for him, in seeking to persuade her to abandon him,

and follow him in his wayward fortunes. Many were the bitter pangs which those reflections cost him; and when he was alone, he at times gave himself up almost entirely to despair. Old Sam Sculler, who had always taken the deepest and most friendly interest in his affairs, did all in his power to console and advise him, and Joe listened to him with all attention, though it was a hard matter to convince him.

"It is evident," said the latter, in the course of one of their conversations upon the subject, "that Mary, instead of loving me, must now ever view me almost as the only barrier to her happiness, and that her whole thoughts must at all times be devoted to Harry, though the greatest distance may separate them, and they may never meet again."

"Say not so, my lad," returned Sculler. "Mary possesses too noble a heart to cherish any thoughts which honour and virtue would not sanction and that in time she will cease to remember the past only as a dream."

"Oh, no," said Tiller, "that is impossible; I feel convinced that the image of Halliyard is too firmly ingrafted in her heart for her ever to tear it from it, and that absence, on the contrary, will but serve to increase her passion, and to make her feel the more painful regret at the fate which has separated them. Could she ever have consented to elope with him, and leave me to all the misery of my fate, had not my surmises been correct?"

"Think not of it, Joe," remarked Sculler; "she knew not what she said or did at the time, depend upon it, and deeply now does she regret it. Besides, is not Harry now at Portsmouth? And in a few days, the vessel on board of which he has entered will set sail, and then all those fears which you now so groundlessly entertain will, I trust, be at an end."

Tiller shook his head, but returned no answer, and it was clear that the observations of Sculler had made but little impression upon him.

"Come, Joe," said the old man, "I must not see you give way to such feelings of despair as those, and which must in fact, only be productive of the greatest evil to yourself and your wife."

"Sculler," returned his companion,

"I feel that a blow is struck at my happiness, from the effects of which I can never recover. But, fool that I was, I might have expected it, when I knew how fondly the heart of Mary was devoted to Halliyard, and that she could never possibly more than esteem me. I must have been mad to consent to become her husband under such circumstances, and now I am only properly punished for it."

"How rashly you talk, Joe; did you not act in obedience with the poor old woman's dying wishes, her most solemn injunctions? And where could Mary have found a more fitting protector than in yourself? You have nothing to reproach yourself with; and though storms have at present gathered over you, they will quickly pass away, and Providence, depend upon it, will not desert you in the hour of you need."

"But to see her, poor thing," sighed Tiller, with the deepest feeling, "wandering about so lonely and wretched, and to know that it is not in my power to console her, but that, on the contrary, the bare sight of me cannot do otherwise than to add to her anguish—alas! that of itself is more torturing than all. Sculler—Sculler, I am bewildered: I know not how to act."

"Be advised be me," replied the old man, "and all will yet be well. But if you suffer Mary to perceive the anguish of your feelings, then, indeed, are the worst consequences to be apprehended, and the fears you at present entertain will in all probability be realised. Come, my lad, I hope better things for you; and should Harry ever return to England, I trust that both himself and Mary will have so far conquered their unfortunate passion as to meet only as old and respected friends."

"Alas!" returned Joe, "I fear that can never be, and, although you express such sanguine hopes, that you do not think what you say. Mary can never cease to love Harry Halliyard less than she does at present, and I am certain that the same sentiments must continue to glow within his heart while he exists. Should they meet again, Heaven only knows what the consequences may be. I dread, I shudder to think of them."

"Would that I could persuade you to think to the contrary," remarked Sculler; "but, at all events, do not give way entirely to despair, but try to hope for the best."

"I know the kind feelings you bear towards me, Sam," replied Joe, "and, believe me, I am not ungrateful for them. I will, indeed, endeavour to follow your advice, though I fear it will be with little success that I shall be able to do so."

After some further conversation they separated, and Joe hastened to his business, but it was with a heavy heart that he did so, and it was in vain that he tried to banish the dismal thoughts that occupied his mind.

At length our heroine was enabled to leave her chamber, but she avoided al society as much as possible; and when she was in the presence of her husband, although she tried to conceal her rea thoughts and feelings, and even at times affected to be cheerful, it was quite evident the anguish of mind she was enduring was most intense, and that her efforts to conceal it only the more added to the agony of her feelings. This could not but increase the misery of poor Joe, while at the same time he pitied her from the very depths of his soul, and could not reproach her for still entertaining those feelings over which she had no control, and which at the same time, it was clear, she was equally anxious to conquer. Whenever Joe was absent from home, Mary would sit for hours, buried in the deepest and most gloomy thought, and would scarcely ever change her attitude, so completely would her mind be absorbed, while the tears would chase each other rapidly down her cheeks, and the most convulsive sobs would escape her bosom.

"Alas—alas!" would she sigh, "what a wretched, what an untoward and insupportable fate is mine, and how much better would it have been had I never been born. I cannot banish from my mind the thoughts that torture it, and yet how guilty am I for encouraging them, how shamefully do I abuse the kindness and affection of Tiller by so doing! He is indeed to be pitied, and certainly deserved a far different fate than that which has befallen him. And yet I find it is impossible for me to banish these thoughts from my mind;

the more I endeavour to do so, the more rapidly do they crowd upon it. Harry Halliyard, so deep is the influence you have obtained over my heart, that nothing whatever, I feel convinced, can subdue it. And shall we never meet again? Oh, no, ere many days, perhaps ere may hours have elapsed, the ocean will far divide us, and it may be his fate either to perish in the tempest, or in the deadly conflict. And but for this unfortunate marriage that might have been avoided, and how happy might we both have been. But were either myself or Tiller to blame? —Oh, no! it was the dispensation of Providence, probably ordained for some wise purpose, and ought we to murmur? We did but act in obedience to the last injunctions of Harry's mother, and she, poor soul, advised everything for the best, and out of the purest good wishes towards me. Alas! how fatal has it proved to be! But who could have foreseen what would happen? though my own heart misgave me, and I revolted and shuddered at the sacrifice which I was about to make of my own feelings. But has not he to whom I have given my hand ever proved himself worthy of me?—He has, indeed, been most kind, affectionate, and most studious of my happiness; and is it not my duty to endeavour to make him all the return for it in my power?—But how have I done so?—Is it not monstrously ungrateful in me to resign myself to the sinful thoughts that at present inhabit my bosom?—Am I not dishonouring him by so doing?—And, good God! into what an abyss of guilt and shame was I about to precipitate myself! I shudder at the recollection! I consented—I was willing to abandon him, and to resign myself to the *protection* of Halliyard! Infamous idea! I must ever reproach myself for having entertained it; and what must be the opinion that Tiller, knowing it, must now entertain of me? He affects to forgive me, but is it possible that he can ever do so in his heart?—Ah, no! when he recalls everything to his mind, he surely must hate and despise me! I blush to meet him, for my conscience too bitterly upbraids me for the wrong I have done him. Would to Heaven that I might be permitted to hide myself in some place far remote from all society, that I

might indulge the heavy sorrows of my heart alone. Oh, Harry! why did we ever know each other, since Heaven has ordained that all the bright and sanguine hopes we had so fondly entertained should be thus annihilated? You might have been happy in the love of some other maiden more worthy of you than myself, and I might have been contented and blessed as the wife of Tiller, nor had a care, a thought, or wish beyond him."

She wrung her hands as she gave utterance to these words, and the agony of her mind increased every moment. She arose from her seat, and traversed the room in the most violent state of agitation, and bitter, indeed, was the anguish of soul that she endured. But at length a passionate flood of tears came to her relief, and she became somewhat more calm.

In the meantime the villain Brandon was not idle, and having kept a strict watch upon the progress of Mary, he matured his plans to get her in his power. Jack Oarsby was his most ready and efficient tool, and being on intimate terms with old Sam Sculler and Joe Tiller (who had not the least idea of the villany of his real character), he was enabled to bring him all the information that he required, and thus to prepare him to put his nefarious designs into execution. He had, as the reader is probably aware, ascertained the fact of Harry Halliyard having gone to Portsmouth, and entered on board of the Porpoise, and he had given instructions to his colleagues there to seize him, if possible, for if he could only get him in his power as well as Mary, his revenge would be gratified tenfold, and his triumph would be complete. At length Oarsby, having brought him word that our heroine had so far recovered as to be able to leave her chamber, though she did not venture from the house, he determined to carry his diabolical designs into effect without the least delay.

"Everything goes on as well as I could wish," he observed, as he was seated one evening with his guilty associates at the old tavern in Westminster, "and if fortune does not jilt me, which I do not expect that she will, in a day or two at the latest this Pretty Poll of Putney, as she is called, the darling of

Harry Halliyard, and the wife of Joe Tiller, will be in my power; and if I can only obtain possession also of the person of the young seaman, I shall consider myself one of the luckiest fellows in existence."

"And so you ought," observed one of the guests, "if she is only half as handsome as she is represented to be."

"Take my word for it," said Brandon, "that I am no judge of female beauty, which, by-the-bye, I flatter myself I am, if she is not one of the most lovely damsels that mortal man ever clapped his eyes upon; and every way worthy to become the mistress of the bold buccanier. Should I also succeed in trepanning Harry Halliyard, it will be one of the most fortunate things, in my estimation, that ever I achieved. But you say that she is able to leave her chamber, Oarsby?"

"Yes," replied the latter, "and that I have seen her."

"Well, that is proof enough, at any rate," said Brandon; "but how does she look?"

"Why, bad enough, you may guess," answered Oarsby; "she seems to have suffered from some severe shock or another."

"No doubt from her interview with Harry Halliyard. Ah, that poor devil, Joe Tiller, is finely duped, and the only thing that surprises me is that Halliyard did not endeavour to persuade her to abandon him, and accompany himself."

"Well," returned Oarsby, "there is no knowing, probably he did; but she must have been a bad one, indeed, had she consented to desert her own lawful husband."

"Husband be d—d!" said the ruffian Brandon; "what matters that, when her heart is another's? Harry Halliyard was betrothed to her from a boy, you know, and if it had not been for the report of his death, they would have been united now, and she would never have married Joe Tiller, though he always had a sneaking regard for her."

"Very true," coincided Oarsby; "but what plan do you propose to adopt to get her in your power? It would not be safe, you know, to venture to make a forcible seizure of her at the house where she resides."

"No," returned Brandon, "I never contemplated that. She must be decoyed away by stratagem."

"But how?"

"Why, I will leave everything to you, and you need not fear that I will reward you handsomely for your trouble."

"Oh, I do not doubt that," said Oarsby; "still, I stand in need of some of your suggestions to know the best manner in which to act. There must be no blundering in the business, or the opportunity may be lost for ever."

"True," coincided Brandon; "then what I propose is this: in the first instance, Joe Tiller must be lured away. You know the house that he usually calls at after he has left his business?"

"Ay, the Crown and Crosier it is called," answered Jack Oarsby.

"Just so," said Brandon. "Now it will be a very easy matter for some of our friends here to be present at that house at his usual time of calling there before he goes home, and by plying him and Sam Sculler with drink, detain them there, while you make your way to the residence of Mary, and by a story of Joe's having met with some accident on the river, and his being taken to some house in this neighbourhood, persuade her to accompany you hither. The plan is simple and easy enough: what think you of it?"

"Why," answered Oarsby, "that it is a very good one, and there is not much fear of its succeeding, especially managed in the way I shall execute it. Mary believes me to be the intimate friend of her husband, and no doubt will place every confidence in my statements. But when do you wish the plot to be carried into execution?"

"Why, the sooner the better," replied Hugh Brandon; "everything here is ready for her reception, and so to-morrow evening the business shall be performed, if you please."

"Agreed," said Oarsby; "and you shall find that I will perform my task with my usual ability."

"Oh, I have not the least doubt of that," returned Brandon; "so that point is settled?"

"It is. But how do you mean to get her on board the Wasp?"

"Oh, that will be a matter of after consideration; only let me get her safely here, and I do not fear the least of being able to accomplish the rest. To-morrow night, then, if fortune does not frown upon me, I may calculate upon having Mary Tiller securely here in my power ?"

"You may," answered Oarsby.

"It will be a glorious triumph," said Brandon, "and I wait impatiently for its accomplishment."

"Well," observed Oarsby, "you will not have to wait long. Mary's fears will be easily worked upon by the story I will concoct to tell her, and she will not hesitate to accompany me to see her husband. You could not have hit upon a better scheme, I think, Brandon."

"No," replied the latter, "and I do not think there is much fear of its success. But you must be careful how you break the news to her, or she will be so overcome that she will not be able to attend you."

"Oh, fear not, leave everything to me, and you shall find that I will act with all the precaution that will be necessary on the occasion. Our friends here must also be cautious how they play their cards with Joe Tiller and Sam Sculler, or their suspicions will be aroused."

"True," returned Brandon; "but, no doubt, they will know how to act. So we have arranged everything ?"

"Yes, I believe we have."

"To-morrow night, then, is fixed for the execution of the plot ?" said Brandon.

"Yes," answered Oarsby, "if nothing particular occurs to render it necessary to defer it."

"What do you mean ?" demanded Brandon.

"Why, Mary might suffer a relapse," said Oarsby ; "and, of course, it would be no use attempting it then."

"Certainly not," coincided Brandon ; "but I hope that no necessity for any such delay will take place."

"I will visit the cottage in the morning," answered Oarsby, "and then I shall be enabled to ascertain if all goes on right."

"Exactly so; and I trust it may, for I must confess that I am all impatience until this plot is carried into full effect, and I have this damsel securely in my power."

"My word for it, your wishes will be gratified to the fullest extent, Brandon," said Oarsby.

"Only do you work well, and I will not fail to reward you handsomely."

"I have no doubt of that; but we will talk of that another time."

"Come, then," said Hugh Brandon, "since this important business is so far arranged, we will enjoy ourselves for an hour or two. Fill your glasses. Here's the health of Pretty Poll of Putney !"

"Bravo !" shouted the whole of the guests, raising the glasses to their lips. "Here's to the health of Pretty Poll of Putney !"

"And may she soon be safe on board the Wasp !" added Brandon.

"And may she soon be safe on board the Wasp!" repeated the men.

"And now, my lads," said Brandon, "I will give you another toast, to which I know you will all most heartily respond. Here's the Saucy Wasp, and may success attend all our future undertakings !"

"The Saucy Wasp !" shouted the guests, "and may success attend all our future undertakings !"

These toasts were drunk with the utmost hilarity, and the spirits passing freely round, the ruffians soon became exhilarated to the utmost pitch of rude and boisterous mirth, and seemed determined to continue their carousal to the latest hour ; Hugh Brandon leading them on, and being one of the first to make the welkin roar again with tumultuous hilarity.

"I am elated, my lads, at the prospect before me. This damsel is no mean prize to covet ; and if I obtain possession of her, which I have no doubt that I shall, I shall consider it as one of the greatest triumphs and gratifications of my revenge that I have ever achieved."

"But," said Oarsby, "do you think there is any probability of Harry Halliyard's being seized ?"

"Any probability !" repeated Brandon; "to be sure there is ; that is, if the lubbers only follow my instructions, I think they cannot very well miss him. He is not yet on board the ship, and lodging in the town, they may have plenty of chances of trepanning him. I shall be very much disappointed if they fail."

"And is it possible that none of the authorities have ever suspected the real character of the Wasp?" asked the landlord, who at that moment had entered the room.

"No," answered Brandon, "I have managed that business too cleverly for them. I have every reason to believe that there is not the slightest suspicion entertained of her."

"It was a bold trick of yours to put in at Portsmouth, in the very midst of his majesty's fleet."

"Ah!" returned Brandon, "I have done many such bold things in my time. The more daring the venture the less chance is there of being detected; at least, so I have always found it."

"Right, captain, right," assented one of the men; "there is nothing like putting a bold front upon everything, and it is almost sure to carry you through."

"But," answered Jack Oarsby, "should you get Harry Halliyard in your power, it will raise a bit of a hubbub in the place, I think, and it will not be safe for you to remain there much longer, lest they should make such inquiries of you as it would not be altogether pleasant to answer."

"True," said Brandon; "but I will not give them much opportunity of doing that, never fear. Harry Halliyard and his pretty Polly once on board the Wasp, and we will set sail in a tangent, and bid defiance to the swiftest craft in all His Majesty's service to overtake us—should their suspicions at last be aroused, and they should give chase to us. Old Tapster," he added, addressing himself to the landlord, "you have prepared everything for the accommodation of my future mistress, I believe, while she remains here?"

"Why, Master Brandon," replied the host, "I believe you are fully aware that I have."

"All right!" said Brandon; "she will probably not remain here many hours, or, at least, no longer than I can make the necessary preparations for her departure to Portsmouth."

"Ah!" said Oarsby, "it puzzles me how you are going to convey her there without fear of being discovered."

"Oh, leave me alone for that," replied Brandon. "I have made all the necessary arrangements, as you will find. There will be a small skiff moored just below bridge in a day or two; I will contrive to administer to Mary a powerful opiate, which will steep her senses in unconsciousness; in that state she may be easily conveyed on board, and then she will be safe enough, and the job will be completed. What think you of that plan?"

"Oh, it will do, there is no doubt, if it is only properly executed," answered Jack Oarsby; "do you intend to convey her direct on board the Wasp?"

"No," returned Brandon. "I do not think it would be exactly prudent to do that. So I have resolved to remove her to the rendezvous at Portsmouth, until we can find an opportunity to convey her direct on board the Wasp without any danger of being discovered. But come, all the business is settled so far, and I think with every prospect of success, so we will at present talk no more upon the subject, but give ourselves up to the pleasures of the glass."

Of course, there was not a dissentient voice raised against this proposition, and the ruffians sat carousing together until a late hour of the morning. The next day Jack Oarsby, according to his promise, paid a visit to the neighbourhood of Mary's cottage, where he made such inquiries as satisfied him that she continued to improve in health, and that there was nothing to prevent the plot being put into execution that evening, which he was most anxious to do, as he knew well that Brandon would well reward him for his trouble, and there would not be much danger in it, as Mary and her husband, he believed, had such a high opinion of his character, that they could not for a moment have any suspicion of his intending them any harm. He returned to the house in Westminster, and informed Brandon of the result of his inquiries.

"All right," said Brandon, "then this night I may expect to have the beauteous Mary securely in my power?"

"Yes," returned Oarsby, "should nothing particular occur to prevent it."

"Pshaw!" ejaculated Brandon, impatiently, "and what is to occur to prevent it, think you, if you only manage your business cleverly?"

"Well," said Oarsby, "you will have

nothing to apprehend on that score. I believe you have tried me often enough before."

"True," answered Brandon, "and you have rendered me some good service. Ben Summers here, and Hal Guernsey will see to taking Joe Tiller and Sculler in tow at the Crown and Crosier, and then all will be ready for action."

"Yes," remarked Oarsby, "but they most be cautious how they act, for Sam Sculler is a shrewd old chap, and it would not take much to arouse his suspicions, I can tell you."

"Oh, leave us alone for that," said Ben Summers, "neither I nor Hal are very green in such matters as that, and we shall manage this business with our usual ability."

"Well," said Oarsby, "I dare say you will; and while you are keeping them in tow, I will be acting my part at the cottage, and no doubt, in due time, have the pleasure of conducting Pretty Poll of Putney to this house."

"Well said," observed Brandon; "I feel as sanguine over this business as if it were already accomplished."

"And you may do so, Brandon," remarked Oarsby, "for I do not see that there is the least chance of its failing. I have got a tale ready for Mary which will be sure to deceive her, and I shall find no difficulty in persuading her to accompany me."

"Well," said Brandon, "I am glad to hear you express so much confidence, for it almost inspires me with redoubled hope."

They now sat down, and seriously arranged the completion of their infamous plans, which being settled to their satisfaction, they separated, agreeing, however, to meet again towards the evening.

Our heroine, however, notwithstanding all that Oarsby had been informed, was far from being so well on the day which had been fixed upon for her abduction as she had been previously; fearful dreams had tortured her imagination during the night, and she could not arouse herself from the effects of them. Fearful misgivings haunted and troubled her mind; something of a painful nature seemed about to happen, and, although she struggled to the utmost, she could not arouse

herself from the dismal feelings that had such powerful possession of her mind. And yet she was at a loss to account for the torturing misgivings that beset her on the present occasion. Strange as it may appear to be, she felt somewhat relieved when Joe took his departure from home in the morning on his usual daily occupation, though at the same time she was anxious and restless, and could almost have wished that he had remained at home for that day, for she could not help apprehending that something of a fearful nature was about to happen to her, which his presence might be the means of preventing. Restless and timid, she paced from room to room, sometimes looking from the window, and at others from the door, in a state of the greatest anxiety, and totally unable to settle her mind to anything. Then she took up a book, but although her eyes glanced over the pages, she was totally unconscious of what she was reading.

"What can be the meaning of this?" she said; "why do these strange and melancholy thoughts and apprehensions haunt and distract my brain?—What have I to fear?—Surely there is nothing more than usual to happen to me! It can only be the effects of the despair and anguish of my feelings, created by the extraordinary and exciting events that have recently taken place. Oh, Harry! fond and faithful, what a cloud has fate cast over our prospects! that which was once so bright and cheerful, so light, so buoyant, and so sunny, is now wrapt in the gloom of the darkest night. All around is gloomy and threatening; and though we have already experienced so many of the rude tempests of untoward, unpropitious fortune, there are other storms gathering in the horizon of our destiny which I feel convinced are about to burst upon us with tenfold fury, and, perhaps, to overwhelm us altogether. Oh, God! I humbly beseech You to be merciful to us, and not to try us beyond our strength to bear!"

She clasped her fair hands together in the most vehement manner as she thus spoke, and raising her eyes towards that fountain of grace to which she so eloquently appealed, the tears flowed fast and involuntarily adown her cheeks.

"And he is now far away from me," she continued, after a pause, "and in a

short time will be once more exposed to all the perils and dangers of the boundless deep, without one hope, without a single hope to cheer him on, or to impart a ray of consolation to his lacerated, his broken heart. All the fond anticipations that formerly buoyed him up, and made him look upon danger with a dauntless heart, are crushed and annihilated for ever; and life, I know, has become an insupportable burthen to him. And I have been the innocent cause of all this. Had I remained faithful to the vows I uttered to him so often, this could not have happened. Even though I believed him dead, the intense love I should have borne his memory, ought to have prevented me from ever becoming the wife of another, and but have rendered my love the more intense in my supposed irremediable bereavement. Then how happy should we both now have been! what a sweet recompense for the cares, the anguish, the despair I had previously endured! Harry would have been my husband, and I could have had no other wish, no other hope to gratify. Wretched, wretched fate! I feel myself as one accursed of God, and —But why do I suffer such guilty thoughts as these to haunt my wild and disordered imagination?—Am I not the wife of another? of one who has ever acted towards me with the most unexampled kindness? who values my happiness even far more than he does his own existence, and who, I am convinced, would willingly lay down his own life to serve me? And since it is the will of Providence that I am so, ought I not to submit without a murmur, and endeavour to the utmost to do my duty towards him, and even to forget that there was ever such an individual as Halliyard existed?—Forget him? oh, that is impossible!—How preposterous is the thought! In spite of reason, justice, honour, everything; notwithstanding all my efforts to the contrary, every moment, every fresh trial, does but ingraft him still more firmly in my heart. Good God! where will this end? —I shudder even to contemplate the miseries that may yet be in store for me; and yet how sincerely do I pity Tiller for the sufferings to which he is so undeservedly exposed. He reproaches me not, he seems to place every confidence in my fidelity, and yet with what feelings of dark suspicion must he view me after what has happened! Alas—alas! I feel that I have been most guilty in yielding for a moment to the persuasions of Harry, and consenting to abandon my husband and to follow him in his wayward fortunes. But I must have been mad!—Reason, for the time, must have forsaken her throne, and I could not have known what I was about, or the dreadful gulf into which I was about to precipitate myself, and upon the very verge of which I stood. May God forgive me, for I feel that I have greatly sinned."

She wrung her hands in the intense agony of her feelings, and again she traversed the apartment in the most disordered manner. It was in vain that she sought for consolation. Every moment she became more restless, and the dismal forebodings that had before occupied her mind, and pressed upon her bosom like a nightmare, increased in strength the more she tried to check the power of their influence. Her head turned giddy; strange and ghastly phantoms seemed to flit before her eyes, and she sank into a chair with a sensation as if she were about to faint. For some time she remained in a kind of stupor, and was scarcely conscious as to where she was; then she suddenly started again to her feet, and gazing wildly around her, exclaimed—

"What terrible spell is this that is thus working its influence upon me?— What awful thoughts and imaginings are these that crowd upon my fevered brain?—What is about to happen, that such an insupportable dread comes over me? I feel as if I had committed some dreadful crime, and that the vengeance of offended Heaven was about to overtake me! God help me, for I scarcely know what I do!"

She pressed her hands upon her burning temples, and bitter sobs of the most uncontrollable anguish escaped her aching bosom. And yet there appeared no cause for all this violent emotion, and that rendered it even the more oppressive and painful. Although it was in the broad bright noon of day, the darkness of midnight seemed to her disordered imagination to surround her, and every trifling object upon which her eyes rested appalled her, and made her tremble. She almost feared to be alone, and yet she had not the courage to leave the house and seek the society of a neighbour, which might have served to dissipate her melancholy, lest she should betray the real feelings that so powerfully agitated her breast, and thus expose herself to the voice of scandal.

"What a weakness is this!" she said at length, making a powerful effort to arouse herself from the malady that affected her, and had so strange an influence over her intellect; "let me arouse myself, and become more firm and confident. What have I to fear? There is no one who can wish to harm me, or to add to the misery that I now endure, and, therefore, must I persevere to conquer this sickly feeling. And yet

I cannot get rid of the impression that something of a serious nature is either about to happen to me or Joe. Heaven preserve him from all danger! I wish he were at home. Nay, how childish are these fears.—What ground is there for them?—None whatever; and therefore should I laugh them to scorn. Ah, no! I may try, but still to accomplish the task I feel to be utterly impossible."

Again she became silent, and meditated deeply; but nothing could remove the extraordinary, and apparently unreasonable misgivings from her mind. And now the dreams that had haunted her imagination in the course of the night recurred to her recollection, and added to her anguish. They had been of the most torturing description, but of so complicated and mysterious a nature that she was unable to form any settled opinion upon them. At one time she had imagined that she beheld her husband struggling for life in the water, and though there were numbers of persons present, they seemed to be all paralysed and transfixed to the spot, and unable to render him the least assistance. She heard his frenzied cries for help—she beheld him sink amidst the gurgling waters—and then he rose again, and with all the desperate energy of death, redoubled his struggles to save himself. Oh, how ghastly and impressive were the mingled looks of agony, supplication, and reproach, that he fixed upon her; but although she thought she tried, and that her heart was full almost to bursting, she was unable to render him any aid, or even to attempt to induce others to do so. And now he seemed to be driven farther and farther away by the current, and in vain struggling to save himself from the awful fate which seemed inevitably to await him, until he was completely lost to her sight; but still his frantic cries for help sounded in her ears: gradually and gradually they became fainter, until they died away, and she awoke, though still she was in a state of unconsciousness.

Again she slept; once more she dreamt; and now the scene was changed, and she imagined herself on a wild and unknown coast, and struggling in the arms of a ruffian of frightful aspect and muscular proportions. In vain she shrieked to him for mercy; the more she did so, the fiercer his determination appeared to become, and the oaths to which he gave utterance were of the most appalling and disgusting description, and she had no recollection of ever having seen him before. She thought she looked despairingly around for help, but there was no one near to render her any assistance, and the wild and solemn echoes of the place alone answered her frantic shrieks for aid. The place on which they stood was a barren rock, against which the stormy ocean beat on every side; and the lightning flashed, and the thunder pealed along the sky, and the wind bellowed in terrific gusts, adding still greater horrors to the scene and the moment. Still she fought desperately with her ferocious enemy, and endeavoured to release herself from his hold, but her efforts were as powerless as those of an infant, and again and again did he pollute her lips with his odious kisses, at the same time rending the air with his hideous laughter of exultation. Gradually and gradually she imagined her strength failed her, until it became completely exhausted, and she sank insensible in the arms of the ruffian who held her. The spell of sleep was broken, and she awoke.

Once more she dreamt; and now the scene of her vision had again changed, and she supposed herself to be wandering in a strange and frightful place, which seemed to be buried deep in the bowels of the earth, and was pregnant with every horror that the most distempered imagination could possibly conjure up. It appeared to be a charnel-house of interminable extent; putrid and festering corpses obstructed her progress on every side; glassy, dead men's eyes glared upon her in the sickly and ghastly light of the place, and the atmosphere she breathed was poisonous and suffocating. She thought she tried to escape from this horrible receptacle of the dead, but the more she did so the more did she become involved in its terrors. And then how piercing cold it was. Every limb of her trembled, and it was with difficulty that she saved herself from sinking amidst the ghastly remains of frail mortality. Suddenly she thought she stumbled over a corpse, and, impelled by a powerful curiosity which she could not restrain, she stooped down and examined it more minutely. Oh, horror upon horror! she gazed upon the disfigured corpse of her husband! And what an awful spectacle did it present. How frightfully distorted were the features! The orbless eyes were half open, and seemed to glare upon her. She recoiled from it with a feeling of disgust and dread, and then she imagined that she endeavoured to call upon his name, but the words were stifled in her throat, and hollow and indistinct mutterings in the air seemed to mock her sufferings. Again she imagined that she tried to escape from the place, but her efforts were all in vain. Fresh terrors accumulated upon her at every step; the mouldering forms seemed to pursue her, and to float before her eyes. She could not shut them out. They were with her, before her at every turn. Her strength gradually left her; she found her limbs failing her, and at length she sank down among a mouldering heap, and again she awoke.

Need we attempt to describe the agony of our heroine's feelings as these terrific and mysterious dreams arose to her recollection? She trembled convulsively in every limb, and the dismal forebodings that had so long haunted and distracted her mind increased every moment. She could almost imagine that the realization of them had taken place; and for a minute or two she looked around her, and could with difficulty conceive where she was, or persuade herself that she was not actually still wandering in the awful precincts of that fearful place which we have just described,

"My God!" she ejaculated, "what can they mean?—What can they portend?—Is it possible they will ever be realized?—Is it indeed my fate to have to experience such unexampled horrors? Oh, no; it would be madness to entertain such a thought. I must at once dismiss it from my mind. But still it seems but too palpably evident that something of a dreadful nature is about to happen to me or Tiller, and I feel as though I were, in a manner of speaking, prepared for the shock, whatever it may be. Oh, Tiller, how cruel is the fate which has befallen you in becoming

united to me. It seems as though a curse attended all those with whom I have unfortunately become connected; and it would be better, far better, if I were dead. Alas—alas! little did I imagine that such a winter of despair and misery would succeed the summer and bright sunshine of my youthful days! How cheerful, how redolent of hope was everything then around me! No cares, no anxieties ever for a moment corroded my heart; I had not a wish ungratified. Harry, too! Oh, how happy was he!—What fond delight bounded at his heart as he breathed to me his vows of love, and received from my lips the pledge of my fidelity. The very face of Nature then seemed to wear a different aspect, and all was bright and smiling. Little did we anticipate the fearful change that was so soon to come over us, and to overwhelm at one fell swoop all our air-built hopes and prospects. Had we done so, we surely could not have survived the shock. Alas—alas! why did cruel and untoward fate ever tear him from me? Had he remained at home, we should now have been united, and supremely happy in each other's love. How dreadful is the contrast of the present with the past! The senses reel and totter, and threaten to leave their throne at the bare reflection. And we have seen each other for the last time. My throbbing heart convinces me that we have, and I am plunged into the very depths of the most abject despair. In vain do I seek to obtain relief in the midst of this misery. There is none for me; Fate is against me, and it is useless for me to murmur or complain, for it will but mock my sufferings, and make more painfully apparent the horrors by which I am on every side surrounded. My God! my God! this anguish of thought is more than I can bear. I am a misery to myself and all those with whom I am connected; and my heart must break beneath the heavy, the insupportable weight that presses upon it and bears me down!"

The most agonising sobs choked her further utterance, and sinking on a seat, and covering her face with her hands, she gave herself up entirely to the frenzy of her feelings; and there were moments even when she was driven to that pitch of distraction that she could have laid violent hands on herself; but Providence fortunately watched over her, and prevented her from committing the rash and fatal deed. At length she sank into a kind of lethargy, and for a time became unconscious of everything around her. It would have been well for her, and been some respite from her anguish, had she remained in this state for some time longer; but she was too soon aroused again to consciousness and thought, and then her misery assumed a still more painful character than before. She arose from her seat, and traversed the room in a state of mind that was bordering on distraction, and the most hysterical sobs escaped her bosom as though her heart would break.

"It is useless," she cried; "I cannot battle with my fate, or struggle with the fierce tempest of the feelings that hold such predominant sway in my breast, and threaten to crush me beneath their powerful influence. I shall go mad! Oh, Heaven! what have I done that I should be punished thus severely?—Do not visit me, I beseech Thee, with more than I have strength to bear. And still those dreadful forebodings! I cannot dismiss them from my brain—they haunt me like grim and grisly phantoms, and seem to point exultingly at that which I dare not contemplate. Fate has marked me for its victim, and there is no escaping from the vortex of misery into which I feel that I am plunged. Would that I could fly from myself!—Would that my agonised mind could become a chaos, and that all recollection of the past and present could vanish from my memory. But, alas! no, there is no oblivion for me, and every moment presents the horrors of my fate more vividly before my fevered and distempered imagination. Oh, Harry, what would be the bitter anguish of your soul could you but form an adequate idea of the intense and insupportable sufferings I am now enduring? But, alas! what is the torture that he himself is fated to experience? Surely, if he still loves me with the ardour that I believe he does, it must be equal to my own; and he has no friend near him to offer one word of consolation, or to sympathise with him in the cruel disappointment of his hopes. I feel that his fate, if it be possible, is even worse than my own, and my poor brain is worked up to a pitch of frenzy at the reflection. God bless him! for without His merciful aid, what, oh what will become of him?"

As these mournful lamentations escaped the unfortunate woman's bosom, the scalding tears gushed rapidly from her aching eyes, and again sinking upon a seat, and clasping her hands together in an agony of feeling that no language can possibly describe, she once more relapsed into a state of unconsciousness.

CHAPTER XVI.

JACK OARSBY ACCOMPLISHES HIS DE-SIGN.—MARY IS TREPANNED TO THE OLD TAVERN IN WESTMINSTER.— WHAT TOOK PLACE THERE.—THE TRIUMPH OF BRANDON.—THE OPIATE, AND THE REMOVAL.

THUS drearily and wretchedly to our unfortunate heroine wore away that eventful day, and she experienced but few intervals of calmness; in fact, her feelings were too powerfully wrought upon for anything easily to do away with the dismal impression that had gained such ascendancy over her reasoning faculties; and as the hours dragged their slow length along, the anxiety of her mind seemed rather to increase than diminish, and apprehensions of she knew not what harassed and distracted her brain. She might have felt somewhat relieved by society, yet had she not the resolution to leave the house, and to seek the company of the good woman who had been so kind to her during her illness. She was afraid to communicate the torturing and conflicting thoughts, and the strange forebodings that besieged her brain to any one; and thus by depriving herself of that sympathy which she would otherwise have excited, she increased her misery tenfold.

And there she sat by the parlour window, looking out upon vacancy, her hands clasped vehemently together, the tears streaming down her pale and careworn cheeks, her bosom heaving with convulsive sighs of the most bitter and poignant despair. What a fearful change had only the last few days wrought in her appearance ! those even who were intimately acquainted with her, but who had not seen her for some time, would scarcely have recognised her. Ten years seemed to have swept with lightning speed over her head; her form was bent and attenuated, her cheeks ghastly pale; her once bright and sparkling eyes now lustreless and sunken; and, in fact, she looked old, haggard, and care-worn altogether. It was indeed melancholy to behold the fearful wreck of one once so lovely and so fascinating.

And now the evening set in; and a dull, chilly, and hazy one it was, but in perfect accordance with the feelings of our hapless heroine. In fact, she took no notice of the weather, for her thoughts were too much occupied another way. It was past the usual time of Tiller leaving his employment, and now Mary became most anxious for his return home; for although she was fearful of his seeing her in the present agitated and excited state of her feelings, yet was she most anxious to behold him in safety, the more particularly when all the dreadful circumstances of her strange and mysterious visions recurred to her memory. She looked more eagerly from the window, but not a human being met her observation, and there was nothing whatever to inspire her with hope. She again arose from her seat, and paced the room backwards and forwards in a state of agitation that was almost unendurable. The time wore on; it was now more than an hour beyond the usual time of Joe's returning home, and she could not imagine what had detained him; for knowing the delicate state of her health, he had latterly been most punctual in returning home as soon as possible. Something surely must have happened to him! She shuddered at the thought; for should cruel fate deprive her of his protection, what would become of her in her present lonely and desolate situation? Several times she was half inclined to leave the cottage, and to wander forth in search of him, but something seemed to prevent her, and she again seated herself at the window, and with the most melancholy feelings looked out upon the gloom of the night. It seemed as though a storm was likely soon to gather, and, as the evening advanced, it became even more cheerless than before. Mary felt cold and nervous, and retired into an inner apartment, and taking up a book, she endeavoured to withdraw her thoughts from the melancholy that engrossed them. How fruitless was the task! she could not distinguish a letter of the page, and, throwing it aside, she once more paced the room in an agitated and bewildered manner.

"What dreadful thoughts are these that continue to rack my brain?" she said. "What fearful spell is it that is upon me? My senses seem to wander, and I know not where I am or what I do. And what is it that detains my husband? He is not wont to be so late in returning home, especially since he knows the melancholy and despair that now beset my mind. Surely something must have happened to him, or he would never tarry thus, knowing the anxiety of mind under which I must labour. Ah! my awful dream! it now rushes with tenfold force upon my memory. Should it be realised!—But no, Providence is too kind and merciful to suffer it to be so. Oh, Tiller! I fully estimate your value; I duly appreciate the uniform kindness and affection with which you have ever behaved towards me, in spite of all the anguish, and regret, and disappointment that I may evince by my conduct, and there is no sacrifice that I would not willingly make as some grateful acknowledgment for all the services that I have experienced from you. I know that I wrong you by still entertaining thoughts of Harry, but I am convinced that from your heart you can and do forgive me; for how can I ever forget one to whom I have been so fondly, so devotedly attached from my earliest days of childhood, and who has endured so much for my sake? Alas! how distressing are these thoughts! and at the same time to know, while I am surrounded by every danger and difficulty, I have no means of extricating myself. Would to Heaven that he would return! that would at least banish some of the terrible feelings that at present distract my mind, and render me one of the most wretched of human beings. It is wrong of him to tarry thus when he knows the terrible state of excitement in which I must be, and that I have no one here from whom I can seek advice or consolation. But no, I am certain that it must be something particular that has detained him, or he would not have remained so long from home as this. It is long past the hour of his leaving business, and, therefore, I know not what to think, what conclusion to arrive at."

She paused, and passing her fair hand across her forehead, she reflected deeply, but still she was quite unable to come to any satisfactory conclusion. In this manner another half-hour passed away, and still Tiller was absent, and now Mary was wrought up to such a pitch of fear and anxiety that she could scarcely contain herself. She traversed the room with still more hasty and disordered footsteps, and wrung her hands in the agony of her feelings, and her mind became so bewildered and so violently agitated, that she scarcely knew what she did. The longer she reflected, the more violently agitated she became, till at last she threw herself on a seat, and covering her face with her hands, she resigned herself entirely to despair.

She was suddenly aroused from this lethargy, however, by hearing a hasty knock at the door, and she started to her feet.

"Ah!" she exclaimed, "thank Heaven it is he!—He has come at last!—Oh, Tiller! had you but known the anxiety and suspense I have been enduring, you surely could never have tarried so long. But I will not reproach him; no—I do not marvel that, wretched and melancholy as I now am, my society should become irksome to him."

The knock was repeated, and Mary, with a trembling and faltering step, and a dread of something which she could not comprehend, approached the door and opened it, and was about to greet her husband, when the light from the lamp which she carried falling upon the person's features, she started back in amazement on beholding that it was not he, but one of Tiller's acquaintances and brother watermen on the river, the man who has been already introduced to the reader, the veritable Jack Oarsby, and the emissary of the villain, Hugh Brandon. Oarsby, without waiting to be invited, entered the room, and ad-

vancing towards our heroine with a well-assumed air of respect, he said—

"You did not expect to see me, Mrs. Tiller, I dare say; and—and I am sorry that circumstances should have compelled me to pay you this unexpected visit, but there was no one who, as the friend of your husband, was considered so well qualified, you see, to impart the painful intelligence to you, as myself, and so——"

"Speak!—speak!" interrupted our heroine, in the most breathless haste, " do not keep me in suspense, I implore you, but let me at once know the worst. What have you to communicate?"

"Do not be alarmed, Mrs. Tiller," said Oarsby, " for it may not be so bad after all, though it certainly looks very doubtful at present."

"What do you mean?" again gasped forth Mary "Why do you still hesitate? This is most torturing! Some accident has taken place, in which I am interested, I feel convinced; but let me know the worst at once."

"Your husband, Joe, poor fellow—he was well not more than an hour ago, and——"

"Well, well!" exclaimed Mary, "what dreadful meaning do your words imply?—What of him now?—Oh, tell me, tell me! or I shall go mad!"

"Why," answered Oarsby, "the worst may as well out first as last. Sam Sculler would have come to have brought you the painful intelligence, but he didn't like to leave him, so he asked me."

"For Heaven's sake!"

"Well then, Mary—Mrs. Tiller, I mean, I ax your pardon—in helping to unload a barge, the cross-chain snapped, it fell on poor Joe, and so seriously injured him, that——"

"Ah!" shrieked our heroine, turning more ghastly pale than she had been before, and sinking into a seat; "my dream! my fatal, my awful dream!—The climax of my misery has arrived!—He is dead!—he is dead!"

"No, no," replied Oarsby; " not so, he is not dead, and I hope that he will recover it, though he is very badly hurt. It was too far to remove him here, so——"

"Where is he?" interrupted Mary, in a voice of the most extreme agitation; "oh, why am I not permitted to see him when he so much requires my attention? Poor, unfortunate Joe! Oh God! whither have you removed him? —Let me fly to him!—A moment's delay, and it may be too late!"

"We took him to the Black Swan, near Millbank," answered Oarsby, "where he is under the attendance of a medical man, and, as you may suppose, most anxious to see you. But do not be excited, for it may not be so bad as it now appears to be, after all. My boat is moored just off the Hard here with Tom Feather in charge of it; so if you will just be so good as to compose yourself a bit, and will only trust to me, which I should think you can, such an old friend as I am of your husband, I will row you over to the house where he is lying in no time at all."

"Yes, yes," replied Mary, in a voice of increased emotion, "I am ready to accompany you. Oh, Joe!—my dream! Good God! how fearful are the trials to which I am subjected!"

She could say no more, for sobs choked her utterance, and covering her face with her hands, she remained for a moment or two in a state of the most indescribable agony; but suddenly arousing herself, starting to her feet, and hastily throwing on her bonnet and cloak, she exclaimed——"

"Duty to my husband calls upon me to act with energy and promptitude.—I am ready to attend you, Mr. Oarsby. Come, come, let us not delay."

The villain Oarsby could not without the greatest difficulty conceal the exultation he felt at the success of his stratagem; which far exceeded his expectations, but he stifled the expression of his feelings as well as he could, and said——"

"I am quite ready, Mrs. Tiller, and we shall soon be there; the Black Swan is not far from Millbank, and it was the most handy house we could take him to. Wrap yourself up warmly, for it is rather cold to-night. But do not alarm yourself; after all, poor Joe may not be so badly hurt as we imagine him to be. Allow me to take your arm, Mrs. Tiller."

Our heroine suffered him to do as he requested, for her brain was so bewildered and distracted that she scarcely knew what she was about; and Oarsby, having first cast a hasty glance out of the window, to ascertain whether or not there was any person coming who was likely to obstruct them, they quitted the cottage, and made their way towards the Hard. But what was the agitation of our heroine as she proceeded with her treacherous guide?—Her worst apprehensions seemed to be realised, and she gave herself up to the most absolute despair. She and Oarsby exchanged no words together as they went on their way, and in a few minutes they arrived at the Hard, where Tom Feather, another of the infamous colleagues of Hugh Brandon, was waiting with a boat to receive them. Oarsby handed her in, and taking a seat by her side, he said, addressing himself to Feather:

"Pull away with all your might, Tom, for there is not a moment to be lost. Poor Mr. Tiller! Well, well, there is no foreseeing accidents of this kind: and we poor fellows on the river are exposed to many of them. But let us hope that this one may not turn out to be quite so bad, after all. It is a dark night, so mind you do not run foul of anything, Tom. It would be rather a serious matter, I reckon, if we were to capsize. Courage, Mrs. Tiller; do not give way to despair altogether; your husband is worth a hundred dead 'uns yet, I hope. Steady, steady, Tom! All right—we shall soon be there!"

"Oh, God! oh, God!" exclaimed Mary, clasping her hands together, and unable to control her agony, "that it should ever come to this! Alas! how prophetic were my forebodings. Unfortunate Joe! there seems to be a fatality attending you. But tell me," she added, appealing to Oarsby, "you have not deceived me?"

"Deceived you, Mrs. Tiller!" replied Oarsby; "do you think that I would? you ought to know me better. I should despise myself if I could thus sport with the feelings of any one."

As Oarsby gave utterance to these words, himself and Tom Feather exchanged hasty glances with each other, which, however, were not observed by our heroine, whose anxious and painful thoughts were too deeply occupied another way, and they secretly exulted at the easy manner in which they had

MARY'S DREAM OF THE CHARNEL-HOUSE.

been enabled, so far, at any rate, to put their villanous designs into effect.

"Pardon me," said Mary, in reply to the observations of Oarsby, "pardon me, Mr. Oarsby, if I have appeared uncharitable by the remarks I just now made, but pray tell me, and do not on account of my feelings hide the truth from me—he is not dead ?"

Jack Oarsby felt momentarily con-

fused by the questions which she so eagerly put to him; but he quickly recovered, and answered—

"Well, Mrs. Tiller, I sincerely hope not, for your husband and I, as you know, are particular old friends, and I should be sorry indeed if he were to die in such a manner as that, though, to tell you the truth, he did seem to be most fearfully injured when I started to your cottage to bring the painful intelligence to you, and—"

"This terrible uncertainty is most torturing and insupportable!" interrupted Mary, again wringing her hands, and tears of the most poignant anguish starting to her eyes. "Your words convince me that I have everything to fear : and, oh, how can I express the anguish and despair of my feelings? Unfortunate husband! how fatally have the dreadful forebodings that for so many hours have occupied my mind been realised. Alas —alas! what a miserable destiny is mine!"

"Nay, Mrs. Tiller," said Oarsby, in the most hypocritical accents, "do not take on so ; it is wrong for us to question the will of Heaven, you know. But suspend your doubts and apprehensions till we arrive at the place of our destination, and I trust that all will yet turn out better than you now anticipate."

Mary attempted to speak, but sobs choked her utterance ; and covering her face with her hands, she gave herself up to all the powerful emotions that struggled in her breast, and from which she could find no relief. Jack Oarsby and his companion again exchanged significant glances with one another, which, if our heroine had noticed, must have excited her worst suspicions, and they then pulled more vigorously at their oars, anxious to reach the rendezvous with their unfortunate victim as quickly as possible.

For several minutes our heroine remained in the same state of overwhelming agony, and she pictured to herself in the most vivid and torturing colours the troubles that were in store for her, and the melancholy bereavement which, in all probability, she was about to experience. Never had she before felt so keenly the value of her husband ; and now that it seemed likely she was so soon to be deprived of him, all the numerous virtues he possessed, and the uniform attention and affection with which he had ever behaved towards her, arose more prominently to her imagination, and she could not help reproaching herself in some measure with not having returned that affection with the warmth that she should have done. And yet, under all the peculiar circumstances of her melancholy fate, surely, she thought,

she was more to be pitied than blamed. But if she was now to be deprived of him, to whom was she to look for consolation and protection? She would be alone in the world, and probably exposed to every danger, for she never expected to behold Harry again, and— but she shuddered at the thought, and endeavoured all that she could to stifle it in her breast. Her anxiety and impatience increased every moment, and at length, again looking up, she hastily demanded—

"Oh, have we much farther to proceed?"

"No, Mrs. Tiller," answered Oarsby, "we shall soon reach the shore, and then a few minutes only will serve to bring us to the old Black Swan. So keep up your spirits, and let us hope on our arrival there that poor Tiller may be found to be not so seriously injured as was expected."

"Yes," she sighed, "after what you have stated, I cannot but fear the worst. Oh, my husband! should Fate, indeed, deprive me of you, what will become of me? To whom can I look for pity or consolation?"

"As for that matter, Mrs. Tiller," remarked the deceitful villain, Oarsby, "who is there that knows you that would not willingly do all in their power to serve you? Oh, do not fear, for, no doubt, if the worst should come to the worst, that you would find plenty of friends."

"Oh, yes, there can be no doubt of that," said Feather.

"Friends!" repeated Mary, in the most melancholy accents; "oh, where can I hope to find a friend like my unfortunate husband?—But tell me, was he able to speak?"

"Yes," replied Oarsby, "and he begged that we would make you acquainted with the melancholy accident which had befallen him as quickly as possible, but to break the painful intelligence to you as gently as we could."

Mary again sobbed bitterly, but returned no answer, and once more resigned herself to the dismal thoughts that occupied her mind, and the boat proceeded rapidly on its way, though the darkness was intense, and objects could scarcely be distinguished at the shortest distance. And now the rain began to descend, and everything gave token of a stormy night, and this, of course, was not at all calculated to ameliorate the anguish of our heroine's feelings, whose brain, indeed, was distracted almost to madness.

"The elements frown despair upon me," she ejaculated, "and I read the horrors that await me in the voice of the tempest. Oh, shall we never reach the shore and arrive at the place of our destination?"

"Patience, patience, Mrs. Tiller," returned Oarsby, "we are proceeding there with all the speed we can; and you may be sure that, for your sake, we will make no more delay than possible."

Mary did not return any answer to this, and her anxiety remained unabated. And now thoughts of a different nature flashed upon her brain, and the most fearful suspicions arose to her imagination. Might not Oarsby and his companion, with some sinister motive, which it was impossible in the present agitated state of her mind to penetrate, have deceived her? She almost regretted that she had been persuaded by them to leave the cottage; and turning suddenly towards Oarsby, and looking earnestly in his face, she said—

"I have placed every confidence in the dreadful tale you have told me, and resigned myself to your care; tell me, I beseech you, have you spoken the truth?"

"Spoken the truth, Mrs. Tiller!" repeated Oarsby, assuming a look of reproach; "and is it possible that you can doubt my word, I who am such a particular friend of your husband? I must be a villain indeed if I could invent such a tale for the purpose of deceiving you, and leading you astray. Besides, what motive could I have for doing so? No, no, Mrs. Tiller, if such are your ideas, you greatly wrong Jack Oarsby, I assure you."

Mary was again deceived by the plausibility of the villain's manner, and she said—

"Pardon me, Mr. Oarsby, if I have indeed wronged you, but I am sure you will be able to make every allowance for the agitation of my feelings on so trying an occasion as this. My mind is so bewildered and distracted that I scarcely know what I say."

"Certainly, Mrs. Tiller, I can and do make every allowance for the excitement of your feelings," replied Oarsby; "but endeavour to muster up all your fortitude, and I trust that the fears which you now so naturally entertain may prove to be groundless."

"God grant that they may," cried our heroine; "but, alas! how is it possible that I can banish them entirely from my mind under such dreadful circumstances?"

"That is very true," observed Oarsby, "and I assure you that, although I have but a plain way of expressing myself, I most sincerely pity you."

"I thank you for your commiseration, Mr. Oarsby," returned Mary, "for Heaven knows how much I stand in need of it under the heavy affliction which it is my hard lot to experience. Alas! little did I think when my husband left his home this morning what was about to happen to him, and even now I can scarcely persuade myself but that it is all a frightful dream. But is he properly attended upon?"

"Oh, yes," answered Oarsby, "you may depend upon that. A surgeon was called in immediately on his being removed to the tavern, and poor old Sam Sculler was attending upon him when we left, with the same anxiety as if he had been his own father."

"And may Heaven reward him for it!" said Mary, fervently, "for already am I much indebted to him for the kindness and friendship which he has ever shown towards myself and those so dear to me."

Oarsby made no observation in reply to this, and Mary, wrapping her cloak closer around her form, in order to shield her in some measure from the storm which was now at its height, endeavoured all that she could to calm her feelings, but that was a task which it was not easy to accomplish, and she awaited with the utmost impatience and apprehension their arrival at the place of their destination, offering up the most fervent prayers to Heaven.

Never had anything appeared so tedious to her as this short passage across the Thames, and she every moment urged her companions to endeavour to quicken their speed, lest her husband should have breathed his last ere she should have the opportunity of seeing him, and of receiving his farewell and blessing. Numerous as were the trials she had experienced, none seemed so severe as the present one, and her heart was full to bursting. As for the villains, Oarsby and Feather, they continued to triumph in the successful manner in which they had managed their diabolical plot, and they had no doubt of the applause they should receive for it from Hugh Brandon. At length the boat reached the shore, and Oarsby having landed, assisted Mary to do so likewise, and Feather having hastily secured the boat, followed them. Mary trembled, and had it not been for the support of Oarsby she must have sunk to the earth. They bent their way through the most lonely and unfrequented streets, where they were not likely to encounter any one, and our heroine proceeded with them for some distance in silence, but at length she suddenly paused, and looking timidly along the dark street through which they were advancing, she said—

"What a wretched place is this! I have never been this way before, and I can't help feeling a sensation of dread to find myself in such dreary precincts. Why have you chosen this way?"

"Quiet your fears, Mrs. Tiller," said Oarsby, "for you are perfectly safe while we are with you. We have chosen this route because it is the nearest to the tavern. Come, come, let us not delay, for every moment is precious."

Mary looked earnestly in his face with an expression of suspicion, and though she could observe nothing in his manner or that of his companion to warrant her apprehensions, her heart almost misgave her.

"Should you seek to deceive me," she remarked, "a heavy curse will most assuredly pursue you."

"Ay," replied Oarsby, "and we should richly deserve it. But why are you so suspicious?—What designs do you think we can have against you?"

"I know not," returned Mary; "but I have now proceeded too far to retrace my footsteps, and must put my trust in Providence. Have we much farther to go?"

"No," said Oarsby, "a few minutes will bring us to the house, and again I tell you that you have nothing to fear."

Our heroine felt far from easy or satisfied; but still the thoughts of her husband urged her on, and she suffered them to lead her from the spot where this brief dialogue had taken place. They continued to traverse the same description of bye-streets and alleys for about a quarter of an hour longer, and they did not meet with a single individual on the way, and all was dark and dreary in the extreme. The houses, too, if such they could be called, were all of them in the most filthy and dilapidated state, and seemed to be inhabited by the very lowest of society, and the doubts and fears of Mary gained strength every moment. At length she again paused, and in a voice of anxiety she said—

"Whither are you leading me? These places look suspicious, and I am not at all satisfied with the integrity of your intentions. I will proceed no farther without an explanation."

"I am surprised to hear you talk thus, Mrs. Tiller, when we are only endeavouring to render you a service," replied Oarsby, in tones of reproach. "I tell you again that we are not seeking to deceive you, and if you are anxious to see your husband in his deplorable situation, you will not for a moment longer hesitate to repose confidence in us. Should you do so, it may be too late, and you will have painful cause to regret it."

The thought of Tiller, and that he might die before she had an opportunity of seeing him, again aroused and emboldened our heroine, and she ejaculated:

"Lead on; I will trust you, let the consequences be whatever they may. Alas! we have delayed too long already, and should he be no more, how bitterly shall I reproach myself."

It was well for Oarsby and his companion that the darkness was so intense, or Mary must have noticed the triumphant expression of their features, and even after having proceeded so far their base designs might have been frustrated; but they returned no answer to her observations, and once more proceeded on their way as fast as they could; and at length they arrived at the tavern, at the door of which they were met by the landlord, and our heroine, in a state of almost breathless excitement, hurried into the passage.

"So, you have returned, Mr. Oarsby," remarked the landlord, fixing upon him a significant look, which Mary was too much agitated to observe. "This is Mrs. Tiller, I presume?"

"Oh, yes, yes!" eagerly ejaculated our heroine; "but my husband! oh, tell me, I beseech you, and do not keep me in suspense—does he still live?"

"He does," answered the landlord, "but he is in a very dangerous state, and——"

"Where is he?" she hastily interrupted. "Oh, let me fly to him! There is not a moment to be lost!"

"Excuse me, ma'am," said the host, in a persuasive voice, "you had better endeavour to compose your feelings in some measure before you see him; for the excitement which your present agitated state might cause him would probably be productive of the most fatal consequences to him."

"No, no!" returned Mary, vehemently, "I must see him immediately. Who shall keep me from him?"

"Come, my good woman," said the landlord, "you must not be rash and obstinate in such a moment of danger as this. I will conduct you to a private room, while we carefully break the news of your arrival to your husband, and probably in a short time you will be sufficiently composed to see him without danger."

"Where is Sculler?" she eagerly demanded.

"He is attending upon his unfortunate friend," replied the landlord; "I will send him to you immediately. Come, come, let me lead you this way."

Mary, scarcely knowing what she did, suffered him to take her arm, and after conducting her up one flight of stairs, he opened a door, and ushered her into a gloomy and old-fashioned apartment, where she sunk in a chair, and became almost in a state of unconsciousness.

"Try to tranquillize your feelings," said the rascally landlord, in an assumed voice of sympathy, "and I will send your friend Sculler to you presently."

With these words he abruptly quitted the room without Mary being aware of his departure, and our unfortunate heroine was thus completely caught in the diabolical snare laid for her by the villain, Hugh Brandon. For some time after he was gone she remained in a state bordering upon insensibility; but at length she suddenly started, and looking around her in a bewildered manner, she exclaimed—

"What strange place is this?—Where am I? Alone! Ah! I remember now; my husband! they told me he was dying, and that he was in this house. Why was I, then, not permitted to see him? Oh, Tiller—Tiller! and are you indeed about to be taken from me?—Must I lose you thus? But why do I remain here, when it may be too late for me to receive his last sigh, and to crave his forgiveness for the neglect and injustice with which I too much fear I have treated him? Let me begone, and try to find him!"

She was interrupted in the midst of these observations by hearing a rude burst of laughter, which evidently proceeded from below, and she started and trembled with mingled feelings of surprise and consternation; and for a moment or two, so sudden was the shock, she could scarcely believe the evidence of her senses.

"Ah! those coarse and riotous sounds," she articulated; "is it thus that they sympathise with the sufferings of the unfortunate, and with one who has been stated to be in his last moments? What dreadful suspicions are these that arise to my mind? Some treachery is at work, and danger threatens me. Let me know the worst at once, and try to escape from it ere it may be too late."

With trembling footsteps she advanced towards the door, and to her horror and dismay she found that it was fastened, and that she was indeed a prisoner. She stood aghast, and her heart palpitated violently against her side, whilst her whole frame was convulsed with the most powerful emotion.

"Betrayed!" she cried at last; "trepanned! Oh, what black plot of villany is this?—What will now become of me? Oh, help—help!"

Frantically she endeavoured to force the door as she thus spoke, and then, worked up to a pitch of frenzy, and completely overpowered by the horror and despair of her feelings, she uttered one piercing shriek, which reverberated through the place, and sunk senseless and inanimate on the floor.

When she again recovered, she looked wildly around her, and her brain was so bewildered and distracted, that for a moment or two she had no recollection as to where she was or what had happened to her; but at length she found herself in the same room into which she had been trepanned by the villanous proprietor of this den of infamy, and looking up, she beheld a woman of the most disagreeable expression of features standing by her side. She staggered instantly to her feet, and fixing upon the woman a look in which astonishment, terror, and indignation were combined, she said—

"Ah! where am I?—who are you? and for what base and brutal purpose am I brought hither? Speak, woman, and do not keep me in a state of suspense which is too horrible, far too horrible to endure."

"You came here of your own free will," replied the woman, "and if you have suffered yourself to be trepanned, you have no one to blame but yourself. However, as you are now here, you must put up with the consequences, for you are the prisoner of those who well know how to take care of you."

"Oh, Heaven!" gasped forth our hapless heroine, and looking with a sensation of the most indescribable horror and disgust upon the woman before her; "then my worst fears and forebodings are realized. I am betrayed, and I have but too much reason to anticipate the most dreadful fate. Oh, what a monstrous outrage is this!—The whole story, then, was a wicked fabrication, and my husband——"

"Is not here," answered the woman, "nor do I know where he is."

"He, then, has not met with any accident?" said Mary, and the feelings that struggled in her breast may be easily imagined. "He still lives? Oh, tell me—tell me!"

"For aught I know to the contrary," replied the woman; and a sarcastic smile overspread her forbidding features.

"Oh, God!" groaned our heroine, and wringing her hands, "how cruelly have I been deceived, and how base must be the mind which could conceive such a brutal plot as this! But who is the guilty wretch who has thus got me in his power?"

"One who has long known you, and marked you for his victim," returned the woman.

"His name? his name?" gasped forth Mary.

"Hugh Brandon!"

"Ah! that name is associated with every vice," cried our heroine; "I shudder with the most uncontrollable horror. Wretched, wretched Mary! you are indeed lost! But let me begone!—Let me fly this den of crime! Who shall dare to detain me?"

"Hold!" cried the woman, pushing her rudely aside, and intercepting her passage to the door; "these paroxysms are of no avail here, so you may as well be calm. Hugh Brandon, the pirate, parts not so easily with those whom he has had so much trouble to obtain possession of, especially when he has revenge as well as other passions to gratify."

"Revenge!" repeated Mary, in a faint voice; "oh, what have I ever done to excite such feelings in his breast?"

"If you have not," the woman replied, "he whom you loved has—Harry Halliyard, I mean; and, as Black Brandon told him, he never forgets an injury."

"Harry Halliyard!" exclaimed Mary, and her bosom swelled with emotions almost too powerful for utterance at the mention of that beloved name; "oh, Harry! had you been near, this outrage would never have been committed; and how terribly, but justly, would you have resented the attempt."

"Becoming words these for one to utter who is the wife of another," observed the woman, with a sarcastic grin; "but you will never behold him again, or if you do, it will be under circumstances which you little expect, and which will not be likely to afford you much gratification."

"Heaven forbid!" ejaculated Mary, who perfectly understood the dark hints which the woman threw out. "But by all my hopes I will not be detained!

Let me pass; or tremble for the consequences that will descend upon your own head. Let me pass, I say!"

As she spoke, she struggled with the old woman, and made a violent effort to reach the door, but she pushed her rudely to the other end of the room, and in a savage voice she exclaimed—

"Fool! of what use, think you, is it to offer any opposition here? You are the prisoner of Brandon, and he will not fail to avail himself, you may be sure, of the advantage he has obtained. But I will leave you to him, and I have no doubt that he will speedily find out the way to tame this turbulent spirit."

"Oh, God!" again cried Mary, beating her breast, "and is there no hope for me? Tiller, Tiller! where are you? Why did you absent yourself so long from home? This would not then have happened."

"You much deceive yourself if you imagine that Brandon would ever have abandoned his designs, or have failed in the ultimate accomplishment of his wishes, even should this scheme have failed," returned the woman. "However, that is no business of mine, and I dare say that he is perfectly satisfied now that he has got you in his power. I wish you joy of the prospects that are before you, and will leave you to ruminate on them at your leisure."

"Monstrous cruelty!" ejaculated our heroine; "my heart will break under this unexpected misfortune. And is there no one who will fly to my assistance, and punish the heartless wretches who have thus mercilessly torn me from my home?"

"What chance is there of that, think you?" demanded her companion; "do you suppose that Brandon would be so silly as to convey you to any other than a place of security? Oh, it was an excellent plot to entrap you without much trouble, and I give him credit for it. No one can form the least idea in whose power you are; and before many days have elapsed you will be safe on board his gallant craft, borne far away from your native land, and compelled to yield submissively to his every will, or take the consequences; and, perhaps, I need scarcely hint to you what the consequences of incurring his vengeance would be?"

"Cruel woman!" said Mary, "if I dare call you by the name; and can you thus take a savage delight in taunting and mocking the sufferings of one who never injured you?"

"You might as well spare yourself the trouble of talking to me in this manner," she replied, "for I am perfectly insensible to any such nonsense. But I only waste my time with you, and will leave you and Brandon to settle the business between you."

"Alas—alas!" sighed Mary, and the tears streamed rapidly down her cheeks as she spoke, "and must I indeed remain a prisoner here, and leave my unfortunate husband in a state of such horrible doubt and suspense as to what has become of me."

"Oh," returned the woman, "I dare say he will soon reconcile himself to your loss; for probably he will only conclude that you have followed the footsteps of his rival, and thus consider that you are unworthy of taking any trouble to discover, or wasting a thought upon, and——"

"Dreadful thought!" hastily interrupted Mary, and every limb trembled with the power of her emotions. "Woman, forbear to give utterance to such torturing words, for they will drive me to madness. Tiller suspect me of infidelity? Oh, that can never be; his heart is too generous and noble for that. And yet, after what has taken place, has he not ample cause to do so? And what can he imagine has become of me, disappearing as I have done in so mysterious a manner? How agonizing is that reflection! Oh, woman! if you have one spark of pity remaining in your breast, you will not persevere in thus torturing one of your own sex, who is an entire stranger to you, and who cannot, therefore, ever have done you any harm either by thought or deed. Suffer me to quit this place, where I am so cruelly and unlawfully detained, and I can then even bless you, notwithstanding the cruelty of your words towards me."

"Suffer you to depart? Ha, ha, ha!" laughed the old woman, scornfully; "a very reasonable idea that, truly. And think you that I am such a fool as to run any such risk for your sake? No, no, not I; I am too much attached to

Brandon to do anything to thwart him in his wishes; and it is not likely that I would take such an interest in the fate of one who is unknown to me. Hither you have suffered yourself to be ensnared, and here you must remain until such time as Brandon thinks proper to remove you to some other place of security, which I dare say will not be long first. As for your husband and your friends, you may now consider them as dead to you, for you will never behold them again, or I am much mistaken."

"Great God of Mercy!" cried Mary, "can I patiently endure this? Oh, look down with pity upon me, and protect my husband from any danger that may threaten him, and give him strength to support this terrible misfortune with fortitude, though I am well convinced that he will never be able to do so with resignation."

Grief choked her utterance; she fixed one imploring look upon the woman; then she once more tried to speak, but could not; her brain seemed to reel, and her heart to sink within her; the most ghastly phantoms appeared to dance before her eyes, and to mock her sufferings, and with one frantic cry of despair, she sank upon the floor in a state of insensibility.

It was some time before she was restored to anything like a degree of consciousness, and then she found herself alone, with a lamp burning upon the table. It would be impossible to do adequate justice to the feelings of agony that racked her bosom, and for several minutes she could only give vent to her emotions in sobs and tears; but at length she started to her feet, and pressing her hands for a second or two upon her burning temples, she continued to gaze vacantly around her, and could scarcely believe in the dreadful reality of her situation. The apartment was a gloomy one, as has been before stated; it contained a bed and a table, and a couple of chairs, and those were the only articles of furniture. There was one window, which was secured; and going to it, she found that it looked upon a wretched rookery, which showed the character of the inhabitants, and thoroughly convinced her that there was no hope of any assistance from them, if even she had an opportunity of making them acquainted with her situation, for probably they were in some way or other connected with the wretches who infested this den, and were more likely to aid them in their nefarious and diabolical designs. She turned away with a sickening feeling of despair, and for some minutes afterwards she again resigned herself to all the anguish of her thoughts. Then she hastened to the door and tried it, but of course, as might have been expected, it was fastened, and she staggered to a seat, on which she sunk, and sobbed and wept bitterly.

"I am, then, indeed a prisoner," she soliloquised, "in this terrible haunt of infamy, and it is no idle dream. Would to Heaven that it were; but, alas! the reality is too fearful and palpable. And to be placed at the mercy of such a man as Brandon, the pirate, too; a man who is inured to every crime, and who, I have no doubt, will take a savage delight in inflicting upon me all the tortures he can invent, and in witnessing my sufferings, on account of the mortal hatred and deadly feelings of revenge that he entertains towards Harry. Oh, this is anguish most insupportable, and my strength of mind will surely sink under it. Oh, Tiller! and what must be your present despair and anguish at my disappearance, and how fruitless all your efforts to discover me. Something seems to convince me that I shall never behold you more, that we shall never meet again. And will you, indeed, believe me false to you, and that I have voluntarily abandoned you, and followed the footsteps of Harry? Alas! I fear that I have given you too much reason to do so; and yet, surely, taking all the peculiar and painful circumstances of my melancholy history into consideration, there is some excuse to be offered for me; I am more to be pitied than censured. Oh, Harry! dear Harry! for in spite of all my efforts to the contrary, I still cannot help viewing you in that character, why did cruel Fate thus frown upon our loves, when the prospects before us were once so bright and cheerful? Oh, God! how fatally were they doomed to be annihilated! Why were we ever separated? then we might have been happy. But,

THE PIRATES ON THE LOOK-OUT TO ENTRAP MARY.

alas! how vain are these lamentations and feelings of regret. There is nothing left for me but to resign myself to despair; and yet that is impossible.

She was compelled to pause, for her strength failed her, and for several minutes she remained in a complete state of apathy, and was, as it were, dead to every sense of feeling. But this did not continue long, for she quickly started again to her feet, as the horrors of her situation were depicted in more vivid colours to her imagination, and she beat her breast and sighed deeply.

The old abbey clock now struck the hour of one, and its tones came dismally to her ears, and made her start and tremble as though she had encountered some fearful apparition. She listened attentively, but all was profoundly still in the house, and it would seem as if all the inmates had retired to rest. Mary was, however, for some time afraid to do so, until at length an irresistible sensation of drowsiness came over her, and scarcely knowing what she did, she threw herself upon the bed, and sleep almost immediately held her under its influence. But her mind could not rest, that was impossible; the imagination was busy at work, and visions of the most painful nature were presented to it, the nature of which the reader will too well imagine to render it necessary to describe them. At length she awoke in a state of the greatest agitation, and she then found that it was still dark, and that she had probably not slept long. Not feeling inclined for sleep again, she arose, and endeavoured to await patiently the arrival of daylight, to see what the result of this painful event would be. But this was no easy task to accomplish, and the longer she reflected upon her situation the greater became the anguish of her feelings, and to which she could find no possible relief.

After the departure of the ruffians on their diabolical errand on this eventful evening, Hugh Brandon, as may be anticipated, waited impatiently to find what would be the result, though he had very little or no doubt as to the success of the nefarious plot, if Joe Tiller and Sculler could be prevailed upon to remain at the Crown and Crosier, for he could place every confidence in Oarsby, having tried him before; and Mary, he was satisfied, would have no suspicion of him, as she believed him to be the friend of her husband, and she would, therefore, believing the tale he would tell her, be easily persuaded to accompany him, and thus there could be but little doubt of her security. Ben Summers and Hall Guernsey he also well knew would execute their part of the business skilfully, so that altogether the villain's anticipations were most sanguine, and he secretly exulted in the prospect of revenge, and the gratification of his base wishes, that was before him.

He was seated in the usual place of rendezvous in the old tavern in Westminster, in the company of old Tapster, the host, and several of his ruffianly crew, and, in expectation of the success of his infamous schemes, was drinking freely, being fully resolved that nothing should be wanting to render his triumph complete.

"Yes," he said, "I think it is almost impossible that this stratagem can fail, and the night will place the beauteous Mary Tiller secure in the power of Hugh Brandon, the pirate, and the deadly enemy of that man to whom her affections are devoted. Oh, what gratification does that thought afford me! You have everything in readiness for her reception, have you not, Master Tapster?"

"I have," answered the latter; "and no one will ever think of looking for her here. What a state of agitation Joe Tiller will be in when he discovers that she has gone."

"Ay, poor devil" coincided Brandon, "he will indeed; and it is not at all unlikely that he will conclude she has voluntarily abandoned him, and followed the footsteps of Harry Halliyard, who, if my comrades at the old tavern at Portsmouth have not failed, is by this time safe on board the Wasp; and should he be so, I shall indeed have every opportunity of gratifying that revenge I have so long sought to the fullest extent, and I cannot help exulting at the thought of what their meeting will be. Oh, I will inflict such tortures upon him as shall harrow up his very soul to madness, and have ample vengeance for all the injuries I have received from him. He shall linger in the greatest misery that it is possible for the human mind to conceive, and what insupportable agony it will be to him to hourly witness the suffering and degradation to which his beloved Mary will be subjected."

"True, captain," observed one of the pirates, "and I only hope that you may not be disappointed. Bullruff and the others, however, must be prompt in their designs, for you know that Halliyard has entered on board the Porpoise, which is to set sail in a few days."

"True," coincided Brandon, "but leave them alone for that; I have very little fear as to the result. Mary must be conveyed to our secret haunt as quickly as possible, and from thence on board the Wasp; then, weighing anchor with no more delay than can be helped, we shall soon be far beyond the reach of danger."

"But have you formed any plan for the safe removal of Mrs. Tiller from hence?" inquired Tapster.

"Yes," answered Brandon, "that can easily be accomplished; your nephew, Bob Rudley, the waggoner, will be of the greatest service to us in this business, and I know we can depend upon him, for he is acquainted with all our secrets, and will be ready to do anything if he is only well paid for his trouble."

"Yes," said the host, "Bob is not at all particular, as you have found upon more than one occasion, eh?"

"Right, right," returned Brandon, "and, therefore, I am not afraid to trust him."

"What is it you propose, then?" demanded the landlord.

"Why," replied the villain, Brandon, "Bob will be here to-morrow night, as usual, with his waggon, I suppose?"

Tapster answered in the affirmative.

"My plan, then, is this," observed the pirate; "by means of a powerful drug, which I will contrive to have administered to her, Mary may be rendered perfectly unconscious of all that is taking place, and powerless to offer any resistance; placed in the waggon, she may then be removed to at least some distance on the road to the place of our destination, and not the least suspicion can possibly be excited. Should she recover, she will be too terrified to create any alarm, and, indeed, I will take good care to prevent her from doing that. What think you of my scheme, Tapster?"

"Why," returned the latter, "it is as good a one as you could have hit upon under the circumstances, and I do not see how it can fail to succeed. You may depend upon it that Bob will perform his part in the business to your satisfaction."

"I do not doubt it," remarked Brandon, "for I have tried him frequently before. Oh, how impatient am I for the accomplishment of my designs. Should I fail, my rage and disappointment will exceed all bounds."

"There is not much fear of that," said Tapster; "and my word for it that Oarsby and his comrade will perform their parts with their usual ability."

"I do not doubt them," replied Brandon; "but should Tiller and Sculler fail to visit the Crown and Crosier as usual this evening, it would mar everything; for it would not do to venture to seize Mary by force."

"True," coincided the landlord, "but a storm is gathering, and, therefore, Tiller and his companion are the more likely to stop at the tavern on their way home till it has abated."

"Ay," observed Brandon, glancing towards the window, "it will be a rough night, I take it, and, therefore, as you say, Tiller and Sculler are the more likely to seek a temporary shelter till the storm has in some measure abated. Come, fill your glass, we must splice the main-brace on this particular occasion. Here's success to my designs, and the Pretty Poll of Putney!"

Tapster and the other friends assembled drank the toast with much cordiality, and Brandon endeavoured to wait patiently the issue of his villanous plans.

"With such a damsel as Mary for my mate on board the Saucy Wasp," he remarked, "who might not have good reason to envy Hugh Brandon, the pirate? As for her scorn and hatred, I will not heed that, and I have no doubt that I will soon find the means of conquering or subduing it, especially when she finds that she is completely at my mercy, and that she has no other alternative but to resign herself to her fate. Oh, Harry! detested foe! should you too fall into my power, my triumph will be indeed complete. But they tarry."

"Oh, fear not," said Tapster, "they will be here anon. Hark! some one knocks."

The landlord hastily opened the door, and Summers and Guernsey, and two or three more of the pirates who had been in disguise to the tavern, entered the room. Brandon eagerly rose to meet them, and impatiently demanded:

"Ah! you have, then, at last returned? How now—what success?"

"So far as the part we had to play in the business, all that you could wish, captain," answered Summers.

"You have seen them, then?" said Brandon.

"We have," replied Summers; "we met them, as we expected, at the Crown and Crosier, insinuated ourselves into their company, secretly contrived to drug their drink, and left them both there in a state of insensibility from which it is not likely that they will quickly recover."

"Well done, my lads," observed Hugh; "you have performed your business cleverly, and if Jack Oarsby is equally successful, it will not be long before Mary will be here. Fortune seems to smile upon me, and I do not much fear the result. I triumph!—I triumph!"

"Ay," coincided Summers; "and I do not fear that Mrs. Tiller will fail to fall into the snare which is laid for her, for Oarsby will know how to perform his task, I dare say."

"Yes," returned Brandon; "and the thought of the dangerous state of her husband will urge her to comply readily with his request, and to accompany him. Ha, ha, ha! it is an excellent plot. But are you certain that Tiller and Sculler did not suspect your real character?"

"Oh, certainly they did not," replied Summers, "or they would have been sure not to have fallen into our snares so readily. They believed us to be honest, jovial fellows, and partook freely with us of the grog which we called for in such abundance."

"Ha, ha, ha!" laughed the villain, Brandon. "Poor fools! how great will be their astonishment and alarm when they are restored to their senses, and discover what has taken place. But it will be necessary, should Oarsby succeed in persuading Mary to accompany him here, to induce her to enter the house before she is made acquainted with the deception which has been practised towards her, or she might create such an alarm as would probably frustrate our plans."

"True," agreed Tapster. "Leave that part of the business to me, and no doubt I shall be able to accomplish it to your satisfaction. I will persuade her to enter the room prepared for her reception, under the pretence of breaking the news of her arrival to her husband as gently as possible, and to prevent the danger which might arise from the sudden excitement of his feelings; and when once there, she will be perfectly secure."

"Well contrived," remarked the pirate approvingly. "Would that they had arrived, for my patience is almost exhausted. Tapster, you proceed to the outer door, and watch there till you see something of them."

With this request the landlord complied, and left the room. Brandon was in a state of the greatest excitement, and paced backwards and forwards with hasty steps, at times pausing to listen, to catch any sounds that might reach his ears, and gratify his wishes. And he was not long kept in suspense, for shortly afterwards he heard the frantic voice of our heroine in the passage, inquiring in the most eager and melancholy accents for her husband, and he could scarcely contain his exultation within the bounds of reason.

"Ah!" he cried, "by all the infernal host, 'tis she! Fortune has smiled upon me, and I triumph! Ha, ha, ha! Oh, Mary! how cleverly have you been ensnared, and how little do you anticipate the fate which is in store for you! Halliyard, could you but be aware of what this night has happened to her whom you so fondly loved, how great would be the agony of your mind! Revenge!—revenge! you are now within my grasp, and by all my hopes I will not fail to avail myself of the opportunity which is afforded me to the fullest extent."

He was interrupted in the midst of these observations by the sudden entrance of Oarsby and Tom Feather, and he hastily advanced towards them and seized them by the hand.

"Ah, then, my brave lads," he cried, "you have triumphed—you have succeeded? Oh, thanks! thanks! Mary, then, is in my power?"

"She is," replied Oarsby; "and I congratulate you on your good fortune, Brandon."

"To you I am indebted for all this," said the latter; "and I know not how to reward you sufficiently for the service you have rendered me. But did you meet with any obstruction?"

"Not the least."

"And you had no difficulty in persuading her to accompany you?" demanded Brandon.

"No," replied Oarsby. "When I informed her that her husband had met with a dreadful accident, she was in a terrible state of excitement, as you may imagine."

"Ha, ha, ha!" laughed the pirate, triumphantly; "the plot was well contrived. What will be her astonishment and terror when she discovers her situation! I must see her directly, that I may exult over the success of my designs, and to convince her of what she has to expect in future."

"No, captain," observed Oarsby, "that would be imprudent at present, and might be attended with the worst consequences, so powerfully excited as her feelings must naturally be at what has taken place. It should be enough for you to know that you have her securely in your power, and you may, therefore, well reserve your final triumph to a future occasion."

"True," coincided Brandon; "but are you certain that you were not watched by any one on your way hither?"

"Oh, I am quite positive of that," answered Jack Oarsby; "we took up the most bye-streets on our landing, and the darkness of the night favoured us. Have Summers and his companions returned?"

"Yes," replied the pirate; "and they managed their business with Tiller and his old friend admirably, and left them both in a state of insensibility."

Oarsby was about to make use of some other observations, when the landlord entered the room and prevented him.

"Well, she is secure," he remarked, "though I had a hard job to persuade her to enter the room until she had seen her husband."

"Her husband! ha, ha, ha!" laughed the villain, Brandon, loudly and triumphantly; "she will never behold him again."

It was this laugh which reached the ears of the unfortunate Mary, as has been before stated, and first led her to the discovery of the fatal truth, and caused her to give utterance to such a piercing cry of terror.

"Ah!" exclaimed Brandon, "that shriek proceeds from her; she has found out that she is a prisoner, and no doubt the terror and excitement of her feelings are almost insupportable. The utmost precaution must be used, or terror may yet deprive me of my prize. Let old Nance hasten to her and see to her recovery immediately; to-morrow I will have an interview with her, and the nature of what that will be I can very well imagine."

Tapster complied with this request, and the old woman was despatched to the room in which the unfortunate Mary was confined, and Brandon sat himself down to exult over the success of his guilty designs, and to arrange fresh plans for the future. So elated was the villain at his triumph, that he resolved that night to give the most unrestrained indulgence to riot and dissipation; and the wine passed freely round, and coarse and ribald jokes were bandied from the pirates one to the other.

"To-morrow," observed Brandon, "we must contrive to administer the opiate to her, and when her senses are steeped in unconsciousness she must be removed from here in the manner I have suggested, which I have not the least doubt can be done in safety; and when I have her on board the Wasp, I may set all attempts to discover her at defiance. Should Halliyard also have been secured, I shall have the full means for the gratification of my revenge in my hands. Oh, he shall yet learn to tremble at the name of Brandon, and to sue to him for mercy! Mercy? Ha, ha, ha! what mercy can the dog expect from me?"

"Such mercy as our enemies generally receive, captain," returned Summers. "We owe him many a grudge for the pranks he has played us, and it is not likely that we shall fail to pay him, should the opportunity ever be afforded us."

"True," said Brandon; "and that it will be afforded us I have very little doubt. But, at any rate, one thing is certain, namely, that his beloved Mary is mine; and that of itself is sufficient satisfaction to me for all that I have experienced from him. Charge your glasses, my lads, and drink to the health of Pretty Poll of Putney, the future mistress of Hugh Brandon, the pirate chief!"

The ruffians immediately complied with this request, and then, raising their glasses towards their lips, they shouted in a breath—

"Pretty Poll of Putney, the future mistress of Hugh Brandon, the pirate chief!"

The most tumultuous noise followed this toast, and it was some time before it subsided, and the pirates seemed determined to carry their revelry to the fullest extent; but at length growing tired of the noise and riot that prevailed, and all the ruffians being in the most disgusting state of inebriation, Brandon having given some instructions respecting Mary, they separated for the night, and silence at last reigned in this den of crime.

CHAPTER XVII.

THE CROWN AND CROSIER.—THE PROSECUTION OF THE DESIGNS AGAINST TILLER AND SCULLER.—THE RECOVERY, RETURN HOME, AND THE FEARFUL DISCOVERY.—THE AGONY OF JOE TILLER.—HIS DESPAIR.—TERRIBLE SUSPICIONS.—ATTEMPTED SUICIDE.

ON the evening that the fatal events recorded in the previous chapter took place, Tiller and his old friend bent their steps towards home, having finished the usual business of the day. It was their custom, as has been shown, to call at the Crown and Crosier on their way home, in order to have a parting glass, but on this occasion, Joe having felt much depressed in spirits during the day, and knowing the delicate situation of his wife, he did not feel inclined to do so, and was anxious to return to his cottage as soon as he could. He knew not how it was, but the most dismal forebodings had continued to haunt his mind throughout the day; and although he exerted himself to the utmost to banish them, he could not do so, nor could all the arguments and persuasions of old Sam Sculler tend to alleviate his anxiety.

"Come, come, Joe," said the old man, "this is sheer weakness and folly; what have you to apprehend? Dismiss such idle thoughts from your mind, and try to persuade yourself that your troubles are all at an end. I know you have had much to distress you and harass your mind of late in the illness of Mary, but she is fast approaching to convalescence now, and will, I trust, in a short time be restored to her former health and spirits."

"Oh, no!" replied Joe, disconsolately, "I dare not flatter myself by encouraging any such hope; I can see too plainly the dreadful struggle she has with her feelings; and I fear that the fatal blow is struck from which she will never be able to recover. Poor girl— poor girl! is it not heartbreaking to see the melancholy change that has come over her, and to know that I have not the power to afford her any relief?"

"Well, well," returned Sam, "it certainly is a severe trial, but you must try to bear up against it, and to rely with confidence in the goodness of Providence. Should you give way to this melancholy, she will think that you inwardly reproach her for what has taken place, and that idea will be sure to render her doubly wretched."

"Oh, Heaven forbid!" ejaculated Joe, fervently; "I love her too well and too sincerely to do that, Sam; but I know not how it is, to-day my mind has been tortured by the most dismal forebodings that something of a fearful nature is about to happen; and in spite of all my efforts I cannot dissipate them."

"Nay," said his companion, "you must persevere, for I see not the least reason for such fears. But come, let us for half an hour only to the Crown and Crosier, where society, and a cheerful glass, may serve to revive you. Mary will not be uneasy at your absence, for no doubt she will seek the company of her neighbour."

"I do not feel at all disposed to go there to-night, Sam," replied Tiller, "and would much rather make the best of my way home."

"Well," remarked Sculler, "I will not seek to persuade you, if such is your wish, though, for my own part, I cannot see the least cause that you have for entertaining these fears."

The storm which had so long been threatening now commenced with much violence, and the rain in a few moments came down in torrents.

"We are close to the Crown and Crosier," observed Sculler, "and it would be folly to get wet through when we can so easily avoid it. Let us, at any rate, go there till the storm has somewhat abated."

As they were some short distance from home Joe reluctantly complied, and they hurried towards the tavern as quickly as they could. They found it, as it usually was in the evening, rather full, and they saw amongst the guests several of their old acquaintances, though there were two or three of them whom they did not remember to have seen before. Among the latter were the ruffians, Ben Summers and Hal Guernsey, who had entered into conversation with the company, and were handing the grog about freely. On seeing Tiller and Sculler enter the room they exchanged significant glances with one another, which were not observed by any one; and they made way for them very politely, so that they might get nearer the fire. It so happened that the only vacant seats in the room were at the same table where the pirates were sitting, and that circumstance favoured their designs, for Joe and his companion took their places opposite to them.

"Ah! Joe Tiller, my worthy friend, I am glad to see you," said Wallit, the landlord; "it is a good job you are here out of the storm, for the rain does come down smartly now."

"Yes," answered Joe, "and I am sorry for it, for I was anxious to get home early this evening."

"Why in such a hurry, Master Tiller?" inquired Wallit; "you cannot fare much better than you will do here, where there is good company, good grog, and a blazing fire; not bad things, I reckon, on such a night as this."

"True," said Sculler, "but Joe is so low spirited this evening that I hardly know what to do with him."

"Low spirited!" repeated Wallit; "oh, that is one of the worst complaints a man can have; you should always try to keep your spirits *up* by pouring spirits *down*, as Watchful Waxend used to say."

"Right, right, my jolly son of Bacchus," cried Ben Summers; "I admire your sentiments; there is nothing like splicing the main brace when we happen to run foul of the quicksands of trouble. But I ax your pardon, young man," he added, addressing himself to Joe; "did I not understand the skipper here to say that your name was Joe Tiller?"

"That is my name," answered the latter.

"Well, splice my timbers!" cried the pirate, "that is strange; who'd ha' thought it?—Why, Joe, my hearty, whoever expected to come in sight of your figure-head again?—Give us your flipper, my lad."

Joe looked at him with amazement, as he said—

"I am much obliged to you for your friendly greeting, but upon my word you have the advantage of me."

"Well, to be sure, hard service, and buffeting about for so many years on the stormy ocean, I dare say, have made some alteration in the appearance of my craft," remarked Summers; "but is it possible, Joe, that you do not recollect me?"

"No, I be hanged if I do," repeated Tiller.

"What, not Tom Newton, who was bred and born in this neighbourhood?"

"I can't say that I have that pleasure," said Joe.

"Well," said Summers, "I remember you as well as if I had seen you only yesterday. Why, we were schoolfellows, Joe."

"Indeed!" said Tiller; "what, did you go to school with me to old Tickletoby's?"

"To be sure I did," answered Summers.

"Well, that is strange," remarked Joe; "and yet I have not the least recollection of any boy of the name of Tom Newton. But wasn't old Tickletoby a rum 'un?"

"You may say that," agreed the pirate. "Well, splice my timbers! I am as glad to see you, Joe, as if you were my own brother. To-morrow I and my shipmate here depart for Portsmouth, in order to join our ship; and as we may never see each other again, why, we will have a jolly night of it."

"Excuse me, Mr. Newton," said Joe, "I would rather not to-night, for I do not feel very well, and I am anxious to get home."

"Avast! avast there, Joe!" said Summers. "Why, you would not shy an old shipmate like that? Besides, it's impossible for you to weigh anchor in such a gale as this. Landlord, let us have a whole cargo of grog aboard, and be quick about it."

"To be sure I will, master," said Wallit. " Now, you're what I call a sensible man, and I feel proud of your company. Come, Joe, cheer up your spirits, you'll find yourself quite another man when you come to have about a dozen glasses of my real old Jamaica into you. I'll be back in the drawing of a cork, Mr. Newton. Sam Sculler, you endeavour to arouse him, will you ?"

Notwithstanding the apparent honest manliness of the disposition of Summers, Joe Tiller could not feel exactly satisfied or easy in his company, and would gladly have declied his invitation, but the storm was still raging with so much violence that it was impossible for them to depart yet from the house, and he knew not what excuse to make.

"This place is strangely altered since I knew it a child," said Summers ; " most of the old people have gone aloft. There was one Dame Halliyard that I remember well ; but she has slipped her cable, poor soul, I take it."

"Yes," answered Sculler, "she is dead, poor old woman."

"She had a son, too, had she not ?" asked the pirate ; "Harry, I think, was his name,—what has become of him ?"

At the mention of that name a feeling of the most painful emotion agitated the breast of poor Joe, and he looked at Sculler to return an answer to the question of the interrogator.

"Why," said the old man, "you see, Harry Halliyard was for some years Joe's partner in a wherry, and he was the pride of Battersea Hard ; but he was pressed, and forced to sea ; and not long since he returned ; but—but there was nothing but trouble awaited him, and where he is gone to now I don't know, poor fellow."

"Ah, I see," remarked Summers, "crossed in love. Well, that is no uncommon thing in this life."

At this moment the landlord returned, much to the relief of Tiller, for the questions that Summers had put were torturing to him.

"There, my friend," said the landlord, placing a tray full of grog on the table ; " you will find that some of the right sort of stuff ; and if you are able to match it in London I'll forfeit my head."

"Well," replied Summers, "belay your palaver, and let us try the quality of it ourselves. Joe Tiller, my boy, take a glass, and do not be afraid of it, for damme, there is plenty more where that came from. And you, my old tar, never flinch from it ; no four-water grog this, I can see ; if it had been, I would not have placed this old brandy nosed figure-head of a gorgon in the bilboes my name is not Tom Newton, of His Majesty's ship, the Defiance ! Joe, my fine fellow, here's your health, an may our wishes for success in whateve we undertake, never be doomed to b disappointed."

" Bravo !" said Wallit, helping him self to a glass without having bee invited, " that's a capital toast, and I' drink it with all my heart. I alway like to give encouragement to business Come, Master Tiller, why are you s tardy ?"

Joe drank the toast, and he did fee the liquor revive him, for the landlor had not forgotten to bring some of th best that his house afforded, and h could not resist the apparent franknes and liberality of Summers.

"Ah !" said the latter, smacking hi lips after he had drunk, " that is some thing like grog, and you will find it th best medicine you can take for you complaint, Master Tiller. Come, do no be afraid of it, for a glass or two wil never do you any harm on such a nigh as this. I will give you another toas Here's to sweethearts and wives !"

Joe drank this toast the same as th other, and Wallit helped himself t another tumbler of the beverage.

" Now this is what I like to see," said the landlord, "for there's som sense in it ; and whenever you com from sea to Battersea, Master Newton if you have not the misfortune to b swallowed by the sharks, I hope you wil not forget to cast anchor (as you nauti cal gentlemen call it) at the Crown an Crosier,"

Summers only smiled, and then h and Guernsey seated themselves by th side of Tiller and Sculler, and engagin them in conversation, they continued t force the drink upon them until thei heads began to feel muddled and stupid

A SCENE IN THE OLD KEN AT WESTMINSTER.

As the fumes of the liquor began to ascend the spirits of Joe Tiller became much more buoyant, and he soon would have become hilarious but for the oft recurring thought of his Mary, whom he could not take a mental glance at without clouding his otherwise bright horizon with sadness and melancholy, which required the utmost tact of the two ruffianly pirates to keep at a distance. It was their fear that he would rush from their presence and seek his home before their confederates had had time to fully act on the susceptible feelings of Mary, if they did not keep him constantly engaged in either drinking toasts, or talking about seafaring exploits, some of which they had never seen, or even heard of. But as their object was to gain time, it was of little consequence to them whether what they stated was true or false, or whether it was believed to be so or not, so long as they en-

chained the unfortunate Joe Tiller's attention, and occupied his time.

"I suppose you are married, Master Tiller?" said Summers, after a brief pause. Joe was rather startled by the question, but he quickly answered in the affirmative.

"And I suppose to some trim craft or other, whom you love fondly?" said the pirate. "But you look melancholy. I hope my question has not disturbed you?"

"No, no!" returned Tiller, in a confused tone, "Heaven knows that a more amiable being than her who is unfortunately my wife it is impossible to exist."

"Unfortunately!" repeated Summers; "how so? But I see that my questions upon that subject annoy you, and I, therefore, will not press them further."

Joe became immersed in deep thought,

and Sculler was also abstracted. The landlord, too, had turned away his head for a minute or two, so that the villain Summers seized the opportunity to pour the drug which he had brought with him into their tumblers, and he then again pressed them to drink heartily, as he said they were going out into the cold, which they did, and Summers and his companion again exchanged significant looks of satisfaction with one another. In a very few minutes the opiate took an effect upon them; their heads became heavy and giddy, an irresistible feeling of drowsiness came over them, and at length their heads sunk upon the table, and they were perfectly insensible.

"Why, bless my soul!" ejaculated Wallit, "did ever you see anything more sudden than that? The liquor has certainly taken most powerful effect on them. That is all owing to my mixing my grog strong."

"Oh, I dare say they will soon sleep off the effects," remarked Summers. "But my time is up, and I must weigh anchor. Come, Hall. Remember me to them when they awake, and tell them that I was sorry I could not wait to bid them good night."

"But you surely are not going yet?" said the landlord; "the grog is not all out, and it is a pity it should be wasted."

"Oh," returned the pirate, with a sarcastic grin, "I have no doubt that you will be able to find some place to stow it away. Good night, my old tar."

With these words Summers and his companion quitted the Crown and Crosier, very well satisfied with the result of their scheme, and made their way towards the old Black Swan in Westminster, fully certain that they should meet with the thanks of Brandon, and not doubting that Oarsby would be able to accomplish his wishes, for it was not likely that Tiller and old Sam would recover for some time.

"Well," remarked Wallit, when the pirates and his other guests, with the exception of Joe and Sculler, were gone; "what a particularly nice fellow that sailor is. If all my customers were only half as liberal as him I should soon make my fortune. But how singular it is that the liquor should have taken such a sudden effect upon

Joe and Sculler. I do not suppose that they will wake in a hurry, and it is no use to disturb them. I wonder what Mary would think of her husband if she were to see him in this state! What is to be done with all this grog? Never mind; as perhaps I sha'n't have any more customers to-night, and it happens to be all paid for, I suppose I may as well try to finish it myself. It will relish a pipe of tobacco nicely; so here goes."

Thus saying, Wallit filled his pipe, drew his chair closer to the fire, and then commenced his attack upon the grog which remained with the utmost vigour and determination; till at length he was overpowered by its effects, and gradually sunk off sound asleep in his chair. How long he had remained in this condition he knew not, but when he again awoke, the fire was out, and Tiller and Sculler were in the same state as they had been before he had gone to sleep.

"Hallo!" cried Wallit; "what, not gone yet, but as insensible as ever?— It must be now past midnight, and it is time that I secured the house. I must endeavour to arouse them, or I fancy they will sleep to all eternity. My goodness! what will Mrs. Tiller say to all this? I expect that he will get a curtain lecture. As for old Sculler, he's his own master, and, therefore, will easily get over it. I cannot help thinking of that Master Newton, as he called himself, what a particularly good-natured man he was, to be sure. I only wish that he was going to stay in this neighbourhood, that's all; for such customers as he are not to be found every day. But I must arouse these sleepers. I wonder how any one can drink so greedily as to get into such a state of intoxication."

Thus saying, he shook Tiller and his companion violently, and after a short time they opened their eyes, and started in stupified amazement to their feet.

"Ah!" ejaculated Joe, staring wildly around him, "where am I?—Sculler here too!"

"Why, don't you know, Joe?" said the landlord; "you are at the Crown and Crosier, to be sure. Do you not recollect drinking with that kind-hearted schoolfellow of yours, Tom Newton?"

"Oh, foolish and imprudent that I

have been!" said Tiller, striking his forehead. "What is now the time?"

"Why, past midnight," replied the landlord.

"Past midnight!" repeated Joe, "and I still away from home! What will be the anguish of Mary at my unaccountable absence?—And how can I excuse myself? The cursed drink! never did I before so commit myself. Oh, Sculler, we have been much to blame.'

"Nay, Joe," replied the old man, "do not excite yourself in this manner. It is unfortunate, but who could foresee what was about to happen? However, it cannot be helped; and fear not, for no harm has befallen Mary."

"Alas!" returned Joe, "how know we that? I cannot forget the dreadful misgivings that beset me all day. Oh, why did you persuade me to come here? —What can I possibly say to Mary?— Dare I reveal to her the disgusting truth? Oh, I am heartily ashamed of myself."

"You reproach yourself too severely," said Sculler. "But come, let us away."

"I dread to return home," remarked Tiller, "for my heart forebodes that something of a terrible nature has happened to my wife during the time I have been away."

"Nay," observed the old man, "this is ridiculous; what can have happened to her? You have no cause to fear that any danger threatened her."

"Would to Heaven that I had never met with those men," said Joe.

"Oh, indeed!" remarked Wallit; "then I must say that I only wish I could meet with them every day, for I fancy that I should soon then be able to retire. But do not alarm yourself, Master Tiller, though I have no doubt that you will have a bit of a curtain lecture, for you are not the first man, you know, who has been a little top-heavy through taking rather too much of my excellent old Jamaica.'

"Idiot!" said Joe, impatiently; "I regret that ever I entered your house. But, come, Sculler, for every moment that we delay may be fraught with danger."

They now hurried from the house, and as they did so a neighbouring clock struck the hour of one.

"Idiot!" repeated the landlord, when they were gone; "humph! rather harsh language, methinks, Master Tiller. But it's excusable; when the liquor's in the wit's out. What a rating he will get from his wife, no doubt, when he gets home; and all through my excellent old Jamaica. But it's time that I closed the house, and retired for the night."

Having thus spoken, he fastened all the doors: and after drinking the remainder of a glass of grog which was standing on the table, he retired to rest.

Tiller and Sculler hastily proceeded on their way towards the cottage, and the nearer they advanced towards it the more did the fears and forebodings of Joe increase, and he dreaded, yet was anxious to know the worst. How cruel it was, he reflected, to leave Mary so long alone, and in the present delicate state of her health. The shock might prove too much for her strength to endure. And in what manner would she be able to account for his absence? She would be inclined to conclude that he had, in all probability, met with some accident; and he could not but anticipate the nature of her feelings on such an occasion. And could he dare venture to explain himself?—to divulge the truth? Oh, no, that was impossible: for how disgusted would she be to hear it.

As they proceeded on their way old Sam Sculler in vain tried to compose his feelings; he had no patience to listen to him, and his apprehensions every moment became stronger.

"There is no excuse which I can offer," he said, "which can possibly expiate my conduct; and I can anticipate nothing but Mary's bitterest reproaches should I ever, indeed, behold her again, which something tells me I shall not."

"What madness is it to talk thus!" said Sculler; "what think you has become of her? As for what has occurred, you will be able to invent some excuse for it."

"And would you have me impose upon her with a falsehood?" demanded Joe, fixing upon him a look of mingled surprise and reproach; "fie, old man; I did not think you were capable of throwing out such a suggestion."

"Well, well," returned Sam, "it is uselesss to argue thus, while all is uncertain. Calm your feelings for the present, and you will, in all probability, find that your fears are groundless. I am, however, at a perfect loss to account for the stupor which so suddenly came over us; and certainly I do not think it was owing to any extraordinary quantity we drank, though I am ready to admit that we had more than our usual allowance."

"There is some mystery in this which I fear that time alone can solve," said Tiller. "My heart forebodes some treachery, and I dread, yet am I so anxious to reach my cottage."

"Treachery!" repeated Sculler; "from whom have you to fear anything of the kind? But this is a mere idle speculation, and unworthy of a second thought. Come, Joe, let us hasten on our way, for the sooner we get rid of these doubts and apprehensions, and quiet the fears of poor Mary, the better."

Joe returned no answer, but it was quite evident from his looks and his demeanour altogether that his excitement rather increased than abated; and although old Sam tried his best to conceal it, his misgivings and apprehensions were almost equal to those of his companion. The strange stupefaction which had come over himself and Joe he could not account for, and in spite of the apparent frankness and cordiality of the two persons whom they had met with at the tavern, especially the so-called Tom Newton, his suspicions were in some degree excited as to their real characters; though, as they were entire strangers to them, at any rate, as they never remembered to have seen them before, he could not imagine what sinister design they could have against them, and he almost upbraided himself for having suffered such strange and apparently unfounded doubts to enter his mind. Notwithstanding, however, he could not but regret, after what had occurred, that he had been the means of persuading Joe to stop at the Crown and Crosier, especially when his own inclination was so much opposed to it.

Such were the thoughts which occupied the minds of both Joe Tiller and old Sam Sculler, as they hastily proceeded on their way; and the former, more particularly, evinced the extreme

agitation under which he laboured, and for which, taking all the peculiar circumstances into consideration, there seemed to be at present so much reason. He had never before been so late from home, and what could Mary think of him? he reflected. Would she not consider him cruel and neglectful, ill and lonely as she was? He felt himself thoroughly degraded by his conduct, and dreaded to meet her, knowing how richly he merited her censure and reproaches.

He and Sculler continued to hurry on their way with breathless haste, and when they came to the entrance of the short lane which led to the little hamlet in which they resided, they were compelled to pause, in order in some measure to try to compose themselves, and to prepare for the worst which it was too probable awaited them.

"Oh, Sculler!" observed Joe, "this is one of the most painful and embarrassing events which ever has happened to me, and I know not how to combat it. You may deem me weak and irresolute, but I feel quite unmanned, and am thoroughly ashamed of myself. I feel like one who has committed some great crime, and tremble to meet the consequences that are attendant upon it."

"Arouse yourself, Joe," said the old man; "you surprise me by the extreme nervousness and self-condemnation you betray. Believe me, the apprehensions that you entertain will not be realised, and we shall be able to come to a satisfactory explanation of the whole unpleasant affair with your wife. She is not blind to truth and reason, and will agree that this accident was quite unexpected and unpremeditated on your part."

"I would fain think so, knowing her generous and unsuspicious nature, but I cannot," answered Tiller; "nay, more, I blush to acknowledge to her the truth; for what excuse is there for drunkenness and dissipation? Oh, it is a sad job!"

"I admit that it is," returned his companion; "but still it has not occurred through wilfulness, and you, therefore, reproach yourself too severely. Come, come, take courage, and depend upon it this slight storm will quickly blow over. Let us not delay here, for that is only adding to the evil, and increasing the painful suspense which at present agitates your bosom."

Joe was again unable to return any answer, and Sam, taking his arm, led him from the spot, and they advanced along the lane. And soon they arrived at the end of it, and within sight of the little cottage in which Joe and our heroine resided. Eagerly they cast their eyes towards it, but it was buried in profound darkness, and not a sound disturbed the dismal silence which reigned around. Everything seemed to forebode evil, and poor old Sam Sculler could not help feeling a sensation of dread stealing over him, and he knew not what to say or what to think.

"My heart sinks within me," said Joe, in a low voice. "all is darkness and gloom within the cottage, and this death-like stillness——"

"Nay," interrupted Sculler, "these forebodings are unreasonable, Joe; remember the lateness of the hour; Mary has, in all probability, tired with watching, fallen off to sleep; and her neighbours, no doubt, have retired to rest some hours since."

"Ah, no!" returned Joe, "it is impossible that anxiety and doubt at the uncertainty of the cause of my unusual absence could have suffered her to rest. There is something more fearful in this than you seem to anticipate. I fear to ascertain the truth."

"This is only adding to your misery," remarked his companion; "better at once to know the truth than to remain in such a torturing state of suspense."

He now urged Tiller forward, and they looked anxiously in at the parlour window, the blind of which was up, and the shutters unfastened, but all was dark and silent, and it would seem that that room, at any rate, was entirely deserted.

"Mary, dear Mary!" cried Joe, in an agitated voice; but no answer was returned, and he beat his breast in despair.

"She hears me not!" he exclaimed; "she is not here! Oh, God!"

"Patience, patience," said Sculler; "she is probably up stairs. Let us knock at the door, and that will, probably, arouse her."

They did so, but still no answer was returned, and the agitation of Joe then exceeded all bounds.

"The cottage is either deserted," he said, "or she is dead. Oh, Mary! and I have been the guilty cause of all this!"

"Be firm," remonstrated Sculler, whose fears were, in fact, as great as those of his companion. "Have you not a key of the door?"

"No," answered Joe, "I never carry one, for I have hitherto been so regular in my time of returning home that the poor girl would always sit up to let me in, except when she was unable to leave her bed through illness, and then, you know, I had always a kind neighbour in attendance upon her. Something dreadful has happened, I feel convinced of it, and I shudder to be convinced of the truth."

Sculler again knocked, more loudly than before, but all remained perfectly silent, and they both stood and gazed at each other for a moment or two in stupified amazement and apprehension. At length a sudden thought struck the old man to try the door, and to their astonishhment and alarm it opened; Mary, in the confusion and excitement of her mind when she had so abruptly and unexpectedly quitted the cottage, having neglected to secure it after her. A cry of terror and anguish escaped Joe on perceiving this, and had it not been for the support of Sculler's arm he must have fallen to the earth.

"Good God!" he exclaimed, "what is the meaning of this? The door unfastened at this time in the morning! My worst fears are realised!—something dreadful has happened! She is either dead, or is not here. Mary—beloved Mary! and I have been the accursed cause of all this! Oh, what a wretch I am! Oh, Sculler, what will now become of me? I shall go mad!"

"Courage, courage," said the old man; "after all it may not be so bad as you anticipate. Mary may only have fallen asleep up stairs, and thus have neglected to fasten the door. Let us search the cottage. Here is a lamp, and here are matches."

He hastily struck a light, Joe, in the meantime, overpowered by his feelings, having sunk in a chair, and his brain so bewildered that he scarcely knew what he was about. They looked eagerly around the parlour, but there was nothing unusual in its appearance, and the book which our heroine had attempted to peruse was lying on the table. They searched the back parlour, but she was not there, and then they hurried to the rooms up stairs, which they found equally deserted, and poor Joe covered his face with his hands and groaned aloud, while the anguish and alarm of Sculler were almost equal to his own.

"God of Heaven!" cried Joe, with a burst of the most indescribable and almost uncontrollable agony, "my misery is complete!—My horrible surmises are confirmed! She is not here!—She is far from me, and I am wretched and accursed for ever! Mary—dear Mary! unfortunate, deeply injured girl! where art thou?—What fiends in human shape have done this?"

He beat his breast and tore his hair in the wild paroxysm of his feelings, and poor old Sculler was so completely astounded and bewildered that for a few minutes he knew not what to say or do. It was quite evident that something dreadful had happened, or Mary would not have been away and left the cottage unsecured; but what the nature of it was he could not imagine, and he was perfectly at a loss how to endeavour to console Joe, or what advice to offer him.

"My cursed neglect and mad infatuation have alone brought about this awful event," groaned Tiller, striking his forehead with the utmost despair; "and I am justly but severely punished. Oh, Mary! how totally unworthy of thee have I proved myself to be! Alarmed at my absence, the poor girl has probably gone forth in search of me, and in the excitement and distraction of her feelings has forgotten to fasten the door. She has fallen into the power of some villains, and I shall never behold her again. Oh, what torture is this! frenzy will certainly seize upon my brain, for this is more, much more than I can endure. It is, indeed, a most mysterious and melancholy affair," said Sculler; "but still, after all, it may not be so bad as it now seems to be. Endeavour to muster up all your fortitude and energy, and to put your trust in the Almighty, who surely will protect one so good and

innocent from the dangers which you apprehend."

"Ah, what madness is it to talk thus!" cried poor Tiller, impatiently, and in accents of the wildest and most insupportable despair; "what is there to abate the horror of my feelings, or to inspire me with hope? Does not everything reveal to me the full extent of my misery?—Is she not gone?—Am I not deserted? And yet you would have me be calm, and bear so dreadful a trial as this with what you are pleased to call fortitude and stoical indifference. Oh, it is a bitter mockery to endeavour to reason with me thus! Sculler, if you are sincerely my friend you will forbear, and rather bid me despair."

"Pardon me, Joe," said the old man; "you greatly wrong me if you think that I mock you, or treat this deplorable event with indifference. Heaven forbid that I should do so. But I would have you struggle against the severe trial with which it has pleased the Almighty to visit you. Come, come, my poor fellow, you must not give way thus. Amiable Mary, whom I regard as fondly as if she were my own daughter, what agony would it cost me should anything fatal have befallen her! But we waste time in useless lamentations, which should be devoted to searching for her. Probably, on finding that you did not return, she has sought the cottage of one of the neighbours, and——"

"Wild and extravagant idea!" hastily interrupted Tiller, again striking his forehead in the frenzy and excitement of his feelings; "think you that she would thus abandon her home? No, she would rather have summoned them here to advise and console her. I am distracted by the terrible and conflicting thoughts that crowd upon my brain, and I know not what to do."

"At any rate," observed Sculler, "we had better make immediate inquiries among the neighbours, and they may be enabled to give us some information respecting her. Come, there is no time to be lost."

"They have all retired to rest," said Joe, "and shall we disturb them at such an hour as this?"

"Oh," answered the old man, "they must be very unfeeling to complain of it. But I am certain that they will all of them be ready to render us any assistance in their power under such painful circumstances. Come."

"Alas!" sighed Tiller, " what hope is there?—None. I see plainly that I have incurred the wrath of Heaven, and that Mary is lost to me for ever."

" Nay, talk not thus, for it is arraigning the mercy and justice of the Supreme to do so," remarked Sculler. " We shall yet be able to discover her, and I trust that Heaven has protected her from all danger. Let us hasten, for to be kept in this horrible state of doubt and suspense is more torturing than all."

" Do with me as you like," ejaculated poor Tiller, in the most melancholy accents, "for I care little what now becomes of me. Oh, Mary! and did I ever think it would come to this?"

The old man took his arm, and he suffered himself to be led from the room, almost unconscious of what he was doing. They quitted the cottage, and hastened to that of the nearest neighbour, the good woman who had so kindly attended upon Mary in her illness, and at the door of which Sculler knocked loudly, whilst Joe leant against the gate in the most desponding and pitiable condition. It was not until the old man had repeated the knock several times that it seemed to arouse the inmates, they consisting of the old woman and her son. But at length a light appeared in the room up stairs, and presently afterwards the casement was opened, and the young man putting his head out inquired who was there, and what they wanted.

"For God's sake open the door, William," said the old waterman.

"Ah! is that you, Mr. Sculler?" asked the young man, " and at this hour of the morning ?— What is the matter ?"

" Oh, something has happened which drives me to madness!" ejaculated Joe; " my——"

"You there, too, Master Tiller?" interrupted William. "Dear, dear, what can have taken place? I will arouse mother, and admit you directly."

With these words he retired from the window, and Sculler and his companion were left in the most painful suspense and agitation.

" It is evident that she is not here," said the former, in a tone of despair.

"Alas, alas! what horror is in store for me ?"

" Be calm," said Sculler; " they may still be able to give us some information respecting her."

Two or three minutes elapsed, when the door was opened, and the old woman and her son made their appearance, and Joe and his companion hastily entered the cottage.

"Bless my soul!" exclaimed the old woman, staring at them with astonishment, " what can have brought you here at this hour of the morning ?"

"My wife! my poor Mary!" gasped forth Tiller, and he staggered to a seat, and stared eagerly and anxiously upon her, without being able at the moment to articulate another word.

" What of her, poor thing?" inquired Mrs. Bromley, hastily; " I hope she is not taken worse? How pale and agitated you look, Joe."

" We were unavoidably detained till a late hour," answered Sculler, and on our return to the cottage we found that the door was unfastened, and that Mrs. Tiller was not there, so we thought—"

" Not there !" repeated the old woman, interrupting him, and with a look of surprise; "gracious me !"

"Have you seen nothing of her?" impatiently inquired Sculler.

"Nothing whatever since the afternoon," replied Mrs. Bromley; "and as she then appeared very melancholy, and expressed a wish to be alone, I left her. Dear me, dear me, how you surprise me! Poor woman, where can she have gone."

"And you heard no disturbance near her cottage? eagerly demanded Sculler.

" Not the least," was the reply.

" Ah !" exclaimed Joe, suddenly starting to his feet, and his whole frame violently convulsed with emotion, " a terrible thought flashes upon my brain! Worked up to a pitch of frenzy by the disappointment of her hopes and the departure of Halliyard, she has committed self-destruction !"

"Hold, Tiller!" remonstrated the old man; " banish so dreadful an idea from your mind. Mary rush unbidden into the presence of her Maker ? Oh, it is impossible !"

"She is lost to me for ever!" groaned the wretched man; " I shall never behold her again ! But I will not survive this awful affliction! What is life now to me but a hateful burthen? Mary is taken from me, and——"

"Forbear!" interrupted Sam Sculler, solemnly; "you wrong her by such cruel suppositions, and hereafter, in your calmer moments, you will bitterly reproach yourself for it. Mary desert you? Oh, that thought is monstrous!"

"And have I not reason to suspect her, after what occurred between her and Harry?" demanded Tiller. "Oh, I could weep like a child! What can afford any relief to my tortured soul?"

"Reliance on Heaven, which never entirely deserts those who put their trust in it," returned Sculler.

"You say right, Master Sculler," agreed Mrs. Bromley. "Come, come, Joe, you must not take on in this manner. To be sure it is a terrible thing, but you must endeavour to exert all your energy, and who knows what may happen to restore you to peace? Poor Mr. Tiller! dear, dear, how astonished and grieved I am! Whatever can be the cause of her mysterious disappearance? But this is a waste of time. You must endeavour to find her out, if there is a probability of so doing, and God will prosper you in your efforts."

"You talk to me in vain," replied the unhappy man. "Whither am I to go in search of her?—What is to guide my footsteps? She is, doubtless, far away by this time, and I can never hope to behold her again! God of Heaven! this trial is too severe, and is surely past all human endurance. I must have been a guilty wretch, or this would never have happened to me. I am accursed of God and man! Why did Fate ever ordain that we should meet if such were to be the sufferings to which we were to be exposed?"

The expression of his eye was wild as he gave utterance to these melancholy words, and the most convulsive sobs escaped his bosom, which excited the deepest commiseration in the breasts of those who heard them.

"Tiller," said his friend, at last, "you reproach yourself too severely. You have not been to blame, and well am I convinced that Mary has nothing to upbraid you with, even if it were not opposed to her gentle nature. But come, let us not delay going in search of her; and gloomy though the prospect before us appears to be, something may yet occur sooner than you expect to guide us to her, and we may find that she has escaped from every harm."

"No, no!" returned Tiller, impatiently, "that is utterly impossible, and it would be little short of madness to entertain any such an idea. How can I but imagine the worst under such dreadful circumstances? Would to Heaven that I were dead, for I see but too plainly that there is no future happiness for me in this world! Mary has abandoned me, and——"

"Hold!" interrupted Sculler; "do not wrong her by such a cruel supposition. Mary is too good, too pure to entertain a thought to your dishonour. But this mystery must be solved, if there is at all a possibility of doing so. Come, my unfortunate friend, let us away in search of her, and perhaps, before the daylight dawns, which it will soon do, success may crown our efforts."

"Ay," observed Mrs. Bromley; "and I'm sure that no one can more sincerely hope that it may do so than myself. Poor Mary! hers is a life of trouble, and most fervently do I pity her. My son shall accompany you, if you think proper, for you might, perhaps, require his assistance."

"Thank you, Mrs. Bromley," replied Sculler; "we will accept your offer, for we might probably find his assistance valuable to us."

"Alas!" said Tiller, rising, "whither can we direct our footsteps? The errand we go upon is a hopeless one, and I see but too plainly that nothing but disappointment awaits us."

"Say not so," returned Sculler. "And shall we remain inactive, and abandon ourselves entirely to despair, when the painful occasion demands the full exercise of all our energies? Come, come, Providence will direct us."

"I will comply with your request," said Tiller, disconsolately, "for it matters now little what becomes of me. Mary!—Mary! thou art lost to me, and I feel myself a wretch more fit to perish than to live."

He sighed deeply as he thus spoke, and Sculler taking him by the arm, led

THE MEETING BETWEEN MARY AND JACK OARSLEY.

him from the cottage, followed by William Bromley.

"Poor fellow!" said the old woman, when they were gone, "this is a severe trial for him, and I do not wonder at the poignant anguish he betrays. Unfortunate Mary! what can have become of you? I fear that the worst has happened to her, though I tried to conceal my apprehensions from her husband. Hers is an unfortunate fate, and no luck has attended her since Harry Halliyard was pressed and went to sea. Had she and Joe never have been united, they might all now have been happy. But they were neither of them to blame; they were not to foresee what was about to happen, and I pity them from my very heart. Joe has been a good husband to her, and she has ever performed the duties of a wife towards him, I am convinced, though her heart is still as fondly devoted to Harry as ever, there can be no doubt. Poor things! poor things! ah, well-a-day!"

With these words the old woman seated herself, and mused deeply upon all that had taken place.

In the meantime Tiller and his two companions made their way to the several cottages in the vicinity, the inmates of which they aroused, and having acquainted them with the unfortunate circumstance that had taken place, they made the strictest inquiries after our hapless heroine; but, as may be expected, they could obtain not the least information which might direct them in their search, though every one expressed their astonishment at what had occurred, and their deep anxiety as to the fate which had befallen Mary, and which was shrouded in so much mystery. Poor Joe! what were now his feelings? They baffled all description, and he excited the sympathy of all who saw him. He raved in the most frantic manner, and again and again he cursed the severity of his fate, and Sam Sculler found it utterly impossible to pacify him; in fact, the old man's feelings were almost as much excited as his own. Again they returned to the cottage, to see whether they could discover anything which was at all likely to throw a light upon this torturing mystery, but they saw nothing whatever to assist them in their search. But Joe now saw that the bonnet and cloak of Mary were gone, and a fearful and maddening thought flashed upon his brain.

"Ah!" he cried, "this is enough to convince me that her departure has been voluntary, and that she has abandoned me. Oh, Mary! cruel, cruel girl! and art thou, indeed, false to me?—thou for whom I would have willingly laid down my very life! Oh, is not this enough to drive me to madness?"

"No, no, Tiller," remonstrated Sculler, "you wrong her, indeed you do; I am convinced you wrong her by such a cruel thought. Mary act so base and deceitful a part! it is impossible. This only confirms me in the belief that, alarmed at your absence, she has gone in search of you, and——"

"And," hastily interrupted Joe, "is not that very idea calculated to excite the most torturing apprehensions in my breast? Should she, indeed, have gone in search of me, had not some terrible accident befallen her, would she not have returned ere this? In whichever way I direct my thoughts I see nothing but despair before me. I shall go distracted! for this terrible uncertainty is enough to crush the stoutest heart!"

He covered his face with his hands, and groaned aloud in the intense agony of his overwhelming emotions. Then again the idea occurred to him that she had committed suicide, and he started to his feet, and in the wildest accents he exclaimed—

"Ah! it is too true; everything convinces me that it is; the disappointment of her hopes, and the disappearance of him on whom alone her heart's fondest affections are fixed, has driven her to frenzy and despair, and she has terminated that existence which so long has become hateful to her. And I have been the indirect cause of this, for had I never have consented to become her husband she might now have been happy, and the wife of him to whom her heart has from the earliest days of childhood been devoted. Fool that I was not to foresee this! I shall never behold her again, unless it be to gaze upon her ghastly corpse."

"Oh, Tiller!" remonstrated his friend "why will you give way to such horrible thoughts as these? Mary could never be guilty of so rash and awful an act as that which you have mentioned, nor have you any cause to reproach her for her conduct towards you since she has been your wife."

"And yet," continued the wretched man, apparently taking no notice of the observations of Sculler, "Heaven knows how fondly I have loved her, and how constantly it has been my study to contribute to her happiness. I knew that her heart was not mine, and I never reproached her with it; but this proves how thoroughly hateful I must have been to her, and makes me look upon myself as a poor degraded wretch, who——"

"Hold, Tiller!" interrupted the old man; "I am shocked to hear you talk thus. Why will you give way to feelings of such excessive grief and despair?"

"And have I not ample reason to do so?" hastily demanded Tiller. "Think you that I can view this dreadful calamity, this awful bereavement, with cold indifference? Bah! I must, indeed, be less than man if I could."

"Arouse yourself from this state of despair!" ejaculated Sculler, "you will behold your wife again, no doubt; she will be restored to your arms, and everything will be explained to your satisfaction."

"Oh, never! never!" cried Tiller. "you seek to buoy me up with false hopes, but I dare not, will not encourage them."

"I am surprised at your want of manly fortitude, Joe," remarked the old man, "even severe as the trial is. Is this the way to discover Mary, by sitting here and giving vent to useless lamentations? See, it is now daylight, and we must renew our search. The inhabitants of the neighbourhood will now be stirring, and from some of them we may obtain all the information we require. Probably, exhausted by fatigue and anxiety, she may have sought shelter in the dwelling of one of them, especially if she should have happened to have gone forth in the storm."

"Oh, no, no!" ejaculated Joe, despairingly. "Such an idea as that which you have just expressed is most improbable, for if she had done so they would have been sure to have sent to my cottage before this to see whether I had returned, and to make me acquainted with her safety. Our search will be fruitless, and whither can we direct our steps? She has gone—she has abandoned me for ever! and perhaps—oh, maddening thought! she has ascertained where Hailiyard is, and, reckless of the misery and despair which it would cost me, has hastened to throw herself in his arms."

"Oh, how cruel and unjust is this!" said Sculler. "Can you believe that Mary could ever act so base a part? You could never have loved her as you profess to have done if you can. Will nothing arouse you, when every moment which we delay is so precious, and may be fraught with danger? Let us away, and my word for it, if we persevere, we shall be successful."

"Well, well," answered Tiller, in a melancholy voice, "do with me as you will; it is now a matter of indifference to me whither I go, or what becomes of me."

Sculler took his arm, without making any reply, and they once more quitted the cottage; but the old man was equally at a loss which way to proceed; and although he had endeavoured to inspire Tiller with hope, he entertained the most dismal doubts and fears himself. They took the way, however, which led to the Crown and Crosier, and on the road they met with several persons whom they knew, whom they made acquainted with what had happened; but they could gain not the least information; no one had seen anything of Mary, and the agitation and despair of Tiller increased. As we have before stated, our heroine was universally respected by all who knew her, and her disappearance in so mysterious a manner caused the deepest sympathy, and every person expressed their willingness to assist them in the search, and endeavoured to impart some degree of consolation to poor Tiller, but with not the least success. At length they reached the Crown and Crosier, at the door of which they saw the landlord standing, and he greeted them in his usual manner.

"But," he continued, "you are up early, after that little affair of last night, and which I should have thought would have caused you to sleep as sound as tops. A rare fellow that Master Newton; capital sort! I wish he was going to visit me again to-day. Now, I shouldn't wonder but that you have come here this morning with an idea of seeing him, and getting a sort of reviver; very necessary after a——"

"Fool!" interrupted Tiller, passionately.

"Fool!" repeated the astonished Wallit. "Not very complimentary, I must say. What's in the wind now eh?"

"Cease, Master Wallit," said Sculler; "we are in no humour to listen to such nonsense as this now. Something has happened which has filled us with anguish and alarm."

"Indeed!" said Wallit. "Well, Master Tiller certainly does look pale and excited, but I thought it might only be the effects of—— no matter. I will say no more about that, since it seems to be disagreeable to you. What is the matter, pray?"

Sculler briefly informed him.

"God bless me!" he ejaculated; "poor Mrs. Tiller disappeared? *Non est inventus*, as Watchful Waxend would say, if he were here. Well, that is a bad job—at least, I suppose Master Tiller thinks so, though I am not quite certain that I should be of the same opinion if I should happen to lose my old woman. Lost, stolen, or strayed, I take it, as they——"

"Insolent, unfeeling brute!" cried Tiller, fiercely, grasping him by the collar, and shaking him violently.

"Oh—oh—oh!" gasped the terrified Wallit, struggling to release himself; "I—I—I say, Master Tiller, I did not wish to ——now—oh—oh—you do not mean to throttle me, surely?"

"Let go your hold, Joe," said Sculler, "and calm yourself. Wallit did not mean to offend you, I dare say; though he should be a little more cautious in his language."

"Offend him!" repeated Wallit; "no, that I am sure I did not, for I am very sorry for him. Come, Joe, have a glass of brandy, and that may serve to relieve you."

"Oh, God!" groaned Tiller, taking no heed of what the landlord said, but throwing himself disconsolately into a seat when they had entered the house; oh, God! what a dreadful trial is this! my senses can never withstand the shock, and would to Heaven that I could become unconscious of all that has happened. Oh, Mary!—Mary!"

"Poor fellow!" said the landlord; "this is, indeed, a melancholy affair for him; but," he added, speaking to Sculler, "have you no idea where Mrs. Tiller is gone, or how, or whether she has been forced away clan*decently* like?"

"Not the least," answered Sculler. "We found the door unfastened, but everything in the cottage as usual. None of her neighbours saw her after the afternoon, nor did they hear any disturbance."

"Well, that is certainly very strange," said the landlord; "I do not know what to think of it; though it certainly appears to me that she must have been forced away against her will."

"And who is there that could have been guilty of so atrocious an act?" said Sculler. "It seems more probable to me that, finding her husband remained from home so unusually long, she had been induced at last to come forth in search of him, thinking——"

"And if she did," interrupted Joe, in an agitated voice, "some accident, surely, must have befallen her. Curses on my folly in coming here at all when my mind was tormented, and had been throughout the day, with so many dismal forebodings."

"Why, as for that matter," remarked the worthy host, "you might have been in many worse places out of the storm than the Crown and Crosier, and especially when you were in such pleasant company as that of your old schoolfellow, Master Newton, and his friend."

"D—n them!" cried Tiller, passionately.

"Nay," remonstrated Wallit, "you should not damn them, Master Joe; you ought rather to blame my extra strong old Jamaica, which certainly had a most wonderful effect on you, for I never saw two men drop off so suddenly in my life. Had your drink been drugged it would scarcely have beat you more quickly."

"Well," observed Sculler, "as you say, friend Wallit, the insensibility which came over us was certainly most strange and sudden, and had we not known you, and that you are incapable of anything of the sort, we might have felt disposed to suspect that you had done something wrong to your liquor, for the purpose of detaining us in your house."

"Not a bit of it, Master Sculler," returned the landlord; "I should despise myself if I could be guilty of any such untradesmanlike action. All fair and above-board with me, unless it is by accident that I happen to have a glass or so too much, and then, you know, if my customers will have me chalk it up, like all other drunken men I am apt to see double."

"Well," said Sculler, "enough of this folly. Did you hear or see anything in the course of the night, or rather morning, after we left your house, to excite your alarm or suspicion?"

"God bless you! no," replied the landlord. "I slept as sound as that fellow they call Bacchus, in a cask of wine. It is a bad job, a very bad job, and I wish it was in my power to render you any assistance, I'm sure I would most willingly do so."

"Do you know anything of those men who were here last night, and who made themselves so familiar with us?" hastily demanded Tiller.

"God bless your soul, no!" answered the landlord; "only that one of them, at least, Master Newton, I mean, your schoolfellow, you know, Joe, is the pleasantest, and the generousest, and the best-heartedest chap as ever I met with, and that his score came to one pound thirteen shillings and fourpence half-penny, upon which, as I like to do the thing as is honourable, I merely satisfied myself by taking a barely living profit. I never remember to have seen them before, but I should be most happy to see them again every day and every hour in the week for the next twelvemonths to come, for they are the sort of men who do my heart, and, by-the-bye, my pocket good, to be in the company of."

"What can make you inquire so particularly about them, Joe?" asked Sculler.

"I have my reasons for doing so," returned Tiller, quickly. "I have my suspicions that they are not the characters they represent themselves to be."

"Suspicions!" repeated Sculler, with a look of surprise; "what mean you?"

"No matter," answered Joe. "I wish I could see them again. I have no recollection of the man who called himself Tom Newton, in that character, but it strikes me that I have seen him before, under different circumstances."

"How? where?" demanded the old man.

"Some years since, in this very neighbourhood. Should my surmises be correct—oh, Mary!—oh, my brain!"

"I do not understand you; explain yourself," said Sculler.

"Oh," replied Joe, "it tortures me to the very soul to do so! Of course you must remember that fatal and eventful day when Halliyard was pressed, and torn away from his home?"

"Ah, well," returned the old man;

"is it possible that I can ever forget it? He and Mary performed for me a noble act of generosity that saved me from a prison. Poor Harry!"

"And that act excited the deadly revenge of the fellow they called Black Brandon," continued Tiller, "and no doubt led to what followed, namely, the impressment of Harry Halliyard."

"Ay, poor fellow! I have too much reason to believe so," said Sculler. "But what then?"

"Why," answered Joe, "one of the ruffians who accompanied Brandon on that occasion very much resembled this man who now calls himself Newton; and should he be the fellow, we have been ensnared, betrayed, and—oh, God! my brain turns giddy at the thought!"

"I am afraid, Master Tiller," observed the landlord, "that your brain has not exactly recovered itself from the effects of my exta strong old Jamaica of last night. That liberal-hearted tar, who spent his money so freely in my house, and didn't care a rush what he paid, the associate and friend of pirates, and all other such rascals? Oh, it is impossible! it is a libel upon honesty to imagine such a thing."

"Hold your nonsense, friend Wallit," said Sculler, "for this is not the time or the occasion for its indulgence. Joe, you must be mistaken, depend upon it you are."

"Oh, no," said Joe, "I feel quite convinced that I am not. The longer I reflect upon his conduct the more do my suspicions increase. Oh, what a blind fool have I been! and I am now justly, though terribly punished for my imprudence. Some vile plot has been at work to entrap Mary, and I shall never behold her again. May eternal curses light upon those who have done this!"

"Be calm, Joe, be calm," expostulated Sculler, "and all will yet be well."

"Ay, so I say, Master Sculler," remarked old Wallit; "it is no use dropping down on one's luck altogether, for that only makes matters worse. But what course do you mean to adopt which is likely to lead to the discovery of Mrs. Tiller?"

"Ask me not!" answered Joe, impatiently, "for I am mad—distracted! Oh, Mary!"

"Pardon me," said the landlord, "for what I am about to take the liberty of suggesting, but had you not better make the magistrate acquainted with all that has happened, and he will, no doubt, take every means to institute a search after her?"

"Ay," replied Sculler, "a good suggestion, Wallit, and I am obliged to you for it; this mystery must be unravelled, and that, too, without delay. Come, Tiller, arouse yourself, and Mary will yet be delivered, I hope and trust, and restored to you uninjured."

"Oh, no!" sighed Joe, "I dare not encourage such a hope; it would be madness for me to do so. Mary is lost to me for ever, and life is now a curse and a misery to me. Some villain has got her in his power for purposes which I shudder to think on, or else she has deceived me, and——"

"Forbear, Tiller!" interrupted the old man; "judge her not so harshly, for well am I convinced that, by doing so you do her the greatest and most cruel injustice. Mary deceive and abandon you? Oh, bethink yourself, and you must be satisfied of the fallacy of your suspicions. Wait patiently, and a short time will, I hope, solve this painful mystery, and remove the anxiety which at present so naturally tortures your mind."

"Wait patiently!" repeated Tiller, bitterly; "oh, how easy is it to talk thus! But it is all a mockery, and I know that you cannot, do not believe in what you say. Whither can we direct our inquiries?—What chance is there of our discovering her?"

"By attending promptly to the suggestion of our friend Wallit," answered Sculler, "and making the proper authorities quickly acquainted with what has taken place. By vigilant measures Mary may soon be discovered—at least, what has become of her may quickly be ascertained. Come, Joe, let us immediately depart to the office of the magistrate, and in the meantime do not abandon yourself entirely to despair."

Tiller was about to make some reply, when he was prevented from doing so by the entrance of some other person, who seemed rather startled and confused on beholding him and Sculler. This individual was no other than the villain, Jack Oarsby, whom Joe believed to be his friend, and who had taken such an active and prominent part in the abduction of Mary. He at once observed the dreadful state of excitement under which Tiller laboured, but which, of course, surprised him not; and he secretly exulted at the success which had attended his nefarious and diabolical schemes. He, however, disguised his real feelings with his usual skill, and advancing in a friendly manner towards the unfortunate man, he said—

"Why Joe, my friend, and you, my worthy Sam Sculler, who would have thought of meeting with you so early at the Crown and Crosier? What's up? —But, eh! you look ill and dejected, Tiller, and——"

"Alas—alas!" interrupted the latter, with a sigh, "I am wretched, distracted, Oarsby!"

"Ah!" ejaculated the villain, with affected surprise and concern: "why, what is the matter?"

"I can scarcely find courage to tell you," answered Joe; "but my wife, my poor Mary!"

"And what of her?" inquired Oarsby; "she is well, I hope?"

"She is gone—torn from me, or abandoned me," groaned Tiller.

"Gone! repeated the hypocrite, with well-affected astonishment and incredulity, "I do not understand you. Are you serious?"

"Alas—alas!" returned Tiller, in the most dismal accents.

"Perhaps you can explain this, Sam," observed Oarsby, "for, indeed, I am most anxious to know."

"Unquestionably," returned the old man. "What poor Joe has said is too true; we were detained here last night until an unusually late hour, in consequence of the storm, and on our return to the cottage we found that Mrs. Tiller was not there, nor have we since been able to gain any intelligence of her."

"This is most strange," said Oarsby; "you astonish me. But now I come to recollect myself, I met Mary yesterday evening about six o'clock, going in the direction of the Hard, and having a small bundle with her."

"Ah!" cried the distracted Joe,

starting to his feet, "this all but confirms my worst suspicions. She has deserted me; the false, the heartless! Oh, Mary, that——"

"Softly, softly, Tiller," interrupted old Sculler; "condemn her not rashly, for you may—you must be deceived. Oh, I can never believe that Mary can have been thus guilty. It would be monstrous and uncharitable to do so.— But are you sure that you were not mistaken, Oarsby?"

"Oh, no," replied the latter, "it is impossible that I could have been so. It was quite light, and I had every opportunity of distinguishing her features."

"But did you speak to her?" hastily demanded Sculler.

"I did," answered Oarsby, "but she seemed to be in great haste and much agitated. She returned me some sort of an answer which I did not understand, and then hurried on her way, and I quickly lost sight of her."

Poor Joe struck his forehead in despair, and groaned aloud in the agony of his feelings; and Sam Sculler was so thunderstruck and bewildered by this unexpected intelligence that he knew not what to think.

"The wretch!" exclaimed Tiller, with a burst of emotion which was pitiable to behold; "there can no longer be any doubt as to the fatal and disgusting truth—the extent of my misery and my dishonour! And have I, indeed, lived to see this day? She has deserted me, and followed the footsteps of Halliyard! Oh, monstrous thought! May curses light upon her, and——"

"Forbear, Tiller!" again interrupted the old man. "Give not utterance to such awful words as these, for, after all, she may be innocent. I do believe her so, and never can I alter that opinion until I have the most satisfactory proof to the contrary."

"Well," remarked Oarsby, "I am sorry that anything I have said should agitate Joe thus; but I thought, after what you had told me, that it was no more than my duty to inform you of what I had seen. But do not take on so, Tiller, for, after all, everything may be explained to your satisfaction, and your wife may be exonerated from all blame, or any criminal intention."

"Oh, no, no!" replied Joe, "I am already satisfied. Where is she now? She has heartlessly deceived me, and probably, at the present time, she is exulting in the misery she has inflicted on me. Oh, God! that I should ever live to experience such degradation as this!"

He could no longer restrain the full expression of his agonizing feelings, and hysterical sobs choked his further utterance, while old Sam Sculler, who was lost in doubt and amazement, knew not what to say to console him.

"I am sorry for you, Tiller," observed the villain Oarsby, who gloried in the misery and anguish of the unfortunate man, and inwardly congratulated himself on the skill with which he had conducted the diabolical business entrusted to his hands; "I am sorry for you, my friend, and only hope that things may not turn out so bad as you expect. But did not your wife leave you any note to apprise you of the business she was gone upon?"

"Ah, no," answered Tiller, "she had not even the humanity to do that. May my heaviest curses pursue her wherever she goes!"

"Say not so," said Oarsby, "for, after all, she may not be so guilty as you imagine. But I must be going, for I have some particular business to attend to. Good bye, Joe, good bye, Sculler; I sincerely hope that your doubts and anxiety will soon be brought to a termination. As for my own part, I will do all in my power to assist you in your endeavours to discover her, which, I firmly hope, will be crowned with success."

"Thanks, Jack," said Sculler, grasping his hand; "for you are an honest, kind-hearted fellow, and I am well aware of the friendship you have always entertained towards poor Joe."

"You do me no more than justice by entertaining that opinion of me, Master Sculler," said the hypocrite; "and if I can do anything to serve him, especially in his present trouble, I'm sure he is most heartily welcome to it. Good morning."

Having thus spoken, Jack Oarsby departed, and when he had got outside the tavern, and was proceeding on his way, he could not help laughing aloud and in exultation at the misery which he had just witnessed, and in which he had pretended so deeply to sympathise.

"The poor fools!" he muttered to himself; "how cleverly and completely have I deceived them. Ha, ha, ha! And they believe me to be a very paragon of honour and Christian humanity. Behold your wife again, Joe Tiller?—oh, no; if you flatter yourself with any such an idea you will be most wofully disappointed. In a few days she will be safe on board the pirate craft, and have fallen a victim to the passions of Hugh Brandon. I shall pocket a rich reward for my share in the business; and that I have succeeded in my designs affords me the more gratification seeing that I have always in secret entertained a feeling of hatred and jealousy towards Tiller, who has ever been my most successful rival on the river. He little suspects with whom I am connected, or what I have done to ruin his hopes and prospects, or how different would be the feelings that he would entertain towards me. However, I have destroyed his happiness for ever, and I am satisfied. I shouldn't wonder if the poor devil were to commit suicide, at the loss of his pretty Polly, for he believes her false to him, and that will be quite sufficient to drive him to despair. How will Hugh Brandon exult when I inform him of what I have witnessed this morning! Ben Summers and Guernsey also performed their business well, for had they not kept Joe and Sculler in tow at the tavern it would have been almost impossible for me to accomplish my purpose. But I must away to the rendezvous, and make Brandon acquainted with all that has taken place."

With these words the hardened and heartless scoundrel hurried on his way; and we will now return to the wretched and unfortunate Tiller. After the departure of Oarsby, he remained for some time in the most deplorable condition, and Sculler in vain tried to console him. The statement of Oarsby confirmed his worst conjectures, and drove him almost mad, and he lamented the severity of his fate in the most melancholy accents. Then he cursed the treachery of Mary, whom he could not but believe had found out the place where Harry Halliyard was, and, forgetting the solemn vows she had plighted with his at the altar, had flown to his arms, and that he should never behold her again.

"Behold her again!" he repeated, wildly; "no, Heaven forbid that she should ever again cross my path, the wanton—the deceiver! The sight of her would be odious and disgusting to me, and in the fury of my wrath I might be tempted to strike her dead at my feet."

"Oh, Joe!" said Sculler, shocked and sincerely grieved at the violence of the unhappy man's manner; "what horrible words are these? You cannot know what you say; bethink yourself; remember, she is your wife, and——"

"My wife?" fiercely interrupted Tiller; "perish the thought! She has abandoned all claim to that sacred title, and henceforth I can only think of her with loathing. Oh, that I should have suffered myself to be so deceived, and to be laughed and mocked at by one whom I had cherished with such unbounded affection, and for whom I would willingly have laid down my life to have rendered happy. But I have been a weak fool, and I am justly punished for my credulity."

"Be more calm, Joe," said his friend; "for of what use is it giving way to these wild paroxysms of grief and despair? My life on it that you will still find her innocent. I cannot believe to the contrary."

"Innocent!" repeated Tiller, with a satirical and unnatural laugh; "oh, what a cruel mockery is it to talk to me thus! I must be worse than an idiot to believe that she is otherwise than the most abandoned of women.—Woman! by Heaven it is a libel upon the sex to call her by that name. What proof is there wanting of her guilt? Is not the statement of Oarsby damning evidence against her?"

"Nay," observed the old man, "you should not place too much confidence in that statement, for it is not at all improbable that he might have been mistaken."

"Mistaken!" said Tiller; "no, no, no! that is impossible, so well as he knows her. Besides, did he not speak to her? Oh, everything is too terribly clear, and confirms the fatal and disgusting truth of my dishonour. Could

BRANDON AND HIS ASSOCIATES IN THE SMUGGLERS' RETREAT.

the poor old woman who was the means of our being united return to life, would she not curse her and her son? Halliyard, he whom I believed to be my warmest friend, he is the guilty author of all this —he is the tempter! Oh, Harry! little did I imagine that you could ever have been guilty of such black-hearted villany; and may the curse of God pursue you for it!"

"Tiller," said his companion, "you wrong the noble-minded youth by entertaining such cruel suspicions against him. Think of what cruel Fate has ordained that he should suffer, and surely, rather than unjustly condemn him, you must pity him. Has he not gone no one knows whither, though probably to sea again, and——"

"No," interrupted Joe, hastily, "I

will not believe it. He has been concealed somewhere until he should have an opportunity of communicating with Mary, and she has now gone to join him and resign herself entirely to his guilty will. Oh, it is in vain that you try to flatter me with any false hopes. She has brought disgrace and misery upon me, and there is no punishment that can overtake her and her guilty paramour which can be too severe for them."

"Do not judge too rashly, Tiller," remonstrated Sculler; "for even though suspicion may appear strong against your unfortunate wife, a short time, perhaps only a few hours, may prove her entire innocence, and then how bitterly must you reproach yourself for having entertained such fearful thoughts to her prejudice."

"Yes," interposed Wallit, "I always like to have full proof, like my spirits, before I condemn any one; though, to be sure, if it is true what Master Oarsby has stated, it does look *rayther* suspicious, to say the least of it. Where could Mrs. Tiller be going in such a hurry, and with a bundle too? And then——"

"Hold! officious fool!" interrupted Joe, sternly; "who asked you for your opinion? and if you study your bones you will not presume to offer it."

"Well, well, Master Tiller," said the landlord, "you need not put yourself in such a passion, and make use of such abusive language, for I'm sure I meant no harm. As for my opinion——"

"It is not wanted," said Sculler, "and, therefore, I beg that you will not force it. I believe you are a good-meaning sort of a man enough; but this is no business of yours, and you must make every allowance for the excitement of poor Joe's feelings on this painful occasion."

"Oh, certainly, I can and do," remarked Wallit; "and I only hope that he may soon be restored to peace of mind, that is all the harm I wish him."

"Thank you," said Sculler, "and pray Heaven that he may be so. But come, Tiller, we do but waste the time here which should be devoted to the prosecution of our inquiries. Let us begone, and God grant that success may crown our efforts."

"No," replied Tiller, disconsolately,

"it is all useless, for the truth is too apparent. She has fled to the arms of another, and will never venture to cross my path again. Should she have the boldness to do so, I will not be answerable for the consequences. Oh, God! how the thought of the baseness with which she has acted towards me, when I believed her to be all goodness and purity, maddens me! May her guilty conscience haunt her like a phantom wherever she goes, and blast all her hopes of happiness."

"Tiller," said the old man, "your language shocks me, and I never thought you capable of judging any one, especially your own wife, so uncharitably as you now do. Poor Mary! how sincerely do I pity her, for I feel well convinced in my own mind that she is perfectly innocent of the base crime of which you suspect her, and that she is rather the victim of some unfortunate accident; and so also, I have no doubt, you will believe, when reason has resumed its sway in your present excited brain, and you can reflect calmly and dispassionately upon all the painful and mysterious circumstances."

"By Heaven, never!" ejaculated the unhappy man. "Too long have I suffered myself to be deceived, but it is over now, the veil is drawn from before my eyes, and I see plainly the wretched tool that I have been made, and I hate and despise myself! But let her go, abandoned and guilty one as she is; and, if she can, while basking in the smiles of her seducer, exult in the misery of him whom she has so heartlessly dishonoured. I will not seek her out—I will not try to—Oh, Heaven! how my very heart bleeds when I think of the cruel fate which has befallen me, and which surely I have never deserved! Mary——"

He could not finish the sentence, for the power of his emotions choked his utterance, and covering his face with his hands, he wept like a child. Sculler was deeply affected, and even old Wallit, albeit he was not accustomed to the melting mood, was moved to pity.

"Come, Tiller," said the old man, at length, "do not thus give way to such excessive grief and distracting thoughts. Fate, it is true, frowns upon you at present, but there are happy days in store for you yet, take my word for it; and when you will be able to bury the gloomy past in oblivion, or to think of it only as a painful dream."

"Oh, never, never!" returned Tiller, with a look of the utmost desair. "The blow is struck which renders me a wretched being for ever! Oh, little did I once think that this would ever be the fate of poor Joe Tiller! I will not honour her with one pang of regret! Henceforth the recollection of her must be as poison to my heart; and her very name must fall odiously and disgustingly upon my ears, for with it is coupled everything that is base and treacherous."

"Ah, no!" said Sculler; "again I tell you how much you wrong her by such a supposition. But the words you have expressed, I am satisfied, do not spring from your heart, and ere long you will regret ever having made use of them."

"Regret!" repeated Joe; "why should I do so? for is not her abandoned conduct deserving of all that I can say or think? Sculler, you must think me mad, if you suppose that I am any longer to be deceived, when all the disgusting facts are placed so clearly before me. The statement of Oarsby is more than sufficient to convince me; and think you that I will not believe one whom I have known as a friend for so many years? What motive could he have for attempting to deceive me? Oh, the more I think of it, the more torturing does it become!"

"All attempt at argument or persuasion for the present, I see, is completely useless," said Sculler; "but I fervently trust that your fears will not be realised. However, it is folly to remain here when so important a duty calls us forth. Come, Tiller, we will talk further upon this painful subject another time; we must now to the magistrate, and procure his assistance to discover the unfortunate Mary."

Tiller looked wildly up at the old man for a moment or two without being able to speak a word, and from the expression of his features it was quite evident that his mind wandered. But at length he said——

"Do with me as you please, for I now care not what becomes of me. Were you to lead me to death it would be no more than performing an act of mercy towards me, for it would release me from those troubles that have now become insupportable to me."

"Psha!" ejaculated the old man; "you surprise me, Tiller; have your firmness and resolution entirely deserted you? Courage, courage, man, and all will yet terminate far more happily than you can now anticipate."

"Still do you seek to buoy me up with false hopes, Sculler," returned Joe; "but you might as well spare yourself the trouble, for they can make no impression on me. The full extent of the misery that is in store for me is fully revealed to my eyes, and I shrink not from it, since all my hopes are annihilated, and all that I valued on earth has proved herself to be a worthless and abandoned woman. Oh, Mary! surely your guilty conscience must, sooner or later, most terribly upbraid you for the heart you have broken. Lead on, my friend, my only sincere and valued friend on earth, for I am ready to accompany you."

Sculler took his arm without saying another word, and bowing to Wallit, he led him from the tavern, followed by William Bromley, who had been a silent, but a deeply affected spectator of all that had passed.

"Poor fellow!" said the landlord, looking after them; "he is in a terrible way, sure enough; quite mad—mad as a March hare, and I do not wonder at it, for the disappearance of his wife certainly looks rather suspicious, to say the least of it, and the statement of Oarsby goes to prove that it is caused by no accident that she has done so. Well, who would have thought that Pretty Poll of Putney would ever have turned out such a character? I only wish my wife would follow her example, I should not take the trouble to advertise after her, I'll warrant. But no, she is not such a fool as that, worse luck. Heigho! What a sensation this circumstance will cause in the neighbourhood! As for poor Joe Tiller, he may say 'Farewell my trim-built wherry,' now. We shall have a crowner's 'quest before long, I shouldn't wonder. Oh, these women, these women! they are the very devil, and that's all about it. But this is a very dry subject, so I think it would be advisable to wet it. Poor Joe Tiller!"

Having thus delivered himself, the worthy landlord mixed himself a strong glass of grog, which he sat down to enjoy with his accustomed relish.

The news of the mysterious disappearance of our unfortunate heroine spread like wildfire, and caused the greatest sensation; and although there were some malicious persons who did not hesitate to give it as their opinion that she had eloped with some gay gallant or other, the majority attributed her disappearance to no voluntary act of her own, but had not the least doubt that she had fallen a victim to some foul conspiracy; and they deeply sympathised with poor Joe Tiller, for they were convinced that he had ever proved a kind and affectionate husband, and he was esteemed by all who knew him. No one, however, could furnish the least intelligence of her, excepting Oarsby, and there were many who placed not the least reliance upon what he had stated.

After wandering about the whole of the day to no purpose, Joe and Sculler, weary, exhausted, and disappointed, returned to the cottage, the former in such a state of mind that it was dangerous to leave him for a moment, and the old man tried all the powers of argument and persuasion he had at his command to pacify him, but with little or no success. How wretched, deserted, and lonely did that cottage appear, which had once been the abode of peace, if not of happiness. Poor old Sculler could not help sighing as these thoughts occurred to his mind, and his anxiety for the fate of Mary increased every moment. His eyes wandered to a portrait of Mary which hung from one portion of the room; and so faithful was the likeness that he could almost have imagined that the fair but unfortunate original was standing before him. It had been painted in her happiest days, and a beauteous smile played around her lips, which seemed to speak of the innocence and happiness of the soul within. Tiller, who had been buried in deep thought, suddenly raised his head, and saw the object on which his attention was fixed, and starting hastily to his feet, in wild accents of despair he exclaimed—

"Ah! it is her portrait! and oh, how like her when she was good and innocent, and deceit was unknown to her heart. And how I loved her then; nay, I worshipped her, and never thought that I should have such bitter cause to change my sentiments towards her. Oh, how altered is she now! Where is that purity of soul which once endeared her to all who knew her? Base, false, and treacherous, she has sunk beneath the level of the most degraded beings. Away with this resemblance of one who has abandoned me to misery and despair, and flown to the arms of some more favoured rival! I cannot gaze upon it; my fevered blood rushes to my brain as I do so. Let me remove it for ever from my sight, or thus destroy it!"

As the wretched man gave utterance to these wild exclamations he snatched up a knife which happened to be lying on the table, and rushing up to the portrait, he would immediately have destroyed it, had not old Sculler grasped him by the arm and arrested him in his mad intent.

"Hold, Tiller!" he exclaimed. "What is it you would do? Are you mad?"

"Mad! mad!" repeated Joe, glaring at him wildly; "yes, I am, and can you wonder at it? Think you that I am more than man, that I can tamely endure the foul injustice which I have received at the hands of the abandoned wretch whom this painting represents? By Heaven, I will not! Oh, may the heaviest curses that can descend upon the head of the guilty pursue her!"

"Horrible!" ejaculated the old man. "Oh, Tiller! it makes me shudder to hear you, and I can scarcely believe that it is you who are standing before me. For Heaven's sake, give not way to these wild paroxysms, but endeavour to be calm."

"Calm!" repeated Joe, with a painful look; "oh, how easy it is for you to preach to me thus! Calm, when I think of my cruel wrongs, so undeserved? My brain's on fire! Oh, that she were now before me, that I might thunder my curses in her ears, and wreak my deadliest vengeance on her guilty head!"

"Forber! forbear!" again remonstrated Sculler, shocked at the wild and frenzied observations his unhappy friend made use of; "such language as this I thought you could never have made use of. Why yield yourself entirely to such frantic emotions, and thus close your ears altogether to the voice of reason? Ah, Joe! how cruelly do you wrong poor Mary by thus severely judging and condemning her. Satisfied I am that her soul would recoil in horror and disgust from the guilt of which you so unjustly suspect her, and that her sudden and mysterious disappearance has been caused by some dark scheme of villany, which I sincerely hope will yet be detected and frustrated, and your wife restored uninjured to your arms."

"Ah, no!" returned Joe, striking his forehead with increased emotion; "that cannot, will not be! I must be a perfect idiot did I not believe that this is her own voluntary act, and that she has long contemplated it. Did she not consent to abandon me and follow the fortunes of Halliyard, notwithstanding the solemn vows she has plighted with mine at the altar? She did, and yet you seek to exonerate her from all blame, and to hold her up as a very paragon of virtue and rectitude. Psha! such a mockery of reason as this is more than human patience can endure. Sculler, if you are sincerely my friend you will no longer seek to delude me by any such fallacious ideas."

"I speak to you only as reason and my own conscientious feelings dictate to me, Tiller," replied the old man. "Heaven forbid that I should judge the unfortunate Mary to be the base and abandoned woman you seem to suspect her to be; for well do I know the cruel injustice I should do her if I did so. Nor can I believe that the words which you have suffered to escape you spring from your heart, but that when the natural tempest of your excited feelings has somewhat calmed down, and reason has assumed its sway, that you will, you must admit how little she deserves the cruel reproaches that you have heaped upon her, and you will most probably regret ever having given expression to them."

"No, no!" cried Joe, passionately; "nothing whatever can alter the opinion I have formed, and the longer I reflect on it the more thoroughly am I convinced that I am correct. Oh, how basely have I been deceived, duped, cajoled! and

now, no doubt, she laughs and mocks at me for my blind credulity. And this is the return I meet with for the unbounded love I ever lavished upon her! Oh, it is monstrous! And not even to condescend to leave me a single line in explanation in deserting me! But I have deserved it all for having been the weak fool to trust her, and to believe her true, and good, and virtuous. Oh, God! what torment, what dreadful, what excruciating torment is this to endure! And yet you would persuade me to bear patiently with it all—not to murmur—to forgive her, and basely to submit to the misery and dishonour which she has brought upon me. Oh, it is most reasonable, truly, to expect any such conduct from me!"

"Tiller," said his companion, in half-reproachful accents, though, at the same time, it was quite evident how sincerely he sympathised with him in his misfortunes, and how glad he would have been to be able to impart to his heavily-afflicted bosom some consolation and hope; "Tiller," he repeated, "do you doubt the sincerity and fervour of my motives? I have known you from a child—I have ever regarded you as my own son, and Heaven knows that there is nothing whatever in my humble power which I would not do to serve you and contribute to your happiness. Do you then believe that I mock you in your misfortunes, or that I seek to inspire you with ideas that I do not entertain myself? No, I should hate and despise myself if I thought that I could thus act the part of the hypocrite, and should, indeed, be unworthy of your friendship or your confidence if I could do so. This is, I own, a most severe trial for you; but exert all your energies, all your fortitude to bear up against it, and depend upon it that Providence will not desert you, that the innocence of Mary will be established beyond a doubt, and that she will, ere long, be restored to you, free from all those dangers which you have now so much reason to apprehend have befallen her."

"Alas, alas!" groaned Tiller, "when I view all the dreadful circumstances, how can I think so?—How dare I indulge in any such sanguine and, I fear, delusive expectations! My mind is racked and tortured to madness! What a terrible change has but a few short hours worked in my very nature! I do not feel to be the same individual! Strange and fearful ideas flash upon my brain, and urge me on to that which at the same time I shudder to think upon! Mary! oh, Mary! cruel, ungrateful woman! what a wretched, lonely being have you made of him whose whole, whose fondest affections were devoted to thee, and who would have thought no sacrifice too great to have rendered thee happy. But it is all over now, thou hast struck the blow which has rendered me hateful and miserable to myself for ever!"

He threw himself in a chair as he thus expressed the anguish of his feelings, and burying his face in his hands, he wept and sobbed like a child. Old Sculler was much moved to witness his sufferings, and he knew not what to say to comfort and tranquillize him. He could not but admit the heaviness of his affliction; but to admit that Mary was really false to him, he could not do so even for an instant, although he was unable to form the least conjecture as to the cause of her singular disappearance, and the longer he sought to do so the more did he become involved in mystery.

"Come, Joe, my poor friend," he at last remarked, advancing towards him, and placing his hand upon his shoulder, "do not thus unman yourself, but endeavour to arouse yourself into firmness and confidence. Retire to rest for a few hours, and that will——"

"Rest! rest!" he wildly interrupted, and again starting hastily to his feet; "oh, what madness it is to talk thus! What rest, think you, can there possibly be for a poor heart-broken wretch like me? Oh, I shall never rest again! Let me forth and wander, and try to hide myself from mortal eye—from myself! I cannot endure this!—I cannot remain here!—It is no longer a home for me, but, on the contrary, has become hateful to me. I will never enter it again! Let me begone—let me begone, I say!"

With these words he was rushing hastily towards the door, when the old man interposed and prevented him.

"What would you do, Joe?" he demanded; "it is now midnight, and the heavens threaten a coming storm. Would you madly wander forth at such a time as this, and in your present state of mind?"

"Yes," returned the wretched man; "for darkness and horror are consonant with my present feelings, and no tempest can equal the one which is raging within my breast. Oh, Mary! to what a state of horror have you reduced your unhappy dupe! May Heaven's curses——"

"Hold! rash man!" interrupted Sculler; "know you what you say? Beware, beware! lest the maledictions which you invoke upon the head of your unfortunate wife should descend upon yourself, and render you still more wretched."

"They have — they have!" hastily ejaculated Tiller; "am I not accursed already? And shall I hesitate to curse her who has been the guilty cause of all that which I am now doomed to endure? My wife! Oh, banish the name from my memory, for it is a bitter mockery to my ears, and only the more thoroughly convinces me of the weak fool that I have been! I have no wife!—I am a poor deserted wretch! despised, hated, loathed by every one! Oh, God! that I should ever live to become thus degraded!"

Again he struck his forehead in despair, and once more sinking into a chair, he abandoned himself entirely to all the violence of his grief. Old Sculler did not seek to interrupt him, for he wisely imagined that, by being permitted to give indulgence to his feelings, he might probably find some relief; and thus he remained for some time when he suddenly again started to his feet, and paced the room backwards and forwards in the most disordered manner, the most painful groans and sobs at intervals escaping from his bosom.

"Gone—gone!" he at length articulated in the most dismal and desponding accents; "left me, and fled to the arms of another! she whom I once believed to be all that was good, and amiable, and pure! Oh, how monstrous! how cruel! how abandoned! I can scarcely believe the evidence of my senses, or that it is not all some frightful dream! Alas! was ever man before so cruelly deceived? Even now she lavishes her warmest caresses on the base paramour to whose arms she has fled, and laughs scornfully at the thoughts of the misery which she knows full well she has inflicted on me. Distracting thought! Oh, that she were now before me! I would wreak my vengeance on her head, and endeavour in her heart's blood at least to wash out my dishonour!"

The expression of his features was fearful as he gave utterance to these words, and Sculler was completely terror-stricken as he gazed upon them.

"Oh, Tiller!" he observed, "how fearful, how revolting are the feelings which you have just now expressed, and which seem to have worked your brain up to madness! For Heaven's sake try to banish them from your mind, and to call reason to your aid! Good God! is it possible that you can for a moment contemplate so foul, so horrible a deed? Would you bathe your hands in the blood of your innocent but unfortunate wife? Oh, awful! my ears are shocked, and my blood freezes in my veins at the thought!"

"Innocent!" repeated the distracted man, with a bitter smile; "oh, what canting nonsense is this, and to repeat to one who is placed in the situation that I am! Oh, most innocent, and pure, and amiable, truly, to abandon me to my fate, and to resign herself to the guilty passions of another! Ha, ha, ha! 'tis well, 'tis very well; but let her not cross my path, let her no more degrade me by her presence, or, by all my hopes I swear——"

"Forbear!" interrupted the old man. "Swear not to anything so diabolical, so guilty, and so horrible; as you value your soul's welfare do not. By Heaven, I can scarcely believe that it is yourself that I am listening to, for never could I have supposed that any such guilty and dreadful thoughts could ever have entered your breast. Persevere, my friend, and you will yet be enabled to await patiently the decree of Fate, and the awful doubts and suspicions which you now suffer to distract your brain will be satisfactorily removed, and you will, you must be convinced how much you have wronged poor Mary by for a moment encouraging them."

"You talk in vain to me, old man," he returned; "I have too long suffered

myself to be deceived, but the mask is now removed, and I see the woman on whom I had placed all my heart's warmest affections in her natural deformity, and hate and despise her accordingly!"

"Alas!" sighed Sculler, "what arguments can I make use of to remove this fatal and cruel prejudice from your mind, and to defend the character of the ill-fated Mary from the foul aspersions that have been cast upon it? Tiller, is it possible that you have become insensible to every feeling of humanity and justice?—Will nothing whatever convince you of the fatal error under which you are now labouring, and which, if persisted in, must be attended by the most fearful consequences? Again I implore you to reflect seriously, and surely you cannot, will not much longer suffer yourself to be so blinded to truth and reason."

"Psha!" exclaimed Tiller, passionately. "Talk not to me of reason, for it is only an insult to my feelings, and can make no impression upon me, unless it be to add to my excitement, and to render my agony still more complete. But I can endure this no longer! My brain is burning, and desperation nerves my arm. Mary, my dying curse be upon your head, for you have been the guilty cause of all this! Oh, God!"

As the wretched man thus spoke he rushed towards the door which conducted to the inner apartment, and the expression of his features plainly showed the fearful and determined purpose of his soul. The alarmed old man laid his hand upon his arm and sought to detain him, as he exclaimed—

"Tiller—Tiller! for Heaven's sake, what is it you would do? Those awful words, and those fearful looks convince me that you have some dreadful design in contemplation, and I will not leave you. Oh, hold—hold! and in the frenzy of your feelings do not that which may condemn your soul to perdition!"

"Unhand me, old man!" cried Tiller; "my purpose is fixed, and let the consequences be whatever they may, I will not be moved from it. What is life now to me but an insupportable burthen, of which the sooner I rid myself the better? Unhand me, I say again!"

"No, no!" cried Sculler, still struggling to detain him; "hear me, Joe. By all your hopes of the future, and——"

"Nay, then," interrupted Tiller, flinging him from him to the floor; "since you are so obstinate, I must e'en use violence. Off!—off! Now, Mary, the completion of your work is at hand!"

He hastily dashed open the door, and rushed into the room as he spoke, and Sculler immediately gathered himself to his feet, and following him, exclaimed—

"Tiller!—Tiller! hold, rash man! Oh, God! what dreadful crime have you determined upon?"

He had no sooner entered the room when he beheld the unfortunate man in the act of taking a loaded pistol from over the mantelpiece, and with a cry of terror, and mustering up all his strength, he rushed upon him, and grasping his arm, endeavoured to force the pistol from him, at the same time calling aloud for help, with the hope of alarming some of the neighbours, and of getting some of them to hasten to his assistance, and thus prevent the fatal catastrophe which might otherwise take place. In the struggle, however, the pistol was accidentally discharged in the air, and thus all immediate danger was prevented.

"Officious fool!" cried the distracted man, fiercely, and again hurling Sculler from him; "why do you interfere to prevent me from the execution of my design? But no, I will not be thwarted; this night, this hour shall witness the termination of all my misery, at any rate, in this world. Stand back, old man—stand back, I say! I would not harm you, but if you attempt to obstruct me you may bitterly repent it!"

In a moment he darted with the air of a madman out of the cottage, and made his way towards the river, the old man hastily following him, and shouting aloud for help as he did so. The report of the pistol, however, had alarmed the neighbours, several of whom rushed out of their dwellings in the greatest consternation, and eagerly inquired of old Sculler what was the matter. He hastily pointed to Tiller, who was flying at the top of his speed, and said, in an agitated voice—

"For Heaven's sake pursue him, or it will be too late to save him! He has already attempted self-destruction,

and—ah! see! he is making his way towards the river! for the love of God, quick!"

They needed no further urging, but as quickly as they could they pursued the footsteps of the wretched maniac, for the desperate and awful design which he contemplated could not be doubted for a moment. He had, however, got so far in advance of them that they feared it would be impossible to overtake him before he reached the banks of the river, and they redoubled their speed, the unfortunate Tiller at the same time making the air resound again with his wild cries. Another instant and he had gained the river's bank, and his pursuers were some short distance from him. They saw him raise his arms above his head; again they heard him shout aloud; and then he plunged head-long into the water, and a cry of horror escaped from poor old Sculler and his companions.

"Unhappy man!" cried Sculler, "he has accomplished his deadly purpose! Oh, hasten—hasten, or it may be too late to save him!"

With the speed of lightning they dashed forward, and in an instant they arrived at the spot, and, by the light of the moon, they beheld the wretched man struggling in the water, but apparently without making the least effort to save himself. William Bromley, who was one of the party, immediately threw off his coat and waistcoat, and boldly plunging into the water, swam towards the drowning man. There happened to be a boat moored alongside the river, into which Sculler and two or three others instantly leapt, and rowed towards the place where they already beheld Bromley and Tiller struggling together, the latter apparently making a most desperate attempt to prevent his being saved, and Bromley equally determined to rescue him, even at the peril of his own life. Twice they had sunk together before the boat succeeded in reaching them, but just as they did so they arose for the third time, and Bromley had a firm hold of Joe, who, being exhausted and insensible, they had no difficulty in dragging him into the boat; the brave fellow, Bromley, followed immediately, and they rowed towards the shore with all the expedition they

MRS. ARNOLD CONSOLING MARY FOR THE ABSENCE OF TILLER.

could. On reaching it, Sculler despatched one of his companions for the assistance of the nearest medical man, and poor Tiller was then conveyed to the cottage, where the doctor was quickly in attendance, and having ordered him to be immediately placed in a warm bed, proceeded to apply such remedies as the emergency of the case required. It was some time, however, before Joe showed any signs of returning life, and then the doctor ordered that he should be kept strictly quiet, and on no account that any person should enter into conversation with him, or to say anything which might be at all calculated to excite him. This precaution was, however, quite unnecessary, for Joe, although he breathed pretty freely, seemed to be quite unconscious of everything that was passing around him, and he remained in the same state of stupor for some time.

Old Sculler and Mrs. Bromley continued to watch him, and to the latter he related all the particulars of what had happened, and to which she listened with much attention and interest.

"Ah!" she observed in a low tone, when he had concluded; "it is a sad affair, sure enough, and I cannot but pity poor Joe most sincerely. Unfortunate man! I am afraid that this shock will have such an effect upon him that he will never more recover his senses. What a providential thing it was that you happened to be with him, or he would certainly have succeeded in the perpetration of the awful crime he contemplated."

"Yes," coincided Sam; "and I shudder to think of it. Nothing can banish from his mind the awful impression that Mary has proved false to him; and all the persuasions I could make use of failed to have the least effect upon him."

"Well," observed Mrs. Bromley; "certainly her disappearance is a most mysterious affair, and I scarcely know what to think of it; but I am inclined to believe that it is the work of villany, for I am well convinced that Mary could never become so abandoned and lost to all sense of shame as to desert her husband, and throw herself into the arms of another."

"Oh, no!" returned Sculler; "it would be monstrous to imagine any such a thing! Poor lass! I am afraid that some terrible fate has overtaken her, and, although I have sought to buoy her husband up with different ideas, I have my doubts as to whether or not she will ever again be discovered."

"Oh, Mr. Sculler!" replied the old woman; "say not so, for that would, indeed, be a dreadful circumstance. But know you of any one from whom she had any cause to apprehend danger?"

"No," answered Sculler; "for Mary was so good and amiable that I thought it was not possible she could have an enemy in the world."

"It is a most mysterious piece of business altogether," remarked Mrs. Bromley, "and the longer I reflect on it the more do I become bewildered. If the statement of Oarsby be correct, it has a more strange appearance still."

"True," said Sculler; "but still I am inclined to think he was mistaken."

"I don't see how he could well be so," said Mrs. Bromley, "so well as he is acquainted with Mrs. Tiller; and especially as he said he spoke to her."

"Well," returned Sculler, "it certainly is rather strange; but still I do not attach much importance to that circumstance. Even if it really was Mary, feeling uneasy at the absence of Joe, she might have left the cottage in search of him."

"But if she had done so," said Mrs. Bromley, "would she not have been sure to have inquired of Oarsby whether he had seen anything of him? Besides, he says that it was early in the evening when he met her, and that she had a bundle with her."

"Oh," answered the old man, "in that he must have been mistaken altogether, for there is nothing missing from the cottage, with the exception of her bonnet and cloak; and that circumstance makes me doubt the whole of his statement."

"Poor lass!" ejaculated Mrs. Bromley; "whatever can have become of her? It makes me quite shudder to think of it. Poor Harry Halliyard, too, I wonder where he is gone? It was a sad disappointment to his hopes, this union of Mary and Joe; but they were neither of them to blame, for who could have thought that the news of Harry's death would turn out to be false?"

"Certainly not," said Sculler. "Ah! theirs has been a cruel fate, and they are much to be pitied."

"Ah, Master Sculler," observed the old woman, "you may say that, and no one can more sincerely feel for them than I do. God grant that everything may terminate much better than we can now anticipate. As for poor Joe, I am afraid that his senses will never be restored, so severe is the shock that his mind has received. It is, indeed, a most severe trial for him, and I wonder not at the excitement he has evinced."

"True," coincided her companion; "he was doatingly fond of poor Mary; and although it is not likely that she could love him with the same fervour as she did Harry, I am well convinced that she honoured and esteemed him for his numerous manly virtues; and, indeed, she could not help doing so, considering the kind and affectionate husband he has ever been to her. It is that which convinces me that her disappearance is no voluntary act of her own, but that she has been forced away, and that she is now in the power of the villains who have committed this outrage."

"Alas!" ejaculated Mrs. Bromley, "it is but too probable; and how painful is the thought! What will become of the poor girl, if such is the fate which has befallen her? How terrible must be the anguish of her mind! But is it not strange that none of the neighbours were alarmed? She would be sure to shriek for help when she found herself thus forcibly seized."

"That point bewilders me," answered the old man; "but there is no knowing what means the villains who probably hold her in their power may have adopted to prevent her. But, hush! Tiller seems to be reviving to consciousness, and he must not overhear us."

The unfortunate man now opened his eyes, raised himself partially in the bed, and gazed vacantly around him for a moment or two, and it was evident that his mind was still wandering, and that his brain was bewildered.

"Joe, my good fellow," said Sculler, in his kindest accents, "how do you feel now? Is there anything that we can do for you?"

"Yes, yes!" repeated Tiller, hastily, grasping the arm of the old man vehemently, and looking with fearful meaning in his face as he spoke; "give me poison —plunge a knife into my heart, and end at once this accursed existence! Oh, why was I recalled to life? It was cruel—it was monstrous!"

"Tiller," said Sculler, "for Heaven's sake do not talk in such a fearful manner, for it cuts me to the heart to hear you. Be thankful that you are saved from the perpetration of so awful a crime as that which you attempted, and——"

"Ah!" interrupted the unhappy man, fiercely, "you, then, are one of those busy fools who interposed between me and death, and who prevented me from obtaining that everlasting rest from the sorrows that overwhelm me, which I sought! Oh, I have reason to curse you for it, for what is life now to me but an earthly pandemonium? and all mankind seek to torture and to persecute me! See, see, where the bold and heartless adultress stands, and smiles in mockery upon my anguish; and you encourage her in her guilt, and would fain persuade me that she is purest of the pure, and would sooner perish than she would deceive me! Ha, ha, ha! Liar! it is false! Think you I am mad—that I am to be cojoled thus by that shameless wanton? Has she not abandoned me—left me to my fate —and do I not now behold her the guilty paramour of another? Yes, there she unblushingly stands, and laughs to scorn the wretched being whose hopes, whose happiness she has so inhumanly destroyed! But I will have revenge! Yes, a terrible revenge! Let me get at her! She shall not escape me! Release your hold of me, or may Heaven's most awful curses descend upon your head! She shall not live to triumph in her guilt, and pander to the brutal passions of another! Woman! deceiver! I have thee now! and thus I——"

As the afflicted man thus wildly raved, he started up in the bed with all the strength of madness, his eyes glaring fearfully, and struggled desperately with Sculler and the old woman, who had the greatest difficulty in holding him. But at length his strength was completely exhausted, and with an hysterical laugh he sank back on his pillow, and again became unconscious of everything around him.

"Oh, what a painful scene is this!" said Mrs. Bromley. "Poor fellow! he will, I fear, never recover from this shock. His senses have entirely left him!"

"Alas!" remarked Sculler, "I fear that is too true. Unfortunate man! how it grieves me to see him reduced to this deplorable condition. Heaven help him! I never thought it would have come to this!"

"What is to be done?" said the old woman. "Oh, what must be the agony of poor Mary, if she can form the least idea of the awful situation of her wretched husband?"

"The thought is most torturing!" returned Sculler, "and I know not what can be done for the best. It is most melancholy to behold the fatal impression which her mysterious and unaccountable disappearance has made upon his mind. God grant him some relief! for without that I tremble to think what the consequences may be."

"All that I imagine can be done for the present," observed Mrs. Bromley, "is to keep him as quiet as possible. Should nothing be heard of Mary, we have every reason to apprehend the worst."

"Alas!" ejaculated old Sculler, "that is too true; and at present there seems to be not the least probability of her being discovered. What, oh, what can have become of her? Would to Heaven that we had returned direct home instead of staying at the tavern, this terrible calamity might then never have happened."

"Yes," coincided the old woman, "it was indeed unfortunate. But who was to foresee what was about to happen? I'm sure I pity them from my very soul."

"And need I say that I do also?" said Sculler. "I have ever been as studious of and as anxious for the happiness and welfare of poor Tiller and his wife as if they were my own offspring. My curses pursue the guilty wretches, whoever they are, who have been the cause of this!"

"The vengeance of Heaven will most assuredly overtake them," remarked Mrs. Bromley. "But what can ever recal that which has happened?"

"No," returned the old man; "and it grieves me to the very soul to think of it. Poor Joe! poor Mary! yours are troubles that it is almost impossible for human nature to withstand."

"Alas!" sighed Mrs. Bromley, "that is too true; and when I reflect upon the dreadful circumstances I cannot but anticipate the worst. But what is now to be done to endeavour to ascertain the fate of Mary?"

"I know not," answered Sculler; "and the more I think of it the more am I bewildered. The only information of her that we have been enabled to obtain has been from Oareby, and upon that I do not place much dependance."

"Had Mary, indeed, voluntarily forsaken her husband, though I cannot believe her to have been so guilty," remarked Mrs. Bromley, "she would surely not have had the heart to do so without leaving him a letter to explain in some measure her conduct."

"True," returned Sculler. "But I cannot entertain such an idea for a moment, for I am convinced that it would be doing her the greatest injustice to do so. Oh, no! I can never believe that of Mary Tiller. God grant that this most terrible mystery may be shortly explained! and if it ever is, I am certain that it will be to exonerate Mary from all blame."

"That, also, is my most fervent hope," said Mrs. Bromley. "But, alas! I see but little prospect of it at present."

Sculler returned no answer to this, and they continued to watch in anxious silence by the sufferer for some time. But little, if any, change took place in his melancholy condition. For hours he remained in a state of stupor, and when he did arouse from this lethargy, the wild ravings to which he gave utterance were quite pitiable to hear. It seemed but too evident that his reason was fled for ever; and, in fact, the medical man gave but very little hopes of him, and feared that one of the violent paroxysms under which he at intervals suffered might prove fatal to him. Old Sculler and Mrs. Bromley were deeply affected to witness his sufferings, and there was nothing which they would not willingly have done to ameliorate them; but of that there seemed not to be the slightest chance. This startling and mysterious event had cast a melancholy gloom over the whole neighbourhood, where our heroine and her husband were universally respected, and every one deeply sympathised with the deplorable situation of poor Joe. As for the disappearance of Mary, it was a mystery which was perfectly impenetrable, and various were the conjectures that were formed on it; but no one was enabled to come to any satisfactory conclusion, though most persons acquitted the unfortunate woman of all criminality, and felt satisfied that she had been forced away from her home by some villain or villains, and they trembled for the fate which had in all probability befallen her. The excitement increased every hour, and every means were adopted that were calculated to discover her, but with very little chance of success; not the least information could be obtained respecting her, and all continued enshrouded in the same state of mystery.

Knowing the melancholy state of mind under which Mary had for some time suffered, there were many persons who apprehended that she might have committed suicide; and that dismal idea gained strength every moment, especially when all the singular and ambiguous circumstances of the case were taken into mature consideration, more particularly if the statement of Jack Oarsby could be relied upon; and he being supposed to be the friend of Tiller, no one could see any reason why it should be doubted.

This idea caused the most painful sensation, and steps were immediately taken to ascertain whether it was well founded or not. The river was dragged in every direction, but all to no purpose; and all remained in the same state of doubt, perplexity, and uncertainty.

CHAPTER XVIII.

THE MISFORTUNES OF MARY INCREASE.— THE DISMAL JOURNEY.—ARRIVAL AT THE SECRET HAUNT OF THE PIRATES. —FEARFUL DISCOVERY.—MARY ON BOARD THE VESSEL OF HUGH BRANDON.

HUGH BRANDON arose at an early hour on the morning following the abduction of our heroine; and, in fact, such was the excitement of his feelings at the success which had attended his nefarious plot that he had been enabled to sleep but little. The first thing he did on joining his companions in the usual place of rendezvous in the old tavern was to send for the old woman, and inquire of her as to the condition of Mary; and from her he learned that she was as wretched as might be expected, but that, at the same time, she considered that she was much less excited than she had been on first dis-

covering the manner in which she had been betrayed.

" 'Tis well," said Brandon, with a look of triumph. " She may as well be calm as not, for she cannot resist the fate to which I have doomed her; and as for there being any chance of escaping from my power, that is utterly out of the question. However, I have changed my mind, and will not seek an interview with her at present, for the excitement which the sight of me might cause her might, perhaps, be attended with danger. Towards the evening we must contrive by some means to administer the opiate to her, and then she can be safely removed from here, and will be soon far beyond the reach of discovery. One of you had better immediately take your departure to the farm, in order to make our comrades aware of what has happened, and that they may be prepared for our arrival. All goes well, and if they have only succeeded in capturing Halliyard my triumph will, indeed, be complete, and I shall have the opportunity of fully gratifying my revenge. Oh, how I exult at the thought !"

He was interrupted by the entrance of Jack Oarsby, who had just come from the Crown and Crosier, where, as the reader is aware, he had seen the unfortunate Tiller and old Sculler, and been full witness of the acute suffering of the former.

" Well, Oarsby," said Brandon ; "any news ?"

" I have seen Tiller and Sculler," answered Oarsby.

" Ah! and what do they seem to think of the disappearance of Mary ?" inquired Brandon.

" Why, Joe is nearly mad, if not quite," replied Oarsby. " He imagines that his wife has eloped from him, and the suspicion I confirmed by informing him that I met Mary yesterday, going in the direction of the Hard, in a great hurry, carrying a bundle, and in a state of great agitation."

" That was a wise plan of yours, Jack," said the pirate, "and I give you full credit for it. Ha, ha, ha ! poor devil ! I pity him ; and the best thing he can do is to cut his throat, or to make away with himself in some way or the other."..

True," said Oarsby ; " and I do not think it will be long before he does something of that kind, for the loss of Mary has driven him completely crazy."

"Well," answered Brandon, " he may make up his mind never to behold her again ; for now that she is securely in my power, her fate is certain. This night she will be removed from here, and before many hours afterwards she will be safe in our secret haunt at Portsmouth ; then on board the Wasp, and all chance of discovering her will be at an end. Have you despatched a messenger to your nephew, Tapster, to make him acquainted with our scheme, and the service we wish him to perform?"

" I have," answered the landlord; "and you may depend upon his readiness to comply with your request. Like myself, he is not over particular what he does for money."

"Ay," observed Brandon, " I believe you ; and I will not fail to reward him well for his trouble. I do not think we could have hit upon a better scheme."

"True," said Tapster ; "and it cannot fail to succeed. He will be here as soon as it is dark in the evening, and by that time, I dare say, the drug which you intend to administer to your victim will have taken effect, and she may be removed without creating any alarm or exciting suspicion."

" Yes," said Brandon, " Fortune, as far as regards her, smiles upon me. She is a rare prize, well worth the trouble it has cost me to obtain possession of her; and should my associates at the farm have been equally successful in securing Halliyard, all my wishes will be gratified, and nothing whatever can exceed my triumph. Oh, how great will be his anguish and despair when he finds that his beloved Mary is in my power, and that she must yield to my will. He will be excited to madness; and to witness his sufferings will be food to my revengeful soul. It will be my delight to torture him, and to laugh at and triumph in his anguish. The destroyer of my brother must not, shall not escape my vengeance !"

" Right, captain," remarked Summers ; "and I hope that when you return to the farm you may find Halliyard safe in the bilboes. But it will be prudent to sail from Portsmouth with all possible expedition, for the disappearance of Halliyard will be sure to cause a great sensation in the neighbourhood, and suspicion might attach to us ; and it would be rather awkward were they to overhawl our craft."

"True," said Brandon ; " but I do not think there is much fear of that. We have hitherto managed to deceive them, and they little imagine that the vessel which they suppose to be the Helen, a fair trader, is no other than the terror of the ocean, the Saucy Wasp, which they have so long tried to capture or destroy to no purpose. However, once more safe on board my gallant craft with my fair prize, we will weigh anchor without delay, and in search of booty, for I long to be on the bright blue waters of the ocean again, and in pursuit of fortune."

" Ay, captain," said Summers ; " I am tired of being laid up in port, for it does not agree with the constitution of such men as us at all. Oh, ours is a merry life, a life of freedom, and I would not change it to be made an emperor."

" Well spoken, Summers," said Brandon ; " you are a man after my own heart, and I am proud of my crew. With such daring spirits we have no occasion to fear to meet any foe, however powerful, for success has never yet failed to attend us."

"And it never will, I hope," returned Summers. " This evening, then, we depart from hence ?"

"Yes," said Brandon ; " myself and you only will accompany Mary in the waggon, and the rest of our comrades must follow in different parties, so as to avoid all suspicion. Old Nance will see to her during the day, and, no doubt, she will be able to administer the drug to her towards the evening. It is a powerful one, and after she has taken it there will not be much fear of her troubling us during the journey. Poor Joe Tiller ! what a state of agony he must be in at the loss of his wife, and how great would be his despair if he knew that she was in the power of Hugh Brandon, the pirate ! Ha, ha, ha ! poor devil ! he will never behold her again, he may make up his mind to that. But you think we may depend upon your nephew, Tapster ?"

"Oh, yes," answered the latter, "I am sure of that. He will be here this evening punctual to the time appointed, never fear; and no doubt he will be glad enough of the job, for he is not over and above rich at present."

"Well," observed Brandon, "only let him perform his business well and faithfully and he shall have no reason to grumble at the manner in which I will reward him."

"That's enough," said Tapster. "You will find him, as I said before, ready enough to do anything for money; for, like his worthy uncle, he is not at all particular, and conscience is not apt to trouble him. But this is a dry subject, Brandon, and I should think that a glass or two of grog, just merely to drink success to your future undertakings, would not hurt us now. I always have an eye to business, you know."

"Right, right, old Brandy-nose," said the pirate; "and you can't say but that we are good customers to you when we are ashore. So, heave a-head, and bring as much grog aboard as you like."

Tapster needed no second order, but left the room anh quickly returned with the liquor, and the ruffians commenced their debauch with avidity, and gave unlimited license to their boisterous mirth, Brandon being elated beyond all measure at the success which had so far attended his diabolical schemes. But we must leave him for the present, and return to our heroine. No language can possibly do adequate justice to the dreadful sufferings she endured that fatal and awful night. At times her mind was worked up to a complete state of frenzy and despair, and the wild lamentations that escaped her were sufficient to have moved the stoutest heart to pity. So fearful, so sudden, and so unexpected was the change that a few short hours had made in her situation, that she could scarcely believe in its reality, or that she was not labouring under the influence of some frightful delusion; but, alas! it was too painfully evident to deceive her, and she beat her breast and tore her hair in the agony of her despair. To think of retiring to rest it was impossible, for how was it likely that she could sleep in that strange and fearful place, and in her present state of mind? Every moment she dreaded the appearance of Brandon, and she shuddered at the thought of what she might expect from him. For some time she paced the room in the most distracted manner, wringing her hands, and giving vent to the extreme agony of her feelings in the most dismal lamentations. Then she would throw herself on her knees, and most fervently implore the protection of the Supreme; but not the least relief could she obtain to her sufferings.

"Oh, God!" she exclaimed, "what a terrible misfortune is this! how cruelly and how fatally have I been insnared, and how awful and how revolting is the fate which is probably in store for me! In the power of this fearful man, what have I not to dread? The blood freezes in my veins at the thought, and I shall go mad with horror and despair! Alas! how have I merited such a calamity as this? And what must now be the sufferings of poor Tiller? He will be distracted at my loss, and at the horrible uncertainty of the fate which has befallen me. And what may not be the fearful suspicions which my mysterious disappearance may excite in his breast? He may believe me faithless—that I have cruelly abandoned him, and flown to the arms of Harry! Dreadful thought! my senses reel beneath it! God of Heaven, look down with mercy on me and him, and give him strength to support with fortitude and resignation a misfortune which it was impossible to foresee. Fortitude! resignation!—oh, is it possible that he can call them to his aid? Ah, no, it would be madness to imagine so! He will believe me false, and, in the frenzy of his despair, invoke curses upon my head! Oh, how fatally have my dismal forebodings been realized! Alas—alas! unless Providence interposes to rescue me I am lost! To be in the power and at the mercy of this guilty man, whose very name inspires me with feelings of horror, what have I not to dread? Oh, wretched — wretched — wretched fate! would that I were dead rather than be exposed to such fearful sufferings as these!"

Again she wrung her hands in despair, whilst the tears flowed fast, and hysterical sobs escaped her overcharged bosom. Then she threw herself into a chair and abandoned herself to all the agony of thought. Ever and anon the rude voices of the pirates, as they shouted in their boisterous mirth, would reach her ears, and make her shudder with a feeling of horror which she found it utterly impossible to resist, and she feared every moment that they would intrude upon her, and that the consequences that might follow she felt certain would be of the most dreadful description. At times she was worked up to such a pitch of frenzy that she would scream aloud for help; but the echo of her own voice was the only answer she received, and she was at once aroused to the terrible certainty that all chance of help was completely hopeless.

"Ah, no!" she ejaculated in the most melancholy accents, "my fate is sealed, and there are no means of avoiding it! Oh, wretched—wretched Mary! what will become of you?—What chance is there of your escaping from the awful doom to which this guilty man will, no doubt, consign you? My God! how my heart trembles at the thought! Little did I anticipate that I should ever be placed in such a terrible situation as this! Heaven help me, or I am lost for ever! And shall I never behold Tiller again? Ah, no! I feel too well convinced that I shall not! He can never survive this dreadful blow. Oh, Tiller! never did I before feel how sincerely I love you till now! Harry, too—oh why do I suffer his image still to enter my mind? It is sinful to do so. And yet it is impossible that I can ever help feeling for him the warmest regard, associated as we have been by the fondest affections from the earliest days of childhood. Alas! why did Providence ordain that all our bright hopes and prospects should be so cruelly annihilated? Unfortunate, noble-hearted Harry! and where are you now? Doubtless again exposed to all the perils and dangers of the ocean, and reckless what becomes of you. And I, too, shall shortly be tossed on the stormy deep, and in the power of those inhuman wretches who are capable of any crime, however monstrous; from whom I can expect no mercy, but who, on the contrary, will take a savage delight in witnessing and mocking at my sufferings.

Dreadful thought! it racks my soul to frenzy! Oh, Harry! could you but be aware of the horrors to which I am at present exposed, and those with which I am threatened, and which must inevitably overtake me, unless kind Providence, in its infinite mercy, shall interpose to save me, what would be the agony and despair of your feelings? But hold my rash tongue! what a cruel injustice am I doing my unfortunate husband by indulging in these reflections. Alas! I fear that I have greatly sinned by thus encouraging my passion for Harry when I am the wife of another, and that this is the terrible punishment awarded to me for it. Almighty God! look down with mercy upon me, poor, erring mortal, and guide me how to act. My brain is bewildered, and I know not what to do. Oh, dreadful fate! surely it is too severe for human nature to support. Would that I were dead, and thus released from my earthly sufferings altogether, for hope has become completely extinguished in my bosom!"

As these thoughts impressed themselves still more powerfully upon her mind her misery and despair became still more torturing and insupportable, and her tears flowed faster than ever. She pictured to herself in the most vivid colours the intense and excruciating agony poor Joe was then enduring, and she felt even more for him than she did for herself. In imagination she saw the horror and despair of his looks, and heard his wild ravings as he called upon her name, and in vain tried to imagine what had become of her—what was the fate which had befallen her. Would he think that she had been forced away from her home, or would he believe that she had voluntarily abandoned him? Alas! taking all the painful and mysterious circumstances into consideration, she had too much reason to fear the latter; and at times she was wrought up to such a pitch of frenzy by that torturing idea, that she could scarcely contain herself.

"But no!" she ejaculated, "he can never be so uncharitable as to believe me to be so base and treacherous! I dare not think of him, for that would drive me mad! Dear Joe! for, indeed, I now feel how truly dear you are to me, may the Almighty give you for-

THE ENGAGEMENT BETWEEN THE POLYPHEMUS AND THE BLACK BET.

titude to support this dreadful trial, and restore me again to your arms; how will I then study by my future conduct to make you happy, and to convince you of my sincerity and affection. Oh, I must be a wretch, indeed, unworthy the name of woman, did I not feel towards thee the most unbounded gratitude for the fond attentions that you have ever bestowed upon me, and the manner in which you have constantly studied to promote my happiness. Should fate ordain that we should meet no more, may you be enabled to resign yourself to my loss, and to meet with some other woman whom you can love as fervently as you have done me. But that, I know, is impossible. And if it is, indeed, the will of Heaven that I should never again be restored to you, I fear that your fate will be sealed, and that life will become insupportable and hateful to you. Alas, alas! how terrible are the prospects that are now spread before me! There is no hope—there is no hope!"

Again the scalding tears chased each other rapidly down her cheeks, and she sobbed as if her heart would break. In vain she exerted herself to the utmost, she could obtain no alleviation to her anguish, and, in fact, it rather increased than abated. And thus the dreary hours rolled on, and our heroine looked forward to the morning with apprehension, for she had no doubt that she would then be visited by Brandon, and what the result of that interview might be she shuddered to think upon, though she had every reason to fear the worst. All was now buried in profound stillness in the house, and that, if possible, added to the gloom and misery of Mary's feelings; and various and overpowering were the thoughts that crowded upon her brain. She threw herself in a chair, and resigned herself entirely to the most dismal meditations, and soon became unconscious to everything else. But she was not long suffered to remain in this condition, all the terrors by which she was at present surrounded, and those that awaited her, rushed with redoubled force upon her imagination, and starting to her feet, she traversed the dismal apartment in which she was confined with disordered steps, and again gave vent to her feelings in the most mournful lamentations. She blamed herself for having been so easily led astray; but still, was it not natural that she should be so when she was led to suppose that some dreadful accident had befallen her husband? And how could she doubt the statement of the crafty and villanous Oarsby, given in so plausible a manner, and when she had ever believed him to have been the friend of Tiller?

"Oh, what a base plot has been laid to ensnare me! and what power had I to guard against it? But the vengeance of the Almighty will surely overtake the wretches who have been guilty of this, and I shall not be permitted altogether to fall the victim to their nefarious and diabolical artifices. Courage, Mary, courage, for threatening and awful as is the situation in which you are at present placed, something may occur when you least expect it to rescue you from the power of your inhuman enemies, and to restore you to liberty and the arms of your unfortunate husband."

These thoughts did for a short time reanimate her with fresh fortitude, but it soon vanished, and she became as wretched and as hopeless as ever. Thus the night passed away, and the unfortunate prisoner never once attempted to obtain a temporary respite to her cares and anxieties in sleep, for that, she well knew, would be a fruitless task; but she was completely worn out with fatigue and anguish of mind. Daylight at length dawned in at the windows of the gloomy apartment; but that afforded her little or no relief, for she had no doubt that she would shortly be visited by Brandon, and she looked forward to the events of the day with the most torturing apprehension, and most earnestly did she supplicate the protection of the Supreme from the dangers that seemed too certainly impending over her. With a heavy heart she walked to the window and looked from it, but the view that she was enabled to obtain from it was only calculated to excite her disgust and to increase her

fears. Nothing, as we have before stated, could be more wretched and desolate than the prospect it commanded. Old and tottering houses, filthy yards, and dark alleys, were all that met her gaze; and the individuals that she beheld occasionally emerge from them were of the lowest grade of society, squalid and savage in their appearance, and the very sight of them was calculated to inspire feelings of terror and disgust. Even could she have made her deplorable situation known to them she felt perfectly satisfied that she could expect no relief or assistance from them; and she turned from the window with a sickly feeling of despair, and again sinking on a seat, and burying her face in her hands, she gave herself up to the most overwhelming grief. She could hear the different persons moving about in the house, and every moment she expected to be intruded upon by the object of her terrors; and she endeavoured, but in vain, to prepare herself for the painful trial. At length she heard some one ascending the stairs towards the room in which she was confined, and she clasped her hands together and awaited the result in a state of the most trembling anxiety. She had not to wait long, for the next moment the room door was unlocked and the old woman entered, bringing with her some provisions. Mary shrank from her with a feeling of terror and disgust; but she appeared to take very little notice of the expression of her countenance, and having placed the food upon the table, she said, in rather more civil and gentle accents than before—

"I have brought you some refreshment, of which I dare say you stand in need. But it seems you have not been to bed, which was rather foolish on your part, for you must have stood in need of a few hours rest, and——"

"Rest!" interrupted our heroine, with a heavy sigh; "alas! how think you it is possible that I can rest in this dreadful situation, and with such a terrible prospect before my eyes? Oh, it is a bitter mockery to talk to me thus!"

"Well," observed old Nance, as she was called, "I have no particular wish to wound your feelings, but as you cannot help yourself it is no use giving way to this excessive grief, and you may as well resign yourself to your fate, which, after all, may not turn out to be so bad as you anticipate."

Oh, God!" ejaculated our distracted heroine, "what mercy or forbearance can I expect from such a villain as he who holds me in his power? Am I not a prisoner—torn away from my home and my husband? Am I to be detained here?"

"For the present you are," replied the old woman; "but I have no doubt that you will soon be removed to some other place of security. It is not likely that Brandon will let you go after he has been at so much trouble to obtain possession of you"

"Heaven look down with mercy upon me!" exclaimed Mary. "Oh, what must be the anguish of my unfortunate husband at my mysterious disappearance! But tell me, I beg of you, have you heard anything of him?—Is he safe?"

"For anything I know to the contrary he is," answered the woman. "He has nothing to fear from Brandon; it is quite enough for him that he has got you in his power; though there is another individual whom I imagine he is determined shall not escape him if he can help it."

"Ah!" cried our heroine, fixing upon her an anxious look, "who mean you?"

"Harry Halliyard."

"Harry!" repeated Mary. "Oh, Heaven forbid! for well do I know what he has to expect from his savage vengeance if he should fall into his power. But I trust that he is now far beyond the reach of any such danger."

"Well," returned old Nance, "it will be lucky for him if he is; but if the plot which Brandon has laid to entrap him does not fail he is already secured."

"Good God!" exclaimed Mary, in astonishment and alarm; "is it possible? Know you, then, where he is?"

"Yes," replied the woman, "at Portsmouth, where the vessel on board of which he has entered, the Porpoise, is lying. But if Fortune smiles upon the designs of Brandon he will find himself on board of a very different craft to that."

"Oh, Harry!" ejaculated our heroine,

"and do such terrible dangers as these threaten you? God protect you, and frustrate the guilty schemes of our brutal enemy!"

"You will stand a chance of seeing your lover again sooner than you expected," said the old woman, with a disagreeable grin; "and perhaps that meeting may reconcile you to the loss of your husband."

"Forbear!" commanded Mary, with a look of indignation, and the crimson blushes of shame mantling in her cheeks; "dare not to insult my ears with any such disgusting remarks! Oh, if you had anything of the feelings of a woman you would pity me, instead of thus mocking my sufferings! But Halliyard will yet escape the diabolical designs of Brandon; and that vengeance which the latter's crimes deserve will at last overtake him."

"It is well for you that you can imagine so," said the old woman; "however, it is no business of mine, so I have nothing more to say upon the subject. I suppose you can dispense with my society, so I will e'en retire, and leave you to settle the matter in your own mind the best way you can."

"Oh, tell me," said Mary, "is it the intention of Brandon to bear me, indeed, from my native land, and to convey me on board his pirate vessel?"

"No doubt of it," answered Nance; "so you may as well prepare yourself for the change."

"Alas—alas!" groaned Mary, wringing her hands; "wretched, dreadful fate! will nothing save me from it? To be placed in such a dreadful and revolting situation, and surrounded by such desperate and heartless ruffians, with no one nigh to assist me, or to avenge the cruel wrongs inflicted on me, my blood freezes with horror at the bare thought! Heaven, I again implore thee to look down with mercy upon me: for how much do I stand in need of thy aid!"

The old woman returned no answer to this; and after fixing a look of significant meaning upon the hapless Mary, she retired from the room. When she was gone the wretched prisoner gave full vent to the feelings of agony and despair which her observations had excited, and it was some time before she could control herself anything within the bounds of reason.

"Oh, this is a fate which I never anticipated would have befallen me!" she ejaculated; "and it is almost too horrible to contemplate! Oh, what have I done that I should thus be made the sport of cruel destiny? To be forced from my home and all that is dear to me, and conveyed on board this fearful vessel to witness nothing else but scenes of bloodshed and horror! My God! how can I ever find strength to endure it? Brandon, too, whose very name is associated with all that is brutal and revolting; to be at his mercy, and forced to submit to his diabolical will! the thought alone will drive me mad! Oh, surely it cannot be! something will yet occur to save me! Oh, that I had been aware of that which threatened me, I would never have survived to meet this fate! Harry, too! Alas! should he unfortunately fall a victim to the guilty plot that is devised against him, how horrible are the tortures that are in store for him! what intense, what insupportable agony will be his when he finds the dreadful situation I am placed in, and knows that he has no power to assist me! God grant that the designs of these savage men may be thwarted, and that he at least may escape their deadly vengeance! My heart sickens at the torturing thoughts that crowd upon my brain, and I feel but too certain that there is no hope for me!"

She paused, for the power of her emotions choked her utterance, and the most heartrending sobs escaped her bosom. It did not seem to be the intention of Brandon, however, to intrude upon her for the present, and that afforded her some slight degree of consolation. In this state of mind she continued for several hours; and the longer she reflected the more hopeless and deplorable her situation appeared to be; and in vain she tried to muster fortitude to support her troubles with any degree of patience. She scarcely dared to think of Tiller, for whenever she did so madness almost seized upon her brain, and she pictured to herself in the most glowing characters the distraction of his feelings, and the wild despair which must have taken possession of him. All the many acts of kindness and affection she had experienced from him, the manly and generous sympathy he had ever evinced for the disappointment which the hopes of herself and Harry had received, rushed to her memory with overwhelming force, and she never felt the extent of the regard which she bore him till then. What a kind protector had he been to her, and how studious had he ever been of her happiness. She feared that she had never made him a sufficient return for his affectionate zeal, and she felt that she owed him a debt of gratitude which she could never repay, even if the opportunity should be afforded her, which she had now too much reason to fear it never would. But to think that she should be torn from him in such a fearful and mysterious manner as must naturally leave doubts and suspicions in his mind was far more torturing than all; and it was in vain that she tried to reconcile herself to it. The more she sought to do so the more truly wretched did she become. At length, worn out with thinking, and bodily as well as mental suffering, she threw herself upon the bed, and without being able to compose her mind to rest she sank into a state of unconsciousness, which was some relief to her, and granted her a short respite from her cares.

In the meantime Brandon and his vile associates, after having indulged in their drunken carouse, made every preparation for their journey in the evening, and the former continued to exult to the fullest extent in the success that had attended his guilty designs, a success which he had no doubt would be rendered complete before long; and he awaited the arrival of dark with some degree of impatience.

"All goes on as well as I could wish," he observed; "and before many hours have elapsed we shall be on the way to the place of our destination, and Mary will be far removed from her native home, and with very little chance of returning to it; for those who once fall within the power of Hugh Brandon are never afforded the opportunity of escaping from it. Should Harry Halliyard also have been secured I shall be doubly gratified. My vengeance will be complete should I have the means of making him witness my triumph over his beloved Mary; and the torture it will be sure to inflict upon him will amply repay me for all that I have suffered from him. Death to all those who provoke the anger of Hugh Brandon, the pirate!"

"Ay, so say I, captain," remarked Ben Summers; "and that is the fate which they seldom fail to meet with. You have, indeed, good cause to exult in having got Mrs. Tiller in your power, and I dare say you will not fail to take advantage of it."

"You may take my word for that," returned Brandon. "I have long had my eye upon her; but now she is mine, and I will take good care that nothing shall rescue her from me."

The old woman, Nance, now entered the room, having just returned from the apartment in which our heroine was confined, and Brandon eagerly inquired respecting her. She informed him of the conversation which had taken place between her and Mary, as described in the previous pages, and the pirate expressed his satisfaction at it, and commended Nance for the manner in which she had treated the fair prisoner during the short time she had been in her charge.

"Her excitement I heed not," he continued, "for it is no more than I had a right to expect. What her feelings will be when she sees me I can very well imagine; but if she flatters herself with the idea that she can by tears or supplications move me to forbearance she will find herself much mistaken, so she may as well make up her mind to the fate which most certainly awaits her. The poor devil, Joe Tiller! I am almost inclined to pity him; for he never did me any harm, and the loss of his wife will no doubt drive him out of his senses. No matter, I have gained the gratification of my wishes, and that is enough for me."·

"To be sure it is," said Summers; "and what matters it who suffers so long as we succeed in our designs?"

"And it is not often that we have failed to do so," observed Brandon. "But it will soon be dark, and your nephew will be here, I suppose, Tapster?"

"He will be sure to be punctual to the time appointed," replied the latter; "he never fails to keep his word, especially when there is a reward in view."

"All right," said Brandon. "Hark ye, Nance; you must contrive to administer the drug to Mary, before long."

"Leave me alone for that," returned the old woman; "I will not fail to accomplish my task, and I will be careful to administer it to her sufficiently strong to take immediate effect, so that she will not be likely to recover from it for some time."

"Enough," said the pirate; "all promises well; success is certain; and in a few hours Mary will be a safe prisoner in the old farm."

"And shortly afterwards on board the Wasp, I presume?" said Summers.

Brandon replied in the affirmative, and he then resumed his preparations for the journey.

Evening was rapidly approaching before Mary was aroused from the lethargy in which we left her, and then her brain was distracted, and she was awakened to a full sense of all the horrors by which she was then surrounded, and those which no doubt awaited her; and the intensity of her emotions may be much better imagined than described. She arose from the bed, and paced the room with trembling footsteps, muttering incoherent sentences to herself, and bewailing in the most piteous accents her cruel fate, all hope of release from which was entirely banished from her mind.

"But a few short hours," she sighed, "and what, then, may not have become of me? Oh, how terrible are the sufferings which I have too much reason to anticipate! All before me is wild and dismal, and my heart sinks within me as I contemplate the fearful prospect. All the tortures that I now endure, I feel convinced, are merely trifling in comparison with those that are in store for me. God give me strength, or I must surely sink under these accumulated miseries! And would it not be a mercy to me were I to do so? It would, for life in such a state can only be a burthen to me!"

She felt sick and faint, and would have given anything for some sooting cordial which might serve to revive her; but of the provisions which the old woman had brought her in the morning she had hitherto had no appetite to partake. It was now almost dark, and the gloom of Mary's spirits increased. She seated herself at the table, and reclining her head upon her hand, she endeavoured again to compose her senses into forgetfulness; but her mind was too busily occupied and agitated to suffer her to do that, and the most fearful thoughts haunted her disordered imagination. She was, however, soon aroused from this state by hearing some one at the room door, and directly afterwards it was opened, and the old woman again made her appearance, bearing in her hand a small decanter containing a liquor which had the appearance of wine. She placed it on the table, and then fixed an earnest gaze upon the countenance of our heroine for a minute or two.

"You have not partaken of any of he refreshments I brought you," she said at last. "How foolish is this! What is the use of remaining thus obstinate?"

"Alas!" replied Mary, with a sigh, "how think you I can eat in the dreadfully agitated state of my mind? My heart is sick!"

"You must, indeed, be faint and exhausted," said the woman, in rather kind accents; "but I have brought you some wine, and a glass of that will, I dare say, revive you."

Mary hesitated for a moment or two, and then fixed a searching glance upon her; but the old woman withstood it coolly, and filled a glass from the decanter, which she handed to our heroine, at the same time saying persuasively—

"Come, come, drink this; it is very nice indeed, and no doubt it will do you good. Surely you can have no objection to that, and you stand much in need of it."

Mary took the glass, but she still hesitated, and something like a feeling of dread and misgiving came over her, and she said—

"I would fain accept your offer, for I am, indeed, faint and heart-sick; but there might be danger, and——"

"Danger!" repeated the old woman, interrupting her. "What! think you that Brandon would take all the trouble

he has done to obtain a prize, and then to cast it thus recklessly away? Your fears are groundless, Mrs. Tiller, and one moment's serious reflection must convince you that they are so."

"No matter," said our heroine, resolutely, "even though it be poison it will be a welcome draught, far preferable to the revolting fate which seems at present impending over me. Heaven watch over and protect my husband and Halliyard, and pardon me!"

As the unfortunate woman thus spoke, she raised her eyes devoutly and solemnly towards that Power which she so earnestly invoked, and then, without uttering another word, drained the contents of the glass to the dregs, the old woman watching her all the time eagerly and impatiently; and when she saw that she had accomplished her vile purpose, she could scarcely refrain from giving expression to her feelings of exultation in a loud laugh. Scarcely, however, had Mary taken the deleterious draught when a strange sensation shot through all her veins, and seemed to communicate to the whole of her system. Her heart throbbed violently—her brain became bewildered—her eyes sparkled with an unnatural lustre; and, in a faint voice, she ejaculated—

"God of Heaven! what have I been prompted to do?—What means this strange feeling which comes over me? Wretch!—woman I will not call you—you have murdered me!—I——"

She could say no more; her strength failed her—her head dropped upon her hand—her faculties seemed enchained as if by some powerful spell; strange and hideous forms danced before her disordered imagination; gradually all objects faded from her sight, and she became perfectly insensible; and but for the heavy palpitation of her heart it might have been supposed that she had indeed swallowed poison, and that she was dead.

"Ha!" exclaimed old Nance, as she gazed at her with looks of almost fiendish exultation; "the draught has taken the most overpowering effect, and much sooner than I expected. Brandon must be satisfied with the manner in which I have performed my task."

She raised the form of the insensible woman in her arms, and after gazing at her for a few minutes with looks of satisfaction she placed her on the bed, and then hastily quitted the room and repaired to the one in which Brandon was anxiously waiting to receive her.

"Ah, Nance!" he said, on her entrance, "you have returned, then?— What success?"

"All that could be wished," replied the old woman. "I have administered the draught, it has taken due effect, and she is quite insensible, and will, no doubt, from the power of the drug, remain so for many hours."

"Ah!" cried the pirate, with a look of the utmost satisfaction, "you have well performed your task, Nance, and I offer you my thanks. There is nothing now to impede the progress of my designs. This is well, and I triumph! But is she quite insensible, say you?"

"Perfectly so," answered Nance.

"I must see her," observed Brandon. "Follow me!"

The old woman obeyed, and they quitted the room together and hastened to the one in which poor Mary was confined. Brandon hurriedly approached the couch on which she was lying, and stood and gazed at the unfortunate woman with looks of the most unspeakable triumph, and at length he exclaimed—

"Ah! there she lies, pale, and unconscious to everything, and little dreaming of where she will be when she awakes to sensibility again. You have, indeed, obeyed my instructions to the very letter, Nance, and again I thank you for it. How beautiful she looks in her state of insensibility! And she is mine! Oh, this is the greatest triumph which Hugh Brandon, the pirate, has ever achieved! In a few hours she will be safe on board my bonny barque, and then, indeed, my success will be complete. Beauteous Mary! thou art, indeed, a prize it were worth running any risk to obtain possession of!"

As the villain thus spoke he stooped down, and dared to pollute the pale lips of our insensible heroine with his odious and unlawful kisses; while the old woman stood by, and watched him with looks of the most malignant satisfaction.

"Nothing will easily arouse her from this state of stupor till the strength of the opiate has evaporated, I think," said Brandon.

"No," answered his companion, "there is no fear of that. She will remain sound enough for several hours; for I took good care to administer the dose strong enough to her."

"Thanks, thanks," said the pirate; "I will not fail to reward you well for your services. It is near the time when Rudley should arrive. It is now quite dark, there is no one about to watch us, and she may be removed in safety. Let me convey her below, to be in readiness."

He raised her from the bed as he spoke, having once more imprinted a kiss upon her lips, and bidding Nance follow him, he quitted the room with his insensible burden and descended to the one below, in which himself and his infamous associates usually assembled when they were at the old tavern, and placing her in a chair, he gazed at her with feelings of admiration and malicious delight.

"There she is!" he ejaculated, "in all her simple and natural beauty! and I feel that I have achieved a triumph which might justly excite the envy of any man."

"Ay, you may say that, Master Brandon," remarked the landlord. "I never saw a more handsome woman, and she well deserves the title she has obtained of 'Pretty Poll of Putney.' Poor Tiller! he will never be able to recover such a loss, I should imagine."

"No," agreed Brandon. "Well, after all, I must say that I pity him; and as his life in future is sure to be a misery to him, why, I say that the sooner he gets rid of it the better. But is it not almost time that your nephew had arrived, Tapster?"

"Oh, never fear," answered the latter; "he will be punctual, for this is a business which just suits him, and it is not the first affair of the kind that he has been engaged in."

"Ay," returned Brandon, with a sarcastic grin. "I have not the least doubt that he will do honour to his worthy relation."

"I thank you for the compliment, Master Brandon," returned Tapster, with equal sarcasm; "coming from a gentleman of your distinguished character, it is highly flattering. Ha, ha, ha! I only wish it would suit my purpose to go a cruise with you in the Wasp, for I cannot help thinking that yours must be a very jovial life."

"A jovial life!" repeated the pirate; "ah, you may say that, my friend. There is not a merrier one under the sun; and a profitable one it is, too, if Fate is only not against us. Hugh Brandon's name has struck terror into many a sturdy breast; and now that he is in possession of such a mistress as Pretty Poll of Putney, he will be incited on to fresh deeds of daring."

"Well, all joking apart," observed Tapster, "you ought to consider yourself a very lucky fellow in the possession of such a damsel, and I wish you success with her."

"Well said—thank you!" returned the pirate. "It will be some time before we shall meet again, I dare say, so we will e'en have a glass at parting."

"With all my heart!" replied the landlord; "it is nothing but natural, you know, when old friends are about to separate. I will be with you in a minute."

He left the room as he spoke, and Brandon once more turning his gaze upon the insensible Mary, and unable to contain his feelings of exultation, said—

"This is one of the greatest triumphs which has ever fallen to my lot. Fortune smiles upon me, and I thank her for it. Oh, Hary Halliyard! did you but know that I have her whom you so fondly love in my power, and the fate which is in store for her, what would be the anguish of your feelings! It is a glorious revenge, and I thank all those who have been the means of enabling me to accomplish it."

"Why, yes, captain," said Summers; "you may, indeed, consider it a triumph, and one which has been achieved most skilfully. There are but few women who, in point of charms, can compete with Mary Tiller; and she is well worthy of being the mistress of Hugh Brandon, the pirate captain."

Old Tapster now entered with the grog, which he placed upon the table, and immediately commenced filling the glasses.

"This is some of my superior sort," he remarked, "which I only serve upon particular occasions. Come, my friends, I will take the liberty of giving you a toast, which I dare say will be agreeable to you. Here's to the daring Wasp, that flies over the broad waste of waters like a sea-mew, and may she never lose her sting!"

This toast was received with the utmost applause, and drunk with the utmost cordiality.

"Well said, Tapster!" observed Brandon; "that is a capital toast, and I thank you for it. As for my gallant barque, I do not fear but that she will long continue her triumphant career, and to be the terror of the ocean. But, come, again we must drink the health of pretty Mary, the future mistress of Hugh Brandon, the buccaneer!"

"Long life to pretty Mary, the future mistress of Hugh Brandon, the buccaneer!" shouted the ruffians, unanimously, and the applause which followed made the place resound again. But great as was the noise which prevailed, our unfortunate heroine remained undisturbed in the same state of death-like stupor.

"Old Nance has performed her task well," remarked Brandon, "and it does not seem likely that Mary will recover from the stupifying effects of the drug she has taken for some time. And even if she should, we can soon find the means to silence her."

"Oh, no," returned Brandon; "only let us once get on the road, and I have no fears as to the result. But I wish that Rudley would arrive, for the sooner we depart the better, as we have everything in readiness. It is now past the hour that he should have been here."

"Do not be impatient," said Tapster, "for he will not fail; you may take my word for that."

It was now completely dark; and the pirates having arranged everything for the journey, they did indeed become impatient at the delay. But at length the heavy rumbling of wheels, and the tinkling of bells was heard approaching towards the house, and old Tapster starting from his seat, observed—

"He is here! that's him, I'll be bound! and you must acknowledge that he is not much behind his time."

"No," replied Brandon, "I am satisfied. Go to the door, Tapster, and

ascertain whether it is really he or not."

"Oh, that's his team," said Tapster, "I could tell it a mile off. However, to satisfy you I will go and see."

He retired from the room accordingly, and Brandon then gave some further instructions to his companions. The sounds approached nearer, and in a few minutes they heard the waggon stop at the door of the tavern, and directly afterwards Tapster re-entered the room, followed by his nephew. He was a coarse, vulgar, clownish-looking fellow, but there was something in the expression of his eyes which showed that the villain lurked in his breast, and that he was just the sort of man to undertake the nefarious business to which he had lent himself. Brandon greeted him on his entrance.

"So, you have come," he said; "you are not far beyond the time appointed."

"Oh, no, master," replied the fellow, "I am generally pretty punctual when I have business to attend to; but I was detained this evening a little beyond my time. But I suppose it does not much matter?"

"No," returned Brandon. "But I suppose you are fully aware of the nature of the service I require of you?"

"Oh, yes," said Rudley; "my uncle has made me understand all about that."

"And you are willing to undertake it?"

"Certainly, or else you would not have seen me here. I am not particular what I do so long as I am well paid for it."

"Well," observed Brandon, "you shall have no reason to grumble on that point. Have you everything in readiness?"

"Yes," answered the man, "the waggon is at the door. This is the young woman, I suppose?"

"Yes," returned the pirate, "and we must, therefore, not delay any longer than possible, while she is in the state of insensibility you now see she is."

"I am quite ready when you please," said Rudley. "Well, she is a handsome young creature, sure enough."

"Ay, ay," replied Brandon, impatiently. "But I may depend upon you, can I not?"

"Oh, yes, you have no reason to doubt me."

"Enough!" said Brandon; "then let us to business at once. Summers and Guernsey, you will accompany me; let the rest follow as quickly as possible, according to my instructions." He then approached the unfortunate victim of his villany, and gazed at her earnestly, as he added—

"She still sleeps soundly; and it is not likely, according to appearances, that she will be aroused to consciousness for some time. Quick, assist me to remove her to the waggon, and let us begone. You will be careful to take the most unfrequented roads, Rudley?"

"Oh, yes," answered the latter: "but there is not much fear of any suspicion being excited, if she only does ot create any alarm."

"I will take good care to prevent that," said Brandon. "By what time do you think that we shall be able to arrive at the place of our destination?"

"Why," answered the man, "I have a capital team of horses, and a change on the road; but I do not think it is possible that we can arrive at the end of our journey before some time to-morrow morning."

"Well, be as expeditious as you can, for you know the urgency of the case."

"You may depend on my doing my best," answered Rudley.

"I am satisfied," remarked Brandon. "Now, then, let us away."

He threw a cloak over the unconscious woman as he spoke, and, Tapster leading the way to see whether or not any person was lurking near the place, he raised her in his arms and carried her from the room, followed by Rudley and the two ruffians whom he had arranged to accompany him.

"All right," said Tapster, looking out when they had arrived at the door, "there is not a soul nigh. Good-bye, Brandon, and success attend you."

"Thank you," replied Brandon; "there is not much fear of that. Good-bye; we shall meet again some time or the other, I dare say."

"I hope so," returned Tapster; "and I hope if ever you come to London again, you will not forget the Black Swan."

"Oh, no, you may depend upon that," answered the pirate, and he then conveyed our heroine from the house, and placed her at the farther end of the waggon. He and his two companions followed, Rudley smacked his whip, and the journey was commenced. The exultation of Brandon now knew no bounds, and placing himself by the side of his unfortunate victim, he again and again polluted her lips with his guilty kisses.

"She is mine! she is mine!" he cried in an ecstacy of delight; "I have surmounted every difficulty that was placed in my way, and she is securely in my power. Oh, how I will luxuriate in the success I have met with! and of what use will all her appeals be to me for mercy and forbearance? None whatever. I hope this insensibility will continue for some time yet, and it seems likely to do so."

"Oh, yes, captain," said Summers, "we have nothing to fear. Even should she revive, we may easily prevent her from creating any alarm."

"True," remarked Brandon. "But what will be her astonishment when she does recover her senses!"

"Ay," returned Summers, "no doubt of it. We could not have hit upon a better scheme."

"No," said Brandon, "the business has been well managed throughout. Should our comrades also have succeeded in capturing Halliyard, all my wishes will be gratified, and I shall have every opportunity of wreaking my vengeance on his head."

"Well," observed Summers, "I hope they may; it will be no fault of theirs if they do not. But I have my doubts as to their success."

"Well, if they fail it cannot be helped; but I firmly believe that I shall one day have him in my power, and then how terrible shall be the tortures I will inflict upon him. The hatred I bear towards him is most deadly!"

"And I do not wonder at it, captain," said Summers. "But, at any rate, you have your revenge in having her whom he so fondly loves in your power."

"Oh, yes," returned Brandon, with a savage expression of countenance, "that thought is food to my soul. Would that Halliyard could be aware of her situation, how great would be his anguish."

"True," said Summers. "But there is not much chance of that, unless he should happen to fall into your hands. But when do you propose to set sail from Portsmouth?"

"As soon as possible after our arrival."

"Ay, it will be perhaps prudent to do so; for something might occur to excite some suspicions in the minds of the land-sharks, and we should then be placed in rather an awkward predicament."

"Oh, we will take good care to prevent that," returned Brandon; "and

I am anxious to be once more upon the blue waters."

"Yes," returned Summers, "we are out of our element on shore."

Brandon returned no answer, and they remained silent for a time. The waggon proceeded at more than its usual speed, and they had soon got far away from the tavern, and out of the noise and bustle of town. Rudley obeyed the instructions he had received, and took the most lonely and unfrequented roads; but even had he not have done so, there would have been nothing to fear, for no suspicions could possibly be excited, and poor Mary gave not the least signs of returning sensibility; and, in fact, the stupor in which she was wrapped almost resembled the sleep of death.

After they had thus travelled for about a couple of hours, Rudley stopped at an old-fashioned roadside public-house, in order to obtain some refreshment, and they then again proceeded on their journey, Brandon and his companions entering but little into conversation on the way. The night was exceedingly dark and cold, and everything was in perfect unison with the guilty deed the villains were performing; but Brandon took no heed of the weather, for his thoughts were fully occupied with his diabolical project, and he continued to exult at the success he had so far met with. They had now got some distance into the country, but still the journey appeared unusually tedious to Brandon, and he frequently called to Rudley to quicken his speed, though the waggon was going at a rate which was quite uncommon for such a ponderous vehicle. They had hitherto seen few persons on the road, and they passed on without taking any notice, so that the confidence of Brandon became stronger, and he looked forward to their safe arrival at the place of their destination as certain. Suddenly, however, he was aroused from a deep train of thought into which he had fallen by hearing our heroine breathe a deep sigh, and he started from the place where he had been seated in considerable excitement and alarm.

"Confusion!" he exclaimed; "she is reviving, and we have not half accomplished our journey. Whats to be done?"

Mary now showed evident signs of returning animation, and opening her eyes, she stared in utter bewilderment around her, but was unable to distinguish anything at first in the darkness.

"Where am I?" she ejaculated: "where have I been all this time? and what strange fears are these that come over me? Tiller! oh, God! I——"

"Silence!" said Brandon, in a hoarse voice, "and no harm will come to you. To make any complaint, or to raise any alarm, will be useless."

"Ah!" she cried, in accents of still greater terror, and endeavouring to scrutinize Brandon as well as she could, "who are you that speak to me? Your voice fills me with terror! Again I command you to inform me where I am?"

"Why," replied Brandon, "if it will be any satisfaction for you to know, you are now far away from the house in which you were lately confined, and journeying to a place where you will be quite secure from discovery."

"Good God! is it possible?" exclaimed the wretched woman, in the most piteous accents. "Brandon!"

"Ay," returned the pirate, triumphantly, "it is even him that you are addressing, and to whose will you must in future submit."

"Horror! horror!" cried the distracted Mary, and endeavouring to rush from the waggon; "am I, indeed, consigned to such a dreadful fate? Release me, villain, or fear the vengeance of Heaven!"

"All this is complete madness, Mary, and will not avail you in the least. You are securely in my power, and it will be utterly impossible for you now to escape. Again I enjoin you to silence, or it may be worse for you."

"Oh, help—help!" shrieked our heroine, as loud as she could; and her cries were re-echoed far around, to the alarm of the ruffian, Brandon, who feared that they might attract the attention of some travellers.

"Rash woman, forbear!" he said, rudely grasping her arm, and holding her down in the waggon. "These cries are useless; there is no one here to assist you. Cease, I say, or tremble for the consequences!"

But his words had no effect upon Mary, and she screamed for help more loudly than before. Brandon now became desperate, especially as Rudley stopped the horses, and coming to the end of the waggon, informed him that he could see two or three persons rapidly approaching, and that the cries of Mary had probably reached their ears. This announcement caused our heroine to redouble her calls for help; and the confusion and dismay of the pirate and his vile associates in crime may be readily imagined,

"D——n!" he cried, fiercely; "we shall be discovered! Cease your cries, rash woman, I again command you!" he added, drawing a knife from his pocket, and pointing it to her breast, "for if you dare to utter another sound beyond a whisper I will bury this in your heart!"

Horror-struck, and overpowered by her emotions and the exertions she had undergone, Mary tried to speak, but she could not; and fixing upon the hardened miscreant, Brandon, a look which was sufficient to move the most stubborn heart, she again sank down in the waggon in a state of utter insensibility.

"She is quiet at last," said the pirate, with a fearful look; "but I am afraid it is too late."

He then called to Rudley, and inquired if the persons whom he had seen were still approaching the waggon. Rudley answered in the affirmative, and added that there were three of them, and that they were men.

"What is to be done?" demanded Summers; "this is a confounded unfortunate affair."

"Be firm," returned Brandon, "and all may yet be well. But should the worst come to the worst, we must resist them boldly; and as we are armed and they are probably not, we shall be more than a match for them. Do not acknowledge that you have any one in the waggon," he added to Rudley, "and be careful what you say to them."

Rudley promised that he would, and soon after the men came up, and, stopping him, inquired whether he had not heard cries for help.

"Yes," he replied, pretending to be deaf, "it be a very cold night, sure enough; and I think it freezes sharply."

"Did you not understand the question we put to you ?" demanded one of the men, impatiently.

"Speak a little louder, if you please," said Rudley, "for I am very deaf."

The man repeated his first question in a voice which was loud enough to awake the dead, and received the following answer:

"Oh, no, you be going quite out of your way; it is just three miles the other road."

"D——n the fellow!" said the man, "he is either drunk or a fool. We shall get nothing out of him. Let us hurry on; I am certain that the cries proceeded not far from this spot, and some poor creature may stand in need of our assistance. Come, my lads."

They then departed, and the crafty Rudley proceeded, whistling on his way, as though nothing had happened.

"Cleverly done, Rudley," said Brandon; "you have completely baffled those fellows, and we are now safe, thanks to our lucky stars. Proceed on your way as fast as you can. I hope Mary may remain insensible the remainder of the journey."

"There is not much chance of that," observed Summers; "but should she revive we must endeavour to intimidate her into silence."

"Yes," said Brandon; "but could I only manage to administer another sleeping potion to her which I have with me we should be safe. This is a tedious journey, especially travelling by such a vehicle as a waggon. But now I recollect myself, a few miles further on is a lonely inn, kept by a man with whom I am well acquainted, for we have often transacted business together; and there we can stop for an hour or so to rest ourselves, and procure a lighter vehicle, that will carry us quickly the remainder of our journey. It is a lucky thought of mine, and I wonder it did not occur to me before."

He then called to Rudley, and directed him which way to go, and informed him that there he should be able to dispense with his further services.

"All right, master," replied Rudley; "a waggon is certainly not the best thing for those who require expedition. But I hope I have given you satisfaction so far?"

"Oh, yes," returned Brandon, "you could not have managed better, and I thank you for it. But get on as fast as you can, lest we should meet with some other mishap. That was a narrow escape that we had just now."

"Ay, you may say that, Master Brandon," remarked Rudley; "and had I not happened to hit upon the scheme that I did, I don't know what might have been the consequence."

"Yes," said Brandon, "you certainly deserve credit for that. But push on your way."

Rudley obeyed, and they proceeded in silence on their way. Mary's feelings had received such a shock that she still remained insensible, and it did not seem likely that she would soon recover. They saw nothing more of the men who had overtaken them, and they therefore concluded that the strange answers that Rudley had given to their questions had completely quieted their suspicions, and that they had nothing more to fear from them; and after travelling in this manner for about an hour they came in sight of the inn, before the door of which they quickly stopped. It was closed, but a light in one of the windows convinced them that all the inmates had not retired to rest; and Brandon having alighted, advanced to the door, and knocked loudly at it. In a few minutes it was opened by a man, whose personal appearance was anything but prepossessing, and who inquired in rather surly tones what he wanted at that hour of the night.

"What, don't you know me, Redford?" demanded Brandon, hastily.

The man thrust the lamp which he carried in the pirate's face, in order that he might scrutinize his features more narrowly, and he then started back in amazement, as he exclaimed—

"What, Brandon, my old particular! is it possible? Why who the devil would have thought of seeing you in these parts?"

"No, I don't suppose you did," replied Brandon; "and it is only a complete accident that has brought me here."

"Why, what's up now?" demanded Redford. Brandon informed him in as few words as possible.

"This is a strange adventure," said Redford, "and I wish you success with all my heart. I am glad to see you, and you know that you are welcome to all the assistance that I can render you. Bring your fair prisoner into the house, and we will see what can be done. There is nobody here but myself and my wife."

Brandon now returned to the waggon, and with the assistance of Summers and Guernsey conveyed Mary into the inn, where they were followed by Rudley; and they found the wife of Redford in the room. Mary was placed on a sofa in the room, and Mrs. Redford could not help gazing with some degree of interest upon her.

"She is remarkably handsome," she said; "and you say that she is a married woman, Brandon?"

"Yes," answered the latter, "but my futue companion and mistress; she will never behold her husband again. I will leave her to your care while I remain here, which must only be for a short time. And, hark ye, should she recover, perhaps you will do me a favour?"

"Name it," said Mrs. Redford.

"I am anxious that she should remain in a state of unconsciousness until we arrive at the end of our journey," observed Hugh. "You may persuade her to take something to revive her, and if you will only mix this potion with what you give her to drink it will have the desired effect."

"I will do so," answered Mrs. Redford, taking the bottle from his hand.

Brandon thanked her, and then he and the landlord, and the others, retired to another room, where refreshments were placed before them.

"Well," observed Redford, "I'm sure you are the last person I expected to see, Brandon. I thought you were far away on the wide ocean at this time. But how goes business?"

"Oh, as successful as usual," replied the pirate. "Fortune generally smiles upon me, you know, and I have no cause to grumble."

"No," said Redford, "thanks to your daring and determined spirit, and your gallant crew. But this is a handsome prize you have got in your possession."

"Ay, you may say that," returned Brandon, "and I am proud of her. But I with I was at the end of my journey. We have hitherto travelled but slowly by the waggon. Have you another vehicle you can accommodate me with?"

"Yes," answered Redford, "I have a light covered cart, and as pretty a little horse as ever was put into shafts, which are at your service. But had you not better remain here till the morning?"

"No," replied Brandon, "there would be danger in delay. The sooner I depart the better. If your wife can only succeed in persuading Mary to take the drug she will remain quiet enough till we arrive at the end of our journey."

"I have no doubt she will do that," said Redford, "so you may set your mind at rest upon that point. But do you mean to take this damsel on board your vessel?"

"Certainly," answered Brandon; "do you think I will ever suffer her to quit my sight again? But you will be careful not to tell any one that you have seen me, or to state that I had her in my power."

"Psha!" ejaculated Redford, impatiently, "what occasion have you to caution me? You know well that I should not be so stupid as to do that."

"Well," remarked Brandon, "I can trust you. Now, Rudley, I can dispense with your further services, since my friend here can accommodate me with another and a more convenient vehicle."

"Very good, master," said Rudley. "However, as it is now so late, and I have no wish to travel any further, I shall stay here till the morning."

"I can depend upon your secrecy in this business, can I not?" interrogated the pirate.

"Of course you can," answered Rudley. "It's not likely that I will say a word of it to anybody. But you don't forget your promise as to the reward you promised me?"

"No," said Brandon, tossing him a purse, "there it is, and I am very well satisfied with what you have done."

Rudley pocketed the purse, and thanked him; and they then continued to converse together for some time, until they were interrupted by the entrance of the landlady.

"Well, Mrs. Redford," eagerly demanded Brandon, "what news?"

"All that you could wish," she answered. "The female did partially revive, but not exactly to consciousness; and not knowing what she did, I easily persuaded her to swallow the draught which you gave me, and she is now in a complete state of insensibility."

"Ah!" ejaculated Brandon, "that is most fortunate; you have my thanks for this piece of service. Now, Redford, if you will oblige me by getting the vehicle ready, we will resume the journey without delay."

"I will do so," answered Redford; and he left the room for that purpoe, and Brandon followed Mrs. Redford into the room where they had left our unfortunate heroine. Brandon approached her and gazed at her earnestly.

"Ah," he said, "she is sound enough, she will not trouble me for the remainder of the journey, I dare say; and altogether I have managed this business in a much better manner than I could even have expected. In two or three hours more she will be safe in my secret retreat."

"Poor thing!" said Mrs. Redford, in something like a tone of pity, "her sufferings must be very great when she comes to her senses. But her husband?"

"Why, he, no doubt, is in a state bordering upon madness at her loss," replied the heartless villain; "but that I cannot help. I had made up my mind to obtain her, and when once I have done that, nothing can move me from my purpose."

Redford now entered the room and informed him that the cart was ready; and with the assistance of Summers, Brandon conveyed Mary to it, and placing her on a rug at the bottom of the vehicle, he covered her over with the cloak, so that she was completely concealed from observation, He and his companions then followed, and after bidding Redford, his wife, and Rudley farewell, the cart was driven off at a rapid pace, and was soon out of sight. They only stopped twice to obtain some refreshment, but by the time they had arrived near the place of their destination the morning had far advanced, though they entered the house without being seen by any one. On beholding their captain and his unfortunate victim, the pirates greeted

him with the loudest acclamations, and all eyes were directed to the insensible Mary, who showed not the slightest signs of recovery.

"Thanks to fortune," said Brandon, "we have arrived safe, and all fear of Mary being discovered is now at an end. I will carry her into another apartment, and Alice will attend upon her. I dare say it will be some time before she will sleep off the effects of the draught she has taken."

He raised the inanimate form of our heroine in his arms as he gave utterance to these words, and carrying her to a chamber up stairs, where he placed her on a bed, he kissed her two or three times exultingly, and then quitted the room, locking the door after him, and returned to the apartment where he had left Harville and the pirates, and whom he found busily discussing the charms of Mary.

"So, captain," said Bullruff, "you have, then, succeeded, and Mary is destined to become your future mistress?"

"Yes," answered Brandon, "and I would not resign her for the universe. What think you of my choice, Bullruff?"

"Why, that it is an excellent one," returned the latter; "and I congratulate you on your success. We have been most anxiously awaiting your return, for it is almost time that we quitted this port, I think."

"True," coincided Brandon; "but has anything happened since I have been away?"

Bullruff replied in the negative.

"But what of Halliyard?" eagerly demanded Brandon.

"He is still at liberty," answered the pirate.

"Ah! how is that?—Have you not obeyed my orders?"

"We have; but Fortune frowned upon us just as success seemed certain. We had Halliyard and his companion in our power, and were conveying them hither, when the cries of that infernal Waxend brought a number of the coastguard to their assistance, and we were compelled to take to immediate flight and to leave them behind, or our lives would probably have been sacrificed."

"Curses light on this misfortune!" said Brandon, passionately. "I had hoped to have found Halliyard secured on my return here, and then my triumph would have been complete. Why did you not boldly face the land-sharks?"

"It would have been madness for us to have done so," replied Bullruff; "for they so far outnumbered us that we should have stood no chance with them."

"Then he has, for the present, escaped me," said Brandon, "and I have lost the opportunity of gratifying my vengeance to the fullest extent. Had you managed your designs as cleverly as I have done mine you would not have met with this failure."

"Do not blame us, captain," said Dogsby, "for it was no fault of ours. Fortune decided against us, and that's the whole truth of the matter."

"I would willingly have given a thousand guineas to have got him in my power, so that I might have wreaked my vengeance on his head," remarked Brandon. "But is the Porpoise still in the harbour?"

"She is," answered Bullruff; "but from what I have heard I believe that she sails the day after to-morrow."

"May every curse attend her and her crew!" cried Brandon, fiercely. "Should I ever by chance encounter her, notwithstanding that she is well manned, and carries such heavy metal, I do not doubt but that she would find the dare-devil Wasp more than a match for her. But think you that the enemy had any suspicion who you were?"

"No," answered Bullruff, "there is not much fear of that, for I do not believe that they had ever seen any of us before."

"And they did not notice whence you came?"

"No, that is not likely, or they would have been sure to have paid us a visit before now."

"Well," observed Brandon, after a pause, "it is an unfortunate affair, but it cannot be helped. I do not despair of yet getting Harry Halliyard in my power; and if I do, let him tremble, for he can expect no mercy at my hands. But what would be his sufferings did he only know the situation of Mary, on whom, notwithstanding she is the wife of another, his affections, I am convinced, are still firmly fixed!"

"True," said Summers; "and you ought to consider yourself fortunate, captain, that at least Mary has not been able to escape you. It was an excellent plot that we laid to entrap her; and nothing could have been managed with greater skill or safety that it was throughout."

"You say right, Ben," coincided Brandon, "and I cannot but congratulate myself upon it; but still I have a cautious game to play. I must endeavour by some means to abate the excitement of Mary, or it may retard the gratification of my wishes."

"Oh, no doubt you will be able to accomplish that," said Summers. "I never knew a woman, let her disposition be ever so stubborn, yet, who was not to be conquered, especially when she became convinced that all opposition would be completely useless. You will, however, I suppose, not delay conveying her on board the Wasp?"

"No," answered Brandon, "as soon as I can find an opportunity of doing so without fear of detection; for we must be cautious of those land-sharks, the coast-guard, and also of the crew of the Porpoise, which is moored so close to us. Once safe on board, we must contrive to slip our cable unseen in the night-time, and once under weigh, and plenty of sea room, they may suspect us as soon as possible, for we may defy pursuit, unless the Porpoise is a much faster sailer than I take her to be."

"Ay," agreed Summers, "and you will then have Mrs. Tiller completely at your mercy, and she will be convinced that she has no means of avoiding her fate."

"She might very well be satisfied of that now," remarked Brandon; "for those whom I once get in my power may be certain that their fate is sealed, and may as well make up their minds to the worst. However, since we have thus far succeeded, and have arrived in safety here, we may as well celebrate it in a social glass."

"With all my heart," said Harville, the pretended farmer; "there is nothing like making merry on such occasions as this; and the bold pirates of the sea should never be sad, even though fortune, at times, may frown upon them."

"Well said, Harville," remarked

Brandon. "For my own part I never felt in better spirits; so bring the grog, and we will make merry for an hour or two. My fair prisoner will not require to be disturbed just yet, I dare say."

"No," said Summers; "and our friend Alice can attend upon her. It will be better for you not to see her to-day, captain, I think, but suffer her to recover in some measure from the shock and terror of the journey."

"Yes," coincided Brandon, "I do indeed think that would be the most prudent plan."

Harville now brought in a plentiful supply of grog and other refreshments, which the pirates sat down with avidity to partake of, and the exhilarating effect of which soon put them in high spirits.

"The removal of Mary on board the Wasp may easily be accomplished without any fear of detection," observed Summers. "This place affords every facility for that; you had forgotten the secret passage which leads near to the cliffs."

"True," replied Brandon; "along which she can be conveyed with safety, at midnight, and thence on board the vessel, we having a boat waiting near the creek for that purpose. It shall be so, and, therefore, that point is settled. To-morrow night, if all goes well, that business shall be accomplished; and then the sooner we set sail the better, when we have the opportunity of doing so without being observed. Should we be discovered while we remain here, we should be placed in a very awkward situation."

"You may say that, captain," observed Ben Summers; "and it was a bold step to lay up in the very port where we are completely surrounded by the enemy."

"Such bold steps are calculated to disarm suspicion," returned Brandon, "and to render the danger of detection less hazardous. They little think what kind of craft the supposed Helen is, or we should soon be all placed in the bilboes, or made food for the sharks. But, come, drink, and make yourselves merry."

The pirates willingly obeyed this order, and they were soon all in a beastly state of intoxication, and were ready for the perpetration of any crime at the command of their captain.

Mary still continued in the same state of insensibility as when she had been brought to the house, and from which it did not seem likely that she would shortly be aroused. Indeed, it was a mercy to her that she was unconscious of the terrible dangers by which she was surrounded; and had she never woke again it would have been better for her, rather than to have had to experience the manifold sufferings that were in store for her. In the course of the day Alice, who was the wife of one of the pirates, frequently looked in upon her, and finding that she slept soundly, and apparently calmly, she did not offer to disturb her. Brandon, too, could not resist the temptation to visit her, in order to gaze upon her, and to triumph over the success of his diabolical plot; and it would be impossible to describe the savage delight with which he contemplated his unfortunate victim, whom he had so remorselessly torn from her home, and consigned to a fate which was horrible to think on."

"How beautiful she looks, even though so pale and care-worn," he ejaculated, folding his arms, and gazing eagerly upon her. "What man is there who need not envy me my lot, possessed of such a mistress as this? Oh, I am amply rewarded for the trouble it has cost me to get her in my power. Sleep on, fair damsel, I will not, for the present, disturb you. Little do you dream, I dare say, of the fate which is in store for you. Oh, I could gaze for ever in admiration upon such charms as these; and even my stern nature seems partly subdued by them, and I feel that I could freely worship where I am the master."

He gazed more earnestly at her as he spoke, and then he ventured several times to imprint his unlawful kisses upon the unconscious woman's lips, and to revel in his triumph.

"But a short time," he continued, after a pause, "and you will be completely mine; the whole of my wishes will be accomplished, and your fate will be decided for ever. With such a woman as this I shall be stimulated to fresh acts of daring, and my success will be greater than ever. But should she die—should her strength sink beneath this heavy trial, all my sanguine expectations will be annihilated, and the bitterest disappointment will be my doom. But, psha! let me not give way to any such idle apprehensions; if I act with my usual precaution I can prevent such a calamity from taking place. I will be firm, and success will no doubt crown my efforts. I feel annoyed, however, at the escape of Halliyard; I was in hopes on my return here to have found him secured, and then what glorious satisfaction would it not have afforded me to witness his anguish, and to add to his tortures by every possible means in my power. Bullruff and the others must have managed it badly, or they could not have failed to have succeeded. But no matter, the time may yet come when he shall fall into my clutches; and then let him beware, for I will amply repay him all the many debts I owe him. He little dreams of the deed which I have already accomplished, or his proud spirit would be crushed, and he would be overwhelmed with anguish and despair. The fate of his beloved Mary is in my hands, and I will not fail to take advantage of it."

He ceased, and after once more kissing the pale cheek of his hapless victim, he slowly retired from the room; and having assumed the disguise which he usually wore when he was on shore, he made his way towards his vessel, in order to make his crew acquainted with his arrival, and to prepare them for the reception of our heroine, probably on the following night. He had proceeded but a short distance on his way when his ears were suddenly saluted by the voices of men in earnest conversation, and presently afterwards two individuals emerged from a dark opening, in whom he immediately recognised Harry Halliyard and his friend, Mr. Watchful Waxend. Hastily Brandon drew himself back into a place where he could not be observed, and watched them eagerly, while the various feelings that agitated his guilty breast at the sight of him whom he so mortally hated, and whose destruction he sought, may be readily imagined.

The two friends stopped at a convenient distance, but within hearing, and the pirate listened attentively to catch what they were so earnestly conversing about. Harry seemed to be in a state of the greatest excitement, and held a newspaper in his hand, upon which his eyes were intently fixed, and his manly bosom seemed to heave with the power of his emotions.

"No, no!" he said at last, "it cannot be—it is all a dream! My top-lights must be getting misty, or else the enemy is hoisting false signals; and yet, here it is all entered in the log as plain as A, B, C. Mys—mysterious disappearance of a female—Suspected murder—Mary Tiller—wife of a Thames waterman, and commonly known by the name of Pretty Poll of Putney—No traces of her have been discovered, and it is strongly suspected that—oh, d——n it, I can read no more!—My upper-works are getting crazy—I am taken all aback! Mary—poor Mary—my Mary! Oh, God! and can this be true? I.—I shall go mad!"

"He pressed his hands upon his forehead as he spoke, and gave himself up entirely to the agitation of his feelings,

"Ah!" muttered Brandon to himself,

with a savage grin of satisfaction, "he has heard it, then; and his torture is complete. Revenge, revenge, thou art sweet."

Again he listened attentively, and presently Waxend observed—

"Ah, it is, indeed, a sad affair! and there can be no doubt that it is, unfortunately, too true. Poor Mrs. Tiller! what can have become of her? Something terrible has befallen her, there is every reason to believe, and that makes out another portion of my dream. Oh, I am very fatal in my dreams, and——"

"Avast, you swab!" interrupted our hero, impatiently; "this is not the time to give utterance to your ridiculous palaver, when the vessel is stranded. Dear, unfortunate Mary! little did I think that such a fate as this was ever in store for you! What, oh what can have become of you? Supposed to have been murdered! Oh, dreadful thought! But no, it cannot be! Providence would never so cruelly desert her! And yet I know not what to think! This is, indeed, the worst news that I have heard for many a day!"

"Poor Joe Tiller, too!" remarked Waxend, "what a state of distraction he must be in at her loss! How greatly do I pity him!"

"Ah, poor fellow!" sighed Harry, "he is, indeed, to be pitied; for the loss of such a mate as Mary is enough to break the heart of any man. But who could think to injure one so good and innocent? Perhaps—perhaps she has been induced to elope from her home, and to endeavour to find me out, and follow my footsteps; or else, in her despair, she has laid violent hands upon herself! Oh, how torturing are these thoughts! I know not what to think—what to do! Mary, dear Mary, you are still all to me, although fate has decreed that you should sail under another captain. And poor Harry is sent adrift, without either rudder or compass to steer by. Oh, I would willingly wander the world in search of her, and would not rest until I had discovered her, but I am fettered, bound, and have no power to do so. Supposed to have been murdered! The thought is madness! It must, indeed, be a black-hearted, cowardly pirate, who could be guilty of such a crime as that!

Oh, what shall I do?—Whither can I go? I am wretched! Would that I had, long ere this could have happened, been food for sharks!"

"Come, come, Harry," expostulated Waxend, "do not take on so; she may not have met with the fate which is apprehended, and she may yet be restored in safety to her home."

"Oh, no!" returned Halliyard, in accents of despair, "there is no chance of that! I see it clearly enough; she has fallen into the hands of some villain, and her fate is all but certain. And the day after to-morrow our vessel sails from these shores, and I shall be deprived of the opportunity of searching for her. To have to endure this state of suspense will be too much for me, and my senses will certainly founder. But I cannot, will not leave the country till I have ascertained what has become of her. I will desert, abandon the ship, and—"

"Hold, Harry!" interrupted Waxend; "know you what you say?—Would you, after all the years of honour that you have experienced, thus disgrace yourself?"

"Disgrace myself!" repeated Halliyard, "by braving that which I consider to be my duty, for the sake of poor Mary? Oh, how think you that I can dare the perils of the ocean with my usual fortitude while I am in this terrible state of fear and uncertainty as to the fate which has befallen her? It is impossible; and my patience becomes exhausted while I think of it!"

"Nay," again remonstrated Waxend, "but you must endeavour to call reason to your aid, and to reflect calmly upon the painful circumstance."

"Reflect calmly!" repeated Harry, in a voice of the greatest emotion; "oh, what a mockery is it to talk to me thus! As well might you attempt to drain the ocean as to calm my feelings on such a dreadful occasion as this! Cruel fate is against me, and every day, every hour brings me fresh trouble, and seems to hold me up to mockery and scorn."

He struck his forehead in the wildness of his agony as he thus spoke, and the villain Brandon could scarcely refrain from laughing aloud.

"Let us to the inn, Halliyard," said Waxend, "and there we can discuss with our friends what is best to be done."

"Lead me where you will, I care not what becomes of me now; I am cast upon a barren shore," replied our hero, in a voice of the utmost despair. "Oh, Mary! poor, ill-fated lass! why did Providence decree that we should ever be separated?"

As he uttered these words he slowly moved away from the spot, accompanied by Waxend. Brandon watched them till they were out of sight, and he then came from the place of his concealment, and in accents of the most savage exultation he exclaimed—

"My wishes are gratified! He has become acquainted with the mysterious disappearance of Mary, and the horrible ideas to which it gives rise in his mind torture him to madness. Ha, ha, ha! what pleasure it afforded me to witness his misery—to listen to his mournful lamentations. And this is but a prelude to that which he has to endure. The despair of his mind will lead him into some breach of duty, and he will bring disgrace and punishment upon his head. I see, I read his fate as clearly as if it were at this moment realised; and all this has been the work of my hands. Again I triumph, although I have failed to get him into my power. Oh, if he knew that I am the author of all this—that Mary is my prisoner, and is doomed to become the victim to my guilty passions, how doubly severe would be the agony of his soul! Harry Halliyard, in spite of your vain boastings, your proud spirit is yet doomed to be crushed, and all through my secret machinations."

Again the villain laughed aloud, and then abandoning the idea of going to the vessel for the present, he retraced his steps towards the farm, where he soon arrived, and made his way to the room where his guilty associates were assembled.

"Why, captain," said Summers, on his entrance, "you have soon returned; has anything particular happened? You seem excited."

"Yes," answered Brandon, "I have seen and heard that which has been as food to my soul. I have seen Halliyard!"

"Ah!" exclaimed Summers, "and did he then behold you?"

"No," returned the pirate, "I took

good care to conceal myself from him and his companion, but I closely watched him, and I overheard sufficient to convince me that he is now one of the most wretched of human beings, and that, at any-rate, is some gratification to my revenge."

"'How? what mean you?" demanded Ben.

"He has become acquainted with the disappearance of Mary," answered Brandon; "it is in the newspapers, and the fact has struck him like a thunder-bolt, and he seems half mad."

"Ay," remarked Summers, "this news is, indeed, most gratifying; but if it is not too much trouble, captain, perhaps you will relate the particulars."

Brandon complied, and the pirates listened to him with much attention and satisfaction, and when he had concluded Bullruff observed—

"This must, indeed, be a terrible shock to Halliyard, and the anguish of his feelings in some measure makes up for the disappointment you experienced at his escape."

"True," coincided Brandon; "but still do I hope some time or another to get him in my power, and then I will inflict upon him such sufferings as it is not easy to conceive. Oh, what delight did it afford me to listen to his dismal lamentations!"

"But did he seem to form any idea as to what had become of her?" inquired Ben.

"Not the least," replied Brandon. "How is it likely that he should?"

"And you say that he and Waxend have gone to the Seaman's Friend?" said Summers.

"They have," answered the coptain.

"Would it not be possible to waylay them on their return, and to bring them hither?"

"No, it might be fraught with danger so soon after the recent attempt. I am perfectly satisfied with what has been done at present, and have no doubt that I shall have some future opportunity of getting him in my power. The day after to-morrow the Porpoise sails, and it will be with a sad heart that Halliyard will go on board. He little suspects that the object of his anxiety is so near him, and that in a few hours she will be on board the very vessel which is moored next to the ship he belongs to, and of which his old and deadly enemy, Hugh Brandon, is the captain. Fortune indeed favours me, and I thank the fickle jade for it. At one moment my feelings were so much excited that I could scarcely help rushing upon him and burying my knife in his heart."

"It would have been a rash act," remarked Summers, "and might have been fraught with danger."

"Very true," assented Brandon; "it was better avoided, and I shall yet have the means of wreaking my vengeance on his head."

"No doubt of it," said Summers. "It is a fortunate thing that neither of them beheld you, for that might have led to discovery."

"True," said Brandon. "But how is my prisoner?"

"In the same state as when you left her."

"'Tis well. When she recovers to sensibility the utmost caution must be used to endeavour to quiet the excitement of her feelings, which I dare say will be very great."

"No doubt of it," replied Ben; "and if you are wise you will not be too precipitate in your advances towards her, for it might be attended by the most fatal conseqences to her, and you might thus deprive yourself of the gratification you desire."

"Oh, never fear," said Brandon; "I value the success I have as yet met with too much for that; and I would not lose the chance of the gratification of my wishes for all the wealth in the world, although that is a bold statement to make. You will go to the ship, Summers, and tell the lads of my arrival here. And let as many of them as can be spared accompany you back, for it is my wish that we should make a jovial night of it on this occasion, especially as we are so soon to depart on another cruise. Do you hear, Ben?"

"Ay, ay, captain," answered the latter, "I will fulfil your orders to the very letter, and will soon return."

Having thus spoken Ben Summers departed, and Brandon then retired to another room to mature his nefarious plans, and to enjoy his malignant feelings of triumph alone.

The agitation of Harry Halliyard at

the fatal intelligence which he had read in the paper by accident, and which had fallen like an electric shock upon him, has been fully described in the dialogue which had taken place between him and Waxend, and which the villain Brandon had listened to with so much satisfaction. But it would be impossible to convey anything like an adequate idea of the real state of his mind as he and his companion took their way towards the 'Seaman's Friend,' an agitation which increased in strength every moment. It was all to no purpose that Waxend exerted himself to the utmost to console him; the spirit of the hardy young seaman was completely subdued—he resigned himself to absolute despair; and when he thought of the probable fate of his still beloved Mary he could have wept like a child. But the mystery in which her fate was involved tortured him more than all, and he in vain racked his brain to fathom it.

"Poor lass—poor lass!" he ejaculated, mournfully, "how cruelly have all your hopes of happiness been wrecked and run down by adversity! And yet 'tis hard that so fair a craft should thus split upon the rock of misfortune! Oh, Mary! your Harry's heart bleeds for you, and he would willingly lay down his own life to save you from further sorrow, and to reverse the evil destiny which has hitherto attended you. But this terrible blow, so sudden and so unexpected, is worse than all! Oh, what can have become of you? Who is the villain that has wrought this mischief, if, indeed, despair has not caused you to precipitate your fate by your own hands? Horrible thought! it drives my brain to frenzy as it occurs to me! But, no, I cannot believe that you would ever be urged to commit so rash and fatal an act! Some villanous plot, from enemies whom I know not, has been at work to destroy you, and too well, alas! I fear, have they succeeded."

"It is a melancholy job, Harry," observed Waxend, "and I feel as much for poor Mrs. Tiller, if possible, as yourself. But do not give way entirely to despair; for, although it appears bad enough at present, after all it may turn out much better than you now anticipate. Poor Tiller's sufferings must, indeed, be great, and I only hope,

for his sake, that she may be discovered, and restored to him uninjured."

"Alas!" returned Halliyard, "there is not much chance of that; for if she has fallen into the hands of some designing miscreant, which it seems but too probable that she has, he will take good care that she does not escape him, for were she to do so it might lead to his detection and punishment, and he would rather sacrifice her life than that such a result should take place."

"That is a fearful idea, Master Halliyard," remarked his companion, with a shudder, "and I hope it may turn out to be unfounded. Who can you suspect of having any designs against Mary?"

"I know not," answered our hero, "for she was too good and amiable to give cause for enmity in any human breast. There is only one man who I believe, if he had the chance, would, from a spirit of deadly revenge which I know he cherishes towards me, be guilty of so foul a crime."

"And who is that, pray?" inquired Waxend.

"Hugh Brandon," replied Halliyard.

"Ah, a most awful fellow," said Waxend, "and I would as soon encounter the devil as him; though, with all his daring, I did manage to settle the business for that rascally brother of his. I am strongly inclined to believe that it was some of his ruffianly crew who lately seized us, and would have borne us off in triumph had it not been for the very fortunate arrival of the coast-guard; and I should not at all wonder if he is nearer to us than we now expect. Ah! all this makes out my dream more than ever."

"D——n your dream!" impatiently cried our hero, "I have no patience to listen to such nonsense."

"Ah!" returned Waxend, "you may call it nonsense if you please, Mr. Halliyard, but I only hope that it may not prove to be too true. But I do not wish to alarm you, and——"

"Alarm me, you lubber!" interrupted Harry; "do you think that I am so chicken-hearted as to be frightened by such a lubberly boy as you? Oh, Mary! how can I express the anguish which I feel at the terrible uncertainty of your fate? May eternal curses pursue the wretch or wretches who have been the cause of it!"

"So I say, with all my heart, Harry," observed Waxend; "for a prettier, or more innocent and virtuous a lass never stood in two shoes, and I flatter myself that I am a pretty good judge in such matters."

"Pretty—innocent—virtuous!" repeated our hero, with the deepest emotion; "oh, yes, she was all these and what description can possibly do justice to her! And she was to have been mine—my own bride! and we should have been so happy! But fate, cruel fate decreed it otherwise, and cast a gloom upon our future prospects which nothing whatever can banish! Oh, God! I certainly shall go mad, for it is impossible for human nature to endure such accumulated miseries as these."

He paused, and again he struck his forehead in despair and anguish, while his manly bosom heaved with the power of his emotions.

"I wish that I could persuade you to tranquillize your feelings, Mr. Halliyard," said Waxend; "it is of no use to excite yourself in this violent manner."

"And I must be less than man could I treat such a calamity as this with indifference," returned Harry; "the more I think of it the more distracted does my brain become. If I had the opportunity to search for her it would be some relief to my mind."

"And whither could you direct your footsteps, if even you had?" inquired Waxend. "I never knew a more mysterious business in the whole course of my experience, and I know not what to make of it. But, come, arouse yourself, Harry, and——"

"Arouse myself!" interrupted the latter, impatiently; "oh, how easy it is to advise! But you know not the nature of my feelings, or you would not talk thus."

"Pardon me, my friend," returned Waxend, "but no one can more fully appreciate your feelings than I do, and I am sorry that it is not in my power to assist you. As for poor Mary, I trust that under all her misfortunes Heaven will still watch over and protect her, and defeat the wicked designs of any secret enemies she may have."

"Most fervently do I pray the same," ejaculated Harry; "but still I cannot indulge the hope, for everything seems against it. Alas! I fear that I shall never behold poor Mary again, and though all chance of her ever becoming mine has long since fled, I care not now what becomes of me. I hope that the next engagement I may happen to be in the cannon's ball will lay me low, and thus terminate a life which has now become hateful to me!"

"Oh, God forbid!" exclaimed his companion. "Come, come, Master Harry, you must not talk so rashly, for I trust that you have yet many years to live, and that you may again be restored to peace and happiness."

"Happiness!" repeated our hero, disconsolately; "ah, no! that can never again be mine, and I do not flatter myself with any such ideas, which can only end in disappointment. My voyage through life has been a rough one, but now I am completely cast away, and everything convinces me it is no use hoisting signals of distress, for there is no friendly being at hand to relieve me. Lord, lord! what a terrible change has come over me within the last few months! How bright and flattering were the hopes I formed of happiness on my return to my native land, after I had been so long absent! How cruelly have they been destroyed! I return home—alas! to what a home do I return! My poor old mother mouldering in the silent grave;—Mary the wife of another;—and now—oh, God! how harrowing is the thought!"

"Do not give way to such dismal reflections," said Waxend, "for it makes me feel quite melancholy to hear you. You have certainly had your share of troubles, and this last is a misfortune of no common description; but still you must endeavour to bear up against it like a man; and gloomy even as everything at present appears to be, you will yet be able to surmount every difficulty, and to look back upon the past with calmness and resignation."

"Ah, no!" returned Halliyard, "while the fate which has befallen poor Mary is so uncertain that is impossible. You talk to me in vain, for I see not the slightest reason to flatter myself with the least degree of hope, and the more I think upon all the dreadful circumstances the more truly wretched do I become."

"Well, I am sorry to hear you talk in this doleful strain, Master Halliyard," said Waxend, "and I only wish it was in my power to relieve you, I would most willingly do so. There are many wonderful changes in the course of a man's life, and who knows what favourable change may shortly be in store for you?"

"I know the goodness of your intentions, my friend," said Harry, "but all the arguments you can possibly make use of are entirely lost upon me. Reason tells me that I have nothing to hope—that I am a marked man; and that a curse seems to pursue me. I fear that I have been most guilty in attempting to persuade Mary to abandon her husband, and that this is the retributive justice which has overtaken me for it."

"Nay, Halliyard," observed his companion, who had seldom before been in so serious a mood, "you censure yourself too severely. Your conduct was wrong, I admit, but you were driven by despair, and the natural excitement of your feelings at the disappointment of your hopes, to know not what you said; and you are more to be pitied than condemned."

"Oh, I have been most culpable," said our hero, "and I am justly, though severely punished for it. Would that I could recall the past, and once more sail with a fair wind—but it is too late now."

Waxend returned no answer, for he was at a loss what argument to make use of; and they having now arrived at the tavern, they entered it, but found nobody there. Our hero threw himself disconsolately on a seat, and resigned himself to his melancholy thoughts, while Waxend, with the hope of reviving his inward man, ordered a stiff glass of grog, and seated himself in the opposite corner.

Harry once more drew the paper from his pocket, and again and again perused the fatal paragraph with increased interest and emotion; Waxend never offering to interrupt him, for he saw that he was in no mood for conversation; and he respected his feelings too much to intrude upon them.

"Alas—alas!" sighed our hero, with his eyes still fixed intently on the paper, "can this indeed be true, or do my senses deceive me! It seems printed in letters of blood, and my brain grows giddy as I peruse it! What a terrible and impenetrable mystery it is, and what chance is there of its ever being unravelled? Mary could never, surely, voluntarily abandon her home, and leave her husband to misery and despair. She must have been forced away, and has fallen into the hands of some desperate villain, and if so, what may not be the awful fate which has befallen her! But who can he be? My brain becomes bewildered in seeking to form a conjecture, and every moment increases the agony of my doubt and suspense. Heaven watch over and help her, for I tremble to think of the suffering she has endured, or is now enduring."

He was interrupted in the midst of these melancholy reflections by the sudden entrance of Ben Bowsprit and two or three shipmates into the room, but still he could not remove his eyes from the paper.

"Well, Harry, my hearty," said the boatswain, advancing towards him, and holding out his hand, "I am glad to get within hail of you, for I feel inclined to splice the main-brace with you, and I do not suppose that you will have any objection to that. What, are you overhauling the log, eh? But, hollo! what's in the wind, now? Why, messmate, you look as dull as a vessel in a fog."

"Ay, Master Ben," replied our hero, "and I have good reason for hoisting signals of distress, if you only knew all. This paper communicates news to me which has taken me all aback. I feel cast on a lea-shore, and I care not how soon I founder altogether."

"Avast there, Harry," said Ben, "you must not talk in that manner while you have still got a timber left to float with. But what has happened to capsize you like this?"

"Read that!" replied Halliyard, handing him the paper, and pointing to the fatal paragraph, "and if you do not say that such news is enough to make a wreck of any man, I hope I may never go afloat again."

Ben Bowsprit hastily, but attentively, perused the passage which our hero had

pointed out to him, and when he had come to the conclusion he said—

"Why, this is a strange and black piece of business, sure enough. Mrs. Tiller! why that is her you called your pretty Poll, and who was to have been spliced to you, and——"

"Yes—yes!" hastily interrupted Harry, with the most violent emotion. "It is her on whom all my hopes were fixed, but which cruel Fate in the first instance crushed, and now she has either fallen into the hands of some rascally pirate, or, driven to despair, has herself slipped the cable of life. Ob, Ben,

the very thought shatters my upper-works, and makes my heart beat at the rate of forty knots an hour. My poor Mary, gone—disappeared, no one knows how, but supposed to be murdered! By all my hopes it quite unmans me, and I could blubber like a child!"

He hastily dashed away the manly tears that started to his eyes in spite of all his efforts to restrain them, and then covering his face with his hands, he gave himself up completely to the insupportable agony of his mind.

"Come, come, Harry," said the boatswain, "you must not take on so;

although it is a bad job, to be sure, and the mystery of it is the worst part about it. But after all it may not turn out so bad as you expect. Mary may yet be discovered, and restored uninjured to her home."

"That's just what I have been telling him, Master Bowsprit," remarked Waxend, "but he will not listen to me. Ah! it makes out my dream to a——"

"Belay your fishing-tackle, you lubber," interrupted Harry, passionately, "or I'll make mincemeat of you in no time! Ben, how can I encourage the hopes you would inspire me with when I take all the circumstances into consideration? What chance is there of discovering her, or of ever learning the fate which has befallen her? Some rascally buccaneer has, I fear, laid his grappling-irons upon her, and has got her secure in the bilboes, or else she has shipped herself to eternity. Oh, Ben! had you but known the poor lass, you would not wonder at the love I bear her, or the despair and anguish of my present feelings. A fairer craft was never launched on the ocean of life; and that she should ever have to encounter such heavy storms as those she has met with is enough to break the stoutest heart to think of."

"Poor woman!" said Ben, compassionately, "I sincerely pity her. But what infernal shark can have been guilty of that which you suspect? Know you of any enemy that she had?"

"Enemy? No!" repeated Halliyard. "Who could have been base enough to entertain any feelings of enmity towards one so good and amiable? I am distracted, and know not what to think!"

"And I am quite at a loss how to advise you," observed Ben. "But do you not think it is possible she may have learnt where you are, and, urged on by the love which she probably yet bears you, that she has formed the resolution of hastening here, in order to bid you a last farewell?"

"Oh, no," answered Harry, "Mary could never have been so guilty—she could never have had the heart to abandon her husband, and without leaving him a line to inform him of her fatal determination. She has been forced away from her home, I am convinced, but by whom I cannot imagine. There is but one villain whom I can believe would be guilty of such an atrocious crime, if he had the opportunity to do so, for it would gratify the deadly feelings of hatred and revenge that I know he bears towards me."

"Ah!" ejaculated Ben Bowsprit, "and who is that?"

"That infernal scoundrel, Hugh Brandon, the pirate," replied our hero.

"He, the swab!" cried Ben; "oh, no, I cannot be of your opinion, Harry. It is not likely that he would venture near these shores, where he would be almost certain to be detected. He is, no doubt, at present, far away at sea; and I only hope that I may encounter him some of these times, for I long to have a breeze with the lubber."

"I know not that," returned Halliyard; "the rascal has a most secret and certain way of accomplishing his designs, and he may even now be nearer to us than we imagine. Who those fellows were that seized me and Waxend I should like to know."

"Ay," said Waxend, "that was a most mysterious piece of business, and a more ferocious looking set of scoundrels I never saw. Who knows but they might be a portion of Brandon's crew? and if so, he himself is not far from us, you may depend upon it."

"Psha!" returned Ben, doubtfully, "that is a very improbable story. However, I should like to discover the fellows, and I cannot imagine what their object was in laying their grappling-irons upon you. But, come, Harry, cheer up, my lad, and take my word for it that Mary will yet escape the breakers, and be towed safe into port."

"Oh, how useless is it to seek to flatter me with any such hopes, Ben," said our hero; "I must indeed be mad to encourage them. Poor lass—poor lass! she is indeed lost to me, and all to whom she is most dear. Oh, would that I were at liberty, there is not a spot on the face of the globe that I would not search for her, and I would not rest until I had discovered her. Oh, Mary! this trial is more than I can bear. Would that I had perished in the battle's heat, or——"

"Avast, Harry!" interrupted Ben, "you must not lower your flag to the enemy, despair, altogether, but try to bear your misfortunes with firmness, for there is no knowing what is in store for you yet. Mary's husband is greatly to be pitied, poor fellow, for his sufferings at the loss of his wife must be very great, and almost past endurance."

"Alas!" sighed our hero, "it is too true; and believe me that I most sincerely commiserate with him. What can he think?—How can he account for the mysterious disappearance of his wife? Knowing the love that she still bears towards me he will probably believe that she has voluntarily deserted him, and hastened to follow my footsteps; and that thought, if possible, tortures me more than all. The day after to-morrow, too, our vessel sets sail, and I shall never more have an opportunity of learning the fate which has befallen her. Oh, I shall go mad!"

Ben Bowsprit knew not what to say to endeavour to console him, and a silence of some time ensued, the despair and anguish of Harry's feelings increasing every moment, until he was worked up to such a pitch of excitement that he knew not how to control himself Ben and the others were at length compelled to leave him, and when he and Waxend were alone he gave free indulgence to the powerful and overwhelming emotions that agitated his bosom, and from which there seemed to be not the least possibility of relief.

"Oh, Mary!" he cried, "if you have not fallen by your own hands, may curses light upon the head of the villain who has been the cause of all this! for a more atrocious deed was never perpetrated. And I have no means of avenging your wrongs, or of ascertaining the fate which has befallen you. So sudden and unexpected is this blow that I can scarcely believe its reality—and yet the fatal truth is too apparent for me to doubt it for a moment. But shall I quit England in this terrible state of uncertainty? No, it is impossible that I can do so! Let whatever may be the consequences I will go in search of her, and if I should fail, what is there then that should any longer render life valuable to me?"

"Oh, Master Halliyard!" observed Waxend, "how can you talk in this manner? Do endeavour to become a little more reasonable, and not to rashly do that which you may afterwards have such bitter cause to regret. Surely you would not bring yourself into disgrace and trouble by abandoning your ship? That would, indeed, be an act unworthy of Harry Halliyard."

"And what care I now for name or honour?" said our hero, despairingly. "It matters not what becomes of me, wrecked and shattered as I am. Mary must and shall be discovered, if there is a possibility of doing so, and at any cost!"

"Be calm," said his companion, "and think of what it is which, in the excitement of your feelings, you would do. No doubt that no means will be left untried to find out what has become of her; and I firmly hope, too, with success. But where could you go in search of her?"

"Providence, surely, would guide me," answered our hero; "but to endure this state of suspense is impossible! What danger is there which I would not fearlessly brave to discover her? But, alas! it may now be too late! She has, probably, already fallen beneath the diabolical designs of some heartless miscreant, and is now pining in that state of misery which it is too awful to contemplate! Unfortunate girl! why did I ever leave you, after my return to England?—Why did I not remain near you, and, with your husband, watch over your safety with a brother's care and anxiety? This, then, would never have happened, and in time we might have learned to reconcile ourselves to the cruel disappointment which our hopes have experienced. Alas! how great and terrible have been the misfortunes that have befallen us!"

"Now, now," again remonstrated Waxend, "do endeavour to compose yourself, and not to give way to this excessive anguish. Brandy-and-water, hot and strong, is an excellent remedy when the mind is disturbed, and if I—"

"Fool!" hastily interrupted Harry, "think you that my anguish is of that trifling nature to be dissipated by maddening drink? Beware! for if you attempt to mock me in my troubles I will make you pay dearly for your boldness!"

"Well, I am sure, Master Halliyard," returned Waxend, "I meant no harm, and only spoke for your good. I know it has a beneficial effect on me whenever my mind is disturbed, and I thought it was likely to do the same with you."

Harry returned no answer, for his mind was too much occupied with his own gloomy and agonizing thoughts to take much notice of what Waxend said; and he remained silent for some time, and resigned himself to all the violence of his emotions; and Waxend did not venture to interrupt him, but endeavoured to content himself with his glass and his pipe, though he really felt deeply for the troubles of our hero.

"What a terrible change has a few short years only wrought in our circumstances!" at length soliloquised Harry. "How bright and cheerful were our prospects, and how fond the hopes which we once cherished! But they are gone now—fled for ever—and misery the most insupportable is our doom. Oh, Mary! much better would it have been for us both had we never known each other! then might we have been spared the misfortunes that have since befallen us, and sorrow might have been a stranger to us. These thoughts distract my brain, and I know not what I am about!"

He struck his forehead in despair as he thus spoke, and his manly bosom heaved with the intensity of the emotions that agitated it; but still he could find no relief, and he was so violently excited that Waxend feared to offer him any advice. He perused and re-perused the fatal paragraph in the newspaper again and again, and the oftener he did so the greater became the horror and anguish of his feelings. He continued in this state during the whole of the day, and his mind was so bewildered that he knew not what he was about. But we must leave him for the present, and once more turn our attention to the situation of our heroine.

For several hours after her removal to the old farm she remained in the same state of insensibility, and was several times visited by the villain Brandon and Alice, the former of whom gave vent to his savage feelings of exultation in the most unmeasured terms. But at length the effects of the opiate were exhausted; she opened her eyes, and with difficulty raising her head from the place on which it was reclining, she looked around her in the greatest bewilderment and alarm. The strangeness of all that she beheld filled her with astonishment and alarm, and her brain was so bewildered that for a moment or two she was unable to recal to her memory what had taken place, and imagined that she was still labouring under the influence of some remarkable dream or wild delusion. But the whole fearful truth flashed suddenly upon her brain, and starting to her feet, she stood transfixed to the spot like a statue with the power of her emotions. She remembered recovering her senses on the journey, and finding herself in the waggon with the wretch Brandon, but what had subsequently happened of course she was ignorant of. She found herself alone, in a room of the same miserable and gloomy description as the one she had been confined in at the old tavern in Westminster, and that Brandon had succeeded in conveying her without detection to the place of his destination she could entertain no doubt. Her first impulse was to rush to the door and try to force it open, but, as may be expected, it was fastened, and she staggered back terrified and distracted.

"Gracious Heaven!" she exclaimed, "it is, then, no dream! Villany has triumphed, and I am borne far away from my friends, and am doomed to become the helpless victim of a wretch who is capable of committing any crime, however atrocious! What strange stupor is this that I have been wrapped in? And why did I ever recover my senses, since it was only to be made aware of the horrors by which I am surrounded, and those that are doubtless in store for me? Oh, wretched Mary! your fate is inevitably sealed, and nothing whatever can save you from it, unless the Almighty shall look down with mercy upon me—and he seems to have entirely deserted me. Where am I now? I shudder to think! Oh, God! oh, God!"

The violence of her emotions choked her utterance, and she sobbed aloud. Then she rushed to the window, and looked from it on the prospect which it commanded, and which was of the most extensive and rather picturesque description. In the distance she caught a view of the harbour, and the different vessels that were lying at anchor there; and when she recalled to her memory the observations that the old woman had made to her at the tavern, the whole truth was rendered apparent to her, and the full extent of her misery was no longer concealed from her.

"Brandon has succeeded!" she ejaculated, "and in a few hours he will probably have me secure on board his pirate vessel, and then my fate is as certain as it is unavoidable! Oh, Heaven! how ever shall I find strength to support such a trial as this? And would it not be a mercy to me could I escape by death from the horrors that otherwise await me? Tiller—Tiller! my unfortunate husband! what is now your fearful situation? And how awful must be the doubt and anxiety you are enduring, and without any one who can impart the least consolation to you, or afford you any relief! That thought of itself is more than sufficient to drive me to distraction, and my brain is burning! But must I remain here?—Is there no one to pity or relieve me? Alas! what pity or relief can I expect in such a place as this, and surrounded as I am by wretches who take a savage delight in the sufferings of their fellow-creatures?"

Again she rushed to the door, against which she kicked violently, and screamed aloud; but at last, completely exhausted by the excitement of her feelings, she sank back in a chair, and became again almost as insensible as she had been before. But she was not long suffered to remain in this state of suspense, for the door was unlocked, and Alice entered.

Alice was a woman who, notwithstanding the guilty situation in which she was placed, and the scenes of crime to which she was inured, was not entirely insensible to every feeling of pity, and she, therefore, felt some commiseration for the misfortunes of our heroine, and was inclined to treat her with all the kindness and indulgence that was in her power; and advancing towards her, she endeavoured by her looks to soothe her in some measure into composure. Our heroine was somewhat encouraged by the expression of her countenance, and in the most expressive accents she said—

"Ah! do I then, indeed, meet with one of my own sex in this abode of crime? Oh, stranger, whoever you are, let not a deeply-injured woman appeal to you in vain! For my sake—for that of my husband, from whose affectionate protection I have been so inhumanly torn, I implore you to take compassion on me!"

"I do pity you," replied Alice; "and could I render you any assistance I would willingly do so, but I am powerless."

"But where am I?" demanded Mary, in a voice of the most extreme agitation. "Whither have they conveyed me?"

"You are now at Portsmouth," answered Alice.

"And in the power of the villain Brandon?" interrogated our heroine.

Alice replied in the affirmative.

"Good God! how torturing is this! What a dreadful fate is it to be consigned to! But, oh tell me, for you do not appear to be devoid entirely of the feelings of humanity, are there no means of escaping from it?"

"Oh, no," said Alice, "I cannot hold out any such hopes to you. The plans of Brandon are well matured, and no doubt in a few hours you will be conveyed secretly on board the pirate vessel, the Wasp, which is at present lying in the harbour, supposed to be a fair trader, of the name of the Helen."

"Alas—alas!" sighed poor Mary, wringing her hands, and tears gushing to her eyes, "then my fate is sealed, and I am lost for ever! Left to the mercy of such a wretch as Brandon and his inhuman crew, what can I expect! Oh, my husband! what a terrible misfortune is this for us both—and one which we never anticipated! We shall never—never behold each other again! May Heaven's heaviest maledictions descend upon the heads of all those who have been engaged in this diabolical plot!"

"It is, indeed, most cruel," observed Alice, "and well worthy of Brandon and his colleagues. Alas! that ever I should become associated with them!"

"Ah!" ejaculated Mary, eagerly, "you do, then, sympathise with me?"

"Most sincerely I do," replied Alice. "But for Heaven's sake be cautious what you say, for there may be listeners, and should we be overheard it would not fail to bring down upon me the vengeance of the pirates, and the consequences might be yet more painful to you than they are at present. Be calm, be firm, and you may yet surmount the dangers by which you are at present surrounded."

"Alas!" cried Mary, "firmness and calmness in such a dreadful situation as mine are impossible. But who are you that, expressing the sentiments you do, I find associated with villains of the blackest dye?"

"Alas!" answered Alice, with a sigh, "I am a poor unfortunate wretch, who has been the sport of evil destiny, and compelled to mingle in scenes of guilt that are revolting to my feelings! My life has long been a burthen to me!"

Our heroine's thoughts were for the moment diverted from her own misfortunes by these observations, and she eagerly inquired—

"Oh, what can have placed you in such a fearful situation?"

"Circumstances which I have not now time to relate," answered Alice; "a forced marriage with one who was believed to be all that is good and honourable, but who too soon I discovered to be a villain of the blackest dye, a pirate, and, I fear, a murderer. He is at present one of Brandon's crew, and thus am I detained a prisoner, and forced to mingle in those terrible scenes that are so repugnant to my nature, and which freezes the very blood in my veins to think of them."

"Fearful idea!" said Mary, "you are, indeed, to be pitied! But, oh, tell me, I beseech you, what are the intentions of the miscreant Brandon towards me?"

"I fain would not shock your feelings by informing you," replied Alice, "but, alas! his intentions, I have too much reason to know, are all that your worst fears can anticipate."

"Oh, God!" groaned our heroine, clasping her hands together in agony, "and must I, indeed, be doomed to such a fate as this? But, Harry Halliyard—oh, tell me, know you anything of him?"

"Yes," replied Alice, "he has entered on board his majesty's ship, the Porpoise, at present lying in this harbour. Last night he was waylaid and seized by the pirates, but afterwards rescued by the coast-guard, who fortunately came to the spot at the critical moment."

"Oh, thank Heaven for that!" cried our heroine, vehemently. "Oh, Harry, you are rescued from the terrible fate with which you were threatened, and for that I am most grateful! Oh, did you but know the fearful situation in which I am placed, how torturing would be your sufferings!"

"From what Brandon by accident discovered to-day," remarked Alice, "he having overheard a conversation between Halliyard and his companion, he has read the account of your mysterious disappearance in the paper; and it is suspected that you have either been murdered, or laid violent hands on yourself."

"Oh, God!" exclaimed our heroine, "is it possible? The thought of the agony which he and my unfortunate husband are now enduring will certainly drive me mad! Oh, Harry, am I indeed so near to you, and yet we cannot meet? But, hear me, my good woman," she added, after a brief pause, "you say that you would be willing to serve me if you had the means? You have now the power to do so; and if you will only comply with my earnest request, may the blessings of Heaven ever attend you!"

"What mean you?" demanded Alice.

"Could you not contrive to see Halliyard, or to communicate with him?" asked Mary. "Once acquainted with the place of my confinement my restoration to liberty would be sure to follow immediately. Oh, do this, and how can I ever sufficiently evince my gratitude? while your reward here and hereafter will be great indeed."

"Alas!" returned Alice, "you ask me that which it is impossible for me to perform, or most readily would I undertake to do so. The pirates will never suffer me to leave this house whenever we are ashore without I am accompanied by one or more of the crew; for they well know my mortal hatred of my present course of life, and how gladly I would escape from it. And as for communicating with any one out of doors, I have not the slightest chance."

"Then there is no hope for me?" said our heroine, fixing upon her a look of anguish.

"I fear not, at present, at any rate."

"And what hope will there be for me afterwards," sighed Mary, "when I am borne far away over the perilous deep, and no one can have the means of ascertaining my fate, or flying to my rescue? God of Heaven! the fate to which You have destined me is far too horrible to think on; and surely no act of my life has merited this severe punishment! My brain is distracted, and my heart sinks within me! Would that I were dead—would that I were dead!"

Hysterical sobs choked her further utterance, and Alice, who was indeed deeply affected, and sincerely sympathised with her, for all her woman's best feelings were aroused, exerted herself to the utmost to tranquillize her feelings, but to no purpose.

"It is no use!" ejaculated Mary; "how can I experience anything but the blackest despair when I contemplate the manifold horrors by which I am surrounded, and those that too plainly await me? My destruction is inevitable! My fortitude entirely forsakes me, and I feel myself but too surely one of the most wretched of human beings!"

"I wish to Heaven that it was in my power to relieve you," remarked Alice, fervently, "you should find that I am no hypocrite, but that I have still the heart to do good, questionable even as my character may seem to be."

"Oh, I believe you!" returned our heroine, grasping her hand, "and most grateful do I feel to you for your sympathy, which is some consolation to me in the midst of my overwhelming troubles. But will you be permitted to accompany me on board this dreaded vessel?"

"Yes," answered Alice; "and no doubt I shall be appointed to attend upon you; and all the kindness and attention I can show to you, you may depend upon."

"Oh, thanks—thanks!" ejaculated Mary. "Heaven will most assuredly reward you for all that you may do for me. But this fearful man, Brandon—oh, how I shudder at the bare mention of his name!"

"He is, indeed, a miscreant of the foulest description," remarked Alice; "and many are the cruelties that I have experienced from him. Would to Heaven that I had the means of escaping from his power, and denouncing him and the whole of his ferocious crew; how gladly would I do so!"

"And he is at present in this house?" interrupted Mary, anxiously.

"He is," replied Alice.

"And no doubt I shall soon see him?"

"I know not—but it is more than probable that you will; and I would advise you to endeavour to muster up all the fortitude you can to meet him."

"Alas! what an arduous task is that!" observed our heroine. "The bare sight of such a monster as he is will be sufficient to fill me with horror; but when I think of the dreadful fate to which he has consigned me my courage entirely fails me, and the weight of my anguish is more, much more than I can bear!"

"Heaven will, I trust, give you strength to do so," returned Alice. "But I must leave you, for Brandon will begin to be impatient at my absence; and should he suspect the sympathy I feel for you, the consequences that would follow I have too much reason to apprehend."

"Oh, do not leave me to my own wretched thoughts!" supplicated Mary. "I feel some relief in your society, and——"

"I will visit you again as soon as I can," interrupted Alice; "and in the meantime I again urge you to try to muster all your fortitude and energy to encounter that which may yet be in store for you, and you may yet triumph."

"Oh, no," said our heroine, disconsolately, "there is no hope of that. My fate is sealed. Oh, what a miserable being I am! And what is now to become of me, placed in this dreadful situation? In a few hours, too, I shall be on board the pirate ship, and then all chance of my escape, if any indeed ever existed, will be at an end. That thought in itself is madness, and the longer I dwell upon it the greater and more insupportable becomes the anguish of my mind!"

"Try to banish it," said Alice, "and not to give way entirely to despair; for, after all, notwithstanding that Brandon appears to have completely triumphed in his diabolical designs, there is no knowing what may yet occur to frustrate them, and to restore you to liberty. You have my heartiest good wishes that such may ultimately be the result."

"Oh, thank you for this kind feeling!" ejaculated Mary. "Your observations do indeed impart some degree of consolation to my deeply afflicted mind. God be praised that I am at least not without one sympathising friend in the midst of my adversity. But, oh, with what feelings of uncontrollable terror do I look forward to the future!"

"Again I say, be firm," urged Alice, "and after all I sincerely hope, notwithstanding your present prospects are so gloomy, that the apprehensions you now so naturally encourage may turn out to be groundless. Farewell, till we meet again, which will be before long."

Mary again grasped her hand, and warmly expressed the gratitude she felt for the kindness she had shown her; and Alice then quitted the room, and she was left to the free indulgence of her own torturing reflections. She sank upon her knees, and with upraised hands and eyes, whilst the tears streamed in torrents down her cheeks, she supplicated the mercy and protection of the Supreme. But one circumstance which indeed afforded her consolation was the kindness and commiseration that Alice had expressed towards her, and which could not fail to make a most favourable impression upon her; and yet when she viewed all the peculiar and awful circumstances in which she was placed, what room was there for hope? Alas! none at all! Brandon had succeeded in all his nefarious plans, and it was not probable, as he had proceeded thus far, that he would suffer anything to occur to frustrate them. This thought alone was more than sufficient to drive her to distraction, and it was not without the greatest difficulty that she could contain herself within the bounds of reason. But to think that she should be so near Halliyard, and without having the opportunity of making him acquainted with her perilous situation, and from which only the lapse of a few hours would render it impossible to release her. Oh, how torturing was that reflection! And he knew of her disappearance—and what must be the perfect frenzy of his feel-

ings at the uncertainty of the fate which had befallen her, but which he would be sure to picture in the most awful characters!

"Alas!" she sighed, "how dreadful it is to be subjected to such a fate as this! and whither can I look for hope and consolation? Everything seems to mock me, and to frown despair upon me! It is in vain that I seek to gain the least respite from my cares and anxieties! Peace will never more be mine! My husband, too, how can he support this terrible calamity? He is perhaps even now stretched upon the bed of death, and he has no one near to soften the anguish of his dying moments. Great God! this visitation is most severe!"

Such were the thoughts that continued to occupy the mind of the unfortunate woman, and she could obtain but little and only transitory relief. Every moment she dreaded the appearance of Brandon, for the sight of him she was convinced would be sufficient to deprive her of what little fortitude she still possessed; and she had every reason to fear that he would not hesitate to go to any lengths in the prosecution of his infamous and odious suit. However, hour after hour passed away and these fears were not realised, and she gradually became a little more calm. It was now night, and the gloom and silence of all around her increased the melancholy and agitation of Mary's mind, and she found it impossible to quiet the excitement under which she naturally laboured. But at length she staggered in a state of great trepidation to her feet as she heard the footsteps of some person approaching the room in which she was confined, and imagining that it was the villain Brandon, and anticipating the horrors that were in store for her, her heart sank within her, and she trembled so violently that she was obliged to lean against a chair for support. Her fears were, however, soon banished, for the room door was opened, and instead of the object of her terror, Alice entered the room, bringing with her a lamp and some refreshments. She greeted her with much kindness, which Mary returned with equal cordiality; and her heart felt a great relief, though she still trembled violently.

"I could not return before," observed Alice, "or I would have done so. But you look pale, and how you tremble! Has anything occurred to alarm you since I have been gone?"

"I thought it was Brandon who was approaching me," answered our heroine, "and that has alarmed me. But I am glad you have again visited me, for I need not tell you how lonely and wretched I was when left to myself. Tell me, have you heard anything more as to the intentions of Brandon since you have been away?"

"Yes," replied Alice. "From all that I have been able to ascertain, it is the intention of Brandon to convey you secretly on board the Wasp at midnight."

"So soon?" ejaculated Mary, with a shudder. "Alas—alas! what will become of me?"

"Be firm," said Alice, "and your fate may be less fearful than that which you now apprehend."

"Ah, no!" sighed our heroine, "how can I encourage any such a delusive hope? The wretch, Brandon, having me now securely in his power, will not fail to carry all his diabolical plans into execution, and I have no possibility of any assistance to release me from the fearful position in which I am placed. Oh, could but Halliyard be made acquainted with the facts, how soon should I be rescued from the fate which is at present impending over me!"

"Would that I could do so," said Alice, "I should feel most happy to accomplish such an object, for it would also be the means of releasing me from a course of life which every hour renders still more revolting and intolerable to me. Oh, Mrs. Tiller (for that I believe is your name,) did you only know what it has been my fate to suffer, you would then be fully aware how well I can appreciate and sympathise with the sufferings of my fellow-creatures."

"I do not doubt it, Alice," replied our heroine, who was already deeply interested with her attendant, " and I feel grateful to you for your kindness to me under my heavy misfortunes. But the thought of the fate which it seems too likely awaits me drives my brain to distraction, and I scarcely know what I say. Is it possible that this pirate vessel can lie in this harbour without exciting any suspicion as to its real character ?"

"Yes," replied Alice; "she is supposed to be the Helen, a fair trader; and so well are the plans of Brandon always laid that it is impossible to defeat him. The men who comprise her crew are daring, ferocious ruffians, completely devoted to Brandon, and ready to perpetrate any crime, however monstrous, which he may order them to do; and it would shock your ears, Mrs. Tiller, were I to relate to you all the fearful scenes I have witnessed on board the pirate vessel."

"Alas !" sighed Mary, " what may I not then expect? Oh, have I not reason to shudder at the prospect before me ?"

"Again I say that I most sincerely pity you, and only regret that it is not in my power to assist you, for I am, in fact, almost as much a prisoner as yourself," remarked Alice. " But I do not believe that Providence will desert you altogether on such a trying occasion as this, and that Brandon will be permitted to triumph completely in his guilty designs; therefore, again I urge you to endeavour to call all your fortitude to your aid, and you may yet escape the dangers which you have now, indeed, so much reason to apprehend. I thank you most fervently for your kind wishes, Alice," said our heroine, " but I dare not flatter myself with any such hopes; and, indeed, I see nothing but destruction before me. Securely as the villain Brandon has got me in his power, and determined as he is in his brutal purpose, what is to prevent him from carrying his diabolical designs into effect? Oh, God ! how I shudder at the thought, and what feelings of horror and disgust fill my bosom at the dreadful prospect before me ! Could Halliyard be made

acquainted with my terrible situation it might yet not be too late to save me."

"But," returned Alice, " unfortunately there is no possibility of doing so, or there is no one who would be more ready to undertake the task than myself. Oh, what would I not willingly give were it in my power to be released from this guilty and disgusting course of life ; for Heaven knows how strongly it is opposed to my nature, and what I have suffered for many years past."

"I do believe you, Alice," said our heroine. " But has your husband treated you with unkindness ?"

"My husband !" repeated Alice ; " oh, how I shudder to call him by that name ! Alas ! he has ever treated me with the greatest barbarity, and I verily believe that he takes a savage delight to torture me."

"Ah !" remarked Mary, " yours, like mine, is indeed a cruel fate, and from the very bottom of my soul I pity you. But, alas ! what is now to become of me ? How my heart sickens when I think of the fate which seems inevitably to await me ! How can I possibly contemplate it without feelings of horror, disgust, and despair ?"

"It is, indeed, most torturing," said Alice, " and I only regret that I have it not in my power to relieve you, or to offer you hope or consolation."

"In a few brief hours, then," ejaculated the hapless prisoner, " I shall be an inmate of the pirate vessel, and then my fate will be sealed, and nothing but the merciful interposition of Providence can rescue me from it !"

"Alas !" returned her companion, " it is too true."

"Oh, God ! oh, God !" groaned Mary, again clasping her hands vehemently together in the most intense agony, " what a wretched being I am ! Would that death might relieve me from my sufferings, for to become the victim of such a blood-stained miscreant as Brandon is too horrible even to reflect upon, and madness must surely seize upon my brain ! Oh, my husband ! oh, Harry ! what must be the agony you are now enduring ? I am lost to you for ever, and am doomed to become a poor degraded being, hateful to myself, and the sport of the wretches who hold me in their power ! Alice," she added, solemnly, and with a fearful expression of countenance, " if you sincerely commiserate with me you will release me from my sufferings, and thwart the monstrous designs of the hardened villain who would be my destroyer."

"How?—What mean you?—What power have I to do so?" eagerly demanded Alice.

"Supply me with the means of terminating that existence which has now become a misery to me," replied our distracted heroine, in still more solemn accents than before.

Alice started, and looked at her appalled.

"And would you have me become an accessary to the awful crime of self-murder?" she said. "Dreadful thought! Oh, arouse yourself from this state of frenzy and despair, and give not way to such horrible and guilty ideas as these."

"And have I not sufficient cause to do so?" hastily interrogated Mary. "Is not death under any circumstances preferable, far preferable to the revolting fate to which my oppressor has doomed me? Oh, Alice! if you really pity me you will comply with my request, and——"

"Forbear — forbear!" interrupted Alice, " I shudder to hear you talk thus. Again I implore you to be firm, and to put your trust in Providence."

"Alas—alas!" groaned Mary, "then there is no escaping from it! Fate mocks me, and I am accursed of God and man!"

She burst into a violent paroxysm of sobs and tears as these mournful expressions escaped her, and it seemed as if her heart would break under the violent conflict of her feelings. Alice tried her utmost to tranquillize her, but with very little success; and at length she suffered her to give indulgence to her emotions without interruption, thinking that probably that might be likely to relieve her.

" It is some distance from here to the place where the vessel is lying, is it not?" she said, at length.

" It is," replied Alice.

"Ah, then," remarked Mary, "in conveying me thither may they not be detected, and——"

"No, no," interrupted Alice, " it would be cruel of me to suffer you to flatter your mind by the encouragement of any such delusive hopes. The pirates have nothing to fear from detection, for all their plans are too well arranged. Beneath this building is a secret subterranean cavern, which leads directly to the harbour, and along that you will be conveyed without any chance of discovery. Before daylight, I have no doubt, the vessel will set sail, for it would not be safe to remain any longer here; and thus you see that there is no prospect of your deliverance from the power of Brandon for the present, at any rate."

"Terrible thought!" exclaimed our heroine; "and you would seek to inspire me with fortitude! Oh, how fruitless is the task, when all is gloom and horror around me! But you will accompany me on board the vessel, and will be suffered to attend upon me, will you not?"

"Yes," answered Alice, I have told you so; and all that I can possibly do to alleviate the miseries of your fate most willingly will I. But in the presence of Brandon and his base associates we must be cautious in our behaviour towards each other, for should he suspect that I feel any commiseration towards you he would probably remove me from you; and the consequences might be of the most painful nature."

" The villain!" cried Mary. "Alas I am too well convinced that he is capable of any atrocity, and that I can expect no mercy from him! And is it for such a fate as this that I have been reserved?—Have I, indeed, so offended against the laws of God that I should be thus severely punished? Have mercy, Heaven, and do not try me more than my strength can bear!"

" I must now again leave you," remarked Alice, " for I have some business to perform, and——"

"Oh, no, no!" hastily interrupted Mary, " you will not leave me thus, in this dreadful and insupportable state of mind?"

" I am compelled to do so," replied her companion; "it is the order of Brandon, and I dare not disobey him. We shall doubtless meet again before long."

"Ah! where?" ejaculated Mary,

with a shudder. "On board that terrible vessel which is doomed to be my future prison, and where I shall be exposed to all the cruel persecutions of the monster Brandon, who will be sure to carry his diabolical designs into effect to the very letter!"

"Again I request you to seek to acquire all the firmness and resolution which you possibly can," said Alice; "for it is only by that that you can hope to surmount the many difficulties by which you are at present surrounded. Farewell for the present, and depend upon it that you have my warmest sympathy and friendship, and that I shall only be too happy should it providentially fall in my power to save you."

Mary pressed her hand most cordially, in gratitude for the humane feelings she expressed towards her; but she was unable to speak, and Alice having fixed upon her a look of the deepest compassion, left the room.

When she was gone the state of Mary's mind may be easily imagined; but for a few minutes she was so bewildered and distracted that she could not arrange her thoughts, and with clasped hands, and tearful eyes, she stood the very image of anguish and despair. But at length all the horrors of that which awaited her rushed upon her brain with the most overwhelming force, and scalding tears chased each other rapidly down her cheeks, whilst hysterical sobs agitated her bosom, and her limbs trembled so violently that had she not supported herself against the back of a chair she must have sunk upon the floor.

"My fate is then drawing to a crisis," she sighed, "and I have nothing left for me but to resign myself to the blackest despair, for there are no means of avoiding it; it would be madness for me to encourage any such an idea, for it could only be followed by the bitterest, the most torturing disappointment. In another hour or two I shall be conveyed on board the pirate ship, and the horrible cruelties and outrages to which I shall then most certainly be subjected are too frightful and revolting to think upon! Oh, would that Harry could discover my situation ere it is too late! how soon should I then be rescued, and

the wretch Brandon and his infamous colleagues be brought to that condign punishment which their atrocious crimes so richly merit. But, oh! no, there is no chance of that! Providence seems to have entirely deserted me, and there is nothing left for me to do but to make up my mind to the worst. And yet 'tis hard that I who have never yet wilfully injured any of my fellow-creatures should be destined to endure such unexampled miseries and injustice as I experience. Oh, All-merciful Father! I beseech you most fervently to look down with an eye of pity upon me, and not to suffer me to become the victim of the brutal designs of this hardened miscreant altogether!"

She sank down on her knees as she thus spoke, and most fervently did she offer up her supplications to the Supreme. But when she took into consideration all the circumstances by which she was surrounded her fortitude entirely forsook her, and she awaited the time when she might expect that Brandon would make his appearance to convey her on board the Wasp in a state of the most trembling anxiety. She could find no relief; and as the time elapsed her fears and uneasiness increased, and she could with difficulty restrain her feelings within the bounds of reason. All was, however, silent in the house, and it seemed as if she were the only inmate, only she was too well convinced to the contrary. She went to the window, and it being a clear, moonlight night, she had a distinct view of objects to some distance. She directed her eyes eagerly towards the harbour, and as the tall masts and rigging of the several vessels lying there met her gaze she sighed deeply as the form of Harry arose to her imagination.

"On board of which of those gallant ships is he?" she questioned herself. "Oh, what are now his thoughts?—what the anguish and despair of his mind? Little does he imagine that I am so near him, and that I am in the power, and left to the mercy of his most deadly enemy, or how speedily would he fly to my rescue. But is it possible that the wretches can convey me on board their ship without attracting the attention, and exciting the suspicions of the other vessels alongside of which it is moored? My piercing shrieks shall raise an alarm, and thus bring assistance to me, and defeat the monstrous plans of Brandon. I will not despair, for it may not yet be too late to escape from the fate with which I am threatened."

These thoughts somewhat inspired her with hope, and she became more calm, but still she awaited the result with the greatest impatience and anxiety. Again and again she offered up her supplications to Heaven, and tried to muster all the fortitude she could for the painful and arduous task which was in store for her. Ten, eleven o'clock arrived, and all in the house remained in the same profound silence; and Mary began to hope that Brandon had abandoned his designs for that night, and that the delay might be productive of some important change in her favour. But these ideas were soon banished, and a trembling sensation came over her, when she suddenly heard heavy footsteps ascending the stairs, and which convinced her that it was not Alice. She clasped her hands in agony together, and gazed with terror towards the door, which was immediately opened, and to her horror Brandon entered the room, followed by Summers and Guernsey, who, folding their arms, stood in one corner of the room, and watched their captain and our heroine with looks of savage satisfaction. Mary gasped for breath, and staggered to the farther end of the room; she averted her looks from the rude and triumphant gaze of her cruel oppressor, who, however, nothing abashed by her conduct, and the hatred and disgust which he was well aware she bore towards him, advanced towards her, and in a bold and confident tone observed—

"So, my pretty Mary, you turn disdainfully from me, do you? and do not seem much to admire the build of my craft? No matter. I am not particular to a shade or two; it is sufficient for me to know that I have got the weather-gauge of you, and that, although no doubt it is much against your inclination, you must strike to me, seeing that I have safely got my grappling-irons upon you, and that you cannot escape from me. Hugh Brandon, the pirate, greets you, Mary, and congratulates himself upon his triumph."

"Taunting villain!" our heroine found strength and energy sufficient to reply; "it is well worthy of your savage and cowardly nature thus to exult over a poor, defenceless woman, whom you have so cruelly torn from her home, and consigned to so monstrous a fate. But think not to crush me altogether—no, I will dare you yet; and though you may now appear to triumph I shall yet escape from you!"

"Ha, ha, ha!" laughed Brandon, scornfully, "what idle talk is this! It only serves to amuse me to listen to it. The pirate chief is not so easily to be defeated as you seem to imagine, and that you will quickly ascertain to your cost. This night—this hour, I bear you on board my gallant craft, where I have destined that you shall reign as my future mistress; therefore you may as well belay all this abusive lingo, and since you cannot help yourself, make up your mind to the fate which is in store for you. Oh, there are many who would be proud to share the wild fortunes of the sea rover, Hugh Brandon."

With what feelings of unspeakable indignation, disgust, and dismay, did the hapless Mary listen to these brutal observations; the more so as she was well aware how fully determined he was to put his threats into execution, and that every attempt at resistance on her part would be entirely useless. She stared at him aghast, while he remained perfectly unmoved, and the power of her emotions for some moments completely choked her utterance; but at length she said—

"And can this be a man who thus addresses me, and disgusts and shocks my ears with his inhuman threats? Oh, no, it would be a monstrous libel on the name of man to call him one. All-merciful God! and will you suffer him to triumph altogether in his guilt?"

"Ha, ha, ha!" again laughed the pirate, ironically. "And of what use, think you, is it giving utterance to such idle cant as that to me? I have triumphed, and, therefore, it is all to no purpose your trying to resist or avoid the fate which awaits you. Harry Halliyard is not present now to stand up in your defence, although he is nearer to you than you perhaps imagine; and if I am not much mistaken, some time or other he also will be in my power, and will then discover what it is to incur the vengeance of Hugh Brandon."

"Oh, Heaven forbid that Halliyard should be so truly unfortunate!" most fervently ejaculated our heroine; "for then too well do I know the fate which would be certain to befal him at the hands of such a villain as you. But, oh, Brandon, what have I done that you should persecute me in this heartless manner?"

"Hark ye, Mary," replied Brandon, "from the first moment that I came in sight of that pretty figure-head of yours I felt as it were completely capsized, and so I determined to crowd all sail in chase of you, and if possible to convey you to some place of safety, intending that you should sail in future under my command. I have succeeded, and you may, therefore, make up your mind, now that I have got you in tow, we will not part company in a hurry, Once on board my gallant bark, and sailing over the bright blue waters of the deep, your fate is sealed, and so you may as well make up your mind to it as not."

"Oh, spare me, Brandon!" implored the unfortunate woman, and the tears at the same time streaming from her eyes.

"Ah!" cried the pirate, with another look of triumph, "and after all the scorn and defiance with which you have affected to treat me. do you now condescend to sue? Oh, this, indeed, affords me increased satisfaction! But you know not my stern and inflexible character yet, or you would be well aware that you supplicate to me in vain. Hugh Brandon never wavered in his resolution, and, therefore, it is but a waste of time and words to seek to move him from his purpose."

"God of Heaven! do not forsake me in this terrible hour of my need!" cried Mary, her bosom swelling with the most powerful emotions, to which it would have been utterly impossible to have given utterance. "Oh, Brandon! your looks and observations strike horror to my soul, and I tremble while I am in your presence! Leave me, and——"

"Leave you!" he interrupted, with an ironical smile, "oh, no; that is not very likely, seeing that I am about to convey you on board the craft; so you may as well prepare yourself. Come, I have delayed too long in idle conversation. This way—this way!"

As Brandon thus spoke he threw a large cloak, which he had brought with him, over Mary's shoulders, and then grasping her by the waist, he tried to hurry her towards the door; but, excited to a pitch of frenzy, she uttered a piercing shriek, and struggled to release herself from his hold with all the strength she could. But, alas! how useless were all her efforts—what resistance could she offer to such a ruffian? And at length, exhausted with the exertions she had made, and overpowered by her feelings, she fainted in his arms, and was thus left entirely at his mercy.

"Ah!" he remarked, "this is well; it will be fortunate if she does not recover till we have got her safe on board the Wasp, and then all danger of discovery will be at an end. But even if she should revive, we have got the means of stifling her cries. All the crew are on board, except Bullruff, who is waiting our arrival with the boat, are they not?"

"They are," answered Summers, "and if fortune does not frown upon us, we shall quickly be on board also."

"Ay, ay," returned Brandon, "there is not much fear of our being discovered. But, quick—quick; follow me!"

With these words he raised the insensible form of our heroine in his arms, and quitted the room, followed by Summers and his companion. They hastily descended the stairs, and when they had got below they turned to the right, and entered a room at the back of the premises, where Harville was awaiting them.

"So," he observed, "she is in a very fit state for your purpose; and if she only remains insensible till——"

"True—true; I know what you would say," impatiently interrupted Brandon; "but there is no time to lose. Open the secret trap, Harville!"

The latter obeyed, and stooping down, with some difficulty raised a trap-door in the flooring boards, of sufficient dimensions to allow the body of a man to pass through. A flight of steps was then revealed to the observation, the bottom of which could not be seen from above, for all below was involved in complete darkness. Summers took up a lamp, and then, on a motion from Brandon, he and Guernsey first passed through the trap, and were immediately followed by the former, bearing his unfortunate and insensible burthen. The steps were winding, and after descending two or three flights they alighted in a vaulted passage, which seemed of vast extent, and the walls of which were damp with unwholesome moisture, and black with age. Along this strange place they proceeded, and after traversing it for about ten minutes they arrived at the extremity. Summers and his companion now removed a large stone which concealed the entrance, and a view of the harbour and the coast for some distance was then obtained. At this moment Mary recovered, and beholding the strange and fearful place she was in, she uttered a loud cry of terror, and again struggled to release herself from the hold of Brandon.

"D——n!" he exclaimed, furiously. "Woman, are you mad?—Think you that you can now escape from me?"

"Oh, help—help!" screamed Mary in a still louder tone than before.

"Gag her! stop her cries!" exclaimed Summers, "or she will betray us!"

This suggestion Brandon availed himself of immediately, and poor Mary, again overpowered by her feelings of terror and despair, once more fainted. At the same moment the dark shadow of a man was seen on the ground at the entrance to the passage, and soon afterwards a human form approached the spot.

"Ah, Bullruff!" demanded the pirate captain, in undertones, "is that you?"

"It is,'" replied Bullruff, in the same low voice. "You have succeeded, then?"

"Of course," returned Brandon; "what was to prevent me? But is the coast clear?"

"Quite," answered Bullruff; "I have not seen a soul since I have been here."

"Quick, then," said the pirate captain; "let us to the boat!"

Summers and Guernsey then replaced the stone before the entrance to the passage in such a manner that it could not excite suspicion, and they all then hurried to the boat, which was moored in a small creek close by. Having placed Mary at the bottom of the boat, they threw the cloak completely over her, so as to conceal her entirely from observation, and then entering it, they pulled away with all their might towards the vessel, which they were not long in arriving at; and the next moment, with their unfortunate prisoner, they were all safe on board, and were greeted by the pirates with the heartiest cheers.

"Convey my prize to the principal cabin," said Brandon, addressing himself to Summers; "and let Alice see to her recovery. I have other business to attend to just now. A thick fog is fast gathering, which will enable us to weigh anchor without any fear of discovery, and before daylight we must be far away from here. Bear her below, I say, and then attend me on deck."

Summers obeyed, and then raising the unconscious Mary in his arms, he conveyed her to a cabin below, where Alice was waiting to receive her.

The fog increased in density, and everything seemed to favour the designs of the pirate, for it was impossible for any of the other vessels to observe what they were about. The most active preparations were immediately made for sailing, which were promptly completed; and in little more than half an hour after Brandon and the others had conveyed our heroine on board, the anchor was weighed, the pirate bark had cleared the harbour, and was soon fairly on its voyage.

CHAPTER XIX.

THE TROUBLES OF OUR HEROINE INCREASE.—THE PIRATE BARK AND ITS CREW.—THE CHASE.

LEAVING the villain Brandon and his savage associates to exult over the success which had hitherto attended them, we will return to Mary, upon whom, after she had been committed to her care, Alice had been attending with the most anxious solicitude and kindness; and deeply did she deplore the cruel fate to which she was exposed, and which now seemed to be quite unavoidable.

It was not, however, until the vessel had got under weigh that Mary was restored to sensibility; and the confused recollection of what had taken place, the motion of the ship, the hollow sound of the billows as they dashed against its side, and the novelty of the place in which she now found herself, so stupified and bewildered her, that for some moments she was completely lost in amazement, and scarcely knew whether she was asleep or awake. But looking up from the place on which she had been reclining, and recognising Alice leaning over her, and watching her with looks of the most earnest compassion, she remembered everything in a moment, and in a voice of extreme anguish she exclaimed—

"Gracious Heaven! the villain, then, has triumphed in his nefarious designs, and my fate is sealed past recal! Oh, Alice! what shall I do? How avoid the horrors that seem to be too surely impending o'er my head?"

"Calm your feelings for the present," replied her attendant, 'and we will discuss that subject together upon a more fitting opportunity."

"Calm my feelings?" said Mary, with a look of despair; "oh, what madness is it to talk to me thus! how is it possible that I can do so when I contemplate the dangers that environ me on every side? Am I not on board the pirate vessel commanded by the blood-stained miscreant, Brandon, who has declared to me the full extent of his monstrous designs?—And what mercy can I expect from one to whom pity is a stranger, and who takes a savage delight in the misfortunes of his fellow-creatures?"

"True," remarked Alice; "your situation is most deplorable, and I scarcely know what to say to comfort you. But call all your resolution to your aid, and there is no knowing how soon something may occur to release you, even though it may at present seem to be ever so impossible."

"Oh, I dare not flatter myself by encouraging any such sanguine ideas," said our heroine, "for reason too well convinces me that they would prove to be delusive. Alas! how I tremble at the thought of again beholding Brandon, after the fearful threats that he has held out to me; and I cannot believe for an instant that, stern and determined as he is, he will act with any forbearance towards me."

"An idea has just struck me," said Alice, after a brief pause, "which, if it should only be realised, may yet be the means of saving you."

"Ah!" cried our heroine, eagerly, "what mean you? Do not keep me in suspense, but explain!"

"The sudden disappearance of the Wasp from the harbour will probably excite suspicion that she is not the fair trader she pretended to be," answered Alice; "and should they pursue her, it is not likely that the pirates would be able to stand against superior numbers. and one of his majesty's ships of war Their destruction would be almost inevitable, and in that case your deliverance would be certain."

"Alas! not so," remarked Mary, with a desponding expression of countenance; "you well know the desperate character of these wretches, and that there is nothing they would hesitate to do in order to gratify their revenge. If such a circumstance as that to which you have alluded should occur, and Brandon should find himself likely to be defeated, then I feel convinced that, sooner than suffer me to escape altogether, he would sacrifice my life, and thus, at any rate, gratify his revenge. Alas! no, I see little or nothing to hope from such an occurrence as that; in fact, as I have often said before, Brandon has me entirely at his mercy, and what that mercy is I need not seek to explain."

Alice was about to return some answer to this, when she was interrupted by hearing the loud shouts of the pirates, who seemed to be giving way to the most boisterous mirth; and directly afterwards the following chorus met their ears, which was shouted in no very harmonious strains:

"Over the dark and boundless deep,
The pirate bark doth proudly sweep;
Let the wind blow high or low,
No fear of danger we e'er know.
Though lightning blazes in the sky,
And surging waves run mountains high,
By no dangers scared are we,
The dauntless rovers of the sea;
Then, hey for the rovers of the sea!"

The chorus ceased, but the acclamations that followed continued for several minutes, and filled the agonised mind of our heroine and her companion with the most unbounded disgust. The chorus having ceased, and the shouts of the desperate and brutal crew subsided, a silence of several minutes ensued, which was only interrupted by the hollow murmuring of the wind, as it swept over the vast ocean upon which they were riding, or the dashing of the waves against the vessel's sides, as it glided swiftly on its way ; and our unfortunate heroine, who was completely heart-sick, and whose agony every moment became the more intense, looked at her companion with an expression of the most indescribable despair, and wringing her hands, in a melancholy voice she ejaculated—

"Oh, God ! how does my terror increase as I listen to the rude mirth of these savage men, and think upon my utter hopeless condition. I see plainly enough that my fate is sealed, and that there is not the least chance of my escaping from it ; and my brain is racked to madness. Alas—alas ! Providence has too surely entirely deserted me !"

"Oh, banish such thoughts from your mind, Mrs. Tiller," returned Alice, in her most gentle and compassionate accents, "and endeavour, in spite of the misery of your present situation, to look forward to the future with confidence and hope."

"Confidence! hope !" repeated Mary; " alas ! how futile is it for me to attempt to do so, for am I not now completely in the power of the villain Brandon, borne far away o'er the foaming billows from my home and all that is dear to me ? and is it at all likely that my brutal persecutor will delay the execution of his diabolical purpose ? Ah, Alice, in vain you seek to tranquillize my feelings ; how can I experience anything but the utmost despair when I contemplate the horrible fate which most certainly awaits me ? Oh, my unfortunate husband ! how intense, how insupportable must be the present anguish of mind that you are enduring ! and what will probably be the fatal conclusion at which you will arrive on my mysterious disappearance ! You

will believe me guilty, false, and treacherous, and perhaps at the present moment your heaviest maledictions are invoked upon my head ; and thus are the horrors of my fate increased, and madness almost seizes upon my brain !"

"Ah, no !" returned Alice ; " do not torture your mind by such reflections as these, for surely they will prove to be unfounded. Your husband can never be so ungenerous or unjust as to imagine you thus guilty and abandoned."

" To what other conclusion can he arrive, without the least clue to the manner in which I have been so cruelly trepanned ?" said our heroine, hastily, "and taking all the unhappy circumstances of the past into consideration ? Was he not fully aware of the fatal passion which I still entertained for Halliyard ?—Did he not know that I had at one time consented to abandon him, and to follow the footsteps of the man to whom I was betrothed ?—And will he not now have too much reason to suspect that I have put those guilty wishes into execution, and that I have brought shame and dishonour upon him ? He will—he will ! And even now I think I behold the wild frenzy of his despair, and hear the dreadful curses and reproaches to which he gives utterance ! Alas—alas ! there is no hope for me—I am accursed of God and man !"

Again she wrung her hands, scalding tears rushed to her eyes, and the most heart-rending sobs of bitter anguish choked her further utterance. She sank back in her seat, and resigned herself to all the intense horror and despair which rushed impetuously through her bosom, and nearly overwhelmed her. Alice knew not what to say that was likely to afford her the least consolation, and she remained silent, but gazed at her with the deepest sympathy and compassion.

The pirate vessel still proceeded swiftly on its way, and every moment hope receded still farther from the unhappy Mary, and the terrible crisis of her fate seemed to be more rapidly approaching. At length she once more started hastily to her feet, and gazing wildly and vacantly around her, she said—

"But shall I remain here to meet a

fate so disgusting and revolting as that with which I am at present threatened?——Shall the wretch, Brandon, be allowed to triumph in his atrocious designs altogether? No, by Heaven he shall not! I have yet the means of escaping from it, and why should I hesitate? Death is far more preferable than disgrace and degradation! Let me escape; the waves will be far more merciful to me than the monster who now holds me in his power. Let me die—let me die! and thus end at once those sorrows that are now completely insupportable!"

As she thus spoke, in the distraction of her feelings she rushed towards the door of the cabin, and the expression of her countenance was quite awful to behold. Alice was deeply affected, and gently arresting her, she again, but in vain, endeavoured to soothe her into composure.

"For Heaven's sake be calm, Mrs. Tiller!" she expostulated, "for by giving way to this overwhelming distraction of feeling you will but increase the misery of your fate. Again I implore you to trust to the Almighty; and He, depend upon it, will not desert you altogether in this terrible hour of your need."

"You mock me," said our heroine, impatiently, and fixing upon her a mingled expression of reproach and despair; "what hope is there for me? Am I not completely in the toils of the destroyer?—his doomed victim, marked out for a fate which is inevitable? and yet you would talk to me of calmness and resignation! Oh, how useless is it! Alice, if you are indeed my friend—if you sincerely feel for me that sympathy which you profess to do, you will not seek to obstruct me in my purpose, but will rather assist me to escape by death from the power of this heartless monster, who would sacrifice me to his brutal and disgusting passions."

"What madness it is to talk thus, Mrs. Tiller!" returned her companion; "would you rush unbidden into the presence of your Maker? But thank Heaven the means are denied you, if even you have the will to do so. Come, come, arouse yourself; and after all it may not turn out to be so bad as you now anticipate. I still cannot believe

that Brandon will be permitted to triumph in his guilty designs altogether."

"And what is to prevent him?" demanded Mary, hastily; "has he not the power to execute his diabolical purpose at any moment that he thinks proper? and think you that he will any longer retard the gratification of his atrocious wishes? Oh, no, most assuredly he will not; and my heart sinks within me, while the blood curdles in my veins with horror and despair!"

She could say no more, for the violence of her grief completely overwhelmed her; and covering her face with her hands, she became almost lost and unconscious to everything that was passing around her. Alice did not offer to arouse her from her lethargy, for she thought that probably silent meditation might serve in some measure to afford her relief, and she stood by and watched her with the most anxious solicitude. She was well convinced that the apprehensions of Mary were too well founded, and that she had nothing to expect from the mercy and forbearance of Brandon, especially as he had succeeded so far, and there was nothing whatever to obstruct him in the accomplishment of his brutal designs; and most deeply did she pity her, and only regretted that it was not in her power to assist her, or to release her from the dreadful situation in which she was placed. Alice possessed an excellent heart, notwithstanding the questionable circumstances by which she was surrounded, but which she had no means of avoiding, and great were the misfortunes it had been her hard lot to experience, and, therefore, it is not to be supposed that she could witness the sufferings of any of her fellow-creatures, especially one of her own sex, with indifference. But the reader will probably be made acquainted with her singular and melancholy history by-and-by. Watching anxiously over our unfortunate heroine we will leave her for the present, and return to Brandon and his villanous crew. He and several more of the pirates were seated on the quarter-deck, and indulging themselves to the most unlimited extent. Ribald jokes were bandied freely from one to the other, and their loud shouts of boisterous mirth rent the air. Brandon's exultation knew no bounds, and he determined to carry out his diabolical purpose to the fullest extent without delay.

"Why should I retard the gratification of my wishes," he exclaimed, "since Mary is now completely under my control, and there is no one near to render her the least assistance, or to thwart me in the execution of my plans? I have her now secure on the dark waters of the ocean, and not all her reproaches, tears, or supplications can save her from the fate to which I have doomed her. Oh, would that I had succeeded in getting Halliyard in my power, that he might be the witness of my triumph! How glorious then would have been my revenge!"

"True, captain," coincided Ben Summers; "but as it is, what the poor devil will have to endure at the mystery of the fate which has attended her will be a severe punishment for him, and the time will yet come, I have no doubt, when you will be able to get him in your clutches; and then I dare say you will know what to do with him."

"Ay, Summers," returned Brandon, "you may well say that. The lubber can expect no mercy from me; and should fortune thus so far favour me, it will be my delight to torture him, and to witness his despair and misery. The death of my brother must and shall be avenged; and, therefore, let Harry Halliyard tremble should he happen to fall in my power. But, come, charge your glasses again, and let us once more drink to the health of Pretty Poll of Putney, the mistress of the pirate chief!"

This command was, of course, immediately and most willingly obeyed, and the toast was drunk with the most boisterous and enthusiastic hilarity.

"In a few hours," resumed Brandon, after a brief pause, "and when I have given her sufficient time to recover herself in some measure from the excitement into which the peculiarity of her situation must naturally have thrown her, I will not fail to complete the task which I have so well and so successfully begun, and in spite of all the consequences that may follow, Mary shall be compelled to yield to my desires, and what is there that can save her?"

"Most true, captain," agreed Ben, "and you should consider yourself a most fortunate man in having surmounted every difficulty which was placed in your way, and obtained possession of so fair a prize, which there are few men that would not envy you. We have hitherto been most fortunate, and this fog has greatly favoured us. What astonishment will our sudden disappearance excite."

"No doubt of it," returned Brandon; "and the lubbers will at length begin to suspect our real character, I dare say. But we are now far out of the reach of pursuit I should think, and have nothing to fear from them."

"Fear from them?" repeated Summers; "certainly not. The daring crew of the Wasp are strangers to fear, for they are a match for the very devil himself, and that many a one has found to his cost. But you do not mean to visit Mary just yet, I suppose?"

"Certainly not," answered Brandon; "it would be imprudent to do so, though I am most anxious to see her, and to gloat over those charms of which I am now the supreme master. I will for the present leave her to the care of Alice, who, no doubt, will know how to deal with her. The poor devil, Tiller! what a state of anguish he is no doubt at the present time enduring at the loss of his wife; and what would be his horror and despair did he but know the fate which is in store for her. Well, I am sorry for him; but, at the same time, I cannot abandon the gratification of my wishes."

"Certainly not," said Summers; "you must be mad to do so, after you have so far succeeded. But it would be as well if this fog would now disperse, since we have so far proceeded on our course without any interruption; for if it continues much longer it might be fraught with danger."

"True," coincided Brandon; "let every man be careful to do his duty, for there is every need of it at the present time."

Thus the villains continued to converse for some time, and in this manner about an hour passed away, and, in spite of the numerous difficulties that presented themselves, the vessel proceeded rapidly on her way, and scudded over the broad billows with the speed of a sea-bird.

At length the fog gradually dispersed, and daylight dawned upon the sea, everything giving token of fine weather, and fortune seeming to favour the pirate crew; but at length the man who was on the look out shouted "a sail astern!" and Brandon and the others starting from their seats, gazed eagerly in the direction which he had intimated, and then beheld a vessel in the distance, which seemed to be advancing rapidly in their wake.

"Ah!" cried Brandon, "it is a vessel, sure enough, and seems to be making way towards us. Can you make her out, Darnton?"

"No, captain," replied the man, "she is too far off at present to do so; but as near as I can judge from her build she is a British craft, and, as the wind is in her favour, she is gaining upon us."

"Our disappearance has probably been discovered," said Brandon; "and we being suspected, this ship is likely enough sent in pursuit of us. We must not encounter her if possible, for she might prove more than a match for us, and I am not inclined for a squall at present. Crowd every stitch of canvas, and, thanks to the well known quality of our gallant craft, we may yet be able to outstrip her."

The orders of the captain were promptly obeyed, and all was confusion and bustle on board the pirate vessel; Brandon continuing to watch the approaching ship with anxious eyes, and giving his orders in a hurried and impatient manner to his crew. But still, notwithstanding all their efforts, the strange vessel evidently continued to gain fast upon them; and presently the loud report of a gun came booming over the ocean, which plainly showed that she was in pursuit of them, and the excitement of Brandon increased.

"Oh!" he exclaimed, "so that is your temper, is it? Well, I am sorry to say that it is not convenient for me to accommodate you. You will have your work to do if you overtake the Wasp."

He now took the glass, and tried to make her out; and he was then satisfied that it was a British vessel of large size, and he had no doubt as to its intentions.

"But you will be deceived, my noble craft, if you think to come athwart our hawse. Ah! see our gallant bark rides swiftly on, and, if fortune favours us, will soon leave her pursuer far behind. Bravo—bravo! we shall triumph yet!"

Swift as an arrow from the bow sped the pirate vessel on its way, and the pursuing ship seemed to have little or no chance to overtake her; and the speed of the Wasp was greatly increased when, in obedience to the orders of Brandon, everything that could possibly be spared was thrown overboard to lighten her. They now altered her course, and did everything to elude the enemy; but that, of course, only served to increase the exertions of the latter, and again it seemed to make way upon her, and once more the loud report of a cannon sounded over the ocean.

"A polite invitation, truly," said Brandon, "but I do not feel at all inclined to accept of it. Steady—steady, my lads, and we shall give her the slip yet; and if we cannot, why, we know what we have to do—fight for it like devils, and we have not much reason to fear the result."

"Ay, ay, captain," shouted two or three of the pirates in a breath, "death or victory! We will never yield while a man of us can wield a sword or fire a musket!"

"Well said, my brave boys," returned Brandon; "I know well your brave and daring spirits, for I have tried them on many occasions before. But they will not have to be put to any such a trial on this occasion, I have no doubt. We must outstrip our pursuer, if possible, for an engagement would be rather inconvenient at present."

The pirates now redoubled their exertions, but again the strange vessel seemed to increase in speed, and all was doubt and anxiety on board the Wasp. All was prepared for action, in case it should turn out that they could not avoid it, and every man was determined to perform his duty with the utmost bravery; and, buoyed up by the thoughts of their former triumphs, they had very little doubt of success on the present occasion.

While this scene was going forward

on deck, the state of excitement and agitation into which our heroine was thrown may be readily imagined. She clasped her hands together, and listened to the loud and confused exclamations of the pirates with mingled feelings of hope and fear, and Alice in vain sought to calm her. The loud report of the guns from the distant vessel startled her still more ; and, unused as she was to such scenes, she could not help trembling with apprehension.

"Oh, God !" she cried, "what will be the result of this ?—What fresh scene of danger now threatens us ?"

"Be not alarmed," said Alice, "for you have more reason to hope; for, from the observations of the pirates, it is evident that this is some vessel in pursuit, which they are anxious to avoid, if possible; and should it overtake us, your deliverance may be nearer than you anticipate."

"But, oh, the horrors of the deadly strife !" ejaculated Mary ; "I shudder to think of it. And should the villain Brandon triumph my fate will then be certain. Alas—alas ! how horrible is this suspense !"

Again the loud report of a gun was heard, and it sounded much nearer than before.

"Hark !" cried Mary, "again that signal ; oh, Heaven defend the right ! and, oh, Harry, if you should happen to be on board this ship, may the Almighty protect you from every danger, and consign me to your friendly care. But, no ; how wildly, how madly I talk ; I dare not indulge in such a hope !"

"Compose your feelings," said Alice, "and I will hasten on deck, and endeavour to ascertain the facts."

Mary returned no answer, for the power of her emotions prevented her ; and Alice quitted the place and hurried to the deck, where such a scene of confusion prevailed. The moment she was gone our heroine sunk on her knees, and, with clasped hands and tearful eyes, she earnestly and fervently implored the mercy and protection of the Supreme, and then awaited in the utmost state of anxiety the return of her attendant.

"All-merciful Father !" she cried, "oh, look down with an eye of pity upon me, defeat the diabolical plans of my deadly enemy, and release me from the dangers by which I am at present surrounded ! Oh, should this vessel, indeed, overtake the one in which I am a prisoner, may conquest crown their efforts, and then I may indeed hope to be again restored to liberty, if not to happiness. But if Brandon should find that he is likely to be defeated, will he not immediately prevent the consummation of my wishes by sacrificing my life to his revenge ? Alas ! it is but too probable, for he will never suffer me to escape. Dreadful thought !—And yet, why should I tremble at the idea of death ? Would it not be far preferable to the awful fate with which he has threatened me ? It would ! I will be firm, and seek to resign myself entirely to the will of Providence. Ah, little did I ever expect to experience such a trial as this !"

The shouts and confusion on the deck of the pirate vessel seemed to increase, and the anxiety and suspense of our heroine became almost insupportable. But at length the door of the cabin in which she was confined was thrown open, and Alice made her appearance.

"Ah !" exclaimed Mary, advancing eagerly towards her, "what news ? Oh, tell me, tell me !"

"It is as I expected," answered Alice ; "a vessel, which has been discovered to be a British man-of-war, has given chase to the pirate."

"But with what chance of success ?" eagerly demanded our heroine.

"I fear 'but little," returned Alice. "At first she seemed to gain upon them, but fortune appears to favour the villains, and they are now fast leaving their pursuers in the distance behind. There are few vessels that can compare with the Wasp for quickness of sailing."

"Alas—alas !" sighed the hapless Mary, again wringing her hands, "then there is no hope; the fate that awaits me is certain ; Providence is against me ! Oh, God ! how dreadful is it to be condemned to suffer thus !"

"Still be firm !" said Alice, "for there is no knowing the turn which may yet take place in your favour."

"Oh, no !" replied our heroine, "I dare not encourage any such an idea. I see plainly that the fates have conspired against me, and there is nothing left for me to do but to abandon myself to complete despair."

She was interrupted by loud shouts of exultation from the men on deck, and then she heard the voice of Brandon exclaim in accents of triumph—

"Hurrah! hurrah! well done, my gallant craft, you have not failed me yet, and never will; you have performed your task well, and fairly defeated the efforts of the enemy. Where is she now? Ha, ha, ha! there is not a speck of her to be seen upon the horizon. We have escaped—we have escaped, and can now proceed without danger on our course!"

"It is all over," sighed our heroine, "the pirates have triumphed, and I am lost! Would to Heaven that I were dead, for never can I find strength to endure the horrors that are in store for me!"

"Would that I could induce you to become more tranquil and resigned," remarked Alice, "for of what avail is it for you to give way to these feelings of abject despair?"

"And how think you I can do otherwise?" emphatically demanded Mary; "how is it possible that I can be otherwise than truly miserable, situated as I am? Alas—alas!" what will become of me? I shall go mad at the bare contemplation of the fate which is but too evidently in store for me! And Brandon, will he not be goaded on by this event to increased determination to complete his infamous designs? and probably but a few hours will complete my doom! How the blood curdles in my veins at the thought! What will become of me?"

She beat her breast as she gave utterance to these words, and Alice was completely at a loss what to say to console her, for she had too much reason to fear that the apprehensions of the unfortunate woman would be realised. But Mary sank into a complete lethargy of despair, and Alice did not attempt to disturb her from it, for she knew well that all her attempts to compose her would be useless, and she could not bear to listen to her dismal lamentations. A dead silence had succeeded the noise and confusion which had lately prevailed upon deck, and the vessel was sailing rapidly on its course, and evidently with-out any other danger threatening it. But at length both Mary and Alice were startled and aroused by hearing a knock at the cabin door; the latter opened it with a trembling hand, and our heroine could not repress a cry of horror when Brandon made his appearance. He fixed upon her a look of fearful meaning, and for a minute or two he stood at the entrance, and seemed to hesitate to advance; but at length he turned abruptly to Alice, and in a peremptory tone commanded her to retire. This aroused Mary, and in a voice of the deepest emotion and earnest solicitation she said—

"Oh, no, no, no! for Heaven's sake do not leave me, Alice! Alone with such a villain as this, what will become of me? Remain here, I beseech you, and protect me from his brutal violence!"

"Psha!" exclaimed Brandon, contemptuously; "of what avail is this appeal? Do as I command you, Alice, or you know the consequences."

"Oh, Brandon!" Alice ventured to interpose, "I beg of you to act with forbearance towards this unfortunate woman, and to take into consideration the dreadful state of mind in which she must at present be placed."

"Begone, I say!" again commanded Brandon, sternly, "nor dare to intercede for her. Shall I submit to have my will called into question by such a being as you? Begone—or fear my wrath!"

Alice fixed upon our heroine a look of the deepest pity and sympathy, and was then forced to obey; and the pirate, after contemplating his wretched victim for a few minutes in silence, and with feelings of exultation, advanced towards her and pronounced her name. At the sound of his voice she started, and a shuddering feeling of horror came over her on finding herself alone with the wretch whom she had so much cause to dread, and of whose monstrous intentions she could not entertain the least doubt; but he viewed her emotions with indifference, if not with satisfaction, and advancing still nearer towards her, he said—

"I am fully prepared for this reception, beauteous Mary, but I heed it not. 1 congratulate myself on the success which has attended my designs, and I come to welcome you on board my gallant craft, of which in future you are destined to rule its supreme mistress."

"All-merciful Heaven!" gasped forth the distracted and disgusted Mary, "and must I be compelled to listen to language such as this? Villain! leave me, and no longer shock and appal my sight by your odious presence!"

"Not so, my fair one," replied the pirate, with a sarcastic smile; "although in many things I am inclined to obey you and acknowledge you as my sole mistress, on certain points I must exercise my free will, and nothing whatever will induce me to alter it. Nay, you may as well restrain your feelings, for here they will be completely thrown away. Again I bid you welcome to my bonny bark, and would persuade you to endeavour to look upon me with more favourable eyes than you do at present, for it is only by that means you can hope to receive from me those indulgences that I am anxious to lavish upon you. Here, as the mistress of my heart, you shall have everything at your command, and——"

"Cease, cease, villain!" interrupted Mary, her bosom swelling with shame and the bitterest resentment; "your words freeze the very blood in my veins with horror, and I can willingly submit to death rather than be exposed to the revolting fate with which you have threatened me, and which I know you are sufficiently heartless and brutal to put into execution, if Providence does not interpose to prevent you. Oh, God! is it not enough that you should tear me from my home, my husband, but that you should still seek to add to my sufferings by this brutal system of persecution?"

"Psha!" returned Brandon, "what have you to regret in the loss of your husband? You never loved him, and though wedded to him, he was unworthy of you."

"Base wretch! forbear to slander that unfortunate man whom you have so deeply injured," said our heroine, indignantly. "Oh, Tiller!"

"Nay," returned Brandon, with a bitter sneer, "methinks you did not always entertain the same feelings towards your husband as you now profess to do, especially when Harry Halliyard arose uppermost in your thoughts."

"Alas—alas!" sighed poor Mary, and the blushes of shame glowing in her cheeks, "this is insupportable! Oh, Halliyard, were you present, how deeply would you resent this brutal insult!"

"Ha, ha, ha!" laughed Brandon, triumphantly, "he is powerless to do me harm, and it will be well for him if he never encounters me. But I tell you, Mary, that you will never behold him again, unless he should happen to fall into my power, which, for the gratification of my revenge, I hope he will."

"Oh, Heaven forbid!" cried Mary fervently, and with a shudder of horror. "Sooner would I that he should perish than that he should be consigned to such a fate as that."

"You may flatter yourself with the hope," observed Brandon, with a malicious grin, "but I feel confident that it will never be realised. But if it is any consolation to you to know, I can inform you that within the last hour or two, Harry Halliyard has been nearer to you than you now imagine."

"No, no, that is impossible!" ejaculated our heroine; "you seek to torture and deceive me!"

"Indeed I do not," answered the pirate. "The vessel which was in pursuit of us was the Porpoise, on board of which he is."

"Good God!" cried our heroine, "and can this indeed be true?"

"It is," answered Brandon; "but I have said enough on that subject, and must come at once to the purport of my visit to you. I have before told you, Mary, that you have excited a most powerful passion in my breast, which I am determined shall be gratified, let the consequences be whatever they may; and as you are completely at my mercy, you will see, no doubt, the wisdom of not attempting to offer any obstinate and futile resistance. Three days from hence you must prepare yourself to yield entirely to my will, for I am fully resolved not to delay the completion of my wishes any longer."

"Oh, no, no, no!" gasped forth our heroine, and every limb was convulsed with the terror of her feelings; "cruel as I know you are, even you cannot

MARY'S INTERVIEW WITH BRANDON AT FARMER HARVILLE'S.

mean what you say. Oh, spare me—spare me!"

"Bah!" cried Brandon, scornfully, "you must think me a weak fool, indeed, were I to suffer myself to be subdued by your supplications. But I waste words in thus cavilling with you. As sure as I now stand within your presence you will find that I will not fail to keep my word; and, therefore,

you will do well to make up your mind to the fate which is in store for you."

"Father of Heaven, I earnestly implore You to interpose to save me," exclaimed Mary, solemnly, "and not to suffer this inhuman miscreant to triumph in his hideous designs!"

"Place confidence in the power you invoke, if you will," returned Brandon, triumphantly, "but you will find that you will be doomed to the most bitter disappointment. In three days hence from the present time, I repeat, you shall be mine ; and situated as you are, what earthly power is there that can save you? Nay, frown not, for frowns ill become a countenance so fair and lovely. You shall reign the pirate queen, and the bold and daring crew who are under my command shall acknowledge thee their mistress, and do you homage. Oh, ours will be a bold life on the ocean deep! a life of freedom and reckless enjoyment, and——"

"Oh, hold, cruel, heartless man!" interrupted our heroine, her bosom swelling still more than ever with the feelings of indignation that agitated it, and crimson blushes of shame glowing in her cheeks, "I must not, will not listen to language such as this, and proceeding from the lips of a villain whose guilty and inhuman soul I am certain will not hesitate at the perpetration of any crime, however hideous. Oh, God! what have I done that I should be subjected to such a fate as this? If there is still one spark of pity left within your breast, Brandon, you will leave me, and no longer shock my ears by your observations, or disgust and appal me by your hateful presence!"

"And is this the sort of language, think you, to conciliate me, or to move me to relent?" demanded the ruffian, sternly. "Beware, beware! I know full well how much you hate me, and that alone will urge me on still more to put my threats into execution. As for your scorn and reproaches, I heed them not. Doubtless I shall soon learn the way to curb your haughty and obstinate spirit, for Hugh Brandon never yet failed to triumph in anything upon which he had fixed his mind, and it is not likely that he will do so now."

"And what a proud thing it will be for you to boast of," retorted Mary, in a voice of the bitterest scorn, "that you have triumphed over a poor defenceless woman, and brought about the destruction of one who never injured you. But, no, I will not believe that the just God above will ever permit you to do so. Certain as you even now appear to be in the success of your atrocious designs I shall yet escape you, and a terrible retribution will descend upon your head for the wrongs you have inflicted on me!"

"You must be mad, indeed," returned Brandon, with a look of exultation, "if you flatter yourself with any such erroneous ideas. What chance have you of avoiding the fate to which I have doomed you? Could I not even this very moment put my threats into execution, and what power have you of resisting me? However, you may thank my forbearance that I do not do so; but be certain that at the time I have mentioned you shall become mine, and that nothing whatever shall be suffered to stand in the way of the accomplishment of my wishes."

"Horrible thought!" again gasped forth our heroine, and raising her hands and eyes imploringly towards Heaven. "Oh, Brandon, once more I beseech your mercy, and implore you not to proceed to the dreadful extremities that you have threatened! Rather consign me to death than to such a frightful and revolting fate as that you have mentioned! Oh, restore me to my home, and——"

"Restore you to your home? Ha, ha, ha!" laughed the hardened wretch, scornfully; "a very reasonable idea, truly, after I have proceeded so far, and my triumph is all but complete. Why, you must think me mad to make such an appeal to me; and to think that I will now abandon all my hopes, and perhaps expose myself to destruction. No, no, Mary, your doom is sealed, and, therefore, there is nothing left for you to do but to submit to it, for there is nothing whatever that can save you from it. Nay, you must learn to love me, though you now view me with loathing and contempt."

"Love you?" repeated our heroine, with a look of the utmost horror and disgust ; "oh, monstrous idea! dare your lips give utterance to it? Brandon, your crimes have already stamped you a villain of the blakest dye ; but for this, depend upon it, however you may affect to scorn my words, the most terrible vengeance of outraged Heaven will descend upon your head, and you will learn to repent when too late of the wrongs you have inflicted on me and so many others of my unfortunate fellow-creatures!"

"Bah!" ejaculated Brandon, with a look of the most ineffable contempt, "of what use is it wasting your breath in thus preaching to one who is perfectly callous to all such feelings as those of which you speak? I am a man of such a stern and inflexible nature that nothing can move me from my purpose, and that, methinks, you should have discovered ere this. But you have heard my determination, and for the present, therefore, I have nothing more to say to you, but will leave you to your own meditations."

"Oh, hear me, Brandon—in mercy!" again supplicated the distracted Mary, clasping her hands together, and tears of anguish starting to her eyes.

"Enough!" he returned, abruptly, and resolutely; "remember my words, and instead of trying to persuade me from my purpose, prepare yourself for that which must inevitably take place."

With these observations, to which our heroine was unable to return any reply, and once more fixing upon her a look of triumph, Brandon retired, and no sooner was he gone than Mary burst into a violent paroxysm of sobs and tears, which for some minutes completely choked her utterance, and nearly overpowered her.

"Heaven have mercy upon me!" she at length ejaculated, "for without thy aid I am, indeed, entirely lost! To appeal to this hardened and brutal miscreant is vain and useless; he will not fail to realise the dreadful threats to which he has given utterance, and no other prospect presents itself to my distracted imagination but the blackest despair and misery! Alas—alas! little did I ever dream that such a dreadful fate as this would ever befal me, and my blood freezes with horror as I contemplate it. But three short days, and then must I become the victim of this fiend in human form. Oh, let me die—let me die before such a horrible fate can overtake me! The many and severe trials I have already experienced have rendered me weary of existence, and death would indeed now be a mercy to me. Oh, my unfortunate husband! we shall never meet again, and what a curse it was that we should ever have beheld each other. Kind Heaven give him fortitude to support this fearful calamity, and do not suffer him to curse me; for, alas! under all the painful and mysterious circumstances, will he not believe me guilty? That thought of itself is more than sufficient to drive me to distraction!"

She now sunk upon her knees, and earnestly and fervently implored the merciful interposition of the Supreme; but not one ray of hope or consolation was admitted to her lacerated bosom, and tears again gushed to her eyes, while she beat her breast in the agony of her feelings. But to think that the vessel which had been in pursuit of the pirates was the very one on which Harry Halliyard was aboard, tortured and distracted her more than all. Had it overtaken the Wasp, it was most probable that the pirates would have been defeated, and she should, perhaps, now have been safe under the protection of Halliyard, and the infamous designs of Brandon would thus have been defeated, and all further danger from him would have been prevented. Alas! what a bitter disappointment was this to the unfortunate woman; and when she reflected upon it she could scarcely control herself within the bounds of reason.

"And should it have come to his knowledge that I am in the power of Brandon, how great must be the anguish and despair which he must now be enduring!" she ejaculated; "for too well will he anticipate the dreadful fate which is in store for me. Oh, Harry! how will your noble heart bleed for me, and what is there which can inspire you with hope and consolation? May Heaven watch over and protect you! and though I cannot hope that it will ever be our fate to meet again in this world, may every blessing attend you, and may you be able to meet with some other woman on whom you can place your affections, and who shall be worthy of you. But, no, too well am I convinced that in the loss of me your hopes are all annihilated, and that you can never love another woman as you have done me. Oh, cruel and untoward fate, which has prevented us from coming together, the terrible misfortunes that have now taken place would probably then not have happened, and we should at the present moment have been happy together. But am I not criminal in entertaining such thoughts as these, since fate has made me the wife of another, and one who has ever bestowed upon me the most unbounded affection and indulgence? I am, and I blush to acknowledge it. Oh, Tiller! unfortunate man! how little have you deserved to be exposed to such sufferings as these; and what would I not give were it in my power to relieve you; but of that there is no chance, no prospect whatever, and the longer I reflect upon all the circumstances connected with my fate the greater does my agony become. Brandon is a determined ruffian; he has everything in his power, and he will not fail to carry his threats into execution to the very letter, and thus the prospect before me is of the most horrible description, and I shrink with terror from it."

She was interrupted in the midst of these melancholy reflections by the opening of the cabin door, and Alice made her appearance, much to the relief and gratification of Mary, who advanced towards her with trembling footsteps, and looked in her face with an expression of countenance which plainly showed the nature of her feelings, if Alice could not previously have anticipated them.

"Alas!" she said, in tones of compassion, "I fear that you have suffered much from this interview with Brandon."

"Suffered, Alice?" repeated our heroine, with a deep sigh; "oh, how is it possible that I can describe my feelings? But three days will be suffered to elapse, and then he has threatened that the crisis of my fate shall be decided; and can I contemplate that without a sensation of the most insupportable horror? Oh, God! what shall I do? Where can I look for relief or consolation?"

"Still endeavour to be firm," said Alice; "for something may yet occur to frustrate the wicked, the diabolical designs of your guilty persecutor, and to restore you to liberty and your home at the very moment when you least expect it."

"Ah, no!" returned Mary, disconsolately; "of what use is it attempting to buoy me up with any such delusive hopes? What is to prevent the accomplishment of Brandon's designs? What can release me from his power?"

"We may encounter some vessel," replied Alice, "which he cannot resist, and then your deliverance would be certain. The vessel which was lately in pursuit of him, although he has for the present outstripped it, may yet overtake him, and then——"

"No, no!" interrupted Mary, hastily, "that hope is gone; but, oh, Alice, what will you say when you hear that that vessel was the very one on which Harry Halliyard was aboard?"

"Is it possible?" said Alice.

"It is true," answered our heroine, "if what Brandon has stated be correct."

"It was, then, indeed, unfortunate that it did not overtake the pirates," observed Alice, "for their defeat would then have been all but certain. It is not likely that they could have resisted so powerful an enemy. But still, as I said before, the pirates may not yet be able to escape, and you must not, therefore, abandon yourself entirely to despair."

"Alas!" sighed Mary, "how is it possible that I can do otherwise, so short as is the time that the villain Brandon has allowed me? And even should he be overtaken, and he finds that his defeat is inevitable, would he not immediately sacrifice me to his savage vengeance rather than I should be suffered to escape? and thus, whichever way I turn my eyes, I see nothing but destruction before me. Oh, Alice, what a truly wretched being I am, and it would be a mercy to me were this moment to prove my last!"

"Talk not thus, Mrs. Tiller," remonstrated Alice, "for it makes me shudder to hear you. Endeavour to call all your fortitude to your aid, and you will, fear not, yet be able to surmount all the numerous difficulties by which you are surrounded."

"Alas!" ejaculated Mary, "it is in vain that I seek to bear with fortitude and resignation the heavy misfortunes to which it is my hard lot to be subjected. And when I think of the threats which Brandon has held out to me, and the all but certainty of his carrying them into effect, my heart sinks within me, and my patience is completely exhausted. In three days from the present, I repeat, he has marked me for the victim of his brutal passions, and death alone can rescue me from the disgusting fate. Torn away from my home and friends, and tossed about on the wide billows of the boundless deep, and surrounded by wretches whose delight is in the perpetration of every dreadful crime, what else have I to look forward to than the utmost misery and degradation? Oh, my poor brain, it is distracted, and madness must most surely ultimately seize upon it! Heaven, in mercy try me not too far, but avert the horrors which I have now too much reason to apprehend!"

She pressed her hands upon her burning temples, and sobbed bitterly, and Alice was at a loss what to say to comfort her, for she was too well convinced within her own mind how utterly hopeless was her situation, and how little reason she had to expect any mercy or forbearance from Brandon.

For some minutes Mary resigned herself completely to the violence of her grief, and the various torturing thoughts that crowded upon her brain distracted and bewildered her. But at length she suddenly started from this lethargy of agony and despair, and clasping her hands together, in the wildest accents she exclaimed—

"But shall I live to endure so horrible a doom?—Must I, indeed, become so lost and degraded?—The mistress of a pirate and a murderer? Forbid it, Heaven! My heart revolts at the bare idea, and my bosom swells to bursting! Alice, if you indeed feel for me the pity and sympathy that you profess to do, you will provide me with the means of terminating a wretched existence which is now insupportable to me."

"Oh, forbear—forbear!" expostulated her attendant. "Banish such dreadful and guilty ideas from your mind, for they make me tremble to listen to them; and I can scarcely believe that you are aware of what you are saying. Be firm; who knows what three days may bring about? At any rate, it is no use to anticipate the worst."

"You talk erroneously, Alice," said our heroine, impatiently. "How can I help anticipating the worst, situated as I am? and would it not be better to die than to become a victim to the brutal passions of such a blood-stained miscreant as Brandon? It would; and all the arguments that you can make use of will not convince me to the contrary."

"Would to Heaven that I could succeed in banishing these torturing thoughts from your mind," returned Alice; "for, indeed, there is no one who can more deeply sympathise with you than myself, or who would more readily release you from the dangers by which you are at present surrounded than I would, were it in my power to do so; but, alas! it is not. And when I assure you how much I regret my inability to do so, you will, I trust, believe me that I speak sincerely?"

"I do, Alice," replied Mary, pressing her hand; "and pardon me, I beseech you, if I have said anything which may appear harsh or ungenerous, but my mind is so bewildered that I scarcely know what my tongue gives utterance to."

"I am well convinced of that," said Alice, "and can make every allowance for it. But I am anxious to see you become more calm, and to put your trust in Providence, who will not desert you in this hour of your severe trial, you may depend upon it."

"Would to Heaven that I could follow your advice, Alice," ejaculated Mary, "but when I take all the circumstances into consideration it is impossible for me to do so. I am shut out from every hope—my fate hangs upon a thread—and but a few hours only will probably snap that thread asunder. My poor husband! can I reflect upon what his sufferings must at present be without feelings of the deepest anguish?"

"He is, indeed, much to be pitied," answered Alice; "but still I hope, even desperate as I must acknowledge your situation now to be, that you will yet be restored to him."

"Restored to him?" repeated Mary; "oh, what chance is there of that? He will never be able to survive my loss, and probably ere this he is no more; and he has died with the fatal impression upon his mind that I have been faithless to him, and in his last moments he has most likely invoked the most terrible curses of Heaven upon my head."

"Oh, no," anwered Alice, "if he sincerely loved you, he could never be so uncharitable and unjust. Do not torture yourself with any such ideas as these, for I trust that they will be proved to be entirely groundless."

"You know not all the circumstances of my melancholy history," returned our heroine, " or you would think differently, Alice. Alas! he has too much reason to doubt and suspect me, and I cannot but believe myself to have been most culpable."

"Oh, no, Mrs. Tiller," remarked Alice, "that is impossible; you must reproach yourself too severely. But, come, arouse yourself from this dismal state of mind, and endeavour to look forward at least with some degree of fortitude to a favourable change in your circumstances; and that, too, before long. If you act with firmness and precaution you may yet be enabled to resist the monstrous designs of Brandon; and every delay that may be caused in the accomplishment of his wishes may tend to release you from his power, and ultimately to restore you to liberty and your former happiness."

"Happiness!" repeated our heroine, shaking her head doubtfully; "alas! that can never again be mine, under any circumstances. But, oh, how serene and blissful were the days of my youth—how little did I anticipate the sad change which was in store for me! I shudder when I contemplate it, and all my courage forsakes me. Oh, what a chequered life has been mine, and what will be the result of it? And what renders it still more torturing is, that I have involved others who were dear to me in my fate, and they are now exposed to sufferings which I shudder to think upon. Oh, Tiller! oh Harry! how my heart bleeds for you!"

She sobbed aloud as she gave utterance to these words; and Alice was deeply affected, and would have given anything could she have succeeded in tranquillizing her feelings. A silence of some minutes ensued, and Mary paced the cabin backwards and forwards in the mose disordered manner. At length she turned hastily to Alice, and said—

"But whither is this vessel bound? How long shall we be exposed to the perils of the deep?"

"I know not," answered Alice; "but probably Brandon will make his way to one of those fastnesses which he possesses in various parts of the globe, and which have rendered it so difficult to detect him."

"Ah!" ejaculated our heroine, "and is he then, indeed, so powerful?"

"Yes," returned her companion; "many years of success have rendered him so, for he has hitherto escaped almost with impunity. But I trust that the time is not far distant when justice shall overtake him, and his career of guilt, and that of his infamous associates, may at last be brought to a termination."

"And yet you say that your husband is one of the crew?" said Mary.

"Most true," answered Alice, with a sigh, " but he is as great a villain as the rest; and think you that it is possible I can view him with any other feelings than those of disgust and horror?"

"What could ever have induced you to become his wife?"

"Because I was most cruelly deceived and betrayed," replied Alice; "and my misguided parents, may Heaven pardon them, sacrificed me to one whom I could not view with esteem, let alone affection."

"It was a hard fate," remarked our heroine, " and I sincerely pity you."

"I thank you for your commiseration, Mrs. Tiller," said Alice, "and should you ever become acquainted with my history, you will acknowledge how much I deserve it. Alas! mine has been a cruel fate indeed, and how often have I prayed to Heaven to release me from it, and from those scenes of horror which it has too often been my hard lot to witness. But why should I obtrude my sorrows upon you, who have already so many of your own to struggle against?"

"Our misfortunes are mutual," said Mary, "and, therefore, can we the more warmly sympathise with each other. I feel grateful that I have at least one friend in you, Alice, who can pity me; for had it not been for you, how tenfold would have been my misery."

"I only regret, Mrs. Tiller," replied Alice, "that it is not in my power to serve you more; for you know, I think, that it is my will to do so. But my means are unfortunately limited, and I cannot do as I could wish."

"I am well convinced of that," returned Mary, "and believe me that I feel most deeply your kindness. Alas! I fear that I shall never be able to make any return for it."

"Mention it not," answered Alice; "your friendship and esteem are all I seek, and to which I trust I shall be able to prove that I am entitled."

"Oh, yes," said our heroine, "you have more than done so already. Alas! I should have sunk entirely beneath the heavy burthen of despair and misery that presses upon my heart ere now, had it not been for you."

Alice returned a suitable answer; and thus they continued to converse for some time longer; and Alice did at last succeed, much better than might have been expected, in tranquillizing her feelings. The pirate vessel sailed on its course without anything occurring to obstruct it, and Brandon and his crew were in high spirits, and did not forget to regale themselves to the fullest extent.

"All goes on as well as could be wished," observed Brandon, "and fortune smiles upon us, and assures us of future success. We have fairly outstripped the Porpoise, and no doubt the officers and crew are greatly disappointed at our having been enabled to give them the slip. The Wasp is a clipper, and it must be a noble craft indeed which is able to compare with her."

"Very true, captain," answered Ben Summers; "but still it is quite as well that we were enabled to avoid an engagement with the Porpoise, for I am inclined to think that she might have proved more than a match for us, and we had little, if anything, to gain by the combat."

"True," coincided Brandon, "she carries too much heavy metal for us, but still we would have had a desperate and determined struggle for the victory; and if fortune should have happened to have been in our favour, it would have been a most glorious triumph for us. And what would have been more gratifying to me than all, is the probability that I should have got Harry Halliyard in my power, and I should have had the means of making him feel the terrible effects of my revenge?"

"Ay, captain, you may say that," returned Ben; "but chance will, perhaps, some time or other throw him in your way, and if it should, you will know how to deal with him."

"Yes," said Brandon, "and soon would he have cause to acknowledge the terrible effects of my revenge. If he has any idea that Mary is in my power his anguish of mind will be complete. As for her, my resolution is fixed, and nothing can move me from it. As I have told her, in three days from the present she must prepare herself to yield to my wishes."

"And a wise resolution, too," remarked Summers, "for you have already delayed quite long enough. Mary, no doubt, is in a state of great excitement at the hopelessness of her situation and I dare say she has not forgotten to heap upon you her reproaches?"

"You may well say that," replied the pirate; "I had to receive a full broadside of her abuse; but, as you may expect, it had not the least effect upon me, for I was fully prepared for it. I shall soon be able to tame her proud spirit, I dare say."

"No doubt of it," returned Summers; "it is not much use remaining obstinate when you once get into the power of Hugh Brandon, the pirate. She is well worthy to become your mistress, captain, and no doubt you will soon be able to reconcile her to her fate."

"It shall be no fault of mine if I am not," said Brandon; "at any rate, it does not much matter whether I am or not, for I have her securely in my power, and it is impossible that she can ever escape from it. But how surprised the lubbers in the harbour must be at our sudden disappearance."

"Yes," said Summers; "and it is quite evident that they at last suspected the real character of our craft, or they would not have sent the Porpoise in pursuit of us."

"Ay," coincided Brandon, "and their vexation and disappointment will, consequently, be all the greater. Come, let us drink confusion and destruction to our enemies."

They did so, and thus the villain Brandon continued to exult. But it is necessary that we should give some explanation as to what led to the pursuit of the pirates by the Porpoise.

Harry Halliyard continued in the same excitement of mind that we have described him to be at the mysterious and unaccountable disappearance of our heroine, and it was with a sad and heavy heart that he went on board the vessel, accompanied by his faithful, though eccentric friend, Mr. Watchful Waxend. For the first time in his life he felt disgusted with his profession, and dreaded the idea of the voyage, as it would prevent him from endeavouring to ascertain the fate of his still beloved Mary, and he feared that he should never behold her again. Several times he had been half resolved to desert from the ship, and go in search of her, but something withheld him from the rash act, though his misery and despair were increased, and all sorts of terrible conjectures haunted his imagination. At one time he feared that she had fallen a victim to some base plot, and at another that she had committed suicide; but the longer he reflected upon all the dismal circumstances the more did he become involved in mystery and perplexity. Previous, however, to his going on board, he wrote a long and feeling letter to Joe Tiller, expressing his deep sorrow at the terrible event which had taken place, endeavouring to exonerate himself from all blame in the mysterious affair, and urging him most earnestly to arouse all his energies and his fortitude, and to exert himself to the utmost to discover the fate which had befallen the unfortunate Mary. Having done this, and forwarded it, Harry did feel his mind, for a short time, somewhat more at ease, and he endeavoured to feel some degree of hope; but this was a most difficult task to accomplish; and, as we said before, it was with a heavy heart that he went on board the vessel. Ben Bowsprit, who was much attached to Harry, did all that he could to console him, but he turned a deaf ear to all his arguments and persuasions, and his courage entirely forsook him.

"Oh, Mary," he said, "how terrible is it to be in this state of suspense as to the fate which has befallen you, and to be compelled to quit these shores in the same state of doubt and uncertainty! Poor girl—poor girl! what a cruel destiny has yours been—and what hope is there now left for me? The villain who has been the cause of this, if, indeed, it is not your own act, has evidently triumphed in his inhuman designs, whatever they may be; and, exposed as I shall be to all the perils of the deep, what prospect is there that I shall ever behold you again? Indeed, since fate has placed an insuperable barrier to our ever coming together, I care not what becomes of me, and only hope that in the first engagement in which it may be my lot to mingle, some friendly ball may lay me low, and rid me of a life which is now completely valueless to me!"

"Oh, don't talk in that manner, Master Halliyard," said Waxend, who happened to be present as he thus soliloquised, "for I am sure you should not be tired of your existence yet; and it is my firm belief that Mary will yet be discovered, and restored to her home, and——"

"What chance is there of that, you lubber?" interrupted Harry, impatiently. "Ah, no, her fate is decided long ere this, and I cannot but fear that it is one of the worst description. Some villain must have torn her from her home, and got her in his power; and if so, to what horrors may she not at the present moment be exposed—and there is no one near to protect her, or to avenge her wrongs! That thought will drive me mad! Mary—dear, unfortunate Mary! how little did I expect that we should ever have been subjected to such misery as this! May eternal curses light upon the head of the miscreant or miscreants who have done this!"

"It is certainly a most mysterious affair," remarked Waxend, "and I know not what to think of it. But who can you suspect? for I never knew that Mary Tiller could have an enemy in the world."

"Oh, how base must that heart be which could entertain feelings of animosity against her," said Harry, "for

MARY IN HER PLACE OF CONFINEMENT AT FARMER HARVILLE'S.

Heaven never formed a more innocent and amiable being; and she never injured any human being, either by word or deed."

"I believe every word of that, Master Halliyard," returned Waxend, "and that makes me the more strongly suspect that she has not been forced away from her home, but that she has voluntarily abandoned it, and——"

"Liar!" interrupted Harry, passionately, and seizing Waxend fiercely by the collar. "Repeat that word again, and, damme, but I will send you to Davy Jones in less time than you could cry for mercy! Mary voluntarily desert her husband and her home? Oh, it is a monstrous libel, and I will not, must not listen to it! Oh, Mary, what can ever remove this terrible weight of suspense from my mind? As for you, you lubber, if I hear any more such lingo escape your ugly mouth, I—I——."

"Now—now, Master Halliyard," interrupted poor Watchful Waxend, in a tone of remonstrance, "you are so very excitable that you explode in a moment. I'm sure I meant no harm; and as for saying anything against the character of poor Mary, I am the last man in the world who would attempt to do so."

"Well, well, I believe you," said Harry, releasing his hold; "but my brain is so bewildered that I scarcely know what I say. But as to hear poor Mary's virtue and integrity impeached, why, I must be an infernal swab to stand by and listen to it."

"Impeach the virtue and integrity of Mary?" repeated Waxend; "why, lord love you, who ever thought of such a thing? If you imagine that I did, Master Halliyard, I can only say that you judge me wrongfully. All that I meant to suggest was, (and yet I am almost afraid to say so,) that the poor lass, overpowered by her feelings, and driven to despair by all the melancholy circumstances connected with her fate, might have laid violent hands upon herself, and——"

"Ah?" cried Harry, striking his forehead with anguish, "it is that idea which maddens me! And, alas! when I recollect the melancholy, the deplorable, and hopeless state in which I left her, do not my fearful surmises appear but too likely to be confirmed? Poor lass! poor lass! why should you thus be made the sport of evil destiny? But still your fate is involved in a mystery which I in vain seek to penetrate. Surely Providence would prevent you from the perpetration of so rash an act. You must have fallen into the power of some desperate villains, who have a design against your happiness, or have some feelings of revenge to gratify. But who can they be? I in vain seek to imagine."

"Ah, Harry, I shall never forget my singular dream, part of which, you must own, has been realised by the attack which was made on you and myself the other night by those ruffians. Should poor Mary have fallen into the power of Brandon, who is the greatest enemy that you have got——"

"Avast—avast there!" interrupted our hero, hastily; "I dare not entertain such a thought as that! My Mary in the power of that infernal shark, Brandon? Oh, it is impossible. Sooner would I believe that she were dead, than to be exposed to such a fate as that, which is far too horrible to contemplate! Would that I had never entered on board this vessel, but had remained near to, and watched over poor Mary; then would this never have happened, for who would have dared to commit such an outrage as this against her while Harry Halliyard was nigh to protect her? And now I am prevented the opportunity of going in search of her. In a few hours we shall set sail, and then all hope of ever hearing of or beholding her again will be at an end. I know not what to do—my brain is distracted."

"Be firm, Master Halliyard," said his companion, "and trust to Providence, for something seems to assure me that, notwithstanding the present dismal aspect of affairs, something will yet occur to restore the unfortunate Mrs. Tiller uninjured to her friends."

"Psha!" exclaimed Harry, impatiently, "you talk erroneously, Waxend, and I am very well convinced that you cannot think as you say. From the time which has elapsed since the disappearance of Mary, what chance is there of discovering her? She is lost, lost for ever, and all my hopes are stranded and crushed. Oh, Mary, what little cause had we at one time to anticipate that such misfortunes as these would ever fall to our lot! Cruel fate has conspired against us, and it would have been better, far better had we never have known each other, or had we been shipped to the port of eternity. I shall never have patience or fortitude to endure this much longer."

Thus did the anguish of our hero increase every minute, and it was in vain that Waxend and Bowsprit sought to tranquillise him, and in this manner the hours wore tediously away. Night came, and, as has been before stated, set in with a dense fog, which rendered it impossible to distinguish objects at any distance, and all was bustle on board the Porpoise, preparing for the commencement of the voyage on the following day; but Harry Halliyard, on retiring to his berth, was too much agitated in his mind by the various thoughts that crowded upon and distracted it to seek his hammock, and he continued to meditate in the most dismal manner upon the peculiar and melancholy circumstances in which he was placed, and to bemoan the fate which attended him and his still beloved Mary. It was in vain that he endeavoured to conjecture what had become of her; and the longer he reflected the more his anguish and anxiety of mind increased.

"Alas!" he sighed, "in a few short hours I shall be borne far away from this place, and all chance of my ascertaining what has become of the poor girl will be at an end. That thought is too torturing for endurance, and will certainly drive me to madness. Some cursed spell is upon us, and everything seems to frown upon us. Was it not enough that we should be so cruelly disappointed in the bright hopes of happiness we had formed, but that now this additional calamity should befal us? If it is the work of some brutal ruffian, may the heaviest curses light upon his head, and bring him to destruction. But who could be guilty of such a diabolical act?—who could entertain a thought to the injury of one so good as my poor Mary?—My Mary? Oh, yes, it is impossible that she can be otherwise than most dear and precious to my heart, though fate has doomed that we should never come together, and that all the bright prospects that our sanguine imaginations had conjured up should be thus so fatally overclouded. And is this the reward I am destined to meet with, after all the many years of peril which it has been my lot to encounter? Had I fallen in the battle's heat, or perished in the stormy deep, it would have been far better for me than to experience the horrible suspense, anxiety and despair which I am now enduring. Poor Joe, too, my old and faithful friend and associate, what a wreck has your happiness experienced, and how sincerely do I pity you. To what cause can you attribute the loss of your wife? Taking all the painful circumstances into consideration, will you not have too much reason to suspect that I have had something to do with it?—to doubt the fidelity of Mary, and to imagine that she has, of her own free accord, abandoned you, and followed my footsteps? Fearful thought! But, no; Tiller can never be so unjust or uncharitable to entertain it; and if he has done so, the letter which I have forwarded to him must convince him to the contrary. Would that I had never entered on board this vessel; how quickly would I hasten to him to assure him of my innocence, and to co-operate with him in his efforts to discover his unfortunate wife. But my precipitation has rendered me completely powerless to act, and tossed about as I shall be on the stormy ocean, I shall have no opportunity of discovering her fate. Oh, most willingly would I lay down my own life, could I by so doing be the means of restoring Mary, unimpaired, to her friends. But it is madness, complete madness for me to entertain such a thought for a moment. Mary is gone, gone for ever, and there is nothing but the darkest despair left for me. And if the statement that Jack Oarsby made to me, of having met Mary on the evening of her disappearance, be correct, to what conclusion can I arrive? It fills my mind with the most terrible apprehensions. But he must have been mistaken. I am completely bewildered, and know not what to think."

He paused, and folding his arms across his chest, paced to and fro in a state of the utmost disorder, and giving way to the most dismal reflections, from which he could not find the slightest relief. At one time he regretted that he had not deserted immediately on hearing the news of the mysterious disappearance of our heroine, that he might have prosecuted a strict search after her; but still his name had never been coupled with one dishonourable act, and had he adopted such a course, it would surely have stamped him with cowardice, and have tarnished the reputation which he had hitherto maintained; and he could not contemplate such a contingency as that without a manly feeling of repugnance.

Thus, as we have said before, the night passed away, and when the morning dawned, the dense fog which had for so many hours prevailed had entirely dispersed, and the clearness of the atmosphere which succeeded betokened fine weather. Hastening on deck, he found that considerable confusion and excitement prevailed there amongst the crew, and he soon ascertained the cause. All eyes were directed to that spot where the supposed ship, the Helen, had been riding at anchor, and all traces of her were gone. During the night, and while the fog had prevailed, she had disappeared in the most mysterious and suspicious manner, and the crew looked at each other with amazement, and gave vent to the various surmises which this circumstance naturally excited in their minds.

"There is something not square and above-board in this," remarked Ben Bowsprit to our hero; "I begin to suspect that this craft was not what she was represented to be, for if she was a fair trader, why should she take the opportunity of the fog which prevailed to set sail in so secret a manner?"

"Ah!" exclaimed Halliyard, "my darkest suspicions are aroused; the savage appearance of the crew, and the way in which the skipper always avoided society, do but serve to strengthen them. Is it possible that any rascally pirate can have been so bold as to anchor in this port, and in the midst of his majesty's fleet? The attack which was made, too, upon me the other night makes it appear the more suspicious. This vessel could not have borne a character that would bear inspection, or she would not have shifted her cable in so secret a manner."

"Damme!" returned Ben Bowsprit, "but I begin to be of your opinion, Harry; and what lubbers we must have been not to have suspected her before. My word for it that we have been lying alongside some shark of a pirate all this time, and that she has now managed to slip through our fingers altogether. If it be as we suspect, this is one of the most daring acts that I have ever witnessed or heard of, and it must have been for the purpose of effecting some important design that they could have been induced to run so great a risk. I am completely bewildered."

"Did you ever see the captain of the Helen, as they call her?" interrogated Harry.

"Yes, once," answered Ben, "and I can tell you that I did not much like his figure-head."

"What kind of a man was he?" asked our hero, eagerly.

"Why he was a stout, robust man," replied Ben, "apparently between forty and fifty years of age, with large, bushy whiskers and eyebrows, quite black, and having a remarkable scar on his left cheek, which seemed to have been occasioned by a cutlass wound."

"Ah!" exclaimed Harry, starting and exhibiting considerable excitement, "by heaven, that description of yours exactly corresponds with that of the villain, Hugh Brandon."

"Hugh Brandon, the bucaneer?" said Ben, hastily.

"The same," answered our hero; "and if it should indeed be he, the vessel which we were led to believe was the Helen was no other than the pirate schooner, the Wasp; and the attack made on me by the ruffians is fairly accounted for. Oh, Mary! and you, too, may be in his power; and if so, the fate which most certainly awaits you is too horrible to think of."

"Ah," said Mr. Watchful Waxend, who was present, "my dream again. It is being realised in every particular."

"Is it possible that our surmises can be correct," said Ben, "and that the villain can have been so near us? We must instantly see the captain, and acquaint him with our suspicions. Should he be of our opinion, no doubt he will give immediate orders to go in pursuit of her; and should we overtake her, the career of the rascals will be brought to a speedy termination."

"Porpoise, a-hoy!" two or three voices were now heard to shout, and a boat containing some of the crew of the vessel, and a stranger, was perceived approaching.

"They are the men I sent on shore an hour or two since," said the captain, whom Harry and Bowsprit had now approached; "but who is the man they have with them?"

The boat now came alongside, and the seamen came on board, conducting with them a man of forbidding aspect, and whose downcast looks were anything but prepossessing.

"Who is this man?" demanded the captain, "and why do you bring him hither?"

"We ax your honour's pardon," said one of the seamen, "but we found this man waiting near the harbour, and on our approach he hailed us, and stating that he had something to communicate to your honour of the utmost importance respecting the Helen, requested us to convey him on board."

"Indeed?" said the captain. "Well, my man, who and what are you? and what is it that you wish to communicate to me?"

"I am a poor guilty wretch," replied

the stranger, "tired of existence, and caring not how soon I get rid of it. I am a pirate—one who has mingled in the most brutal scenes, but am now stung with remorse, and therefore resign myself into your hands, to dispose of me as you think proper, and as my crimes deserve."

"A pirate!" said the captain, with a look of surprise.

"Ay," answered the man firmly, "and lately one of the desperate crew of the vessel which has so suddenly disappeared, and which you knew only by the name of the Helen."

"Ah!" exclaimed the captain, "were we then deceived? You are not speaking falsely to me, stranger?"

"Of what interest could it be for me to do so?" demanded the man. "I tell you the truth, so that there may be some chance of the guilty wretches with whom for so many years I have been connected being brought to justice. As for myself, I care not what my fate may be, for I am heartily sick of life. Hear me, captain, while I inform you that the vessel which you knew only by the name of the Helen was no other than the notorious pirate ship, the Wasp, commanded by the daring Hugh Brandon."

"Ah!" cried Harry, in a voice of the greatest agitation, "my worst suspicions are then confirmed."

"True, Harry Halliyard," replied the man, "for that I believe is your name; it was by the orders of Brandon, who wished to get you in his power, that the attack was made on you and your companion; and you may think yourself lucky that you escaped. But I have much more to tell to you, which you will, no doubt, be equally surprised to hear."

"Speak out then, and be quick," said the captain, impatiently.

"Mrs. Tiller was trepanned from her home on the night of her disappearance by a false tale of her husband having met with a serious accident, and that he had been removed in a dying state to the nearest public-house; in this manner she was inveigled to a notorious house in Westminster, the resort of the worst and most desperate of characters; there Brandon was waiting to receive her, and from thence she was conveyed to Portsmouth, to our secret rendezvous.

She is now on board the Wasp, and completely in the power of Brandon."

"Oh, God!" groaned the wretched Halliyard, "then her fate is certain, and there are no means of rescuing her from it."

"Just as I expected it would turn out to be," remonstrated Waxend; "there is my dream realised almost to the very letter. Poor Mrs. Tiller!"

"Is this statement you have made strictly true, I again demand?" asked the captain of the man.

"It is," answered the latter; "and now I feel more at ease than I have done for some time before, since I have thus relieved my conscience."

"Then," said the captain, "there is no time to be lost; we will give immediate chase to the pirate, and if the speed of our vessel is to be depended upon, it may not be too late to overtake her. To business, my lads, and let us set sail with all possible despatch; if fortune favours us, the career of the villain Brandon and his rascally crew will shortly be terminated. Halliyard, it seems that you have the deepest interest in the capture of this daring bucaneer?"

"Oh, yes, your honour," replied our hero, "all that I value on earth is in the power of the pirate; and I care not if I risk my life in endeavouring to rescue her. Oh, your honour, if it should be only my good fortune to come athwart the bows of that rascally shark, Brandon, I will pour such a broadside in upon him as shall shiver his vessel to splinters. Pardon me, captain, but for heaven's sake do not delay giving chase to the villains. This man can probably instruct us in the course they have taken."

"Ay," replied the captain; "what's your name, my man?"

"Ned Darrel," answered the pirate.

"Well, mark me, Master Ned Darrel," observed the captain, "on your own conduct depends your life; but should I find that you have deceived us, I will have you strung up to the yard-arm immediately."

"Your honour is at perfect liberty to do with me as you think proper," said Darrel, carelessly; "I am willing and anxious to afford you all the assistance I can; and you will find that I have spoken the truth."

"Enough," said the captain; "see to him, my lads; I must immediately see the admiral, and obtain his sanction for the chase. Lower the gig, and during my absence, which will only be brief, make every preparation for weighing anchor immediately."

"Ay, ay, your honour," replied several of the seamen, and the gig being hastily lowered, the captain stepped into it, followed by two or three of the crew, and put off with all expedition towards the admiral's ship.

We need not attempt to describe the state of excitement and anxiety which our hero laboured under, and every moment of delay appeared to him an age. He approached Ned Darrel, and fixing upon him a look of the most earnest penetration, he said—

"Darrel, according to your own admission, you have been a guilty man, but if you act an honest part on the present occasion, you may depend upon being dealt with mercifully. But have you spoken the truth?"

"Why should you doubt me?" asked the pirate; "have I not placed myself in your power? What, then, could I expect to gain by telling you a falsehood? I have spoken to you nothing but facts, and I am ready to abide by the consequences."

"And Mrs. Tiller, my—my Mary," said Harry, in a voice of great agitation, "is really in the power of the ruffian, Brandon?"

"She is," answered Darrel, "and is now on board the Wasp; it is Brandon's determination that she shall become his future mistress, and he is not the sort of man to abandon anything on which he has fixed his mind, as you must know well yourself."

"Alas! alas!" groaned our hero, "what an awful situation is hers! Poor Mary, my heart bleeds for you. But think you that there is any chance of our overtaking the Wasp?"

"Why," replied the pirate, "of course that greatly depends upon the expedition you use, for the Wasp is a very quick sailer, and she has had two or three hours the start of you; but I only hope that you may be successful, and then there is not much fear, from the superior character of your ship, and the number you have on board, that you will defeat the pirates, though you will find them desperate fellows to deal with."

"Oh, Brandon, guilty and inhuman wretch," ejaculated Harry, "you have indeed hitherto triumphed; and should we fail to overtake you, the fate of Mary is certain. Kind heaven, in mercy avert it! But you say that the villains have a secret rendezvous at Portsmouth, and that there Mrs. Tiller was confined previous to her being taken on board the pirate ship. Is it so?"

"It is true," answered Darrel; "and that secret retret is the farm occupied by the man known by the name of Harville."

"Is it possible?" exclaimed Harry; "and I to be moored so close to the poor lass and to know nothing at all about it! Oh, why did you not denounce the villains previous to their departure?"

"Because they had some suspicion of me," answered the pirate, "and kept too strict a watch over my actions, or else my will was heartily good to do so; for I have long been tired of the guilty course of life I was pursuing, and was anxious to escape from it, but I could not find an opportunity."

"And is the poor girl left entirely to the mercy of those wretches?" demanded Harry; "has she not one of her own sex to attend upon her, and to sympathise with her?"

"Yes," answered Darrel, "she is under the care of the wife of one of the pirates."

"The wife of one of the pirates?" repeated our hero; "then she has little kindness or pity to expect from her, poor girl."

"You are mistaken," returned Darrel. "There is no one who is more strongly opposed to the savage proceedings of Brandon and his crew than Alice. She possesses a kind and humane heart, and Mrs. Tiller will, no doubt, experience every attention and commiseration from her."

"Oh, thank Heaven for that!" said Harry; "but how was Mary trepanned from her home?"

"Why, the whole affair was managed by Jack Oarsby, whom I believe you know."

"Jack Oarsby the waterman, and the pretended friend of myself and Joe Tiller ?" said Halliyard, with a look of astonishment and incredulity.

"The same," replied Darrel. "He has long been connected with Brandon and his crew, though he never accompanied them to sea. Tiller and his friend Sam Sculler were detained at the Crown and Crosier by two other of the pirates; their drink was drugged, they became insensible for many hours, and in the meantime poor Mrs. Tiller was safely inveigled to the old tavern in Westminster."

"Monstrous!" cried our hero, striking his forehead passionately; "and Jack Oarsby to be one of the principals in this infamous plot! Oh, the villain! Should I ever again encounter him, most dearly shall he pay for this. The statement he made respecting poor Mary is now sufficiently accounted for. But this delay is most torturing; the wretches will most surely escape us, and then my misery will be complete. Mary, if we do not succeed in rescuing you, I will not long survive the dreadful disappointment."

At this moment the captain returned to the ship, and all being in readiness, the chase commenced, after the captain had consulted with Darrel, and received some farther instructions from him. The impatience and anxiety of Harry increased every moment, and he could scarcely control himself. Never had the gallant ship appeared to him to sail so sluggishly, and hope gradually faded from his breast. Oh, how eagerly did he strain his eyes across the broad expanse of the ocean, but nothing whatever met their gaze to gratify his wishes, and considering the time which had elapsed since the Wasp had departed from the harbour, and after the account which Darrel had given of her sailing qualities, there seemed to be but little chance indeed of overtaking her, and therefore did his anguish and anxiety of mind every instant gain strength.

"It is all useless," he exclaimed; "fate is against us, and we might as well abandon the pursuit, for we shall never be able to overtake the villains. Poor Mary, your fate is sealed; and probably even now the villain Brandon has taken advantage of the opportunity he has obtained, and you are lost for ever. Oh, dreadful thought! it drives me to madness as it rushes across my brain!"

"Come, come, Harry," said Ben Bowsprit, who was standing by his side, "you must not be cast down thus, for you will be able to escape the breakers of despair never fear, and your pretty Poll, as you still call her, will yet be rescued."

"Ah, no!" returned Halliyard; "I cannot, dare not entertain such a thought. The pirates have all the advantage, having had the start of us for some hours; and if all be true that this man hath told us, and we have not any reason to doubt it, they are by this time far on their voyage."

"The wind is in our favour," remarked Bowsprit, "and our gallant ship is proceeding at a most rapid rate. It cannot be long before we shall come in sight of the Wasp."

Halliyard shook his head, and returned no answer, and he then folded his arms upon his chest, and watched eagerly the progress of the vessel, which, however, to his perturbed imagination, had never appeared to proceed so slowly. They, notwithstanding, crowded all sail, and her captain and crew determined to exert all their energies to achieve their object, and were most sanguine of success. How anxiously did poor Halliyard strain his eyes across the ocean, and pray for the success of their undertaking; but despair was upon his heart, and Ben Bowsprit failed in his efforts to inspire him with confidence.

"It is a fruitless task," said our hero, in accents of despair; "villany will be permitted to triumph, and I shall never again behold the unfortunate Mary; she will become the hapless victim of one of the most atrocious wretches that ever disgraced the form of man. Oh, how dreadful must her sufferings already be; and she has no one near her who can afford her the least ray of hope or consolation. My fortitude entirely forsakes me when I reflect on it."

"Avast, Harry," said Bowsprit, "and do not be throwing out those signals of distress, when, perhaps, there is no occasion to do so. Our noble vessel never yet performed her duty more gallantly, and there is, therefore, every chance of our overtaking these rascally pirates, notwithstanding the long start they have had of us."

"Our ship must indeed be a wonder if she is enabled to accomplish such a feat," replied our hero; "but for my own part I entertain no such ideas, for I feel certain that they would only end in disappointment."

"Well, we must wait patiently," said Bowsprit, "and see whether fortune smiles upon us or not; but I must say that I am most sanguine upon the subject, and only hope that it may fall to our lot to have a brush with these rascals, who have so long carried on their daring proceedings with impunity; and should we do so, every man of them is doomed for Davy Jones's locker as sure as my name's Ben Bowsprit."

In this manner another hour elapsed, and the Porpoise continued to make all the sail she could, but with very little prospect of success, and the anguish and despair of Hallivard now became almost insupportable. The fog had now entirely disappeared, and they had a clear view for miles across the ocean, but for some time nothing at all to gratify their wishes met their sight, and the captain himself began to think that it was a hopeless case. As for Halliyard, he had fully made up his mind, and he gave himself up entirely to all the intense agony of his feelings.

"Unfortunate Mary!" he sighed, "how little did I imagine that you would ever be consigned to such a dreadful fate as this! To become the victim of such a monster as Hugh Brandon—the thought is maddening! Oh, may the heaviest curses of Heaven descend upon his head, and crush him in the midst of his iniquities. Had I but been aware of where she was confined previous to her being conveyed on board the pirate's craft, she might have been saved, and I should then have been comparatively happy; but now—Oh, I shudder to think of it! How horrible must be the torture of mind that she is enduring when she contemplates the disgusting and revolting fate which seems to be inevitably in store for her! She will never find strength or fortitude sufficient to support such a dreadful trial. And how will the inhuman villain, Brandon, exult at the success of his infamous designs, and mock her sufferings! She can expect no mercy or forbearance from him; and perhaps ere now he has accomplished his diabolical wishes, and the misery of poor Mary is complete. I dare not think of it, for the blood curdles in my veins as I do so, and my brain is worked up to a pitch of complete frenzy."

He became silent, and he paced the deck of the vessel to and fro with disordered and uneven steps, and almost unconscious of all that was passing around. But at length he was suddenly aroused from this state of lethargy by loud cries from several of the crew of "A sail! a sail! ahead!" and starting forward, and looking anxiously, he saw the faint shadow of a vessel in the distance, but at such a distance that it seemed almost impossible that anything could overtake it.

"She is too far off at present to make her out," remarked the captain. "What is your opinion of her, my man?" he added, speaking to Darrel.

"Why," answered the latter, "I have not the least doubt that it is the Wasp, your honour."

"Ah!" replied the captain, "should your conjectures turn out to be correct, it will be most fortunate, for notwithstanding she is at present so far ahead of us, I have no doubt that we shall yet be able to overtake her. Stretch every stitch of canvas, for the pirates must not be suffered to escape us, if possible."

The captain's orders were obeyed, and the Porpoise sailed on her way almost with the rapidity of lightning. But with what eager eyes, and mingled hopes and fears, did Halliyard watch the distant vessel; and his impatience increased to such a degree that he could scarcely control himself within the bounds of reason.

"We can never overtake the villains," he said, "and they may laugh in mockery, contempt, and defiance at us. And are you indeed a prisoner in yonder ship, unfortunate Mary, and I so near to you, and without the prospect of saving you? Alas! how torturing is this. And how slowly our vessel drags her way along, as if the Fates had conspired to thwart us in our wishes. We cannot succeed, and it would be madness to think that we could."

Again he fixed his eyes steadfastly on the ship, and his agitation became more powerful every moment. But whatever

THE ATTACK UPON HALLIYARD BY THE SMUGGLERS.

might be the ideas of Harry, it was evident that they were fast gaining upon the pirate craft, and the captain was now enabled, through the glass, to make the vessel out.

"It is the craft of which we are in pursuit," he said; "even at this distance I could swear to her build. Come hither, Darrel, and let us have your opinion."

Darrel obeyed the command of the captain, and putting the glass to his eye, he said—

"It is the Wasp; you need no longer entertain any doubt of that," he remarked; "and thus you see that I have not deceived you."

"True, true," returned the captain, "and you shall have no cause to repent of it. We gain upon her, too; and if all continues as favourable as it does at present for another hour, the fate of the rascals is sealed."

With anxious eyes did our hero continue to watch the progress of the vessel, and the agitation of his mind may be readily conceived; and mentally did he pray to Heaven to crown their efforts with success. But still the most terrible apprehensions crossed his mind, if even they should overtake the pirate ship; for he well knew the revengeful and determined spirit of Brandon; and he had too much reason to believe that if he found that he must inevitably be defeated, he would immediately sacrifice the life of the unfortunate Mary, rather than that she should again be placed under the protection of her friends. That thought made him shudder with horror, and again despair took possession of his heart, and his excitement became so great that it was not without considerable difficulty that he could contain himself at all within the bounds of reason. Ned Darrel also seemed to watch the event with no less anxiety and impatience than the rest, for it was evident that he had a feeling of revenge to gratify in the extermination of the pirates, and he added his endeavours to those of Ben Bowsprit and Waxend to flatter our hero with the hope that they would be successful, and that Brandon and his crew would not be able to escape from them.

"The Wasp is certainly a clipper," he remarked, "and skims over the ocean with the speed of an arrow; but fortune seems to smile upon us at present, and I entertain the most sanguine hopes as to the result. Only let me witness the destruction of Brandon and his daring and blood-stained crew, and I care not if I am strung to the yardarm the next moment."

"Avast there, shipmate," said Ben; "that is not the way in which you will be rewarded for the service you have rendered, you may depend upon it. Your conduct will be fairly represented to the lords of the admiralty, and no doubt you will receive a free pardon, and I only hope that you may prove yourself to be an honest man for the future."

"Yes," said Darrel, "it shall be my study to do so."

"But Mary!" said Halliyard; "alas, I fear that there will be but little chance of rescuing her; for desperate and savage as Brandon is, if he sees that he is likely to be overpowered, will he not immediately sacrifice her to his vengeance?"

"Why, as for the matter of that," replied Darrel, "he is monster enough for anything. But do not despair, young man, for there is a Power above far greater than his which watches over the innocent of heart, and will arrest his arm."

"Well spoken," said Ben Bowsprit; "those are just the sentiments of my mind. So courage, Harry, courage; and my word for it that in a short time Mrs. Tiller will be safe on board our vessel, and all fears of her cruel enemy will be at an end."

Our hero shook his head, and in vain he tried to encourage those hopes with which Ben and the others sought to inspire him. The Porpoise still continued to gain upon the pirate craft, the crew exerting themselves to the utmost; and at length they got so near her that they had a distinct view of her, and the captain ordered a gun to be fired, so as to bring her to. How that was answered by the pirates has already been shown,

and the Wasp seemed suddenly to redouble its speed, and again it darted ahead of them with the quickness of lightning.

"The rascals evidently do not fancy an engagement with us," observed the captain, "and seem determined to fly for it. But they must not be suffered to give us the slip in this manner, if possible. I would not be disappointed in this object for a trifle."

The Porpoise continued the chase with unabated spirit, but the fears of Halliyard every moment increased, and the feelings that agitated his breast may be much better imagined than described. All hope of rescuing Mary seemed gradually to be fading from him; and the energy which usually characterised him almost forsook him. On, on the pirate vessel sped, with greater and greater rapidity, until she again became little more than a speck upon the horizon, and all chance of overtaking her seemed to be nearly at an end.

"By Heaven she will escape us now!" exclaimed the captain; "and that too when fortune for a time seemed to favour us. See! She has changed her tack; the wind, too, veers; d—n it! are we indeed to be foiled in this manner?"

"There is no hope—there is no chance!" said Harry, in melancholy and disconsolate accents; "the villains mock our efforts, and their triumph is complete. Ah, Mary, most unfortunate of women, your fate is sealed, and you are lost for ever. Alas, alas! how terrible must be the sufferings that you are now enduring!"

He struck his forehead in despair, and it was in vain that Bowsprit tried to arouse his fortitude, and to calm his apprehensions. In a few minutes afterwards the Wasp was entirely hidden from the view, and it was evident that all chance of overtaking her was at an end. Harry's emotions were almost too powerful for utterance; and when he thought of the deplorable situation of poor Mary he could have wept like a child.

"By heavens!" exclaimed the captain, "to be disappointed in this manner, when we were so close upon the enemy, is almost past endurance. But still the rascals must not be suffered thus to have the laugh at us, if possible. We will continue the chase, while they, probably thinking that we have abandoned it, may slacken their speed. Should we again come in sight of them, the game shall be ours, at all hazards."

"Ah, your honour," said our hero, " I fear that all our efforts will be fruitless; we can never overcome the advantage which they have gained over us. The wretches have triumphed, and the unfortunate victim whom they hold in their power is doomed to destruction."

"Nay," said the captain, " it shall not be so, if courage and perseverance can accomplish anything. At any rate, we will not relinquish our task without an effort. Shall it be said that one of his majesty's vessels shall thus be set at defiance by those infernal sharks, who have so long infested the seas, and committed such savage and daring outrages? No, I would sooner forfeit anything than it should be so."

Halliyard returned no answer, for his feelings overpowered him, and never had he felt more truly wretched and desponding. He pictured to himself in the most vivid and painful colours the dreadful anguish of mind which Mary must now be experiencing from the disappointment of the hopes that had probably been excited in her breast at the prospect of deliverance; and the savage exultation of the villain Brandon over his hapless victim, and the idea of the fate which seemed inevitably to await her, and which had probably already overtaken her, drove him almost to distraction.

"Why should the cruel Fates thus conspire against her?" he said. "What has she ever done that she should thus be consigned to a fate which is far too horrible and revolting to think upon? Oh, it would have been a mercy to her had death ere now put a period to her sufferings. Alas, alas! how does remorseless destiny seem to mock at her misery, and to render the designs of her brutal oppressor triumphant. And how much more terrible and insupportable would be the anguish of her feelings did she but know how near I have been to her, and how cruelly have my hopes of rescuing her from the power of her inhuman enemies been disappointed! Brandon, you may well exult, for you have now the means of gratifying your

sanguinary vengeance to the fullest extent, and I have not the least doubt that you will do so without delay. Oh, I could endure anything, methinks, but the horror of that thought!"

"Come, come, Halliyard, my lad," remonstrated Bowsprit, "you must not abandon the sheet-anchor of hope altogether in this manner, for though you have all the tempests of misfortune to encounter at present, who knows how soon a calm may succeed, and the remainder of the voyage of Mary and yourself through life be blest with favouring gales? I cannot believe, somehow, that this Brandon and his guilty crew will be long permitted to escape, though for a time they may triumph. As for Mrs. Tiller, providence will protect her, although, to be sure, her situation is a most perilous one at present."

"A perilous one!" repeated Harry, impatiently. "Oh, it is a most hopeless one, for what mercy can she expect from such a remorseless, hardened wretch as Brandon? And will he not be more than ever goaded on to the execution of his diabolical designs by this pursuit? I see nothing but destruction before her, and my brain is driven to madness when I contemplate it. Oh, how willingly would I sacrifice my own life, could it but be the means of saving her!"

"Avast, avast, my lad," said Bowsprit, "there will be no occasion for you to do that, or I am much mistaken. But be calm, and endeavour to look forward to the best."

"Oh, how vainly do you talk to me of calmness!" returned Harry; "I must be less than a man could I be so under such circumstances. Be calm, and to know at the same time that Mary is in the power of a villain who is capable of any monstrous crime? It is impossible; and the more I think of it the greater become my feelings of horror and despair. What means has she of resisting him? And think you that he will be diverted from his purpose by all the reproaches or remonstrances which she may heap upon his head? Oh, no! He possesses too callous and hardened a heart to do so, and therefore is her doom sealed, and poor Mary is rendered a wretched and degraded being for ever. And she that was so innocent, so lovely, and so amiable, thus to fall a victim to the infernal designs of a miscreant who has been guilty of every diabolical crime! How dreadful is the thought, and how can I possibly encourage any other feeling than that of the most absolute despair, when I know the utter impossibility of my averting it? Alas, Mary! how different were the prospects that were spread before us in our more youthful days! How little did either of us anticipate that such a terrible change as this would ever have come over us!"

He sighed deeply as he thus spoke, and it was in vain that he struggled to conquer the deep and sad emotions that preyed upon his heart, and rendered him entirely deaf to the voice of consolation.

The chase was continued for about a couple of hours longer, but still without their discovering any signs of the pirate ship, and it now became but too certain that she had escaped them, and that there was no chance of getting upon her tack again; and, disappointed and vexed, the captain determined to make for the nearest port, in order that they may wait the arrival of the fleet; and Harry, who was completely heart-sick, and lost to every feeling of hope, seized the first opportunity of hastening below, where he could give free indulgence to the gloomy thoughts that beset him, and where he was soon afterwards joined by Ben Bowsprit and Waxend, who exerted themselves to the utmost to appease the anguish of his mind, but with little or no effect, and his misery of mind rather increased than abated.

CHAPTER XX.

THE SUFFERINGS OF MARY.—THE STORY OF ALICE.—THE STORM.

RETURN we now to Mary in the pirate vessel, whose anguish of mind during the late events we have been describing has been already depicted to the reader. But the interview she had had with the villain Brandon, and the monstrous threats he had held out to her, crowned her misery, and she resigned herself to the most abject and insupportable state of despair. Alice never left her society for a minute; and had it not been for the kind sympathy which she so earnestly evinced in her misfortunes, she must have sunk down altogether; and even as it was, at times she might be said to be more dead than living, and her brain was in such a state of distraction that she scarcely knew what she was doing, or what was passing around her; and it required all the energies of Alice to sustain her.

"Oh, surely," sighed the wretched woman, "I am one of the most truly unfortunate of human beings, and to have to endure such a life as this is a curse to me. Providence seems to have entirely deserted me, and to have abandoned me to that awful fate which it now appears but too certain that it will be impossible for me to avoid. How short is the time allowed me ere my fate must be consummated; but three days, and the miscreant Brandon will triumph, and I shall be rendered a poor wretched being, hateful to myself and despised by others."

"Forbear, Mrs. Tiller," expostulated Alice; "how dreadful is the picture which your disordered imagination conjures up. Try to banish it from your mind, and—"

"Ah! how vainly you talk," hastily interrupted our heroine. "How is it possible that I can do so? What right have I to anticipate other than what I do? Have I not heard the determination of Brandon, and have I any reason for a moment to imagine that anything will move him to abandon it? Oh, no! I must be mad to think so; and it is useless for you to seek to persuade me to the contrary."

"Oh, how glad should I be could I but succeed in doing so," remarked Alice; "but indeed you must not imagine your fate to be entirely hopeless, or to suppose that providence has deserted you in the manner you have expressed yourself. Who knows what the interval of those three days may produce? Deliverance may be nearer at hand than you may imagine."

"Ah, no!" sighed Mary, "I dare not flatter myself with any such ideas. When I beheld the vessel in pursuit, I must own that I did feel some degree of hope; but how soon was that destined to be annihilated, and Providence seemed but too surely to have abandoned me to despair, and to mock at my sufferings, and yet how fervently and devoutly did I pray to it for mercy and pretection."

"Nay, Mrs. Tiller," said her kind-hearted companion, "arraign not the wisdom or justice of the Supreme, for who shall attempt to penetrate His motives, or to question His will? He ordains everything for the best, and sooner or later He will release you from your present dangers and sufferings, if you put your trust in Him."

"But to think that the vessel which was in pursuit of the pirates should be the very one on which poor Harry Halli-yard is on board!" said our heroine. "Oh, had they succeeded in their designs, and Brandon and his inhuman crew had been defeated, how safe should I have been under his protection, and how quickly should I have been restored to my husband and my home. But now that chance is at an end, and the fate which awaits me is too awfully certain. Alas! what must be the anguish of despair under which poor Harry now labours at this terrible disappointment, should he be aware that I am in the power of Brandon!"

"I do not see how it is scarcely possible that he can have obtained that knowledge," observed Alice; "but be that as it may, the ship may not yet abandon the pursuit, although it has at present lost sight of the pirates; and should it be fortunate enough to over-take them, there cannot be much doubt as to which side the conquest will be. Courage, courage, Mrs. Tiller, for I am still of the firmest opinion that you will be rescued from the inhuman fate which now seems but too certainly impending over your head."

"Alas!" returned Mary, "Brandon will, I am convinced, take good care to prevent that; he would not hesitate, if he were driven to the last extremity, to sacrifice my life, rather than that I should fall into the hands of his enemies. In whichever way I direct my eyes, all is dark and dismal; and I must still believe that there is not an individual in the world who has ever been exposed to half the heavy trials and vicissitudes that I have been."

"Ah, Mrs. Tiller," returned Alice, and a deep sigh escaped her bosom as she spoke, "you would, I am certain, think differently where you acquainted with the melancholy circumstances of my history, and must be ready to admit that there are others in the world who have suffered equal misfortunes with yourself. Alas! I have drained the cup of sorrow to the very dregs; and when I reflect upon what it has been my hard lot to undergo, I marvel that I have had strength sufficient to support it. But enough of this: you are in no state of mind to listen to those direful lamentations, and why should I seek to obtrude my sorrows upon you who have so many of your own?"

"Your observations interest me, Alice, and I am certain that one who possesses so kind a heart and so generous a disposition, must have suffered from some sad perversity of fate to have been driven into the painful and humiliating situation in which you are now so unfortunately placed."

"You conjecture rightly, Mrs. Tiller," replied Alice. "Heaven knows how I strove by my conduct to merit a far different destiny, and what I have had to encounter in the hard battle of life. But I endeavour to resign myself to my fate, since I now see no prospect of my being enabled to escape from it."

"You promised to make me acquainted with the particulars of your history," remarked Mary, "and I must request you not to forget your promise."

"True," replied Alice; "but it is a sad story, and you are not in a state of mind to listen to it now."

"Oh, yes I am," replied Mary, "and I am most anxious to hear it; it might serve to divert my thoughts for a time from the melancholy subjects that at present engross them."

"Think you so?" said Alice. "Well, then, if it only affords you even that temporary relief, I will endeavour to comply, premising that you will be the only individual to whom I shall have ventured to confide my sorrows; and when you have heard them, as I said before, I think you will acknowledge that, however great your misfortunes have most unquestionably been, mine, at any rate, have been fully equal to them. But allow me for a few minutes to collect my thoughts, for when I attempt to recall the sad events of the past, my brain seems for awhile to be bewildered."

Our heroine nodded assent, and after a few brief moments Alice commenced her history in the following words :—

THE STORY OF THE PIRATE'S BRIDE.

"My narrative commences at a period of nearly twenty years back, although when I look through the dark vista of time, and recall to my memory the startling events that have befallen me, it seems multiplied into a century, and I wonder how I can have lived so long—that my heart should not have broken under the heavy weight of care which has pressed upon it for so long, and banished peace and happiness entirely from my breast.

"At that time I was a happy girl, although my lot in life was humble, and I envied not those of my more fortunate fellow-creatures whom Providence had placed in the most elevated position of society. I had all that my humble wishes aspired to, and I therefore could not dream that there could be any more fortunate station of life than my own, and serenity and content constantly gladdened my heart, and endowed me with health and vigour. Thus was I, a happy girl of sixteen, and would to Heaven that I had always remained so ! But, alas ! it was not to be ; and let me not now waste my time, or annoy your ears by any useless lamentations over my fate.

"As I said before, my origin was of the most humble description, and myself and a brother, two years older than me, were the only children of my parents, who brought us up with the greatest care and affection, and gave us as good an education as their limited means would allow.

"We inhabited a neat little cottage on the Sussex coast, and my father followed the occupation of a fisherman, though at the time of his marriage to my mother his circumstances in life, I was given to understand, were very different, and he had been reduced by a series of unavoidable misfortunes to his present situation.

"He was a man of naturally good understanding, but the truth compels me to say that he had many foibles, which, if possible, more than counterbalanced his numerous good qualities. He was covetous, and inflexible upon any point on which his mind was fixed, and his obstinacy frequently led him into errors which I have no doubt, in his more sober moments, he deeply regretted. He was also at times morose and repulsive in his manners, which I have no doubt was caused by his temper being soured by the unfortunate reverses he had met with in life, and which could not fail frequently to harass his memory. My mother was a poor, weak, simple woman, who had endured much illness; and she was guided by everything he did, and never ventured to contradict anything he said, let it be ever so opposed to reason, and she submitted to his will, however extravagant it may have been, and never for a moment attempted to murmur at it.

"As my brother increased in years he exhibited a good deal of the disposition of his father, and at times a recklessness and levity of conduct which was extremely unbecoming and unpleasant.

"I have been thus particular in describing them, because it may in some measure account for the cruel treatment which I afterwards received at their hands.

"I had no companions but the sons and daughters of our neighbours, who most of them followed the same avocation as my father, and in their society I passed the whole of my youthful days, and knew nothing of the great world beyond the neighbourhood in which we resided. My brother, of course, assisted my father in his business, while my time was principally occupied in attending to the domestic duties of the house. Although it is not to be expected that we could ever acquire riches, we lived comfortably, and, as I said before, I coveted no more ; in fact, I knew not that there was anything more to wish for beyond it, and therefore it was impossible for any one to enjoy a greater share of peace and sweet contentment than I did myself.

"Among all our neighbours with whom we were probably more particularly intimate than the rest was the family of the Seytons, who resided in the next cottage to us, and had done so the same number of years as my parents. Mr. and Mrs. Seyton had no other offspring but a son, a young man about my own age, and possessing a fine, manly figure, and a handsome and intelligent countenance. He was a gay, generous-hearted, and well-behaved youth, and was generally esteemed by all who knew him. He and myself had been companions from the earliest days of childhood, and I had been accustomed to look upon him in the light of a second brother—a feeling which was encouraged by my parents, and which Walter seemed proud and happy to have bestowed upon him. Ah, Walter, dear Walter! even at this distant period of time, can I cease to dwell upon you with feelings of the deepest emotion and fondest regard, and most bitterly to lament the cruel circumstances that separated us, and which rendered us miserable for ever?

"As we grew older the sentiments we had from our earliest days entertained towards each other ripened into a passion of a far warmer description, and it was soon evident to us both that we loved each other with an ardour that nothing whatever could subdue; and unable to conceal our thoughts, we confessed our sentiments, and under every circumstance vowed eternal constancy towards each other. We threw ourselves at the feet of our parents, and acknowledging the feelings that held such powerful possession of our hearts, besought them in the most earnest manner to sanction our addresses with their approbation; and our happiness was rendered all but complete when we found them yield a ready compliance with our wishes; and they promised us that when we had arrived at years of greater maturity the vows we had so frequently plighted to each other should be solemnized at the altar. How shall I now seek to describe the feelings of transport that now took possession of our bosoms, and added fresh sunshine to the prospects that were spread before us? We knew not how to give expression to our emotions, and again and again we poured forth our gratitude to our beloved parents for having rendered us so very happy. We had nothing left to wish for, and we looked forward to the time which would unite our fates in the indissoluble bonds of matrimony with the most unbounded delight, and with the greatest impatience.

"From that time I and Walter were together even more frequently than before; in fact, we lost no opportunity of being so, and we felt uneasy and anxious whenever we were not in each other's society. We drew the most glowing pictures of the happiness which was in store for us, and never for an instant anticipated that anything could occur to prevent our union from taking place; but, alas! poor short-sighted mortals as we were, even at that moment, in the midst of our most sanguine expectations, the tempest was fast gathering which was ultimately destined to burst upon our heads and overwhelm us. The finger of Fate was pointed towards us, and ere long all those hopes which we had so fondly entertained were destined to be annihilated, and misery the most insupportable was destined to be our portion. I cannot look back upon this without a feeling of the most poignant anguish, and shuddering with horror at the recollection of the dreadful events that were about to take place; and how torturing are the feelings of regret that rack my bosom when I contrast my present life with that which I experienced in my youthful days.

"In this manner six months passed away without anything particular occurring, and every succeeding day seemed to bring more happiness than the preceding one, for it shortened the time which was to intervene before the realization of our hopes, and seemed fraught with every promise of future bliss. Every day the noble qualities of Walter's mind became the more apparent to me, and it was quite evident that his love for me hourly increased in strength. How sweet were the evening walks we took together, when, unrestrained by the presence of any one, we could give the most uninterrupted indulgence to the feelings that throbbed at our hearts, and breathe those vows of love which were as sincere as they were fervent. We considered that there could not possibly be two happier beings in existence than ourselves; and in that blissful state of delusion we suffered not one anxious thought to enter our minds.

"About this period there came to reside in the neighbourhood a young fisherman of the name of Richard Drayton. He was a single man, and had no parents; but he seemed considerably better off than ourselves or our neighbours, for he had three or four boats of his own, and employed two or three men to assist him in his business. This young man, as soon as he came to the neighbourhood, seemed to take great interest in my father, and showed his anxiety to establish an intimacy by every means in his power. My father appeared flattered by Drayton's advances; and giving him every encouragement, he was soon almost a constant visitor at our cottage. From the first moment that I saw him, I know not how it was, I could not help but form an unfavourable opinion of him, and I felt uneasy whenever I was in his presence. There was a boldness and familiarity in his demeanour towards me which greatly annoyed and embarrassed me; and Walter also partook of the same feelings that I did, and began to view him with jealous and suspicious eyes, especially when his visits to the cottage of my parents every day became more frequent, and my father gave him every encouragement, and paid him the most marked attention, which from the short time they had been acquainted seemed both strange and unreasonable. When Drayton was absent, my father was most lavish in his praises of him; and according to the manner in which he expressd himself, he seemed to consider him one of the most worthy, intelligent, and amiable young men he had ever met with. Every eulogism that he passed upon him filled my bosom with misgivings and apprehensions, for it seemed to me to forebode no good; and when Walter and I were alone, and we freely communicated our thoughts to each other, I found that he was of the same opinion. It seemed to us both that my father was completely dazzled by the superiority of his circumstances, and was flattered by his friendship; and we could not but imagine that since we had become acquainted with Drayton, his behavious towards Walter had been less warm than it had previously been, and that frequently his reception of him was of the most distant description, and he allowed us fewer opportunities than formerly of being alone together, and all these circumstances cast a gloom upon the hopes and prospects we had hitherto indulged in, and which we found it impossible to conquer. My brother, too, seemed to be greatly prepossessed in his favour, and was his constant companion at every opportunity, and was always ready to reiterate the fulsome encomiums which my father bestowed upon him, and which served not a little to increase our suspicions and apprehensions, and to cool the ardour of our former feelings, though nothing whatever could alter the sentiments that we entertained towards each other.

"Thus several weeks passed away, and the sentiments of Richard Drayton towards me, and the encouragement given to them by my father, every day became of a more marked character, while his conduct to my lover was more cold and distant, and, in fact, it sometimes was even repulsive. It was now for the first time in my life that I felt the anguish of care, doubt, and anxiety, and the most painful forebodings took possession of my mind, which I found it impossible to banish. The advances which Drayton made towards me, the boldness of his words whenever he addressed himself to me, and the confidence which he appeared to gain by the manner in which he was encouraged by my father, was such as I could not possibly misunderstand, and I saw plainly that some misfortune was about to overtake myself and Walter which we had never any reason before to apprehend, and which would entirely overcloud those bright prospects which we had so fondly pictured to our imaginations. The presence of Drayton every day became more painful and disgusting to me, and I would fain have avoided it, but I had no means of doing so, and my father would not allow me and Walter many opportunities of being alone, so that we now had far less means than formerly of communicating our thoughts to each other; but when we were alone, we gave free vent to our feelings, and in vain endeavoured to banish from each other's minds the apprehensions that had taken possession of them, and to indulge in those sanguine hopes which had hitherto rendered us so happy. But what had we to fear? we tried to argue; was not our love encouraged and sanctioned by my father? Were we not betrothed to each other? and surely he could never be so cruel or unjust as to break a promise which had

THE DEATH OF ZINGA.

been so solemnly made. We, therefore, sought to banish our doubts and fears, and still to look forward with the brightest expectations to the time when we should be united in the indissoluble bonds of matrimony ; but that was a task which, as you may imagine under all the circumstances, was not easy of accomplishment, and we could not, with all our endeavours, obtain but little, if any, relief from our anxiety of mind. But the time was fast approaching when all our doubts were to be set at rest, and the true misery of the fate which was in store for us was made fully and unmistakably apparent to us. One afternoon, Walter being away from home in the prosecution of his business, and feeling melancholy and restless, and unfitted for the society of my parents, whose conversation was principally confined to the most extravagant praises of the character and personal attractions of Drayton, which I need not tell you were most painful, disgusting, and embarrassing to me, I was glad to avail myself of the opportunity which was afforded me of taking a solitary ramble by the sea-side, and freely indulging alone in the dismal and torturing thoughts that crowded upon my mind, and in seeking to tranquillise my feelings. The afternoon was particularly fine; and, completely absorbed in meditation, I wandered further than I had at first intended, until I was suddenly aroused by the shades of evening descending upon the earth, and thinking that my parents would feel somewhat surprised and uneasy at my protracted absence, I prepared to retrace my footsteps towards our dwelling, still in the same melancholy state of mind that I had been on starting from the cottage. I had not proceeded far on my way when I was startled from my meditations by hearing approaching footsteps, and looking up, I beheld by the light of the moon, which had now risen, Drayton advancing towards me hastily. I could not help trembling with dismal feelings of apprehension when I saw him, and would fain have avoided him; but that was impossible, for he had evidently perceived me, and made to me a sign of recognition. Overpowered by my feelings, I paused, and immediately afterwards he came up to me, and with a familiarity which disgusted me, and made me shudder, he took hold of my hand, and pressed it warmly within his own.

"'Oh, Miss Alice,' he remarked, 'how glad I am to think that I have met with you. Your parents and myself have been very uneasy at your absence, and I could not rest any longer until I had come in search of you. Really I am half inclined to chide you for being such a little truant; and yet I am glad of the opportunity of being alone with you, for I have something of importance to communicate to you which I have long been anxious to reveal to you, and which has cost me many a restless hour.'

"'Something to communicate to me, Mr. Drayton?' I replied, in a tremulous voice, and my heart foreboding the worst, while I feared to encounter the bold and fervent gaze which I felt certain he was at that time fixing upon me, and trying, but in vain, to disengage my hand.

"'Do not start, Alice,' he said; 'although you may be little prepared for that which I am about to say, and I fear you will consider me bold and presumptuous; but, let the consequences be whatever they may, I cannot any longer keep the secret confined to my own breast.'

"You may imagine what my feelings were as I listened to these observations, Mrs. Tiller, and which it was impossible for me to misunderstand. My bosom heaved with mingled feelings of emotion, and the crimson blushes of shame and offended modesty glowed in my cheeks. For a moment or two I felt so bewildered that I could not return any answer; but at length I said—

"'What mean you, Mr. Drayton? Your words surprise me. What can you have to communicate to me in private, or that it would be proper for me to listen to out of the presence of my parents?'

"'Nay, Alice,' he returned, an without relinquishing his hold of my hand, 'I must still claim your indulgence, and relieve my mind from a weight of anxiety, doubt, and hope, which has long pressed heavily upon it; nay, more, I have the permission of your parents for that which I am about to declare. Oh, Alice, you surely cannot have failed to perceive from the first moment that introduced me to you the powerful impression that your numerous charms, both intrinsic and personal, have made upon my heart, and—'

"'Hold, Mr. Drayton,' I interrupted, in a voice of indignation, and with a feeling of the most powerful disgust, which communicated itself to the expression of my eyes, and could not fail to meet his observation; 'surely you must forget yourself to venture to address such language to me, especially when you know how I am situated, and the sentiments that exist towards each other between myself and Walter Seyton.'

"'Walter Seyton!' he repeated, in a passionate voice; 'oh, mention not his name to me, for it is hateful to my ears.'

"'Your observations shock me,' I replied, with a look of the keenest reproach. 'Leave me, sir, and let me proceed unmolested on my way, and to try to forget, if that be possible, that you could ever thus insult and wound my feelings.'

" 'Insult—wound your feelings?' he repeated. 'Ah, Alice, you much mistake my real character, and do me also a great injustice, if you imagine I am capable of doing that. But I must reveal the secret of my heart, let the consequences be whatever they may. I love you, Alice—love you to adoration; and it is impossible that anything can ever extinguish the fierce flame which your surpassing beauty and the angelic purity of your soul have kindled in my bosom. Nay, frown not, most lovely of women, nor fix upon me such looks of bitter scorn; I utter but the fervent sentiments of my heart, and throw myself upon your mercy and indulgence; my fate is in your hands, and—'

" 'Cease, bold and unfeeling man,' I again hastily interrupted, and the feelings that rushed tumultuously to my brain were almost overwhelming; 'is this honourable? is it just? is it manly? You would not dare thus to insult me if Walter Seyton or my parents were present.'

" 'Insult you, Alice?' repeated the hypocrite. 'Heaven forbid that I should do so. But think not that I have presumed to reveal to you my sentiments without the full sanction of both your parents.'

" 'The sanction of my parents?' I reiterated, with a look of astonishment and incredulity. 'Oh, no, no, no, that is impossible! You seek to deceive me, Drayton; my father could never be so cruel and unjust towards me and Walter. Has he not given us his solemn promise? And what could ever induce him to abandon his word, especially where the happiness of his only daughter is so completely involved? Oh, no, I will not believe you, for thoroughly convinced am I that your statement is not founded in truth.'

" 'You will find that what I have stated is strictly correct,' returned Drayton. 'Your father approves of my passion, and repents of the promise which he made to you and Walter Seyton; so, why should you remain obstinate? What is there so superior about him that he should monopolize your affections? Try to forget him, for he can never love you with half the ardour and sincerity that I do; and there is nothing that I am not willingly prepared to do, no sacrifice that I will hesitate to make, which will in any way contribute to your comfort and happiness.'

" 'Oh, monstrous thought!' I ejaculated, 'I can scarcely believe the evidence of my senses as I listen to your observations. Forget Walter — break those solemn vows I have so often plighted with his, and for you? Oh, Heaven! how revolting, how disgusting is that idea; and—'

" 'And is there anything so remarkably disgusting and hateful in my appearance and manners,' interrupted Drayton, and a slight frown passed over his features, 'that you can view me with such repugnance and scorn? But no, I will not yet despair. Time will prove to you the sincerity of the vows which I have made to you, and you will, I trust, yet view me with far different feelings than those which you have just now expressed. Oh, Alice, did you but know the real sentiments that glow in my bosom towards you, and which nothing can ever possibly eradicate, methinks you would not turn away from me with such feelings of repugnance, but that you would consider me worthy a far more tender regard than that of mere friendship and esteem. Never did I know truly what it was to love until I beheld you; and I am prepared to worship you, to look upon you as the empress of my soul, and to have no will but yours, to have no hope, no wish beyond you. Give me, then, some reason to hope that I may yet be able to make a favourable, a lasting impression upon your heart, and you will thus render me one of the happiest beings in existence.'

" 'Cruel man!' I exclaimed, and the crimson blushes of shame mantled in my cheeks, while my bosom swelled with the almost insupportable feelings of resentment, 'and dare you thus presume, when you know that my heart is irrevocably devoted to another? Oh, forbear, forbear! Such conduct as this, if persisted in, must deprive you of my esteem; but to love you—oh, there is horror in the very thought!'

" 'You will do well to reflect seriously upon this,' returned Drayton, 'ere you come to a final decision. I imagine that I have only to remind you that your father approves of and sanctions my addresses to you, to cause you to pause, and to see the misery which you are likely to bring down upon yourself by any obstinate resistance.'

"'My father!' I ejaculated; 'and can you have become so completely lost to every feeling of reason and justice as to have acted thus? And would you thus annihilate the hopes, and destroy the happiness of your child, and him on whom her whole affections are rivetted, and to whom you have betrothed me? I will not believe it; it is false, and you seek to deceive me and lead me astray. Let me begone, for I can no longer venture or even endure to remain in your company.'

"'Nay, Alice,' said Drayton, still retaining his hold of my hand, 'you must not leave me thus. I have spoken the truth; and notwithstanding the scorn and hatred with which you at present seem to regard me, I do not despair of yet being able to move your heart to relent, and to treat my passion with far opposite feelings than those of indifference. If you will but learn to love me, my whole study shall be to promote your happiness; and there is not a wish that you can entertain that shall remain ungratified. Forget Walter Seyton, for after what your father has said to me you can never become his bride; and surely you can never have the moral courage as to be so unmindful of your duty to your parent as to seek to oppose his will?'

"'My father can never act in so cruel a manner as that you have intimated towards me,' I returned; 'and it is a base libel on his character to make such an unfounded statement. Mr. Drayton, from this time you and myself must be as strangers to each other, for after the sentiments you have expressed, I dare not trust myself in your society. If you have any respect for my feelings you will no longer detain me, but will suffer me to return home alone, and to endeavour to forget that you have ever so grossly committed yourself. Unhand me, sir, I beg of you.'

"'Why, what a coy little vixen it is, to be sure,' he remarked, with the most insulting rudeness, and affecting to smile. 'But you cannot mean what you say, Alice, and I am not to be daunted by the present reception which you have given to my vows. Faint heart never won fair lady, as the saying has it, and so I am determined to persevere, let the result be whatever it may. As for suffering you to return home alone, I cannot think of such a thing, and I should be very ungallant indeed to do so. So, come, my sweet girl, one delicious kiss from those ruddy, pouting lips, and then—'

"'Villain!' I exclaimed in a voice of the most indescribable disgust, and by a violent effort freeing my hand from his grasp, and retreating from him; 'can your insolent presumption carry you so far? Have you no respect for my sex, and the delicate situation in which I am placed? Forbear—forbear! or you may have full cause to repent of what you have done, and expose yourself to the vengeance of those whom you so deeply wrong by these disgusting advances towards one who can now only in future look upon you with fear and utter repugnance.'

"'And shall I be defeated, despised, and threatened thus?' he cried, 'and when my passion is authorized by your parents, and I have all the means of gratifying my wishes at my command? By Heaven, I will not! Alice, I love you, worship you, ardently and sincerely, and thus do I seal the vows that I now utter to you.'

"As he thus spoke he again rushed towards me, and the expression of his features plainly showed the feelings of excitement under which he laboured at the moment. He threw his arms around my waist, and pressed me vehemently to his bosom, while, in spite of all my endeavours to prevent him, he covered my cheeks with his odious and disgusting kisses. How shall I describe the nature of my feelings at that moment? You, my unfortunate friend, can much better imagine than I can possibly portray them. I was filled with shame, indignation, and terror; I rent the air with my cries for help, and desperately I struggled to release myself from his hold, but it was all to no purpose—my resistance only seemed to goad him on to fresh acts of violence, and my strength was almost exhausted, when there was a loud shout from behind the spot on which we struggled, when the form of a man turned abruptly round the angle of a cliff adjacent, and rushed hastily towards us.

Drayton, dismayed and confused, and, muttering a curse between his teeth, released his hold of me, and I darted towards the man; but you may judge of my mingled feelings of astonishment, fear, and joy, when I found myself in the arms of Walter. As for Drayton, he was perfectly paralyzed to the spot with rage and confusion; and Walter, fixing upon him a look of the most indescribable indignation, and clenching his fist, exclaimed—

"'My beloved Alice, and is it indeed you whose cries for help have brought me to this spot? Villain! what daring act of outrage have you attempted to commit?'

"'Villain in your teeth, beggarly cur!' cried Drayton fiercely, and at the same time he dealt my lover a violent blow, which brought the blood into his face.

"'Ah!' exclaimed Walter, in a hoarse voice, and his manly bosom swelling with resentment; 'struck! and that, too, by such a man as Richard Drayton? Nay, then, by all my hopes, I will have an ample revenge!'

"With these words he released me from his arms, and rushing with a desperate and determined air upon his guilty rival, they closed together, and a fearful struggle commenced, while I rent the air with my cries, and in vain tried to interpose between them. This did not last many minutes. Violent blows were freely exchanged between them; but at length Drayton succeeded in felling his antagonist to the earth, and I was so overcome with terror at all that had passed that I fainted.

"I know not how long I had remained in this condition, but when I was restored to my senses I found myself in the parlour of the cottage, and my parents attending upon me, but neither Walter nor Drayton were present.

"'Oh, God!' I exclaimed, as the recollection of what had passed flashed across my brain, 'to what horrors, to what insults have I been exposed! But where is Walter? Where is the villain, Drayton?'

"'Hold!' said my father, sternly; 'be more choice in the language you apply to Mr. Drayton, for he is not worthy of it. Be calm, Alice, for I have much to say to you on a future occasion, and you will do well if in the meantime you endeavour to look upon him with different feelings than those you have evinced towards him.'

"'Gracious Heaven!' I gasped forth, and fixing upon him a look of astonishment and terror, 'and can it be my father who thus addresses me? I can scarcely believe the evidence of my senses; I must be labouring under some fearful delusion. Alas! alas! then it is but too likely that Drayton spoke the truth when he said that you approved of and sanctioned his odious addresses to me, and that you had made up your mind to break the solemn promise which you had pledged to me and Walter. Oh, I implore you to remove those torturing doubts and fears from my mind, and assure me that it is not so.'

"'I repeat,' replied my father, 'that this is not the time to discuss this subject; but I will take the earliest opportunity of explaining everything to you. In the meantime you will do well to endeavour to banish this childish affection for Walter Seyton from your heart, which I was perhaps wrong for encouraging.'

"'Ah, then,' I cried, clasping my hands together in agony, 'my worst apprehensions are realized. You do not deny it; you are determined to annihilate all my fondest hopes, and to render me miserable for ever! Forget Walter? abandon all my hopes of becoming his bride, and which you have so warmly encouraged? Oh, dreadful thought! But you cannot mean what you say. Oh, my father, bethink yourself; consider the terrible fate you would inflict upon me, and recal your harsh and cruel decree.'

"'Be calm, Alice,' he said, 'I again enjoin you, and await patiently until I think proper to explain the motives that have induced me to adopt the course which I think of pursuing. I have your welfare at heart, and nothing shall persuade me to deviate from anything which may be the means of promoting it. Let that assurance satisfy you, my child, and for the present endeavour to rest contented.'

"'You have, then, resolved to break your promise to me and Walter,' I ejaculated, 'and to sacrifice me to a man whom I can never look upon with any other feelings than those of aversion and disgust, especially after his outrageous conduct towards me this evening. Oh, this is most cruel, and what I could never have believed my father capable of. But can you, my dear mother, lend yourself to such an unnatural design? Will you not, at least, intercede for me?'

" ' It is no use for you to appeal to your mother,' said my father; 'she has no power to avert that upon which I have fixed my mind. It is her duty, and she must obey my will.'

" 'Alas—alas!' I sighed, 'what will become of me? Oh, my father, and is it possible that you can encourage the odious addresses of a man who has behaved in the brutal and outrageous manner that Richard Drayton has done to me this evening? Such a thought is too terrible for encouragement, and I would fain dismiss it from my mind. Oh, what has poor Walter Seyton done that he should deserve such treatment at your hands?'

" 'Euongh,' returned my father, impatiently; 'it does not please me to say more just now. Conduct her to her chamber, dame, and probably the morning may find her in a more reasonable state of mind.'

" I tried to return some answer, but my feelings overpowered me and I could not, and my mother taking my arm, and assisting me to rise, I resigned myself passively to her care, and she led me from the room, and to my own chamber, almost in a state of unconsciousness.

"On reaching my room, and sinking into a chair, I covered my face with my hands, and burst into a violent paroxysm of sobs and tears, which my mother did not attempt to interrupt; and in that condition I remained for several minutes. But at length I looked up with an imploring look towards my mother, and in a voice of the deepest emotion, I said—

" 'Alas! alas! what a dreadful blow is this to all the bright visions of future happiness which I have hitherto so freely and so fondly indulged in! Forget Walter?—love such a being as Drayton? Oh, how terrible is the thought! To indulge in it would be sufficient to rack my brain to madness. But oh! my mother, you surely cannot coincide with the cruel intentions of my father, who must be labouring under some fatal infatuation, or he could never make up his mind to act in the manner which he has threatened. You will endeavour to move him from his harsh and unnatural purpose?'

" 'As your father has said,' she replied, ' I think that he has your interest and welfare alone at heart, and you know full well that I have no power to move him to change his resolution. Richard Drayton has acknowledged that he loves you, and we have no reason to doubt his assertions. He is well to do in the world ; he is young, good looking, sensible, and amiable ; and taking all these things into consideration, I do not see what objection you can reasonably raise to becoming his wife.'

" ' Become the wife of such a man as Drayton ?' I emphatically exclaimed. ' Never! By Heaven! I would sooner perish first. And is it possible that you can talk thus, my mother? Do you not know how warmly, how devotedly my heart is attached to Walter? Do you not remember the solemn promises which my father has so frequently made that we should be united? And would you have him now repudiate those vows, and consign us both to that state of misery and despair which it is frightful to contemplate? Oh, you cannot, you surely do not mean what you say, and you will intercede to save me from a fate which I have so little deserved, and which, if persisted in, can only end in my destruction, and entail the bitterest remorse and regret both upon my father and yourself.'

" ' My dear child,' she returned, ' you must be convinced, I think, that I have your happiness alone at heart, and that I would not do anything which might be at all likely to prevent it. But in this respect I cannot help thinking that you are in error, and that the prejudice which you seem to entertain against Richard Drayton is an unjust one. It is true that his conduct towards you this evening may have been rash and impetuous ; but every allowance must be made for the violence of his love, and that which he has to contend with in your opposition. But time, no doubt, will remove all those objections ; and when you come to be better acquainted you will be able more duly to appreciate those good qualities which I feel convinced he possesses, and to stifle the childish passion which you now entertain for Walter Seyton.'

" 'Oh, never! never!' I replied, with a flood of tears; 'I should loathe and despise myself if I thought I could. Oh, Walter, dearest Walter! how little did we anticipate the troubles and the disappointments that are in store for us! Why did fate ever bring this man, Drayton, to this neighbourhood? But to love him—to look upon him as my future husband—it is impossible! The very thought chills the blood in my veins. But where is Walter now? I saw him struck to the earth like a dog by the ferocious hand of Drayton. What has now become of him?'

" 'Fear not,' answered my mother; 'he was merely stunned by the blow which Richard Drayton, as I have understood, was compelled to deal him in self-defence. In the meantime Drayton conveyed you home; and after relating the particulars of the event, in which he did not attempt to excuse himself, he took his departure. Walter shortly afterwards arrived at the cottage, in a state of the greatest excitement; but after some time we persuaded him to retire, your father promising to give him every explanation to-morrow.'

" 'Alas!' I ejaculated, wringing my hands in the power of my emotions, 'and what a terrible explanation will that be for him! But my father will surely relent—he can never make up his mind to consign me to a fate which is worse, far worse than death. My dear mother, and will you not exert yourself in my favour?'

" 'And what can I do, my child, when your father is determined?' she replied. 'But try to tranquillise your feelings, and to await patiently till you see him again. Some arrangement may then possibly be come to, and circumstances may not turn out to be so bad as you now seem to anticipate.'

" 'And what have I to expect but the worst,' I demanded, 'after what my father has said to me, and so inflexible as he seems? Little did I imagine that he could ever become so reckless of my happiness as to crush at once the hopes which he himself had raised. This is indeed a trial which I never expected it would fall to my lot to experience; and if he persists in his designs, and should cruelly sacrifice me to Richard Drayton, it is impossible that I can long survive it. And oh, how bitterly will my misguided father then have cause to repent of his harsh and inexorable conduct towards me, and how severely must he reproach himself.'

" 'Nay, my child,' observed my mother, 'your father, I am convinced, does everything for the best, however unjust and cruel his conduct may at present appear to you, and so you will, I think, afterwards acknowledge. To be sure, yourself and Walter having been acquainted from childhood, and suffered to indulge in hopes which, perhaps, when everything is taken into consideration, it was wrong to encourage, you will for a time probably feel the disappointment severely. But you must call all your energies and your reasoning faculties to your aid, and you will no doubt at length be able to conquer your present passion, and to look upon one another with no other feelings than those of friendship.'

" 'And can you,' I said, fixing upon my mother a look of surprise and gentle reproach, 'can you thus coolly argue upon a subject of such vital importance to me? for in it all my future welfare and hopes of happiness are involved. Did not my father willingly, readily give his consent to the addresses of Walter Seyton, and hold out to him the most flattering promises to him and myself? and that renders his present rash determination the more cruel and insupportable. And how have we deserved to be thus tampered with and deceived? Has my father discovered anything in the recent conduct of Walter that he should thus discard him from his good opinion, annihilate his hopes, and doom him to future misery and despair? Will not his character bear the strictest investigation? Has he not ever proved himself to be good and honourable—honest and industrious?'

" 'Oh, yes,' my mother replied, 'he is all that you have represented him to be. Heaven forbid that I should attempt to say anything at all derogatory to his character.'

" 'Then why is he thus abruptly rejected, after the solemn promise that was made to him?' I hastily demanded. 'What can possibly justify such conduct as that?'

" 'Walter is very poor,' replied my mother, 'and he has but little prospect of being enabled to support a wife, and a marriage with poverty can only be productive of misery. Richard Drayton, on the contrary, is well to do in the world, and——'

" 'Oh,' I interrupted, with a look of surprise and remonstrance, 'and is it possible that my father's conduct in this painful affair can be guided by any such mean and sordid motives? What am I that I should aspire to anything beyond the humble station in which it has pleased Providence to place me? Is not Walter thrifty and industrious, and with perseverance able to support himself and me with comfort, if not affluence? I covet not riches; my ambition soars not above the humble station in which it has pleased Heaven to place me, and even poverty with Walter Seyton would be bliss, indeed, compared with wealth and any other man, especially such a man as Richard Drayton, whom I can now only look upon with fear and aversion."

" ' Endeavour to banish those thoughts from your mind, Alice, and to entertain a different opinion of Drayton, for whatever may be the prejudice which you may at present entertain against him, I am convinced that you will find that he is undeserving of it.'

" 'And think you then,' I demanded, 'that such a man as Drayton will be ever able to supplant Walter in my affections? Oh, no, I should indeed hate and despise myself, if I thought I could ever thus act towards one to whom my heart is solemnly pledged, and who, I am satisfied, returns my love with equal fervour and sincerity. But as for Drayton, by Heaven, I cannot even think upon his name without a shudder of horror and disgust, for I am certain, notwithstanding all his plausible manners, and by which he has unfortunately been able to obtain such a powerful influence over my father, he is at heart a villain, who——"

" 'Alice,' interrupted my mother, with a look of gentle reproof, 'forbear to make use of observations such as these. Know you what you say? Surely it is unjust to entertain such a severe opinion of one whose conduct has hitherto never given occasion for it.'

" 'And what can justify his rude and brutal outrage against my feelings this evening?' I demanded. 'Think you after that I can ever look upon him with any other feelings than those of fear and disgust?'

" 'Why,' answered my mother, 'that was certainly wrong; but, as I said before, it is to be accounted for by the impetuosity of his passion, and the scorn with which you received his vows.'

" 'And must he not be base and dishonourable to a degree,' I interrogated, 'when he knew that I was already betrothed to another, one who had been my companion from the earliest days of childhood, to seek to wean my affections from him, and to drive him and myself to misery and despair? Oh, the more I think of him the greater become the feelings of absolute abhorrence with which I cannot help viewing him; and there is no horror to which I may be subjected that can be half so bad as a union with him. But it shall never be. Heaven, I am convinced, will never permit it, and sooner, far sooner would I die than be consigned to such a fate as that. If my father should persist in his rash and cruel determination, then will he most certainly afterwards have reason to bitterly rue the consequences. But he will think better of it. I cannot believe that he will thus recklessly sacrifice me, and break the solemn promises he has made to me and Walter. It would indeed be unworthy of him to do so.'

" 'Wait patiently till you see him upon the subject to-morrow, my dear Alice,' said my mother, 'and then be prepared to listen calmly to that which he will doubtless have to say to you. I trust that his arguments will convince you that what he proposes is for your good, and however painful for a time the trial may be, you will try to submit to his will, and to banish from your bosom the unfortunate passion which you now entertain for Walter Seyton.'

" 'Stifle that passion which has glowed within my breast from the earliest springtide of my existence!' I ejaculated vehemently, and my bosom swelled almost to bursting with the various

ALICE'S INTERVIEW WITH RICHARD DRAYTON.

powerful and conflicting feelings that agitated it; 'by all my hopes here and hereafter, that is impossible. Oh, how extravagant and unreasonable is that idea! My father may force me to the altar with Richard Drayton, and the sacred ceremony, in the eye of the law, may make me his wife; but never, no never shall my heart acknowledge him for my husband; never can I experience any other feelings towards him than those of loathing and disgust. My heart can never acknowledge any other master than Walter Seyton, to whom I am affianced by ties that no human power can dissolve.'

"'Alice,' observed my mother, 'your words alarm and agitate me. Be not rash and obstinate, I implore you, but weigh this important subject maturely and dispassionately in your mind before you come to any decision. You cannot, I should think, doubt for a moment the affection of myself and your father towards you, or the anxious solicitude we have for your welfare; but still we must be firm in opposing your inclinations, when they are at variance with our judgment. I would not appear harsh, my child, but such—

"'Oh, my mother,' I interrupted, with a passionate flood of tears, 'I know too well what you would say, and I am both shocked and surprised to think that you should have been able to come to such a determination, which I can designate no other way than as cruel and severe in the extreme, when all the circumstances of my connection with Walter are taken into serious consideration. What has he done that he should be thus discarded as though he were something loathsome? Is it a crime in him to be poor—to have nothing more to depend upon than his own honest industry? If it indeed be so in your opinion and that of my father, why was he not rejected in the first instance when he solicited your sanction to his addresses? Why have you thus so cruelly sported with his feeling, by not only holding out hopes to him, which you could never mean should be realised, but by buoying him up and deluding him with promises which were only intended to be broken?'

"'You judge me and your father too severely and unjustly,' she answered; 'and so, I have no doubt, time will convince you. But you are not now in a fit state of mind to discuss the subject, and I will, therefore, urge it no further. To-morrow you will see your father, and I trust that he will be able to justify his conduct in your opinion, and to reconcile you to his determination. Till then I will leave you, and may kind Heaven watch over and protect you in the meantime.'

"I sighed deeply, and shook my head disconsolately, but I returned no answer, for I well knew that it was useless to argue with her upon the subject, for, as I said before, she was a simple, easy woman, who was influenced and guided by all that my father said or did, and never for a moment thought of or attempted to oppose his will; and shortly afterwards she quitted the room, and left me to my own gloomy reflections. When she was gone I threw myself into a chair, and gave full vent to the grief which overwhelmed my bosom in a violent paroxysm of sobs and tears. It was impossible that I could control my agony.

I fully anticipated the tempest which was about to burst upon my devoted head, and which seemed certain to overwhelm me and my lover in misery and destruction, and I shuddered at the thought, and my faculties almost forsook me. I could not but lament my fate in the most mournful accents; and bitterly did I reproach my father for the cruel and unnatural determination he had come to, and from which, well knowing his stubborn disposition, I was convinced that nothing would move him. I became every moment more inconsolable and wretched, and my brain was so bewildered by the variety of conflicting thoughts that crowded in such rapid and overwhelming succession upon it, that I scarcely knew what I was about. And what a shock would this unexpected blow prove to Walter! What would be the perfect frenzy of his feelings to find how shamefully my father had deceived him, and that he had resolved not only to forfeit his word, given with such apparent earnestness and sincerity to us both, but also to compel me to become the wife of such a man as Drayton, of whose real character he had, like myself, previous to this fatal evening, entertained the strongest suspicions? I felt for what I was certain it would be his lot to endure even more than myself; and many were the tears I shed, and convulsive were the sobs that escaped my bosom. I could scarcely persuade myself that it was not all some frightful dream; but, alas! there was no stifling the fatal truth, and the longer I reflected the more hopeless and wretched did my fate appear to be. What could my father say in extenuation of his conduct? What could he offer in reply to the remonstrances and reproaches he would be sure to lavish upon his head? And what would be the agony of the next, and probably the last meeting between us? I trembled to think of it; and in the distraction of my feelings I almost wished that it could be avoided; and yet the dreadful idea that we might never meet again drove me almost to madness.

"But I should completely fail were I to attempt to give anything like an adequate description of the horrors it was my cruel lot to endure on that fatal night, and I must, therefore, leave it to your imagination, my unfortunate friend, well convinced as I am that you can fully appreciate and conjecture what my sufferings must have been. It was not for many hours after I had quitted the presence of my parents that I ventured to seek my couch, and then it was not to sleep, or, if I did at intervals sink into a dose, it was only to be startled from it again by some terrific vision, which took such an effect upon my faculties that I almost feared to be alone; and at length I arose from my couch, and throwing myself disconsolately in a chair, I abandoned myself to the most dismal and torturing reflections. Then I started to my feet, and traversed the room in the most disordered manner, unable to find the least relief any way. At times I was driven to such a state of despair, that I was half induced to abandon the cottage, and to resign myself to any fate which might befal me, totally indifferent, as I was, as to what might become of me, for since my father had so harshly decreed that I should not become the wife of the only man who did or ever could possess my affections, life would henceforth become a curse to me instead of a blessing, and I considered that the sooner I was rid of it the better. I pictured to myself the agony and despair of my lover, and trembled when I reflected on the future prospects that opened before him, and to what act of desperation he might, in the frenzy of his feelings, be driven. He could never find fortitude sufficient to support the painful, the cruel, and unexpected destruction of his hopes; but to see me the bride of another, and that, too, of Drayton, would be sufficient to drive him to madness. I had, as I have before stated, from the first moment that I had beheld Drayton, entertained the strongest suspicions as to his real character, and now his coarse and brutal behaviour to me on the previous evening, and the dishonourable manner in which he sought to supplant Walter in my affections, and to force me into a union which was so revolting to my feelings, confirmed them, and made me view him with tenfold disgust and repugnance. That such a man could really feel the sacred passion of love I could not believe, and, therefore, even if I could reconcile myself to a union with him, which was totally impossible, what could I expect but the greatest misery that it could ever fall to the lot of any unfortunate being to experience? The very blood curdled in my veins as I contemplated such a dreadful, such a hopeless fate, and my fortitude entirely forsook me. But to think that my father could ever yield himself to the wishes of such a man, even to the certain sacrifice of the happiness of his only daughter, seemed to me to be so monstrous that I could scarcely persuade myself that it was true. It was evident that he was guided and influenced by the most sordid and mercenary motives; and when I reflected upon all the darker features of his character, I was thoroughly convinced that all the persuasions, the supplications, or arguments that I could possibly make use of would fail to move him from his purpose, and thus the fate which was now impending over me was inevitable.

" 'Cruel parent,' I sighed, ' you could never have loved me, or you would shrink with horror from the bare contemplation of such a fate as that to which you have now condemned me, and would have rejected the daring advances of Drayton with scorn and reprobation. Oh, how bitterly will you have cause to regret, when it is too late, the fatal course you have been persuaded by this man to adopt. But it is impossible that I can long survive such a fate, and must not your future days then become those of the most poignant misery and remorse? Accursed was the hour that ever introduced Drayton to us, for till then nothing ever occurred to interrupt my happiness, and all my hopes were bright and sanguine. But now, alas! how mournful is the change! and what I now experience is, I am convinced, but a prelude to that which is yet in store for me. Sanctioned by my father, Drayton will become even more bold and confident; he will turn a deaf ear to my supplications, all resistance on my part will be in vain, and my fate will as surely be sealed as if it were accomplished already. Alas! how completely destroyed are now all the hopes which myself and Walter formerly indulged in, and in which my father encouraged us. Little did we imagine that he could ever have the heart to deceive us thus, after all the promises that he had held out to us, and which we could not believe that anything could induce him to forfeit. Oh, Walter, what a terrible disappointment is this to you! And how can you ever find strength of mind or patience sufficient to support it? And to-morrow we shall behold each other again, probably for the last time. But what a meeting will that be! I almost fear to encounter it. And can my father remain unmoved, stern, and inexorable, on witnessing our agony? Will he indeed turn a deaf ear to all our prayers and supplications? He must possess a heart of adamant if he does. And yet, after what he has said, what reason have I to expect anything to the contrary? Oh, no, he is too much dazzled by the property which Drayton is supposed to possess, to be tempted to abandon his purpose. And can he be so mean and mercenary, so totally lost to principal and the natural feelings of a father, as to sacrifice his only daughter for gold? The idea seems too monstrous to be encouraged; and yet, have I not too much reason to fear that it will be realised? Alas! there is no escaping from it! But I have surely deserved a far different fate to this. All-bounteous Heaven, I throw myself upon your mercy, and humbly, but, oh, most earnestly do I implore you to avert the miseries that are now impending over me, and rather to suffer me to die than to have to encounter that from which every feeling of my nature revolts with horror.'

"I could say no more, for my feelings had arrived to that pitch of excitement that they completely overpowered me, and again I sunk back in my chair, and my mind became totally lost in the confusion and anguish of my thoughts. And thus that wretched night passed away, and the morning of that day which I almost dreaded at length dawned. But I endeavoured to arouse all the fortitude I could, and to prepare myself to meet my father with firmness and resolution, so that I might make such an appeal to him as was likely to have the most powerful effect upon his feelings, though I could hardly venture to hope to meet with the most trifling, if any success. I offered up a prayer to Heaven, and then I did become some-what more calm and confident. My mother shortly afterwards entered the room, bringing with her my morning repast, in case that I should feel myself too much indisposed to leave my chamber, and she made the most tender and anxious inquiries after my health, to which I replied by a deep sigh, and a melancholy expressive look, which was even more significant than words, and seemed to affect her deeply.

"'Believe me, my dear child,' she said, 'that I pity you sincerely, and would that I could do anything to ameliorate your grief, and to encourage you to hope, but the latter, I know, is impossible, and I should only be deceiving you were I to endeavour to do so. Let me beg of you to calm your feelings and to try to submit to your fate with fortitude and resignation.'

"'Resignation?' I repeated; 'oh, how fruitless would be that task, situated as I am, and with such a fearful prospect before me. But does my father then still remain firm in the fatal and unnatural resolution he has formed?'

"'He does,' she answered, 'and I feel convinced that nothing will have the power to persuade him to alter it. He is greatly prejudiced in favour of Drayton, and considers that he would not be doing his duty, or studying your welfare, were he to reject his suit.'

"'Oh, strange, most outrageous and fatal perversion of feeling,' I ejaculated, 'how can he believe but that he is condemning me to the greatest misery and despair, by thus compelling me to become the wife of a man whom I now cannot view with any other feeling than abhorrence, and when he knows that my affections are immovably fixed upon Walter? But he loves me not, or he would be more studious of my happiness, and not thus sport with my feelings.'

"'Hold, Alice,' said my mother, 'you accuse your father wrongfully. His ideas may be erroneous, but believe me that he has no other object in view than your future welfare.'

"'And yet he has determined on the very course which is certain to prevent it,' I returned. 'But it is evident that he discards poor Walter on account of his poverty, and that he would *sell* me to his rival merely to gratify his own ambitious views. Oh, never did I believe that he could have been guilty of conduct so unjust and mercenary as this.'

"'Alice,' said my mother, 'I cannot listen to language such as this applied in reference to your father; you forget yourself when you make use of it, and I must enjoin you to banish all such erroneous and uncharitable ideas from your mind, and to meet him as becomes you, and to listen to the observations he will have to address to you with calmness and patience, for it is only by that that you can expect to arrive at anything like a satisfactory arrangement.'

"'Satisfactory arrangement!' I repeated; 'oh, my mother, methinks those are strange words to imply on such a subject. Think you, then, that I will ever consent to compromise my own honour or happiness by passively yielding to that which is so repugnant to my feelings, and so opposed to reason and justice? I should indeed be unworthy of the love of Walter Seyton if I could. No, let whatever may be the consequences, I will resist with all my power the fearful and revolting sacrifice which my father would make of me.'

"'And of what will that avail you, so determined as your father is? On the contrary, it will only serve to excite his wrath, and to hasten that fate which you seem to dread so much. But I am inclined to believe that time will alter your opinion of Richard Drayton, and that you will then discover the many noble and manly qualities which I am certain he possesses, and forgetting your childish love, which was engendered before you had arrived at sufficient years of maturity to understand its nature, you will yield a ready compliance with that which you now so strenuously oppose.'

"'Mother, dear mother,' I ejaculated, fixing upon her a look of astonishment, 'what cruel injustice you do me, if you entertain such an opinion of me as that you have just expressed. Is it possible, think you, that I can ever banish Walter from my heart, and replace him by such a being as Richard Drayton? The very idea fills my bosom with shame and indignation. I may be forced to resign my hand to the latter, (though fervently I beseech the most High to avert such

a fate,) but never, oh, never can he possess my heart; nor ever can I look upon him but with the utmost loathing and contempt. Had he possessed the slightest particle of honourable feelings, even though I might have excited a hopeless and unfortunate passion in his breast, he would have struggled with manly fortitude to subdue it, knowing that I was betrothed to another, who is so every way worthy of me, and on whom my affections are so firmly fixed that my heart must cease to beat ere they can be removed. But no, his conduct proves to me beyond all doubt that, however Richard Drayton may try to conceal his real character under a mask of hypocrisy, his heart his mean, selfish, and dishonourable, and that there is no length to which he would not go to accomplish his guilty and presumptuous wishes. Such is my opinion of him, and time, I am certain, will prove that I am correct."

"'I see plainly that it is useless to argue with you,' remarked my mother, 'since the prejudice you entertain against him is so strong. Yet would I advise you to reflect seriously ere you decide entirely. You will probably see him to-day, and I hope that you will meet him with that respect which, at any rate, is due to him, and give a dispassionate hearing to that which he may have to say to you.'

"'Oh, Heaven forbid that I should see him,' I exclaimed, 'for when I take all the painful circumstances into consideration, and behold him in the character of my persecutor, and the destroyer of my hopes, my feelings will surely overpower me, and how is it possible that I can look upon him without a shudder of horror? Can I forget the gross insult he offered to me last night? And yet my father can tolerate, if not even applaud such infamous conduct. Oh, my breast is filled with shame and indignation.'

"'Give not way to those sentiments, Alice,' she said, 'for they cannot possibly effect you any good, but, on the contrary, may serve to add to your anguish of mind. Arouse yourself, for your father will probably be anxious to see you before long.'

"'And if he any longer entertains any regard for me,' I rejoined, 'or would not consign me to misery the most insupportable, he will listen to my appeal, and at once abandon the cruel designs which he has suffered to enter his mind, and no longer give any encouragement to the hated suit of Drayton, which, if persevered in, must inevitably entail shame and misery upon us all.'

" 'It would be wrong of me to hold out any such hopes to you,' replied my mother, 'for I feel but too certain they would be doomed to disappointment.'

" 'And why did my father ever encourage the love of myself and Walter,' I demanded, 'if it was ever his intention to crush our hopes? Surely he cannot reconcile such conduct with his sense of truth and justice.'

" 'I am at a loss how to reply to you,' said my mother, 'and must leave the discussion of that question to yourself and your father. God grant that all may yet terminate more happily than you now seem to anticipate.'

" 'Alas! I fear that can never be,' I replied; 'if my father remains obstinate there is no other prospect before me than one which I shudder to contemplate; and I pray Heaven sincerely that I may die e'er I experience it, for what can ever reconcile me to the revolting fate which shall make me the wife of such a detestable being as Richard Drayton? And then to know the misery and despair which my beloved Walter must be enduring!'

" 'When he finds that all his hopes of possessing you are at an end, he will struggle with his feelings of disappointment, and will soon learn to forget you, and to fix his affections upon some other woman.'

" 'Cease, mother,' I ejaculated, fixing upon her a look of reproach, 'cease to make use of those observations. Oh, how little do you know of the real character of Walter Seyton, if such is the opinion you entertain of him! Cease to love me—fix his affections upon some other woman? Oh, what a base calumny is there in the very thought! Ah, no! Walter may behold me the bride of another, but it is impossible that he can long survive the dreadful blow. Should such a terrible fate be in store for me, naught but despair and death await him. Alas! alas! and are there no means of avoiding those horrors? Will my father indeed persist in his cruel determination? And you, my mother, you also seem to approve of it; have you, indeed, no sympathy, no consideration for your unhappy child?'

" 'Alice,' she said, 'have I not ever lavished upon you all a mother's care and fondest affection? Why, then, should you thus express those doubts of me? But you view everything on the darkest side, and torture yourself without a cause.'

" 'Torture myself without a cause?' I repeated. 'Must I not indeed possess a callous heart were I to remain indifferent while I am threatened with such a horrible and disgusting fate as that which is impending o'er me? But I see too plainly that you coincide with my father, and that it is useless to appeal to you. My only hope, then, is in the goodness and mercy of the Supreme, and He I humbly but earnestly trust will not desert me in this the most fearful hour of my need. But shall I again see Walter to-day?'

" 'No doubt of it,' answered my mother, 'for your father treated him with kindness and consideration when he came to our cottage after his affray with Richard Drayton, and invited him to come here to-day, when he promised to discuss this painful subject calmly and patiently with him, and to explain to him his reasons for the sudden resolution he has come to.'

" 'And what excuse can he possibly make for conduct so harsh and unjust?' I ejaculated. 'And, oh, what must be the agony of poor Walter's feelings? He has inflicted a blow upon us both from which we can never recover; and mark my words, the time will come, and that much sooner than he probably expects, when he will deeply repent it. Richard Drayton, too—should he succeed in obtaining possession of my hand may think his triumph complete; but his dishonourable and treacherous conduct will most assuredly recoil upon himself. What happiness can he possibly expect to experience in a union with one whom he must be convinced looks upon him both with hatred and scorn, and while the bitterest curses of the deeply injured Walter will be sure to be invoked upon his head? And then, when it is too late, and when he sees the destruction he has caused, will come the misery and remorse of my misguided father, and how anxiously will he wish that he could recal the past. Would to Heaven that he would calmly reflect upon all this before he proceeds any further with the designs which he has at present unfortunately in contemplation, for if he does not, all that I have now mentioned to you will be most assuredly realised.'

"'Heaven forbid,' ejaculated my mother; 'but I will leave you for the present, and I hope that in an hour or so you will be prepared to meet your father, for I know that he is most anxious to see you.'

"'God give me fortitude for the interview,' I said, solemnly, 'and change his heart towards me. I have never disobeyed his will, but have always behaved towards him with reverence and affection, and why, then, should he thus seek to make me so truly wretched, and to destroy all my hopes?'

"'Such is farthest from his wishes,' returned my mother, 'and of that you will be convinced before long. God grant, I repeat, that all may terminate more happily than you now anticipate.'

"'And most solemnly and heartily do I respond to that prayer,' I said; 'but happiness can never be mine while the hateful addresses of William Drayton are encouraged, and I am threatened with a fate more terrible than the most lingering death of torment.'

"'You will see what effect your arguments will have upon your father,' she replied, 'and till then I will leave you.'

"With these words she retired from the room, and when she was gone I once more knelt down, and with streaming eyes I solemnly invoked the protection of the Almighty, for my situation, I could plainly see, was a most desperate one, and without His aid my fate seemed certain. The observations of my mother had given me little room to hope, and I almost dreaded the approaching interview, and heartily wished that it was over, though what the result of it would be I could very well imagine. But oh, what would be the agony of my feelings at my meeting with my lover? And probably this would be the last time that

we should be permitted to see each other, and what his future fate might be I shuddered even to think. How torturing was that reflection! My brain was wrought up to a pitch bordering upon madness as it rushed upon it, and I beat my breast in the extreme anguish and distraction of my feelings, whilst the tears chased each other rapidly down my cheeks.

"'Heaven give him fortitude to support this dreadful and unexpected blow,' I exclaimed, 'and, oh! may he be able to resign himself to his fate, and to think of me in future only as a dear sister or friend. But, oh! how extravagant and preposterous is that thought; as well might I expect the ocean to stay its course, as for Walter to reconcile himself to his destiny, or to cease to love me with the same ardour and devotion that he does at present. And could I for a moment believe that he would ever place his affections on another, and to unite his fate to hers also? I should then indeed be truly wretched, and then tenfold curses of Heaven would seem to descend upon my head. And even now am I not deserted by the Almighty, and left to the sport of cruel destiny, without one single hope to cheer me or to ameliorate my sufferings? Gracious Heaven, how hard this is to bear, and yet how useless is it for me to murmur at it, since I cannot alter the decrees of fate. And of what value is life to me under such circumstances as these? Would that I were rid of it, since remorseless destiny has cast so heavy a gloom over my future prospects, and annihilated all those scenes of bliss which the sanguine imagination of myself and Walter had conjured up. Oh, my father, you will most assuredly have much to answer for, for the part which you have acted, and the heartless manner in which you have deceived us.'

"My tears flowed faster than ever as these painful thoughts occurred to me, and every moment my anguish rather increased than abated, and it was in vain that I endeavoured to find some ray of consolation. But I will not tire your patience, Mrs. Tiller, by particularising all my thoughts upon that painful occasion; you who are, unfortunately, so well and bitterly experienced in the school of adversity can, I well know, form an adequate conception of them. The crisis of my fate seemed to be rapidly approaching, and I had not sufficient strength to bear up against it. But more, much more than all did I dread to meet Drayton, for, after his conduct on the previous evening, and the bold observations he had made use of, which my parents excused, what could I expect from him? Certainly neither pity nor forbearance, but, on the contrary, he would be sure to take every advantage of the encouragement he received from them, and in spite of my tears, my supplications, my remonstrances and reproaches, would persist in his detested suit with increased boldness, and exult in his cowardly triumph. Had not his heart been base and mean to a degree, even though I have excited a fatal passion in his bosom, knowing my situation, and how devotedly my heart was fixed upon another, he would have struggled to stifle his love in its infancy, and have hastened from the neighbourhood in which I resided, most studiously avoided my presence, rather than have fanned the flame in his bosom, and boldly advanced his suit even to the destruction of all my hopes of happiness. And what a lamentable weakness has my father betrayed, by thus so readily yielding to his wishes, and so cruelly forfeiting his word to myself and Walter. I can scarcely believe that it is true; but when the dreadful certainty becomes too painfully apparent to me, I am driven to distraction, and scarcely know what I am about. Oh, my father, you must, you will have bitter cause to repent of your conduct, if you thus persist in your fatal determination.'

"I ceased, for my thoughts were exhausted, and a kind of apathy seized upon my mind, and the whole appeared as if I had been suffering under the influence of some painful dream, for the circumstances by which I now was surrounded seemed of too dreadful and overwhelming a character to be real. In this state of excitement and mental agony an hour elapsed after my mother had quitted the room, and my feelings underwent no change. I walked at last to the window of my chamber, and looked from it, almost expecting, but dreading to behold Drayton approaching; and I could not believe, even heartless

though I supposed him to be, that he would have the effrontery or the cruelty to obtrude himself again upon my presence for a day or two, or until after I had had an interview with my father, and received the final decision from his lips.

"From my chamber window I had a distinct view of the cottage in which my lover resided, and you may judge of my feelings as I gazed mournfully upon it, and pictured to myself the sufferings he was then enduring. Oh, how anxious was I, and yet how I trembled to behold him again—to listen to the beloved tones of his voice—to hear his vows of undiminished love, and to receive the assurances of my constancy, though remorseless fate should now ordain that we should never come together; but I saw nothing of him or his parents, and the most dismal and fearful forebodings took possession of my mind, and made me one of the most wretched of human beings it is possible to imagine.

"It was a dark and dreary morning, and everything seemed to betoken a coming storm; but the weather was in unison with my feelings, and I heeded it not. As I gazed upon the dark waters of the ocean, how frequently did I wish that, with my lover, I were transported far beyond it, for, so that my fate should be united to his, I cared not what danger I might have to encounter, or how great the poverty it might be my lot to experience. Walter, he was everything to me, and most willingly would I have laid down my life for his sake; but now I was about to be torn from him altogether, and the curse of Heaven seemed, most undoubtedly to pursue me, although I had never to my knowledge, by word, or thought, or deed, offended its sacred laws. I trembled, for should my father persist in that which he threatened, might not Walter, in the frenzy of his despair, be urged into the perpetration of some desperate act? Alas! it was but too probable, and the most dismal and insupportable forebodings took possession of my mind, and which were too soon most awfully destined to be realised. I shudder with horror when I recal to my mind that which I afterwards suffered, and the dreadful fate which was impending over the fate of my beloved Walter. Oh, God! even at this distance of time,

THE VOW OF LOVE BETWEEN ALICE AND WALTER SEYTON.

my feelings completely overpower me when I reflect upon it, and I seem to experience my misfortunes over again. But I fear that I am becoming tedious."

"Oh, no," answered our heroine, "your narrative deeply interests me, and divests my thoughts, for a time, from my own sorrows. Your troubles have indeed been great, and most deeply and sincerely do I commiserate with you."

"Alas! I have indeed been the victim of a cruel destiny," sighed Alice, "and

Heaven only knows how I have had fortitude to support them for so many years. But to proceed: I continued at the window for some time longer, wrapt in such gloomy reflections as those I have described, but I saw nothing either of Walter or his parents, and the cottage seemed to be entirely deserted. This also excited in my breast a feeling of alarm, and I became more uneasy every minute. But at length I was interrupted in the midst of these meditations by the re-entrance of my mother, and I started, and looked anxiously towards her, and the expression of my countenance fully revealed to her what I wished to inquire.

" 'Your father is now prepared to see you, Alice,' she observed, 'and I hope that you will remember my injunctions, and endeavour to meet him with that calmness by which alone this important subject can be fairly discussed. No doubt, however, that he is disposed to make every allowance for the feelings of excitement under which you must naturally labour.'

" 'Oh, tell me,' I demanded, anxiously, 'does he seem to relent? Will he recal his words, and no longer threaten me with a fate so dreadful and revolting?'

" My mother shook her head significantly, as she answered—

" 'It would be wrong of me to hold out to you any such hopes, Alice, which could only be doomed to disappointment.'

" 'Heaven help me, then!' I cried, despairingly, 'for without its aid my fate is sealed, and I see no opportunity of escaping from it. Oh, my father, and can you have become so entirely lost to reason and to justice? Alas—alas! what dreadful infatuation has taken possession of you? Oh, you could never have loved me, or you would shrink with horror and disgust from the bare idea of consigning me so remorselessly to such endless misery.'

" 'Suspend your judgment, Alice,' said my mother, 'until after you have heard the arguments and explanation of your father, and I do not fear that you will continue to entertain the same opinion which you seem to do now.'

" 'And how can I alter it?' I impatiently demanded; 'has he not determined to crush the hopes of myself and Walter, and to force me to become the wife of a man whom I cannot esteem, much more love, and who, I am satisfied, must be at heart a villain, or he would never thus seek to destroy the happiness of a poor defenceless girl?'

" 'You judge too severely of Richard Drayton, I am convinced,' observed my mother; 'in whatever character he may appear to your prejudiced eye, I am satisfied that he possesses a manly and generous heart, and that he sincerely loves you.'

" 'Loves me?' I repeated, with a look of scorn; 'oh! what a bitter mockery —what a pitiful perversion of common-sense it is to talk thus! The sacred and holy passion of love must be a stranger to his breast, or he could never act in the manner he is now doing. But I will resist his bold and presumptuous advances to the utmost of my power. Nature, honour, justice, everything is opposed to the unholy alliance, and I will not passively become a sacrifice to his villainy, and the cupidity (for I can call it by no milder term) of my father.'

" 'Nay, Alice,' she said, 'reflect seriously upon what you say, and think of the consequences which any obstinate resistance on your part may be productive of to you. Your father is determined, and it is not likely, therefore, that he will suffer himself to be intimidated from his purpose.'

" 'May Heaven forgive him, then,' I solemnly ejaculated, 'for he will, by his cruel conduct, consign his hapless child to destruction. It would be much more merciful of him to plunge a knife in my heart, and thus at once rid me of an existence which must in future become so truly wretched and insupportable to m'

" 'Horrible thought!' said my mother, 'forbear to encourage it, for it can be productive of no good to you. But this is a waste of time: arouse yourself from this lethargy of despair, and prepare to accompany me to the presence of your father, who now most anxiously awaits you.'

" 'God help me!' I again ejaculated in the most mournful accents; and sinking on my knees, I implored the Almighty to inspire me with fortitude to support the painful trial I had to undergo, and to move the heart of my misguided parent to pity and forbearance. I did then feel somewhat more firm and composed, and suffered my mother to take my arm; she led me from the chamber, and down the stairs into the room in which my father was awaiting me. I trembled as I entered, and a deathly sickness came over me, but my mother encouraged me by a look, and I quickly recovered myself. My father was standing at the window on my entrance, with his back turned towards me, but he quickly turned on hearing me, and advanced. I again trembled at his approach, but he was evidently prepared for my emotion, and taking my hand, fixed upon me a look of kindness as he said—

"'My dear Alice, you may believe me when I assure you that it grieves me sincerely to be placed in the embarrassing and painful situation which I now occupy, or that I should be the means of causing you a single pang of regret. But Heaven knows that I only act for the best, and with an earnest desire to promote your future happiness and prosperity beyond a doubt.'

"'Oh, my dear father,' I sighed, 'why then seek to annihilate at one fell swoop the hopes that you yourself had raised? Why break the solemn promise which you have made to myself and Walter? And why wish to sacrifice me to a man whom I cannot look upon with any other feeling than one almost amounting to abhorrence?'

"'I own that the sudden resolution to which I have come may appear harsh and unjust,' he replied, 'and that such an unexpected disappointment to your wishes must, for the present, cause you considerable excitement and pain. But I have not done so, believe me, without due deliberation, and some hesitation; but your future interests and prospects in life must supersede every other consideration, and there is nothing left me but to follow the course I have determined upon.'

"'Oh, my father,' I cried, clasping my hands together, and looking appealingly in his face, 'you cannot surely be so cruel—you will not consign me to a fate which appears far too dreadful for me to contemplate? Oh, consider the solemn promise you have made to Walter Seyton in the face of Heaven—recollect his numerous noble and manly qualities—the many, many years that we have been acquainted, and I beseech you most earnestly to abandon the rash and fatal designs which you now have in contemplation.'

"'I admit that Walter is all that you have represented him to be,' returned my father, 'and that as far as the qualities of his head and heart go, he is every way worthy of you. But love and poverty but seldom, if ever, agree together; Walter is very poor, and his future prospects are cheerless and hopeless. Richard Drayton, on the contrary, is well to do in the world already; and from the manner in which he is connected, it is not at all unlikely that he may become a wealthy man at no distant period; he has confessed to me that he loves you, and I have no doubt that he is sincere. He is good looking and accomplished beyond his station in life, and, therefore, I know of no man who is more worthy to become the husband of my Alice than he is.'

"'Oh, never—never!' I exclaimed, with a burst of the most intense emotion; 'forbid it, Heaven! for sooner would I perish than that I should be thus sacrificed, and made the victim of a man whom I loathe and despise. His conduct to me last night was sufficient to confirm my suspicions of his real character, and I cannot think of it without a mingled feeling of disgust and indignation.'

"'You must learn to banish such feelings from your bosom, Alice,' returned my father, 'for, notwithstanding the manner in which you are at present prejudiced against Richard Drayton, he is totally unworthy of the opinion you have formed of him. As for the rudeness of which you complain, I am satisfied that he meant no harm by it, and that it was only the scornful manner in which you treated him that excited him to it.'

"'Oh, my father,' I said, with a look of reproach and gentle remonstrance, 'then it seems from your observations that the superior circumstances of Richard Drayton to those of Walter have dazzled you, and that you are prepared to sacrifice your daughter's happiness for lucre? Oh, how unworthy of you is that idea! Never, never did I imagine that my father could encourage such sordid principles.'

"'Alas!' he cried, with a look of vexation, though at the same time he could not conceal his confusion, 'Alice, your words are bold and severe, and such as should never be applied to a parent by those who know their duty. But I can make every allowance for you, for in the present excitement of your feelings you know not what you say. However, I would advise you to become calm—to try to conquer the passion you now entertain for Walter Seyton—to think of him only as a friend, and to receive the addresses of Richard Drayton with that encouragement and respect which they deserve.'

"'Oh!' I ejaculated, hastily and impatiently, 'that is impossible. Banish Walter from my heart, and replace him by Richard Drayton? The very idea is maddening and disgusting! Drayton can now never possess even my esteem, much more my love; and the sight of him must every day become more odious to me.'

"'Be not rash, Alice,' he said, sternly. 'Recal your words, and learn to obey my injunctions, as you dread my wrath, and lest you should have bitter cause to repent of your obstinacy. My determination, however, is fixed; I revoke the promise which, in a moment of thoughtlessness, I made to you and Walter; you must and shall become the wife of Richard Drayton, let the consequences be whatever they may. I have given him my word to that effect, and nothing whatever shall induce me to break it.'

"'Oh, God, then!' I groaned, and tears gushed in torrents to my eyes as I spoke, 'you have determined on my destruction, and must have discarded me from the place which your only daughter should occupy. Oh, this is most cruel and unnatural! But here, on my knees, I supplicate your pity, your mercy, and forbearance. Consider the misery into which you must inevitably plunge me by such a course, and abandon your designs. Oh, what a hardened and reckless heart must Drayton possess if he persists in those addresses which are so hateful and repugnant to my feelings. Father, dear father, I never offered to disobey your will before, but nature revolts at the idea of a union with such a man as Drayton, while my heart is so firmly, so fondly devoted to another; the blood freezes in my veins at the very thought, and I must oppose it to the last by every means in my power, and which virtue, honour, everything justify.'

"'How madly you talk, Alice,' he returned, with a look of anger and impatience; 'of what use will be all the opposition you can offer? Think you that it will succeed, or that I will suffer myself to be thwarted in the gratification of my wishes? You entertain certain notions and prejudices which it would be well for you to conquer; I act only as reason and prudence dictate, and I have only your interest at heart, I repeat, in so doing.'

"'Alas! what a mockery of the word is it to talk thus!' I returned. 'Of what value is wealth if unaccompanied by happiness? And such, I am certain, can never be my fate if I am compelled to become the wife of Richard Drayton. Would to Heaven that we had never known him, then probably I should never have been exposed to such a fate as that which I now experience, and the more dreadful one which seems to be in store for me. Oh, my dear father, and can you behold the insupportable agony of my feelings unmoved? Will you still obstinately persist in placing me in a position which is too awful and revolting to think on?'

"'You have heard the decision I have come to,' he answered, with stern inflexibility, 'and not all the arguments you can make use of can induce me to alter it. Richard Drayton is not a match that should be despised or hastily rejected; he is every way worthy of you, and I am too solicitous for your welfare not to resolve that he shall become your husband.'

"'Dreadful thought!' I exclaimed, and my heart sunk within me as I spoke, 'is there no hope for me? Oh, wretched, wretched, ill-fated Alice! why have you ever been suffered to live to experience such misery as this?'

"The power of my emotions choked my further utterance, and sinking in a chair I resigned myself to all the agony of my grief. My father folded his arms across his chest, and stood gazing at me for a few minutes in silence; but my agony seemed not to have made any favourable impression upon his heart, and what else was there left for me to do than to abandon myself to despair? But at length approaching me nearer, and laying his hand upon my shoulder, he said—

"'Come, Alice, you must not thus abandon yourself to grief; why will you persist in thus torturing yourself so unnecessarily? It needs but energy and perseverance, and you will soon learn to conquer your hopeless passion for Walter Seyton, and which it was wrong to encourage, and reason will convince you that the decision which I have come to is one of all others which is the most likely to promote your happiness.'

"'Oh, my father,' I cried, 'forbear! for your words do but serve to increase my anguish. Happiness with Drayton, and knowing the despair which the unfortunate Walter is enduring? That is impossible; and I must be mad to entertain such an idea. Think of the numerous virtues possessed by him whom you now so cruelly and shamefully reject, and render him that act of justice which is due to him and me. You have registered a solemn oath in Heaven to unite our fates together; and will you, by the base artifices of a designing man, be induced to break that vow, and to stand self-confessed a perjurer? Oh, bethink yourself before it is too late, for I shudder to think of the dreadful consequences which your conduct will be almost certain to be productive of.'

"'Psha!' exclaimed my father, impatiently, 'you talk wildly, Alice; and again I tell you that all you may say in opposition to my will can have no effect on me. But enough of this—I have given you the explanation I promised you, with which you must rest satisfied, and I have nothing more at present to say to you upon the subject. Reflect seriously and calmly upon what I have said to you when you are alone, and I trust that when next we meet I may find you in a very different state of mind to what you are now.'

"'And think you that I can ever reconcile myself to the cruel fate to which you have condemned me?' I returned, and fixing upon him a look of reproach. 'No, that is utterly impossible, and I should hate myself if I thought that I could. You may drag me to the altar—you may force me to become the bride of Drayton, but you can never change the sentiments I entertain towards him, which are those of the utmost abhorrence, and which must increase every moment that I think upon him.'

"'Rash girl!' said my father, sternly, 'and think you to benefit your cause by language such as this? I command you, on pain of my future displeasure, to learn submission, and when you again behold Drayton, which no doubt you shortly will, to receive him with that respect which is his due.'

"'Oh, God!' I cried, wringing my hands, 'how is it possible for me to do so, when I take all the melancholy circumstances of my case into consideration? Oh, my father, you would impose upon me a task which it is not likely at all that I can ever accomplish. I am no hypocrite, and, therefore, let the consequences be whatever they may, I cannot disguise my real feelings from the dreaded object who has excited them. But do not, I implore you, at present put me to such a severe trial as an interview with my persecutor would be!'

"'Your persecutor?' he repeated, with a look of anger.

"'Yes,' I repeated, firmly, 'in what other character can I behold him, when I take his conduct towards me into consideration? If he possessed the least feeling of honour or humanity he would desist from persecuting his hateful suit, and no longer seek to involve me in a fate which must render me one of the most miserable and hopeless beings in existence.'

"'You talk erroneously, Alice,' returned my father, 'and time must convince you of the truth of what I say, notwithstanding the prejudice which you now entertain against him. Again I tell you that he loves you, I am satisfied, with a passion as ardent as it is sincere, and his whole study will be to contribute to your happiness, and to leave not a wish that you can entertain ungratified. Why, then, should you feel such a repugnance to become his bride, and——'

"'And what a wayward and treacherous heart you must suppose me to possess,' I hastily interrupted, 'if you imagine that I can so easily transfer my affections from Walter, the beloved companion of my childhood, to him, and to leave him to whom I am betrothed to misery, scorn, and despair. I must be a wretch unworthy of the name of woman if I could do so, and surely, my father, you do me a cruel injustice by entertaining such an opinion of me.'

"'Psha!' he replied, 'these are only the observations of a thoughtless and inexperienced girl, and as such I take no heed of them. You will, however, do well by strictly attending to my injunctions, for I can admit of no obstinate opposition, and it can effect you no good. But this conversation has lasted long enough, and I am tired of it. Retire, and reflect upon all the circumstances with a calm and dispassionate mind, which will doubtless enable you to come to a just and satisfactory conclusion.'

" 'Alas, then,' I sighed, 'I see that it is useless to appeal to you any further for pity and forbearance, and I am miserable and distracted. Heaven help me, for surely this is a trial which requires more than human fortitude to endure.'

" 'These fruitless lamentations,' returned my father, 'will not enable you to do so, at any rate. But you must arouse yourself from this state of weakness, and learn to act with energy and decision.'

" 'How vain is such advice to a poor wretched being situated as I am,' I replied; 'how can I contemplate the horrors that seem too surely in store for me without fear and trembling? Heaven forgive you, my father, for you must certainly, at some future time, have bitter cause to regret the harsh, the unjustifiable and cruel conduct which you are now pursuing.'

" 'Enough,' he said; 'I will listen no more to your observations; you have heard my determination, and you must abide by it. Away!'

"I fixed upon him such a look as he gave utterance to these words as was sufficient to penetrate to his heart, and to move him to pity if he had not stifled every feeling of compassion or remorse in his bosom; but I returned no answer, for I knew that it would be useless to do so, and that it might only serve to exasperate him; and sighing deeply, and taking the proffered arm of my mother, who had remained silent all this time, she led me from the room, and once more conducted me to my own chamber. Here I sank into a chair, and overwhelmed by the powerful nature of my feelings, which, on this painful interview, had been put to such a severe test, I burst into a violent paroxysm of grief, which I found it impossible for some time to subdue, and which indeed afforded my overcharged bosom some

relief. My mother seemed to be greatly moved by my anguish, and she stood watching me with anxious looks of commiseration, but did not offer to obtrude any observation upon me. It was now quite evident to me that there was no hope, and that my father would inexorably persist in carrying his threats into execution, and that, therefore, any resistance which I might offer to his wishes would be unavailing. This conviction was of itself sufficient to drive me to distraction, and it was all to no purpose that I endeavoured to calm my feelings, for the longer I reflected upon them the more dreadful and appalling did my prospects appear to be. But from my own sufferings my thoughts wandered to those which I was too painfully convinced Walter must at that time be enduring; and when I thought of the reception he was likely to meet with from my father, should he visit the cottage—which no doubt he would do before long—my anxiety and anguish of mind increased to such a degree that it was not without the greatest difficulty I could restrain myself within the bounds of reason.

" 'Alas!' I sighed, 'after the cruel observations my father has made to me, and the stern determination he has expressed, what can I expect? He will treat the appeal of poor Walter with equal scorn and indifference, and probably add insult to injustice. And then the outrage which was committed by Drayton upon him last night; will Walter fail to resent it? Too well do I know his brave and manly spirit to imagine for a moment that he will; and whenever they meet again, which they are sure to do, I tremble for the consequences, especially goaded on as Walter will be by the disappointment of his hopes, and the dishonourable and despicable conduct of his guilty rival. Heaven protect him, for I plainly perceive that the troubles which I have so long foreboded have only just begun, and that there is that in store for me and Walter which will be sufficient even to crush the stoutest spirit. And you, my father, have been the principal cause of all this. Oh, how keenly must your conscience reproach you for it afterwards.'

" 'Not so,' observed my mother; 'your father's conscience is prompted only by the purest motives, and you do him wrong, Alice, by supposing anything to the contrary. You have accused him of sordidness and avarice in this painful affair, but calm and serious reflection must surely convince you of the gross injustice of such an opinion.'

" 'Heaven forbid that I should judge him wrongfully,' I answered; 'but to what other conclusion can I possibly come, when he states that one of his principal reasons for accepting Drayton, and breaking his promise to Walter, is the superior pecuniary circumstances of the former? A parent who had his child's future happiness sincerely at heart would never for such reasons think of sacrificing her to a man whom she must ever view with disgust and abhorrence, and whose conduct proves how utterly unworthy he is of her.'

" 'Would that I could persuade you to dismiss those false prejudices from your mind,' observed my mother, 'and to view the conduct of your father and Richard Drayton with a more impartial eye.'

" 'When I take all the circumstances into consideration, how is it possible that I can do so?' I demanded; 'and can you, my mother, approve of that which most assuredly dooms your daughter to future misery and despair? Alas! where, then, am I to look for hope and consolation, since those from whom I have a right to expect it, deny it me?'

" 'Will nothing whatever persuade you to become more calm and reasonable, patient and resigned?' she said.

" 'And what better is it than a cruel mockery to talk to me thus, threatened as I am, and all those bright prospects which myself and Walter had so freely indulged in thus blighted for ever?' I returned. 'Patience and resignation! Oh, how extravagant and disgusting do the words sound in my ears, after what has happened, and that which I have a right to expect is awaiting me. If my father persists in his cruel designs, there will be no peace for me but the silent grave, and I care not how soon it covers my cold remains.'

" 'Talk not in that dismal and desponding manner, my child,' said my mother, 'for how it pains me to hear you. Be firm, and you will, I am convinced, by perseverance, be able to conquer the objections which now present themselves to your excited and disordered imagination, and to entertain a far different opinion of the character of the man whom your father has destined for your future husband than that which you now so warmly express.'

" 'And think you then so little of me,' I demanded, 'as to suppose that Richard Drayton can ever hold possession of my heart, and that Walter Seyton will be banished from it as though he had been guilty of some crime, which can only render him worthy of my scorn, my disgust and hatred? Oh, how unworthy of the name of woman should I be if I could act thus! Indeed, my mother, if you speak sincerely, you do me a cruel wrong by suffering such an idea to enter your mind even for a moment. But alas! I see but too clearly that I have no one to sympathise with me, and there is nothing left for me but to bear my sorrows alone, and to put my trust in the goodness and mercy of Providence, to interpose to save me from the horrors with which I am threatened, and which will be far too great for human fortitude to bear. Beloved Walter! may Heaven watch over you and guard you from the dangers which I too fearfully anticipate, for never, I am certain, can you pardon the blow which you received from the guilty Drayton.'

" 'It was done only in the excitement of the moment, if I understand rightly,' observed my mother, 'and in self-defence.'

" 'And think you, then,' I demanded, with a look of astonishment and indignation, 'think you that Walter could stand tamely by and witness the insult which was offered to my feelings by his daring and presumptuous rival? Such observations as these make it appear that you sanction the conduct of Drayton, and that——'

" 'Hold! Alice,' interrupted my mother, 'encourage no such ideas as these, for they are not only unjust but fallacious. You misunderstood me; I acknowledge that Drayton was wrong, and no doubt that he himself now most deeply regrets it, but, as I have said before, he, no doubt, was excited by the scorn and reproach with which you treated him, and was urged on to do that which in his more sober senses he would have shrunk from. He will, no doubt, make you an ample apology when he sees you again.'

" 'An apology!' I repeated, with a look of contempt; 'and think you, then, that a mere apology will reconcile me to such an outrage? No, I must indeed be insensible to every proper feeling could I ever forgive so gross an insult. But if anything were wanting to do so, his conduct on that occasion has fully confirmed my worst suspicions of the character of the man, and convinces me that there is no length to which he will hesitate to go in order to gratify his nefarious wishes. And such is the man who has the presumption to think he can supplant dear Walter in my affections, and whom my father has chosen for my future husband! Oh, most monstrous and unholy thought!—forbid it, Heaven! But surely it will never permit me to become the victim of such a villain.'

" 'Restrain the violence of your language, Alice,' said my mother, 'for surely such epithets as that you have just now made use of ill become you, especially when applied to Richard Drayton. He has hitherto done nothing that should render him deserving of such a name. But you will think better of this, and I trust that the time will come when you will be ready to admit and to regret the injustice which you have done him.'

" 'Never can I entertain a different opinion of Richard Drayton,' I remarked, 'unless he should abandon his hateful and hopeless suit, and endeavour to make me and Walter all the reparation in his power for the misery that he has caused us.'

" 'Powerful as is the passion which I am convinced he entertains for you,' said my mother, 'I do not believe that it will be possible for him to conquer it, or to resign his hopes; and if you suffer such an idea to enter your mind, I fear that it will only end in disappointment. But I see it is useless to argue the subject with you at present, violently excited as you are, and so little disposed as you seem to be to listen to the voice of reason. I will, therefore, leave you to your own reflections, with a sincere hope that you may be able to obtain that firmness and patience which you so much

require on so important and trying an occasion.'

" I fixed upon her a look of gentle reproach and remonstrance as she uttered those words, but I did not offer to make any reply, for I saw the utter uselessness of doing so, and in a few minutes afterwards she left the room, and I was left to all the misery of my own gloomy and torturing thoughts. I remembered every word that my inexorable father had said to me; they were stamped most indelibly upon my memory, and they filled my breast with the bitterest and most insupportable feelings of anguish and despair. I could obtain little or no relief to my care and anxiety, and most drearily and painfully did the hours pass away, until the afternoon had far advanced, and still my lover came not to the cottage, and I was unable to form even the slightest conjecture as to the cause of the delay. The most terrible ideas at times crowded upon my distracted brain. Sometimes I imagined that the blow which Walter had received from Drayton was of a much more violent and serious nature than had been represented to me by my parents, and that he was now confined to his bed, and perhaps placed in a situation of the greatest danger. Then I feared that he had most probably demanded satisfaction of his guilty rival, and if so, what the consequences might be I shuddered to think upon. These conflicting thoughts bewildered and agonised my brain, and I gave vent to the grief and anxiety of my mind in the most mournful lamentations. I walked to the window of my chamber, and looked anxiously from it towards his dwelling; but I saw nothing of him, or anything to inspire me with hope, and my doubts and apprehensions increased to such a degree that I could scarcely contain myself. It must surely be something of a most important nature, I reflected, to prevent him from visiting our cottage as soon as possible, to receive the promised explanations from my father, and to have, if possible, an interview with me; and the longer I reflected the more I became lost and perplexed, and the more difficult did I find it to come to some satisfactory conclusion.

" The weather continued gloomy and cheerless, and it was evident from the appearance of the heavens that a storm

THE ATTACK OF THE PIRATES UPON THE BRIG.

was gathering; but I viewed it with indifference, for my mind was too busily occupied with my own wretched thoughts to suffer me to dwell upon anything else. There was one circumstance, however, which afforded some slight relief to my mind, and that was that Drayton did not visit the cottage, for I need not tell you how much I dreaded to meet him again, and to be compelled to listen to those odious vows in which he would be encouraged by my father.

"In this manner another hour passed away, and I still continued seated at the window, and with my eyes fixed upon the humble abode of him who was so dear to my heart, and of whose present sufferings I could form so adequate an idea. At length my attention was attracted to the shadow of an approaching form, which seemed to come from a different direction to the dwelling of Walter, and appeared to be advancing with a slow and measured step towards our cottage; but at present it was too far distant to enable me to distinguish

more than that it was the form of a man. I did not remove my eyes for an instant from it, and my heart throbbed with anxiety and suspense; but a very few minutes seemed to convince me that it was Walter, and you may very well imagine what was the agitation of my feelings. His eyes were cast to the ground, and it was quite evident from his whole demeanour the state of mind under which he was suffering, and which I could so well and so painfully imagine. I could have rushed from the cottage, and flying to his arms, have wept my sorrows upon his bosom; but I knew that my father would prevent that, and I therefore endeavoured to await with patience and fortitude the result of the interview which would doubtless shortly take place between us. Alas! what a torturing one would it be—what a severe and agonising trial to us both! It was not at all likely that all the arguments and remonstrances that Walter could make use of would be able to move my father from his stern determination, and therefore, what awaited us but the blackest despair? These thoughts passed rapidly in my mind as my lover approached the cottage with his eyes still bent upon the ground, and his mind evidently lost to everything but the agony of his own thoughts. When he had arrived at within a few yards of the cottage he suddenly paused, and I beheld him strike his forehead with his clenched fist, as if in the anguish of the bitterest despair, a feeling which I need not say I so fully participated in, and tears gushed to my eyes and almost blinded me. He suddenly raised his head and looked towards the cottage, and I then had a distinct view of his countenance, and could plainly see the paleness of his features, and the wild and melancholy expression of his eyes. Oh, what a tale of misery did they seem to tell, and how my heart palpitated with the violence of my emotions as I contemplated them. Again he moved towards the cottage, at which he quickly arrived, and was then hidden from my view.

"I now sank on my knees, and offered up my supplications to Heaven, at the same time I awaited with the most trembling suspense my meeting with my unfortunate lover. After this I opened the room door and walked gently on to the landing. I endeavoured to catch what was passing below. For a few minutes my wishes were not gratified; but at length the voice of Walter, in tones of the utmost melancholy and despair, and evidently making an earnest and pathetic appeal to my obdurate parent, reached my ears, and thrilled to my heart, though I could only catch a word here and there of what he said. A silence of a few minutes succeeded, when I overheard the following words from my father, addressed to the unhappy Walter—

"'You appeal to me in vain, Walter, for I am more than ever convinced of the prudence and propriety of that conduct which you so severely condemn as cruel and unjust. I must request that, for the present, you refrain from visiting the cottage, or throwing yourself in the way of Alice, and that for your own sake, as well as hers, you will endeavour to conquer the sentiments you now entertain towards her, and try to fix your affections on some other damsel who

may be equally worthy of you. But although I am compelled to disappoint your hopes, and you can never become the husband of my daughter, believe me, I shall ever be proud and happy to acknowledge you as a friend, and to do anything which may be in my power to serve you.'

"Oh, how every word of this cruel speech, in which the fate which too plainly awaited me was set forth, went to my heart, and how torturing were the emotions that agitated my bosom! But I could not hear what reply Walter made to it; and unable any longer to endure my suspense, I darted down the stairs in a state of excitement I cannot describe, I burst open the door, and with a wild cry of agony I rushed into the room, and into the arms of my lover. The scene which followed I must leave to your imagination; but never can I forget it, and even now it is as fresh and vivid in my memory as if it had occurred but yesterday. How did Walter and myself sob and weep upon each other's bosom, and what pathetic appeals did we make to my father, and implore him not to drive us both to a state of misery and despair which it was impossible that we could ever find strength sufficient to endure. It was all to no purpose, he remained inexorable, and at length, his patience being exhausted, he commanded Walter to leave the cottage, and not to venture to visit it again without his permission. This cruel mandate excited me to a perfect pitch of frenzy; I clung desperately to my lover, and by turns reproached and supplicated my obstinate and inflexible parent. But at length my feelings were quite overpowered by the intensity of my agony, and with a loud cry I sank insensible in Walter's arms."

———

CHAPTER XXI.

ALICE CONCLUDES HER HISTORY.—THE RIVALS.—THE FORCED MARRIAGE.—THE AWFUL SUICIDE IN THE CHUCH.—THE PIRATE.—THE MURDER.

"WHEN I recovered my senses," continued Alice, "I found myself alone in my chamber, and stretched upon the bed, and my brain was so bewildered and distracted, that for a few minutes I was unable to recal to my memory what had taken place; but when I did so, the state of my mind was of the most deplorable description that can well be imagined. It seemed evident that I had remained in a state of unconsciousness for some time, for it was now night, and the storm which had been threatening all day now raged violently. I arose hastily from the bed, and went to the door with the intention of listening to ascertain whether or not Walter had departed from the cottage; but you may guess, Mrs. Tiller, what my astonishment and alarm must have been when I found that it was fastened, and it was thus evident that my father had determined to prevent the possibility of my leaving the cottage, and thus seeking the presence of my lover, by making me a prisoner. My misery was now complete, and I wrung my hands in the bitterness and extreme anguish of my feelings.

"'Cruel, cruel parent!' I ejaculated, while sighs almost choked my utterance, 'how can you thus seem to delight to torture me? What have I ever done that you should punish me in this awful manner? Will nothing induce you to look with an eye of compassion and forbearance upon me? and are you determined to sacrifice me to your avarice, and the evil passions of that man who has gained such powerful and extraordinary influence over you? Most certainly will you sooner or later have cause to repent the course which you are at present pursuing, and most bitterly will your conscience upbraid you for the cruelty you have practised towards me. But were now is Walter? What must be the maddening torture of his feelings now he has heard the determination of my misguided father, and he knows that all our hopes are crushed and destroyed for ever, and that I am destined to become the wretched wife of that man who must possess the heart of a villain, or he could never have acted as he has done? And probably we have met for the last time, and what in the frenzy and wild despair of his feelings may not poor Walter be tempted to do? My heart sinks within me at the thought, and a hundred vultures seem to be gnawing at my brain! How can I ever support those accumulated miseries? I shall certainly go mad!'

"I could say no more, for the hysterical sobs that agitated my wretched bosom completely choked my utterance, and scalding tears chased each other rapidly down my cheeks. It was some time before I could at all tranquillise my feelings in the slightest degree, and then I again advanced to the door and listened attentively to ascertain what was passing below. All, however, was perfectly quiet in the cottage, and I was half inclined to think that my parents had retired to rest, for I could form no idea what the time was. In order, if possible, to try to divert my mind from the dismal thoughts that engrossed it, I once more seated myself by the window, but the scene on which my eyes rested was far from calculated to dissipate the melancholy of my feelings. It was a fearful night, and a more awful tempest which at that time battled in the heavens I had seldom before witnessed. Thunder, lightning, rain, lent their fury to add terrors to the scene; and the roaring of the ocean might be heard even above the voice of the storm. All was buried in the most impenetrable darkness, save when at intervals the fierce lightning darted across the sky, and for an instant illumined everything with a lurid and ghastly glare. But I gazed with perfect indifference at the raging storm, and at times I could almost wish that the lightning's flash would strike me a corpse, and thus put an end to my earthly miseries. I seemed attracted by some unaccountable spell to the window, and I could not remove myself from it, while a dismal foreboding took possession of my mind that something of an appalling nature was about to happen to me, and which strange feeling I found it utterly impossible to conquer.

"In this manner some time elapsed, and I heard the clock of a neighbouring church strike the hour of ten. My thoughts were still fixed on Walter, and I pictured to myself in the most painful and vivid colours the sufferings he must now be experiencing and those that were probably yet in store for him. It was in vain that I tried to obtain some relief and consolation; alas! there was none for me, and every moment which elapsed only served to make my situation appear the more hopeless and terrible. But why should I particularise thus? for certain I am how well you can imagine what the agony of my feelings must have been on that most trying occasion. What would poor Walter now do, banished as he was for ever from me, and with the horrible certainty of the revolting fate which was impending o'er me? I shuddered to think, and all kinds of fearful misgivings distracted my brain.

"The storm had now in some measure abated, but the thunder still roared, and the lightning vividly flashed at intervals. No one offered to approach my chamber, and from the silence which prevailed, I again imagined that my parents had retired to rest; but I could not think of doing so, for how could I expect to sleep with such a weight of insupportable care upon my mind? I remained at the window, and strained my eyes to penetrate through the darkness to endeavour to catch a glimpse of the dwelling of my unfortunate lover, which, I thought, would afford me a dismal sort of satisfaction; but it was only now and then that my wishes were gratified, and then only for an instant by the glare of the lightning, and the most torturing conjectures as to the probable situation in which he was placed continued to harass my mind. Perhaps he had never returned home after the painful interview he had had with my father, I reflected, and even now he might be wandering he knew or cared not whither, in all the horrors of the storm, and worked up to that pitch of frenzy which might lead him to the perpetration of some rash and awful deed! That thought caused me the greatest agony, but still I could not remove the painful impression from my mind. The storm now resumed all its former fury, and the lightning became more vivid and incessant, so that I had almost constantly a clear view of objects at a distance, and my attention was soon attracted to the form of a man who was advancing hastily towards the cottage, and who was habited, as near as I could distinguish, in the garb of a fisherman. My heart again beat violently against my side with some fearful and unaccountable foreboding, and I watched the stranger as narrowly as the flashes of lightning at intervals would permit

me; but I could soon perceive that it was not Walter, for the man was much taller than him, and the thought suddenly struck me that it might be Drayton, and I trembled as it occurred to me. But yet it was a strange hour for him to come to the cottage, I reflected, and I must, therefore, be mistaken. Still I could not remove my eyes from him, and the nearer he approached the more strongly did I suspect that it was indeed Drayton. A few minutes afterwards I saw the dark shadow of another man in the distance, who seemed to be cautiously following him; but he was too far off for me to distinguish him more particularly, and directly afterwards an interval of darkness hid them from my sight altogether, and the next instant the loud report of a pistol saluted my ears, and when the lightning again glared, neither of the men were to be seen; they had vanished as if by magic. A trembling sensation of horror came over me, and I gasped for breath; but still I was unable to move from the window, and as I gazed into the darkness without, I seemed to be completely rivetted to the spot.

"'Good God!' I exclaimed, 'what can be the meaning of all this? Murder, I fear, has been committed, but by whom?'

"The most dreadful thoughts crowded with astonishing rapidity on my brain, and I awaited in the greatest suspense until the painful mystery should haply be solved, though it did not seem very probable that I should learn the facts of the case. I was aroused from these reflections by hearing a confused noise from below, and then it appeared evident to me that my parents had not been to rest, as I had at first conjectured, and that the report of the gun or pistol had disturbed them. Directly afterwards I heard the cottage door opened, and my father issued from it, carrying a lantern in one hand and a gun in the other; and he directed his way towards the spot where I saw the strangers, and from whence the sound of the firearms seemed to proceed. My agitation and suspense now increased, and I knocked and kicked loudly at the door of my room, and called upon the name of my mother. In the space of a minute or two I heard her ascending the stairs, and the next moment she opened the door and entered the room.

" ' Oh, what is the meaning of this ?' I exclaimed; 'can you form any idea, mother ?'

" ' You, then, heard the report ?' she said. 'Your father has ventured forth to endeavour to ascertain the cause, and God grant that no harm has come to him; but I fear that murder has either been attempted or committed.'

" I shuddered, and again a most fearful foreboding came over me which I found it impossible to banish from my imagination. I related to my mother, in as few words as possible, what I had seen, and she listened to me with the most earnest attention and the deepest curiosity; and when I had concluded, she said—

" ' The description you give of one of those men, Alice, exactly corresponds with that of Richard Drayton; but Heaven forbid that any calamity should have befallen him, and I do not believe that he would have been out at such an hour of the night, and in such a furious tempest as that which has been for some hours raging.'

" ' And where is poor Walter ?' I interrogated with a deep sigh.

" ' At home, I should imagine,' replied my mother, 'for he left here almost immediately after you had fainted. But why do you ask that question ?'

" ' Because,' I faltered, and scarcely knowing what I said, for my brain was so bewildered and distracted—'because —but no, no; I know not what I say; heed me not.'

" ' Ah !' ejaculated my mother, 'a terrible thought strikes me. Should one of the men you saw indeed be Drayton, and any calamity has befallen him, on whom could suspicion so reasonably alight as Walter Seyton, considering the feelings of revenge which he, no doubt, entertains towards his rival ?'

" ' Oh, horror !' I gasped forth, 'forbear to give utterance to such dark and cruel surmises. Drayton has deeply, irreparably wronged him, and no wonder if he should feel towards him the most powerful and unconquerable animosity; but dare you for a moment imagine that Walter Seyton would ever become a murderer ? Oh, shame, shame, mother, to suffer such cruel and uncharitable

thoughts for a moment to enter your breast.'

" ' Heaven forbid that I should ever suspect any person wrongfully of so hideous a crime,' she returned, 'especially one whom I have ever respected so much as I have Walter Seyton; but he was in a state of the greatest excitement when he left our cottage after his interview with your father, and—'

" ' And can his excitement be wondered at, after the treatment he has received ?' I hastily interrupted, and my bosom swelled with mingled feelings of anguish, shame, fear, and indignation; 'even should he most severely resent the wrongs he has received from Drayton, could it be wondered at ? But to suppose him capable of such a desperate act as this is monstrous, and makes me shudder with horror while I think of it. Oh, God, most earnestly do I beseech you to watch over him, and to give him strength and fortitude to support the dreadful trials to which he is at present subjected, although they are, alas! almost too much for even the stoutest heart to endure with fortitude and resignation.'

" ' And most fervently and sincerely do I respond to that wish, my dear child,' remarked my mother; 'but pray endeavour to tranquillise your feelings, and to await patiently the result of this fearful adventure.'

" Before I could return any answer to this, still gazing eagerly and anxiously from the window, I beheld by the glare of the lightning two persons slowly approaching the cottage, in one of whom I recognised my father, who was with difficulty supporting another man, whom I concluded was the wounded stranger, and a more terrible feeling of apprehension than ever came over me. On seeing them my mother immediately rushed from the room, and in a state of agitation which I need not seek to describe, but which almost overpowered me, I followed her, and we made our way to the parlour of the cottage, which they had just entered, and my father was supporting the wounded man, who was groaning heavily, in a chair, and the expression of his features plainly showed the excitement under which he was labouring. Hastily I advanced towards the injured man, who was bleeding profusely, apparently from a wound inflicted in his side; but I uttered an exclamation of astonishment and horror when I saw that it was indeed Richard Drayton! The sound of my voice seemed to arouse him, and he raised his eyes towards me, and with a ghastly expression of countenance which I can never forget, he with difficulty faltered out—

"'Walter Seyton, the villain—the—the secret assassin, it is he who has done this!'

"I heard no more—my brain seemed to reel—the blood curdled in my veins, and with a frantic cry of despair and horror, I sunk insensible and inanimate in the arms of my mother.

"Fain would I pass over the horrors which it was my lot to endure after this fearful catastrophe, and the consummation of all my worst fears and surmises, for surely they were much more terrible than had often been the fate of any unfortunate being to experience. How long I remained in this state of unconsciousness I knew not, but it would indeed have been a mercy to me had I never recovered; but when I was restored to my senses I found myself in bed, and my mother anxiously watching over me, while the paleness of her features, and the melancholy expression of her eyes showed the anguish of her mind. The whole terrible truth rushed upon my memory like a thunderbolt, and in a voice half choked by the power of my emotion, I exclaimed—

"'Where is he? oh, where is the unfortunate Walter? It is not true that he has been guilty of this rash and fearful crime—oh, tell me that he has not, but that my senses have been labouring under some frightful delusion only. But Drayton, he is not dead, he——'

"'Be firm, my poor child,' interrupted my mother, in a voice of the deepest compassion and agitation; 'for you have much to endure, and it will require all your energy to do so. The unfortunate Richard Drayton has been removed to his own residence, and your father is now with him. He is severely, though, I trust, not mortally wounded; but Walter——"

"'Ah! what of him? For the love of Heaven do not keep me in suspense!'

"'It is, alas! too true, misguided, headstrong youth,' she returned, 'that

it was his hand which inflicted the injury, and has been the cause of so much misery to all who are connected with him, and of probable ruin to himself. He has fled, and no one knows what has become of him, and his parents, as it was very natural to expect, are in a state of mind bordering on distraction, and most sincerely do I feel for them.'

"'Great God of Heaven!' I cried, with a groan of the most intense and insupportable agony, 'this is too much! Oh, why did you ever suffer me to live to experience such accumulated and indescribable horrors as these? And you, my wretched and misguided father, have been the cause of all this! Walter, dear, dear, but unfortunate, ill-fated Walter! oh, why were you led into the perpetration of such a fatal deed? I shall go mad—I shall go mad! Heaven help me, or terminate at once my wretched existence.'

"Hysterical sobs now choked my further utterance, and overpowered by the intense misery of my feelings I again sank into a state of complete unconsciousness, and in which melancholy condition I remained for two or three days. Would to God that I had never been aroused from it; but the sufferings I had hitherto experienced were trifling compared with those that I was yet destined to undergo.

"When I again recovered, the state of my mind may easily be conjectured, and my mother tried in vain to tranquillise my feelings. I was unable to leave my bed, and my dreary hours were passed in the most dismal lamentations on the cruelty of my fate, and in the bitterest reproaches of my father, who I could not but look upon as the primary cause of all this horror and misery; but he still remained inexorable, and I could but too plainly see that this fearful event had but served to goad him on, and that should Drayton recover, which there was now every probability that he would, it was his firm resolve that I should be compelled to become his wife with as little delay as possible; and the bare idea of that was sufficient to excite my distracted brain to a pitch bordering upon frenzy. But, oh! what was the dreadful anxiety of mind I endured as to the fate which had befallen my lover? Was it not but too probable that in the horror of his despair, after the rash and fatal act which he had so unfortunately been tempted to commit, he had rushed upon some untimely fate, and that I should never behold him again or hear what had become of him? This idea was by far too reasonable for me easily to banish it from my mind, and the horror of my feelings every hour, every moment became the more insupportable. Oh, how bitterly did I regret that he should ever have permitted his feelings of revenge to so overpower him; and yet, taking all the painful circumstances of the case into consideration, was there not every excuse to be offered for him? And were his parents ignorant of what had become of him? I could not believe that he would ever abandon them without making them aware of whither he was gone, and what were his future intentions, and how great must be the anguish of mind they must be enduring, and what bitter cause had they to reproach and deprecate the cruel and unjust conduct of my father. How anxious was I to see them, that I might hear from them all the particulars, and to receive their advice and consolation; but I was well convinced that my father would prevent me from having any such an opportunity.

"In this deplorable manner several days passed away, and I was still too weak to leave my bed, and the terrible agony and excitement of my mind had suffered but little, if any abatement. My father but seldom visited me, and when he did so, his presence was painful to me, and I could not help reproaching him severely for the cruel wrongs that he had inflicted upon me and Walter, and the terrible misfortunes he had been the cause of bringing about. It was not often that he mentioned the name of Drayton, and whenever he did I could not help shuddering with horror and trembling with fear, and the most dismal forebodings; for it was but too evident that he was fully determined to sacrifice me to him, and such a fate was enough to make my heart sink within me with despair and disgust. I heard from my mother, however, that Drayton's wound had proved to be not so severe as it was first imagined to be, and that he was rapidly recovering. This I was glad to hear, for, had he died, how

much more terrible would have been the stigma which would have rested upon the character or the memory of poor Walter, if he no longer continued to exist? But could he have the daring and presumption to persevere in his odious addresses to me, especially after what had happened? Alas! I now knew his character too well to imagine that he would ever abandon his designs, and I saw at once that unless Providence should in some miraculous manner interpose to save me there was no hope, and that my doom would be inevitably sealed. This thought increased my agony tenfold, and naturally retarded my recovery, and, in fact, the blow was struck which must destroy my peace of mind for ever, and render me in future one of the most wretched of human beings in existence, an existence which I now heartily prayed to be brought to a termination. Nothing whatever had yet been heard of Walter, and my most terrible fears that he had rushed upon an untimely fate were all but confirmed. How was it possible that I could control the anguish of my feelings when those dreadful thoughts flashed upon my brain in the most overwhelming confusion, and at times I was perfectly delirious, and raved in the most fearful manner. My mother was constantly in attendance upon me, and did all that she could to appease the agony of my mind; but her efforts were almost fruitless, and I could see that she entertained the worst apprehensions as to what would be the result.

"At length I learned that Drayton had so far recovered as to be able to leave his chamber, and then my apprehensions increased, for I felt convinced that he would not long refrain from obtruding himself upon my presence, especially encouraged as he would sure to be by my father, and what could I expect but that they would put their designs against me into execution with as little delay as possible? I did not wish to be able to leave the room, for I knew that then I should be shortly disgusted with his presence, and how I could find strength to meet him I could not imagine, and I shrank from the task. But youth and a strong constitution at length overcame everything, in spite of my wishes to the contrary, and I was enabled to leave my chamber and to eet my father in the room below. He :ceived me with much apparent affec-on and sympathy; but I was over-helmed with emotion, and covering my ce with my hands, I could only give ent to my feelings by convulsive sobs and ars, to which he for a short time llowed me to give indulgence without ffering to interrupt me.

" 'My dear Alice,' he at length said, believe me, though you may at present iink to the contrary, that I sincerely ympathise with you, and deeply regret o see the heavy affliction of mind under vhich you labour; but you must exert ll your energies, and endeavour to rouse yourself from it, for of what avail is it giving way to this violence of grief? There is happiness yet in store for you, f you will not obstinately reject it, nd——'

" 'Oh, my father,' I ejaculated, fixing ipon him a look of the keenest reproach, ind my bosom swelling with rage and ndignation, 'and is it possible that, while you pretend to sympathise with me, you can talk thus? It is but a cruel mockery on the sufferings you have in-licted upon me already, and the misery and utter ruin into which you have plunged the unfortunate Walter.'

" 'Hold, Alice,' he returned, sternly, 'I cannot allow you to give utterance to language such as that which has just escaped your lips. Your forget the duty you owe to me by heaping upon me such reproaches. It is true that I have broken the promise I had made to Walter Seyton, and his recent outrage-ous and guilty conduct convinces me of the wisdom and propriety of my having done so.'

" 'Oh, upbraid him not,' I cried, 'for although I deeply regret the rash act of which he has been guilty, have not you and Drayton got yourselves alone to blame? Was there not every allowance to be made for the excitement of the feelings under which he naturally la-boured, when he found all his fondest hopes annihilated at one feel swoop, and when Drayton added insult to the many wrongs which he had inflicted on him?'

" 'And were those sufficient,' de-manded my father, sternly, 'to induce him to become the cold-blooded and midnight assassin?'

"'Fobear—forbear!' I cried, with a shudder of horror, 'call not the deeply-injured and ill-fated Walter by such fearful names as those, for how little does he deserve them. Oh, my father, could you but form anything like an adequate idea of the agony of mind I am enduring, if you have not become totally insensible to every proper feeling, you would pity me, and act with more for-bearance. Alas! how do I shudder with horror and despair when I think of the dreadful fate which has in all probability befallen him, and how happy we might both of us now have been had Richard Drayton never have entered this neigh-bourhood, and you had fulfilled that promise which you had so solemnly made to us, and which was ratified by Heaven. Oh, my father, if you still remain obdurate, what bitter cause will you not have to repent it when it is too late.'

"'Psha! girl,' he replied, impa-tiently, 'you talk erroneously, and tor-ture yourself to no purpose. Richard Drayton is every way worthy of you, and so, I am convinced, you will ultimately be compelled to acknowledge, notwith-standing the many and powerful pre-judices that you now entertain against him. As for Walter Seyton, you must banish him from your memory altogether, for it is not at all probable that you will ever behold him again, and if you should, as the bride of his more deserving rival, you can never hope to become his.'

" 'As the wife of Drayton?' I re-peated, and clasping my hands vehe-mently together, in the anguish and excitement of my emotions—'oh, never! Sooner, much sooner would I die the most horrible of deaths than to be con-signed to so revolting a fate as that? But is it possible that neither my tears nor entreaties can move you to relent? Have you become so entirely destitute of feeling as to sacrifice me to that man on whom I cannot now look upon with common respect, much more love? The bare idea is monstrous, and will reflect everlasting shame upon your memory. Reflect then seriously, I implore you, before you do anything so cruel and so unnatural. Suffer me to remain as I am, rather than force me to become the wretched wife of Richard Drayton.'

" ' I have already reflected maturely upon the important subject, Alice,' he

WALTER'S REMORSE ON THE REJECTION OF HIS SUIT.

replied, 'and I see nothing whatever to induce me to alter the determination I have come to; nor will all the arguments that you can make use of persuade me to do so.'

"'Then are my worst fears confirmed,' I returned, 'and you discard me entirely from your heart. Oh, God! how torturing and insupportable is this; and what have I ever done to deserve this severity? It has been my constant study to obey your will, and to convince you of my affection and reverence; and this is the return I get for it! Alas—alas! you try my fortitude too far, and sooner or later you must most deeply regret the sufferings you have inflicted upon me. But Drayton, will he have the boldness to persist in his suit when he knows how hateful it is to me? Oh, no, surely, if he possesses the least spark of manly feeling in his breast he will not.'

"'I should despise him if I thought

he could ever act in the manner which you say,' replied my father; 'but I know full well that he will not, and you will act more wisely if you do not give encouragement to any such hopes. It is fortunate that the injury which he received from the hands of Walter in so cowardly a manner was not so serious as we at first imagined ; he has now all but recovered, and I would therefore have you prepare yourself to meet him, Alice, and that, too, in a very different manner to what you have heretofore done.'

" 'Alas !' I sighed, 'how is it at all possible that I can do so? Spare me this dreadful trial, father, and let not my ears be again shocked and insulted by his odious and disgusting vows.'

" 'Nay, Alice,' he returned, 'you talk ridiculously, and you should by this time be convinced that all you can say can make no impression whatever upon me. You are young and inexperienced in the world, and I should not be strictly performing my duty if I suffered you to follow the bent of your own inclinations entirely. But I have said enough to convince you, I should think, of the folly of your offering any obstinate resistance, which can have no other effect than that of precipitating your fate.'

" 'Then you have remorselessly and recklessly resolved on my destruction,' I ejaculated, 'and it is evident that you must have closed your heart against me altogether, and care not in future what becomes of me so that I am made to yield to your stern and inexorable will. Oh, cruel, cruel parent ! how bitterly must you have cause at some future period to repent of the course you are now pursuing, and which must cast such a heavy reproach upon your character, however different you may now affect to think.'

" 'You are a thoughtless, foolish girl,' he returned, 'and it is almost a waste of time for me to argue with you. However, get you gone to your chamber, for I have nothing more to say to you at present. In a day or two Drayton will probably be able to revisit the cottage, and then you must be prepared to meet him in a far different manner to that which you have hitherto done, if you would not incur my utmost wrath and indignation.'

" 'Heaven help me !' I sighed, 'for this is a trial which it requires the utmost courage to endure, and one to which I ought never to have been subjected.'

" 'Begone !' commanded my father, sternly and abruptly, 'and learn to conquer the childish feelings that now hold possession of your breast. You will find that if you become dutiful and submissive to my will there is no indulgence which you shall not receive at my hands, but if you act to the contrary you must take the consequences, and will have no one to blame but yourself.'

" 'And this is my father who can talk thus !' I said, and my looks were fully expressive of the mingled and violent emotions that occupied my mind; 'but I will not remonstrate or expostulate, but only trust that the Almighty will bring you to a full sense of the injustice of your conduct, and that you will still alter your determination, notwithstanding the firmness to adhere to it which you now evince. God forgive you for the misery which you have already caused, and save me from that fate with which I am now threatened.'

" My father did not return any answer to this, but it was evident that he was somewhat confused and abashed by my observations, and impatiently motioning me to retire, I did so, and again seeking my solitary room, I resigned myself to all the anguish of the most dismal reflection.

" If my misery had been great before, it was now all but complete, and it was all to no purpose that I tried to gain some relief from it. The cruel observations of my father, and the utter indifference which he had shown to the anguish of my feelings, thoroughly convinced me that there was nothing to hope from his forbearance, and these recollections were stamped upon my memory in characters which nothing could ever obliterate, and which, the longer I reflected, became the more torturing. Never could I have imagined him capable of such cruelty and injustice, and it was impossible that I could otherwise than attribute his conduct to motives of avarice, after what he said to me on a former occasion.

" 'And he would sell me to one who cannot possibly have any sincere regard for me, or he would never consent to accept me on any such terms,' I ejaculated, in the most melancholy accents, and as I paced my room with disordered steps, and unable to control my feelings within the bounds of reason—' he can so close his heart against me as to force me to the altar with one whose conduct has rendered him so truly hateful to me, and towards whom it is impossible that I can ever perform the duty of a wife. A wife, coupled with the name of Drayton—what horrible thoughts does it excite within my breast! But shall such indeed be my fate?—and what reason have I to suppose that it will not? It is not possible that I can continue to live to endure such unexampled misery, and will not my death then be on the head of my inexorable parent? It will, indeed, and I shudder to think what must be the dreadful remorse of feelings he will then have to endure. Oh, would that he might be awakened to reason, and to a knowledge of the fearful precipice, on the very brink of which he now stands, before it is too late; but alas! I fear that such is the powerful influence which Drayton has obtained over him that he will not, and that he is, therefore, working the way for his own destruction as well as that of his unhappy child. And how can I ever find courage sufficient to meet Drayton, after the dreadful occurrence which has so recently taken place, and convinced, as I am, of the guilty thoughts he entertains towards me, and his deadly hatred of the unhappy Walter? I tremble to anticipate it, and would to Heaven that it could be avoided, but I know too well that it cannot, and that I must prepare to have my feelings outraged and insulted by the hateful and disgusting vows in which he is so warmly encouraged by my father. But I will persevere, and endeavour to meet him with firmness and determination, and not to suffer for one moment any idea to enter his mind that I feel towards him any other sentiments than those of abhorrence and horror. Alas! dear Walter, what has become of you? Are you still living or dead? and why did you suffer your feelings of resentment to gain the upper hand of you, as to urge you into the perpetration of a crime which has cast a foul stigma on your hitherto un-

sullied name, and which must be the cause of adding so greatly to your misery? Oh, it was a most unfortunate, a melancholy affair; but surely you had had sufficient to excite you to it, and, after all, you were not so much to blame. I shall no more behold you, I am convinced of that, and that thought is of itself enough to drive me to madness.'

"I ceased, for my emotions became too powerful for utterance, and I could only give vent to them by sobs and tears. But I should become tedious were I to particularise all the various reflections that crossed my mind; let it suffice to state that they were of the most poignant description, and that I could not find the least ray of consolation. My mother did not offer to visit me very often, for my sufferings were greater than she seemed to have strength of mind sufficient to contemplate; nor could she venture to condemn the conduct of my father, and to encourage me to a firm resistance to his will, lest she should incur his wrath, of which she had ever stood in the greatest dread, and showed as much submission to him as a child. However, I did not regret her absence, for I had too much to occupy my own mind not to render me anxious to be alone, and I awaited the result of my fate in a state of the most trembling anxiety and impatience, and that crisis was rapidly approaching.

"Two days after the interview between my father and myself which I have just described, being seated at the window, wrapped in deep meditation, and my eyes vacantly wandering to the scenery beyond, I was suddenly startled from my lethargy by beholding Drayton approaching towards the cottage slowly, and appearing still to be very weak and ill. He raised his eyes towards the window at which I was seated; but I hastily withdrew myself, and the fear and agitation that came over me at the sight of him were so great, that it was not without difficulty I could save myself from fainting. I clasped my hands together and offered up a fervent prayer to Heaven for its protection, and then I endeavoured to await the issue with fortitude, but I only succeeded indifferently. In this painful state of suspense I was kept for about half an hour, and I began to hope that

Drayton would leave the cottage without desiring to have an interview with me for the present; but at length that idea was banished from my mind when heard footsteps ascending the stairs, and my room door being opened, my mother entered.

" 'Oh, my mother,' I exclaimed, 'he has come, then, and I shall once more be exposed to his insults; but does he desire to see me?'

" ' He does, my child,' she answered, 'and your father has sent me for you. But calm the agitation of your feelings, for, depend upon it, notwithstanding what has occurred, Richard Drayton will treat you with every attention and respect.'

" 'It would only be a waste of time, and I should exhaust your patience,' continued Alice, 'where I to enlarge upon the violent struggle I had with my feelings before I could muster sufficient fortitude to meet the man whom I so much dreaded; but at length I managed to acquire much more firmness than might have been expected under the circumstances, and, in obedience to the commands of my father, I repaired to the room in which he and Drayton were anxiously awaiting me. The latter was seated in a remote corner of the room on my entrance, and I did not at first observe him; but my father having motioned my mother to leave the room, which she obeyed directly, Drayton came forward with a hesitating step, and a pale and abashed expression of countenance, and advancing towards me, introduced by my father, he bowed to me with an assumption of the most profound respect and admiration. My heart palpitated violently against my side—I averted my looks from him with a sensation of the most unconquerable disgust, and I trembled with apprehension to know myself in the presence of the man who had already been the cause of so much misery to me, and from whom I had every reason to fear so much. Venturing to raise my eyes towards the countenance of my father, I perceived that he was eyeing me narrowly, and that a frown of displeasure was upon his brow; but I was fully prepared for the storm which I felt convinced was about to burst upon my devoted head, and I endeavoured to arouse myself in order that I might meet it with becoming firmness and resistance. He could, no doubt, easily read the thoughts which were passing in my mind; and as he had determined upon the course which he should pursue, he probably in his heart treated my opposition as a matter of course, and with perfect indifference; but on Drayton it doubtless had an effect which was anything but gratifying to his feelings, though he exerted himself to the utmost to conceal them. A silence of two or three minutes ensued, for neither my father nor Drayton seemed to know exactly how to open the painful business, and during this brief interval I had sufficiently composed and collected myself to bear with patience and fortitude that to which I was fully aware I was about to be subjected. But I was not much longer kept in this state of painful suspense, for my father, taking my hand, said—

" 'My dear Alice, I need not assure you of the sincere gratification it affords me to introduce Mr. Drayton again to you, after the great danger from which he has so providentially recovered, and I trust that you feel the same pleasure, and will receive him accordingly. But I will leave you to yourselves for a short time, and—'

" ' Oh, my father,' I hastily interrupted, and at the same time looking up in his face with an expression of fear and supplication, 'I implore you to remain, and not to leave me in so embarrassing and painful a situation. Surely there is nothing which Mr. Drayton can have to say to me which should not be spoken in your presence.'

" 'Nay, Alice,' he returned, again frowning, and with a look which convinced me, if I could even before have entertained any doubt upon the subject, that his mind was made up, and that I had nothing whatever to hope from his forbearance—'nay, Alice, you will do well to remember what I have said to you, and to act accordingly. You know the consequences if you disobey my injunctions.' And whispering some words in the ear of Drayton, who nodded significantly, he abruptly quitted the room, and I was left alone with my persecutor. Again a trembling sensation came over me, and my heart sunk within me; I staggered to a chair, and covering my face with my hands, awaited with the greatest trepidation and anxiety of mind for Drayton to begin, never for a moment during that torturing interval venturing to raise my eyes towards him, and he seeming not less confused, and at a loss how to commence. At length he approached close to me and took my hand, which made me start and shudder as if some venomous reptile had stung me, and the most insupportable feelings of disgust nearly overwhelmed me.

" 'Beauteous Alice,' he ejaculated in a voice of mingled tenderness and reproach, 'and is this the reception I meet with from you after what I have suffered, and the danger from which I have so narrowly escaped for your sake? Surely I am not worthy of such cold and disdainful treatment as this. What, not a single word? This is, indeed, most cruel.'

" 'Mr. Drayton,' I replied, mustering up all my firmness and determination for the occasion, 'I know not what answer to your observations you have a right to expect from me. If I were to say that I do not most painfully regret the dreadful and unfortunate circumstance which has taken place, and which has brought such irremediable misery upon myself and one who is far more precious to me than mine own existence, I should tell an untruth; but as regards yourself, candour and justice compel me to declare that, for whatever inconvenience or suffering to which you may have been put, you have yourself alone to blame.'

" 'Ah!' he exclaimed, passionately, 'and am I then so detestible in your eyes that you can approve of a monstrous and cowardly outrage which might have cost me my life, and which would have made Walter Seyton, he whom in your innocence and inexperience of mankind you foolishly believe to be all perfection, a murderer?'

" 'Hold, sir!' I ejaculated, rising from my chair, and fixing upon him a look of the most ineffable scorn and indignation, 'dare you seek to stigmatize the unsullied name of the man you have so cruelly wronged by such a foul epithet? Has not your conduct been base and dishonourable in the extreme, and think you that I can ever view the author of so much misery—the destroyer of my hopes,

with any other feelings than those of contempt, if not actual abhorrence? Leave me, sir, for your observations shock me, and I shudder in your presence.'

" He bit is lips as I thus spoke, and I could well perceive the feelings of rage and mortified pride that filled his bosom; but I beheld it all unmoved, for I had now called all my energies into action, and was determined to resist his hateful importunities to the utmost of my power.

" 'Beauteous Alice,' he at length said, assuming as much calmness and forbearance as he could; 'why apply such harsh and cruel observations to me? Indeed, much as you may at present be prejudiced against my character, I deserve them not. Leave you, and in this state of mind? Oh, that is impossible; and I do not fear that before I go I shall be able to move you in my favour, and to convince you that I am not the unworthy and contemptible being you now suppose me to be.'

" 'Presumptuous man, forbear!' I exclaimed. 'If you would indeed convince me that you are not entirely destitute of every proper feeling, you will no longer insult my ears by language as disgusting as it is revolting to me.'

" 'Oh, Alice,' said the hypocrite, sinking upon one knee, and fixing upon me a look of the most tender persuasion, which, of course, was intended to have the most powerful effect upon me, 'how is it possible that I can leave you thus, and without revealing to you the fond thoughts and wishes that have so long occupied my mind? I love you, Alice, I repeat, I love you to distraction, and on you alone my future happiness depends; from the first moment I beheld you my heart was yours, and while the purple current of life continues to circulate through my veins, that passion must remain the same; no other woman can ever supplant you in my affections, and without you, existence can no longer be tolerable. It is true that I knew your affections were placed upon another, but still I found it impossible to abandon myself to despair; I could not remove your fair image from my heart, or turn my thoughts to another woman. Divest your mind, I implore you, of the false prejudice you now unfortunately entertain against me —bury the past in oblivion—view my character in its proper light, and I do not doubt that——'

"'Hold!' I interrupted, 'bold and reckless man, from whom I have to date all my misfortunes and those of the ill-fated, the deeply injured Walter—I cannot allow you to proceed further, and I wonder that shame and remorse do not tie your tongue, and prevent you from doing so. Think you that one who has acted in the base and dishonourable manner which you have done can ever make any favourable impression on my heart? Oh, the bare idea is most revolting, and the very blood curdles in my veins with indignation as it occurs to me. Are you not the destroyer of Walter Seyton, he to whom I was solemnly betrothed, and dare you suppose that I can ever discard him from my heart and replace him by you? Oh, I should indeed be unworthy of the name of woman if I could so debase myself. But rest assured that you can never now possess the esteem, much more the love of Alice Beresford.'

"'This disdainful rejection of my vows is almost unbearable!' he returned rising from his knees, and unable to conceal his wrath; 'but you will find it necessary to conquer this obstinate spirit, which can only be productive of the most painful consequences to you. Your father approves of and sanctions my love, and surely you will not venture to oppose his will.'

"'Alas!' I returned, 'how harsh and unjust is my misguided parent acting; but even though he may compel me to become your wife, (and the thought excites feelings of the greatest horror within my breast) you can never, oh! never possess my heart, and the cruel sacrifice will but serve to hasten me to a premature grave, for life will then have become hateful and insupportable to me.'

"'Oh, why will you thus torture yourself, Alice,' he said, 'when there is no necessity for it? What is there so hateful in me that you should look upon a union with me with such horror and disgust? My whole study shall be to contribute to your happiness, and there shall not be a wish that you can entertain which shall remain ungratified. What could Walter Seyton do more? What——'

"'Mention not his name,' I indignantly interrupted, 'for have you not proved yourself to be his bitterest, his most cowardly enemy; and are you not the man who has destroyed his happiness, and annihilated all his hopes for ever? But I degrade myself by thus condescending to argue with one whom I am convinced is destitute of every proper feeling, and whose conduct, I am satisfied, is dictated by the basest of motives.'

"'These are harsh and uncharitable words, Alice,' he said, endeavouring to conceal his chagrin, but with little success; 'however, I know myself to be unworthy of them, and, therefore, heed them not. A short time will, I trust, convince you of this, and you will yet view me as I deserve, and divest your mind of the prejudices which at present occupy it.'

"'No,' I ejaculated, 'that can never be, unless you abandon the unnatural hopes and designs you now encourage, and endeavour to make me some atonement for the miseries and the injuries you have caused me. Oh, Mr. Drayton, if you have but one spark of humanity left within your breast, you will cease this cruel persecution of me, and no more insult and torture me by those addresses which can never be anything but most odious and disgusting to me.'

"He folded his arms across his chest as I thus spoke, and took two or three hasty strides across the room, evidently in a state of the greatest excitement, and at a loss what answer to make; then he suddenly returned to me, and endeavouring once more to take my hand, which, however, I hastily withdrew from him, he said—

"'Rash and obstinate girl, will nothing whatever arouse you to a conviction of the folly of your conduct? Am I not, at any rate, deserving of more respect than this? But in spite of all you may say I cannot abandon my suit; it is impossible that the love which I now entertain towards you can ever suffer any abatement, and while I have the sanction and the approbation of your father I will not despair.'

"'Cruel man!' I returned with a look of the bitterest reproach, 'then it is evident that you are perfectly indifferent to my happiness, and that you care not what misery you inflict upon me so that you obtain the gratification of your guilty wishes! Oh, reflect and forbear—consider the wrongs you have already done, and endeavour by repentance to obtain forgiveness.'

"'Repent?' he repeated; 'what have I to repent of? Is it, then, a crime to love one so sincerely as I do you?'

"'Yes,' I hastily replied 'when you know full well that that heart which you seek to obtain possession of is already devoted to another—nay, more, that I was solemnly betrothed to him, and, but for you, nothing would have occurred to prevent the consummation of our wishes. Oh, Drayton, how mean, how despicable, how dishonourable is the part you have acted, and yet now, with an effrontery which is quite unpardonable, you seek to justify your conduct! But leave me, sir, and, at any rate, show that you have some little regard for my feelings, and the delicate and painful situation in which I am placed.'

"'No, Alice,' he answered, 'it is impossible for me to leave you thus; my fate is in your hands, the love I bear you can never decay, and at least let me hear you declare that I may not abandon every hope.'

"'Presumptuous idea!' I cried, and the crimson blushes of shame and offended pride glowed in my cheeks; 'what a hypocrite I must be to hold out to you any such fallacious ideas. No, Drayton, you have heard my candid sentiments, and my fixed determination, and not all the arguments or persuasions that you can make use of can move me from it; why, then, persist in that which only reflects the utmost discredit upon you, and which can but torture me?'

"'By Heaven!' he exclaimed, passionately, 'this scorn is insupportable, and my patience is completely exhausted. Alice, you must, you shall become mine, and, therefore, all your obstinate resistance is in vain, and does but serve to increase the ardour of my passion. Your parents encourage my addresses, and, therefore, why should I abandon my wishes? It shall not be; I should despise myself as a weak idiot if I could do so, and by this fond embrace—this

kiss of rapture, do I pledge myself to the solemn fulfilment of my words.'

"'Unhand me, ruffian!' I exclaimed, as he threw his arms around my waist, and endeavoured to put his revolting threats into execution; 'dare you thus insult me beneath the very roof of my parents? Oh, hold—hold! or even defenceless woman as I am, you may have reason to repent of this monstrous outrage.'

"But he heeded not my remonstrances and reproaches; in vain I struggled to release myself, and again and again he polluted my lips with his kisses. Filled with disgust, indignation, and terror, I screamed aloud, and it was not until my father hastily entered the room that he release me, and I staggered, almost fainting, to his arms.

"How now, Alice?' he demanded, 'what is the meaning of all this uproar?'

"'Oh, my father!' I gasped forth, in reply, 'and can you possibly sanction so brutal an outrage as that which has been committed against me by this man?'

"'Pardon me, Mr. Beresford,' said Drayton, 'I may have been wrong, but Heaven knows it was farthest from my thoughts to wound or insult the feelings of your daughter. But the scorn with which she received my addresses, and the reproaches and bitter invectives that she lavished upon me, naturally excited me, and probably led me into excesses I should otherwise not have thought of. I——'

"'There needs no apology, Mr. Drayton,' interrupted my father, 'for I am fully aware that you could do nothing which you should be ashamed to acknowledge. Alice, you have disobeyed my injunctions, and if you persist in such conduct, you cannot but excite my greatest resentment.'

"'Oh, father,' I sobbed, 'it is impossible that you can talk thus upon a subject in which my happiness is so deeply involved. Oh, do not, I beseech you, deny me your pity and forbearance. Oh, how shamefully have I been insulted by this man, and——'

"'I declare again, most solemnly,' interrupted Drayton, 'that I would sooner perish than offer the least insult to your daughter, Mr. Beresford, for too powerful is the love I bear her to suffer me to do so.'

" 'I believe you, Drayton,' replied my father, ' and trust that you will excuse the rash and obstinate conduct of this foolish girl. Calm reflection will teach her better, and in the meantime it may be satisfactory for you to know that the promises I have made to you shall be fulfilled to the very letter.'

" 'And can it be my parent who talks thus?' I cried, reproachfully. 'Oh, how cruel, how unnatural is this! Alas—alas! what will become of me? Father, think upon what you would do, and abandon your harsh and unjust designs ere it is too late, and you shall have bitter cause to regret the manner in which you will have sacrificed the happiness of that poor child who has ever behaved towards you with such duty and affection. You would not have me act the part of a hypocrite, I am sure you would not; and therefore do I repeat, and in his presence, that Mr. Drayton can never possess my love, and if he persists in his present conduct it is impossible that he can ever excite in my breast any other feelings than those of disgust and abhorrence.'

" Drayton bit his lips, and I could perceive that the rage and chagrin of my father was equal to his own, and that it was not without the greatest difficulty he could prevent them from bursting forth in the most unmeasured terms.

" 'Hold! bold and obdurate girl,' he at last exclaimed, 'or fear the consequences. But heed not what she says, Mr. Drayton, for we will soon learn the way of conquering her present feelings, and of making her yield to our will. You have nothing to fear, since you may depend upon me. Retire to your room, Alice, and learn obedience to my wishes.'

" I was indeed most ready and anxious to obey his commands, and to be left to the indulgence of my own sorrows, for how hateful was the presence of Drayton to me. Fixing upon my inexorable parent a look which it was impossible he could misunderstand, but which I was too well convinced would fail to make any favourable impression upon him, I was about to leave the room, without venturing to say a word, when Drayton advanced boldly towards me, and, encouraged by the presence of my father, taking my hand in his, he said—

" 'And will the beauteous Alice leave me thus, without saying one word of kindness at parting? Will she not give me at least some reason to hope that she will in time endeavour to view me with the same ardent and sincere sentiments of affection which I now entertain towards her, and which nothing can ever eradicate from my bosom?'

" 'Unhand me, Mr. Drayton,' I replied, scornfully and indignantly. 'You have heard my decision, and nothing whatever can alter it. At any rate, the system of unmanly persecution which you at present pursue towards me is not at all calculated to do so.'

" 'Beware, Alice,' said my father, sternly, 'for language such as this cannot be productive of any good to you. But it is useless to argue with her just now, Mr. Drayton. I must have some private conversation with her, and when next you meet I trust you will find her in a far different state of mind to what she is at present. Retire, Alice, and prepare to see me anon.'

" I needed no second command, and Drayton having raised my hand to his lips, no longer sought to detain me, and hastening from the room as fast as my trembling limbs would permit me, I left my father and him alone. When I had got into my own room I threw myself in a chair, and burying my face in my hands, I burst into a violent paroxysm of tears, which greatly relieved my overcharged bosom. But you will readily be able to conjecture what were the powerful emotions that agitated my breast when I reflected on what had taken place at the interview, and contemplated the fate which seemed to be too inevitably awaiting me. But the inexorable conduct of my father filled my bosom with the most unutterable anguish and despair, and it was in vain that for some time after I had been suffered to retire that I could at all tranquillise my feelings. It was evident that such was the fatal influence which Drayton had obtained over my father, that he could persuade him as he thought proper, and that any opposition offered on my part would be entirely fruitless; and that, consequently, there was nothing left for me to do than to look forward in the most fearful anticipation to the worst; and this, coupled with the awful mystery

DRAYTON ENCOURAGED IN HIS IMPORTUNITIES BY ALICE'S FATHER.

in which the fate of poor Walter was enveloped, was sufficient to drive me to distraction. In vain did I try to conjecture what had become of him, and the most frightful ideas continued to haunt and to torture my imagination, and from which I could gain no relief. It seemed but too probable that we should never behold each other again; I believed that he was already no more, and it was a wonder, with all those fearful thoughts racking my brain, how I could retain my senses, or that I could at all survive it. How fervently did I offer up my prayers to Heaven to avert that which I dreaded to take place, and the insupportable and intense agony of my feelings increased every moment. Most heartily did I wish that I were dead, for how horrible was the fate to which my father seemed resolved to consign me, and from which there appeared not the least chance of escaping; and thus in the greatest misery did I pass upwards of an hour after I had quitted the presence of my father and Drayton, and no ne offered to intrude upon me—a circumstance which I did not at all regret, as I was thus left to the uninterrupted indulgence of my own reflections, and was in no disposition to converse with any one. At length, hearing the outer door of the cottage close, I went to the window, and I then beheld Drayton issue forth, and make his way to his own dwelling. This afforded me considerable satisfaction, which, however was not doomed to last long, for my mother entered my room directly afterwards with a message from my father to attend him immediately, and I well knew what I had to expect from that interview. My mother, however, endeavoured to console and encourage me, and at length I followed her down below to the room in which my father was seated, and who received me with a stern expression of countenance, for which, however, I was fully prepared. It is needless for me to relate what took place at that meeting; it is sufficient to say that my father remained invulnerable, and severely censured me for the manner in which I had behaved towards Drayton, whom he represented as a very paragon of perfection, and again and again repeated his determination to compel me, in spite of whatever the consequences might be, to become his wife. All my prayers, my tears and entreaties were lost upon him, and I returned to my chamber in a state of mind which any language of mine must fail to give an adequate idea of. Such was the effect which these painful trials had upon my health, that I was again confined to my bed, and for a few days I was in a state of complete delirium; but even all this, and the fatal consequences which it seemed too probable would follow his obstinacy, it failed to move my father to relent, and it seemed as if he had banished every proper feeling from his breast. I will, however, pass hastily over this part of my narrative, and come as speedily as possible to the more dismal and fatal events that were in store for me. It was, as I said before, several days before I was again able to leave my bed, and then a most extraordinary and fearful change had come over me, and which I scarcely know how to describe. A sort of a pathetic feeling had taken possession of my faculties, and despair had obtained

such a powerful ascendancy over me that I was quite lost and insensible, and perfectly indifferent as to what might become of me. It appeared evident to me that Walter was no more, and I flattered myself with the melancholy hope that I was soon destined to join him, so I cared but little what it might be my fate to suffer while I remained in this world. I frequently saw Drayton, who urged his suit with all the energy he was master of, backed by the arguments and persuasions of my father, and I no longer offered any resistance, but resigned myself passively to their will; so that they flattered themselves with the idea that they had at length triumphed over all my scruples, and treated me with every kindness and indulgence. I must have been mad; but certainly I seemed to walked about constantly in a kind of waking dream, and from which nothing appeared likely at all to arouse me. But frequently, when I was alone, I had my intervals of consciousness, and how dreadful was the agony I then endured, and how many were the tears I shed, as I contemplated the awful and revolting fate which inevitably awaited me, and which I could then too plainly see I had no possible means of averting. How many and how fervent were the prayers that I offered up to the memory of my beloved Walter, and how solemnly did I invoke his spirit to intercede with the Almighty in my behalf. But these moments of reason were only brief, and I again relapsed into that singular state of apathy which I have before described, and I was almost unconscious of what was passing around me.

"At length the day was fixed for my union with the hated Drayton, and I looked forward to it with the same indifference and apparent resignation which I had lately evinced, and Drayton seemed to be in ecstasies at the idea of his approaching triumph, and never for a moment appeared to suspect the real feelings towards him that occupied my mind. The parents of Walter had suddenly quitted the neighbourhood, and no one knew what had become of them; and in one sense of the word I was not sorry for it, for how great must have been the anguish of their feelings had they been aware of my approaching nuptials with the destroyer of their son, and how bitterly must they have reproached me for my imagined infidelity. Drayton had been making great preparations for the day which was to seal my fate, and at length that fatal day arrived ; and as if as a forewarning of the awful events that were about to take place, the morning set in dark and tempestuous, and all around presented the most dismal aspect. But, strange to say, I remained in the same state of indifference, and received the attentions of Drayton and my father in passive silence. In fact, at times I could not persuade myself that what was passing around me was real, but imagined that I was under the influence of some remarkable dream ; and when the procession moved towards the church, I walked with a steady and composed air, and my eyes were fixed on vacancy. Most of the neighbours had assembled in the church, and they seemed to watch the proceedings with the deepest interest, and I have no doubt many of them read the real feelings that were passing in my mind at the time, and deeply sympathised in the fate to which I was about to be consigned. We stood before the altar—the solemn ceremony commenced—every eye was fixed upon me with the most profound attention, but still not the least change took place in my demeanour, and I stood as inanimate as a statue, with my eyes fixed solemnly and steadfastly on the holy man who officiated in the performance of the sacred rites, and almost unconscious as to where I was, or what was taking place ; in fact, the depth of my despair might be said to have completely stupified my senses, and it was actually monstrous for all the parties concerned to sacrifice me under such circumstances. No doubt, however, that Drayton and my parents attributed my conduct to far different motives, and flattered themselves with the idea that they had at length succeeded in conquering my scruples and the repugnance I had evinced and felt to a union with such a man as Drayton, and that I was at last resigned to my fate. Alas! what a wrong and unreasonable, as well as ungenerous estimate must they have formed of my real character, if they could do so! Little did they imagine that my heart was breaking while I

seemed so perfectly cold and indifferent to what was taking place.

" 'The fatal ceremony was completed —I was the wife of the hated Drayton, and my parents were about to congratulate and embrace me, when suddenly a confused noise was heard from the farther end of the sacred building, and all eyes were instantly directed towards the spot from whence it proceeded, and an exclamation of astonishment and alarm burst simultaneously from the lips of the persons assembled, who separated on both sides, as if to make way for the approach of some one. I also gazed vacantly and in stupified amazement in the same direction to which all eyes were turned. The report of a pistol was now heard, and Drayton staggered back a few paces, though it was evident he had escaped the injury which was, no doubt, intended for him ; the next moment, Walter, pale, wild, and distracted, and with an exclamation which even after the lapse of so many years still seems to ring in my ears, rushed up to the altar, and confronted me and Drayton and my parents! I uttered a loud shriek, but still my senses left me not. Ah! no ; it was cruelly destined that I should be a witness of the awful and tragic scene which followed ; and all those who were present were so completely taken by surprise and consternation at the unexpected occurrence, that they had not the least power to interfere. But one fearful interval of a moment followed, during which the wretched and ill-fated Walter fixed his hollow and blood-shot eyes upon my countenance with a mingled expression of pity and reproach, and then, in accents which were scarcely earthly, so wild was their tone, he exclaimed—

" 'The work of villany, then, is accomplished, and the last fearful moment has arrived. Mr. Beresford, oh! can you exult at the cruel work of your hands? And you, Alice, oh, God!— But no, I will not reproach you, my still beloved one. Richard Drayton, traitor, villain! think you that you will thus be allowed to triumph, and to laugh at the misery and desolation you have caused? No, by all my hopes hereafter you shall not! Revenge, or, rather, a just retribution for such unexampled treachery, is still mine, and thus hypocrite, unmanly miscreant, do I wreak it upon you! Die, wretch, and—'

"As he thus spoke he drew a knife from his pocket and aimed a deadly blow at Drayton, which he, however, avoided, and two or three of the persons present were about to seize upon Walter, when in an instant, and fixing one look of the most indescribable agony upon me, he plunged the fatal blade to the hilt in his own breast, and with one dying groan sunk bleeding and lifeless on the ground.

"A wild shriek of horror and despair escaped me, and I fell totally insensible on the bleeding form of my ill-fated lover.

"How can I dwell upon this awful event, or give any adequate idea of my sufferings? Even now they are almost as acute as they were at the time when this frightful tragedy took place, and I could almost fancy that I see it re-enacted before my eyes. Oh, Walter! what a dreadful fate was yours; and is it not wonderful that I could have survived it so long, especially considering the manifold sufferings, the cruelties, and the degradation it has been my hard lot to endure? But pardon me, Mrs. Tiller, I must pause for awhile in my dismal story to give indulgence to the painful feelings that now torture me, and to try to collect my thoughts. It is impossible to recal such dreadful and torturing events to my memory without emotions of the deepest anguish."

"Oh, most true, Alice," replied our heroine, "yours has indeed been a hard fate, even more severe, if possible, than my own, and most sincerely do I sympathise with you, and hope that the time will yet come when you will be restored to something like peace and happiness."

"Ah! no," returned Alice, "that can never be; and it would be little short of madness to entertain any such an idea. My hopes have long since been buried in the grave of the unfortunate Walter, and death alone can release me from my misery, to which, Heaven knows, I have long looked forward to with anxiety and impatience. But I have not yet related half of the troubles it has been my fate to encounter, and which I know not how I have ever found fortitude sufficient to bear up against. But I must be allowed a few minutes to collect my scattered thoughts, though I fear that I have already almost exhausted your patience by the tediousness of my story."

"Oh, no," answered Mary, "believe me that I listen to it with the deepest interest and sympathy, and that I would fain offer you all the consolation in my power under such unparalleled misfortunes. But if the recital of them causes you so much pain, as they must naturally be expected to do, I beg of you to proceed no further."

"Oh, yes," said Alice, "knowing the kind sympathy that you feel towards me, it is a relief to my mind, and I will, therefore, in a few minutes proceed to the conclusion."

Mary returned no answer to this, and Alice remained silent for a short time, and seemed to be buried in the most profound meditation, and to be indulging in the most melancholy retrospections. All was pretty still upon deck; the vessel was proceeding swiftly on its way, and it did not seem as though they were likely to be interrupted; but although the interesting though melancholy narrative of Alice had in some degree diverted the thoughts of our heroine from her own immediate misfortunes, they now returned upon her with full force, and she could not look forward to that which was too probably yet in store for her without the most fearful apprehensions, and she shuddered when she reflected how completely she was in the power of the villain Brandon, and the terrible and revolting fate to which he had consigned her, and from which she could not possibly escape without some merciful and miraculous interposition of Providence. In about a quarter of an hour, however, Alice seemed to have recovered her composure, and turning to our heroine, she said—

"I will now proceed with my dismal story, Mrs. Tiller, if it be agreeable to you, and bring it to a conclusion as soon as I can. You may imagine the painful sensation the awful tragedy which I have been describing created in the breasts of all those that witnessed it; poor Walter, as I afterwards was informed, died immediately after he had inflicted the fatal injury on himself, and his corpse was removed to the nearest house, there to await the coroner's inquest, but as for myself I recollected no more till some days afterwards, when, on recovering my senses, I found myself in bed in one of the apartments of my new residence, and with Drayton and my parents watching anxiously by my side. The sight of the former excited in my bosom an indescribable feeling of horror, and I averted my looks from his countenance as though they had encountered some frightful apparition; for the whole horrible truth flashed upon my recollection with the most overwhelming force, and I could not look upon him, who was now my husband, in any other light than that of a murderer. His rage and confusion were apparent, and he could not conceal his feelings, for in a moment he read the thoughts that were passing in my mind, and he seemed to reproach himself for the part he had acted, and the irreparable misery which he had been the means of bringing about. He seemed, however, to be about to address me, but my father motioned him aside, and after holding him in conversation in an under tone for a few minutes, he advanced towards the bed on which I was lying, and taking my hand, he raised it to his lips in silence, and then abruptly quitted the room, fixing upon me a peculiar and impressive look as he departed, which made me shudder, and could only fill my breast with increased feelings of disgust and hatred towards him. My parents now advanced towards me, and spoke some words of kindness and consolation to me, but which fell harsh and discordant upon my ears, and calling upon the name of Walter, a deathlike sickness came over me—I trembled convulsively in every limb—my brain seemed to be on fire—the most frightful phantoms danced before my disordered imagination, and my senses again left me.

"In this deplorable condition it appears that I remained for several days, and it was feared that I should never again recover; would to Heaven that I had not, for it would have been a mercy to me to have rescued me from those sufferings which it was afterwards my fate to experience. What the anguish and anxiety of my parents was during that time, of course, I had no means of knowing exactly, but I had every reason to believe that they regretted the cruel and unjust course they had pursued in compelling me to become the wife of Drayton, and which had already been productive of such dreadful and fatal consequences. The parents of poor Walter, I was given to understand, immediately came forward on learning the melancholy catastrophe, which had thus in so untimely a manner deprived them of a beloved son, but after the interment of his remains they again departed from the neighbourhood, and no one was aware whither they had gone.

"How the next few days and weeks passed away, I can scarcely give an adequate idea of, but you may well imagine the horrible state of my mind, and that all attempts to console me were completely fruitless—and, in fact, only served to add to the intensity of my despair. Drayton ventured to visit me every day, and appeared to feel the greatest anxiety and sympathy for my melancholy situation; but the sight of him, as you may suppose, was now more odious to me than ever, and every word that he uttered fell upon my ears with a sensation which it would have been quite useless for me to attempt to conquer, or even to control. The form of the unfortunate Walter was constantly present to my imagination, and the dismal lamentations to which I constantly gave utterance must have been most pitiable to hear. Wonderful it is that my heart did not break under such an accumulation of unexampled horrors; but I was reserved for still greater misery, and it seemed as if Providence had entirely deserted me; but to know myself to be the wife of that man who had been the means of bringing all those terrible events about was more torturing than all, and my strength of mind nearly gave way under it. Drayton tried by every means in his power to do away with the feelings I entertained towards him, but the more he exerted himself to do so the stronger and the more insupportable they became. Whenever I mentioned the name of poor Walter Seyton in his presence, his conscience seemed to smite him, a deathly paleness would overspread his features, and trembling in every limb, he would abruptly quit the room; and I must acknowledge that to see him suffer from remorse and terror afforded me the most infinite satisfaction, and was a gratification to the feelings of revenge that I could not but entertain towards him. My father, however, would venture to remonstrate with me in the most gentle manner; but I turned a deaf ear to all he could say; and when I thought of the harsh and inexorable conduct he had pursued towards me it was impossible that I could help reproaching him, and look upon him as one of the principal instruments for the destruction of my happiness and that of my ill-fated lover.

"In this manner several weeks wore away, and without effecting scarcely any change in my health. During this time I received the best of advice, and the utmost attention; but everything failed to make a favourable impression upon me, and every day made Drayton appear still more hateful and disgusting to me, though I seemed to receive his attentions with the most calm forbearance and indifference. In fact, I now cared little how circumstances went, or what became of me, and I could scarcely be said to live at all; my existence was one continuous fearful dream, which kept my imagination constantly bewildered and on the rack. But at length youth and a naturally vigorous constitution in some degree triumphed over my malady, and I was enabled to leave my bed, and to walk in the little garden which was attached to our residence, and which served to refresh me greatly; but nothing whatever could remove the weight of care that pressed upon my heart, and it was only in seclusion that I could find the smallest relief, and give free indulgence to the feelings that constantly agitated my bosom.

"Drayton tried all that he could to wean me from this melancholy state of mind, and to convince me of the affection he felt towards me; but it was all to no purpose, although I invariably received his attentions with the most perfect indifference, and never once offered to reprove or reproach him for the misery he had brought upon me. At times my mind completely wandered, and I knew not what I was about, and then my melancholy ravings and lamentations were, no doubt, most painful to hear. If Drayton had ever been mad enough to flatter himself with the idea that our union would be productive of happiness to himself, he must now be most bitterly disappointed, and tho-

roughly convinced that it was quite impossible that he could ever make any favourable impression upon my heart; and I could not help thinking, from the conduct of my father, that he at length deeply regretted that our nuptials had ever taken place, although he had hitherto nothing to complain of in the conduct of my husband towards me, which was uniformly kind and attentive.

"One thing which, if possible, annoyed me more than all was the restrictions which Drayton placed upon me, by not allowing me, on any account or pretext whatever, to leave the house, which was a most torturing circumstance to me, for could I have had but an opportunity of visiting the grave of the ill-fated Walter daily, it would have afforded me some degree of consolation. But, no doubt, he feared that such was the abhorrence with which I viewed him, if he thus indulged me, I should take the earliest opportunity of making my escape, and thus all the trouble he had been at would be sacrificed in vain. This served, as may be expected, to add to the anguish of my mind, and every day I became more wretched and restless. The visits of my parents to the house in which we resided also became less frequent than they had previously been, a circumstance which somewhat surprised me, though I concluded that Drayton had his motives for preventing them, for I could not help thinking that it was in obedience to his wishes that they acted. There was something about his conduct, too, which frequently excited my suspicions as to his real character, and in some measure increased my alarm. He appeared to depend but little on the occupation of a fisherman, though he was frequently absent from home for hours together; and when he returned, which was frequently not till after midnight, I have watched him enter the house accompanied by several men of the most ferocious and forbidding appearance, and with whom he would remain in noisy revelry sometimes till daylight. But I never ventured to question him upon such matters, for I felt well convinced as to the return I should have met with if I had done so. His treatment of me soon became very different to what it had previously been;

his patience seemed to be exhausted by the scorn and indifference which I had always evinced towards him, and he was frequently stern in his conduct towards me. This change, however, had but little if, indeed, any effect upon me, and I never once offered to give utterance to a murmur of complaint—in fact, I was not in the least disappointed, for it was no more that I fully expected from such a man as I believed Drayton to be. But why should I become so tedious by explaining so minutely the thoughts and feelings that beset my mind, and which I know, Mrs. Tiller, you can so thoroughly appreciate and sympathise with? Let me rather hasten to the conclusion of my narrative, which has already been too much prolonged.

"Several months I passed in the greatest misery that can well be imagined, when another calamity occurred to me, which you may be certain only served to render my situation the more torturing, and added to the anguish of my mind. This was the accidental death of my father and brother, who being overtaken by a terrific storm, while in the pursaance of their occupation, were wrecked, even within sight of their own cottage.

"Notwithstanding the unnatural and cruel severity and injustice of my father's behaviour towards me, it was impossible that this melancholy catastrophe should fail to make a most painful impression upon me, and it was some time before I could recover from the violent shock which it caused me. My mother now took up her residence at our house, but she never again held up her head after this dreadful calamity; and only a few weeks after it had occurred she also breathed her last, and thus I was left entirely at the mercy of that hated man in whose hands my fate had been placed.

"Soon after the death of my parents he threw aside the disguise he had before assumed to conceal his real character, and his conduct towards me became changed altogether. He no longer condescended to sue, but commanded; and he soon convinced me that he looked upon me rather in the character of a slave than his wife, and that it was completely useless for me to attempt to offer any resistance to his wishes, however monstrous and unreasonable they might

be. If ever I ventured to murmur or expostulate with him, he would heap the most brutal language upon me, and threaten me with even greater severity if I dared to exasperate him. Alas! I wonder how I could ever find strength sufficient to support such an accumulation of misery; but it was no more than I had been previously prepared for, and I was, therefore, not by any means disappointed. And now the suspicions that I had formerly entertained were all but confirmed, for Drayton frequently invited several of the men of whom I have before spoken to the house, and would sometimes compel me to be present, and he seemed to take a savage delight in witnessing the anguish and the feelings of disgust which it caused me. These men, as I have before said, were of the most ruffianly description, and the language they made use of was sufficient to shock the ears of any one who was not entirely lost to every feeling of shame, for it was most coarse and brutal in the extreme, and thoroughly satisfied me that they were men of the very worst character. And these were the particular associates, and apparently the most intimate friends of my husband; if, then, I could have entertained any doubt before of his character, what could I think now? Must not all conjectures be entirely removed? They were, and I viewed him with redoubled horror and repugnance, and only longed for an opportunity to escape from him; how gladly, how gratefully would I have availed myself of it! though, alas, friendless in the world as I was, I knew not where to go. But great as the misery was which I then experienced, there was still much more in store for me. But I was not much longer to be kept in suspense. It was on a stormy night that I was seated in one of the apartments of the house in which we resided, and buried in the most gloomy meditations upon the troubles it had hitherto been my lot to experience, and those which but too probably were yet in store for me; while I listened attentively to the voice of the tempest, which raged so fiercely without. Drayton had been from home since the morning, and had not yet returned, although is was now past midnight, and I began to imagine that some accident had happened to him, and I cannot but acknowledge, though I am almost ashamed to do so, that the idea created no sort of emotion in my breast; on the contrary, something almost amounting to a wish that my surmises might prove to be correct took possession of me. I watched from the window of the room the progress of the storm, and certainly it was one of the most fearful nights that I had ever witnessed; and as I contemplated the horrors that reigned around, the most dismal forebodings crossed my mind that some fresh calamity was about to befal me, though I felt satisfied that nothing could now occur to me half so dreadful as that which I had already experienced. Then all the horrors of the past rushed upon my memory with the most overwhelming force, and it was not without the greatest difficulty that I could control my faculties within the bounds of reason. Again did I imagine that I saw the unfortunate Walter, as he appeared before me in the chapel on the fatal day of my marriage; once more I observed the wild, despairing anguish of his looks, and listened to the words which he had given utterance to on that never to be forgotten occasion. Then I beheld re-enacted the horrible tragedy which I have already so minutely described; I saw my lover plunge the fatal blade into his breast—beheld the ghastly distortion of his features—the gaping wound from which his life's blood so copiously streamed, and heard that last dying groan of agony which it is impossible that I can ever forget, even to the very latest moment of my existence; and my imagination was wrought up to such a pitch that I could scarcely contain myself. But I, was interrupted in the midst of these reflections by beholding the dark shadow of a man coming towards the house, and in which, when it approached nearer, I recognised my husband, and, I therefore, prepared myself to meet him with all the firmness I could, though it was seldom that I had felt a greater dread of him than I did on this occasion. He soon entered the room, and appeared to be wet to the skin, and in not one of the best of humours; but I was afraid to make use of any observation to him, and he took a seat before the fire, which was blazing cheerfully. I could see that there was some-

thing which he wished to say to me, for he frequently looked earnestly in my face, and seemed about to speak, but he again hesitated, and remained silent for a few minutes, all the time I was apprehending that something of a disagreeable nature was about to happen to me, and in which I was, alas! fated not to be disappointed.

" ' Bring me my great coat,' he said, in a stern voice.

" ' What want you with it to-night?' I ventured to inquire.

" ' What should I want with it but to wear?' he demanded, morosely, and fixing upon me a stern look. ' Do as I tell you, and ask no questions!'

" I obeyed in silence, and when I had returned with the coat, he put it on over his wet clothes, and arose from his chair.

" ' Surely you are not going forth again to-night, Drayton?' I interrogated.

" ' Yes, I am,' he replied, ' and what is more, you must accompany me.'

" I started at the mention of these words, and gazed with astonishment and incredulity upon him.

" ' I—I accompany you,' I faltered out, ' at such an hour, too, and in such a storm as this?'

" ' Yes,' he returned, ' and you must not hesitate about it, either, for we have no time for delay. This night we must leave here for ever.'

" ' Leave here?' I repeated, with increased astonishment and trepidation; ' what can be the cause of this sudden resolution, and whither are you going to take me?'

" ' You will soon know all about it,' remarked Drayton.

" ' Your words alarm me,' I cried— ' going from here to return no more? This suspense is most painful. I beg of you to explain yourself, Drayton.'

" ' Well,' he returned, ' it is time that you and I understood each other, Alice, and you might as well know the truth first as last. The fact of it is, I have deceived you, and I am a far different man to what I represented myself to be.'

" ' Ah!' I ejaculated, and fixing upon him an earnest look of mingled fear and reproach, ' it is no more than I all along suspected. But who and what are you?'

THE DEATH OF ALICE'S FATHER AND BROTHER.

"He again hesitated, and I could perceive that, notwithstanding the air of indifference he had assumed, he almost dreaded to divulge the fatal secret, and I repeated the question I had put to him more urgently than before.

"'The whole of it is, Alice,' he at length replied, 'that you are the wife of a bold rover of the sea, and that this night we must on board the craft which is destined to become our future home.'

"'The wife of a pirate? Great Heaven! is it possible?' I exclaimed. 'Alas! alas! then my fate is indeed sealed, and I am truly wretched. Oh, Drayton, what a villanous part is the one you have acted, and how basely was my poor misguided father deceived! Heaven pardon him for the misery, the shame, and degradation he has brought upon his unhappy child. But, Drayton, is your mind so totally insensible to every feeling of pity and compunction? You will not surely put your threats into execution, and compel me to go on board this pirate vessel?'

"'And where should a wife be but with her husband?' he demanded.

"'Alas!' I sighed, 'I am indeed your wife, weak, friendless, and defenceless, Heaven help me; but—'

"'Come, come,' he interrupted, impatiently, 'there must be no hesitation in the business; the ship now awaits us but a short distance from hence; and if we are not soon on board we shall incur the anger of the skipper, and that is rather a dangerous thing to arouse, I can tell you.'

"'Oh, spare me, spare me, Drayton,' I implored, and clasping my hands together vehemently. 'See how fearfully the storm rages, and—'

"'No more!' he again interrupted, impatiently; 'you know me now, and it is useless for you to offer any resistance to my will. Let it be storm or let it be calm, what matters it to me? The fierce battling of the elements is but amusement to the hardy and reckless rover of the seas. Come, I say again, we do but waste time; there are those who await our coming, and are anxious to give to the fair pirate's bride a hearty welcome. You have lavished on me your utmost scorn and hatred, but I told you I should triumph yet, and you will find that Richard Drayton never fails to keep his word. We see this place no more. Away with you, I am weary of waiting, and henceforth you will know from experience the folly and danger of attempting to disobey my commands.'

" 'Are you indeed a man?' I eagerly demanded, in a voice of the greatest agitation, and sinking on my knees at his feet, while I looked in his face with an expression of the most earnest supplication; 'if so, you will take pity and compassion on me, and not consign me to a fate which is by far too horrible to think on. It is true I am, unfortunately, your wife, but the union is unsanctioned by Heaven, and never will I submit to take part in those guilty proceedings that are so revolting to my heart, and which the bare idea of makes the life blood curdle in my veins to dwell upon. I will resist the horrible fate to which you would condemn me even with my latest breath.'

"Fool!' he cried, passionately, and grasping me fiercely by the wrist, 'and how can you help yourself, situated as you are, and since it is my will? But again I say that I waste time with you, and become impatient. Rise, and follow me immediately, or by the infernal host I swear, let the consequences be whatever they may, I will drag you hence by force, and you will afterwards have bitter reason to repent the opposition which you have offered to my will. Already have I brooked too much from your obduracy, but I am determined to act the hypocrite no longer, and henceforth you must learn to look upon me as your master, and to obey me as my slave. This way, woman; through storm and tempest I will drag you, no power on earth or in heaven shall prevent me from carrying my designs fully into purpose.'

"As the hardened and brutal miscreant thus ejaculated, unmindful of my pitiful looks, regardless of my prayers, my tears and supplications, he seized me still more fiercely and determinedly by the arm, and dragged me to my feet. Again I attempted to speak and implore

his mercy, but my voice failed me, and the sternness of his looks filled me with terror and dismay; the thunder, too, in the most deafening peals, seemed to mock my agony and despair; my senses reeled—my limbs tottered beneath me—all my faculties at once seemed to desert me, and with one faint cry of anguish I became unconscious to all around me.

"What afterwards took place I know not; how I was removed from the house I had no means of knowing, and cared not to inquire; but when I again was restored to my senses, I found myself on board this vessel in one of the cabins, with an old woman, who then acted as an attendant upon the lawless crew, but who has been for may years dead, standing by my side, and apparently most anxiously awaiting my recovery. You may imagine, Mrs. Tiller, the horror and the agony of my feelings as the whole dreadful facts of what had happened to me flashed with the most overwhelming force upon my memory, and I knew myself lost for ever. I stared aghast around me at the novelty of the scene which presented itself to my gaze, and I tried to speak, but all my faculties were bound up in terror, and utterance was denied me, and I could see from the aspect of the old woman, that all appeal to her for pity or sympathy would have been in vain. The storm still raged with terrific fury, the vessel was tossed about at the mercy of the waves, and the shouts and oaths of the crew, coupled with the noise of the battling elements, completely paralysed my senses, and made me almost afraid to look around me. The old woman, on seeing me recover, approached me, and in a voice which seemed more harsh and disagreeable than anything which I had ever heard, she said—

" 'So you nave awoke at last, young woman, have you? You have had a long rest, and it is well for you that you can sleep so soundly in such a storm as this, and when we are likely enough to go to Davy Jones every moment. Well I am an old sailor, and many's the rough gale that I have weathered, but I must say that——'

" 'Oh, for God's sake,' I interrupted, 'do not talk thus to one who is placed in the horrible situation that I am, but tell me, where am I, and what is it they intend to do with me?'

" 'Why,' returned my unfeeling attendant, ' those questions, for the matter of that, are very soon answered. In the first instance you are on board the pirate schooner, the Wasp, as trim a craft as ever ploughed the billows, or bid defiance to the foe. In the next place it is the intention of Dick Drayton, your husband, and the rest of our crew, to initiate you into the rover's life, and to make you useful, as you should be; and if you are wise you will not be dull of learning, that's all I have to say to you. For obstinacy and disobedience are duly punished on board this vessel, I can tell you.'

" 'Oh, God!' I cried, clasping my hands, and raising my eyes in despair, ' and has it indeed come to this? Have my worst forebodings been so fearfully realised, and is there no hope for me? Gracious Heaven, what will become of me? But where is Drayton?—he, the villain who has betrayed me to destruction, and consigned me to a fate than which death would have been far preferable? Is he on board this vessel?'

" 'Oh, yes,' replied the old woman, ' you may be sure of that, and that you will also see him anon. He is one of the boldest of our crew, and has done much service. I admire the choice he has made, and the clever manner in which he has accomplished his designs. But I must leave you for awhile to your own thoughts, and see how we are getting on, for, to tell the truth, I am rather fearful as to the result of this tempest, which is one of the wildest and most severe that I ever remember. I dare say you can dispense with my services for a time.'

" With these words she hastily departed from the cabin, and left me in a state of stupified amazement and horror, All the terrible apprehensions that had suggested themselves to my mind were now fully realised, and most earnestly did I pray that death would at once put a period to my sufferings, which were now far too severe for human nature to endure. What added to the intense horror and anguish of my feelings was the melancholy fact that I was about to become a mother; and when I thought of the shame and misery to which my unfortunate and innocent offspring would be born, and the fearful career of crime to which his guilty father would no doubt train him, I shuddered with terror and disgust, and most sincerely did I wish that it might please the Almighty to take me and it together. Left to myself, I could give the most unrestrained indulgence to my emotions, the power and the nature of which it would be almost impossible, while it is quite unnecessary for me to describe.

"The storm increased in violence every moment, and the vessel was tossed about like a straw at the mercy of the mountainous and angry waves, while the shouts and imprecations of the crew fully convinced me of the danger which prevailed; but I regarded it almost with indifference, for, situated as I was, I cared but little what became of me. It was night, but the vivid flashes of lightning that shot in such rapid succession across the sky rendered it as light as day, and made the dreadful scene which reigned around still more awfully impressive. I threw myself on my knees, and with clasped hands, and earnestly upturned eyes, I committed myself to the care of Heaven, expecting and wishing, as I sincerely did, that every moment would prove my last. But my prayer was not granted, for I was unfortunately reserved for even worse troubles, if possible, than those which it had already been my lot to undergo. Thus more than an hour passed away, and no one offered to interrupt me. The pirate barque weathered the storm bravely, and it was evident, from the observations of the crew that reached my ears, that they firmly believed they should be able to surmount every danger, and that the prolongation of my misery to an indefinite period was certain.

" 'Alas—alas!' I sighed, ' what a wretched, what an insupportable fate is mine, and in whichever way I turn my thoughts, I see not the least probable means of my being enabled to avoid it. Oh, God, why have you suffered me to live to endure this? But I must not arraign your Almighty will, but endeavour to put my trust in your mercy. Oh, Drayton, what a villanous, and treacherous, and inhuman part have you acted towards me; and how was my unfortunate and misguided father misled in being thus deceived by you. But let me not reproach his memory, but only hope that Heaven has pardoned him for his cruel and unnatural conduct towards me. To know myself to be the wife of this man of crime, and to contemplate the frightful prospect, should my existence be prolonged to any length of time, which is spread before me, is surely enough to unnerve me, and to render me one of the most wretched of human beings. And you, my innocent, unborn babe—alas! how dreadful will be your destiny, should the Almighty ordain that you should live, and arrive at years of knowledge and maturity! Inured from childhood to crime, what can you become but a blot upon humanity, and a curse to your fellow creatures? Heaven grant that you may never see the light of day, but that together with your wretched parent you may be rescued from those miseries that otherwise are in store for us.'

"How long I might have continued to give vent to my feelings in the same melancholy strain I know not, but at length I was aroused from them by the return of the old woman, whose name was Beatrice, to the cabin, and feeling satisfied from the behaviour which I had hitherto experienced from her how completely useless it would be for me to appeal to or expect any sympathy from her, I controlled my feelings as well as I could, and sought to appear composed and resigned to my fate, though God knows the tempest of anguish and despair that at the same time was raging within my breast, and which worked up my feelings almost to a pitch of frenzy.

"'Thanks to our lucky stars,' said Beatrice, 'and our gallant craft, than which a better never yet ploughed the broad waters of the deep, or battled with the angry elements, we shall yet surmount every danger, and remain to triumph in our career of freedom for many a year to come. The wind has lulled, the storm is rapidly subsiding, and ere long we shall again ride over the white-crested billows as free from danger as the wild sea-mew. But you look pale and agitated, Mrs. Drayton.'

"'Alas!' I sighed, 'how is it possible that I can be otherwise to find myself in the dreadful situation in which I am?'

"'Oh!' replied the old woman, in the most unfeeling accents, 'you must learn to conquer these childish fears, for you will, no doubt, have to encounter far greater dangers than those you have this night experienced, now that you have become one of us, and I dare say that you will become inured to them, and learn to think nothing of them. The pirate's life is one of peril, but we are amply repaid for it by the rich booty which we so frequently obtain, and the freedom and independence that fall to our share. Few free-traders have met with greater success than the Wasp.'

"'Heaven help me!' I ejaculated, and clasping my hands vehemently together in the intense agony and despair of my feelings; 'but has Drayton long been connected with these lawless and desperate men?'

"'Ay,' returned Beatrice, 'from a lad, and his father before him.'

"'Oh, God! then,' I exclaimed, shuddering, 'in how many scenes of crime and horror has he doubtless been engaged!'

"'Yes, you may say that,' returned the old woman with a savage look of satisfaction, 'and no doubt he prides himself on the occasion, and hopes that it may be his good fortune to be connected with many more.'

"'Oh, dreadful and revolting thought!' I cried; 'to think, too, that to such a hardened wretch as this my happiness has been sacrificed. And can you exult in the recollection of such atrocities as those to which you have alluded?'

"'Certainly,' she answered, and an expression passed over her aged and wrinkled features that were at any time most forbidding. 'I should be unworthy of the situation which I hold on board this vessel, and the many years of uninterrupted enjoyment I have experienced, if I did not.'

"'And who is the principal of this lawless crew?' I interrogated.

"'Hugh Brandon is the skipper of this ship,' replied Beatrice; 'but he and his brother, Black Brandon, as he is commonly called, are the masters of this and several other vessels, that have for years swept the ocean, and set defeat at defiance. No weak boys are they, but desperate and determined men, and so their enemies have found out times out of number to their cost. You may consider yourself favoured, for it is not every female who is admitted on board this craft, for we have generally found them more trouble than they were worth. Ah, many's the fair thing I have seen, after she has been made the victim of Brandon, and others of the crew, who has been consigned to the deep.'

"'Good heavens!' I exclaimed, with a shuddering sensation of terror which I find it impossible to convey an adequate idea of, 'and is it possible that there can be such inhuman wretches in existence?'

"'You will find that I have spoken nothing but the truth,' returned the old woman, 'for I can have no possible reason for attempting to deceive you, seeing that I should gain nothing by doing so. But let me caution you to be more choice and guarded in the terms which you apply to the crew, for though it matters little to them what you call them, it cannot fail to bring down upon your head their vengeance, which would be far more terrible than you can possibly form the least conception of. You are the wife of Dick Drayton, and as such must learn to obey him and the rest of the crew in everything.'

"I looked at her with an expression of disgust and terror as she gave utterance to those brutal observations which I feel at a loss to describe in language sufficiently powerful or appropriate; but she treated my looks, and the thoughts which were evidently passing within my mind, with the utmost indifference; and feeling how perfectly useless it was to argue or to remonstrate with her, I remained silent, while my bosom at the same time heaved with the most violent and overwhelming emotions. I saw plainly the horrors of the fate which was in store for me, the utter impossibility of my escaping from it, and my brain was racked almost to madness. The presence of old Beatrice, who was evidently, from her conversation, so deeply inured to crime, did but serve to increase the anguish of my mind, and it was not without the greatest difficulty that I could control myself within the bounds of reason. She, however, at length once

more left me, and I was thus permitted to indulge the intense agony of my feelings alone. The storm had now entirely ceased, and all on deck was quiet; but I awaited in dread and suspense the most insupportable expecting every moment the appearance of Drayton, and whom I could not now look upon without tenfold horror and apprehension. But time wore on, in the most dismal and torturing manner that can be conceived, and still he came not; and at length, worn out with thinking, and my brain bewildered by the many and fearful ideas that crowded upon it, I sunk into a kind of lethargy, and became almost unconscious of what had happened, or the situation in which I was placed; and happy indeed would it have been for me had I remained so. The motion of the vessel, however, and deadly sickness that came over me, disturbed me, and aroused me to a full recollection of everything; and bursting into a violent paroxysm of sobs and tears, I paced the narrow confines of the cabin in which I was a prisoner in the most disordered state, and at the same time gave vent to my feeling in the most dismal lamentations, but found it utterly impossible to gain any relief to my sufferings.

"'I am lost—lost entirely!' I ejaculated, wringing my hands; 'the Almighty has evidently abandoned me; I have, unknowingly, incurred His most terrible wrath, and what hope is there for me? None, none whatever! Oh, wretched Alice, why were you ever born to encounter such a cruel and revolting destiny as this? But what use is it my lamenting, since it is quite impossible for me to avoid the horrors that are now impending over me? Love could never have found a place in the hardened bosom of the man to whom I have been so remorselessly sacrificed; and knowing the feelings which I entertain towards him, and which I have never been hypocrite enough to endeavour to conceal, what else can I expect from him but the greatest cruelty? Alas! unfortunate and beloved Walter! oh, may your sainted spirit be permitted to plead to the Supreme for mercy to me and my unborn babe! Why was not I suffered to die at the same time that you sealed your fate for ever? And can I ever look upon the man whom I cannot but consider as indirectly your murderer, with any other feelings than those of the most unspeakable horror and hatred? And he is my husband, and has me completely in his power and at his mercy. Dreadful idea! the blood curdles in my veins as I think of it, and all my energies fail me. Oh, when will there be an end to this insupportable misery? When will my soul be at peace? He has been from childhood inured to crime, and must, therefore, be insensible to every proper feeling; and knowing the sentiments that I must entertain towards him, he will feel a savage delight in witnessing the terrible sufferings which he will inflict upon me. And what can I expect from the guilty wretches with whom he is associated? Alas! there is no one to sympathise with me, to offer me one word of consolation, or to stand up in my defence. Nothing whatever can equal the horrors to which I am subjected; and the longer I reflect upon them the more acute becomes the anguish of my despair. Have pity on me, kind Heaven, for without your merciful interposition what is to become of me?'

"I could say no more, for grief entirely choked my further utterance, and I abandoned myself to the dismal thoughts that had taken such strong hold on my senses, and from which nothing whatever seemed likely to afford me any relief. In this manner the night passed away, and it was such a one as I had not often experienced, and Beatrice did not again visit me, which, however, I was not sorry for, for her behaviour, as far as I had experienced, was most repulsive and painful to my feelings. I felt surprised that Drayton did not come near me, but I could not expect that he would long neglect doing so, and I looked forward to my interview with him with the greatest apprehension, for I was thoroughly convinced that the agony of my sufferings would make no other impression upon him than to cause him to exult, and excite his derision and contempt. To endeavour to obtain a short respite from my miseries in sleep I knew would be a fruitless task, and I, therefore, made no effort to do so, but continued to pace the cabin backwards and forwards in the same manner that I had done for hours, and to listen to the voices of the pirates, which occasionally met my ears,

in the greatest agitation and suspense. How I was enabled to keep about at all I cannot imagine; but at length morning dawned, and soon afterwards Beatrice made her appearance, bringing with her some provisions, which she spread before me, and motioned me to partake of, but my heart was far too full to permit me to eat, and with a deep sigh I averted my looks, for I liked not the sinister expression of her eyes, which, I perceived, were earnestly fixed upon me, and I found no difficulty in penetrating the thoughts that occupied her mind. I felt disgusted and uneasy in her presence, and would have been glad if she had not troubled me with it; but she seemed not at all in any hurry to depart, and I was, therefore, compelled to bear with it in the best manner I could, and did not offer to make use of any observation.

"'So,' she said, at last, 'you are still gloomy and abstracted; but of what use is it to give way to such feelings? Here you are safe on board the pirate vessel, and as there is no chance of your escaping from it, you may as well resign yourself to your fate, for such conduct as this is not at all calculated to conciliate your husband.'

"'Alas!' I sighed, 'too well do I know that. Too strongly am I convinced that I have nothing whatever to expect from his mercy and forbearance. But is it possible that you can approve of his conduct, and——'

"'And what reason have I to disapprove of it?' she hastily interrupted; 'he would disgrace his character were he to act otherwise. We must have no chicken hearts in the profession to which he belongs, and Drayton has ever proved himself to be one of the bravest and most daring of the crew.'

"'Oh, God!' I exclaimed, shuddering, 'and that I should be the wife of such an inhuman miscreant.'

"'Rather a harsh epithet to apply to your husband, methinks, young woman,' observed Beatrice; 'but I would advise you not to let him hear you do so, or you may have cause to repent it.'

"'And how is it possible, think you, that I can look upon him in any other character, after what I have already experienced from him, and what I have so much cause to anticipate?' I demanded.

'My husband?—oh! I can never acknowledge him as such; my heart revolts at the disgusting and fearful idea.'

"'You will do well to conquer those feelings, which cannot be productive of any good to you,' returned Beatrice, 'though, for the matter of that, knowing that he has you completely in his power, I don't suppose that he cares much about the feelings you entertain towards him.'

"'Alas, no!' I replied, 'and therefore does the sense of the horror of my situation, and the utter despair by which I am surrounded, become the more acute. Oh, Beatrice, have you not one spark of feeling remaining in your breast, that you can thus view the misery to which I am remorselessly subjected with such stolid indifference?'

"'And what business is it of mine?' she interrogated; 'were I to presume to question the conduct of Drayton, or any other of the pirates, I should have enough to do. No, young woman, you much mistake my character if you imagine such a thing.'

"'Cruel woman!' I cried, 'and can you possibly make use of such brutal and disgusting language towards one of your own sex, and whom fate has placed in a situation which should command the deepest sympathy? Your words shock me, and I can scarcely believe that it is a woman who is speaking to me, and who can give utterance to sentiments that are so disgusting and revolting.'

"'Well,' returned Beatrice, 'you may talk on, for I care nothing at all about the opinion you entertain of me, and so you will find when you know me better.'

"'I see too clearly,' I returned, 'that your heart is invulnerable to every feeling of pity, and that you are a fit instrument in the hands of the guilty wretches with whom you are associated, to carry out their diabolical views.'

"'Thank you for the compliment,' said the wicked old woman, with a look of derision and contempt; 'had I proved myself otherwise, I should not now have been here to tell it you. Brandon and his colleagues have a very ready and summary way of quieting those who may render themselves obnoxious to them, and I would advise you not to incur the danger which I hint to you.'

"'I care not for their vengeance,' I replied, boldly; 'no fate can be half so dreadful as that with which I am threatened. Life has now become hateful to me, and even if I were rid of it this moment, it would be a mercy to me.'

"'Indeed!' sneered Beatrice; 'however, I do not expect, if such are your wishes, that they will be gratified. Drayton has much to do before he can make up his mind to lose you; therefore you may as well await your fate with patience and forbearance.'

"'Cruel words,' I sighed, fixing upon her a look of the keenest reproach, 'and must I be compelled to listen to them, and to have my ears thus insulted? But I only waste my time in thus addressing you, for it is evident that you take a savage delight in witnesssig my sufferings. Leave me, woman, and no longer torture me with your brutal and degrading remarks.'

"'Oh, most willingly,' she replied, 'I will leave you, and give place to the society of your husband, which, probably, you may find more agreeable to you. I dare say,' she added, sarcastically, 'that you are most anxious to see him, and he will probably, therefore, be here anon.'

"'Oh, would to Heaven that I could avoid him altogether,' I ejaculated, with a shudder. 'God help me, for the dreadful trial to which I am subjected is almost too much to bear.'

"'Well,' returned Beatrice, and a malicious expression overspread her features, 'that is no business of mine, and I do not, therefore, feel the least interest in it, so I wish you good morning.'

"As she thus spoke, she curtseyed to me with mock solemnity and respect, and without waiting to receive any answer from me, had I even been so inclined, she quitted the place, and I was again left to my own dismal meditations, the nature of which, Mrs. Tiller, you can better conceive than I could portray them to you. When she was gone I remained for a few minutes in a state of stupor, but from which I was at length aroused, and sinking on my knees, I fervently supplicated the merciful interposition of Heaven in my behalf, but I could obtain no relief. I felt most keenly the fearful truth of all that she had said, and it was in vain that I endeavoured to encourage the least ray of hope that I should be enabled to obtain any mitigation of the sufferings with which I was threatened, and which Drayton seemed to take such a savage delight to inflict upon me. I listened attentively to catch every sound, fearing every moment the appearance of my brutal husband, and I was not long kept in suspense, for presently the cabin door was thrown open, and Drayton stood before me. I could not help giving utterance to a cry of terror when I behold him, as if by so doing I could avoid his presence. He was, however, evidently quite unmoved by the emotion I evinced, and with an expression of brutal exultation he advanced towards me, and in a stern and commanding tone of voice repeated my name. I started involuntarily at the sound, and trembled in every limb; but, nothing daunted, he roughly grasped me by the wrist, and in stern accents, drawing me towards him, he addressed me. What took place at this meeting I will not attempt to particularise; it may be sufficient to state that it was one of the most painful nature, as I had fully expected it would be, and that Drayton treated me with the most harsh and cruel indifference, openly exulting at the manner in which he had deceived me, and gave me every reason to fear what sufferings would be inflicted upon me, and how completely hopeless it would be for me to imagine that I could escape from the fate to which he had destined me. Could I ever previously have entertained any doubt, how thoroughly convinced I must now be of the consummate villain he was, and with what tenfold disgust and abhorrence did I view him. But, alas! what were the horrors I was yet doomed to experience from him? Even now, as I recal them to my memory, from which it is impossible they can ever be effaced, my very soul sinks within me, and I marvel how it is that I have ever existed so long, or that my senses have not left me, with all those dreadful thoughts constantly crowding upon and distracting my brain. But I will be as brief as possible in recounting the further particulars of my melancholy history, for I fear that I have already detained you too long, and that I may become tedious. From that time my situation, if possible, became more

dreadful than before, and even my delicate state failed to move my brutal husband to relent, or to relax in the least the cruel severity of his treatment towards me. The guilty scenes that I was compelled to witness on board the Wasp struck terror to my breast, and every hour added to my despair. Oh, how earnestly did I pray to Heaven that it would be mercifully pleased to release me from my sufferings, and never permit my poor child to see the light of day, for, alas! how terrible was the prospect to which it would be born, and what scenes of crime would it be compelled to mingle in. This thought was almost too painful to endure, and I have often wondered since, how I found strength of mind sufficient to bear up against it. But fate had marked me for its victim, and it was in vain that I might seek to evade the horrors that were in store for me.

"In this dismal and hopeless manner several weeks wore away, and at length the hour of my accouchement arrived, and surrounded by the greatest misery that can well be imagined, but which you, no doubt, can form a pretty adequate conjecture of, and with only the attendance of the stern and unfeeling old woman, Beatrice, I gave birth to a lovely boy. Would to God that we had both perished immediately afterwards, for what numerous and unparalleled miseries would it have been the means of preventing. Any one would have thought that this event would, at least, have moved Drayton to relent in his behaviour towards me, but, alas! it was far from doing so, for he was totally insensible to every proper feeling of humanity —and, in fact, he seemed rather to view my little innocent with feelings of repugnance, and offered me not one word of kindness or consolation in my painful situation. What scalding tears of the most poignant anguish and regret did I shed over my poor babe, and how terrible were the anticipations that haunted my mind as to that which was in store for him and myself. But oh! how little did I imagine the awful and untimely fate to which that poor child was born, or doubly should I have lamented the hour when it first saw the light of day. One thing, however, struck and agitated me more than all, and that was the ex-

THE PIRATE, DRAYTON.

traordinary resemblance which the features of my infant bore to those of the unfortunate Walter, and which became the more painfully and remarkably apparent the longer that I gazed upon it. Had it really been his own child, the likeness could not have been more wonfully or powerfully striking, and you may well imagine the nature of my feelings as I gazed upon it and wept for hours over it, as though my heart would break. I could not but believe that Drayton was struck with the same idea, for whenever he gazed upon the infant, it was with an expression of hatred, and he would then turn abruptly away, and pacing the cabin to and fro with hasty strides, mutter some unintelligible words and execrations between his teeth, and which plainly showed the guilty thoughts that were passing in his mind, and increased the agony of my feelings, which were already almost too much to bear. On one occasion, when I thought to move him to some degree of tenderness and compassion, I presented the infant to him, and appealed to him in the most impressive and eloquent manner in its behalf; but no sooner had I done so, than a tempest of the most furious passions seemed to take possession of his bosom, and in the most fierce accents, and pushing me and the child abruptly from him, he exclaimed in a hoarse voice—

"'Alice, do you presume to mock me, by holding up to me the likeness of one whom I had so much cause to loathe? Away with the brat! the sight of it is hateful to me!'

"Thus saying, and again spurning him from him, he abruptly quitted the place, and left me in a state of agitation which there is no necessity for me to attempt to describe. Day after day passed on, and still there was no abatement of my misery, and, in fact, it was, if possible, increased, and my brutal husband seemed to take a savage delight in making me as wretched as possible, and from old Beatrice, who acted entirely by his instructions, I experienced the same insolent and unfeeling treatment which she had from the first evinced towards me. You may readily conceive, then, Mrs. Tiller, what the excruciating, the almost insupportable anguish of my mind must have been, and how totally impossible it was for me to find any relief or consolation. Alas! it would have been little short of madness for me to attempt to do so, and I could only resign myself to despair; for to my distracted imagination it would seem that Omnipotence had entirely abandoned me, and that my inhuman husband would be permitted to triumph in all his atrocious designs. Every day the remarkable likeness which the infant bore to the ill-fated Walter Seyton became the more apparent, and it seemed as though it had been so ordained by Providence to keep me in a constant state of agony, and to add to the guilty and malignant feelings of my husband, who, whenever he gazed upon its inno-

cent features, it was with an expression of countenance which made me shudder, and filled my bosom with the most horrible apprehensions. Oh, had I known the real thoughts which at that time occupied his mind, how doubly fearful would have been my sufferings, and what madness must have seized upon my brain! Monster as he was, to conceive even the awful crime which he then had in contemplation! Oh, why did not the Almighty, in his infinite mercy, avert his arm, and thus have prevented the perpetration of one of the most hideous and unnatural of crimes that ever entered the mind of a demon?

"I had now been some months on board the pirate vessel, and during that time the dreadful scenes that I had been compelled to witness, and in which my husband took so active a part, were enough to shock even the most stout and insensible heart; and what rendered my misery the more complete was the certainty that I should never be permitted to escape from it, and that all the torture which Drayton could inflict on me he seemed resolved to do. But, above all, his hatred of the poor child evidently every day increased, and I could not help oftentimes shuddering with horror as I marked the expression of his countenance, and reflected what the result of the thoughts it was too evident he encouraged might be. But I must now come to one of the most horrible and revolting parts of my dismal tale, and I almost shrink from the execution of the painful task which I have imposed upon myself.

"It was night, and worn out with fatigue of mind, on seeking my bed, I had quickly dropped off to sleep with my child nestled in my bosom; but still my rest was broken and disturbed by painful dreams, the nature of which, however, could only serve to distract and bewilder my brain in my waking moments. But at length I was aroused from my slumbers by the cries of my child, and starting up, I was astonished and alarmed to find that it was removed from my bosom, though I still heard its cries, which convinced me that it was not far from me. There was a light in the cabin, and casting my eyes in the direction of the place from whence the cries of the infant proceeded, I was somewhat startled and surprised to behold my husband standing in the cabin with the infant in his arms, and which he seemed to be about to convey from the place; but he appeared to be greatly confused and abashed on beholding that he had awakened me. The light fell full upon his features, and the expression of them, which was savage in the extreme, made me shudder, and filled my mind with the most dismal forebodings. I started hastily towards him with a cry of astonishment and alarm, and endeavouring to snatch the child from his arms, I exclaimed—

"'Drayton, this strange interview at such an hour—what means it? The most anxious fears, of which it is impossible to divest it, seize upon my mind, and a cold shudder comes over me. Your frightful looks, and — the child! my innocent babe! Oh, why have you taken it from my bosom? What would you do with it? Speak, and no longer keep me in this horrible state of suspense, I conjure you.'

"'Alice,' he replied, in a tone of voice which made me tremble, and which indeed convinced me that I had the worst to dread—'Alice,' he repeated, and still holding the child in his arms, 'it is true that you should be made acquainted with my full determination, and learn to submit to it, for you have not the slightest power, as you must be aware, to move me from my purpose; and any attempt to resist me will be only certain to be visited by my heaviest vengeance.'

"'Oh, God!' I ejaculated, staring at him with a wild expression of terror and astonishment, 'what mean those dreadful and mysterious words, I again demand? And what fresh deed of guilt do you contemplate? What do you with the child? Your looks forebode no good, so give it to me and begone.'

"'Come, come,' returned the villain, impatiently, 'enough of this; I come not here to listen to such idle nonsense, but rather to act with promptitude and determination. Alice, I want no brats no call me father, and to serve you merely as a plaything. The hardy pirate has another and much more fitting employment for his wife than that, and you must prepare yourself, therefore, to take a much more active part in the business of the crew than you have hitherto done.

As for this youngster I hate it, and cannot look upon it without disgust and uneasiness, for in its countenance do I not behold the exact counterpart of he who was my rival, and for whom you treated me with such contempt and hatred? The brat shall no longer annoy me, and I will save you the trouble of nursing it. You now gaze upon it for the last time.'

"'Horror! horror!' I gasped forth, and as I spoke my brain seemed to be on fire, and such emotions agitated my bosom which I feel at a loss to describe properly. 'Brutal man! what dreadful, what unnatural thoughts have taken possession of your mind, and what awful deed is it that you would now do? Give me my child—my innocent babe, for the words to which you have given utterance inspire me with the greatest terror, and I almost shudder to look upon you. Oh, my child—my child!'

"As I thus spoke, I rushed frantically forward and endeavoured to snatch my infant from his arms; but it was all to no purpose that I did so—he spurned me aside, and in a voice which showed still more forcibly and terribly his fierce determination, he exclaimed—

"'Fool! forbear! Of what use is it for you to try to prevent me from the execution of my purposes? You have often regretted that the brat should ever have seen the light of day, and why, then, should you now be so particular as to what becomes of it? However, it matters not to me whether you do or not, for I am fully determined to release you from your anxiety, so far as regards the child.'

"'God of Heaven!' I again cried, and all my faculties bound up to a pitch of madness, 'can I hear aright, or do my senses deceive me? Drayton, what do the horrible words that you have so heartlessly spoken imply? My child!—your child!—Oh, horror! you would not, you cannot murder him!'

"'Ay,' returned the brutal miscreant, with the utmost coolness and indifference, 'it would be a mercy to rescue the boy from the shame and the suffering which I know you anticipate for him, and it will soon be over; this hour he dies!'

"'Wretch! villain! fiend in human shape!' I gasped forth, in the wildest accents, and my veins swelling as if they would burst with the power of my emotions; 'hold! Dare not to proceed in your monstrous and unnatural purpose, or dread the most terrible vengeance of that Almighty Being whose laws you have frequently and so fearfully outraged. Give me my child, I say, and abandon the hideous design which you have had in contemplation, or I will invoke the most awful curses upon your head! My boy! my own little one!—I—I——'

"I could say no more. Once more I made a frantic and desperate effort to snatch my unfortunate babe from his hold, but I failed; he seemed to mock my frenzy, and overpowered completely by the tumultuous feelings that rushed in such rapid succession upon my brain, I uttered a groan of the most intense agony and despair, and my senses left me. Oh, God! why did you ever permit me to revive? Why did you not in your infinite mercy suffer me to perish at the same moment as my innocent child?"

"But is it possible," said our heroine, with a look of astonishment, horror, and incredulity, "that your husband could ever have had the heart to put his fiendish threat into execution?"

"Alas!" replied Alice, "it is too true. He murdered the poor babe by tossing it into the sea, and—"

"Gracious Heaven!" interrupted our heroine, "and is it possible that there can be such a monster in existence? Alas! my good woman, if all that you have stated to me be true, you have indeed suffered most severely, and I marvel much that you should ever have found strength sufficient to endure it."

"Heaven only knows how I have done so," returned Alice; "and it would have been much better for me if I had not, for you must at once imagine how unspeakable must have been my sufferings after what it had been my cruel lot to have to encounter, and to be compelled to remain with that man who had been guilty of such numerous and dreadful crimes.—But to continue: When I once more recovered I found myself in my own cabin, at least the one in which I had been confined since I had been on board the vessel, and that old Beatrice was in attendance upon me. My first act was to look anxiously round for Drayton and the infant, but they were not in the cabin, and the whole of the dreadful truth flashed upon my memory with the most overwhelming force, and in the most delirious accents I demanded of Beatrice what had become of my infant. Although she did not return any direct answer, her looks were sufficient to confirm my most terrible apprehensions, and with a loud skriek, I again became insensible.

"For weeks and months after this my situation was most deplorable, and I was completely delirious. No doubt the treatment I received on board the pirate vessel during this painful interval was anything but kind; but youth and a vigorous constitution at length served partially to restore me, and I became acquainted with all the dreadful particulars that had taken place. What was the horror, the insupportable agony and frenzy of my feelings as I listened to them; and how many and fearful were the curses that I invoked upon the head of the monster Drayton. But how much more intense were those powerful feelings when I first saw him after my restoration to my senses! How bitter were the reproaches that I heaped upon his head! But he listened with the utmost indifference to them, and they made not the least impression on him. From that time not the least change might be said to have taken place in my destiny, and there is nothing more which it is worth the while for me to take the least trouble to relate; years have in some measure blunted the edge of my sorrows, but it is impossible that I can ever again know what peace and happiness are while I remain in the present painful and degrading situation into which I have unfortunately for so many years been plunged, and from which death would afford me such a happy release."

CHAPTER XXII.

MORE PERILS.—THE TEMPEST.—THE RENEWED CHASE.—THE ENGAGEMENT.—DESTRUCTION OF THE PIRATE SHIP.

Thus Alice concluded her eventful story, which from the startling nature of some of its incidents had greatly interested our heroine, while at the same time it had excited her warmest sympathy for the many heavy misfortunes which it had been her hard lot to encounter.

"Your troubles have certainly been far greater than my own, Alice," said our heroine, "and I wonder that you did not entirely sink under such an accumulation of terrors. What an inhuman wretch must the man be to whom you are united! But do you really believe that he sacrificed the life of your child in the manner which he threatened?"

"Alas!" answered Alice, with a shudder, as she recalled the dreadful circumstance to her memory, but from which it could never be eradicated, "there can be no doubt of it; and Drayton seemed to take a savage delight in talking of it in my presence afterwards."

"How agonising it must have been to you to be compelled to remain in the power and at the mercy of such a miscreant," remarked Mary.

"Ah, Mrs. Tiller, you may say that," returned Alice. "What language can possibly convey an adequate idea of my sufferings?"

"You must indeed view him with horror and disgust," said Mary. "But has the opportunity never presented itself to you to escape from him?"

"Ah, no," replied Alice; "the villains, who know well what they would have a right to expect should I obtain my liberty, will take good care of that. And, in fact, so great is the number of years that have elapsed since the pirates have held me in their power, that I have become almost resigned to my fate, though it is quite impossible for me ever to forget the dreadful past, or to look back upon it without the blood freezing within my veins. But I fear that you are weary after having listened so long to my tedious narrative, and I will, therefore, retire, and leave you to endeavour to gain an hour or two's repose. I do not suppose that you have anything to fear from the intrusion of Brandon at present."

"God grant that I may not," said Mary fervently; "but, alas, I fear that I have now a right to anticipate the worst, after the cruel and revolting threats that he has held out to me."

"Keep up your spirits, Mrs. Tiller," advised her kind-hearted companion, "and I trust that fortune may smile upon you much sooner than you now seem to anticipate. Should the vessel which Harry Halliyard is on board again come in sight of us, they will, no doubt, exert themselves to the utmost to overtake us; and should they do so, from their superior force, there can be little, if any doubt which way the victory will be decided."

"Ah, Alice," returned our heroine, "I cannot flatter myself with any such an idea; and even if the Porpoise should be likely to bear down upon this ship and to obtain a victory, I feel most terribly satisfied that, sooner than I should fall into the power of my friends, the villain Brandon will at once put a period to my existence, and thus all the hopes of Halliyard will be destroyed, and he will be left to even still greater misery than that which he now doubtless is enduring."

"Well, Mrs. Tiller," remarked Alice, "it will be much better for you not to abandon yourself altogether to those feelings of despair, but still to try to put your trust in Providence, who, you may depend upon it, will not desert you, but will yet bring you safe through all the dangers by which you are surrounded, however dismal and cheerless your prospects may for the present appear to be."

"I thank you for the words of encouragement you offer me," said Mary, "and believe me I will endeavour to indulge in them. Should it turn out as you predict, how sincerely grateful must I ever feel to the Almighty for the mercy He will have extended towards me."

Alice returned no answer, but she again encouraged our heroine with a smile, and then quitted the cabin. When she was gone, Mary resigned herself to those thoughts that so busily occupied her mind, and upon which she was unable to come to any decidedly satisfactory conclusion. The circumstances which Alice had related in her narrative were of such a peculiar nature that they excited her deepest interest, and she could not but feel the greatest pity towards her, and to look upon the misfortunes she had had to encounter as far more terrible than her own. At length, however, feeling indeed somewhat fatigued, she sought to compose herself to sleep for an hour or two, and, as all was silent on board the vessel, she succeeded in doing so, and in this state she continued for some time, until she was once more aroused by the return of Alice, who brought with her some refreshments, and in reply to her eager inquiries she informed her that she might make her mind quite easy for that day, as she had overheard Brandon declare that it was not his intention to visit her. This, as the reader may expect, afforded her much satisfaction, and she became more calm and contented in her mind. The day passed away without anything particularly worthy of notice taking place; but as the evening approached, ponderous clouds gathered upon the horizon, the sea-bird sent forth his melancholy cry, and everything gave token of an approaching storm, much to the discomfiture of our heroine, who looked forward to its terrors with much alarm and anxiety. She was not long kept in a state of suspense, for presently the waters became violently agitated, the wind blew a stiff gale from the north, and the black clouds which had so long hung over the broad waters of the ocean like funeral palls, burst and discharged their contents in torrents of rain, while the loud voice of the thunder, and the flashing of the lightning added their horrors to the scene.

Mary felt a terrible presentiment at her heart; but still her thoughts were more powerfully fixed upon the danger to which Harry would be exposed, and the grief and disappointment he would experience at the escape of the pirates, in whose power he had probably ascertained that she was.

"Heaven protect you, poor Harry," she exclaimed, "and bring you quite safe through all the perils by which you probably are at present surrounded. Alas! too well I know how great your anguish must be when you reflect upon the uncertainty of my fate, and the little chance there is of our ever beholding each other again. Oh, were the fond hopes we had encouraged in our more youthful days never doomed to be realised? and if so, better, much butter would it have been for both of us had we never beheld each other. Oh, Harry, I feel that, let whatever may be the consequence, your image is fixed so firmly in my heart that nothing can ever erase it. And yet am I not a guilty wretch to encourage such thoughts at these? Unfortunate Joe, you who have ever been so kind to me, and who must at the present time be suffering so much at my mysterious disappearance, how greatly are you to be pitied, and what a cruel injustice do I do you by still encouraging my fatal and hopeless passion for another now that I am your wife. The misfortunes that have since befallen me are only a just punishment for the errors I have committed; and oh, how I shudder with horror when I reflect upon those that are doubtless yet in store for me."

The howling of the winds, the noise of the rattling thunder, the crash of falling spars, and the oaths of the pirates as they rushed hurriedly to and fro above her head in the performance of their various duties, now became completely deafening; and ever and anon, as the lightning flashed athwart the dark sky, and rendered the terrors of the scene still more awfully visible, our heroine's heart sunk within her, her courage entirely forsook her, and covering her face with her hands, for a few moments she could only give vent to the powerful emotions that struggled at her breast in the most convulsive sobs and tears. Unused as she was to such terrific scenes as that which then prevailed, the reader may easily form a just idea of the feelings of mingled horror and despair that at that moment agitated her. In truth it was a fearful storm, such a one as probably not one of the oldest seamen had seldom, if ever before experienced, and no wonder, therefore, that it should have such an effect upon one of the delicate nature of our heroine. But at length she sunk upon her knees, and most fervently did she offer up her prayers to Heaven for mercy for herself, for Harry, and for all those unfortunate beings who were exposed to such imminent and fearful dangers. She then endeavoured to become more calm, but that was a task which it was impossible for her easily to accomplish, and she almost gave it up in despair. She was interrupted in her dismal and almost insupportable thoughts by the abrupt entrance of Alice, the expression of whose features plainly showed that she was labouring under feelings almost of as great excitement as her own.

"Oh, Alice," she exclaimed, "what a horrible storm is this! Heaven in its wrath frowns upon us, and the crisis of our fate is evidently approaching."

"Do not give way to this violent state of agitation, Mrs. Tiller, I beseech you," returned Alice, "for great though I admit the dangers by which we are at present surrounded to be, we shall yet, I trust, be able to surmount them. Be calm—be calm."

"Calm!" repeated Mary, and she shuddered—"oh! how is it possible that I can be so when I contemplate this frightful scene? The guilty wretches, too, that compose the crew of this vessel, what mercy can they expect? Alas! our fate is sealed; but why should I repine or tremble? Is not death far more preferable than the revolting fate to which the miscreant Brandon would consign me? It is!—Almighty God, your will be done, I resign myself into your hands; pardon me for the errors I have committed, watch over and protect my husband and Halliyard, and suffer my soul to be at rest."

Sobs choked her further utterance, and again covering her face with her hands, she gave herself up to all the violence of her emotions. Alice did not offer any observations for some time, but suffered her to give free and uninterrupted indulgence to her feelings—in fact, she seemed to be at a loss what advice or consolation to offer under the peculiar circumstances, for she was nearly in as great a state of alarm and agitation as herself, and stood watching the progress of the storm in the greatest anxiety. Every moment did that fearful tempest increase in violence, and from the wild and fearful expressions of the guilty crew, which might be plainly heard above the furious voice of the tempest, it was perfectly clear that they thought their situation to be most desperate, and were nearly in a state of as great alarm as themselves. The sea, to use a common observation, ran mountains high, all the efforts of the pirates were comparatively ineffectual, and notwithstanding that their vessel was an excellent craft, and had surmounted innumerable perils of the most awful description during the many years it had been afloat, it was quite evident that unless the storm shortly abated, it would be almost impossible for it to live, and as they viewed the impending danger by which they every moment became more and more surrounded, the crew seemed to be worked up to a pitch of excitement which rendered them almost incapable of performing the extra duties which had devolved upon them, and, therefore, made the situation of all those on board still more critical and fearful. Alice viewed the anguish of our heroine with the deepest sympathy, and almost forgot her own danger in the anxiety she experienced for her—and, indeed, so great were the troubles she had for so many years experienced, and from which she now saw not the least probability of any deliverance, that she was almost enabled to view death with indifference, as a happy release from the sufferings and the degredations to which she was now and had been so long exposed. She, however, devoutly offered up her prayers to the Almighty, and endeavoured to muster up all the fortitude she could in order to impart some degree of consolation and confidence to her fellow-sufferer. A loud crash on deck, which seemed to proclaim the occurrence of some fresh and fearful disaster, aroused Mary from the lethargy of despair into which she had fallen; this was succeeded immediately by the most terrific flashes of lightning, and deafening peals of thunder, and completely astounded, confused, and dismayed, our heroine started from the spot on which she had been supporting herself, and staggering to the arms of Alice, with a cry of terror, she stared in her face aghast, and, for a second or two, she was so much overpowered by her feelings that she was completely unable to utter a syllable. At length, however, she said—

"Great God of Heaven! what does that awful sound portend? Our fearful doom is sealed. What will become of us?"

"Courage, dear Mrs. Tiller," replied the kind-hearted Alice, "for much, if not everything depends upon your firmness on this, as I must admit, most trying occasion. With the blessing of Heaven, notwithstanding the awful dangers by which we are at present surrounded, we shall yet be saved from the untimely fate which now seems to be so inevitably impending o'er our heads."

"Ah, no!" ejaculated Mary, "I dare not encourage such a hope, for what room is there for it under the dreadful circumstances? But believe me, it is not for my own fate that I so much suffer (for life has now but little or no value for me), as for the dangers to which those who are far more precious to me than my own existence are exposed. Oh, Halliyard, in such a storm as that which now prevails, and which threatens to sacrifice all those who are unfortunately exposed to its fury, what will become of you? If we were only permitted to meet again, though death should almost immediately be our portion, methinks I could meet my fate with fortitude and calm resignation to the will of Heaven. My wretched husband, too—alas! I fear that we have beheld each other for the last time, and to know, to feel, at least, convinced that you will consider me guilty of infidelity, from the mysterious manner of my disappearance, is, if possible, far more torturing than all. Oh, God! these accumulated feelings of excruciating agony nearly drive my brain to madness, and I scarcely know what I am about."

Convulsive sobs choked her further utterance, and she leant upon the shoulder of Alice for support, and wept aloud. That equally unfortunate woman was at a loss what to say to her, for her despair was as great as her own, and a silence of several minutes ensued, during which interval the danger of their situation every moment became more painfully imminent. The vessel was tossed about like a straw, now being almost engulphed in the waters of the deep, and anon, as it were, dashed to the summit of the loftiest rocks, and threatened every instant to go to pieces. In the agony and delirium of her feelings, our heroine would have hastened upon deck, and at once have become a spectator of all the horrors of her situation, had she not been prevented by Alice, who exerted herself to the utmost to pacify her, though it was with very little success indeed that she did so; and, in fact, the task which had so pain-

fully devolved upon her was a most hopeless one, and one which it required almost superhuman skill to accomplish, and it was wonderful how she was enabled to act with the fortitude and presence of mind that she did, which would have completely disheartened many persons, who might have been supposed to possess more moral courage and energy than she did. But she struggled with her own feelings in a most marvellous manner, and assuming a degree of composure which she was far from experiencing, she tendered to our heroine such advice and consolation as were necessary under the dreadful and trying circumstances. But, unfortunately, such was the despair which had settled upon the heart of Mary, that all that she could say to her was nearly to no purpose, and as every succeeding minute rendered their danger still more appallingly apparent, that despair naturally increased to a degree that was quite insupportable.

"All is lost!" exclaimed our distracted heroine, as she clasped her hands together vehemently, and gazed wildly upon Alice in the most indescribable agony; "Heaven announces our fate in the hoarse voice of the tempest, and how puny and unavailing are all our efforts to avoid it. Why should I thus prolong my misery, since there is no hope? Let me hasten to precipitate my fate, and by plunging at once into the angry deep, terminate the sufferings which I am now, and have been for so long a time enduring. Release me, Alice; if you are indeed sincerely my friend, you will no longer detain me from the execution of my purpose."

"Oh, what madness is this," replied her companion, forcibly holding her, and endeavouring by all the means in her power, and by the expression of her features to pacify her, though she saw but too much reason for the wildness of that despair to which she gave utterance, "for Heaven's sake, my dear Mrs. Tiller, do endeavour to tranquillise your feelings now that there is so much reason for calmness and fortitude, under the fearful circumstances in which it has pleased Providence to place us. Would you, in the frenzy of your despair, commit an act which might afterwards doom your soul to perdition? Again I im-

ALICE'S ILLNESS ON THE DEATH OF WALTER SEYTON.

plore you to be firm, and to seek to resign yourself to the will of Heaven, which, depend upon it, will not desert you in this the terrible hour of your need."

"Firmness—resignation !" said Mary, with an impatient and despairing look; "oh, how wildly and how uselessly do you talk to me. What hope is there for us? Does not Heaven, I say again, frown upon us, and in the voice of the tempest bid us despair? Why, then, should we procrastinate that fate which must so shortly overtake u how the thunder rattles alon vault of Heaven—how the our vessel shiver in the blast mountainous wave which swe is a fearful herald of appro of that frighful doom whicl impossible for us to avoid of the Most High is up vain we may seek to strug solemn and almighty decr ful execrations of the g tel our inevitable doom, s? Hark the high timbers of , and every eps its deck .ching death, it is utterly .. The curse .n us, and in le against His ee. The fear- ilty crew fore- and add to the terrors which it is impossible for human nature to support. And now methinks I behold the gallant ship on which poor Halliyard is aboard battling in vain with the angry and fearful elements. What form is that which wildly rushes upon the deck, and stretches forth its arms towards me? It is that of him to whom my heart must ever be devoted, but whom cruel fate so sternly decreed should ne'er become mine! Even above the loud voice of the tempest I can hear him call frantically and despairingly upon my name; and oh, how vainly does he supplicate to Heaven for mercy! And now still fiercer rages the tempest, wave after wave sweeps over the deck, washing numbers of the unfortunate crew to an ocean grave. One simultaneous and appalling shriek, and the ill-fated vessel has disappeared in the angry sea with which she has so long and so vainly battled, and the whole of the wretched beings who were on board of her have perished. And shall I still continue to live when he who was so precious to me has met with so awful and untimely a fate? No, no, it shall not be! Release your hold of me, woman, or dread the consequences. Dear Harry! I hasten to join you in eternity!"

With these wild words, and with an expression of countenance which was truly awful to behold, she forcibly released herself from the arms of Alice, who was so bewildered that she scarcely knew what she was about, and hurried towards the door of the cabin with all the air of a maniac; but, overpowered by the excitement of her feelings, she uttered one piercing cry of despair and agony, and sunk insensible upon the floor.

Alice gazed upon her for a few moments with the greatest pity, and then raising her in her arms, she placed her in a seat, and supported her as well as the violent motion of the vessel would permit her.

"Unfortunate woman," she ejaculated, "too well, I fear, have you predicted the awful fate that awaits us, and which, unless it is prevented by some merciful and almost miraculous interposition of providence, it will be impossible for us to avoid. How fiercely does the storm continue in its fury, and how vainly do the puny efforts of man seek to combat it, and to stay that fate which appears at present too probable it will be impossible for them to avert. Heaven help us, and receive our souls, if it be its almighty will that we should thus untimely perish."

She could say no more, for the horrors of the scene which reigned around, and the confusion which prevailed on deck, completely bewildered and stupified her, and she was in that state of agitation that she scarcely knew what she was about. Nothing could surely equal the terrors of that moment, and every one that elapsed seemed to be fraught with accumulated danger, and to frown additional despair. It seemed as though the fate which awaited them was indeed inevitable; and it appeared little short of madness to seek to combat against it; but still it was evident that the daring crew were unabated in their efforts to weather the storm, and Alice could hear from their hurried and wild exclamations that, like most men in their painful situation, they alternated between hope and despair, though the latter feeling no doubt predominated. The heart of Alice, even although she had been accustomed to such scenes, sunk within her as she contemplated the frightful dangers by which they were surrounded, and she did not attempt to restore Mary to sensibility, for she considered that, under present circumstances, unconsciousness was a mercy to her; but most fervently did she offer up her prayers to Heaven for mercy, and continued to watch in a state of the greatest anxiety and dread the progress of the storm, but for some time without perceiving anything whatever to excite her hopes.

In this manner about half an hour passed away, and although our heroine breathed freely, she still remained insensible, such was the powerful effects which her over-excited feelings had taken upon her. But, at length, a sudden and unexpected change came over the scene, so sudden, indeed, that it seemed almost miraculous, and Alice could scarcely believe the evidence of her senses. The violence of the storm, as the wind suddenly changed, abated in a considerable degree, the lightning flashed less frequently, and not so vividly and intensely as it had before done; the thunder gradually murmured off in the distance, the rain no longer descended in the same overwhelming torrents which it had previously done, the waves were less violently agitated, the dangers of the tempest appeared to be all but over, and everything betokened a coming calm.

What an extraordinary and almost incredible change was this to take place, when but a few minutes before grim death seemed to stalk most threateningly before them, and Alice could not but view it with the utmost astonishment and incredulity, while at the same time her heart overflowed with gratitude to the Supreme for the unbounded mercy He had extended towards them, a mercy which the villain, Brandon, and the guilty wretches who were under his command so little deserved, and hope again revived in her bosom, though her feelings of thankfulness were the more excited for the preservation of our heroine than the prolongation of her own life, which for so many years had been an insupportable burthen to her. The noise and confusion which for so many hours had prevailed upon deck now all but subsided, and Alice imagined, though she had no doubt that the vessel had received much injury in the storm, that the crew considered the dangers that had before so fearfully threatened them were past, and that they would again abandon themselves to their usual state of recklessness and dissipation, for they were not the sort of men upon whom the warning which they had received was likely to work any beneficial effect, but, on the contrary, was calculated to inspire them with fresh confidence and daring.

Mary still remained in the same state of insensibility, and from which she did not seem likely soon to recover, but she was perfectly calm, and Alice considered that her unconsciousness was all for the best, and she had no doubt what the effect of the sudden and fortunate change would have upon her spirits when she should revive to a knowledge of it. She sank upon her knees, and raising her hands and her eyes energetically towards Heaven, she poured forth her heartfelt thanks to it for their truly providential preservation, and then awaited calmly the recovery of her unfortunate and insensible companion, but whom she was determined not to leave for a minute.

"Oh, what a happy and unexpected change is this," she ejaculated, "and from what a dreadful state of agony will it relieve her when she becomes conscious of what has taken place. Poor woman, she is indeed the victim of a most cruel fate, and would to Heaven that I had the means of rescuing her from it; but alas! I am as powerless as herself, and any promise of that kind on my part would not only be cruel but fallacious. May the Almighty watch over and protect her, for I fear that she has many troubles and persecutions yet to experience from the guilty Brandon. The hardened wretch, there are no means of moving him to pity or remorse, and to encourage any hopes of the kind would be mad and futile. The threats he has held out to her he will not fail to carry into effect, and it will afford him the most savage satisfaction to witness her anguish and despair. Heaven help her, I most fervently say again, for without that she will indeed be lost."

Such were the thoughts and wishes that so strangely occupied the mind of the kind-hearted Alice, and so great was the sympathy which she felt towards her, that it completely superseded the anxiety and care which her own misfortunes would otherwise have caused her. She was, however, shortly aroused from these reflections by the sound of approaching footsteps, and soon afterwards the door was thrown open, and she was thrown into some confusion and dismay when the villain Brandon entered the cabin. He advanced hastily towards the spot where our heroine was reclining, and gazed eagerly and with a slight expression of alarm upon her, and then turning to Alice, in a stern voice he demanded—

"Why, how is this? What ails my fair prisoner? Speak!"

"The terrors of the storm that lately raged have been too great for her," answered Alice, "and she has fainted."

"Ay," repeated the pirate, "I wonder not at it, for a more terrific tempest, while it lasted, I have not experienced for many a day, and I fully expected that we should all have been food for the sharks before this. But, thanks to our gallant barque, we have weathered it bravely; it has now subsided, and all danger is at an end. But I must see what I can do to restore this damsel to her senses. Leave me, Alice, for I must have no intruders at our interview."

"Pardon me, Brandon," said Alice, timidly, "but surely it will be most imprudent for you to see her on the present occasion, and when her mind is naturally so much excited and agitated by the horrors that have taken place; I would advise——"

"You advise?" interrupted Brandon, fiercely—"fool! dare you so much presume? Begone, I say, or you may excite my wrath, and I need not tell you, I imagine, that that will be worse for you."

Alice looked anxiously and compassionately towards our heroine, and still hesitated to obey the stern and imperious commands of the brutal ruffian, but a look from him convinced her of the danger of any useless opposition on her part, and without venturing to say another word, she hastily quitted the cabin, and left the pirate captain with his unfortunate victim with a sad heart, anticipating the worst, and deeply lamenting that she had no power to assist her. When she was gone, Brandon stood and gazed earnestly upon our insensible heroine for a few minutes in silence, and it was quite evident, from the dark expression that overspread his stern and forbidding features, the guilty thoughts that occupied his mind, and how unshaken was the cruel determination he had formed to work her destruction. She still remained in the same inanimate and insensible condition, and from which it did not seem likely that she would at present recover, and the villain had, therefore, the opportunity of feasting his eyes to the full extent of his gratification.

"She is a lovely creature," he soliloquised, "and the longer I gaze upon her the more does my admiration increase, and the greater become the feelings of exultation I experience at my triumph. Oh, what moments of transport are in store for me! and what man is there who would not envy me my happiness? And yet I was fearful that the storm would deprive me of the gratification of my wishes, and that we should all of us ere this have been sent to Davy Jones. However, it seems that no such fate awaits the Saucy Wasp; and how gallantly has she been able to surmount every danger. Thanks to fortune, who has not yet deserted me and my daring crew, and, I trust, never will, the storm has now subsided, and our trim craft has escaped with far less damage than might have been expected. We shall see good service in her yet. But these perils are not at all fit for one of the tender and delicate nature of my victim to have to encounter, and I wonder not that it should have such an effect upon her, and that her fears should overpower her. Time, however, will doubtless inure her to them, and it shall be no fault of mine if I do not wean her entirely to my will. How beautiful she looks, even in her insensibility; her transcendent charms have completely captivated my senses, and I am half inclined to think that she has excited feelings of love in my hitherto stubborn heart. Ha—ha—ha! it would be something novel indeed to see Hugh Brandon, the pirate, the slave to a woman's heart! And yet, the sentiments with which she has inspired me, I feel convinced, amount to something more than mere admiration. No matter, she is mine, and in spite of the feelings of disgust and abhorrence which I know she entertains towards me, she must yield to my will, though it should break her heart afterwards. Break her heart? —psha! I talk like a fool; women's hearts, notwithstanding all they may affect, are not made of such fragile materials, I am satisfied, and I am not the sort of man to be intimidated from my purpose by any such idle and ridiculous consideration; and of that fixed resolve I will soon convince her, should she indeed entertain any doubt upon the subject, which I do not think she is likely to do. No, Mary, all your remonstrances, your tears and supplications will be in vain, for nothing whatever can rescue you from the fate to which I have consigned you, and in the anticipation of which I experience so much proud delight."

The villain paused, but he still continued to gaze with gloating eyes upon the unfortunate woman before him, and every instant his guilty and revolting passion increased in strength. But at length, unable to control his disgusting feelings, he stooped down over the inanimate form of our heroine, and impriated the most unlawful kisses upon her lips, while the expression of his eyes fully revealed the brutal determination he had come to, and how little poor Mary had to hope from his mercy and forbearance.

"Unconscious beauty," he again soliloquised, "how little do you dream who now stands in your presence, and has sipped the honey from your lips. But the length of this insensibility is most extraordinary, and I wish she would recover, though I am fully prepared for the shock she will experience at my presence, and can expect nothing less that that she will lavish her bitterest reproaches upon my head. But what matters it to me? What reason have I to heed them? All that she can say to me can have no possible effect upon me, or frustrate me in my purpose, and I may, therefore, well allow her full scope to her abuse."

Such were the guilty thoughts that continued to occupy the mind of the villain Brandon, and he again ventured to pollute her lips with his kisses. He watched her restoration to sensibility with the utmost anxiety and impatience, and paced the cabin backwards and forwards with hasty steps; but for some time she evinced not the least signs of recovery; and had it not been for her breathing so freely, and the expression of her countenance being so calm, he would have been under some apprehension as to the result, but as it was, he awaited with all the patience he could, and fully prepared himself for the reception he was sure to meet with from her. He had not to wait in suspense much longer; the effects of the strange state of lethargy which had so long steeped her senses evaporated, and suddenly heaving a deep sigh, she started from the place on which she had been reclining, and looked anxiously but vacantly around her, evidently for a moment or two unconscious of where she was, and not beholding Brandon, who had retired cautiously to a remote corner of the cabin, until she had sufficiently recovered for him to address her. She pressed her hands upon her temples, and seeming to endeavour to recal her scattered senses, at length, in wild and mournful accents of despair, she exclaimed—

"Where am I? What a strange and fearful dream I have had. But no, it was no dream; and hark! still howls the tempest! The rattling thunder and the flashing lightning mock my despair, and far outrival the tempest of feelings that rage within my breast. Husband! Harry! where are ye now? Ah! Halliyard, I see you! The frail vessel in which you sailed has gone to pieces, and you are struggling with the waves betwixt life and eternity! God! how they foam, and roar, and mock his efforts! Hark! he calls upon my name! he casts his eyes towards Heaven, and oh, what despair is there in his looks! Cowards! why do you all thus stand helplessly by? Is there no one who can render him any aid, and try to rescue him from the jaws of death? Have ye all become worse than infants? Nay, then, I, a poor weak woman, will boldly make the effort, and put ye all to the blush. Harry, dear husband of my soul, I come to save you, or to perish with you!"

As she gave utterance to these wild words she extended her arms, and with a frantic exclamation, but still not observing Brandon, she rushed towards the door of the cabin, but the violence of her distressed feelings overpowered her, and she sunk down again almost in a state of insensibility.

Even the villain Brandon was somewhat moved by her sufferings, and stood for a few moments and contemplated her in silence, half induced to leave the place, and abandon the idea of the interview which he had contemplated. But in a few moments Mary again started to her feet, and gazing vacantly around her, she exclaimed, in accents that were sufficient to make an impression even upon the most insensible heart—

"Ah! he still is battling with the merciless waves, and stretches forth his arms in vain towards me! Oh, what heartless monsters must ye all be not to make one effort to rescue from the jaws of death one so good, so noble, and so generous! He must not, shall not perish thus! Why do you hold me back when he calls upon me for aid in this his last extremity? I come to save you, or to die with you!"

With these frantic and delirious words

she once more rushed forwards, but at that moment her eyes caught the figure of the hated miscreant Brandon, and with an exclamation of fear she started back, and gazed at him with an expression of the most indescribable disgust, but was unable for a moment or two to give utterance to even a single syllable. Brandon, also, for a moment or two felt confused and abashed, and knew not what to say or how to act; but he quickly recovered himself, and advancing towards her, and laying his hand upon her arm, he ventured to utter her name in a more subdued tone than he was in the habit of doing. She started at the sound of his voice, and recoiled from him as if he had been something hideous, and then in tones the most thrilling, and which spoke at once the strong torrent of feeling that raged within her breast, she cried—

"Ah! fiend in human shape! murderer! pirate! monster! you here? You come to mock me in my agony, and to inflict fresh tortures upon me? Then it was no dream, and I am indeed truly wretched! Oh, why has not death relieved me from my sufferings? Why am I still left here to battle with such accumulated miseries that it makes the very soul shudder and freezes the blood within the veins to think upon them? Miscreant, begone, and leave me to my despair, or if you have one spark of pity remaining unextinguished in your insensible and guilty bosom, plunge your dagger to my heart, and end at once that life which has now become an intolerable burthen and so hateful to me."

"Psha!" exclaimed Brandon, sternly, "these heroics are all useless, and perhaps it is unnecessary for me to inform you that they will have not the slightest effect upon me. You may as well abandon them, and endeavour to act and to talk a little reasonable. You have nothing to fear, if you will only act according to my will, and resistance, I should think by this time you must be convinced, is little better than madness. The storm has now subsided, and, thanks to fortune, the saucy Wasp has been enabled to weather it gallantly; so come, Mary, away with this nonsense—become firm, and turn your thoughts alone to love and me, for here you are destined to reign the queen of as brave and loyal a set of subjects as ever owned the sovereign sway of beauty. You are from henceforth the pirate's bride—the mistress of the fearless rover of the seas; and as such, I, your lord and master, and all those who sail under my command, and dare not even to disobey my nod, are ready to pay homage to you. One sweet embrace in token of—"

"Monster!" cried the disgusted and horrorstruck woman, recoiling from him as he advanced towards her and endeavoured to put his threat into execution, "dare to approach me, or to pollute me by your touch, or, even powerful and secure as you may think yourself, the retribution of an outraged Heaven will descend upon your head and crush you. Oh, God! and must I then indeed be thus tortured and insulted? Death would indeed be a mercy to me, rather than to be subjected to such a fate as that which now threatens me. Brandon, you may pride yourself upon your present power and security, and think that you may set the vengeance of Heaven at defiance, and carry your brutality to the most unlimited extent; but beware of what you do, for—"

"Bah!" interrupted the pirate, hastily, "and think you that I heed such idle threats as these? No, I scorn, I defy them, and you may, therefore, save yourself the trouble of giving utterance to them, for there is nothing whatever that shall prevent the accomplishment of my wishes, and to obtain which I have been at so much trouble. A few hours only, and you must become mine, and henceforth become the willing partner of the rover's fortunes."

"Oh, horrible idea!" groaned our heroine, clasping her hands together, and looking despairingly around her, "are there no means of avoiding so fearful and revolting a fate? Oh, why did I not perish in the storm? Why did I ever again awaken to life, rather than I should meet with so terrible and apparently inevitable a doom as this?"

"Mary," said the villain Brandon, in a tone of affected gentleness, "if you are wise you will seek to tranquillise your feelings, and try to resign yourself to that which is in store for you, and from which nothing whatever can rescue you. Remember, that the treatment you will receive will depend entirely upon your own conduct. To remain obstinate where you have no power to oppose my will would be little short of madness, and would be sure to excite my indignation and revenge. But why should you view the prospect before you with such feelings of horror and disgust? To be sure, the change of life is new to you, and you are not yet inured to the perils of the deep; but, no doubt, by care and perseverance you will soon become used to it, and it shall be my constant study to afford you every means of enjoyment and happiness in my power, and which will leave you no cause to regret those from whom you are separated, and whom you probably will never behold again. So, come, my fair mistress, banish those gloomy feelings of despair and misery from your breast, and learn to enjoy those pleasures which it is in my power to bestow upon you. You will find a life on the ocean wave, and especially on board of such a gallant craft as the Wasp, and with such bold and fearless fellows for your subjects, much better than being compelled to be the partner of the poor, drivelling waterman, whom I am well convinced you do not love."

"Miscreant!" ejaculated Mary, her bosom swelling with feelings of the utmost resentment, "dare not to shock my ears by language so disgusting as that which has just escaped your lips; for, although you do indeed most unfortunately hold me in your power, and my fate appears to be inevitable, you will find me firm and resolute, and Heaven will yet, I trust, give me the power to resist your infamous, your diabolical designs."

"Ha—ha—ha!" laughed Brandon, "these are indeed bold words, Mary; but I can well afford to smile at them. Your resistance? Psha! the very idea is ridiculous, and you know but little of my character if you imagine that they can excite any thing but my utmost scorn. Fate has made you mine, and I will not fail, you may depend upon it, to take every advantage of it. You may, therefore, as well prepare yourself for that which I have promised you, and which will most assuredly take place, and that in a few hours."

"Mercy! mercy!—spare me, oh, spare me, Brandon," earnestly suppli-

cated our heroine, and tears of anguish starting to her eyes, "you cannot surely contemplate so dreadful, so monstrous an outrage;—oh, forbear, and even great as is the misery and the cruel wrongs you have inflicted upon me, I can yet forgive you for the past, and——"

"Forgive me?" interrupted the hardened villain, with a look of the greatest contempt; "and what, think you, do I value your forgiveness, knowing how completely I have you at my mercy?"

"Alas—alas!" sighed our heroine, "I know too well how completely useless it is to appeal to a wretch who is quite insensible to every feeling of humanity, and who takes a fiendish delight in witnessing the misfortunes and the sufferings of his poor, defenceless fellow creatures. But surely it is most brave, it is most manly to persecute a helpless woman, whom evil destiny has placed in your power, and to exult over the anguish which your villany has caused."

"You are at liberty to reproach me as much as you think proper," replied the pirate, coolly, "for I shall take no heed of it. I would, however, merely warn you that such observations as those you have just now made use of are not at all calculated to move me in your favour, but, on the contrary, they will only serve to strengthen my determination. You may as well banish the imagine of Harry Halliyard from your mind, for under the circumstances in which you are placed, it is not at all likely that you will ever behold him again, unless he should happen to fall into my power, a circumstance which, I imagine, knowing the feelings that I entertain towards him, would not afford you much satisfaction."

"Oh, Heaven forbid that such a fate should befal the noble-hearted but unfortunate Halliyard," cried Mary, fervently, and tears again gushing to her eyes, "for better, far better would it be for him should the angry waters of the ocean form his grave. Oh, Harry, what a cruel destiny is that to which you are now exposed, and how fearfully have all those fond and sanguine hopes of happiness that you formed been annihilated."

"As," said the pirate, with a sardonic grin, "they have, and that thought affords me some satisfaction, and also tends in no small measure to gratify my revenge."

"Hold, monster!" exclaimed our heroine, "and dare not thus to speak of one so noble and so generous. Oh, Brandon, you may proceed too far in your iniquitous designs, and foil yourself at the very moment when you imagine your triumph most certain."

"Bah!" returned the ruffian, impatiently, "I am not to be intimidated by observations such as these, and you do but waste your time in giving utterance to them. What, think you, have I to fear? What difficulties have I to surmount? Even this very moment I could put my threats into execution, and, poor weak woman as you are, how could you help yourself? But I will act with more forbearance to you than the scorn with which you treat me deserves, and will at least give you the time I have before mentioned to reflect upon what I have said, and to prepare yourself to meet that fate which most inevitably awaits you."

"Oh, monstrous!" groaned the distracted Mary, wringing her hands in an agony of anguish and despair. "All-merciful God, I most humbly but earnestly implore you to look down with pity upon me, and not to suffer this heartless miscreant to triumph altogether in his atrocious designs. Brandon, again I tell you to beware, and not to proceed to the dreadful extent which you have threatened, for assuredly, if you do, the most terrible vengeance of outraged Heaven, which ever watches over the innocent, will descend upon your head, and crush you in the midst of your guilty career."

"Ha—ha—ha!" again laughed Brandon, scornfully, "what an excellent sermon, and from what a pretty, pouting pair of lips does it proceed; I am sure it is quite enough to fascinate any one to listen to it. But, unfortunately, I am composed of such different materials to those which other men are, that I cannot duly appreciate it, especially when I have the entire gratification of my wishes at my command, and, therefore, you do but waste your time in exercising your eloquence upon me. No, Mary, you may depend upon it that Hugh Brandon, the pirate, is not the drivelling fool to waver in any purpose, or to be moved either by reproaches or supplications; and you may, therefore, as well make up your mind to the worst."

"Alas—alas!" groaned our heroine, "I feel that what you have said is too true, and my heart shudders with horror when I reflect upon it. Oh, what have I ever done to merit such a dreadful fate as this? Brandon, again I implore you in mercy to plunge your dagger to my heart, and terminate this wretched existence, rather than consign me to such a cruel destiny as that with which you have so inhumanly threatened me."

"Woman," returned the villain, sternly and determinedly, "you talk madly; sacrifice your life? No, no, I have reserved you for a far different fate, and one from which no human power can rescue you, so you will do well not to flatter yourself with any delusive hopes, for it would be worse than madness to anticipate that they could ever be realised."

"Oh, man of iron heart," said poor Mary, fixing upon him a look which was enough to penetrate to even the most guilty soul; "surely you will, notwithstanding your at present stern indifference, have bitter cause to repent such brutality as that which you are now practising towards me, a poor, defenceless woman. But my words are lost upon you; I should ere this have been convinced that your black heart is completely callous to every feeling of humanity, and I will no longer appeal to you. God of Heaven, I again beseech you to look down upon me, and not to suffer me to fall a victim to a fate which is too horrible, too disgusting, and too revolting to think upon."

She clasped her hands together, and again the scalding tears chased each other down her pale cheeks. Brandon stood by, and contemplated her for some minutes in silence; but he remained completely unmoved by her powerful emotion, and, on the contrary, exulted in the certain triumph of his atrocious designs, and which he was fully determined he would not delay putting into execution. But, at length, advancing nearer towards her, and again attempting to take her hand, which, however, she resisted, he said—

ALICE'S FATHER BEARING THE WOUNDED DRAYTON INTO THE COTTAGE.

"Come, Mary, these tears are useless, and I would, therefore, advise you to conquer your grief, and to resign yourself calmly to your fate, which, after all, you may not find to be half so terrible as you now seem to anticipate."

"Resign myself to my fate?" repeated our heroine, with a shudder; "oh! monstrous, most outrageous idea! How is it possible for me to do so with such a dreadful prospect as that which is now spread before me? But your triumph will be brief; never can I long survive such insupportable misery and degradation, or madness must surely seize upon my brain. Oh, Brandon, think upon what it is you would do, and abandon your wicked and diabolical designs ere it is too late."

"Abandon my designs," returned the pirate, "and when there is nothing to prevent their accomplishment? I must be an arrant fool to do so; and if you flatter yourself with any such preposterous ideas, you will find that they will only be doomed to be disappointed. In a few days I have no doubt that I shall reach one of my strongholds, and there my future mistress must prepare herself to yield to my wishes, and to offer no foolish resistance, which can only serve to exasperate me, and will have no power to alter her condition the least in the world."

"All-merciful Father, help me, then!" cried our heroine, emphatically, "for without your aid nothing but inevitable destruction awaits me. Oh, God, that I should ever have lived to experience such horrors as these, and to have no one near to assist me, or to sympathise in my most unmerited misfortunes. Brandon, you are a villain of the blackest dye, and the curse of Heaven will most surely one day descend most heavily upon your head, and crush you in the midst of your atrocious career of crime."

"I scorn, I defy the power you invoke," said the hardened wretch, "for I put no faith in it, and know full well that nothing whatever can thwart me in my plans. Of that you will be shortly convinced, if you any longer entertain any doubts upon the subject."

"Alas!" groaned the hapless Mary, "what terror do your words convey; but yet, oh, how much reason have I to fear that they will be realised, unless providence should interpose to rescue me at the eleventh hour. God grant that such may be the case, for even should I perish the next moment, it will be far more preferable to being made the wretched victim of such a hardened and odious miscreant as you."

"You would act wiser," said Brandon, with a frown, "if you were to be more choice in the language you venture to address to me. But it matters not; I am a villain, and I do not disown or feel ashamed of the title, and I have not the least doubt that I shall ever do justice to it. But mark me, Mary, and you must be convinced that when speaking of this business I do not state anything erroneously, the future mistress, the wife in all but the name of that villain you are doomed to be, and therefore will my triumph, at any rate, be complete, and all your remonstrances and reproaches will be entirely unavailing. You say true, there is indeed no one near who can render you the least assistance, or who will venture to sympathise with you, lest they should incur my vengeance, and consequently I can gratify my wishes to the fullest extent, and without any fear of interruption."

"What horrible words are these!" gasped forth our heroine, "and yet do I keenly feel how true they are, and that how powerless I am to help myself. Oh, my unfortunate husband, how dreadful would be your sufferings did you know the awful situation in which I am at present placed, and the fate which is impending o'er me!"

"Poor devil!" said the pirate, "no doubt he is not in a very comfortable state of mind at your strange disappearance; but you had better banish him from your mind, for it is not very likely that you will ever behold him again; and I dare say, considering that he was never the man of your choice, you will find no great difficulty in doing that."

"Hold!" said our heroine, fixing upon him a look of the utmost disgust and resentment; "dare not thus to mock and insult me. Oh, this is most cruel, and Heaven only knows how I shall find strength to support it. But leave me, Brandon, to the misery of my own torturing and dismal thoughts, for I cannot look upon or listen to your brutal observations without a shudder of horror. Leave me, I say, and endeavour, if possible, to encourage some slight feelings of humanity towards that unhappy and unfortunate woman whom you have so cruelly persecuted."

"Well," returned the pirate, coolly, "I consider that this interview has lasted long enough, and I will, therefore, comply with your request, and retire; but remember, when next we meet your fate will doubtless be decided."

"Oh, God!" gasped forth the unhappy woman, in accents of the greatest agitation, "and must it indeed be so? Is there no hope for me?"

"None whatever," answered the ruffian, with a malicious look of triumph; "on that you may depend, so you need not flatter yourself with any delusive ideas, which only a few hours, in all probability, will serve to dissipate. Remember my words, and prepare yourself for that which will most certainly take place."

Poor Mary again vehemently clasped her hands together in the intense agony of her feelings, and raising her eyes towards Heaven she exclaimed—

"Almighty God, I commit myself to your keeping, and fearful though the prospect which is spread before me at present appears to be, I do trust that, in Your mercy, You will not desert me in this dreadful hour of trial, and when I am threatened with destruction. But I will be firm, and not give way to despair; so great a villain as he who holds me in his power, and takes a savage delight in inflicting such miseries upon me, will not be permitted to triumph altogether; it would indeed be monstrous to suppose so."

"Ha! ha! ha!" laughed Brandon, "how it amuses me to hear you make use of such observations. But continue to indulge in such idea, if you think proper, for it matters not to me; in a very short time you will know whether or not they are doomed to be disappointed. As for myself, my mind is fully made up, and that is, therefore, quite enough for me."

"Brandon," said Mary, looking earnestly in his face, "and is it possible that you can remain inexorable? Oh, reflect upon that which you would do, and—"

"I have already reflected enough," impetuously interrupted the pirate, "and I think I have given you indulgence enough, in thus so long delaying the accomplishment of my wishes; but more you must not expect, for, as certain as you now breathe, at the time which I have stated, you must yield to my will, and all your supplications to avert your fate will be completely thrown away."

Mary groaned, and gazed at him with an expression of countenance that was sufficient to move the most stubborn heart, but it made not the least impression upon him, and, in fact, her agony, as we have said before, seemed rather to afford him satisfaction.

"Oh, God!" she cried at last, "and is it possible that there can be such a hardened miscreant in existence? And will he be allowed to accomplish his villanous designs with impunity? I cannot believe that he will, but that something will yet occur to relieve me from his power, and that, too, at a moment when it might be least expected. But why do I degrade myself by talking to him? The very sight of him is odious to me, and—"

"Odious as it is," interrupted Brandon, "you will ere long have constantly to endure it, and cannot help yourself. Farewell; when next we meet you may, perhaps, be convinced that I am at length a man of my word, and that I have promised nothing which I am not willing and fully enabled to perform."

Our heroine returned no answer, for her agitation was too great to suffer her to do so, and the villain Brandon having thus expressed himself, and fixing upon her once more a look of exultation, quitted the cabin, and left her to indulge in those thoughts that naturally crowded upon her mind, though she did feel somewhat relieved after he had retired from her presence. For some moments she remained silent, and transfixed to the spot on which he had left her; but at length all that had passed at this painful interview rushed with overwhelming force upon her memory, and the anguish of her mind can much better be conceived than any language could possibly portray it.

"Merciful Heaven!" she cried, and the blood seemed to curdle in her veins as she spoke, "in what a terrible and hopeless situation I am placed, and how dreadful is it even to contemplate. I am standing upon the very brink of destruction, and it is only by the kind interposition of Providence that I can hope to be saved. Oh, what an awful miscreant is he who holds me in his power, and what crime is there, however hideous, which he will hesitate to commit? How my soul shudders when those dark and torturing thoughts arise to my mind. Would to God that I had never again awakened to consciousness, but that I had perished in the tempest which lately so frightfully raged, then indeed all my cares would have been at rest; but now, great though and terrible as have been the miseries I have already endured, what tenfold troubles are yet in store for me! How is it possible that I can ever find fortitude sufficient to encounter them? and what resistance can I offer to such a desperate villain as Brandon? None, none whatever that can be of any avail. Alas! he has said truly that his triumph is all but certain, and now what is there left for me to do but to abandon myself to the most abject despair? Husband, unfortunate husband, and you, my still beloved Harry, we shall never meet again ; or, if we should indeed do so, under what dreadful circumstances would it be ! But, alas! when I reflect upon Halliyard, my heart misgives me, and I cannot help thinking that he has perished in the storm which recently raged with such fearful violence. Oh, that he should be so near me, and yet unable to come to my rescue ! Had the vessel on which he is aboard been successful in the pursuit, the pirates would, in all probability, have been defeated, and I should now most likely have been at liberty, and safe under the protection of him to whom my heart is still so fondly attached. Oh, how terrible is this disappointment, and it ought to convince me, if anything were wanting to do so, that the fates have conspired against me, and that I am doomed to nothing but misery and despair. What human fortitude can ever endure all this ?"

She paused, for convulsive sobs choked her utterance, and she paced the cabin backwards and forwards with those poignant feelings of emotion that almost overpowered her.

"But a few short hours, he said," she resumed at last, "and then he is resolved that the brutal wishes he has so long entertained shall, in spite of the consequences that may follow, be accomplished. Oh, God ! how terrible is that reflection ; and yet, at present, there seems not to be the least probability of anything occurring to prevent it, and the fate which awaits me appears to be inevitable. What is to be done ? I know not, and the longer I dwell upon it, the more dark and certain seems to be the doom which is in store for me."

She was interrupted in the midst of these melancholy reflections by the sudden opening of the cabin-boor, and Alice entered and advanced eagerly towards her, and gazed with the utmost anxiety in her face.

"Thank Heaven, this painful interview is over," said the kind-hearted woman, "and that I am once more permitted to come near you, for I have no doubt you much need my consolation and advice. You look pale and agitated, and I fear you have suffered much ; but has anything more particular occurred to alarm you ?"

"Oh, Alice," replied our heroine, "I have indeed much to distract and to torture my mind, and no wonder that misery and despair should settle upon my heart, when the crisis of my fate seems to be so rapidly and so inevitably approaching. Oh, Alice, did you but know the painful and disgusting interview which I have just had with my cruel and remorseless persecutor, you must, you would indeed pity me."

"I am fully certain, Mrs. Tiller," returned Alice, "that you will do me the justice to believe that I sincerely sympathise with you in your misfortunes, and only regret that it is not in my power to render you any assistance ; still, I would not have you give way to despair, for, dismal though your prospects at present probably appear to be, I trust that something will shortly occur to release you from your present sufferings, and to avert those dangers which you now so naturally apprehend."

"Alas !" sighed Mary, "how dare I encourage that hope, when, in a few short hours only, the villain Brandon has threatened to carry the diabolical designs he has against me into execution ? Oh, Alice, how my soul trembles and recoils when I reflect upon that, and see not the least chance of my avoiding the cruel and revolting fate which is impending over me. Would to Heaven that I had perished in the tempest which recently raged so furiously ; then would my troubles have been at an end, for life under the circumstances in which I am placed is an insupportable burthen to me."

"Talk not so, my unfortunate friend," said her kind-hearted companion, "for it grieves me to hear you. The Almighty will not desert you in your hour of need, depend upon it ; and He will not suffer the brutal ruffian Brandon to triumph altogether in his guilty designs. He will be foiled, depend upon it, and you will again be restored to liberty and happiness."

"Oh, Alice," said Mary, "in vain you try to inspire me with hope, and I cannot believe that you think what you say, for what cause is there for it in the prospect that is at present before me ? The miscreant who has me in his power is insensible to every feeling of humanity and justice, and takes a savage delight in witnessing my anguish; what, then can I do but apprehend the worst? Oh, God! how terrible is the thought, and I wonder how I have so long been able to withstand the dreadful trials to which I have been subjected. But to anticipate that which is in store for me, to become the degraded mistress of such a guilty miscreant as Brandon, oh, Heaven! the bare thought alone harrows up my very soul; and had I but the means, sooner than encounter such a fate, I would at once terminate my existence."

"Calm your feelings, my dear friend," said Alice, "and do not give way to such fearful thoughts as those to which you have just now given utterance. There is no knowing what a few hours may bring forth. Should the pirates encounter an enemy it might prove too powerful for them, and then you would be released from the dangers by which you are at present surrounded, and be restored to your home and your friends."

"Blissful thought!" ejaculated our heroine; "but, alas! I dare not encourage it, for too well do I feel convince that it would only be doomed to disappointment. The cruel fates seem to have conspired against me, and I see no prospect whatever of any deliverance from my present misery. Had the vessel on board of which is Halliyard succeeded in overtaking the pirates, there might have been some chance of my deliverance. But, even then, I fear that the hardened and inexorable Brandon would have sacrificed me to his vengeance, when he saw that he was likely to be defeated, rather than that I should again have been restored to liberty. What is there that such a blood-stained miscreant as he is would hesitate to do?"

"He is indeed a villain of the blackest dye," coincided Alice, "and Heaven knows what I have suffered at his hands. But still the retribution of outraged Heaven is sure, and it may overtake him much sooner than you anticipate. Muster all the fortitude you can, and you will yet be able to surmount the dangers and difficulties by which you are at present surrounded."

"Would to Heaven that I could think so," returned Mary, "but it is impossible for me to indulge in any such hopes

when I take all the circumstances of my situation into consideration. In whatever direction I turn my thoughts, nothing but despair meets my imagination. The threats that Brandon has held out to me are dreadful, and what can I expect from a man who is so entirely callous to every proper feeling as he is? Alas—alas! how terrible must be the sufferings that my unfortunate husband is now enduring; how awful the uncertainty that he must be in concerning the fate which has befallen me. Will he believe me false to him, and think that I have abandoned him to follow the fortunes of Halliyard? Dreadful idea! and yet it is too probable for me to banish it altogether from my mind."

"Try to do so," said Alice, "for it is only torturing your mind unnecessarily. Your husband will, I trust, not be so uncharitable as to judge thus harshly of you."

"You know not all the melancholy circumstances of my history," said our heroine, "or I am afraid you would think differently. Oh, I feel that I have acted with cruel injustice towards him in still encouraging the passion which I entertain towards that man to whom I was betrothed, but whom fate decreed should never become mine. But in vain do I endeavour to stifle the fatal and hopeless sentiments in my breast. Oh, what a fearful destiny has ours been. And shall we never meet again? Alas! there seems to be no prospect of it, and even if we should, under what circumstances will it be? The brutal wretch, Brandon, will probably then have accomplished his atrocious designs, and I shall have become a poor degraded being, hateful to myself and despised by all my fellow creatures. It would have been much better for me had the Almighty long ere this have taken me to himself, rather than reserve me for a fate which is far too dreadful to contemplate, but from which I see not the least possibility of escaping."

The most agonising sobs and tears choked her further utterance, and throwing herself back on her seat, and burying her face in her hands, she abandoned herself to all the anguish of her feelings, and every moment her despair became greater and more insupportable. Alice did her utmost to console her, but that was a most difficult task to accomplish, and she succeeded but indifferently. In fact, she was at a loss what to say, for she could not but view the prospect before poor Mary with the same melancholy and despairing eyes that she did, knowing so well as she did the brutal and determined character of Brandon, and that nothing whatever would have the power to move him from anything on which he had fixed his mind, especially when goaded on by a spirit of revenge, as well as the gratification of his guilty passions.

"Would to Heaven," she said, "that it was in my power to rescue you from your present danger, or to alleviate your sufferings; there is no sacrifice that I would not make, no risk that I would not willingly run to do so."

"I feel certain that you speak the truth," returned Mary, "and most sincerely grateful do I feel to you for it; but, alas! I feel too keenly that my fate is sealed, and that nothing whatever can release me from it; how is it possible, then, that I can be any otherwise than wretched?"

"True," coincided Alice, "I deeply appreciate your feelings under the desperate and melancholy situation in which you are placed, and I am certain that I need not again assure you that I fully and deeply commiserate your sufferings, and hope that the retribution of Heaven will at last overtake your brutal oppressor. Certain though his success now indeed appears to be, I cannot believe that he will be allowed to triumph altogether in his nefarious and diabolical designs."

Mary shook her head dismally, and it was in vain that she endeavoured to think as Alice suggested, who she felt convinced did not breathe the real sentiments of her mind; in fact, taking all the melancholy circumstances of her situation into consideration, she did not see how it was possible that she could do so. She remained silent for some time, and abandoned herself to the most dismal thoughts, and Alice did not offer to interrupt her; in fact, she was at a loss what to say which was at all calculated to tranquillise her feelings; and thus some considerable time passed drearily away.

The pirate barque was now proceeding at a rapid rate over the deep waters of the ocean, propelled by a favouring breeze, and the excitement which had prevailed amongst the crew during the time of the raging of the storm had now ceased, and the rude and boisterous mirth of the ruffians frequently saluted and shocked the ears of our unfortunate heroine, and made the terrors of her fate, if possible, more apparent. It was in vain that she strove to obtain any relief from her anguish of mind, and almost overwhelming were the thoughts hatt crowded upon her brain, and drove her almost to madness. In this dismal manner the day passed away, and Alice only left her for a short time, and did all that she could to arouse her from the state of despair under which she suffered, but all the arguments that she could make use of had but little, if indeed any effect upon her. With what melancholy feelings of agony and despair did she watch from the windows of the cabin in which she was confined, the rolling of the billows, and picture to herself the dismal fate which was in store for her, and from which there seemed not to be the least chance of escaping, and when she thought of the cruel destiny to which she was consigned, and remembered the threats that Brandon had held out to her, and which there could not be the least doubt that he would not fail to put into execution, and that, too, at the time which he had promised, her heart sunk within her, and the anguish of her feelings was so great that she could not contain herself, and she wrung her hands in despair, and scalding tears chased each other down her cheeks. Alice was deeply affected, and still she exerted herself to the utmost to calm the violent agitation of her mind, and to inspire her with hope; but her words fell ineffectively upon the ears of our heroine, and every moment her anguish became, if possible, more terrible and insupportable.

"There is no hope—there is no hope for me!" she sighe, "and I must be mad if I were to to indulge in it. Alas! what a wretched and unfortunate being I am, and how can I look forward to the future with any other feelings than those of horror. But a few hours, and the miscreant who holds me in his power, and who seems to take a savage delight in witnessing my sufferings, will put his awful threats into execution, and then what a poor degraded being shall I be. Oh, God! how I shudder when I contemplate the fearful fate which is impending over my head, and which I see not the least possibility of avoiding. Why am I permitted to live if I am doomed to such misery and degradation as that?"

"Would to Heaven that anything I could say could impart consolation to you, and banish those torturing feelings of despair from your mind," observed Alice. "Pray exert yourself, and acquire all the energy you can, and all may not terminate so bad as you now anticipate."

"Alas?" returned Mary, "what room have I to think so. No supplications on my part can possibly make any impression upon the villain, Brandon, for, inured to crime as he is, and taking a malicious pleasure in working the misery of his fellow-creatures, his heart is entirely insensible to every feeling of pity."

"But Providence may yet interpose to rescue you from his power," said Alice, "which I fervently hope and trust it will, for from the wretch Brandon, I am fully aware that you can expect no mercy. But much depends upon your firmness, and if you make a determined resistance to his will——"

"Oh, of what use will be any resistance that I, a poor defenceless woman, can offer to such a desperate and determined ruffian?" interrupted Mary, with a look of the utmost despair; "he will but mock at my opposition, exulting in the power which he knows so well he holds over me, and nothing whatever, I am convinced, after what he has said, will induce him to abandon his atrocious designs. Ah! no, I see too plainly the awful fate which is inevitably before me, and the longer I reflect on it, the more torturing do my feelings become."

Alice was at a loss what argument to make use of that might be calculated to banish those gloomy thoughts from her mind, for under the present circumstances in which she was placed, she could not but see the probability of her worst fears being realised; and most deeply did she deplore the wretched fate which seemed so quickly to await the unfortunate woman, and sincerely did she regret that she had no power to save her from it.

The hours passed dismally away, and Brandon did not offer to intrude again upon her; but his coarse voice frequently met her ears as he issued his orders to his crew, and it imparted a sensation of horror to her which she found it difficult to conquer. Night came, and that only brought additional misery to her, as the crisis of her fate seemed to be rapidly approaching, and all prospect of deliverance was banished from her mind —in fact, it would have been little short of madness to have encouraged any such futile hopes, and she could only anticipate the horrors that awaited her with feelings of the most unconquerable and insupportable dread.

Alice did not leave her for a minute, and she in vain tried to persuade her to retire to rest; to sleep in the present agitation of her feelings she knew would be utterly impossible, and she did not even encourage the thought for a minute, but continued for some time to traverse the cabin backwards and forwards in a state of the most painful disorder, and which the reader may easily form an idea of. Then she would throw herself disconsolately on a seat, and covering her face with her hands abandon herself to those agonising thoughts which it was only natural should crowd upon and distract her mind, whilst her bosom heaved with the most convulsive sobs, and the tears chased each other rapidly down her cheeks. Alice watched her with the most anxious solicitude, and most happy would she have been could she have afforded her any relief; but she knew too well that it would be useless to attempt to do so, and she, therefore, abandoned the idea, though she tried by conversing on different subjects to divert her thoughts from the melancholy subjects that engrossed them; but that was a fruitless task, and in that effort she also failed.

We need not attempt to describe how wretchedly that night passed away, but as morning approached, Mary was completely worn out, and did at last sink into a broken slumber, which was anything but refreshing; for, as might have been expected, her imagination was disturbed by the most fearful dreams, and she frequently started up in the greatest agitation and terror, and Alice, who remained watching by her side, had the greatest difficulty to pacify her in the slightest degree, or to persuade her that what she had dreamt had not really taken place. At length, finding that it was impossible for her to obtain any rest, she arose and once more paced the cabin in the same state of agony which she had so long experienced, and which nothing seemed to have the power to alleviate. Another wretched day had now dawned upon her, and still the dismal prospect before her remained unchanged, and hope was as distant from her bosom as ever. In fact, as the time which she so much dreaded approached nearer, the anguish and despair of her feelings naturally increased, and she became so utterly dejected that it was not without the greatest difficulty that she could support herself at all, and Alice had to exert all her energies to sustain her with very little, or no effect.

"In vain you seek to tranquillise my feelings, or to banish the thoughts that crowd upon my mind," she said, "though I know full well the humane motives that prompts you. My fate is sealed, that is certain, and nothing seems likely to be able to avert it. The time rapidly approaches, and then I am lost for ever. But never can I survive the monstrous fate with which I am threatened. And I should feel happy if death would release me from my sufferings before the villain could accomplish his diabolical purpose."

"Oh, no," said Alice, in the most persuasive accents, "I cannot yet banish the idea from my mind that Providence will never suffer you to fall a victim to the brutal passions of such a guilty miscreant as Brandon. Come, my unfortunate friend, try to arouse yourself from this state of despair, for there is no knowing what a few hours may produce, even situated as you are at present. May the Almighty interpose to save you, and to bring the villain from whom you have suffered so much to that punishment which the many abominable crimes he has committed so richly merit."

"I am grateful to you, Alice," an-swered our heroine, "for your kind wishes, which I am certain come from your heart, but although I would fain do so, it is impossible for me to entertain any such hopes, which reason too well convinces me could only end in disappointment. Heaven seems to have deserted me altogether, and what can, therefore, possibly alleviate my misery and despair.

"Oh, say not so," returned Alice, "for it grieves me to hear you talk so despondingly. What have you ever done that you should be thus abandoned by the Almighty? Take courage, and you will yet triumph over all the troubles by which you are at present surrounded."

"Would to God that I could think so, and that such hopes should be realised," ejaculated Mary, "how grateful should I be, and how readily could I bury the past in oblivion, and seek to find tranquillity in the future, if I could not realise happiness. But oh, how fruitless are all my efforts to do so, and every moment makes me feel doubly wretched. I am one of the most unfortunate and miserable of beings, and it is in vain that I endeavour to find some degree of consolation ; there is none for me, and it is useless for me to seek it."

"Yours is indeed a hard fate," said Alice, "and it requires all your fortitude to be able to support it with any degree of patience ; but God is good and merciful, and He, I hope will, ere long, interpose to save you from your present sufferings, and the dangers with which you are threatened. Who knows what this day may produce? You may think me foolish, and that I am endeavouring to excite delusive hopes in your bosom, but still I cannot divest my mind of the impression that something is about to happen to rescue you from that state of misery by which you are at present surrounded."

"Oh, what reason is there for any such hopes?" demanded Mary, with a melancholy look; "I dare not encourage it, for the disappointment which would be almost sure to follow would be nearly as terrible to bear as the reality. No, Alice, I look in vain for some prospect of relief. All is darkness and despair before me, and every moment my ter-

MRS. TILLER'S DISTURBED MIND CONJURES UP A PHANTOM.

rors become more powerful and insup-portable."

Alice returned no answer, and a silence of some minutes ensued, during which time Mary was gazing with melancholy and anxious looks from the window of the cabin, and the expression of her countenance plainly showed the anguish of mind she was enduring. Alice was compelled to leave her for a few minutes, and Mary was thus left to the indulgence of her own dismal thoughts, which were of that torturing description that they almost overwhelmed her.

The weather still remained favourable, and the vessel sped lightly over the sea. It was with a sad heart that our heroine looked upon the prospect before her, and all the many sufferings which it had been her lot to endure recurred to her mind with redoubled force. But what were they compared with those which she imagined were yet in store for her? The bare thought almost overpowered her, and the tears started to her eyes, whilst her bosom heaved with the most convulsive emotions.

"Alas!" she sighed, "how little did I anticipate that such a fate as this would ever befal me, or never could I have lived to endure it; and even now how can I hope to find fortitude suffi-cient to support it. Happy indeed would it be for me could I perish before the wretch whom I have so much cause to dread, and who has heaped upon me such misery, could accomplish his brutal designs. Almighty God have mercy upon me, and do not abandon me altogether."

She raised her eyes fervently and devoutly towards Heaven as she gave utterance to those words, and the anguish of her feelings increased to an insupportable degree. She was aroused from her gloomy and torturing reflections by the return of Alice, who brought her some refreshments; but she was too sick at heart to suffer her to eat, and the meal remained untouched, notwithstanding it was so many hours since she had partaken of any food. She inquired eagerly of Alice if she had seen Brandon, and she replied in the affirmative, but added that she did not imagine that she had any reason to fear that he would trouble her with his presence that day, and that she might, therefore, make her mind as easy as her position would allow her on that point.

"And did he inquire after me?" asked Mary.

"He did," answered her companion, "and I did not fail to assure him of the agitated state of your mind, which I thought might induce him to defer the execution of his guilty designs for a time, at any rate, and in the meanwhile something may occur to frustrate them altogether, and to rescue you from his power."

"Oh, that it would," returned our heroine, fervently, "how grateful should I be! But, alas! I fear that to indulge in such a hope would be useless, and I must, therefore, not give way to it."

"And why should you thus abandon yourself entirely to despair?" said Alice. "I will never believe that so great a miscreant as Brandon will be suffered to accomplish the brutal designs he has against you. Reason and justice revolt at the thought."

"And yet, how is it possible for me to think otherwise, situated as I am?" demanded Mary. "I feel satisfied that Brandon will not delay the execution of his guilty purpose longer than he has stated, and what can possibly, therefore, calm the anguish and despair of my feelings? Oh, Alice, did you but know

the real state of my mind, how sincerely would you pity me."

"And think you, Mrs. Tiller," returned Alice, "that I cannot understand exactly what your feelings must be? Oh, yes, most fervently do I enter into them, and deeply do I sympathise with you, as I have often before assured you, in all the misfortunes which it is your hard lot to have to endure. God grant that they may be quickly terminated, and that you may be restored to that peace and tranquillity of mind from which you have been so long and so unfortunately estranged."

"Alas!" sighed our heroine in reply, "I fear that can never be, and yet Heaven knows how little have I deserved to be subjected to such suffering. Oh, what a monster is this man, Brandon, and I cannot even think of his name without a shudder of horror."

"He is indeed a heartless and inhuman villain," said Alice, "and terrible are the crimes he has committed in the course of his guilty career, and which, sooner or later, must bring down upon him the vengeance of offended Heaven. Oh, my poor friend and companion in misfortune, did you but know all the dreadful scenes that I have been compelled to witness on board this vessel, it would curdle the blood in your veins to hear them. But I will not shock your ears, nor harrow up your feelings by relating them. May it never be your lot to experience the same."

Our heroine was about to return some reply, when she was prevented by a confused noise upon deck, and then they heard the loud voice of Brandon, who seemed to be greatly excited at something, and gave utterance to several fearful oaths, which struck terror and disgust to the gentle bosom of poor Mary, who trembled, and fixed an anxious look on Alice.

"What has happened?" she said; "it must be something particular, or Brandon would not be excited in so powerful manner."

"I have a presentiment that something particular is about to occur," replied Alice; "and that it will be the means of saving you from the fate with which you are at present threatened."

"Oh, Heaven, should it, indeed, be so," cried our heroine, in an agitated voice—"but no, I dare not flatter myself with the hope, which it seems but too probable will never be realised."

"And why should it not?" demanded Alice. Courage, courage, and you may yet be rescued from the hands of your cruel enemies. But I will go and ascertain what has occurred."

"Oh, do not be long," said Mary, for you may imagine how anxious I am to know."

"I will return to you in a few minutes," replied Alice, "and I hope to bring you good news."

With these words she quitted the cabin, and left our heroine in a state of suspense and anxiety which may be readily imagined. While she was absent Mary listened with the most profound attention, to endeavour to catch what the pirates said; but she could only distinguish a word now and then, and that was not sufficient to make her understand the nature of what they were talking about. The confusion, however, every moment increased, and she was well convinced that something of an important, and to the pirates, an alarming nature had taken place, and her heart palpitated violently against her side with mingled hopes and fears. But she was not long kept in suspense, for Alice returned to the cabin, and she could see from the expression of her countenance that she had something of importance to communicate.

"Oh, Alice," said our heroine, "relieve the anxiety of my mind, I beseech you, and tell me what has happened?"

"Courage, Mrs. Tiller," replied Alice, "and, with the blessing of heaven, you will yet be saved. A vessel has again appeared in sight at no very great distance, and seems to be making rapidly towards us."

"Oh, Heaven be praised!" cried Mary, vehemently, and clasping her hands together; "this does, indeed, revive my hopes. Should it prove to be a friend, and too powerful for the pirates to cope with, I may yet be rescued. But did you say that it seems to be in pursuit of us?"

"Yes," answered Alice, "it is evidently giving chase, and Brandon is in a terrible state of alarm and rage, for the Wasp has been so much damaged in the late storm that it can make but little

speed, so that it is not unlikely that the strange vessel will shortly overtake it."

"God grant that it may!" said our heroine, "and that it may be enabled to defeat the wretches who hold me in their power, then, indeed, may I be saved from the fate with which I am now threatened. But have the pirates yet been able to make out what she is?"

"No," replied Alice, "for she is yet too far off for them to make her out distinctly; but it is a large vessel apparently, and, as well as they can guess, a British ship. But Brandon would not suffer me to remain any longer on deck, and ordered me below. I never saw him exhibit so much alarm before, and I sincerely trust it is not without good reason."

"Oh, should it again prove to be the vessel that Halliyard is aboard of," said Mary, eagerly, and her heart throbbed more violently than before; "but I dare not encourage the thought, lest I should be doomed to a sad disappointment."

"It is not at all unlikely that it is the Porpoise," remarked Alice; "and from some observations which I heard Brandon make use of, I imagine that he thinks so too. But a short time will decide that; for if the Wasp is not able to make any more speed that she does at present, it will soon be down upon us."

"Oh, how I tremble for the result," ejaculated Mary; "for should the pirates triumph, my fate will then most surely be decided, and all hope will be at an end."

"Be firm, Mrs. Tiller," replied Alice, "for something seems to assure me that all will be well, and that should an engagement take place, the pirates will be defeated. But a short time, and I trust to heaven that you will be at liberty."

"Ah! should your sanguine expectations be realised," said our heroine, "and I should be rescued from that dreadful fate which now is impending over my head, how grateful to Heaven shall I be for its merciful interposition. But should the villain, Brandon, find that he is likely to be defeated, may he not sacrifice me to his vengeance?"

"Entertain no such fears," returned her companion, "for the Almighty will never permit the perpetration of so monstrous a deed, and you will yet be able to triumph over your cruel enemy. Let us implore the mercy and protection of Heaven."

Mary and Alice immediately sunk upon their knees, and in the most fervent tones they offered up their supplisations to the Supreme, and after that our heroine felt her breast inspired with more confidence, and awaited the result of this important event with the greatest anxiety and impatience.

The noise and confusion on deck increased, and Mary could imagine, from the terrible execrations which she frequently heard Brandon give utterance to, that he was suffering under the greatest excitement and alarm. In this manner several minutes elapsed, and the suspense of our heroine became greater, while she alternated between hope and fear, and urged Alice to go again upon deck to try to ascertain some further particulars. But Alice was afraid to so, as Brandon had given her such strict injunctions to remain below, and she feared to excite his resentment, well knowing what the consequences of her doing so would be. However, she endeavoured to calm the agitation of Mary's feelings, and succeeded rather better than might have been expected. But we must leave them for a time, and relate what was passing at that moment on the deck of the pirate vessel.

Hugh Brandon was in a state of the greatest possible excitement, and paced the deck backwards and forwards with hasty and disordered steps, and gave his orders in a hurried tone, uttering the most fearful oaths at intervals, and keeping his eyes almost constantly fixed upon the approaching vessel, which was evidently in pursuit of them, and gained upon them rapidly, for, as has been before stated, the Wasp had suffered so much damage in the recent storm that she could make but little speed, notwithstanding all the exertions of the daring and hardy crew.

"By the infernal host!" cried Brandon, in a hoarse voice, "fortune frowns upon us, and we shall never be able to give this d—d craft the slip. She darts over the deep with the swiftness of an arrow, while our ship seems to have taken the sulks and makes no way at all. I can nearly make her out," he added, gazing eagerly towards the ship through his glass, "and from what I can see of her, she seems to be a large vessel, and probably carries some heavy metal, besides a number of hands. From what I can see of her build she seems to be familiar to me. We must avoid her if possible, for we are in no condition for fighting at present."

"True, captain," said Summers, "and I am rather fearful of the consequences, should she happen to overtake us, which, at the speed she is now sailing, she seems not at all unlikely to do. Should it turn out to be the Porpoise again, I would not give much for our chance."

"D——n!" exclaimed Brandon, passionately, "what put such a thought as that in your head? The Porpoise? Psha! it cant be; and yet, if it should, and it should happen to overtake us, we shall have our work to do, sure enough. Strain every nerve, we must leave no means untried to escape her; and yet, our sluggard ship seems to mock us, and to give every advantage to the approaching enemy. Curses light on this misfortune! The ship approaches nearer every moment. However, if it does overtake us, they shall find that they have no children to deal with."

"True, captain," returned Summers, "though, if I may judge from her appearance, I am afraid that she would prove more than a match for us."

"Psha!" cried the pirate, with another oath; "we are not to be daunted, nevertheless, and there is no knowing what we might be able to do under such desperate circumstances."

"Ay," said Summers, "we have never been conquered yet, and it shall not be our fault if we are on the present occasion; however, it would be better to avoid an engagement with such an enemy, if possible. See, how she scuds along—she gains upon us every minute, and I can now make out her build. She is a large man-of-war, and, d—n it! can it be?—yes, I am not mistaken. Do you not see, Brandon? By all that is unfortunate, it is the Porpoise!"

"Confusion!" exclaimed the pirate, as he gazed towards the ship, "the Porpoise? It is so; I see it plain enough now! What devil's luck blew her here, after we had once before so narrowly escaped her? If she overtakes us, it is all up with us, I am afraid, for we shall never be able to stand against such a superior force; and Mary, too— But let the worst come to the worst, she shall not escape me. D——n! she comes on faster and faster, and we shall never be able to escape her! Curses light on the tempest which has so disabled our gallant barque, which before could skim the ocean like a bird! Let every man be prepared for action, for I imagine that we shall have hot work of it presently; and mark me, we must conquer or die!"

"Ah, ay, captain," shouted several of the daring crew; "we will not fail to do our duty!"

Brandon continued to pace the deck in the most disordered manner, and the expression of this coarse features showed the violent excitement of his mind, and notwithstanding he tried to conceal it, it was evident that he feared what the result of this adventure would be. All chance of their escaping the approaching vessel, however, now seemed to be at end, and it had gained so rapidly upon them that they could see it distinctly, and could no longer entertain any doubts as to its being the porpoise. Desperate were the efforts of the pirates to escape; but fortune evidently frowned upon them, and there seemed to be no alternative but for them to come to an engagement, the result of which, however, could not be very doubtful. Brandon's agitation increased every moment, and the oaths that escaped his lips were quite frightful to listen to. His thoughts were fixed upon our heroine, and he formed the most desperate resolution respecting her, but still he could not venture to move from the deck for a minute, and he continued to watch the approaching enemy with the most anxious eyes. The loud report of a gun was now heard, which was the signal from the Porpoise for them to heave to, a command which the villain Brandon was by no means inclined to obey, though he was aware that an engagement was unavoidable, and in spite of all his efforts to the contrary, he trembled for the result.

"May destruction overtake her," he cried fiercely, "and all those who are on board of her; I had hoped that we had escaped her altogether; but it seems that I reckoned without my host. However, if they do conquer us, they shall do so dearly, and they shall find that it is to no power that Hugh Brandon the pirate will yield. As for Mary, her fate is sealed, she shall not escape me. No doubt her agitation is now great, and she flatters herself that she is about to be delivered from my power. But she will find herself most woefully deceived. Hugh Brandon is not to be thus foiled in his designs. But is this to be the finish of my career? and that too, at the very moment when I fancied that my success was complete? It is a confounded shame that fortune should have deserted me in this manner. But no matter, I will die as I have lived, a desperate and determined man."

Having given utterance to these words, he folded his arms across his chest, and then gave some further instructions to his crew, who were prepared for action.

All was bustle and excitement on board the Porpoise, and Harry Halliyard was in a state of agitation which the reader may very easily imagine as the probability of the speedy rescue of his beloved Mary from the power of her cruel enemy occurred to him. Since the time when the Porpoise had failed in its pursuit after the pirate, the despair and anguish which Halliyard had endured was of the most violent description, and he had made up his mind that the fate of Mary was decided, and that he should never behold her again. It was in vain that he tried to arouse himself from this state of melancholy, and the more he did so the worse he became; and such was the nature of his feelings that he was almost incapable to attend to his duty, though the captain and the whole of the crew, knowing the painful circumstances of the case, heartily pitied him, and regretted that they had not an opportunity of punishing the miscreant, Brandon, and the ruffians under his command, as their crimes so justly merited. None more deeply sympathised with the noble-hearted but unfortunate seaman than old Ben Bowsprit, who was with him at every opportunity, and tried to arouse him from the state of melancholy and despair he was in, but with very little success; for knowing the dreadful situation that Mary was in, and the character of the heartless miscreant in whose power she was, he saw plainly that the fate which awaited her was of the most revolting description, and that without some miraculous interposition of Providence it was also inevitable; and that reflection of itself was almost enough to drive him to madness.

"Poor lass—poor lass!" he would cry, in the agony of his feelings, "little did I think, when we were so happy together in our loves, that such a cruel destiny was in store for you, or the very anticipation of it would have been sufficient to have driven me mad. And she so good and innocent, too! Oh, surely Heaven has been most unjust towards her. And must she become the victim of that atrocious ruffian Brandon? Forbid it, oh Heaven! And yet, what chance is there of her escaping now he holds her so completely in his power, and can put his inhuman designs into execution whenever he thinks proper? Nay, perhaps, even ere this he has accomplished his infernal wishes, and Mary has become the wretched victim of his guilty and brutal passions. Oh, the anguish of that thought! Brandon —wretch!—fiend in human form, if I should ever come in contact with you, how terrible is the vengeance that I will wreak upon your head!"

"Well, Harry," said Ben Bowsprit, who was present when he gave utterance to those words, "I hope that you will have an opportunity of punishing the infernal shark as he deserves; for a greater scoundrel never remained unhung, and I only regret that he has this time slipped through our fingers; but we shall come athwart his hawse some of these times, never fear, and then let him look out, for he will have to pay rather dearly for the tricks he has played. As for Mrs. Tiller, I hardly know what to think of her situation. Certainly it is a most fearful one, for Brandon is not the sort of man from whom she can expect much mercy; but still he must be a most cowardly ruffian if he can take advantage of a poor defenceles woman."

"And think you, then, that anything will restrain him?" demanded Harry—

"do you imagine for a moment that he will hesitate to put his infamous designs into execution, now that he has her completely in his power? Oh, no; it would be preposterous to entertain such an idea, for it is opposed to all reason. Already, no doubt, she has fallen, and the thought is sufficient to drive my brain to distraction."

Ben still endeavoured to console him, but it was to no purpose, and he gave up the task and left poor Harry to his own reflections, the nature of which the reader can, no doubt, very well imagine.

It was the intention of the commander of the Porpoise, as we stated in a previous chapter, to join the fleet, but contrary winds drove the vessel out of its latitude, and the storm then coming on, they were tossed about for some hours in a state of the greatest danger, and expecting every moment that the vessel would founder. The anguish and anxiety of Harry Halliyard's mind increased, as he pictured to himself what the sufferings of poor Mary must be, exposed as she was to such horrors, and probably doomed to perish in the deep; but even that, awful though it was, he considered, was preferable to the fate with which she was threatened from the atrocious designs of the miscreant, Brandon. What he suffered during the time the storm lasted, we must leave to the imagination of the reader, and it was such as quite to unman him. He prayed most fervently to Heaven to watch over and protect her, though he never now for a moment anticipated that he should ever behold her again, and when he thought of the cruel manner in which all their fondest hopes had been annihilated, his emotions became so great that they almost overpowered him, and he could have wept like a child.

"Oh, would to Heaven," he ejaculated, in the most melancholy accents, "would to Heaven that I had perished years since in the stormy deep or in the battle's heat, rather than have lived to endure this misery. Fate has frowned upon me, and life must henceforth be a burthen to me that I would fain get rid of. Oh, Mary, had you never known me, you might never have been exposed to the miseries, the horrible sufferings it is now your hard lot to experience, but might have been happy in the love of some other man; but now, alas!——— But oh! I dare not reflect upon it; the very idea is enough to madden my brain."

He struck his forehead in despair as he gave utterance to these dismal lamentations, and it was in vain that he tried to gain any relief to the anguish of his mind—in fact, the more he endeavoured to do so, the greater his sufferings became. But to think that he had been so near her, and yet had failed to rescue her. Had the vessel succeeded in overtaking the pirates, he had no doubt that they would have been defeated, and then it might not have been too late to save her; but now he could not but consider that all hope was at an end, and that the opportunity would never again be afforded him.

"The miscreant Brandon has indeed triumphed," he said, "and terrible is the revenge which he has taken. But why should he thus pursue a poor defenceless woman? She never injured him, and, therefore, should have escaped his cruelty. But what could be expected from a heartless wretch like him, especially when goaded on by his guilty passions? I can feel no surprise at any lengths to which he may go, and can only shudder with horror and disgust when I reflect upon him. May the curses of outraged Heaven descend upon his head and crush him."

Thus did poor Harry continue to ruminate, and he looked forward to the future with the most poignant anguish and despair.

The storm at length subsided, and they found that they had been driven out of their course, and determined to make for the nearest island in order that they might repair the damage which the vessel had received, but which, however, was not of a serious nature. After sailing for a few hours, the man who was on the watch suddenly exclaimed—"A sail a-head!" and as a feeling of renewed hope sprung up in his breast, Harry hastened on deck, and quickly beheld the vessel at a distance which the seaman had intimated, and the appearance of which immediately excited his suspicions.

"Your honour," he said, addressing himself to the captain, "if my eyes do not deceive me, that is no other than the rascally pirate of which we were before in pursuit."

"Ah!" said the captain, looking through his glass, "by Jupiter! I think you are right, Halliyard; and if so, I do not think she will be able this time to escape us, for the wind is in our favour, and she does not seem to be proceeding very rapidly. Now I look at her again, I am certain that I am not mistaken. It is the Wasp, sure enough; so crowd all sail, and we shall be down upon her in the turning of a handspike."

"Heaven send that it may not be too late to save poor Mary," cried Halliyard fervently. "Oh, I feel that I could perform wonders to rescue her from her present terrible situation."

"We have had a specimen of the sailing capabilities of the Wasp," observed the captain, "so there is not a moment to be lost. We must not suffer her to give us the slip this time."

Quickly all was in motion, and the Porpoise was soon gliding rapidly over the ocean, and it seemed probable that she would soon be able to overtake the pirate, whose progress was uncommonly slow in comparison with what it had been on the former occasion. The suspense and anxiety of Harry's mind was now most intense, and he alternated between hope and fear, though the former feeling at that time predominated, and he mentally, but most earnestly prayed to heaven that he might not be doomed to disappointment. Never, to his disordered imagination, had the vessel seemed to be so tardy in its progress, and he became painfully impatient. But he trembled when he reflected upon what Brandon might be tempted to do when he found that he could not escape, and that there was no chance for him. He might sacrifice the unfortunate Mary to his fury, and thus every hope would be annihilated, but he endeavoured to banish those fears from his mind, and to hope that she would escape uninjured, though it was almost impossible to imagine that she could do so, considering the time that she had been in the power of her heartless persecutor, and the fierce determination he had no doubt formed against her. However, he continued to watch the vessel, which contained all that was so dear to him, most anxiously, and felt relieved from a weight of care when he found that the Porpoise was gaining fast upon her, and there could be· very little doubt that the pirates could not escape them, and their defeat, considering the superior force they had to contend against, was also equally certain. Having got to within a short distance of her, the captain ordered a gun to be fired as a command for her to heave to, but of this the pirate took no notice, but seemed to try to redouble its speed, though without the least probability of success.

"The daring rascals," said the captain, "they seemed resolved to brave the worst; but it strikes me that their game is almost up, for it is not at all likely that they can stand long against such a vessel as the Porpoise. We must secure this fellow, Brandon, alive, if possible."

They had now got so near to it that they could perceive the pirates busily engaged upon the deck, and apparently making every necessary precaution for that engagement from which they must now be thoroughly convinced it would be impossible for them to escape, and from among the rest the eager eye of Halliyard quickly singled out the ruffian Brandon. The activity which prevailed on board the pirate ship became more apparent every moment, and it was quite evident that they were fully resolved to make a most desperate resistance, seeing that it was impossible they could avoid coming to an engagement; but what the result of that engagement would be, taking into consideration the superiority of the Porpoise, and the numbers with which she was manned, there could be very little, if any doubt; and the whole of the brave crew were most eager and anxious for the fray, by which they hoped to exterminate a host of blood-thirsty and desperate wretches, who had been guilty of so many atrocious crimes, who had been the complete terror of the ocean. But the suspense which our hero experienced as to the probable fate of poor Mary, and whether she would be rescued uninjured from the power of the miscreant, Brandon, was almost insupportable, and as his eyes rested on the tall and powerful form of that man who had wrought himself and all those who were so truly dear to him so much misery, his excitement became greater, and the utmost indignation swelled his breast.

A very short time, however, would probably decide this important and painful business, for the Porpoise gained rapidly on the enemy every instant, and all was prepared for the determined struggle which was sure to follow. Mentally and fervently did Halliyard invoke the protection of the Supreme for his beloved Mary, and he then endeavoured to muster all the confidence he could, and to look forward to the issue of this most important event with the most sanguine hopes, and in which he trusted that he should not be doomed to be disappointed. He was further encouraged by Ben Bowsprit, who deeply sympathised with his feelings, and was as anxious for the fray as he was.

"Courage, shipmate," he said, " the fate of those infernal sharks will soon be decided; no doubt though, I dare say, we shall have warm work of it, for they are not the sort of fellows to yield without a determined struggle. As for your pretty Mary, I trust that she will shortly be moored safe and sound again in your arms."

"But, alas!" returned Harry, with a doubtful look, "when I think of the time which the poor lass has been in the power of that atrocious scoundrel, Brandon, the worst fears beset my mind, and even now, seeing the chances that are against him, may he not sacrifice her to his vengeance, rather than that she should be restored to liberty, and thus all his diabolical plans defeated ?"

"Those fears will not be realised, take my word for it," replied Ben; " but come, this is not the moment to indulge in any such thoughts. The moment of action approaches, and the great Commander aloft will, no doubt, defend the right, and bring the inhuman career of these wretches to an end."

To this our hero returned no answer, but he impatiently awaited the battle, and, as he watched with the most eager eyes the motions of the pirates on the deck of their vessel, and which were now clearly discernible, his courage gained strength, and he most fervently

THE ATTACK OF THE PORPOISE UPON THE PIRATE VESSEL.

wished that it might be his lot to encounter Brandon, on whose guilty head he wished to wreak his vengeance, and he had no doubt that Providence would enable him to do so, and thus to rid society of a monster who had inflicted upon it so many atrocious outrages, and for so many years had carried on his guilty career with complete impunity.

And now the important moment on which so much depended arrived, and the Porpoise having got within gun-shot of her desperate foe, commenced business immediately, seeing that parleying would be of no avail, and poured in a heavy broadside, which seemed to shake the Wasp immensely, and to throw the pirates into some confusion, from which, however, they quickly appeared to recover themselves, and returned the compliment with much spirit, though it told with little effect upon the Porpoise.

"If we continue this game we must soon blow her out of the water," remarked the captain; "but that is not exactly my object. We must board her, and secure Brandon and as many of his crew as possible, and also restore such prisoners as he probably has in his power to liberty."

To this Harry Halliyard most heartily responded, and when the smoke had in some measure dispersed he gazed eagerly towards the pirate vessel, and beheld Brandon in the midst of his crew, and busily engaged in giving his orders, and directing the movements of the fight.

The scene that followed was terrific in the extreme; the pirates fought with desperate courage, and returned the fire of their more powerful assailants with the most consummate skill and energy, seeming resolved never to yield but with death. The shouts and execrations of the wretches rent the air, and might be heard above the roaring of the cannons, and the doubts and anxiety of Harry Halliyard, in spite of all his efforts to the contrary, increased every moment. For a minute or two he lost sight of Brandon, but his gaunt form was soon again distinguishable from among the rest, and the agony and alarm of the young seaman may be readily imagined when he beheld that on one arm he supported the insensible form of a female, and in whom he immediately recognised her for whose safety and restoration to liberty he was so anxious, and whose fate now evidently hung upon a thread. He could not help giving utterance to an exclamation of horror, and such was the excitement of his feelings that he was almost inclined to leap into the sea, in the desperate hope of forcing his way alone on board the pirate bark, and rescuing the unfortunate Mary or perish in the bold attempt. But the attitude of the miscreant Brandon was menacing and exulting, and he stood in that prominent part of the deck where he could be most distinctly seen, and where himself and his wretched victim were exposed to the greatest danger, seeming resolved that if he fell, she should also perish with him. The worst fears of Harry Halliyard were now almost realised, and as he gazed with frenzied eyes at the awful situation of poor Mary, his courage nearly forsook him, and he gave utterance to an exclamation of despair.

A pause of a minute or two now took place in the deadly strife, and the captain and the other officials on board, seeing the critical situation of our heroine, and the threatening attitude of Brandon, hesitated what to do.

"The villain seems to defy us," said the captain, "and we must alter our tactics, for this unfortunate woman must be saved, if possible. Our only course is by boarding them, and let that be done without delay. Destruction to the pirates, and may British courage prove triumphant!"

The gallant crew responded to this sentiment with a loud shout, and the orders of the captain being promptly obeyed, by a skilful manœuvre, which, however, seemed partly to have been anticipated by the ruffians on board the Wasp, the next moment the two vessels were yard-arm and yard-arm, and the sailors, led on by the captain, and who was closely followed by our hero, rushed on the enemy's deck, with a determination to decide the struggle without delay. And now the dreadful scene of slaughter which followed baffles description; the pirates fought with the ferocity and determination of wild beasts, and the slaughter which took place on both sides was terrific. The shouts of the combatants, and the dreadful execrations of the pirates, mingled with the groans of the wounded and the dying, were appalling to hear, and for some time it seemed doubtful, notwithstanding the superior and overwhelming numbers of the crew of the Porpoise, which way the deadly conflict would terminate. Harry Halliyard performed wonders, and dealt destruction around him, but for a minute or two he had lost sight of Brandon and our heroine, and his agonising fears for her fate may be readily imagined. But at length he encountered him, and he found that he still supported the insensible form of our heroine on his arm, while his other hand grasped his cutlass, and his attitude showed the fierce and determined feelings that raged within his guilty bosom. For a moment Brandon and our hero stood and eyed each other with looks of hatred and revenge, and the expression of Brandon's features was scarcely human.

"Halliyard," the ruffian said at length, "you whom I so heartily hate and despise, at last we meet in deadly combat, and this moment decides our fate; but the triumph shall not be altogether yours, for though I perish, yourself and her whom you seek to rescue shall also perish with me. Look to yourself, for in me you will find no child to contend with."

"Villain! monster!" exclaimed our hero, as he rushed upon him, and tried to rescue Mary from his hold; "your threats I scorn, and thus do I bring that retribution upon your guilty head which your numerous and atrocious crimes have so long merited."

A hoarse laugh of defiance was the only answer which Brandon gave, and the combat commenced with desperate valour on both sides, but they were so equally matched that it seemed doubtful which would gain the advantage. For some minutes this continued, but at length the sword of Brandon was struck from his hand, at the same moment our hero succeeded in releasing Mary from his hold, and pressed her to his bosom. Brandon's eyes flashed fire, he was bleeding from several wounds he had received in the combat, and with a fearful oath he snatched a pistol from his belt before Halliyard could sufficiently recover himself to stand upon his defence, and was about to discharge the contents at his head, when Ben Bowsprit at that critical moment rushed suddenly forward, and plunging his sword twice in the body of the guilty ruffian, with a loud cry of agony Hugh Brandon, the pirate, fell upon the deck a ghastly corpse. His death had an immediate and powerful effect upon those of his crew who had survived the slaughter, who were very few; they instantly yielded, and the loud shouts of the gallant crew of the Porpoise proclaimed the victory they had obtained. An exclamation of terror in the voice of a female now attracted the attention of all those who were present,

and immediately afterwards Alice rushed on deck, and approaching the spot where Halliyard was standing, fondly supporting the inanimate form of Mary in his arms, sunk on her knees, almost overpowered by the violence of her emotions, and the terrors she had for some time been enduring.

"The vessel is sinking," she ejaculated; "oh, save me from death, and rescue me from those dreadful horrors which it has so long been my hard lot to experience."

"See to her safety," said the captain, addressing himself to some of his crew; "and quick to the ship—we have accomplished our task, and the wretches who have so long spread dismay around them are destroyed. Halliyard, you have acted bravely, and you are well rewarded for it."

"Ah, your honour," replied our hero, "I am indeed. Oh, Mary, and do I indeed once more clasp you to my bosom, and gaze upon your beloved features, which I never expected to behold again? But oh, how pale and careworn does she look. Good God! should the miscreant Brandon have accomplished his diabolical designs—"

"Fear not, Mr. Halliyard," interrupted Alice; "thank Heaven you have come in time to rescue her from the dreadful and revolting fate with which she was threatened; though had it been a few hours later Brandon would, no doubt, have carried his threats into execution."

"Ah, then," cried Halliyard, in tones of gratitude and delight, "the wretch has been defeated, and Mary is still pure and unsullied, and may yet be restored to peace and tranquillity, if she cannot be to happiness. God of Heaven, for this I thank you, for it has removed a weight of care and anxiety from my mind which was almost too heavy to bear. Dear Mary! with what fond transport do I gaze upon you. Bless you, bless you, a thousand times, and may all those trials which it has been your hard destiny to have to encounter now be at an end."

He raised her insensible form in his arms as she spoke, and once more went to the vessel, followed by Alice, whose brutal husband was one who had perished in the combat, and the crew. In a few minutes after they had reached the ship the pirate vessel rapidly filled, and immediately sunk beneath those waters on the surface of which it had lately so fearlessly sailed, and not a vestige of it remained to tell that it had ever been.

CHAPTER XXIII.

THE INTERVIEW BETWEEN HARRY AND OUR HEROINE. — ANTICIPATIONS OF THE FUTURE. — FRESH TROUBLES THREATEN. — THE SHIPWRECK.

THIS startling event having terminated in the manner we have described in the previous chapter, the gallant ship, the Porpoise, proceeded on its way, and the crew were allowed to regale themselves after the gallant victory that they had obtained, and for which they had so bravely fought.

Every attention was paid to the females, especially Mary, who, however, still remained in a state of torpor, and was attended upon by the faithful and kind-hearted Alice, though Harry never left her for a moment, except when his duties compelled him, and he watched over her with mingled feelings of anxiety and transport. So sudden and unexpected had been her restoration to him, and all the circumstances that had taken place, that he could scarcely persuade himself that it was real, or that he was not at that moment labouring under some delusion ; but when the facts became quite apparent to him, the nature of the feelings that he experienced may be readily imagined. His heart swelled with gratitude to Heaven ; but when he heard from Alice the brief particulars of what she had suffered from the cruelty and oppression of Brandon during the time she had been in his power, his emotion increased, and while he execrated the villany of the wretch whose guilty career was at length fortunately terminated, his feelings of commiseration with Mary in the sufferings she had had to encounter, and the dreadful fate from which she had so narrowly escaped. Again and again did he press the fondest kisses upon her lips, and manly tears started to his eyes as he gazed upon her pale features, and recalled to his memory all the manifold and unmerited troubles she had undergone, and the melancholy way in which her hopes and his had been annihilated, and that, too, at the very time when they seemed so certain of being realised.

"Poor lass ! poor lass !" he sighed, as he still hung anxiously and affectionately over her, "yours has indeed been a hard fate, and it is wonderful how you have ever had sufficient fortitude or energy of mind to support it. And do I then indeed again behold you, and know that you have escaped from the horrors by which you were encompassed ? I can scarcely believe the evidence of my senses ; and yet I cannot be deceived —it is true, and how can I be sufficiently grateful to Heaven for it ? Oh, may your future days be those of peace and tranquillity. But her husband ! Oh, that name, it casts a gloom of despair upon my heart which nothing can disperse. Those bright visions of future bliss which we at one time so fondly indulged in can never be realised—she can never be mine, and even now it is criminal in me to encourage the thoughts that at present hold possession of my mind. Yes, we must abandon all hopes of each other, and perhaps it would be more prudent and better for us both should we avoid each other's presence, lest we should be led into some act of indiscretion which we might afterwards have so much cause to regret. But now that you are restored to me, how can I bear to exist if deprived of your presence ? The trial is a hard one, and I know not how I shall be able to accomplish it."

He paused, for, in spite of his efforts to the contrary, his feeling almost overpowered him, and he felt ashamed of the weakness he had betrayed, and the thoughts which held possession of his mind. He still continued to gaze upon her pale face, the melancholy expression of which revealed such a tale of suffering ; and, if possible, the anguish of his feelings increased in strength, and his mind was so bewildered by the various and perplexing thoughts that crowded in such rapid succession upon it, that he scarcely knew what he was about. But the death of the miscreant Brandon, and the restoration of Mary to liberty, gave to him much satisfaction ; and that which

Alice had told him had removed a weight of care and anxiety from his mind which had been almost overwhelming, and he felt inexpressibly grateful to Omnipotence for Its merciful interposition.

"Had the villain Brandon triumphed altogether," he said, with a shudder, "how terrible would her fate have been, and how hateful and insupportable would her future existence have been. I tremble when I think of what she has so providentially escaped, and can scarcely believe that she is once more restored to liberty."

"Ah, Mr. Halliyard," said Alice, "it is indeed a most fortunate job, when the desperate and brutal character of Brandon is taken into consideration; and you must feel grateful to Heaven for it. Poor woman, her sufferings have been great, and had it not been for the sympathy I felt for her misfortunes, she would never, I am convinced, have been able to support them."

"My good woman," said Harry, "to you I feel much indebted; and if I can only be the means of rewarding you for your invaluable services, you will find me most ready and happy to do so."

"Pardon me, Mr. Halliyard," replied Alice, "but I seek no reward; what I did came from my heart, and I only feel too happy to think that I was enabled to assist her. But see, she revives; had you not better leave for awhile, until I have explained to her what has so fortunately taken place? Your sudden and unexpected appearance might excite her feelings to a dangerous degree."

"True," coincided our hero, "and I will do as you suggest, and will leave everything to you. Oh, Mary, what will be your feelings when you are made acquainted with what has taken place, and find yourself not only rescued from the awful and disgusting fate which was impending over you, but that I am near you? I dare scarcely trust myself with the thought."

With these words, after gazing once more affectionately and anxiously upon her, he quitted the cabin, and left her to the care of Alice.

Mary now gave evident signs of returning sensibility, and at length she opened her eyes and gazed eagerly around her, and perceiving Alice, for a moment or two she had no recollection of what had taken place, but imagined that she was still a prisoner on board the pirate vessel, and that the fate with which she had been threatened was about to overtake her.

"Oh, God!" she cried, "and am I then still here, and in the power of that cruel man? Methought that something had occurred to release me from it; but it could only have been a delusive dream, and there is no hope for me. And yet," she added, again looking around her, "this place seems strange to me, and the impression is still strong upon my mind that something particular has taken place, and that I—Ah, Alice, you here? Then my hopes are all futile, and I have suffered my disordered imagination to deceive me."

"My dear Mrs. Tiller," replied Alice, "I beg of you to compose your feelings, and prepare yourself to hear that which must greatly relieve your mind from that terror and despair which must have before tortured it. You have been labouring under no delusion. The heartless miscreant from whom you experienced so much suffering is no more, his vessel, and nearly the whole his daring crew are destroyed, and you are now safe, and have, I trust, nothing in future to apprehend."

"Ah!" cried our heroine, eagerly, "can you speak the truth, or do you seek to flatter me with false hopes?"

"Indeed you do me an injustice," returned Alice, "if you suppose for a moment that I could have the heartlessness thus to sport with your feelings. All that I have told you is strictly true."

"I can scarcely believe the evidence of my ears," ejaculated Mary; "and yet I have a dreamy recollection of something of importance taking place, and all that I now behold is strange and novel to me. Where am I?"

"On board his majesty's ship, the Porpoise," answered Alice.

"Ah! is it possible?" exclaimed our heroine, clasping her hands together, and her heart palpitated violently against her side with the power of her emotions, "on board the same vessel which contains Halliyard? Oh, the news is too blissful to be true."

"My dear friend," said her companion, "doubt not the truth of what I have said; but you will soon be convinced of it. Mr. Halliyard rescued you from the hands of your brutal persecutor, at the risk of his own life, and you are now on board the same vessel with him, and free from all those dangers by which you were before surrounded."

"God of Heaven!" exclaimed our heroine, in a voice of the most indescribable emotion, and again clasping her hands together, "for this I thank You! Saved!—saved! and that too by him to whom my heart is so fondly devoted? Oh, joy the most unspeakable! But where is he? Why do I not behold him? Alas! I fear that in the dreadful combat, which I can now so vividly picture to my imagination, he has met with some fatal accident, and that I shall never behold him again."

"Let not your fears thus alarm you, Mrs. Tiller, for I assure you that they are quite without foundation. Mr. Halliyard was here but a few minutes since, and he has escaped from the combat entirely uninjured."

"Oh, thank Heaven for that!" emphatically exclaimed our heroine, and the feelings of transport that agitated her breast were quite indescribable; "Halliyard safe and I am happy. But why is he not here to remove all doubt and suspense from my mind, and to receive the expression of my unbounded gratitude for the inestimable service he has rendered me? Oh, Harry, and after our long and painful separation, shall we meet again, and under such peculiar circumstances? But whither do my thoughts guide me? Must I not rather tremble in his presence when I think of my unfortunate husband? Fate has ordained that we should never come together, and yet, to banish his image altogether from my heart I feel to be utterly impossible, and, therefore, it is little short of madness to make the attempt."

"And indeed there is no occasion for you to do so," remarked Alice, "you love each other with a sentiment pure and harmless, I am convinced, and though for a time your hopes have been doomed to be blighted, I trust that ultimately they will be realised, and that you will be happy together."

"Ah, Alice," ejaculated Mary, "and

should your predictions indeed be verified, what happiness will be mine, and how amply shall I be rewarded for the troubles of the past. But I dare not indulge in such a thought, which, under all the circumstances, I have too much reason to fear will be doomed to be disappointed. And if my unfortunate husband still lives, is it not criminal in me to encourage any such ideas?"

"Endeavour to banish these gloomy thoughts from your mind, Mrs. Tiller," said her companion, "and to trust to the goodness and mercy of Providence as to the result of the future. Thank Heaven, you are at last released from the terrible fate with which you were threatened, and are safe from every danger."

"Oh, yes," replied Mary, "and my heart overflows with gratitude to the Supreme for my unexpected preservation, when all hope seemed to be at an end; but could my husband be assured of my safety, and the horrors from which I have escaped, I should be content. Alas! the sufferings he has had to endure at the uncertainty of the fate which has befallen me, and the doubts and suspicions that I have too much reason to fear have haunted his mind, must have been terrible indeed."

"Try to conquer those feelings, Mrs. Tiller," said Alice, "and to believe that Providence has sustained him under the severe trials it has been his hard lot to have to encounter. He surely cannot have been so uncharitable as to entertain any suspicions as derogatory to your character."

"Alas! what could he think, mysterious as my disappearance was," said our heroine, "and knowing, as he did, the love which I still cherished for Halliyard? My heart almost misgives me when I think of it, and, anxious as I am, I almost dread to meet him, lest I should not be able to banish from his mind the dark and fatal impressions which I so much fear he has suffered to take possession of it. I feel convinced that, notwithstanding I am rescued from the power of my brutal enemy, my troubles are not yet at an end."

"Try to conquer such feelings, Mrs. Tiller," said her companion, "and to look forward with hope to the future, for indeed I cannot believe that such apprehensions as those you have just now expressed will ever be fated to be realised. Your husband, if he truly loves you, can never entertain so cruel and unjust an opinion of you, and when you meet again, which I trust you shortly will, all will be explained to your mutual satisfaction."

"Oh, Alice," returned our heroine, "how much obliged do I feel for the generous interest which you evince in my welfare, and the kind attention which you ever paid to me since I have been acquainted with you; had it not been for you, and the kind sympathy which you have ever shown me under the dreadful misfortunes it has been my lot to have to encounter from the persecution of that heartless man who tore me from my home, never could I have found strength sufficient to have supported them; I owe you a debt of gratitude which I much fear it will never be in my power to repay."

"Do not mention it, I beg of you," answered Alice; "I require no reward for that which it has been in my humble power to do, and I can only feel too happy and sufficiently repaid in knowing that I have been able to perform my duty. I should indeed have loathed and despised myself, and considered myself unworthy the name of woman, could I have neglected to commiserate with and to assist an unfortunate fellow-creature in such a painful situation, especially one of my own sex. So let that subject trouble you no more, I beg, for I do not consider you are under any obligation to me, and what I did emanated from my heart, and was prompted by the best of motives."

"Oh, yes," ejaculated Mary, "full well am I convinced of that, and I must ever look upon you with feelings of the most unfeigned and unbounded respect for the kindness I have experienced from you. God will reward you, for I cannot; but I do sincerely hope that your troubles are now all at an end, and that your future days will be those of tranquillity and happiness."

"Thank you, Mrs. Tiller," replied Alice, "for your kind wishes, which, I am satisfied, spring from your heart, but although, with the blessing of Heaven, I may be enabled to obtain tranquillity, true happiness I can never

expect will ever fall to my lot to experience."

"Say not so," observed our heroine, "for Providence will surely reward you for the patience and the resignation with which you have endured the heavy trials to which you have for so many years been exposed, and which, I am certain, you so little deserved to suffer. But your guilty husband—say, has he perished?"

"He has," answered Alice; "he has at last paid the fearful penalty of all the numerous crimes he has committed, and may Heaven have mercy on his guilty soul."

Mary pressed her hands upon her burning and aching temples, and she remained silent for a minute or two.

"All that has recently happened," she said, at length, "is so extraordinary and so unexpected that I can scarcely persuade myself it is anything more but some torturing dream, and from which I shall quickly be awakened to fresh troubles. Oh, God, from what a terrible fate have I been rescued, and when I thought that my destruction was inevitable. I shudder to think of it. But where is Halliyard? Why does he not visit me, and by his presence convince me that my senses are not labouring under some fearful delusion."

"I tell you again, Mrs. Tiller," replied her companion, "that Mr. Halliyard was here but a few minutes since, and that he is now most anxious to introduce himself to your presence, and to congratulate you on your fortunate deliverance from the revolting fate which was so long impending over your head, and from which it seemed at one time that nothing could save you; but do you think that you shall be able sufficiently to calm your feelings for the interview?"

"Oh, yes," said Mary, "how can I be otherwise than calm now that I know that I am for the present in safety, that the miscreant Brandon is destroyed, and I have nothing more to dread from him, and that I am so near to him to whom my heart is still so fondly devoted, although Providence has ordained that the bright hopes which we once so fondly entertained should not be realised? Dear Harry, noble and courageous youth, I cannot help still encouraging the same sentiments that I have ever done towards you, though my conscience assures me that it is almost criminal in me to do so. Heaven pardon me if I am acting wrong, but in spite of all my efforts to the contrary, I find it impossible to conquer or subdue the feelings that at present hold such powerful ascendancy over my mind. And to think that to him I should owe my deliverance from that misery and destruction with which the wretch, Brandon, had threatened me! There seems to be a fatality attending it, and that, in spite of the many and apparently insurmountable obstacles by which we are now surrounded, we shall yet be united in those bonds of love which naught but death can sever. But let not my thoughts dwell too much upon that subject, or I may be led to give encouragement to hopes that, after all, may never be suffered to be realised."

"You may believe me when I assure you that I most sincerely and fervently hope they may," said Alice. "The troubles and the painful disappointments you have had the misfortune to experience, and which were enough to subdue even much stronger spirits than those you possess, are now, I firmly believe, all over, and that your future days will be those of sunshine and peace."

"Oh, my kind friend," exclaimed Mary, "should your expectations come true, how sincerely happy shall I be, and how easily, I am convinced, shall I be able to bury the past in oblivion, and to look forward to the future with contentment and hope. But let me not wait longer in this state of anxiety and suspense; let me behold Halliyard, and be convinced from his lips of my safety, and I shall then indeed be comparatively happy, and can anticipate the future with the most sanguine expectations."

"Your wishes shall soon be gratified," returned Alice; "calm your feelings for the joyful occasion, and I will immediately bring Mr. Halliyard into your presence, for he, no doubt, is waiting with the utmost anxiety and impatience to see you."

"Oh, do not then delay a minute," said Mary, "and I promise you that my conduct on the important occasion shall be all that could be wished, and which must be expected."

Alice returned no answer, but fixing upon our heroine an encouraging look, she immediately quitted the cabin. When she was gone, Mary instantly sunk down upon her knees, and with tearful eyes, and upraised hands, she gave full vent to the feelings that struggled in her breast in prayers and thanks to the Supreme for His merciful interposition in her favour when she thought that all chance of her deliverance from so awful and disgusting a fate was at an end. Having done this she felt more calm and confident, and rising from her knees she awaited with anxiety and impatience the appearance of Halliyard, fully prepared as she was for the interesting and affecting meeting that was to take place.

She was not long kept in suspense, for the next moment the cabin door was thrown suddenly open, and Halliyard made his appearance; Mary, with an exclamation of delight, sunk insensible in his arms, while he was almost in the same state of agitation and excitement as herself, and pressed her to his bosom with such feelings of transport and gratitude that may be better imagined than even the most eloquent pen could do justice to by description.

Mary looked up in his face with an expression of the most unbounded affection, and her tears of joy almost blinded her.

"Dear Mary," at length he found words to ejaculate, and at the same time he strained her delicate and lovely form still more close to his bosom, "and do I indeed again behold you in safety, and hold your beloved form to that breast which in spite of all the dismal circumstances of the case, and the misfortunes and disappointments that have befallen us, is still so fondly and so lastingly devoted to you, and which can never own any other mistress than yourself? I can scarcely persuade myself that such bliss is mine, or that it is not all some flattering dream, some wild delusion of my brain. And yet I cannot be deceived; no, I feel your heart beat responsive with my own; I look again into that beauteous countenance which has never been absent from my imagination; and to know, to feel convinced that you are rescued from that dreadful fate to which the basest villany had consigned you, is almost too much for my feelings to en-

THE COMBAT ON BOARD THE PIRATE VESSEL.

dure with calmness. God of Heaven, for this Your mercy, receive, I beseech You, my most unbounded, my most inexpressible gratitude. Oh, Mary, what a feeling of transport is this, and one that I had scarcely ever dared to flatter myself with the hope that I should ever experience. Speak to me, my poor lass, for how anxiously do I await to hear the heavenly music of your voice, which has so often ravished my senses, and which I had feared that I should never have been permitted to listen to again."

"Harry, dear Harry!" gasped forth poor Mary, and overpowered by her emotions, she laid her head upon his shoulder, and gave the most unrestrained indulgence to the tumultuous feelings that rushed to her heart, and which it would have been utterly impossible for her to control. As for Harry, he scarcely knew what he was about, and again he kissed her lips and cheeks, while his heart palpitated so violently against his side that he could scarcely control himself.

"Oh, Mary," he said at last, "may this be an augury of future happiness; and may all those black and ponderous clouds that have so long obscured the horizon of our fate at length be dispersed, and the hopes which we once so fondly indulged in at length be gratified. And yet," he added, with a shudder, and looking with a melancholy expression of regret and despair in her pale face, "what presumptuous, if not guilty, thoughts are these which I thus suffer to enter my mind? We can never be more to each other than we are at present, for are you not the wife of another, and one who has ever bestowed upon you the greatest affection, and whom it is your duty to regard in return? How dare I then to give utterance to language such as that which has just escaped my lips?"

"Alas—alas!" sighed our heroine, and her eyes filled with tears as she spoke. "torturing thought! And yet, how can I resist the feelings which, in spite of all my efforts to the contrary, now occupy my breast? Oh, Halliyard, what a melancholy fate is ours."

"Most true," he returned "and yet Heaven knows how pure and sincere are the sentiments that I entertain towards you, Mary, and how remote it is from my thoughts or wishes to wrong poor Tiller by word or deed. On the contrary, no one can more deeply sympathise with him that I do, and I ardently hope that nothing will occur to prevent me from restoring you to his arms."

"Oh, Halliyard," replied Mary "most ardently do I believe you, and you may well imagine that there is no one who can more duly appreciate your feelings than myself. But under all the painful and peculiar circumstances, and notwithstanding my anxiety to convince him of my safety, I cannot but anticipate my meeting with my unfortunate husband with any other feelings than those of dread and misgiving; for I fear that the mysterious manner in which I disappeared from my home has excited some fearful suspicions to my prejudice in his breast, and that he will——"

"Banish such torturing thoughts from your breast, Mary," interrupted Halliyard, hastily, "for Joe can never be so uncharitable or so unjust as to think thus cruelly of you; and should he have done so, which I cannot believe, how soon will it be in my power to convince him to the contrary. Come, come, cheer up, Mary; your cruel enemy is destroyed—you are now safe under my protection, and all will yet be well. Who knows what may yet occur to

realise our wishes, notwithstanding the many disappointments to which we have already been subjected, and the numerous obstacles by which we are at present surrounded? It is in vain to attempt to conceal the sentiments we entertain towards each other, and which spring from so pure and so holy a source, that, even situated as we are, why should we be ashamed to acknowledge them? Oh, Mary, I feel that I never loved you half so fondly as I do at present; and could I think that your sentiments towards me could ever have undergone any change, I should indeed be one of the most wretched beings in existence, and life would no longer be supportable to me."

"Oh, Harry," said our heroine, while crimson blushes glowed in her cheeks, and the most agonising feelings agitated her breast, "and think you that anything can ever alter my feelings towards you, or that, although fate seems to frown upon our hopes and wishes, I can ever love you with less fervour than I have hitherto done? Oh, no, that is utterly impossible; and let the consequences be whatever they may, that passion must remain the same to the last moment of my existence."

"Blessed words!" cried our hero, with a look of transport, and straining the beloved form of Mary still more warmly to his bosom; "what ecstasy do they impart to my soul, and what a weight of care and anxiety do they remove from my breast. Oh, Mary, did you but know what I have suffered since we have been separated, you would indeed pity me; but now to know that you are released from the frightful dangers by which you were before surrounded, and that you still love me, is happiness to my soul to which no language can possibly do adequate justice. The cruel fates will surely not always conspire against us, and we may yet hope that the love we entertain towards each other will ultimately be rewarded."

"Heaven grant that it may," said Mary fervently, and the expression of her features fully showed the feelings that agitated her breast; "but," she added, suddenly seeming to recollect herself, and blushing deeply, "what am I suffering my truant and imprudent tongue to give utterance to? Oh, my unfortune husband, what a cruel injustice do I do you, and how should I blush so encourage such thoughts? Spare me, Harry, you know my feelings, and will pity me accordingly."

"Know your feelings, dear Mary?" repeated Halliyard; "oh, yes, who can better do so than myself? and I call Heaven to witness how much, how deeply I respect them, and how I should hate and despise myself could I harbour a single thought against your happiness, or to cherish an idea which the most virtuous and honourable should feel ashamed to acknowledge. But I am certain that I need not attempt to convince you of the truth of that assertion, and I will, therefore, say no more upon the subject. Oh, it is indeed many a long day since I have been so truly happy as I am at present. You are safe, Mary, and I trust that the time is not far distant when you will be restored to your native land, and that nothing more will occur to interrupt your happiness."

"Heaven grant that your wishes may not be disappointed," said Mary; "but still, how can I expect to be restored to my home for some time to come? This vessel is one of the fleet which has to meet the enemies of our native land, and oh, when I think of the horrors and dangers to which you, Harry, will probably be exposed, my heart sinks within me, and the hopes that I had before suffered to take possession of me are nearly annihilated in my breast."

"Oh, fear not, my beloved Mary," returned our hero, "Providence will, I have no doubt, not desert me, and there is no knowing what may happen to hasten our wishes, and to spare us those dangers which you seem to apprehend. As for this vessel, it is the intention of the captain to put into the nearest port in order to repair the damages received in the storm and in the late engagement, and then an opportunity will probably be afforded us of forwarding letters to England, apprising Joe and our friends of our safety, and that will remove all anxiety from their minds. Before we left Portsmouth I despatched a letter to Tiller, making him acquainted with such particulars as to what had become of you as had come to my knowledge, and he would thus be convinced that your disappearance in so sudden and mysterious a manner was no fault of yours."

"Oh, thank you for that, dear Harry," she ejaculated; "but, alas! how terrible must have been the anguish of my husband on learning that I was in the power of such a desperate and inhuman wretch as Brandon, and what little chance there was of my ever being rescued from it, at least, until after he had accomplished his diabolical designs. But how did you become acquainted with my fearful situation, Halliyard?"

"From one of the pirate crew who is now on board this ship," answered our hero, "and who, being stung with remorse, surrendered himself on the morning after the Wasp had so suddenly disappeared. When I think of all the horrors to which you must have been exposed, Mary, it makes me shudder, and never can I feel sufficiently grateful to Omnipotence, who gave you fortitude to support such dreadful trials, and successfully to resist the diabolical designs of the monster who held you in his power, and whom it seems almost a miracle should have suffered himself thus to be thwarted."

"Oh, yes," said Mary; "Heaven only knows how I was enabled to support myself, and to oppose the brutal designs of the miscreant Brandon in the successful manner that I did. You may well imagine the painful situation I was in; and had it not been for the kind attentions bestowed upon me by Alice, and to whom I am so greatly indebted, I know not what would have become of me."

"May Heaven reward her for it," said Halliyard emphatically. "I shall never cease to remember her with gratitude; and if there is anything which I can do to serve her, I will most willingly do so; but if it will not pain and fatigue you too much, relate to me all the particulars of that which has happened to you since last we met in England, and when I never expected it would be our lot to meet each other again, especially under the peculiar circumstances that have taken place."

"It is a melancholy tale," said Mary; "but as I am certain that you will feel anxious to learn the whole of the dismal facts, I will relate them in as few words as possible."

Our hero seated himself by her side, and looking affectionately in her face, he listened with the most breathless attention while she proceeded to detail those particulars with which the reader is already acquainted. But how did his manly bosom swell with indignation as he listened to the insults and miseries that the villain Brandon had inflicted upon her, and he was frequently obliged to interrupt her, so that he might give free expression to his feelings.

"The monster!" he exclaimed, when she had concluded, "to take such a delight in insulting one so good and innocent; and what a mercy it was that he was not permitted to triumph altogether in his atrocious designs. Oh, from what a fate have you escaped; and there must have been a special Providence in enabling you to oppose the diabolical will of the miscreant, when he had everything in his power."

"Oh, yes," said Mary, "but hope was entirely banished from my bosom, and had not the Almighty again fortunately brought this vessel upon the track of the pirates, in a very few hours more, in all probability, and it would have been too late to save me. The wretch Brandon, I am convinced, would not have failed to carry his designs into execution at the time he had threatened."

"He would not, doubtlessly," agreed Halliyard, "and I cannot help shuddering when I think of what the fearful consequences would have been. Thank Heaven the villain has at last paid the penalty of his crimes, and we are at last released from a cruel and determined enemy whom we had so much cause to dread."

"True," coincided Mary; "but you will perceive that had it not been for the kind sympathy which Alice evinced in my fate, and the consolation and advice which she offered me, my strength must have failed me, and then no doubt Brandon's triumph would have been completed."

"Dreadful and revolting thought!" said Harry. "Alice is deserving of every praise for her conduct throughout this painful business, and she shall not go unrewarded for her kindness. Unfortunate woman, if all that she has told to you be true, she has also suffered considerably, and she is sincerely to be pitied."

"She is indeed," said Mary; "and I am certain that the virtues which she possess are worthy of a far different fate to that which she has experienced."

"Ay, I do believe so," said Halliyard in reply. "But oh, Mary, how can I give utterance to the feelings of delight which now occupy my mind when I see you once more in safety, and listen to the soft and gentle tones of your voice, which I never expected to hear again? So great and sudden is the change from despair to the most unbounded joy, that I can scarcely believe in its reality. Heaven be thanked for its merciful interposition, and may all those troubles by which we were before surrounded now be at an end."

To that wish our heroine most heartily responded, and for some few minutes afterwards a silence ensued, during which time Halliyard continued to gaze with feelings of rapture, such as we need not attempt to describe, at Mary, the expression of whose countenance showed that her emotions were as powerful as his own; but at length it became necessary that they should separate, for Harry's duties called him on deck, and having once more fondly embraced her, and promised to rejoin her as soon as he could, he retired from her presence, and left her to her own meditations, which, as the reader may easily conjecture, were now of a very far different nature to what they had previously been —in fact, so extraordinary and unexpected was the change in her situation from one of the most absolute terror and despair to that of safety and hope, that it was not without considerable difficulty she could persuade herself that it had really taken place; but it was impossible that she could be labouring under so singular a delusion, and her emotions of joy and gratitude naturally knew no bounds; still, when she reflected on the delicate and peculiar circumstances under which herself and Harry Halliyard were placed, she could not help feeling somewhat uneasy and embarrassed, especially when she thought of the sufferings to which her unfortunate husband had been exposed, and recalled to her memory the many acts of kindness and devoted affection she had experienced from him, and which, at any rate, entitled him to her utmost respect, though while Harry held such a powerful influence over her heart, and which she knew full well that he must ever continue to do, it was impossible that she could love him or any other man. How wayward and unfortunate had been the circumstances connected with her fate—how sadly had the fond hopes she had formed been disappointed—how fearfully had those bright prospects which had once been spread before her imagination been overclouded. It did indeed seem as though the fates had conspired against her happiness, and him who was so dear to her; and as these thoughts crowded upon her mind, her spirits drooped, and she found it impossible entirely to divest her mind of a dismal presentiment that her troubles were not yet entirely at an end, notwithstanding that those brutal enemies whom she had so much reason to dread were now destroyed, and she knew not any one whom she should have any cause to apprehend.

When she recalled to her memory all the terrors she had had to undergo, the fearful dangers by which she had been surrounded, and the disgusting insults that had been heaped upon her by the miscreant Brandon, she wondered how she could have found fortitude to support them, or to surmount those difficulties that were sufficient to crush even the stoutest spirit; but they were past now, and she endeavoured to the utmost to look forward to the future with hope and confidence.

With feelings of the most fervent and inexpressible gratitude, she poured forth her thanks to the Supreme, when Halliyard had quitted her presence, and then tried all that was in her power to regain her composure, and in which effort she succeeded much better than might have been expected.

"Yes," she said, "I will be firm, and not give way to such sad forebodings, which can only serve to torture my mind and to depress my energies. Providence has in its mercy interposed to rescue me from that dreadful fate which was so long impending over my head, and from which there seemed to be no possibility of my escaping, so completely had the villain Brandon got me in his power; and why should I anticipate fresh evils, when it has already been my lot to experience so many trials and misfortunes, and which I have supported with such patience and resignation? I will

not give way to such feelings, but place my firmest reliance on the goodness and mercy of the Supreme, who will not suffer my hopes to be disappointed. Oh, Harry, may Heaven continue to watch over and protect us, and to guide us in our future conduct, so that we may be enabled to look back upon the past without remorse, and not to reproach ourselves for the future."

Such were the feelings that now took possession of the bosom of our heroine, and she gradually became more calm, so that when Alice returned to the cabin, which she did shortly after Halliyard had taken his departure, she found her in much better spirits than she had been for some time, and she heartily congratulated her upon the subject.

"Oh, Mrs. Tiller," she remarked, "brighter days, take my word for it, are now in store for you, and you will be enabled to look back upon the past, I hope, almost without regret, or, at any rate, only as some painful dream."

"God grant that I may," replied our heroine, "for Heaven knows that I have suffered enough."

"You have indeed," coincided Alice, "and the fortitude with which you have supported all the heavy trials that have been inflicted on you is deserving of a bright reward, which no doubt you will receive."

"And you, my friend," said Mary, "oh, what am I not indebted to you for the kindness I have ever experienced from you? But for the generous sympathy which you evinced in my fate, I doubt much whether or not I must have sunk under the cruel persecutions that were inflicted on me by my remorseless enemy."

"And how happy am I to think that I had it in my power to afford you any degree of fortitude or consolation in the midst of the dangers and difficulties by which you were surrounded," answered Alice, in accents which fully bespoke her sincerity; "I must indeed have been possessed of a most callous nature, and unworthy of the name of woman, could I have acted otherwise than I did; but I am sufficiently rewarded already in the approval of my own conscience, and I hope that the time is not far distant when you will be restored in safety to that home and those friends from which you have been so long and so painfully estranged."

Our heroine again returned her warmest thanks to her kind-hearted companion, and then they continued to converse for some time, and to picture to themselves in the most glowing colours that they could that which was in future in store for them. But it is useless to detain the reader by entering into those particulars. Harry Halliyard was out of her society no more than he could possibly help, and she received every respectful attention from the captain and the other officers on board, who deeply commiserated with her in the many misfortunes she had experienced, and congratulated themselves on having been the means of rescuing her from the dreadful fate with which the hard-hearted ruffian, Brandon, had threatened her, and which he would, no doubt, have accomplished had they not so fortunately come to her rescue in the very hour of her greatest peril.

Thus two or three days passed away without anything particular taking place, and Mary had become calm and hopeful, and the favourable change which the recent circumstances had so quickly wrought in her appearance was most remarkable, though her thoughts frequently wandered most anxiously to her husband, and she could not but have some misgivings as to the reception she would meet with from him, should it be her fate to reach England in safety. But her troubles were not yet at an end, as the reader will soon perceive.

The whether, which since the destruction of the pirates had been particularly fine and favourable, now suddenly changed, and the vessel was driven by contrary winds out of its course; these going down, the signs of an approaching storm were but too evident. Black and ponderous clouds obscured the horizon, and occasionally peals of thunder rattled through the heavens, and broad flashes of lightning lent their terrors to the sky. The ocean became convulsed, and foamed and bubbled in sullen wrath, and every one became perfectly conscious of the fearful dangers to which they were so shortly to be exposed; but the hardy seamen, used to such scenes, and strangers to fear,

viewed it almost with indifference, and prepared themselves to counteract by every means in their power the perils with which they were so darkly threatened.

And now the wind rose again in all its might, it blew great guns, and soon the squall came on with the most terrific fury; every rag on board yielded to its fearful power, and was rent into tatters; the rain descended in torrents, and poured with irresistible force through every crevice, and the vivid flashes of the lightning become more frequent and more awful. Still the courage of the gallant crew never for an instant failed them, and they exerted themselves with tenfold energy, but, at the same time, with very little, if any effect.

And what was now the state of our heroine's mind? The reader may imagine it, but we fear that we should fail in attempting to describe it. With clasped hands, and looks of terror and despair, she stood and gazed upon the frightful scene and listened with breathless horror to the voices of the crew, as they hurried on in their desperate struggles against that death which seemed too surely to await them. All those sanguine hopes which she had recently so fondly indulged in were now almost extinguished in her breast, and an approaching sensation, which grew stronger every moment, and which she found it impossible to conquer, came over her, and almost overwhelmed her with its intensity. Halliyard was only enabled to snatch a few minutes at intervals with her, and then he tried all he could to calm her terrors and to inspire her with hope; but it was all to little or no purpose—and, indeed, the fury of the storm was such that it was almost impossible that any one could hope to escape it, unless some immediate and miraculous change should take place, but of which there seemed, at present, to be not the smallest possibility.

"Oh no, Halliyard," she sighed, as she rested her head, almost fainting, on his shoulder, "in vain you seek to inspire me with those hopes that I feel convinced, under the awful circumstances, you cannot yourself entertain. Our doom is certain, I see it plain enough, and Heaven prepare our souls to meet it. Oh, how presumptuous must I have been to flatter myself with the idea that I should avoid the fate which it is the will of the Supreme should befal me; still, had I been suffered to return to my native land, and once more to behold my unfortunate husband—torturing thought! my brain is racked to madness and despair as it occurs to me, and——"

Sobs of the most poignant anguish choked her further utterance, and she could not finish the sentence. And oh, what were the feelings of agony which at that moment racked the manly bosom of our hero, but more especially when he gazed upon the excruciating and almost insupportable sufferings of her whom he so fondly loved? It was with the greatest difficulty that he was enabled to restrain them to at all within the bounds of reason, for he saw too plainly that there was but little cause for hope, and that unless Providence interposed to save them, a very short time must decide their fate.

"My poor lass," he ejaculated, in his tenderest and most sympathising accents, "for the love of Heaven endeavour to banish those awful thoughts from your mind, and to put your trust in Providence, who will not yet desert us. Oh, that you should be exposed to such terrible dangers as these, and especially after the awful and unmerited sufferings from which you have but just escaped. What can I say to comfort you? How can I act to calm your fears, and to arouse you to fortitude and hope?"

"Dear Harry," she said, "torture yourself not so much on my account, for after the many trials I have encountered, it is not death that I dread to meet. You may yet be saved, though it may be my fate to perish, and——"

"No, no, no!" interrupted Halliyard hastily, and with the deepest emotion, "that shall never be; we will both be saved, or we will die together. Think you that I could ever endure to live after you had met with so awful and untimely a death? By Heaven, never! Sooner would I—"

He was interrupted by receiving a hasty summons to go on deck, and turning to Mary with a look of the most indescribable anguish and despair, he said—

"I must leave you, my beloved Mary. My duty calls me hence, and I dare not disobey; but I will return to you again as soon as possible, and in the meantime may Heaven watch over and sustain you. God bless you, my poor lass, God bless you!"

Sobs choked his further utterance, and frantically kissing her lips, her cheeks, and her forehead, with a desperate resolution he tore himself away, and she sank insensible in the arms of the faithful Alice.

With what feelings of pity did that kind-hearted friend gaze upon her, and how happy would she have been could she have done anything to afford her some degree of consolation, or to have averted the fate which now seemed so rapidly and inevitably approaching them; but, alas! that was unfortunately quite impossible.

"Ill-fated woman," she ejaculated, "how agonising is it to witness your sorrows, and to know that there are no means of relieving them. I had indeed hoped that after you had escaped from the power of the villain Brandon that her troubles were at an end, but, alas! how has that hope been disappointed."

She still held her in her arms, and tried to restore her to sensibility, but still it would almost have been a mercy to suffer her to remain in a state of unconsciousness rather than that she should have been alive to all the terrors that prevailed around, and which every instant increased in magnitude, and which plainly showed that it was utterly impossible that the vessel could long weather the fury of the storm. But it is impossible better to describe the dreadful scene than in the words of the immortal Byron:—

"As day advanced the weather seem'd to abate,
And then the leak they reckon'd to reduce,
And keep the ship afloat, though three feet yet
  Kept two hand and one chain-pump still
    in use.
The wind blew fresh again; as it grew late
  A squall came on, and while some guns broke
    loose,
A gush, which all descriptive power transcends,
Laid with one blast the ship on her beam ends.

"There she lay motionless, and seemed upset,
  The water left the hold and wash'd the decks,
And made a scene men did not soon forget,
  For they remember battles, fires, and wrecks.

*   *   *

" Immediately the masts were cut away,
   Both main and mizen ; first the mizen went,
Then mainmast followed ; but the ship still lay
   Like a mere log, and baffled their intent.
The mast and bowsprit were cut down, and they
   Eas'd her at least, although they never meant
To part with all till ev'ry hope was blighted,
And then with violence the old ship righted."

We will not attempt to describe the feelings of the hapless persons on board, especially our hero, while this dreadful scene was taking place ; but as for poor Mary, she was in a kind of stupor, and did not seem to be conscious as to what was taking place. Notwithstanding that the vessel had righted, it was evident from the damage it had received that it must shortly go to pieces, and the boats were immediately lowered, into the first of which our hero instantly sprang, bearing the insensible form of Mary in his arms, and was quickly followed by Alice, Watchful Waxend, Ben Bowsprit, the captain, mate, and several others of the crew ; but the second boat was so loaded, and the unfortunate beings who had crowded into it were in such a state of confusion that it immediately capsized, and the whole of them perished.

The other boat now put off with all speed, their eyes directed towards the vessel, to which several poor wretches were clinging, and rending the air with their wild cries of despair.   And it was well that they did so, for—

"At half-past eight o'clock, booms, hencoops,
     spars,
   And all things for a chance, had been cast
     loose,
That still could keep afloat the struggling tars,
   For yet they strove, although of no great use :
There was no light in heaven, save a few stars,
   The boats put off o'ercrowded with their
     crews;
She gave a reel and then a lurch to port,
And going down head-foremost—sunk in short.

" Then rose from sea to sky the wild farewell,
   Then shriek'd the timid, and stood still the
     brave,
Then some leap'd overboard with dreadful yell,
   As eager to anticipate their grave ;
And the sea yawn'd around her like a hell,
   And down she suck'd with her the whirling
     wave,
Like one who grapples with his enemy,
And tries to strangle him before he die.

" And first one universal skriek there rushed,
   Louder than the loud ocean—like a crash
Of echoing thunder ; and then all was hush'd,
   Save the wild wind and the remorseless dash
Of billows ; but at intervals there gush'd,
   Accompanied with a convulsive splash,
A solitary shriek, the bubbling cry
Of some strong swimmer in his agony."

But the situation of the individuals in the boat was scarcely less hopeless than before, for the storm had very little abated, and the wind was so piercingly cold that their limbs were completely numbed, independently of which the boat was so overcrowded that it threatened every moment to capsize.   Still they exerted themselves to the utmost, for what will not men do in the desperate situation in which they were placed ? They constructed a mast out of a broken spar, attaching a blanket to it for a sail, and they then took every precaution in their power to keep the boat righted, which they could only accomplish by continuing to bale the water out of her ; and then with sad and heavy hearts they committed themselves to the care of Providence, and awaited anxiously for daylight in the hope of meeting with some means of deliverance from their present awful situation.

Poor Mary was quite insensible, and the agony of Harry, as he held her in his arms, and tried to shelter her delicate and shivering form from the cold, defies the power of the most eloquent language properly to portray it.   If they did not meet with speedy relief, of which there was at present not the least prospect, she must perish, and even should they be thus fortunate enough, it seemed all but certain that the terrible shock, independent of the sufferings she had previously undergone, would prove too much for her tender frame to bear up against. As those thoughts rushed wildly through his brain, he was worked up almost to a pitch of frenzy, and, in spite of his efforts to the contrary, he could not help the tears starting to his eyes.   But every one was too much occupied with his own dismal thoughts to notice him, and the ghastly and despairing looks which they fixed upon each other were awful to behold, at least as far as they could be seen in the darkness of the night.   A dreary silence reigned amongst them, which was only broken by the howling of the tem-

THE DEATH OF HUGH BRANDON.

pest, and that rendered the moment still more appalling.

Such had been the hurry in which they had been compelled to abandon the sinking vessel, that they had only had time to secure a few biscuits and two kegs of fresh water, so that if they remained any length of time in their present situation, especially exhausted as they already were, they must inevitably perish of hunger, and such a fate as that was too horrible even to contemplate.

What they suffered during that night it is impossible for any language to con-

vey an idea of. Our heroine remained in a state of insensibility, and there were moments when Halliyard feared she was dead, and at such times his agony was so great that he was worked up to a pitch bordering upon madness. At length the wind grew dull, the rain no longer descended, the billows ceased to roar with their recent fury, and the storm was evidently fast ceasing, which seemed to impart some small degree of consolation and hope to the poor sufferers. But still their situation was most desperate and deplorable, and without Providence should send them some speedy relief their fate was certain.

Daylight at length came, and eagerly they strained their eyes in all directions in the hope of perceiving land, or some vessel that might afford them assistance, but no such relief appeared in sight, and their despair increased, for they were now all so weak and exhausted that they could scarcely exert themselves at all to guide the boat, and they had not the slightest idea as to whither they were steering. Mary remained in the same melancholy state, and it was only by a slight breathing that Halliyard could convince himself that she still existed at all. How dreadful were the apprehensions which he formed as to what her ultimate fate would be, though it was quite certain that she could not possibly long survive in her present condition, and he, therefore, abandoned himself to the most absolute and insupportable feelings of despair, which we will not attempt to describe, but leave it to the imagination of our readers. And thus did that day pass away, and all the horrors of another night seemed most assuredly to await them; but as the afternoon advanced a vessel appeared in sight at no great distance, and a loud shout of frantic delight and gratitude arose from the persons in the boat, which rent the air, and might have been heard for some distance; and while some wept with delirious joy, others offered up their prayers to Heaven at the prospect of their deliverance. But the emotions of our hero were almost too powerful for utterance—he could scarcely believe the evidence of his eyes, and he could have wept like a child. He pressed his lips fervently upon the pale cheeks of Mary, and then in a voice which fully showed the feelings that agitated his breast at that moment, he exclaimed—

"God be praised! Mary, dear Mary, you shall yet be saved!"

Resigning her still insensible form to the care of Alice, who had borne the dreadful sufferings which they had had for so many hours to undergo with the most exemplary fortitude, he prepared to render what assistance he could in this emergency. His companions were so frantic at the prospect of escaping from the jaws of death that, although the vessel was yet too far off, they shouted aloud at the top of their voices, in the wild idea that they could be heard by those on board; but they hoisted one of the seamen's shirts as high as they could as a signal of distress, and then exerted themselves to the utmost to steer the boat in the proper direction. They had the gratification to observe that the ship was bearing right down upon them, and as far as they could distinguish from her build she appeared to be a merchant vessel, and in a very few minutes their joy was increased, for the loud report of a gun from the ship, which came booming over the sea, was sufficient to convince them that they were seen, and directly afterwards they saw two boats put off, and make rapidly towards them, so that all their doubts, if they had entertained any, were at once removed, and a simultaneous prayer of gratitude burst spontaneously from the lips of those unfortunate individuals who had but a very short time before looked upon the fate which seemed to await them as quite inevitable.

Rapidly the boats approached the hapless sufferers, and they could then perceive that each of them was manned by four seamen. Oh, what would Halliyard not then have given could poor Mary have awakened to consciousness, and to know that she was once more saved from the jaws of death? But still he feared that the sudden shock might be productive of the most dangerous consequences, and he therefore considered that it was much better as it was, and looked forward to the future with renewed hope and fortitude.

In the course of a very few minutes more the boats had arrived close to them, and they had then the double gratification to discover by the features and dress of the men that they were their own countrymen. But they had no time now for questions at present, and immediately the whole of them were assisted into the boats, which then put off towards the ship.

They learned that it was the Swiftsure trading vessel from the coast of Africa, and homeward bound, and were assured that they would be treated with the tenderest sympathy and kindness by the captain, which they found to be no more than the truth, for on the boats getting alongside of the ship, and their being assisted on board, they were met by Captain Robertson, who proved to be an intimate friend of the captain of the unfortunate ship, Porpoise, and treated with all that humanity and commiseration which is so admirably characteristic of the British seaman to any of his fellow creatures in distress.

Particular attention was paid to poor Mary and her female companion, who were removed to one of the best cabins, and every means were immediately tried to restore Mary to her senses, Halliyard, notwithstanding his exhausted condition from the fatigue and suffering he had undergone, refusing to leave her even for a minute, and watching over her with the utmost anxiety, and with mingled feelings of delight and gratitude. Their preservation did indeed seem to him as all but miraculous, and he could scarcely believe the evidence of his senses, so sudden and unexpected was the change.

"Thank Heaven!" he cried, "she is again saved from a dreadful fate, from which there seemed to be no possibility of escaping, and, if Providence still continues to watch over her, she will at last be restored to her native land and to happiness. Poor Mary, what have you not had to suffer? And, oh, is it not wonderful that your strength has not sunk under it long ere this? But now I trust that your troubles are at last all at an end, and that henceforth your days may be those of peace and tranquillity. But your husband! Oh, let me not encourage that thought. Dear Mary, we must resign ourselves to the will of fate, and Providence will doubless order everything for the best; you are saved, and I am happy."

As he gave utterance to these words he kissed her tenderly, and then again stood by and watched most anxiously for her recovery. He was not much longer kept in suspense, for presently she gave signs of returning life, and directly afterwards she opened her eyes, and with an exclamation of delight Harry Halliyard rushed towards her and enfolded her in his arms.

"Ah!" she exclaimed, looking incredulously at him—"Harry here? It was all a mockery then, and we are not exposed to all those horrors that were so dreadful to witness?"

"No, dearest Mary," he replied, joyfully, "thank Heaven, we have escaped from them—we are all saved."

"Saved!" she repeated, pressing her hands upon her temples, as if to recall her recollection, and looking vacantly in his face, "what mean you? Were we not saved before? Ah, that fearful storm. But where are we now?"

"Safe on board an English merchant vessel, and bound for our native land," answered Harry.

"Oh, can this be true?" ejaculated our heroine, "and am I once more rescued from the jaws of death?"

"You are indeed, my poor lass," returned Halliyard, "and with the blessing of Providence, you will not again be exposed to those dangers from which you have just so fortunately escaped. Oh, what a relief it is to me to listen once more to the beloved tones of your voice; I was afraid that you would never again awaken to life. But let me not prolong this interview in your present naturally excited state. Our friend Alice, here, will explain everything to you, and see to your requirements. Heaven bless you, my poor lass, and may that which you have so Providentially escaped from be the last of the perils you will have to encounter. I will see you again shortly, and hope then to see you recovered from the shock which your system must have sustained from the severe test to which it has been put."

Our heroine fixed upon him a look of gratitude, without returning any answer, but which, however, expressed much more than words could possibly have done, and Harry having embraced her affectionately, they separated, and Mary was left in a state of emotion which it needs no language of ours to convey to the imagination of the reader.

For some minutes after the departure of Halliyard, Alice did not offer to interrupt her meditations, but at length she gently prevailed upon her to take such restoratives as were so necessary to her in her present exhausted condition, previous to her entering into any conversation or explanation upon the wonderful and providential escape which they had experienced from what appeared to be certain death. Having complied with her kind companion's request, Mary felt much relieved, and then asked Alice to relate those particulars which she, of course, was so anxious to hear. Alice did so as concisely as possible, and our heroine listened to them with mingled feelings of astonishment, awe, and gratitude to that Supreme Power which had so mercifully watched over them in the most imminent hour of their peril, and had so often interposed to save her when her fate appeared to be inevitable.

"Oh, Alice," she observed when the former had concluded "how eternally gateful ought I to be to that All-merciful Being who has watched over and protected me through so many awful trials, and enabled me to bear up against them. And what confidence ought I not to place in his future protection. Let me no more murmur at His will, for what presumptuous mortal shall dare to say that all He wills is not for the best?"

"Most true, my dear friend," replied Alice, "and I feel convinced that the patience and resignation with which you have endured those trials of which you now speak, will ultimately be rewarded by that happiness which you so well deserve to enjoy."

"Ah!" sighed out heroine, as a melancholy idea, in spite of her efforts to the contrary, came over her, "fain would I think as you have just now expressed yourself; but when I take all the peculiar and painful circumstances connected with my most extraordinary history into consideration, I find it impossible to do so. True happiness can never be mine, unless (and it is sinful to wish it) that one dark cloud which has obscured the horizon of my youthful hopes shall be dispersed."

"I understand you, Mrs. Tiller," replied Alice, "and, believe me, I fully appreciate your feelings; but let us talk no more upon that subject for the present, at any rate, for it can only serve to create thoughts and retrospections that must be most torturing to your mind. You are now once more safe, and under the protection of one who treasures your happiness and welfare, I am satisfied, more than he does his own existence, and let us hope that, whatever may be your present forebodings, all will terminate as happily as you could wish."

"Thank you, my dear companion in misfortune, for your kind solicitude in my welfare, for I know the sentiments that you have just now expressed emanate from your heart," answered Mary; "I will indeed endeavour to do as you advise me, and trust that, by perseverance, I shall be able to succeed. But you cannot but be aware that I must feel most anxious to know what is the present situation of my unfortunate husband (who, believe me, I respect and reverence as a wife ought to do) and what has been the impression which my mysterious and sudden disappearance has made upon his mind."

"Of course," coincided her companion, "it is no more than natural that you should do so; but do not let any dismal forebodings torture your mind, for if your husband is the kind of man that you have described him to me to be he can never be so uncharitable as to suppose that there has been anything criminal towards him on your part, especially after the information which Mr. Halliyard says he forwarded to him, previous to the departure of the Porpoise from Portsmouth."

"God grant that there may not," said our heroine, fervently, "for Heaven knows the cruel injustice he would do me by harbouring such a thought. And yet, alas! has not fate so conspired against me that there has, unfortunately, been quite sufficient to excite his suspicions, and to distract his mind into a wrong channel? When I reflect upon all this, surely it is not surprising that it should make me doubtful and fearful. God grant that my fears may not be realised, for though it is impossible for me ever to stifle the first love which was engendered in my breast, and which only untoward fate prevented from being gratified, never, never will I be guilty of an act towards my husband which innocence and purity should be ashamed to acknowledge."

"Oh, my unfortunate friend," remarked Alice, "most sincerely do I believe you; but I beg of you not to distress your mind upon so painful and delicate a subject, but endeavour to look forward to the best, and depend upon it that all will terminate more happily than you now seem to anticipate."

Mary made no reply, but she endeavoured to think as Alice had expressed herself, though, in spite of her efforts to the contrary, the most painful doubts and suspicions would crowd upon her mind. A silence of some time ensued, which Alice did not offer to interrupt, for she thought that our heroine would be much better left to her own reflections; but at length the latter was enabled somewhat to calm her feelings, and she inquired more particularly into the nature of the vessel on which they were aboard, and such account as Alice was enabled to give her of it, and the kindness nnd courtesy which the captain had at present evinced towards them afforded her the utmost satisfaction, and inspired in her feelings of the most unbounded gratitude.

"Oh, how fortunate," she said, "was it that Providence sent us such assistance in the terrible hour of our emergency, and thus preserved us, for a time, at any rate, from a fate for which we were all of us, doubtless, so ill prepared. What horrors must you all have endured, and what an infinite mercy it was to me that I was rendered unconscious of them."

"True," answered Alice, "but I will not harrow up your feelings by a recital of them. Thank Heaven, we are now safe, and I sincerely trust that no fresh calamity will occur to blight our prospects, or to interrupt our progress to our native land."

To this wish Mary most heartily responded, and struggling with the fears that had before assailed her mind, she became once more firm and confident. After some further conversation with Alice, and another interview with Halliyard, which was of the same affectionate character as the one we have previously described, she was persuaded to retire to rest, and after a few hours she felt more refreshed and invigorated than she had done for many a day.

The weather was now beautifully fine, there was not the least trace of the late terrific storm, and the vessel proceeded on her homeward passage with every prospect of its arriving at the place of its destination in safety. What happy moments were those that our heroine and Halliyard now enjoyed together! They were enabled by degrees to refer to the past without those painful emotions that had before tortured their minds, and to look forward to the future

with hope and confidence. Alice was their principal companion and friend, and the longer they were in her society the better were they enabled duly to appreciate those amiable qualities that were inherent in her breast, and to commiserate with her in the misfortunes it had been her hard lot to endure throughout so many years, and which were of that peculiar and painful nature which were scarcely to be paralleled in the history of any human being.

"I think my fate to have been a cruel one," said Mary one day when they were conversing upon the subject, "but what is it compared with that which you have had to encounter, Alice? Why should I murmur when I see others who have had to encounter far greater vicissitudes than myself, and equally as undeserving of them? I wonder indeed that you should ever have had the fortitude that you have displayed to support them."

"Heaven only knows, Mrs. Tiller," replied Alice, "how I have; but at times I have been driven almost to madness, and I almost marvel that in the distraction of my feelings I did not put an end to my wretched existence, but some inscrutable Power always prevented me. Had I indeed died years ago, it would have been a happy release to me from my misery, for what is now to become of me, poor destitute creature as I am, without a friend in the world?"

"Avast! avast there, my good Mistress Alice," said our hero. "I have plenty of money, and mean to lay up in port for the rest of my days, if it is my good fortune ever to reach old England again. You must think me an ungrateful scoundrel if you suppose that I can ever forget your kindness to this poor lass, whom I prize far more than my own existence. No, no, while Harry Halliyard exists you shall never want a sincere friend and a brother, and all that I can possibly do for you I am convinced can never repay the heavy debt of gratitude which I owe you."

"Spoken like yourself, dear Halliyard," said Mary, fixing upon the noble hearted young seaman one of her sweetest looks of approbation. "Had it not been for Alice, it is more than probable that we should never have seen each other again, for without her sympathy and consolation I feel convinced that I must have sunk under the heavy trials to which I was subjected. How, then, can I ever sufficiently evince my gratitude for services rendered so disinterestedly, and under circumstances of such a desperate and peculiar nature? Henceforward no circumstances whatever can possibly divide our friendship, and I must be as studious of her happiness as my own."

"Ah, my respected friends," said the poor woman, scarcely able to refrain from tears, "you completely overwhelm me by this unexampled kindness, of which I am so unworthy. I must have been a wretch indeed could I have acted otherwise than I did towards an unfortunate fellow-creature, and more especially one of my own sex; and I often regretted that it was not in my power to assist her in defeating the atrocious designs of the heartless miscreant in whose power she was. But do not estimate my humble services more than they deserve. I do indeed most gratefully accept your friendship, and it shall be my constant study to endeavour to prove to you that I am not unworthy of it."

"That I am sure it will," remarked Halliyard, "so there is an end of the matter. Oh, I do not despair that there are yet happy days in store for us all."

"God grant that there may be," said Mary, vehemently, "and that in the peace and tranquillity of the future we may be able to bury the painful past in oblivion."

"So I say, my lass," observed Harry, "and something confidently assures me that our hopes will not be disappointed. Oh, Mary, how do I long once more to tread the shores of my native land, and to cast anchor in the port of tranquillity. Even though those hopes which we so fondly entertained should never be fated to be realised, when I behold you once more on shore, and know that your bitter enemy is no more, I shall be content, and will endeavour to resign me to that fate which is no doubt ordained by Providence as the best. So come, Mary, away with sad thoughts, put on the same sunny smiles that you once did, and endeavour to anticipate future peace and tranquillity."

Mary shook her head mournfully, but at the same time she endeavoured to conquer the dismal forebodings that would, in spite of herself, steal upon her mind, and after a few more observations the conversation dropped, and Harry quitted the cabin.

CHAPTER XXIV.

THE CROWN AND CROSIER AGAIN.—OLD FRIENDS.—STARTLING NEWS.—SUDDEN ARRIVAL OF WAKEFUL WAXEND.

IT is now necessary that we should return to old scenes, and renew our acquaintance with some of those individuals to whom we have not adverted for some time. There was no change in the Crown and Crosier—it had the same quaint and comfortable appearance as when we first introduced it to the notice of the reader. Most of its old customers visited it as usual, and the worthy host, Will Wallit, carried as rubicund a nasal organ as formerly, drank as much of his own beverage, used the same quantity of double-chalk, and cracked his jokes with his guests with just the same spirit that he had ever done.

It was evening, and several persons were assembled in the parlour of this old homestead, enjoying themselves with their pipe and glass, and discussing the various topics of the day, and the landlord was seated in the chimney corner, looking as jovial and as happy and contented as a landlord well can do, and occasionally taking part in the conversation when he considered that the force of his eloquence was required.

"It is just twelve months this very day," remarked one of the company, "since Pretty Poll of Putney disappeared in such a mysterious way from her home."

"Ay," said Wallit, "that was indeed a mysterious affair, and it has been a terrible blow for poor Joe Tiller; he has never been in his right senses since, and if all the accounts that are given of him be correct, which there is no reason to doubt they are, he will never more leave his bed alive."

"No, poor fellow," remarked the man who had first spoken, "and taking all the circumstances into consideration, I do not wonder at it. It was no trifling matter to lose such a woman as Mary Tiller, and Harry Halliyard must have felt it most keenly when his hopes were so painfully disappointed. But do you really think it is true that she has fallen into the power of that desperate rascal, Hugh Brandon, the pirate?"

"Certainly I do," replied the landlord, "what reason is there to doubt it? Was it not discovered that the vessel known as the Helen was no other than the Wasp, on board of which Mary had been conveyed from the pirate's secret retreat on shore, and did not the Porpoise give chase to it? But whether they succeeded or not has not been ascertained, nor has anything been heard of it, so that there is too much reason to fear that some accident has befallen her."

"Well, then," said another of the guests, "one thing, at any rate, is certain, and that is—if Mrs. Tiller has indeed fallen into such desperate hands, her destruction is all but inevitable. Brandon is a most daring and inhuman villain, and it is not at all likely that he will be moved to abandon his brutal designs. Poor Mary! she was worthy of a better fate."

"Ay, that she was, poor lass," coincided Wallit, "and there is no one who can more sincerely pity her than I do. This neighbourhood has not seemed like the same since she has been taken from it, and we have lost so many of our old friends and acquaintances. Harry Halliyard, the pride of Battersea Hard, Watchful Waxend, the bishop of Battersea, (ah! I do indeed miss him, for he was a thirsty soul), Abigail Holdforth, and several others that I could mention. There used to be some life here when they resided in the neighbourhood, but now—ah! it makes me quite melancholy when I think of it. What a wicked plot it was which caused the abduction of Mary, and what a painful sensation it caused at the time."

"Yes," returned one of the company, "and who would have thought that Jack Oarsby should have been one of the principal actors in the plot?"

"The d—d rascal!" said Wallit, "it's a great pity that he has hitherto escaped, for if ever a fellow deserved punishment he certainly did. However, justice will at last overtake him, I hope.

Harry Halliyard, too, I wonder what will be his fate. He is a fine fellow—a noble-hearted fellow, and deserves all the happiness and prosperity that can fall to the share of any human being."

"You may say that," answered one of the guests, "and I hope it may yet be his lot, though he has had his share of misfortunes."

"Ah, poor fellow, he has, indeed," replied Wallit; "the disappointment to his hopes in finding that his pretty Mary had become the wife of another was a severe blow to him, but to know that she is in the power of such a wretch as Brandon, and that, in all probability, she has become his victim, will, I am certain, prove too much for him altogether."

"Well," said the man who had before spoken, "let us hope that, after all, it may not turn out to be so bad as we at present apprehend. But see, here comes old Sam Sculler; now, he is a sincere friend, if you please, and I don't know what would have become of Joe Tiller before this, if it had not been for him."

"True," agreed Wallit, "and I respect him for it, and he shall always be welcome to the best my house can afford while I have the means in my power. But here he is."

Sam Sculler now entered the room, and was welcomed most cordially by every one present. The old man looked much the same in health as usual; though dull and anxious, and he received the honest greetings of his friends with every kindness and respect.

"Ah, my old friend Sculler, I am very glad to see you," remarked Wallit; "here's your old seat, and I will quickly supply you with your favourite beverage and your pipe, for I know you do not feel yourself exactly at home at the Crown and Crosier without them. As we were saying before you came in, it is just twelve months this very evening since poor Mary was torn from her home, and——"

"Ah, poor lass," interrupted Sculler, in melancholy accents, "it is a sad recollection, and I fear that her fate is sealed, and that we shall never behold her again. That infernal shark, Brandon, may the just retribution of outraged Heaven pursue him! Poor Harry, too, what has become of him? It looks strange and ominous that no tidings have yet been heard of the gallant vessel on which he is aboard; I fear that some calamity has befallen her, that she has either perished in one of those severe gales that have been so prevalent of late, or that she has fallen into the hands of the enemy."

"Let us hope that such fears may prove to be groundless, Master Sculler," said Wallit, "though, to be sure, it is a long time to elapse without receiving any intelligence of the ship. But how is your patient this evening?"

"Ah, poor fellow," answered Sam, "he is very bad—very bad indeed; almost as bad as he can be to be alive. I do not believe that it is possible for him to hold out much longer, for his strength is almost exhausted, and taking all the circumstances into consideration, I must say that it would be a happy release for him."

"Well," remarked the landlord, "seeing how great a sufferer he is, probably it would; but still, after all, I cannot help trusting that matters will turn out much better than we now anticipate. But is his mind in the same wandering state?"

"Why," answered Sculler, "at times he has his lucid intervals, but then the extreme agony and despair of his feelings are quite painful to witness. One thing, however, appears to me certain —that he cannot possibly recover; and could he only be assured of the safety of his wife before his death, that, at least, would be some consolation to him in his dying moments. I had a singular dream last night, and should it only be realised, I shall indeed feel most happy."

"A dream, Master Sculler?" said Wallit. "And what might the nature of that have been?"

"Why," answered Sam, "I thought that I was seated in this very parlour, on a beautiful sunshiny morning, when suddenly the church bells rang forth a merry peal, and going to the door, I saw a bridal procession just emerging from the old porch and make its way towards this house. Eagerly I looked to catch a sight of the happy bride and bridegroom, and what was my astonishment and delight when I recognised in them Harry Halliyard and Mary, who were looking all smiles and cheerfulness, just as they used to do when their hopes were bright and young, and sorrow was unknown to them."

"Ah," ejaculated the landlord, "that was indeed a pleasant dream, and I only hope that it may turn out to be prophetic. And who knows but it may do so, notwithstanding the present gloomy prospects? Oh, it is no use to give way to despair; and do you know, Master Sculler, that I cannot divest my mind of the impression that poor Mary will yet be restored uninjured to her friends, and all those that are dear to her, though of course she must have suffered much from being placed in the terrible situation that she has been, and exposed to the cruel persecution of such an inhuman wretch as Brandon."

"Very true," coincided Sculler, "and may Heaven watch over and protect her, and defeat the diabolical plans of her brutal and remorseless enemy. But I came here principally to have a look at the newspaper, for I am always anxious to look at the shipping intelligence, with the hope of seeing something about the Porpoise."

"Ay, no wonder at that," said the landlord, "so here it is, and if you should find any good news in it, why of course you will not fail to read it out to us?"

"Certainly," replied Sculler, and taking the paper from the hand of Wallit, he turned to the column which he wished to peruse.

"Ah!" he exclaimed in a tone of excitement, and suddenly springing to his feet, as his eyes hastily fell upon a certain paragraph, "can I believe my senses, or am I only dreaming? This— this—no, it is no mistake; here it is all as clear and distinct as the light of day. Oh, thank Heaven!"

"My good old friend," said the landlord, impatiently, "what in the name of wonder can excite you in this remarkable manner? Do not keep me longer in suspense."

"Listen, listen," said the old man in an agitated voice. "Oh, who would ever have believed this? But let me read. Thus runs the paragraph: 'The Emerald, Captain Fordyce, on the morning of the 16th ult., spoke the Swiftsure, Captain Robertson, homeward bound

[THE WRECK OF THE PORPOISE.]

from the coast of Africa. Crew and passengers all well. From this we receive the unfortunate intelligence of the total wreck of H. M. S. the Porpoise, on the night of March 4th. Two hundred souls on board perished, but one boat's crew were happily picked up by the Swiftsure, and are on their way to England. Among them are two females, rescued from the notorious pirate ship Wasp, which was completely destroyed by the Porpoise three days before the wreck. The subjoined is a list of the persons saved: The captain and mate, Henry Halliyard, purser, Mary Tiller, rescued from——.' ''

"Hurrah! hurrah!" shouted Wallit, and the whole of the persons present. "They are saved! they are saved! Hurrah!"

"Hurrah!" shouted old Sam at the top of his voice, "here's joyful news for you! My dream! Oh, I shall go mad with joy! Poor Mary—poor Harry—poor Joe! Oh, dear! what shall I do? How can I express myself? Saved! saved! It seems scarcely possible! I—I—"

And overpowered by his feelings, the poor old man could not finish the sentence, but bursting into tears he wept like a child. It was some minutes ere he could recover himself in the slightest degree, and he then perused the paragraph again and again, fearful that he might have been mistaken.

"I am completely taken by surprise," he said at last. "Poor Mary, may you indeed have escaped entirely from the dreadful fate to which the miscreant Brandon had consigned you. If the weather is fine, it cannot be many days before this vessel will arrive. I know not how to act, I am so completely bewildered. How can I break this important intelligence to the unfortunate Joe? for I fear, in his present state of mind, and so much exhausted by long suffering as he is, the shock will be too much for him. And yet he must be made acquainted with it at all risks."

"True, poor fellow," said Wallit, "it is indispensably necessary that he should be so, but the utmost precaution must be used. I was never half so overjoyed in my life. I wonder if our old friend, Watchful Waxend, is among those that are saved?"

"Yes," answered Sculler, "his name is on the list."

"Well, I am rejoiced to hear that," said Wallit; "oh, I thought that he would never meet his death by water, unless it was brandy-and-water. I have no doubt that we shall again pass many happy hours together again, and——"

"House — house!" now shouted a familiar voice, and interrupting him. "Will Wallit ahoy! Damme, are you all deaf, or is there no one on board? Where's the skipper? Ship ahoy!"

"Hallo!" said Wallit, "who have we here in such a hurry? I should know that voice, and——"

Before he could finish the sentence the new customer entered, and the amazement of all present (but especially that of old Sam) may readily be imagined, when they recognised their old friend and companion, Mr. Watchful Waxend, who looked as though he had just come off a long journey. We need not attempt to describe the scene which followed ; Waxend shook hands again and again with every one, and laughed and wept alternately like a child, and it was some minutes before any one could recover from the state of excitement into which they were naturally thrown, and then they could scarcely believe the evidence of their senses, so extraordinary were the circumstances which had so suddenly and unexpectedly taken place.

"Ah, my old veteran, my respected friend," said Waxend, still grasping the hand of Sam Sculler cordially and fervently, "how it glads my heart to see you, especially after the many perils and dangers I have had to encounter. But poor Joe, tell me, he is not dead?"

"No, unfortunate man," replied Sculler, "he is not dead—but, alas! how fearful is his condition. Mary, Harry, how is it they are not with you? for we have just read the news in the paper, and——"

"Oh, thank Heaven," interrupted Waxend, "they are both safe. The vessel arrived at Portsmouth yesterday, and Harry sent me on in order that I might prepare you for their reception, and break the news to poor Joe, if he should be still living. In a few hours they will doubtless be here."

"But the miscreant Brandon?" hastily interrogated Sculler.

"The black shark and the whole of his guilty crew are destroyed," answered Waxend, "and Mary was enabled successfully to resist his brutal designs."

"Thank Heaven for that," said poor old Sculler, fervently, "for it has been indeed most merciful to us. Oh, Mary, what must be your feelings when you behold the melancholy situation of your unfortunate husband."

"Poor fellow!" said Watchful, compassionately ; "but does he believe her innocent?"

"Oh, yes, in his moments of reason he does," replied Sam ; "but relate to me in as few words as you can the circumstances that have taken place during this long and fearful interval, and then I must return to Tiller, and try to prepare him for the trying scene which is in store for him."

Waxend without any hesitation complied with this request, and we need not seek to describe the interest and attention with which Sam Sculler listened to him ; and when he had concluded, he again expressed his most fervent feelings of gratitude to the Supreme for the merciful protection which our heroine had received, and the fortitude and patience with which He had enabled her to support the many trials to which she had been subjected. After some further conversation, Sculler took his departure towards the residence of Tiller, his bosom agitated by a variety of contending thoughts and feelings which he found it a difficult task to arrange. As for Mr. Watchful Waxend, he betook himself to his pipe and glass, it being his intention to stop at the Crown and Crosier for the night, and he amused his wondering listeners with various marvellous recitals of the perilous adventures he had encountered since they had last met.

CHAPTER XXV.

THE LAST SCENE IN OUR DRAMA.

THE news of the return of Harry Halliyard and Mary to their native land, after so many hair-breadth escapes, flew with astonishing rapidity over the neighbourhood, and, as might naturally enough have been expected, it caused the greatest excitement in the minds of all those who were acquainted with them.

Their friends were abundant in the professions of their hearty welcome, and were quite ready to tender their assistance in every way that would tend to the comfort of those friends who had been so long from their native shores, and whom they had despaired of ever seeing again.

Old Sam Sculler had a most difficult task to accomplish to break the intelligence to poor Joe, who was evidently sinking fast; but he succeeded much better than might have been expected. The mind of Tiller fortunately no longer wandered, and he was, therefore, perfectly conscious of all that his old and faithful friend was saying to him, though the sudden surprise was almost too much for him, and his emotions were so great that for a few minutes they nearly overpowered him. But at length he clasped his hands vehemently together, and raising his eyes devoutly towards Heaven, he ejaculated—

"All-merciful God, I thank You that You have at last heard my prayes, and restored my unfortunate wife to liberty, and rescued her from those frightful dangers with which she was threatened. Oh, suffer me but to live to invoke my blessing upon her head, and to assure her how fondly and how truly I have loved her, and I can then die content, and without a single murmur of regret."

He continued in much the same state throughout the night, and awaited calmly and patiently the issue of all, which was now so rapidly approaching, and Sculler never left him for a minute, but watched him with the utmost care and anxiety. But we must now return to Mary and Harry Halliyard.

It would be a difficult task to portray the feelings of our heroine when the vessel neared the shores of her native land; they were almost too powerful for utterance, and it was only by the untiring exertions of Halliyard that she was enabled to combat the many doubts and fears that, in spite of all her efforts, still continued to hold possession of her mind, as regarded her husband. At length they reached Portsmouth, and having put up at a respectable hotel, as has been seen, they despatched Watchful Waxend to Battersea, to apprise Sculler of the facts, and intending to follow themselves immediately. The next day they accordingly set forward by the coach, and in due time they arrived in that neighbourhood from which they had been so long away, and under such pain-

ful and peculiar circumstances. And now the emotions of our heroine increased, especially when they heard from Watchful Waxend the melancholy situation of Tiller, and knew the dreadful sufferings he must have experienced. It was some time ere they could sufficiently compose themselves to depart towards the cottage; and as they did so, everything that their eyes encountered brought with it the most melancholy recollections. It had been agreed between them and Sculler that they should not enter until he gave them the signal, and they, therefore, stood near the door, and awaited the moment of the said interview with feelings of the most torturing anxiety.

Poor Joe Tiller was evidently sinking rapidly, but his demeanour was calm and resigned.

"Have they not come yet?" he said at length in a faint voice, but in a tone of impatience, "or have you deceived me?"

"Deceived you, my poor friend?" repeated Sculler. "God forbid that I should do so. Have you strength to support the meeting?"

"Yes, yes," replied the poor sufferer, eagerly. "But I feel that my moments are numbered—that I am dying fast; the least delay, and it will be too late. Mary, my wife, my—"

"Husband—unfortunate husband! I am here!" exclaimed poor Mary, and rushing into the room, followed by Halliyard, she sunk on her knees by the side of the couch of the dying man.

"Mary—Harry!" he gasped forth in accents that were sufficient to thrill to the very soul, "do you forgive me the anguish I have caused you? For the suspicions which I have dared to entertain towards you?"

"We do! we do!" fervently ejaculated our heroine and Halliyard in a breath.

"Then I am happy!" ejaculated poor Joe, with a sweet smile. "Harry, she—she is now yours—I am dying—Bless you!—Mary!—Harry!"

With these words he pulled their hands together, joined them before him, and then almost without a sigh he died across them.

"He is dead!" shrieked Mary, and sinking down she became insensible.

*　　*　　*　　*

Twelve months were suffered to elapse after the occurrence of the melancholy event which has just been recorded, when Harry Halliyard led his beloved Mary to the altar; and on the same day, and in the same church, they having long before this effected a reconciliation, Mr. Watchful Waxend was united to his old sweetheart, the loquacious Abigail Holdforth.

Need we say that every happiness was destined in future to be the reward of our hero and heroine for the many misfortunes and severe trials they had experienced, and that a numerous family of lovely and virtuous children increased the blessings of their lot? Old Sam Sculler and Alice resided with them for the rest of their days, sharing with them in all their many comforts, and went to their graves respected and lamented.

THE END.